P9-DMT-961

MAY 0 1 2009

Sunnyside

Also by Glen David Gold

Carter Beats the Devil

Sunnyside

GLEN DAVID GOLD

Alfred A. Knopf New York 2009

This Is a Borzoi Book Published by Alfred A. Knopf

www.aaknopf.com

Knopf, Borzoi Books, and the colophon are registered trademarks
of Random House, Inc.

Library of Congress Cataloging-in-Publication Data
Gold, Glen David, [date]
Sunnyside / by Glen David Gold.—1st ed.
p. cm.
ISBN 978-0-307-27068-9 (alk. paper)
1. Chaplin, Charlie, 1889–1977—Fiction.   2. Motion picture actors
and actresses—Fiction.   3. Soldiers—Fiction.   4. Fame—Fiction.
5. Hollywood (Los Angeles, Calif.)—Fiction.   6. Popular culture—
United States—History—20th century—Fiction.   I. Title.

PS3607.O43S86 2009
813'.6—dc22   2009003804

Manufactured in the United States of America
First Edition

For Alice

I was loved.

—Mary Pickford

This Evening's Entertainment

Newsreel for November 12, 1916: A Day's Pleasure

☆

Travelogue: Unter dem Licht der westlichen Sterne

☆

Two-Reel Comedy: Cupid and the Millionaire

☆

Serial: The Winking Idol

☆

Our Feature Presentation: Three Blue Lights

☆

Sing-Along: "Smile"

Credits

Starring

Leland Wheeler. . . . . a hero
Emily Wheeler . . . . his mother
Hugo Black . . . . a soldier
Rebecca Golod . . . . a little girl
Edna Purviance. . . . . a comedienne
Burton Holmes . . . . a travelogian
Percy Bysshe Duncan . . . . Wild Duncan Cody
Wilhelm II . . . . the Kaiser
George Barnes . . . . a cameraman
Syd (Sid) Chaplin . . . . a brother
Douglas Fairbanks . . . . a friend
Mary Pickford . . . . an enemy
Ashes, Mut, Buttons, etc.. . . . . dogs
Alf, Maverick, Carlyle, Rhiannon, Eddie, etc.. . . . . staff
Frances Marion. . . . . a scenario writer
Mildred Harris. . . . . an ingénue
William Gibbs McAdoo . . . . a businessman
T. H. Münsterberg . . . . a professor
Andrea Pike . . . . a baby vamp
Mr. Pike. . . . . her father
Mordecai Golod. . . . . a crook
Officer McKinney . . . . a square cop
Detective Collins . . . . a straight cop
Major General Frederick C. Poole . . . . a buffoon
Wodziczko. . . . . a fan
Lieutenant Gordon . . . . a drunk
Goose, Banjo, et al.. . . . . war dogs
Lieutenant Ripley. . . . . a pilot
Lenore . . . . his wife
Harry. . . . . a dog trainer

Starring

Nikolai Chaikovsky...................................a politician
General Edmund Ironside ....a leader
Pishkoff...his valet
Adolph Zukor...a mogul
Zasu Pitts ....a comedienne
Tatiana...a witch
Aarne....................................a wizened old man
Anna ....a nervous princess
Maria...................................a gracious princess
Vasilisa ....a nihilist princess
Hannah Chaplin ....a mother
Norman Chaplin ...."the little mouse"

and

Charles Chaplin ....himself

Newsreel for
November 12, 1916

A Day's Pleasure

. . . .

It was quite a large war. It was stupendously big and very distant. The public really was not inclined to pay much attention to it. . . . We had grown used to the shouting. This perfectly understandable and honest public attitude was reflected more accurately and frankly in the motion picture than in any other institution.

—Terry Ramsaye
film historian and publicist (1925)

. . . .

1

At its northernmost limit, the California coastline suffered a winter of brutal winds pitched against iron-clad fog, and roiling seas whose whiplash could scar a man's cheek as quickly as a cat-o'-nine-tails. Since the Gold Rush, mariners had run aground, and those who survived the splintering impact were often pulped when the tides tore them across the terrible strata of the volcanic landscape. For protection, the State had erected a score of lighthouses staffed with teams of three or four families who rotated duties that lasted into the day and into the night. The changing of the guard, as it were, was especially treacherous in some locations, such as Crescent City, accessible only by a tombolo that was flooded in high tide, or Point Bonita, whose wooden walkway, even after the mildest storm, tended to faint dead away from the loose soil of its mountaintop and tumble into the sea.

Until the advent of navigational radio, communication with the mainland was spotty. God help the man who broke his leg on the Farallon Islands between the weekly supply-ship visits. But the peril of the European War had meant Crosley crystal-receiver radio sets and quenched spark systems with an eight-hundred-mile range for all who lived and worked on the coastlines, and so, on Sunday, November 12, 1916, just below the Oregon border, at the St. George Reef Lighthouse, eight miles off the California coast, there began an explosion of radio, telephone, and telegraph operations unprecedented in American history.

At high tide, roughly five o'clock in the morning, it was over an hour before dawn. The sweeping eighty-thousand-candlepower light from the third-order lens cast the frothing sea from shore to horizon into the high contrast of white against black for some moments, then back into full pitch-darkness. Two strong men in caps and slickers rowed the station boat toward the crown of stone upon which the lighthouse stood. Their passenger, her corpulent form bundled beneath a treated canvas sail, her arms crossed around her morning pitcher of coffee, was the Second Assistant Keeper, Emily Wheeler. As the light rotated, there was a stroboscopic effect which illuminated her progress cutting across the sea foam that lay like frosting above the crags and crevasses of the ancient reef.

Emily Wheeler, in the third generation of a family of California lighthouse keepers, was a difficult woman, but, as with all difficult women who could demand such isolated work, her desire was immediately granted. Of course, send her to a rock miles off the coastline, go with the governor's blessings.

But, unlike other such women, she had thought to make her own uniform. She wore it under the sail and her layers of slickers and inflatable vests. It was navy wool, with simple gold braid at the throat, and there was a smart, matching cap under which she tucked the foundry-steel braid of her hair. After considerable thought about stripes—she didn't want to seem conceited, yet she also wanted to acknowledge her duties—she had given herself the rank of sergeant.

Her lighthouse was the world's most expensive, nine years in the making, a cylindrical housing hewn from living granite, a 115-foot caisson tower as sturdy as a medieval fortress, its imposing skin interrupted only by the balistrariac slits of loophole windows. And at the very top, capped with iron painted a brilliant red, was its lantern room, in which rotated the Fresnel lens, as faceted as a sultana's engagement diamond, and which, like the eye of Argus, was chambered myriad ways, as close to omniscience as technology could dare. There was no better light in America.

To be the sergeant sharing charge of such a great beast was an honor and a responsibility to which Emily Wheeler was equal, and to be a woman superior to men was a life she made no secret of enjoying. In fact, to gain their confidence, she was known to pander to their prejudices, in effect putting her own gender up for sale. ("Gentlemen," she said on her first day, "I do not give the orders. The sea gives the orders, and we are at the mercy of *her* unpredictable ways.")

She was clearheaded in a crisis, and had organized the rescue of many a wayward sailor. However, it was her habit in the boring hours to engineer small crises herself. A twitching filament on the reserve lantern was occasion for much shouting; cleaning the fog signal's air compressor meant at least three separate fits of panic. It was thus the curse of her men to wish on every shift for an actual disaster.

Since no one could live comfortably at the station for more than a week, the four keeper families passed much of their lives in cottage-style du-plexes on the coast, on the dunes just above the shoreline. Husbands and wives and children were eternally, twice a day, with the waxing and waning tides, handing off hot meals and kissing each other goodbye.

Eight miles from shore, the station boat now settled into place on the leeward side of the lighthouse, which made a wedge-shaped windscreen, a small pool of calm. The men in the boat flashed their tiny lantern, and in response there was a groan from the crane housing overhead, and a winch dropped down a cargo net, into which Sergeant Wheeler stepped. Another exchange of lights, and then the crane withdrew, bringing her aloft. It was during the long moments when she swung in the wind, and the spray of the sea managed to slap at her face and neck, that she most enjoyed her job at the very edge of the map. "I am the westernmost woman in the country"— an idea she extinguished when the cargo net placed her on granite. Trouble.

Leland, her assistant, helped her unbuckle the harness and step out of the cargo net. "We have a problem, Mom."

Leland was always on duty at the same time she was, less a personal choice than a request of the other families. He was twenty-four years old, talk at the lighthouse had deemed him "unfairly handsome," and he had wrecked two surreys on the dunes near the cottages while impressing girls. Further, he had a propensity for mail-ordering sheet music from San Fran-cisco, *jazz rags,* which he insisted on playing on the clarinet most after-noons, and he was known to visit the picture show three consecutive days to memorize the details of photoplays rather than stay at home and help his grandmother, who had the vapors. It was hoped Sergeant Wheeler would provide discipline.

"What's wrong?"

"Craft adrift. About a mile west-northwest."

"Anyone on it?"

Leland hesitated. He was generally quick with a quip, which melted Emily's heart too much and prevented any actual discipline from occur-ring. So now she looked at him not just as a sergeant, but as a worried mother. Finally, he said, "You should come see."

They passed through the portico into the engine room and took the ele-vator to the cramped observation chamber just below the lantern room. It shared common glass with the lightbox one story above. There were two men already present, a father and a son of the Field family, pushing each other away from their only telescope worth a damn, the Alvan Clark with a two-inch lens. While Emily removed her slicker, and polished the wet from her glasses, two more assistants came into the room, having heard excitement was brewing.

"Where's the craft?" Emily asked.

"It's ten o'clock, a mile out," answered the elder Field.

"And it's manned?"

Field looked to his son, who looked to Leland, who nodded.

"Is it the invasion?" For this had been a topic of discussion, at first hypothetically and of late a grim certainty.

"No, it's just one man. Alone."

Frowning, Emily pulled the phone from the wall and called to the lantern room, asking them to fix the lens so that it shone at ten o'clock, and to send up the code flags, prepare for a series of two-flag signals, and notify all surrounding vessels via radio telephony that a rescue was in progress.

The engine ground down with the easing of a clock spring, and the white light went steady upon the churning seas. The fog, which most days was a woolen overcoat, this morning was but a beaded mist easily torn through, and even without the telescope, Emily could see a small boat bobbing in the swells.

"Lord! It's just a skiff, an open skiff," she whispered. She made fluttering gestures to push back the group around the Alvan Clark, and they exchanged glances of anticipation. This was either a real crisis or one about to be shouted into existence. Emily applied her eye to the eyepiece, blinked, and ran her fingers along the reeded focus knob, making a blur, and then, in a perfectly circular iris, she saw, with a clarity that made her gasp, Charlie Chaplin.

She jolted a step backward, looking to the window without the aid of magnification, as if the telescope might have somehow fabricated this vision. She could see the boat, now rocking on the crests of ever-increasing waves as it came closer, and there was indeed a solitary figure aboard. He was dressed in baggy black trousers, a tight morning coat. He had a mustache. A cane. A derby.

"Is that . . ." She swallowed.

"We were thinking it looks like Charlie Chaplin," Leland said, with the shame of a boy caught believing in fairies.

Emily gulped coffee, searching for it to kick like gin, and then she looked again through the telescope. The lighthouse provided a brilliant spotlight that swept away all color in the flood of illumination, casting its view into glowing white or penumbral mystery; there was no missing the open skiff, its single sail patched and sagging, its occupant shuffling from stem to stern, toes out, gingerly leaping over each oarlock's thwart. He was rubbing his chin, and waggling his mustache as if itched by a puzzling thought, and in the several seconds Emily watched speechlessly, a gust of wind swung the ruined sail so that it hit him in his rear end, causing him to jump in place. He realized what had hit him, he tipped his hat as if he and the sail were engaged in polite social discourse, and he returned to his bowlegged pacing.

"We have to rescue him," Leland finally said.

"Yes," Emily whispered.

"Could it be someone *dressed* as Charlie Chaplin?" asked the elder Field, who always saw the blank physics of a situation, but even his voice had doubts. Each assistant took turns looking at the little fellow in the skiff, and each had to agree, one could certainly dress like Chaplin, and even act like Chaplin—there were contests and so on—but in the view of their telescope's eye, there were no hesitations, no awkward attempts to remain graceful. This man was not pretending or attempting to convince them of his identity. Further, they were battling against logic with their desire to believe it was true. In the end, what was right before their eyes won.

"Well," Leland said, helplessly showing off what he knew from the magazines, "that is definitely Charles Spencer Chaplin." Then he whispered, "Son of a gun. There's a hole in the hull."

He knew this because Chaplin was now using a tin cup to bail out water. As the boat drifted closer to the rocks, waves dumped over the bowl, so the bailing was useless and frantic. Chaplin removed his hat to use it as a ladle, and now both his arms became pistons flinging water away as the sea drew his boat closer and closer to its doom.

Emily's hand went to her mouth. "There's a hole in his derby, too!"

"Perhaps he's making a movie here," suggested Field.

"I'm going," Leland said. Before his mother had a chance to object, he had shot to the exit, and his boots made the authoritative peal of cathedral bells as he sprinted down the circular metal staircase.

"Leland, come back," she cried, as mothers have always called to their children who in turn were called to the brutal seas, but in truth she hardly wanted to stop him. To stop him smacked of that phantom discipline she could not muster. Moreover, he was going to aid a helpless sailor, an act that throbbed with responsibility.

For his own part, Leland could not have been dissuaded, because the chance to rescue Charlie Chaplin would never come again. On the porch where the launch boats hung, he slipped into his flotation vest and jumped into the rowboat behind Johnson, who always wore a cameo of the Blessed Virgin on the outside of his protective clothing. With Johnson in first position, Leland took second position in the oarlocks, and signaled to the crane house to drop them to the sea.

For long minutes, two pairs of youthful arms rowed in splendid unison, threading the boat between spires and jags until it faced the open sea. Leland spotted the skiff ahead; it was drifting toward *la pared de la muerte*. Many points along the coast were known as the Wall of Death; this one had reasons for the name so convincing that the antediluvian Tolowa fishermen had described it thusly, and centuries later the Russian otter-hunters had agreed—*stayna greebel*, of course—for, no matter the tide, a wicked current drew anything in its grip magnetically shoreward, with unexpected speed. When you were still in the swells a quarter mile away from the obvious rocks, in the sickening drop of a trough, the half-submerged wall would be thrown erect before you, and there was a vortex into which all boats would be sucked down, then spat up against it, dashing what remained into bits.

Sergeant Emily Wheeler watched with pride and fear as her boy's rescue boat rose and fell with the ocean, oars moving it foot by foot toward Chaplin's skiff. She was anticipating the outcome—the shoreline, sunrise, seagulls chasing the spindrift, Chaplin on a driftwood log with a blanket draped over his shoulders, sipping coffee laced with brandy, and shaking from the fear and pleasure of having been rescued.

At the same time, arms fatigued and cold, Leland was staring through his partner, Johnson, considering the shape that the gratitude of Mr. Charlie Chaplin might take. He imagined lecturing Chaplin; he had read *Motion Picture Weekly*, and he knew the difference between pretending to be on a dinghy in the movies, and testing your luck on such spirited seas as those near St. George Reef. "But you know, Mr. Chaplin," he would say, "this does make quite a scenario, don't you think?" And how else could Charlie respond but to stand from his log, place one arm up on Wheeler's solid shoulder, pump his hand, and say, "I hadn't considered it, Leland Wheeler, but you're right," and "Leland Wheeler is a splendid kind of name. Come to the studio—we need strong arms and strong jawlines," and Leland constructed and reconstructed these statements with different kinds of English accents, from Ascot-races lordly to cockney chauffeur, since he wasn't quite sure what Chaplin sounded like, eventually settling on the accent he'd heard a slapstick comedian use at the Redding Music

Hall, British with a Jewish or Gypsy tint, he didn't really know the specifics; but such speculation swirled in its own vortices, and he concluded first that this rescue might be his own salvation, then: might there be a filmed re-enactment, but this time with *bathing beauties*?

It is the nature of wishes and their potential fulfillment to travel faster than anything shackled to earth, especially a rowboat straining against a current that all but groaned in its desire to blow into *la pared de la muerte*. So Leland Wheeler's mind could travel from sea to shore to the road leading seven hundred miles south to the bare ankles of the engaging backlot sirens who fluttered and yawned at the Mutual Studios of Los Angeles, in the approximate time it took Chaplin's boat to be sucked into the whirlpool and begin an awful, irresistible spin.

Leland was calling out to Johnson, who called back; Leland could hear just the harder consonants of a prayer. Chaplin noticed them—he visibly perked up, stood, and leaned forward until the boat tipped, and he was forced, hands on hat, to lean back. He smiled, recognizing not the danger but the rescue, and he again tipped his hat, face breaking into the smile of one about to be saved. But his boat was already turning, turning slowly, turning almost gently, in obedience to Coriolis, and the men in the rowboat were shouting themselves hoarse, and Chaplin, in order to keep them in sight, began to march in place, counterclockwise. He was in effect stationary, even as the boat was beginning to spin under his feet. Leland shouted, "No!"

Chaplin cocked his ear as if trying to listen, holding to his temple his useless tin cup as if it were an ear trumpet, and, with the boat's rotation increasing, he stepped up his own counterrotations until he was all but a blur.

The swells drew back. The boat stopped, Chaplin continuing to spin until he toppled over. With acrobatic momentum, the tumble carried him upright, and he stood, arms in fists at his sides, looking as if he had just triumphed over the sea. He did not see what loomed behind. With the weight of a mudslide, a wave crashed down upon the boat, and Charlie Chaplin was blown below the surface.

Pressure mounting against it like the thumb and forefinger of Uranus, the hull of the skiff rocketed out of the depths, sailed six feet over the waves, and crashed into shards like a wine bottle against the Wall of Death.

The sun was beginning to rise; there wasn't yet its actual glow or warmth, but instead the gray promise of daylight. The lighthouse beam was thus fading in comparison with natural light, and the many colors of the sea were being restored: the olive bulbs of kelp atop the rich obsidian rocks, the emerald nightmare that was the sea, the lapis of the dawn skies. Leland and his companion rowed in place. They had lost their spirit. How terrible it was that God had created in humans the urge for compassion, a sensation that nature itself withheld.

The simplest pairs of code flags rode up the station's monkey pole, the blue-and-white "A" and yellow "Q," then the powder flag and St. George's Cross: boat lost, man overboard. An emotionless message, all was lost, all was lost. The St. George Reef telegraph operator, weeping, began to tap out a note to the naval station to the south, and to all the ships at sea, a spotty and impressionistic account whose clarity was far outweighed by its emotional devastation. And yet, at the same time, he was receiving something that was not a response, that made no sense, a message of dots and dashes from the east.

From *la pared de la muerte* there was a quick bubbling, and Leland pointed, just as his mother, eyes red and wet with tears, swung the telescope to see what he witnessed: surfacing, dome up, the battered black derby, with a single strand of seaweed, like a rose upon a coffin.

Then rained down the next wave, and the hat was lost forever.

2

Three thousand four hundred miles eastward, it was nine o'clock in the morning. The autumn sun stretched thinly over Manhattan, and yet, as per local legend, it had still arranged itself so that 350 Fifth Avenue, the Waldorf=Astoria, did not fall into shadow.

At the Waldorf, breakfast was served. In its block-long kitchens, steam rose from copper kettles, Florida oranges rolled down pipe shafts to be cleaved for the juicer, the alchemical preparations for champagne truffles brought gourmet Pierre Revel from his usual tufted seat in the Hamilton Lounge into the kitchen for consultations on proper mincing of the negretto, a platoon of mushroom-hatted chefs from Brussels frowned as they tasted hollandaise sauce puddled on greenbrier-wood ladles, and a legion of metal whisks fluffed up sauces for the orders of eggs Benedict that Park Avenue doctors now prescribed as a morning antidote for the social side of the night before.

Then there was the sound of three chimes.

Cups froze, suspended in the air. A single chime meant a message for a guest in a room the size of a suite or smaller. Two chimes meant the message was for a guest in the Maidenhead Suite or even one of the penthouses. Conversations now began to dissolve like honey in warm water, for no one could quite remember having heard *three* chimes before.

A pageboy in white chinoise-silk gloves again struck the soft rubber mallet against his three-note glockenspiel. He called out, "Mr. Chaplin. Paging Charlie Chaplin." Which, in an instant, caused a ripple. Heads craned, and then, upon realizing what their owners had done, cheeks reddened.

And then the pageboy was gone, down the speckled Bidjar runner and into the lobby, where he again struck his three tones, and called out the name of Mr. Chaplin.

In the Colorado Rockies, at the Grand Imperial Hotel, which had indeed looked imperial in its mining days, the manager uncorked the intercom tube that, in theory, addressed all public areas—in practice, it worked about as well as stretching two tin cans along a length of string—and called, in a voice whose transposition along the ether made it shimmer like a mirage, "Will Charlie Chaplin please come to the lobby?"

And in the Alexandria Hotel of Los Angeles, California, a boy in a red pillbox hat cupped his hand to his jaw and cried, "Paging Charlie Chaplin. Charlie Chaplin, please report to the concierge desk." In a boarding house on the slopes of Butte, Montana, a landlady gingerly knocked on the door of the large bunk room, and cleared her throat so that the men in every dank cot could hear. "Is there a Charlie Chaplin here this morning?"

From the languid playpens of the Florida Gables to the great clapboard Outer Bank inns, from the flophouses of the Bowery to the pilgrims' resorts near the Great Salt Lake, there were pages for Mr. Charlie Chaplin. According to the *Boston Globe*, Chaplin was sought that morning in over eight hundred hotels.

3

Also that morning, on iron tracks through which sifted the East Texas dust, a sturdy 4-6-2 steam locomotive chugged eastward at forty miles per hour, towing its coal tender, four passenger cars, and caboose on the main route of the Beaumont, Sour Lake and Western Railway line. This was nick-named among those who knew it best the Belch, Slow Leak and Wheeze. Constructed during a flurry of interest in connecting the Midwest to the Gulf (the morning the line opened, its Missouri station was proclaimed "The Port of Kansas City"), it had been bought and sold and gone into receivership so often that the workers now demanded to be paid in cash. Still, service was mostly friendly, a "what the hey" camaraderie which accepted as a noble truth that, should you have business aboard the Belch, Slow Leak and Wheeze, you deserved commiseration.

On the train today were a handful of passengers, an engineer, his assis-tant, a conductor, two soused brakemen, an indolent fireman, and a seething porter who continually flipped a coin to determine if his sweet-heart had been faithless.

In the very rear, facing the receding horizon, alone, feet dangling through the iron rails of the caboose, eyes disconsolate and ill-focused, moped one Hugo Black. He was twenty-three years old. He wore the brown-and-elephant-gray overalls of the Beaumont, Sour Lake and West-ern Railway junior engineering staff as if they were prisoner's stripes.

Below a pencil-thin mustache, his mouth was moving; one schooled in the art of lip-reading would find that Hugo was silently pronouncing vil-lainous curses upon the world. In café French. His mastery of the idiom was astonishing, especially in that he had never been to France. He was mourning how moments ago the ill-glued spine of his Flaubert had caught in the wind. As the train rattled past Batson, pages of *Madame Bovary* scattered behind, fluttering into brambles as if brilliant French literature were simply a by-product of steam locomotion.

Hugo no longer had business on this train. He was the son of a professor at the University of Michigan. Hugo Black *père* was a scholar of mechanics, specializing in the design of railway trains. "I am an engineer of engineers," he had said, often, with the eternal hope that he might be found witty, and his son, after cringing through many summers of local railway work, had upon his graduation from college spread his wings as far from home as adventure allowed, seeking at first distant colleagues of his father's on the Chicago, Milwaukee & St. Paul, then the Lehigh Valley, and even two weeks on the Sinnemahoning tending to the needs of a splendid Mikado locomotive. But he consistently found his services were no longer required.

Between jobs, he returned to Michigan for cotillion season, tall and striking in a dinner jacket, with or without vents, executing flashy scarlet waltzes or Viennese rumbas. His family lived not quite in Grosse Pointe, or even quite on Jefferson Avenue, but two blocks away from the Immortals, in a house not quite as fine as the rest. This left his mother eternally vigilant as to class, grace, and aesthetic choices.

Hugo was unsure exactly when he lost his fellow employees on the Belch, Slow Leak and Wheeze, though no one had appreciated the wreath of prairie roses he had braided himself and hung over the staff lockers. Even after he had explained they were created in accordance with William Morris's principles of workplace ablative motifs, his fellow workers could not be said to embrace him. He understood and he tried to be patient, for he wanted to be helpful. But when he volunteered to while away the hours by reading aloud from John Ruskin, they asked that he no longer assist with the boiler, the wheel maintenance, the loading and unloading of baggage, but sit in the back and please be quiet. It was the "please" that killed. His rejection so complete it inspired *politeness*.

There, on the lonely caboose, with the last of the pages gone, and the book binding empty as a corn husk, Hugo considered whether he could at least announce he'd been reading Flaubert in the original French. He had no one to say it to, and so, instead, he let his heels smack against the car's empty coupling until he felt the vibrations ping up his shins, and he slumped while the train found the final slow curve along the Neches River, into the disaster awaiting them at Beaumont.

If the train cut through any particular atmosphere, it was the same suspended tension throughout the forty-eight states, an indrawn breath not yet expelled. The last week's presidential election had been fraught. There were recounts and challenges, and long days later, Woodrow Wilson was declared the winner, and the relief was palpable. America was still at peace.

Sunnyside

But when there was a long-enough lull—all it took was another day or so, news from Europe drifting onto the front pages again—it wasn't really silent anymore. Wayward winds blew to shore the terrible sounds of mortar fire, cries of wounded men, the lacquer tang of poison gas. America was on edge, everywhere, as if every man were glancing toward his rifle and then toward the neighboring barn, hearing cries of pain at sunset, and knowing that before morning came he was charged with the responsibility of shooting the family horse. One day—but when?—America would have to put old Europe out of its misery.

In the meantime, today, Sunday, the surprise guest, the picnic—this came as not just a respite but a blessing for the citizens of Beaumont, Texas. At the Beaumont train station, the burbling crowd drowned out the purple mourning doves cooing on the statues to Progress and Industry. Church bells were swinging as ineffectively as if the clappers had been stolen, for no one was at church.

There was a crow's nest fifty feet west of the station, and in it was a twelve-year-old girl who had courage and a spyglass. She wore exceptionally clean overalls and boots that had never known mud, and she had wind-burned skin, a brown-eyed stare pegged to eternity, and black hair that went easily into pigtails, and this was the single obedient part of her.

Her name was Rebecca Golod, and her fertile kin, all of them industrious, energetic, and argumentative, had come to Texas from the steppes of Russia ten years before, with stops in Toronto (not very friendly), Detroit (the same), Chicago (too many other Jews—it was like Russia all over again), and Biloxi (who wanted to live in Biloxi?). The Golods owned an entire block of Beaumont stores now, with cousins and nieces and nephews who flowed through the Russia-to-Texas pipeline as efficiently as any light sweet crude. Had there been a family crest, it would have shown two rampant hawks with beaks pinching each other's necks.

Roughly half of the family was crooked. The shady half was perpetually blackmailing the noble half to pay off gambling debts, drinking bills, schemes to open opium dens. Rebecca's spyglass was the only keepsake her grandfather had successfully smuggled out of Russia, having lost even the family samovar to guards at the Austrian border. She had determined that, among the screaming and shouting, she could distinguish herself, and still induce the kind of rage that seemed to mean that your parents truly loved you, by becoming the quietest, most humble, and most *honest* of all Golods. The type of girl who had organized her dolls by height (then, as she assigned them personalities, in order of their self-discipline), she decided she could be entrusted with delicate things, and so the spyglass was freed from Grandfather's closet and now comfortably dangled on a chain around her neck.

As one relative, then another spotted her in the crow's nest, each wailed as if hit in the foot with a mallet, looked for someone else in the family to blame, then called for her to come down and hand the spyglass back to Grandfather, but Rebecca put her finger to her lips, looked piqued, as if they were embarrassing her, and returned to looking for the 8:16 train.

On the platform, the Marine Band rehearsed "When the Saints Go Marching In" and its tricky segue to the "Spindletop Fight Song" near a table covered with checked cotton cloth, and on it chicken salad, baked beans, and, finally, their surfaces domed and ready to burst like volcanoes, perhaps a quarter acre of freshly baked pies. The finest people in town, those who had built their homes in The Oaks, lingered by their chauffeur-driven automobiles, for they had their own plans to spirit the guest toward private luncheons with blue-etched china plates shipped from Dresden and on them the amazing fact of tiny, round sandwiches that had *no crusts*.

Beaumont was home to the Spindletop gusher, whose eruption in 1901 had spilled a million barrels of oil even before it was capped. This was exciting to everyone, from the local boys who had found that dancing in the geyser was a fantastic method of causing their mothers to faint, to the petroleum companies—Humble, Gulf, Texas—who had generated wealth beyond reason.

"Thus," Mayor Knight whispered, rehearsing, finger in the air as if slicing through prevailing winds, bringing insight and prosperity, "were Texas a giant, you could lay her upon the bosom of Europe. And, with her head in repose upon the mountains of Norway, with London resting in one palm and Warsaw in the other, she could easily bathe her ponderous feet in the blue waters of the Mediterranean Sea. So, on behalf of the people of Beaumont, proud home of the Spindletop gusher"—he considered the delightful morning he'd had at the Pine Tree Café—"*and* home to the tastiest flapjacks in Jefferson County, we invite you, Charlie Chaplin, to take light refreshment and a morning drink with us."

"TRAIN'S COMING!" The yell came up from a fleet of boys running down the track. Rebecca frowned. With the naked eye, she could clearly see the steam from the smokebox chimney that floated over a locomotive shimmering in the distance, and yet she hadn't been able to see it through the spyglass. And then she saw that the lens was host to a wicked, spidery crack. She was tempted to shout down that the family heirloom was a piece of junk. Instead, she capped the lens, wondering with increasing anger how long her grandfather had kept its obsolescence from them; how betrayed she felt, what a *farbrekher* he was; then, lowering the spyglass into its protective leather satchel, she was chilled. Wasn't there a moment, climbing up, when she'd felt it strike the lodgepole-pine stand? Hard?

Since she was always so careful, she decided that this hadn't actually happened.

The band assembled into neat rows flanking the strongest boy in the twelfth grade, who wore a bass drum strapped to his belly, and who beat on it with a joyous rhythm from the heart of East Texas. There were last-minute panicked repinnings of bunting that had diabolically chosen this moment to sag, and all the town spilled onto the platform in a mass, from the patients at the Ralston Confederate Retirement Home in their wicker-strap wheelchairs to the girls who had turned out in their best dresses, dresses so fine that when the newspaper accounts described the catastrophe to come, they still spent inches serenading local color ("Miss Kate Ogden, pink albatross and white velvet; Miss Fannie Stewart, pink velvet; Miss Hattie Chapman, pale-lavender teatime dress"), and all the girls, no matter how much they hated the others' high-handed ways, stood linking arms so that—hang your light refreshment and a morning drink—*they* would be the most inviting sight for Chaplin's eye.

The 8:16 eased into the station with a belch and slow leak of steam, and then, as promised, a wheeze of ancient brakes. The conductor stood at the exit door, watch heavy in his hand, as if his weighing the correct time might explain this massive crowd.

Rebecca threaded her way between adults until she was in sight of the caboose, where there stood a young man with a razor's-edge mustache and a baroque nose. He put his hands on his hips and fixed the crowd with an angry, disappointed look. Rebecca almost gasped. She thought he had the condemning weight of storybook nobility, a landowner ashamed of his serfs. She wondered if Charlie Chaplin traveled with, among his many friends, royalty.

The band launched into "Over There," which annoyed Mayor Knight: there had been discussion of why exactly Chaplin hadn't enlisted, and he wanted to extend the feeling of welcome rather than guilt. "Play something else! Anything!" he yelled.

"There he is!" The cry came from the throat of a sensible man, Dr. Franklin, and the crowd pressed forward, and a figure appeared at the head of a passenger car. That it was Eugenia Burkhardt in her daisy poke-bonnet, returning from her trip to Houston, in no way diminished Beaumont's enthusiasm. Eugenia, who had never thought much of Beaumont, ignored the hands pulling at her, and the questions of where Chaplin was, until she finally rapped her umbrella against Bethyl Taylor, who was trying to hug her.

By the caboose, Rebecca tentatively waved at her elegant stranger, who was of course Hugo Black, in the hope he might wave back. She had a hunch, which had crept up on her as hunches did for children in folktales who listened to the advice given by magic mirrors or voices whispering from wells: the multitudes around her were missing an actual prince in their midst.

"That's him!" This time the cry came from many places. Nonetheless, the person leaving the train was only mournful Joe Nailer, in his only good suit, who waved glumly, as if crowds greeted him every day of his life.

Whenever there was motion inside the train, ripples went through the crowds on the platform, and Rebecca was jostled, which required her to give narrow looks to many of her neighbors. A conductor in a sharp black cap yelled at her prince, who snapped to attention as no prince ever would.

From here, it was a small leap for her to suspect that Charlie Chaplin wasn't really on the train.

When the porter opened the baggage compartment, a half dozen people fell over, trying to see inside, as if Chaplin—of course!—were traveling under the train like a railway rat, perhaps to surprise them in costume.

"Folks! Folks, stand back from the train!" This was obeyed easily enough—they had to give him some room, that was understandable. Still, it took some time, and the conductor continued, "The train cannot leave the station until there is room, so please stand back."

The crowd did not stand back: they were here to see Chaplin, who was here to see them.

"Where's Charlie?" a girlish voice cried. It was Rebecca Golod. The question took seed. "Where's Charlie?" It was an easy name to join in on, two syllables, and it seemed so friendly at first, "Char-lie, Char-lie, Char-lie."

The conductor consulted with the engineer, and two redcaps stepped up to see what was the matter. Rebecca noticed her young man join them. Within moments, the uniformed men had finally found a use for their imperious-looking college-educated charge, Hugo Black: it was his job to disperse the crowd.

This Hugo took to with vigor, fluttering the backs of his hands at the crowd as if shooing an insistent hobo's dog away from a freshly glazed ham. The chant of "Char-lie, Char-lie, Char-lie" went darker.

The engineer blew the steam whistle, readying the train to go. Farmhands lifted their friends onto their shoulders, and they beat against the train, drumming their palms on the sheet metal in an apoplectic dissonance that caused Hugo to wince. Bravely, he began to lecture from the iron steps of the passenger car, adapting freely from a *Ladies' Home Journal* essay he'd read by Mrs. Alfred Astor about how easily sidewalk etiquette was achieved on Park Avenue, and he explained into the din how those simple lessons of common courtesy dictated that the crowd should disperse. Remembering the impact of the word, he added, "Please!"

He saw just one person looking his way: a little girl. He cocked his head and raised his eyebrows, and he smiled. Humbly, he thought. Her own eyebrows went south, eyes narrowing as if squeezing the last of daylight from them.

Hugo then saw what was around her neck. It was so incongruous his voice spoke on its own accord. "Good grief! Is that a Zeiss Optical spyglass?"

His heartbeat, which had been hammering in nervousness, mellowed. To see this in Texas made the rest of the world oblique; he felt suspended in a bubble outside of which all was blurred and vague. A Zeiss Optical spyglass was the pride of European technology, a salute to Old World charm and warmth, a slender fluted slide with a reeded edge calibrated for sensitive fingers. His father had one, calling it "too sweet for the workaday," and they had used it on weekends together, looking for birds. He remembered his father's hand on his shoulder. "Pardon," he asked, for the girl had said something.

"It's my grandfather's," she whispered again. He could just barely hear her voice, though she had tiptoed closer, two strides away from his stairs.

"I'm sure it is, but——" He broke off, for his own voice was submerged by the tuba player of the band, who had let out an emotive blat of frustration. Hugo swallowed. "I have one, too. At home. I'll be careful."

Hugo had been forgotten by everyone, save Rebecca. Somewhere behind her, someone dropped a bottle, which caused her to look over her shoulder to see one of the hoodlum children, an enormous sixth-grader who was rumored to be twenty-two years old, picking up a hank of broken railway tie and testing for tensile strength by whacking it against one of his callused palms.

As Rebecca approached, Hugo glanced toward the exits, since it was apparent people were walking away. He thought his lecture had worked. But there were actually two distressing developments. First, people were linking arms on the track ahead (putting down blankets so they could sit without dirtying themselves), and, second, the departing Beaumont citizens were only walking as far as the brickyard, where the proprietor, jangling his ring of keys, waved them in.

Hugo, innocent of this view, whispered to Rebecca, "May I hold your Zeiss Optical spyglass?"

There was no reason to let this man touch such a valuable object, but Rebecca realized with a merciless crackle up her spine that such thinking did not become a Golod. Wordlessly, she removed the spyglass from its case, and then took the chain from around her neck, like slipping off a bridle.

Rebecca felt as light and generous as if supported by angels, and Hugo reached for it, cupping his hand as Rebecca confidently, with a determination beyond her years, dropped the spyglass, lens first, onto the concrete platform.

It rolled in a semicircle.

Rebecca found her voice. It was a low, almost subsonic moan that ascended in volume and timbre until it sounded as epic and awful as the misery of a garroted winter wolf.

"You—broke—my—spyglass!"

She was aware, without turning, of the shadow behind her, the way any animal could sense the presence of kin. It was the shadow of someone huge. Hugo was so transfixed by the squalling girl that he went dimwitted. He caught a blur: a left hand that had, on the bitter spring mornings on the steppes of Drohitchen, during troubled whelpings, pulled calves from their mothers' wombs with a single tug, found Hugo's shirt collar. It yanked him forward and off the train.

This was excellent news, briefly, in that the first brick hurtling through the air missed Hugo. It thudded against the train cab stairs just as Hugo's entire field of vision filled with a permafrost of impenetrable white beard surrounding a pit of angry teeth that had known only Russian frontier dentists. This was Abraham Golod, Rebecca's grandfather, owner of the spyglass, and as his left fist continued to reel in Hugo by the collar, his right fist, black as an ironmonger's mallet, punched him in the face. Hugo's head snapped back, his legs buckled under his weight as if they were blades of grass, he heard warbling birds and gamboling children, and he wanted to tell them hello, but he was already unconscious.

Rebecca stood wide-eyed, nostrils flaring and mouth open as if every sense were eager to take in all available wisdom from this moment. Had she actually blamed her tarnished prince for the spyglass? How awful of her! Had that resulted in her slithering out of trouble? How not-quite-awful. Her grandfather grabbed her by the arm. When she resisted, he threw her over his shoulder and strode through the crowd toward their Ford flatbed truck, his shattered spyglass now in one fist.

"Today you ride in the back!"

"But, Grandpa—"

"With the vegetables. In the back!"

Their discussion went unnoticed, the air already gone dusty red, a convocation of bricks soaring in parabolas, colliding with the train, bouncing off sheet metal, cracking windows.

"Char-lie! Char-lie! Char-lie!"

While ranchers clambered in through the window frames, wildcat workers fanned into a passenger car, coughing the name like bloodhounds treeing a fugitive. Luggage compartments were thrown open, and each successive valise, portmanteau, and Dutch satchel that was discovered not to be Charlie Chaplin was heaved out the window, until the skies over the platform were heavy with the rain of neckties, trousers, crêpe de chine smocks. Travelers and train workers were marched down the aisles and to the platform, where the crowds demanded, "Where is he?" and did not listen to the answers.

The portmanteaux and satchels were thrown back first, and, in a savage response to the man who had so terribly dismissed their hospitality, came the light refreshments and pitchers of beer. And then a single pie. It half disintegrated on the way, crust and filling slapping against the train like an upsplash of mud.

Hugo, who could not account for several recent minutes, was crawling, bloody as an anchorite, from the train and toward daylight at the edge of the mob. He arose near the picnic tables. His face felt as if he'd slept on a clothes iron.

He watched the crowd swarm over the train: passenger-car seats were ripped open, their straw stuffing used as kindling, and then, with a careful sprinkle of the God-given, plentiful, and rich local gasoline, the train was set afire.

The rest of the assault—pipes beating on the train, bricks, harassment of passengers—came to a halt, for the spectacle of the burning train was impressive. Hugo had never actually seen a mob before, but this certainly confirmed all he had heard about them. There was a stiff crackle, and he flinched before a sound like rivets popping, the fire finding a cache of ammunition in someone's suitcase.

But passenger cars made poor targets for arson; once the seats and wallpaper were consumed, there was just a no-longer-exciting trickle of smoke going skyward. By then, word had passed through the crowd that perhaps they had made a mistake and it would be best to go home.

When a horde lost its purpose, it was like the sun disappearing in a fog bank. The entire town brushed past Hugo, finding fascinating objects in the middle of the lowlands to stare at. He looked to the picnic tables, where there still sat the quarter acre of pies. His eye was swelling shut, his nose was clotting with blood, there was a bruise that throbbed from his jaw to his cheekbone, and he was running his tongue from tooth to tooth, testing them all for number and fixity.

And yet the pies smelled delicious. The nearest was sweating, its vents swollen with a deep-blueberry ooze. Hugo wondered how a person decided to throw a pie. And why was that supposed to be funny?

With a flick of his eyes, he grabbed a pie in each hand. He limped with determination to a pillar draped with bunting, where he carefully sat with a groan, cross-legged. The pies were slightly warm, and the smell of strawberries and rhubarb was overwhelming. He excavated a palmful of custard filling. The taste was glorious, tempered only by the trouble he had working his jaw. Then he took another pawful of the sticky fruit and crust, and closed his eyes. Heaven.

The train had been destroyed, but he laughed, for he had hated everyone on the train. He glanced toward the station-agent cottage, alive with telegraph activity. As soon as they were done reporting the damages to the company, he would need to wire his father. He put a sticky fist under his chin. He realized, with a shudder, that he needed another goddamned job.

Meanwhile, in the station-agent cottage, the telegraph operator was taking notes with confusion while men all around gave combative monologues punctuated with foul gestures. Beyond the current emergency was something far larger. The engineer, cheek smeared with soot, was telephoning other train operators down the line. On railways across the country that did not link to East Texas, Chaplin *had also been expected*!

Further, the railways were not the only places people had gathered and been disappointed. There were riots on the docks of the Gulf of Mexico, and in Rye, New York, at an airstrip, a mob had tipped over an airplane he was supposed to be on, snapping off the propeller and rolling it down a muddy hillside.

The next week's *Beaumont Sentinel* ran a full account with photos of the unfortunate event. After a chronology of the riot, Beaumont's first, was a statement from Mayor French admitting they had been confused. "What we are trying to ascertain is why we all thought Chaplin was coming. I would swear the Widow Candless said so, but she says she heard it from me."

So Beaumont, in the course of a few hours, had gone from prosperity and the prospect of fame, to being the home of a burnt-out shell of a passenger train. The cars sat on the siding with occasional wisps of smoke and ash rising into the air, and when the winds carried toward town, people would stiffen in embarrassment, then continue on their way.

They were not alone. The next day, the *Kansas City Star* asked in its headline, "HAD YOU THE CHAPLIN-ITIS?" There was an account of his being paged in over eight hundred hotels, the failed rescue at sea off the California coast, his anticipated arrival at train stations, and below was an artist's conception of that day's commotion in Kansas City, when Chaplin had been seen wreaking havoc at the baseball field, knocking down an outfielder as he dove for a fly ball. He stumbled through a church picnic in Knoxville, and in New York City, at 31st and Sixth Avenue, he tied up traffic during a manic boxing match with a hotheaded bruiser of a cop. He was seen clutching the mane of a horse galloping across a field in West Virginia, and falling into a vat of offal in a Chicago stockyard. And then he was gone.

☆　☆　☆

Such is the nature of the inexplicable that, as long as it does not involve money, it can be ignored. Within several weeks, the Chaplin-itis was forgotten, except for one small report.

A circular was issued by the American Society for Psychical Research, a group founded in 1885 in Boston by curious men, including, as they never failed to mention, William James, dean of skeptical inquiry and father of America psychology. After his death, it had become much more satisfying for the remaining founders to *believe* than to *evaluate,* and currently the Society was tilting toward defense of the ethereal world. The circular on Chaplin was written by a Professor Bamfylde Moore Carew ("the Bohemian rhapsodist," as he was known).

Charlie Chaplin, Professor Carew wrote,

> has become an American obsession, and among young and active minds, Chaplin is a subject of constantly recurrent thought. We find beyond peradventure that on Nov. 12 there existed a Chaplin impulse, which extended the length and breadth of the continent.

After several expository paragraphs (including a rhetorical blackjack taken to the knees of his enemies in physics, psychology, and *Scientific American*), Carew concluded:

> There is a new medium which we do not yet understand the psychology behind, the filmed photoplay. For the first time, our "hero" has fame not predicated on his presence before us, but upon a technology that renders him both real and imaginary. Not since the days of the prophets have we all so swiftly agreed that a single entity, one suffering many of life's mishaps, can answer so many of our needs. We needed Charlie Chaplin to be our alter ego—or perhaps simply our ego itself—and so he came to us. Psychologists, those alarmists, call it mass hysteria. I call it a shared dream, a fairy tale, the birth of a myth. Today is a new beginning.

There Professor Carew's argument finished, never to be examined or expanded. He did not indicate what exactly was beginning. No one seems to have inquired. Instead, the moment was over, and the world and all its inhabitants could move on.

Unless, of course, you happened to be one particular person.

His start was rocky. In his first films, age twenty-four, 1914, Keystone Studios, he ambles into shots as if thrown from the wings and unsure where his audience is hiding. His gaze is distant and calculating, that of a boxer sizing up opponents whose looming shadows no one can quite see.

Sunnyside

Only a year later, already making $1,250 a week, he is a different man. Footage of his first day of work at Essanay, Chicago, January 1915, survives. In front of his new cast, crew, and bosses, in a shabby but honest suit of welterweight dark wool, he performs a ninety-second clog dance, hands on hips in mock concentration, gathering speed and flinging off flop sweat as if terrified he isn't dazzling enough. Then he jumps in place like a drunk in a barroom dodging the bullets of savage cowboys, executing each recoil with such expertise you can almost see splinters and the shock of sawdust from six-guns firing into the floor. And then, miming rescue, he radiates bounteous joy by loping like a fawn in the woods. He finishes by tossing daisies (where did he find daisies in the Chicago winter?) to the assemblage; in just three seconds, he shifts his shoulders, goes *en pointe*, performs a curtsy, and falls flat on his behind.

The last moment is almost but not quite a blur: he springs back into position with the shy grin of an undersized youth at his first day of work, and then, eyes flicking darkly to each and every person, awaits their terrible judgment; he gives a start of realization, his finger goes across his throat for the cameraman, and the rest of the entr'acte is unrecorded.

A year after that, twenty-six months after his first film, he is earning over ten thousand dollars a week, making him the highest-paid man in America (the president of United States Steel, upon learning this, was said to have gone to the foundry, reviewed his empire of cooling girders, and mused that the continent was built on more things than he yet understood).

The interviews with *Photoplay* and *Motion Picture Weekly* and *Footlights* began to contain moral instruction. He wished to be known no longer just as a comedian but also as an expert tennis player, composer, pugilist, a clever dancer, golfer, motorist (though never at excessive speeds), and, most of all, "a stickler for poetry." He visited the chiropodist, spent hours reading fan mail, and was in bed nightly by ten p.m. "after a cool shower," a code clear to anyone: he was a man who lived the cleanest of lives. Shockingly, there was not a single lie in it (he never claimed, for instance, to *answer* his fan mail).

He assured the National Board of Review that his dramatics would no longer be vulgar: "I shall steer clear of the Elizabethan style and strive toward the more subtle and the fine. Not all films must end with a climactic pie fight." At a Hippodrome Theatre benefit for the wounded of Belgium, he eschewed comedy, conducting instead a piece of music he had composed, "The Peace Patrol," which he introduced as a celebration of the dove. The reception was so frosty—the audience had expected a knuckle-dusting march of revenge—he reluctantly churned the air with a baton-as-cane, turned out his toes, and did "the walk" until, as he later said, "they no longer wanted to kill me."

The dreary performance, a sodden winter rain, caused questions to spring up like dandelions. Did he not support the Allies, including his own native country of England? Did he mean to enlist? And why wasn't he funny that evening?

He was driven to explain himself in *Photoplay.* "I was born in a hotel in Fontainebleau, where my parents were performing. My father was Spanish, and I never knew him before he passed on. But my mother was a saint, it must be said. Wherever we lived around Lambeth, no matter how poor we were, even if she had to break us from the workhouse to do it, she used to sit me down in Kennington Park and have me watch the people. 'What are they thinking? What are they like? How do they act?' We never had money, so we had to make our own entertainment, and she was the best mimic I have known. Her death . . ." And here he left the table, choking back tears reported as "dragged forth by a gravity previously unsuspected in the buoyant man who makes a million others laugh." Who is to say an ocean of laughs did not seep from a secret source, a font of tears?

Fifty million eyes welled up. Every ditchdigger knew a happy drunk whose life was misery, every soldier in France had death branded on his own still-beating heart, every critic remembered his Versio Vulgata, *Medice, cura te ipsum,* and who was the Little Tramp's master but the physic of laughter who could never heal himself?

As of November 12, 1916, there were fifty-seven films, each one a cry from a broken heart. And here was the irony: for everyone on earth, everyone excluding him, every film was tonic for the soul beset by life's frustrations writ small, by its disasters gone epic, and, of course, by the distant thunder, the lightning over the hill, of the European War.

The Los Angeles Athletic Club boasted a waiting list of every bachelor in the city who could afford its well-tended rooms. It sported the finest gymnasium, boxing ring, wrestlers' mats, spa, and Olympic pool. For socializing, there was a chummy English clubroom whose dark oak walls positively groaned with baleful-looking game animals gazing upon a snooker table that was said to be from Windsor Castle, though it was likely that royalty's snooker tables wouldn't divot so easily, and anyone indisposed enough to spend time beneath it would see grease pencil noting its retirement from the Triangle Studios. Still, it was agreed upon not to discuss too harshly the charms of the snooker table.

The Athletic Club's suites on the third floor were designed for escape, rest, and meditation. They were airy and well insulated. No music was allowed, though a recent exception had been made for violin. It was a concession on behalf of one particular bachelor, in Suite E. His violin playing was agreed upon by management and fellow boarders to be on a par with Mischa Elman, perhaps—the violinist himself despaired as much—in the same vein as their agreement about the origins of the snooker table. He was a courteous fellow, batting away compliments, preferring instead to compare golf swings or uppercuts, to speculate about marlin fishing, or risk a vague but sophisticated comment about the exquisite quality of local women. But then, always, at ten o'clock, hours before the rest had settled down, he vanished to his suite.

And in the conversations that followed, prompted by the young men who filled the game room after eleven o'clock, the questions would begin. "But what's he like?"

"He's nice" was the universal response, universally found wanting. "Nice" was hardly even an adjective. The round-robin comments (Is he funny? Is he conceited? Who's his sweetheart? Has he done anything funny? I know the man who told him to make a crêpe mustache. He's not that funny) echoed out of the game room and up the mezzanine to the second flight of stairs, where, long after he said he'd gone to bed, a small figure sat at the head of the stairs with a violin across his lap, plucking at the strings, reversed for a left-handed player, and debating with himself about whether just to go down these two flights of stairs and join everyone. He never joined everyone.

His suite had piles of books borrowed from the library downstairs, and exposure to the distant ocean, and, at its opposite exposure, the chaparral of the local hills. At night, you could see signs of tiny settlements poking up among the orange groves, the distant lights of Hollywood like a diamond bar pin, and the nearer lights, those of all downtown Los Angeles, the thriving center of culture, commerce, and transportation, were an unimpressive haul of jewels, not quite as many as could be purchased by looting the treasury of any prairie town. Los Angeles had not yet found its own identity, though its supporters were sure that day was coming; as of yet, it had the soul of the Midwest. Since it hadn't cultivated any morals of its own, it borrowed those of the Midwest, too. There were few dinner parties, no frenzies in the street about the local movie stars (Los Angeles was unsure if it wanted to be known for either frenzy or movies); no bookstores sold *Harper's* or other upsetting magazines, clergy ate for free at cafés that otherwise discouraged dawdling over coffee and pie, and the beds at the Club were single bunks. Everyone seemed to know and care about one another's business.

When the winds were blowing properly, the bachelor in Suite E, blessed with exposures on both sides, could put down his violin and his books and lie awake for hours, listening to the songs of coyotes among the smells of sage and orange blossoms. Dawn came accompanied by gulls and the tang of sea spray. But he rarely slept through the night, staying awake instead and thinking that if Los Angeles were a village, then, by definition, he was the village idiot.

Nine blocks away, on a side street whose name no married man could quite recall when asked, was the Engstrom, the ladies' hotel. Its manager, its owner, and its detectives were recent émigrés with talent not just for hospitality but also for tact and continental decorum. Once, a newly hired night manager had turned from a woman who had just signed the register to the man escorting her, and said, "It's amazing, Miss Jones, how much your uncle looks like Adolph Zukor," and he was promptly sacked, driven to the railway station, and never heard from again.

It was a quiet place. Thus it was without precedent that at dawn on Sunday morning, November 12, 1916, a woman ran screaming through the lobby, and, still screaming, to the street. That it was Edna Purviance, an actress with something of a reputation to keep, made it even more surprising.

She ran, one hand to her mouth, the other holding shut her wrapper, which she had thrown on over an explosion of whatever had come to hand first—men's wool trousers from the Mutual wardrobe department, a pajama top, boots.

At the corner of 3rd and Figueroa, she paused to catch her breath. Tears ran down her face; she sniffled and attempted to hold them back. She then proceeded to walk at a steady clip. She was rarely like this. Normally, Edna strolled through life with a faint smile on her face, as if she had heard a terrific joke, and would repeat it if you wanted, and even though she might get the details confused, and the punch line inverted, the two of you would be laughing so hard by then it hardly mattered. She had an orphan child's expressive eyes that were as warm and round as pancakes, and a Junoesque body whose curves seemed seductive in a cabaret scene, comic if dunked under water, and matronly in the fadeout, when she had romanced the hero.

Although not a great beauty by local standards, which were rising by the day, she was known as a good sport. She was never the first to suggest a day at the lake, but she did keep a swimsuit by her makeup table. Level-headed, unambitious, in no hurry to marry, a fine actress in the two-reelers, she had only one character flaw—a propensity to, when ignored at parties, faint dead away into the arms of the closest handsome man.

She had been acting for two years, neither rising nor falling in stature, but consistent in that her only leading man had been Charlie Chaplin. Whose death in a skiff off St. George Reef had just been reported to her by telephone.

So now she rocked on the heels of her worn leather boots at the corner of 6th and Olive, a block away from the Athletic Club. The wide avenues were deserted, built for crowds who hadn't yet arrived. Los Angeles barely had Saturday nights, and Sunday mornings, unless you were a farmer, were equally desolate. It was too early for church or the fish market. The trolley cars were still in their barn. The sky was brightening and throwing shadows so deep they seemed to carry their own echoes. The architecture of the lumpen four-story Federal-style buildings—banks, offices, city departments—was safe, borrowed from other cities, as if the locals were still looking for permission actually to build here.

Edna thought this was the least picturesque corner in all of Los Angeles. Not a single girl in the whole of the United States would see this corner in a film and decide to throw off Atlanta or Omaha or Rochester. Nor, Edna thought, would she have come, not today, from Lovelock, Nevada. She clutched at her wrap as a brief, shockingly cold November wind harassed its edges. Three weeks before, she had turned twenty-one years old.

She returned to walking, step by step, on the recently poured sidewalk. The Athletic Club was right before her, flags of the world undulating above its four concrete pillars. But this was awful—she couldn't go through the lobby, the receptionist would stop her. "Let me through—I know he's dead"—it sounded like a line some girl would use to see him.

When they were apart for more than a week, she would send him a note that read, "Be good, and if you can't be good, be careful." After the first time, he'd just held up the old note, to show he'd kept it. And when he'd returned to her the next time, he held up a subtitle card he'd written himself. On a black background, wreathed by the Mutual Studios wheat-sheathing, It just read, "Good." She lived in mild fear of the reunion when he would hold up a card that read, "Careful."

Edna walked to the alleyway that ran behind the Club, and found the white linens-truck that was always parked in a tactically advantageous place in the early morning (she wasn't the first person in the history of the Club who might need to use a discreet entrance). Tossing the wrapper to the ground, she stepped up to the truck cab, and from there was able to grasp the lowest rung of the fire escape.

Her boots caused the slats on the ladder to ring like a pitchfork, until she learned how to muffle her step. It was quick work, up two switchbacks, and then she was outside Charlie's window. There was his work desk, with the neatly tied piles of correspondence that he had never answered. Stacks of books on the dustless floor. There was his standing wardrobe. His upright piano, which he had moved in after the violin had been approved. And there was his bed, empty.

She held her fist to her mouth, teeth biting into her knuckles. The windowpane was beginning to glow pink, then orange with the sun. She could hear pigeons. And, on streets far away, the clomping of horses' hooves, and an impatient car horn. She squinted harshly toward the sounds—how could the world go on if Charlie was gone?

"We're like a couple of lost dogs who like each other," he'd said on a picnic, down on the deserted beach near Balboa. He had tried to braid her a necklace of kelp; she had saved a single bead of it and meant to keep it, but she lost it almost immediately, when they were still kissing. When he was about to go before the camera, she would call out, "Go on, be cute," which punctured his balloon quite nicely, and thinking of it now made her stomach clench into a knot, and she wept. "Oh, Charlie," she whispered, looking again into his window.

She wiped her large eyes with the back of her wrist. For she noticed two things: First, the bed had been made, quickly, not in any professional manner. And, second, the pigeons were not just cooing; there was an excited mass of fluttering wings nearby. The roof.

Sunnyside

She ascended the fire escape, which jutted over the crowning cornice. Hand over hand, step by step upward, until her watering eyes were level with the tarpaper and composite, which was beginning to warm and glitter.

The distant orange hills made a cradle behind the Club's sparkling roof, where the caps of many airshafts made flamboyant spires, and among them were eccentric weathervanes hewn from copper gone green—ships, roosters, nude women, and witches on brooms—squawking as the wind turned them.

The pigeon coop in the center of the roof, its already faded and chipped paint a mural of bizarre abstract winged figures, was a gift from the same man who'd made the weathervanes, Pablo Picasso of Paris, France, a man in love with *las palomas,* fantail pigeons. In a letter sent to the Mutual Studios, he had compared how he felt when observing their motion in flight to how he felt when watching a Charlie Chaplin film.

As Edna could see, the coop was bursting with excitement, the rock doves of gray and white, the racing banded blue checks and blue bars, all crying and wings beating furiously, for there were cats everywhere.

The Athletic Club had three expert mousers, and they were here, but there were a half dozen more, orange and white and tabby, come from God-knew-where, circling a solitary half-broken Queen Anne chair before the pigeon coop. They were rubbing up against its chipped legs, clawing at the stuffing that escaped from its torn velvet arms. Sitting in the chair was Charlie.

He slouched in his orange bathrobe, hair a nest of black, slept-on curls. Two cats sat in his lap, grooming themselves, and another was taking tentative steps across his shoulders.

Edna could not speak. She climbed over the railing and trotted clumsily across the roof, and there, bathed in light already so bright that the sun and Los Angeles could see every move, her excitement scattering cats and causing a ruckus in the pigeon house, she fell on him and smothered him with kisses.

She plunked down into his lap, which jarred the chair to its limits, but it held, and she laughed, mauling his hair and pecking at his forehead. He seemed a wreck. He was holding a telegram, and even when he finally began to smile in confusion and pleasure, saying, "Now, now, you'll turn my head, gal," he did not let go of it.

"You're all right?"

"Shouldn't I be?"

"I don't know," she said. "I heard the most remarkable thing. . . ." She looked to the telegram.

He shrugged. "It's nothing. What's wrong, Lovelock?"

"I heard you drowned."

"Pardon me?"

"At sea."

He laughed. He hugged her. They were just about the only people in the country who weren't involved in the rest, and so their rooftop was a little Shangri-La, in its way. For a few more minutes, while it was still quiet.

"I keep thinking"—she swallowed—"you're about to leave." She kissed him again. "And I'll find you gone."

"I'm not going anywhere."

"If you have to go, be careful."

"I'm very careful. And good—you know that."

She nodded, but vaguely, for he knew how to act like a man who was sincere. "What's in the telegram?"

"My mother is coming to America," he said.

"Your mother?" She searched his eyes in confusion. "I thought she died, years ago."

"Yes. I said that." And he looked at her in a way not formerly in their lovers' repertoire. His shoulders were stiff, and he was remote—that had happened before—but it was as if he were on a ship, as if he were about to call out in a foreign language and hope the natives ashore spoke it, too. "She's alive. And coming here."

"That's wonderful?"

He shifted his weight under hers. He began to accept her caresses, and leaned his head against her side. It had hardly been the right thing to say, she realized, but the rising inflection at the end had kept it from being entirely wrong. He reached between the buttons of her flannel pajama top to touch her skin. With the other hand, he folded and refolded the telegram perfectly, edges lining up as sharply as a knife blade.

He smiled. "I like that you never wear a corset."

She wondered who he knew that wore a corset, but instead she asked, "Why are you up here?"

He had come because, an hour earlier, his valet had handed him the telegram that announced his mother was coming. Churning with it, pacing, he had come to the roof. And so had missed the other news of the day, his visitations. He had scratched an ever-changing troupe of cats behind the ears and calmed down. Just because his mother was coming didn't mean she would bring chaos with her.

Right now, Chaplin was at peace. Because he was not answering his phone, because the operator at the Club did not know where he was, there were others besides Edna on their way. Soon there would be a rush up the street, soon the sidewalk would be overflowing with his brother, his newly hired secretary, his newly hired publicist, his technical directors, financiers, friends, starlets who knew him, starlets who didn't. They would be on the sidewalk, they would mount the fire escape as if they were ants climbing over one another, heads would pop out of every window on the street. And when he appeared, standing on the roof's edge and looking down on the street to give a pleasant wave and to pretend to fall off, to recover, they would laugh with relief, and then they would stare at him for a moment longer in a way different from ever before. And he would notice this. But not yet. These were the last moments when Chaplin could still think of himself in a certain way.

"What are you thinking, Charlie?" Edna kissed his hand.

He ran a finger down her top and flicked open a button like picking a rose. He whispered, "I'm thinking about love," and Edna looked left and right to see if she and Charlie could be seen by anyone; they couldn't, and so she smiled, and, with the rising street noise, the shouts of paper boys and grocers and movie folk below them, Chaplin thought and rethought, as if practicing the same four measures on his violin, that the only way to keep a person's love was to be unworthy of it, and he watched how the lovely local light caught Edna's eyes before they closed for him.

Travelogue

Unter dem Licht der westlichen Sterne

Viewed as a drama, the war is in some ways disappointing.

—D. W. Griffith (1916)

1

In the 1890s, Crescent City, California, was no longer a paradise of mines and copper ore, and the age in which the local acres of redwood could support an economy had not quite dawned. So all there was—was the sea. Which meant that daily life depended on the harbor, the canvas sails and forged steel rudders of boats and ships and steamers, the songs of the fishermen, how Elk Creek dumped into the ocean, the way diving pelicans gave up schools of feeder fish, how terns pecked for sand dollars beside the salt water. There were perhaps eight hundred souls here, and all of them respected Emily Wheeler because of her lighthouse, which everyone depended on.

When Leland Wheeler was small, he walked with his mother across the tidepool line. She told him there were tides twice a day, and never to play when the water touched Serpent Rock, because it meant you would be trapped in Timber Cove, with no way to get out.

Once, before dinner, while she was shredding carrots with a knife she'd sharpened herself on a whetstone she'd conditioned herself, she declared, "You'd have to cling to the rock all night long, and I would have to find you."

He was seven years old. He considered what his mother was saying. "Maybe you couldn't find me."

"I'd find you," she said.

"You didn't find the sailors from that frigate."

She put down the knife. "They were stupid," she said. She resumed her shredding. "And they weren't my son."

She introduced him to starfish and abalone, and how to pry them away from the rocks with a hunting knife, which he wasn't allowed to touch. And here were hermit crabs and there were fiddler crabs and sea anemones ("If you put a finger in there, they will suck it in and it will never come out." "Could you get it out?" "I could. But it would be very dangerous") and sea urchins, the last of which he was allowed to take home if the spines were falling out, for that meant they were dead.

He grew up believing that the world was a place that invited his mother's rescue. And between the ages of six and ten, he touched hermit crabs, put his finger in sea anemones, removed living urchins from their beds, and even stole the hunting knife from its hiding place in the broom closet.

The first time he was trapped in Timber Cove by high water, he was sure he was doomed, but was also curious whether his mother would somehow sense it, like a high whine only a dog could hear, and whether the station-house boat would appear on shore, with her in her uniform to scoop him up. He was surprised to see that, even though the waves were crashing against Serpent Rock, he could wade through them, and then he was on the other side, safe.

The next several times he trapped himself there, he had a great deal of time on his hands (for a child, a half hour spent waiting for the tide to rise might as well be six weeks). He speculated on how angry his mother would be. He could do her voice, rising, announcing his luck at having her for a mother.

He had never seen her row. So he populated the boat with aides and ensigns, and he did their voices, too, and he sat on the sand, rowing in place, giving himself stern orders that he dared not disobey, for he was going to rescue Sergeant Wheeler's little boy, who was always in trouble.

No matter how often he put himself in harm's way, Emily never needed to rescue him.

Here was the conversation Leland and his mother had most often:

"Lee? Lee!"

"Mom?"

"Are you all right?"

"Yes, Mom."

Then, always, a turn of the head so that one supernaturally clever eye could determine whether he knew what he was talking about.

When he was very small, he had to consider—if his mother wondered, perhaps he wasn't well. But then he learned to answer quickly, "I'm all right." Said with exasperation, until he learned that impatience was treated with castor oil.

He never cried as a child. He sensed it wasn't worth it. The "I'm all right" was delivered with a flat demeanor. He learned how to vary "all right" with "well," or a wise nod as if he were weighing many complex feelings, or, when he wanted to make her laugh, "adequate."

When he was playing outside, he could feel her eyes upon him. He didn't mind; the attention was flattering. When he climbed trees, he would hang upside down from a low branch. He took to waving fondly, even if she wasn't there, as if he had an audience.

Emily was impressed, then baffled, then concerned by the progression of Leland's "Why?"s. His questions evolved from "Why do we live in a lighthouse sometimes?" and "Why does the current change twice a day?" to, when he was about eleven, "Why are we alive?"

The first time he asked this was after dinner at his grandparents' cottage, which was about a hundred yards from their own. He and his mother were walking home along the sandy pathway, and he blurted it out. She seized on her first thought: See that wave in the distance? We're here to see how lovely it is. God wants us to see beauty and to make the lives of others better. And there's a pleasure in responsibility.

For the next weeks, he asked it repeatedly, in different ways, in questions about ambition, about existence: Why was she a lighthouse keeper? Why not just stay in bed all day? Why do chores when nothing actually mattered, if you thought about it?

"You should go play," she said in exasperation.

"But I'm plagued by feelings of unreality." He wasn't looking to get smacked; he was perfectly serious.

"Lee, you have a reason to exist."

"What?"

"You have to trust me on that."

The look on his face chilled her. He tried to look exuberant, but it was as if a bright shroud lay over a wounded animal. His serious eyes took on a melancholy bent that she recognized from long before, which frightened her and made her miss someone, and then they were back to being an eleven-year-old's.

Three weeks in a row, he failed his mathematics tests. The subject was geometry, for which he had no use, and his mind was beginning to wander outside the confines of the town. This week, it was possible he was meant to be a hobo. He was learning from his friends how to read hobo language.

Secretly he had put the marks on his porch that meant "Nice woman lives here," but so far no hoboes had appeared at the door.

Emily had been cleaning the house with lavender soap. She had read in a women's magazine that most ladies used lavender products, and so the table was oiled with lavender, the dishes squeaked from lavender essence. When Leland opened the door, he smelled the blast of lavender. She was sitting in a kitchen chair. His last three geometry tests were in front of her, squared neatly. There was a full glass of milk and a plate with two cookies.

"Sit down," Emily said.

He had a list of excuses prepared, but he didn't begin them. Instead, he put his bookstrap down and sat as asked, face impassive, almost—at age eleven—weathered.

"Are you angry with me, Lee?"

An instinct as primitive as hunting mastodons made him neither nod nor shake his head.

"Because you know how to do geometry. I imagine it like this: you sit down to take the test, and instead of all the numbers and angles and formulas, you just think about ways to punish me. I can almost see it on your face. I think it simmers in there, and you want to hurt me by failing your mathematics tests. Have a cookie."

He picked up the iced sugar cookie and chewed. He listened to his mother narrate how she thought his day went. She imagined him strolling past shopkeepers' houses, striking a stick against the gate, thinking lovely thoughts on the surface, for he was a genuinely good boy, she said, but underneath, she thought he was churning with resentments that, if not checked, would become bitterness when he was an adult, and, for now, yielded poor results in geometry.

"I can see you on your wedding day, Lee," Emily said, "ready to kiss your bride, but if I'm there, I suspect that deep in your heart will still be—"

"Where's my father?" Leland asked.

The story stopped. She looked startled. She had actually been guessing quite well, almost perfectly.

She kissed him on the forehead, announced it was late (it was only four-thirty), and left the room. He looked up at the wooden planks in the ceiling, listening, feeling his heart constrict. He wanted to find something she liked, a rock he would paint for her. He wanted to do a funny voice that would make her laugh. No two times had she told it the same way.

His father sold cultured pearls. His father worked the trees. His father worked the mines. His father knew how to cook meals of fourteen courses. His father traveled in a submarine, loathed oppression, and felt contempt for surface dwellers, and, Lord, he was handsome. His father had been imprisoned for stealing a loaf of bread—a *pain bagnet,* in fact—and, having escaped, was implacably pursued by the authorities, who were on the lookout for a man with a yellow passport. Why did Leland want a father when he had a mother like Emily Wheeler?

He heard the kitchen door open, and he shuffled across the room to the window, and he saw his mother standing on the porch, gazing out to sea. He had hurt her feelings. He swore he would never do so again. Which did not last (how could it?), but it helped him regain his math skills and made him wonder whether—if he was good enough—his father would ever come back.

"Careful by that ridge," his mother said. It was spring of 1904; he was twelve years old now, and they were spending yet another Sunday at the tidepools. He was too old for this, and resenting his mother having repeated this phrase for perhaps the four hundredth time. But he gave his *considering* nod, as if he hadn't thought before about being careful, thank you for having suggested it. He imagined he had an audience for such things; his audience had grown from the time he was young and hanging upside down from the trees. He felt that his life was being recorded some—

His mother was gone.

Water was washing over his feet, flooding into the tidepools, and stirring up pockets of sand. Plumes of ocean water spilling up the side of rocks, and retreating. Then he saw her—she was on her hands and knees in the water, and one hand was held to her mouth. She had slipped. She took her hand from her mouth, and it came away bloody. "I'm all right. Be careful on that ridge."

He rushed to help her up, aid that she accepted.

"Walk me back toward the house. We have tincture of iodine there. I cut my lip, but my teeth are all there. We'll have a lot of blood, and my tongue is going to swell, so I'll sound odd, but otherwise I think I'll be fine." She talked this way, and at first he held her hand, which she disengaged from, as if she needed both hands to balance while walking across the volcanic rocks. "Are you all right, Lee?"

"I'm fine."

"Because this could be frightening to you."

"I'm not frightened," he said. Although he was frightened, he suspected that, like crying, mentioning this wouldn't be worth it.

When they were home, he raced to the medicine chest, and his mother treated her wounds quickly and with great efficiency, saying only, every few minutes, "That was an exciting one," and then, "We can talk about you being frightened, if you want."

"Do I look frightened?" His voice sounded as if it had been measured from a recipe: exactly one-half cup of concern.

"Look at me." She was holding a chip of ice wrapped in cloth to her jaw. "Honestly, you're a handsome boy," she said. "I think you're feeling anxious," and then she had to rest.

Leland opened the back door as quietly as he could. He ran and then walked. On the sands of Timber Cove, he remembered his mother falling. At no time had his father come to save her. It hadn't escaped his attention that in twelve years his father hadn't yet managed to pay him a visit. There were awful fathers in town; his mother was never shy about pointing them out.

He had seen a few motion pictures by now, each of them a minute or two long. They had little effect on him at first, seeming to be aimed at someone stupider than himself. But then he'd noticed that the cowboy in one picture was a bricklayer in another. A strange frisson went down Leland's spine as he watched, and, sure enough, the next week, the same person was now a jewel thief in a one-minute adventure in which he was hit with a frying pan. Perhaps his father could be all those things his mother had claimed.

"I will save you," he said, with a stage actor's projection, sweeping his hand before the ocean as if he owned it. "I will save you," he cried, though he wasn't referring to his mother, for he understood that being saved would only annoy her. Instead, he was saving a pretty girl who had a blank oval for a face. If he was good enough, and wanted it enough, his father would join him.

Above him, on bluffs dotted with clumps of ice plant that kept the dunes from collapsing, was a painful sunlit glint he did not see: the eye of a Bioscope camera. A crank was turning. The operator was muttering, "This is good, this is good, don't turn around, this is good." Then he stopped cranking, smiled, and congratulated himself on this bit of serendipity, a force he had encountered as far away as Java and as recently as an hour beforehand.

Five minutes later, the camera was packed up and ready to go to its next vista, and Lee was still stepping into the waves, throwing punches to pirates, and rescuing things that didn't quite exist.

☆   ☆   ☆

In Detroit, Michigan, Hugo Black was a different child from Lee Wheeler. He did not wander or challenge his mother. He heeded the fairy-tale injunction to obey, always finding fault with those storybook children who wandered under bridges only to be eaten by ogres, for they had clearly been given instruction. And yet real children in his neighborhood were disobedient, and nothing happened. Hugo thus grew disenchanted with what he had seen of life. His mother, hearing his morose pronouncements, met them with faint and approving nods, the equivalent of warm rain and rich topsoil.

Mrs. Black herself seemed burdened by an unnamed offense perpetrated by the world, as if, on a certain spring day long past, she had flown down a dock with her parasol and two well-packed suitcases, only to find that the ship had sailed. There it was, receding into the distance, lovely chamber music playing, handsome men of the highest classes making excellent conversation over a formal meal, and the folly of blown champagne corks echoing over Lake Erie without her.

For reasons never enumerated, this was apparently Mr. Black's fault. Hugo's father, the professor of engineering who enjoyed railway trains, did not go by "Dr. Black," which gave Mrs. Black headaches from which she refused to recover until he left for work in the mornings. Further, Mr. Black showed enthusiasm for mechanical devices, equations, thrilling uses of electricity, parlor games, puzzles—in other words, the minor traps of the material world that Mrs. Black endured.

Quietly, Mr. Black took Hugo to the vaudeville house ("Don't tell Mother"), the Electric Park ("What are we going to do?" "Not tell Mother?" "Good boy"), and the waxworks, the Theater of Blood on Woodward Avenue, where Mr. Black got on one knee to show Hugo where the signs of wax casting were still found, to show that this wasn't really a dead person but, rather, technology and artistry. Mr. Black did not take him to the nickel dumps of the picture show. Hugo said he did not wish to go, for he'd heard that the working class (he did not know what this was) used the darkness for illicit advances upon each other's person (he thought this meant they tickled each other, something he definitely would campaign against).

When Hugo was nine, and as rigid and duty-bound if he were forty-five, Mr. Black asked, "Would you like a job?"

Hugo hesitated. When he was confused, he tended to rely on an aloofness. *"Peut-être."*

"Right," Mr. Black sighed. "It involves Jefferson Avenue."

Which sealed it. The best people lived on Jefferson, and with proximity, Hugo could report back to his mother about their comings and goings, as she called them. The Avenue was paved with cedar blocks that were sealed together with pitch. A single ash from a prosperous cigar would set the whole street on fire. Hugo's job was to sit at the corner with a bucket of water and keep an eagle eye. There was never a fire, but if he saw what looked like a spark, he was quick with his bucket. Sometimes, when a private car was driving by, he dumped water into the cedar as if he were Johnny-on-the-spot. Sometimes he received a dime. He told his mother whom he had seen, and her languid, fading smiles were the best part of working.

Detroit was blessed by a library constructed on the river during the height of the City Beautiful movement. Surrounded by lush gardens planted with every herb mentioned in Shakespeare (the histories only), the library had a dock so the upper caste could return their books by boat. If you returned a book by boat, the fines were waived. There were lectures on Sunday.

For Mr. Black, the idea of a lecture on Sunday at the library was as exciting as a barrel of whey. In this he was not alone. Sunday lectures were looked upon as enlightening and educational, and, regardless of what the "Comings and Goings" column in the *Free Press* said, the smart set was more likely to have *claimed* attendance than to have attended.

The Blacks were the only family to learn about travels to the Canary Islands by plank or errors in Athanasius Kircher's description of the catotrophic lamp. And yet Mrs. Black was determined that culture would infuse her son. What the world had to offer would find its way into him even if someone had to use a hammer and stone chisel.

But the presentations of Mr. Burton Holmes were promising. He was the only lecturer in the United States since Stoddard to sometimes attract an audience. Clever, he did not use the words "educational" and "lecture." His current lecture promised "Bilibid, Sing Sing of the Philippines."

"That sounds interesting," Mrs. Black said.

"It does not." Then Mr. Black saw the rest of the advertisement. Below

"Discus Catching with the Barmanou" and "Kongamato of Bangweulu" was an explanation that Mr. Holmes was bringing *films*. With a heretofore unseen projector. "Perhaps we should see these."

Mrs. Black swung to a different column. Films played at nickelodeons. The working class, as any nine-year-old could tell you, used the darkness for illicit advances upon each other's person. But Benguet . . . Mindanao . . . She wanted to be convinced otherwise. She read the text below:

> Make no mistake, these are moving pictures. But I, Burton Holmes, your far-flung correspondent, bring you neither travel show nor monologue. It is described by a word I have created: the *travelogue*.

"A travelogue sounds appropriate," she concluded.

Holmes, a handsome man with a civil beard and facile eyes, had traveled the world, first with a 60mm Demeny that sat like a boulder on a cast-iron tripod, then replacing it with a more agile 35mm Bioscope that rode an adjustable swivelhead. Europe, Japan, and South America had fallen like dominoes. Siberia and the Spice Islands likewise. He hadn't an ounce of theory in his soul. Theory took too much time.

In Detroit, he began as he always did, explaining, "To travel is to possess the world. But you are no monopolist. It is not yours alone." This was deep enough for him. What did it mean when his very presence made a place no longer remote? When the objective eye of the lens rendered subjectivity antique, what would the new century become?

He didn't ask, because he didn't care. He cared about sharing what he'd seen. Today, in Detroit, he showed jungles. Natives. More jungles. Ceremonies involving natives swinging on vines found in jungles.

It was interesting for about two minutes for young eyes that had never seen anything of the world, and certainly nothing in motion like this. Then young Hugo got itchy and peevish, for he was indoors on a nice day that he could have better spent with his bucket on Jefferson Avenue. What if it had caught fire in his absence? He smelled for smoke. The library's grand lecture hall had seats so comfortable as to rival a ducal palace in the transalpine monarchies. Heavy tapestries cut out all light, the room was overly warm, and Burton Holmes was speaking like a cello, ponderous and asking for nothing in return, and the problem was, a correspondent, no matter how far-flung, is not quite a hero. When his third film, about the condor-sized bats, began to unspool, the entire audience—three-eighths of them the Black family—were sound asleep. "We begin to return to our own shores as before," he said, undiscouraged. "Professor Byrd, the one in the canoe, says that such return, enlivened by experience, is *epanalepsis.*"

Hugo Black's eyes flickered open. He was drowsy and happy, and feeling safe the way only a boy dozing between dozing parents can feel. He had seen, between dreams, his first motion pictures, jungles, birds sitting on the tattooed shoulders of smiling natives. Everything looked as it had in his picture books and encyclopedias. All was well.

"To bring it to our own shores, an educational moment for you, Detroit. The ocean!" Burton proclaimed.

The screen showed previously unseen motion of waves towering, light passing through, sunlight glinting off of them, kelp suspended within salt water, then crashing down.

"This is Crescent City, California, our own country. But have any of you seen something like this?"

Hugo stood. Tapped his fingers against his father's thigh, to no response. The motion! He had no words for it. This was an experience he was having all by himself. His skin chilled. He had heard of the ocean, but seeing it was an entirely different matter; it was like seeing an elephant after someone has mentioned one in passing. He wanted to sing.

There was wonder in the world, and he realized he did not yet understand it. Perhaps there was a word in French for this feeling. Then he noticed onscreen a boy slightly older and probably taller than himself standing on the shoreline, moving his arms as if he were directing the currents.

"Oh," he whispered. He walked forward several steps, unaware he was doing so. The shot took up a number of seconds, so Hugo drew very close to the screen, close enough that his eyes began to smart, and yet the waves were just as real as before, the boy's motion was as enchanting. Had Hugo known how to play, he could have played with this other boy. This was as close as he would ever come to Leland Wheeler or to the California shore.

There were two forces in the world—education and fear—and they always fought, and Burton Holmes, with his lantern, was a proponent of the former long before the rest of the world decided a motion picture could teach any sort of lesson.

"After my trip to Crescent City," Burton Holmes intoned in his friendly voice, "I returned to the hotel, to nap before the fire, to end on a moment of happy reflection and anticipation of further happy purpose. With that, a good ni—"

It happened quickly. The next image was the fireplace. It was an extreme close-up. The flames were taller than Hugo, whose nose was almost against the screen.

"Fire!" Hugo cried. And with the quick wit and trigger finger he had restrained all summer long, he and his bucket on Jefferson Avenue, Hugo knocked the screen onto the ground. "Fire! Fire!" He stomped on it with his good shoes, and several long seconds later realized someone somewhere had made a mistake.

It was his last family visit to a travelogue. He grew up with an antipathy to motion pictures that—many years from now—would invite disastrous consequence.

In 1917, a few months after his attempt to rescue Chaplin at sea, Leland, now twenty-five and strong, tall, often silent, went to Eureka, lying to his mother about the purpose. He told her he was bringing linens to invalids, and to that end he actually canvassed Crescent City, collecting quilts and so forth, and piling them in the back of the truck.

He hadn't thought what to do with the heaped sets of sheets donated in good faith, but conscience spoke to him. When he reached Eureka, he presented them to a local church, which thanked him profusely (it turned out the local shut-ins really did need them, and the reverend shook his hand and complimented his grip, and the woman who mopped the floors and lit the candles told him he was the most handsome boy they'd ever seen).

He had brought a small advertisement from the back of *Photoplay* which indicated that the great cameraman George Barnes (credited with *Betsy's Fatal Slip*, *Traditions of the Tartans*, *The Woodsman and the Fall*, etc., etc.) would be traveling by automobile from location to location to seek new talent. Leland hadn't heard of Barnes, and was embarrassed to think of the other lapses in his education, what with being at sea so many weeks of the year. Luckily, Barnes's advertisement said he did not care for know-it-alls; he wanted *talent*. He would accept professionally composed photographs, and if the applicant was deemed to have potential, he would shoot twenty seconds of film and send it to his contacts at a Hollywood studio whose identity he could not divulge for, he said, obvious reasons.

Leland also brought the five-dollar processing fee, which would be refunded when a studio called for his services.

The office in which they met was a room off the kitchen in a boardinghouse, with a sign on the door that said, "George Barnes, Talent Discoveries," a sign that was scarred and gouged from having been removed in haste more than once.

Barnes wore a tweed cap and jodhpurs, but was otherwise a man of neither discernible traits nor outstanding features. "If he were to rob a bank," Leland thought, "you'd arrest half the town before you found him." He was unsure of the whole setup, which now struck him as possibly a dupe. But then he learned that Barnes was delighted by his photograph.

Barnes pointed at certain features, such as the diamond stickpin and the top hat, and then, encouraged, Leland talked about how he had achieved them. "I borrowed the clothes. As far as that expression on my face, I just thought about a girl I know," he said. "The rest was easy. You like it? Honest?" The photograph was his "elegant" pose, showing him in a black dinner jacket and white tie, chin up, hair slicked back with Macassar, gazing with brilliant eyes toward the unknown—perhaps even destiny—with resolve and wisdom.

Measuring his words, Leland said, "I also have a cowboy photograph."

"No! Do you realize how few people have that kind of range?"

A few moments later, Leland had handed over his five dollars, and he and Barnes were on the roof of the boardinghouse, where there was an Ernemann camera on a tripod, and behind it a grim, slouching man whose gin blossoms were radiant in the noonday sun. "Ray, this is Leland Wheeler," Barnes exclaimed. "He's both a roué and a cowpoke."

"Charmed," said Ray. "Take off your jacket, walk to the end of the roof and back, and then nod at me."

"Certainly . . ." But Leland was torn. He wanted to obey, because those who didn't obey were said to build immediate and horrible reputations. Yet he couldn't help indicating that he was no rube. "Say, friend . . . what f-stop are you using?"

Ray's gaze shifted into something like the point of a knife, then went hazy again. "F-8. Unless it gets sunnier."

"Of course." Leland rubbed his chin. "Now, if I nod at you, what should my attitude be?"

"Your attitude," Ray said slowly, "is that you want to be famous."

"I've always thought if you want something enough—"

"Uh-huh."

"Do you mind if I rehearse? Just once?"

Ray's eyes flicked to Barnes, who shook his head. "That would ruin your natural instincts."

So, while Ray turned the crank at two revolutions per second, Leland shook off his jacket, flung it over one shoulder, and strolled across the roof as if he were on a jaunt to a belle's house. When he got to the edge, he spun on one heel and returned, whistling to himself. He finished by nodding, and then, without prompting, gave the camera a knee-buckling wink.

When Ray stopped cranking, Barnes slapped Leland on the back and congratulated him on his performance.

"Did you like my wink at the end?"

"Especially liked the wink."

"Because you didn't tell me to."

"Not everyone can wink like that, so I don't tell them to do it. Your mother must know how to wink."

"Hmm. Not particularly."

"It's inherited. Most people can't even make the walk back and the nod look so confident," Barnes said, guiding Leland back through the window into the boardinghouse.

Leland filled out a form with his home address, also indicating what frequencies the lighthouse listened to, if the studios were too desperate for him to return to dry land.

He wished Barnes might comment on the lighthouse (it wasn't as if everyone lived in a lighthouse, and this was an interesting gimmick for exploitation), but Barnes said nothing about it. Instead, he ripped an eight of diamonds down the middle and handed over one half. "This is your receipt," he said.

Leland thanked him, and was most of the way out the door before he thought to ask, "Mr. Barnes?"

"Yes?"

"Leland Wheeler. Do you think I should change my name?"

Barnes smiled at him, and made a pistol with his thumb and forefinger. "I like how you think. You've got what it takes."

Leland whistled halfway back to Crescent City, interviewing himself as he drove. "Did you know, on that day, how your bright future awaited you?"

"I did." Then he reconsidered. "No, of course not." But he reconsidered again, and answered, cheerfully, "Oh, of course I knew. The moment I saw that eight of diamonds, and can you believe it was just an eight of diamonds he handed me? I would have to be quite an idiot to trust that, you know." But this line of thought led him to furrow his brow and consider the road more carefully, so he instead went toward the lighthearted, the personal checklists. "Your religion?"

"Gin and tonic."

"Your favorite music?"

"Gin and tonic."

He would be excellent at answering questions.

A week later, there had been no news, but still Leland whistled happily while rowing to the station, or puttering in the engineering room. When people came by and poked their heads in to see what he was doing, it was as if he'd been caught eating cookies. His face went slate-stoic, he became polite, he was unreadable. He considered changing his name to Jackson Wheeler, in case Southern gothics were going to be big again. He wondered, as his cowboy photograph gazed back at him, whether he should begin to answer to the nickname "Jangles."

There were two impediments to Leland's plans for becoming a famous motion-picture actor.

First was his location. No matter how enthusiastic studios might be about his twenty seconds of screen test, it was possible that there were men of abilities greater than his, men found only minutes from Famous Players' front gates. The more he considered it, the more it made his stomach hurt. He began to plot his escape from the lighthouse.

There was a second concern, in that the United States declared war on Germany.

For several weeks, there were excited feelings about the war, but then it occurred to the people of Crescent City and its surrounding areas—and in fact the whole country—that someone would be called on to *fight* it. Naturally, thoughts of the *Lusitania* made the blood boil, but so did the idea of the federal government's demanding the able bodies of America's sons. Even the government itself wasn't quite sure how to coax ten million boys into uniform without causing, as it had during the Civil War, riots in the streets.

The solution came from Enoch Crowder, a vicious Washington, D.C., bureaucrat, a cynical bachelor who hated work, a man whose morning constitutional involved a brief walk in the park, where he would beat a baseball bat against a tree and scream as loudly as he could.

"We will put the people to work," he reported to his staff after one such session, bat in hand, sweat pasting his workshirt to his underwear. "We will appeal to honor, and when that fails, as it will, we will appeal to *shame*," he added.

American men were to report to neighborhood registration boards, which they would find staffed by "their friends and neighbors." Thus failure to appear would be not so much an act of disobedience to a vast economic authority as a tearful slap in the face to your pediatrician, your minister, your grocer.

There were no riots.

Semantics dissolved, and it was no longer a "draft." Tender care was taken to remove all traces of arm-twisting, to replace them instead with decency. In a speech to Congress, President Wilson explained that, when called, the people "had volunteered in mass."

In Crescent City, population eight hundred, there were about a hundred eligible men, fifteen of whom were medically unfit through flat feet, barbers' itch, or varicose veins. There were also three men whose jobs were deemed "crucial to the war effort," and all of them worked in the lighthouse. Which caused Leland a mistaken sort of relief.

Through 1917, Leland worked in shifts at the lighthouse, helped his mother can preserves, joined a volunteer fire brigade on the mainland, wrapped bandages for the Red Cross, and, in a patch of soil that was really too close to the ocean for such things, grew weak stalks of corn to use for flour. He also rehearsed on the dunes alone at dusk, bought an épée and learned as much fencing as he could without a partner, and found that, with the threat of imminent death, and a dwindling pool of beaux, the local girls' interpretation of what constituted light petting had significantly expanded. And here was yet another skill he had: pleasing women.

Except his mother.

One rare morning, there was time to linger over breakfast at the government bungalow, and Leland and Emily sat in the window seat with cups of coffee. He had the current *Motion Picture Magazine,* and was annotating it with a pen. "Antonio Moreno is highly overrated," he said.

The next article was about how to be your own publicity manager. It was written for actresses, but it had a tone that made Leland circle paragraph after paragraph.

> If you have elected to become a vampire, don't answer the doorbell in the flannel dressing-sack in which you have been darning your stockings. If you are the youngest star in motion pictures, send your granddaughter to the park on the day of your big interview. Do not under any consideration have the wonderful jewels given you by the deposed King of Honolulu stolen from your dressing-room. That is quite out of date and is rapidly being superseded by the lawsuit. A lawsuit is very effective and can be worked in so many ways and on any member of your family.

There was more of this, all written to suggest that both author and reader were aware of hidden information: All human endeavor was for personal gain. Everything, including this very magazine, was a grifter's game. Hollywood drank champagne because no one there had real pain.

Seeing the bluffs spelled out in this column was like having the keys to the bank tossed through the mail slot. Leland now wanted to be his own publicist. There were so many good things to lie about. For rugged actors who were just beginning, such as himself, a background of either poverty or crime was essential. Claiming poverty was an insult to his mother, but an air of danger and fisticuffs struck him as entirely possible. A visit to local girls was in order; he would tell them he was a wanted man. Although it would take some finesse to explain who, of the eight hundred people who lived in Crescent City, might be his mortal enemy.

"Mom," he said, for he had a fascinating new fact to impart, but it would have to wait: she burst into tears.

She put her face in her hands, and she sobbed, shoulders hunched forward as if she were protecting herself from rain.

"Mom, what's wrong? What happened?"

She sniffled. She used the edge of a napkin to wipe at her eyes. "Leland, you shouldn't be an actor."

She had never sounded enthusiastic; it was why he had hidden his trip to Eureka. But he had become good at this argument when he imagined it. "You're right. I definitely can't. Not living here." This was the beginning of his proposal to move south for six months. Rhetorically, it was iron-clad, almost Miltonic, but it was still no match for what Emily did next, which was to continue with full, racking sobs.

She didn't even put her hands over her face, but just let herself weep openly. Tears had never been part of her arsenal, as if she had been saving them for twenty-five years. Even she seemed surprised: she started laughing, pointing at herself, and then crying again.

He patted her on the shoulder, awkwardly. She blew her nose. He wanted to tell her that everything would be okay, but he wasn't sure what she was crying about, and he was willing to step through many waterfalls of a mother's tears in order to make his dreams come true.

Emily caught her breath. She had calmed down, and now she tried to catch her reflection in a mirror on the wall. "Oh, look at me," she whispered. "I hate crying."

"You cried when we saw *Widow's Lament*. Which reminds me—"

"I haven't denied you very much in your life. Mrs. Field says I've spoiled you." She held up her hand. "Let me finish." She took in a breath. When she spoke, it was as if reciting an oath. "I don't want you to be an actor."

"But we haven't really talked this through."

"We don't need to. It's been obvious when I look out the window and see you on the sand dunes, pretending you're in a movie. It was sweet at first." She looked at her thumbs, which she'd lined up atop her hands, which nested in her lap.

Not only had his mother been watching him, she had concluded he was something of a moron. He wished she was at least angry at him. But she was attempting to discipline him, and so she was hesitant, a tack that always made him want to protect her, in this case from himself.

"You see," she said, seeming to straighten her shoulders, cast off motherhood, and assume the mantle of sergeant, "people who perform antics for a living are, objectively, immoral."

He had never heard her say anything like this. "But, Mom, the stories you hear about parties and all that, they're exaggerated. You should— The article I was just reading about how to be your own press agent, let me read you—"

"No, no," she said quietly. She had found a place to stand. "I don't mean that. You have a good head on your shoulders, Lee. There's a war on, and that changes everything. I have no feeling one way or the other about how actors behave, neither motion-picture nor stage nor circus nor . . ."

Sunnyside

She tried for reasons that will eventually become obvious to think of a performance other than "Wild West show" and could retrieve nothing, so she plowed on. "It's neither here nor there. The profession itself is disturbing, and I don't want you to have anything to do with it while soldiers are actually dying."

"I don't understand. What does one thing have to do with the other?"

"Oh, how could someone pretend to be a colonel in the army when there are real soldiers, *giving their lives*," she said, and her voice cracked again.

He was baffled. "Do you mean me?" he whispered.

"I want you to do something that's actually important in the world."

"Acting is doing something important."

"Acting is acting like you're doing something important." She shook her head. Her next words were distinct and commanding. "All right, my son. You love acting," she said. "What else?"

He had in mind nests of young robins, otters too weak to cross streams, girls abandoned at the mouth of a silver mine, the love of friends he hadn't made yet. But he sensed such things were the antithesis of what it took to succeed as a star—*Photoplay* would have told him so.

"Leland," she whispered. "The war will make you a better person."

"Then me being exempt is a problem," he said.

"You aren't exempt."

"Lighthouse—"

"I filed a reversal."

"You—you what? How can my mother file a reversal?"

"Your mother can't," Emily said, for the first time all day beginning to smile, "but your employer can."

He didn't believe her, but she then pulled from between the couch cushions a crumpled letter from the Bureau of Lighthouses, San Francisco, allowing him to be entered into registration. There was more discussion, mostly from Emily, which became the echoes from a beehive. She was explaining how he should enlist in the aero program—she thought it was called that—because enlisted men there didn't see combat. She was offering him true experience, she explained, a chance to actually help the world, see life outside of the beach and the dunes and the reef.

He was supposed to say something. She had in her eyes the calm she always did when she felt she had boxed off a crisis. And in that gaze was, horribly, love.

"You're sending me to the war," he whispered. "To make me a better person. All right." At no time did the expression on his face change.

"I think that makes you feel angry."

"No."

"Bitter?"

"No."

"I can't read you anymore."

"Hmm."

Emily started, several times, to say something, but instead she finally left the room and went upstairs. Leland could hear her bedroom door scraping shut, for the wood had expanded in the ocean air, and Emily always meant to plane it down but never seemed to have the time.

Leland left the house carefully, and he walked along the dunes. Time was now ticking. He could get a letter of induction any day. As he walked, he talked to himself. His speaking voice was excellent, a baritone he had in fact inherited along with his awesome ability to wink. Firemen, he explained to the gulls, were excluded from the draft. So were policemen. And men in positions important to the public good. Why not an actor? Leland imagined an actor who could say, "For the good of the troops, I will continue to act," and he knew this was impossible. His mother was right: acting was not that important.

Why could he not stop interviewing himself, then?

"Cocktail of choice?"

"A woman's tears."

"Your one true love?"

"Injuring my mother."

"How do you feel?"

"All right."

"How does your mother feel?"

"Good. Nervous. Bad."

"How does your father feel?"

". . ."

"And how did you know you wanted to be famous?"

Somehow, with his mother's many stories about his father, and his father's complete absence, Leland had decided he was as real as a motion picture star. It wasn't something he'd articulated, or even understood; the idea was half-conscious. There was something eternal in his father's almost-but-not-quite presence. Like Dustin Farnum or Chaplin, perhaps, his father was an imaginary friend who might finally appear by his side if only he, Leland, had been good enough and in love enough and loyal enough to him.

When they asked, and they would ask, about his childhood, he would tell them that the worst and the best day of his life were one and the same. He would tell this with no embellishment, but strictly how it had happened, for that was dramatic enough: That his mother and he had been walking along the tidepools, and that she had slipped and fallen. She had knocked herself unconscious, and he had no way to carry her, and then there was a disturbance in the waters, a heaving of bubbles to the surface, which broke open so Leland could see first a length of hose, then the metal cap, and finally the whole suit of a deep-sea diver, who had been hunting for octopi.

Off came the helmet and—it was his father! His father carried his mother to safety, they had a fine lunch together, he told Leland how tall he was getting, and then he had to get back to the *Nautilus,* for the men would wonder where he had gone. Before he left, he gave Leland a smooth turquoise bottle he had found on the bottom of the ocean.

4

His father wasn't actually Captain Nemo, nor was he the hero of *Les Misérables.* He was something else entirely, the last practitioner of a scruffy kind of performance, a handsome man, a man born to wink, a man whose ambition might have been a roadmap or a cautionary tale for young Leland.

Stage performers, who excel at tales of misfortune, were hard-pressed to top the story of the demise of Colonel Wild Duncan Cody's 101 Wild West Extravaganza Western Roundup. It was an ending so apocalyptic its extinction coincided with many other endings, from which the balance of our tale will flow.

Wild Duncan Cody's given name was Percy Bysshe Duncan, which did not pop with heroics. Though he could rope and ride with great precision, and he had made legitimate Indian friends, he had no real business running a Wild West show. A drunk, a cad with the ladies, unable to hold ten complete dollars in his hand for ten consecutive minutes, he was untrustworthy to the core of his character—even those who liked him best sought a second opinion after asking him what time it was.

And yet, after many a poker game in which he had lost every tangible cent and more, he could throw his arm around his former opponent and now creditor, and make every moment of his future—now *their* future—sound like a party-in-waiting.

"Think of it," he had said one summer dawn, his fingers spread as if they could contain all the purpling Arkansas sky, "think of the crowds who will come to see rugged pioneers and Onondaga Indians throwing rocks at one another!"

"Real rocks?"

"It's important that they seem perfectly real."

For much of his life, he genuinely wanted to present innovations, though the marketplace demanded only that Duncan parrot Buffalo Bill Cody: Indians storming a settlers' village; Indians attacking the overland mail coach; Indians re-enacting the capture of White Feather. Just when Duncan had determined that he likely needed Indians in his show, Buffalo Bill outmaneuvered him by featuring the antics of scimitar-waving Cossacks, anticipating the audience's previously untapped excitement for all things Russian.

Duncan knew he could spend his entire career being dragged behind Buffalo Bill's nimble phaeton. To save his pride, in a blinding flash of mediocrity, his mind made a peculiarly American jump of faith, equating conviction with talent: his own ideas were good because they were *his*.

Except they weren't. "Real New Mexico cactus with deadly spines" lasted half a season, supplanted by a hard-to-defend demonstration of fruitless gold-panning ("just like it was in the Old West"). Giant rocks? A failure. Which depressed him. Why were Buffalo Bill's ideas successful? What did Cossacks have to do with the Wild West? Nothing!

It was a show that needed a rest as badly as any real Indian scout. Duncan was not a reflective man, but even he knew the moment his life had shambled down the wrong path. A summer in Sacramento, a county fair, one hour of roping and riding three times a day among the American Landrace judging and the pavilions of textile witchery. There had been a girl. She had been beautiful and domineering and suspicious. He had been tall, and he smelled appealingly of saddle soap, overpowering her domineering and suspicious parts. She had never met any sort of cowboy, for she had grown up in a lighthouse.

The long dusks were romantic, and there were walks along the Delta, his boasting and her laughter, the accompaniment of crickets and bull-frogs, which led from one thing to another. "You're equal parts headstrong and feisty," he said to her. "Equal parts difficult and difficult." Which was fun, at first.

At the end of the week, they loathed each other. He began to think of her with fondness as soon as he left. No one had ever successfully loathed him. He even thought of writing her.

She—Emily Wheeler, of course—returned to Crescent City and the lighthouse, where she worked the lantern room, rebuilding the hydraulic pumps from scratch, and occasionally, if bothered while welding, throwing cauterized pipe at her parents, should they dare to voice an opinion.

Her judgment of her absent beau rose and fell. She wrote him once to announce her pregnancy, and then she awaited a response. Meanwhile, she still loathed him, she missed him, he angered her, she missed him, and as weeks became eight or so months and he never wrote her, her course went fixed: she hated him.

She sent him an announcement of Leland's birth, the only letter he ever answered. Emily sent back the five dollars, adding that he would never see her or her son, "but know Leland will be brought up to embrace responsi-bilities and to stay away from degenerate influences," which a tiny piece of her heart hoped would cause Percy Duncan to return.

The separation hardly depressed Duncan, for he never really thought of his son as a creature that would crawl, then walk, then go to school and reel in his emotions and play crafty, and desire to be good enough to have his dreams come true. Instead, he every so often imagined a future drink-ing partner, strong, quick, a slayer of the ladies. They would meet, it would be a hootenanny, and then they would part again.

The entire future was a hootenanny to Duncan, every new tour a chance to make up for the last tour. Even members of his company who had been on the disastrous Georgia tour of 1907 (floods), or the Southwest-ern tour of 1909 (brush fires, train wreck), continued to trust the twinkle in his eye as he declared their next destinations—Spokane! Coeur d'Alene! The Montana Highline!—and made them sound like villages made of candy.

Which is how, in the summer of 1914, with the entire continental

United States dried up and no longer booking his antique entertainment, Wild Duncan Cody took his show, each and every one of his twenty-two cast members, the hangdog cowboys and Onondaga Indians nursing knots on their heads, and all of their wives and children, to the final place on earth still starved for the attentions that only a Wild West show could provide.

He took them to Berlin.

If, in July 1914, you asked the average Berliner which was coming first, rain or war, he might look to the slate-colored sky and note that at least no rain was expected today. With countries lining up to defend one another from blows no one had yet inflicted, all the nations of Europe were like children at the dinner table, waiting for Father to get the belt.

Berlin was a hard town, designed with cold stone tools and a mason's cautious hand, its low buildings in rigid symmetry. It was said that on each Saturnalia the Goddess of Victory drove her chariot from the Brandenburg Gate down Unter den Linden, to hesitate beseechingly before Frederick's statue, which smacked her stone cheek to bring tears to her eyes.

There were first-aid drills in the streets. The sound of a car backfiring caused pigeons on the Ku'dammstrasse to bolt into the sky, then scream back to earth, ready to peck at schoolgirls. On July 27, the Café Kranzler, the only café with ice cream acceptable to Berlin dinner parties, was alarmingly out of ice cream, and that evening, families began sewing diamonds into the hems of their servants' frocks.

"And such a dark country, if you think about it, is desperate for entertainment," chirped Cody to his troupe as they waved at the crowds of Berlin.

This was their promenade and ballyhoo, five covered wagons rolling through the center of the city. Normally the sight of such rolling anachronisms brought automobiles and pedestrians to a halt, especially since one wagon was asprawl with Onondaga Indians, the women in beaded finery reminiscent of wampum, and the men in full but ragged ceremonial headdresses won in poker games from ruined members of various Plains tribes.

Duncan winked at two spotless little boys, who stared at him frostily. He stood to take a bow, because a bow was known to generate applause. There were, at the street corner fronting the grand Tietz department store, three nannies with strollers, and upon seeing the hanging fringe of his buckskin jacket, his downswept Stetson, his long salt-and-pepper hair tossing in the wind, and, above all, his wink as he returned upright, they lit up like houses on fire.

But then, on the sidewalk, a man with muttonchops flanking his florid face held a hand out to stop the women from clapping.

"Er ist nicht *Buffalo Bill,"* he explained.

Duncan returned to the reins grimly, shaking hands with an undertaker. Buffalo Goddamned Bill played for kings and queens and came away each time with jeweled cigarette cases, high tea, engraved silver-stocked imperial rifles. Buffalo Bill was so confident, he stopped advertising exactly who he was—his posters showed a buffalo charging toward the west, with Buffalo Bill's iconic visage—the whiskers, the hat, the braided leather vest—branded upon its side, and below it the phrase "I'm coming," or, as when he played Germany, *"Ich komme."* The world bent to Colonel Buffalo Bill Cody. Unlike Duncan, he really was a colonel, for instance.

But Duncan still felt a faint hope that this time he had something good enough. Something to tempt the Kaiser himself to attend the opening show. It was not impossible. The Kaiser loved the Wild West. He had read Karl May and Zane Grey and James Fenimore Cooper. He had attended Wild West shows. Annie Oakley had once shot a lit cigarette from his lips.

The act had to be better than Cossacks or re-enacting Little Big Horn. It had to be better than Annie Oakley. Duncan hadn't put a female sharp-shooter on the program in years, for he had learned that the pleasures of such talented women were obliterated by their ability to draw firearms on him.

The act likely should involve shooting. Which he wasn't that good at. Then he considered that his posters could mention only the shooting, not that any particular shot would hit its target. Wasn't it impressive enough to see him *try* to hit six glass balls at once? Wasn't his failure at least poignant?

But even the scruples of Percy Bysshe Duncan smarted from too hard a spur in the flank. Standing at the printer broker's office in Tenafly, text design form before him, fingers drumming on the zinc counter, pen to his chapped lips, he had it: a phrase describing an act to amaze anyone who came to his show, something he could execute himself, three terrible words, a legend he could live up to: "Shooting While Drunk."

5

Tempelhofer Field, upon which the Ruhleben racetrack was built, was a monumental arena of parched grass reserved for military spectacles and any performances the royal family might attend (all of which in the past twelvemonth had been, ominously, military spectacles).

The entryway's iron gates creaked reluctantly when Duncan's team came to erect their modest, temporary village: a lighting plant, a canvas tent for costume changes, a chow wagon, a shop for the man who was both blacksmith and veterinarian (and, recently, a reluctant Cossack). The Onondaga women who did the Longhouse dances were raking over the ground with poles and brooms, to dislodge stones or fill in rabbit holes that might trip them up. A score of horses were given their freedom in a sandy paddock. Rather than kick up their heels and expel gas, they huddled together silently. They didn't even flutter their lips, as if nervous about disclosing their location.

The setting reminded Duncan of the Roman Colosseum, which he almost mentioned aloud, since this comparison would of course make his troupe gladiators. It was a thought that was jolly but not, if followed to its logical conclusion, *that* jolly.

Around four in the afternoon, there was the briefest of summer showers, ten minutes of warm rain, whose droplets massaged the weary skin. It was like stepping through a waterfall and into a more gracious time of day. Businessmen in bowlers, carrying umbrellas by the handle in the British style, regarded the city kiosks and designated poster boards with puzzlement. A man with a rifle? Doing what?

" *'Schießen, während Sie getrunken werden'?"* They muttered, *"Der muß ein Fehler sein."*

So off to the racetrack they went. Soldiers and sailors came in casual dress. Students in red caps and self-inflicted dueling scars that were kept fresh with repeated applications of salt tried to catch the eye of pretty au pairs. Wet nurses, *Spreewalderinnen,* in huge white headdresses and skirts that could catch the breeze, pushed strollers sturdy as battle cruisers past vendors who had set up in the aisles to sell tree cake, *Pfefferkuchen,* and marzipan to children who ran back and forth, smacking the tops of one another's heads in merry games of *Kaiser, König, Edelmann.* The crowd yelled out for beer, for pickles, for ham on rolls, with a Pantagruelian mass appetite.

It was July 30, 1914, a Thursday, the last possible moment to watch a certain kind of era before it winked over the vanishing point of the horizon. By six o'clock, the racetrack bleachers were at capacity.

Duncan, alone in his tent, removed his comb from its jar of Blue-Vue sanitizer, swept it through his hair, splashed his face with water. He took a tug of whiskey, for luck. The noises of the crowd made his heart rise, briefly, but he knew the Kaiser had men to advise him. They would surely have told him by now, *"Er ist* nicht *Buffalo Bill."*

At some point, Duncan had ceased to believe in fairy-tale endings and imprisoned princesses and the course of ambition. He scratched his horse Betsy between the eyes, and said aloud, "When was that, old girl?" and knew it was the moment someone had first genuinely disliked him: Emily Wheeler. He had been running by rote since then, a train stopping at stations where the towns were deserted. Or so he said now; it was hard to remember when that had actually started.

The central space on the stands, the Imperial Row, was empty. It was two minutes after six, time for the show to begin. At Duncan's signal, the son of the farrier, a pale and dirty-looking boy with blond curls, marched onto the field. He wore an accordion on a torn leather harness. He looked ten, but was about thirteen, and he sported a blue silk stovepipe hat and a tunic with stars and stripes cut off a flag that had fallen on hard times. This was Edmund, one of the children whose parents were in the troupe.

He had learned to play his instrument with the same joyless precision that barefoot waifs exercised in stoking the coal fires of a debtors' prison. Edmund's fingers stumbled across the cracked ivory keys as his twin brother, Edgar, similarly dressed—stars, stripes, hat—approached from the other side. Edgar played his tuba. They were playing "Dixie," possibly, knees pumping in the air, as if fearing they would be sold to pirates.

Duncan touched his spurs to Betsy's flanks, sending her forward in a lope until they stopped at the center of the stands. He cast a solemn gaze across the audience. "The West," he exclaimed. "The Old West. In Europe, forty years can pass, the seasons turn, the harvest comes and goes, and a son becomes the man his father was, exactly, no different. But in the vast land that is the territories, forty years is the difference between one way of life and another."

There was no translation. And yet Duncan, crushed by worries only moments before, was in communion. There was a universal language, emotional, that conducted like electricity.

"Here tonight, the traditions and the pageantry, the glory and the spectacle, the passion and the battles, the skills and the beauty that made America worth winning." He paused here, for the first performers were Onondagas, who could not be accused of winning. "There will also be Cossacks." Behind him, his company was flowing onto the field in preparation, so he finished with a bow and trotted away to no applause.

Edgar came dutifully from the corrals, clutching his tuba and playing the bass part to "The Rubber Rose Polka," tapping his foot in the dust in a way that he prayed inspired festivity.

"Mexico!" Duncan cried. Programs swayed as people fanned themselves, eyes turning toward the still-empty Imperial stands. "Old Mexico, land of desperadoes!" A wind had come up, and it brought to Duncan's ears a couple of coughs, the sipping of beer, chewing of sausage—could he hear the crowd *glare* at him? He said, "Yee-haw?"

Then the digging of spurs into horses' flanks, the percussive upkick of dust, and the clicking of tongues from a pair of genuine *vaqueros* beginning their trick-riding segment. Excitement swept the crowd, but to Duncan's consternation, all eyes had left the field and were turning toward the reviewing stand. Duncan's view was impressionistic, a white-and-red rustling of silk flowers spilling out of a cornucopia. In fact, it was a late arrival of—of whom? The men were all still wearing their hats. So it was not the Kaiser.

Attendants and ladies-in-waiting came first, fussing over the seating and ensuring that pillows with the royal crest were strapped in place. A pair of military guards gave a signal to the company on the field: the performance should halt, for Prince Joachim was arriving.

There was a polite reverence in the crowd, the type of excitement well-coached children would generate on Christmas morning when the gift turned out to be mittens. Joachim returned the nods and waves with equal politeness, as if he understood—he was only Joachim, for which he apologized. He found his seat just as—and this caused a kind of snapping-to—Princes Eitel Friedrich and Adalbert arrived together. It was rare to have three princes traveling together, though Eitel Friedrich and Adalbert were inseparable. Horsemen, lovers of armament, the first to join a hunt, and rumored to have broken the hearts of many noblewomen, they made this a gayer affair.

Then a woman in the highest risers shouted "Oskar," and she was shushed, for it was impossible that Prince Oskar was here: he was known to be suffering from the gout. And yet here he was, easing down the aisle and leaning gratefully on a cane. Four princes!

Duncan attempted to interpret what four princes meant to him. He had no scale to guide him until he considered that he would be jealous of a rival who had four princes attend a show. With a smile, he took a lucky draw on his saddle-blanket flask, and then another. Luckily, he had another flask in his boot.

Then portly August Wilhelm arrived, followed by the even beefier Wilhelm III, each of them ruddy with perspiration, glancing back and forth among their siblings with discomfort, as if trapped in a long receiving line. The crowd barely had time to analyze their clothing, their choice of hats and campaign decorations, before everyone realized the entire generation had come, including the most beloved: last in line, holding her own skirts, was Vickie, Princess Viktoria Luise, the youngest of the Hohenzollerns.

This was unbelievable—the audience fell into an almost nonsensical *walla*, storekeepers in the distant seats turning to servant girls sitting beside them to confirm what they were seeing. Princess Viktoria Luise! Her cameo resplendent in shopwindows, her method of hair braid (*die diplomatische Wellung*) imitated but never perfectly, Viktoria Luise had once shed a single tear and caused her father to tear apart the Transvaal Republic to find her a perfect blue diamond. Which she now wore in a band that went around her finger, as did everything else. She issued a challenging look at Percy Duncan, who shored up his spine to become Wild Duncan Cody. He gave her a courtly nod, which she did not return. He considered this a draw.

There were six princes and a princess. He did not think to ask why there were so many. He noted again there was no Kaiser, and this somehow made him relaxed. No one had yet botched a cue, the most thrilling acts were to come, the seven royal siblings might as well have come from a folktale, and Duncan had drained only two of his flasks.

But wait! A single proudly mustached figure strutted down the aisle in a blue uniform piped in silver. It was the equerry. He carried under his arm a plumed helmet, which he placed in the empty center seat of the royal stands. All the men in the area removed their hats.

Duncan, too, removed his hat, as did the other players.

It was as silent as a racetrack could be in a city, the distant roadway noise echoing and oceanic, as Kaiser Wilhelm II and Kaiserin Victoria paraded down the central aisle. She concerned herself with every step, resplendent in crème-de-menthe cottons (she despised the feeling of silk) and her Roman wax pearls, a sign she was shunning ostentation today. As the ladies made *knix* toward her, Victoria, known as Dona, brushed the air with small waving motions that at once acknowledged the ritual and begged off further display.

Wilhelm smartly returned each salute with a brilliant snap of his wrist, meeting every eye until the other person looked away. His cape covered him from throat to knee. The crowd scrutinized him even more closely than usual today to look for clues; no fortune-teller knew what was actually coming, but if beneath his cape Wilhelm was wearing full military attire, his chest blindingly decked with medals, there would be no rest for Berlin tonight or for many nights to come.

He knew of the intensity of their gazes. He was used to being such an object; it was part of what made him royalty. Hesitating before his seat, Wilhelm waited for the equerry to remove the helmet that had reserved it, and then, with a motion of unveiling, he let his cape go to reveal a tweed jacket buttoned up to the throat, a sash belt buckled above the waist. A groom handed him a homburg, which he tilted rakishly, inserting in its grosgrain band a single feather from a red-tailed hawk.

A hunting jacket! Brilliant! It was a sartorial choice that called for interpretation: he was informal and at leisure, which, being the Kaiser's version of leisure, meant he was in no way relaxing. Instead, he was ready for sport and for the scent of foxes and deer and, if necessary, *Serbs*.

The hat was the bow that tied off all speculation: he was bringing back the style of homburg that Edward VII had spirited away and declared a hat for the English. What was removed from Germany came back to Germany, even if it took thirty years.

Duncan, who was not a party to these thoughts, let his mind bubble, hoping wit and charm would come to the surface. Once, Buffalo Bill had performed for the kings of Denmark, Greece, Saxony, and Belgium. They asked if he'd ever before done such a thing, knowing he hadn't; no one had. Bill had responded, "Surely. But I never held such a royal flush as this against four kings."

Duncan could think of nothing. It was less about a real royal family than the idea of one. Who knew if one was fat actually or if another wept himself to sleep. That word "royalty" was more important than its servant word "reality." Seven royal siblings, a Kaiser, a Kaiserin—no puns or allusions came to mind. "If I had but seven chances to . . ." he thought. "Behold, the seven ages of . . . Were there seven seas upon which, as you see, plus of course your parents . . ."

"Please, Cody, do go on, old chap."

The Kaiser had spoken quickly, with a slight deflective ring to it, as if dismissing his own importance. Duncan nodded, so that his hat came down below his eyeline.

"Old Mexico! Yee-haw!"

All went well for many pleasant minutes. Duncan engrossed himself in the role of ringmaster, focusing so hard on his acts that he hardly paid attention to his own mind except when he was surprised to find the flask at his lips. Mexican riders brandished lariats on swivel *hondas* that they made rise and fall about their bodies, dangerous and obedient like cobra snakes, and the audience leaned forward to watch how the Kaiser leaned forward to watch.

There was a page standing next to the Kaiser; he seemed to have simply materialized. The page passed the Kaiser a paper on a silver tray embellished with the royal crest. It was a telegram from Tsar Nicholas II of Russia. It read, in English, "I beg you in the name of our old friendship to do what you can to stop your allies from going too far," and it was signed "Nicky."

The previous several days had been terrible ones, of course. Serbia had entirely buckled to Austrian demands, and, to Wilhelm's thinking, there was no longer a reason for a war. But Serbia, while making the most humiliating concessions, was also mobilizing its armies, for Austria had declared war on the Serbs. Prince Henry of Germany felt England would be neutral, unless Russia came into the fray, and then what about France?

The night before, Russia had partially mobilized its forces, without expressly declaring its intentions. Then it stood them down. Or it hadn't— the Kaiser had heard both. He had no idea how to respond to Nicholas, so instead he whispered to the page, quickly, that a telegram of support, vague and probing, should be sent to Constantine of Greece, who had been waiting since noon for word from him.

"Peachy," Viktoria Luise murmured, a word favored lately by the young; the Kaiser saw that two Rough Riders had just switched horses at a dead run. He had often felt he was built for philosophical inquiry, sport, and artistic pursuit, not diplomatic frenzy. His famous temper only flared up, he thought, when he wasn't allowed to do what he wanted, which was to enjoy life like a poem. He heard the crowd gasp while he was dictating a new message to a contact in London, and he realized he had missed something, but he had no idea what it was.

A messenger boy from the Admiralty appeared. Great Britain was *unsure* what it was going to do.

"Miserable shopkeeper rabble," he hissed in English, which caused several of his children to look down the row toward him. He told them to look at the show and to ignore him. This was an outing he would not spoil. He wanted them to see Indians.

He drummed his fingers upon his oak armrest, into which palmettes had been carved. What the world needed, the Kaiser frequently said in those dark days, was to calm down. On the other hand, perhaps he could turn India against Britain. With the stub of a pencil he'd found in his hunting jacket, he wrote a telegram in English for the Tsar. "I am exerting my utmost influence to induce the Austrians to deal straightly to arrive at a satisfactory understanding with you." He looked back at the Tsar's cognomen and signed this message "Willie."

He sat back with satisfaction, only to note that the field before him was completely empty. *"Sind die Inder schon gekommen?"* he asked, and then, when he received no answer, "Have I missed the Indians? The Onondagas? I rather hope not."

He had not missed the Indians. He had missed the Arabs and the South American gauchos. Another telegram had crossed wires with one he'd just sent: the Tsar had tried to cancel the mobilization, but it had been impossible; the Russian army was on full alert.

Wilhelm crushed the news in his right hand. The full chill of disaster sat on his shoulders. A great dreadnought had launched, its engines had engaged, and there was no one left to throw down the anchor. A phrase came to him in English, one good enough to be his own, he thought— *looking down the barrel of history*—and, with his mind emptying into despair, he regarded the racetrack, which now flooded with Cossacks.

He did not breathe. Or blink. Cossacks? There, gaudy and preening like show pheasants, in beige-and-silk-girdled *zhupan*s, flowing *sharovary* flouncing as the wind rushed up their legs, shod in high Morocco boots, wearing fur caps that showed off their *oseledet*s, and ululating their wild rebellious cry of "*Yi! Yi! Yiyiyi!*," was a platoon of Cossacks. Wilhelm wondered: Wasn't this a Wild West show? What did Cossacks have to do with the Wild West?

He consulted the program he had long ago pleated with anxiousness.

The Cossacks were the midpoint of the program, and were to perform trick riding, *dzhigitovka,* a form quite familiar to him. This was but a demonstration. It was not, he decided, an assassination attempt. Wilhelm raised a single finger, and an attendant associated with the treasury shimmered to his side. He asked how much gold was in reserve at the Julius *Strum* in Spandau. Then he frowned again at the riding ring before him.

"Cossacks!" Duncan called to the crowd. "Freemen and adventurers! These stalwart cowboys of the Russian steppes!" He was supposed to continue his patter, but the whiskey had finally begun to behave, and the next words, tricky in their alliteration, came forth thickly. "Independent as Americans, frontiersmen, freemen, the cowboys of the Caucasus, Plainsmen of St. Petersburg, the 7th Calvary of Siberia."

Americans had once seen them as suppressors of uprisings, torturers of Jews. Then Buffalo Bill had gotten hold of them. It had taken months of newspaper accounts saluting their fierce independence, their love of Christ. There was no Cossack profession except warrior, an existence that reminded Americans of their own Indians, who were no longer dangerous.

The Kaiser folded his arms. When the sabers came out in Wild Duncan Cody's Wild West show, they came with the harsh scrape and clatter of silverware falling from dinner plates.

"These are not Cossacks," he hissed to Viktoria Luise.

"You think too much, Papa," she responded. Wilhelm turned toward Dona, but knew better; she lacked his sense of poetry. He glared at the "Cossacks" until he intuited that they were actually Onondaga Indians.

Ah, the Red Men. The Kaiser—when he was still just five-year-old Little Willie of the withered arm—received strict tutelage under the skeletal Herr Hinzpeter, who had ordered him to treat all frivolity like an insidious disease. He was never praised, was taught to pursue perfection and to understand that he would never achieve it, and never to eat dessert, even when it was his turn to cut the cake at teatime. He was allowed to play, as long as his games involved diplomacy or, better, war. Hence his love for James Fenimore Cooper. *The Last of the Mohicans,* wholeheartedly approved by the pedant Hinzpeter, was about war, and yet it was also—a secret Wilhelm would take to his grave—*fun.*

Upon learning that there were actual American children in Potsdam, he ordered them to play with him, to play Indians. Some days, he was the Deerslayer; on others, Chingachgook; but on every Saturday afternoon, Willie was no longer Friedrich Wilhelm Victor Albert Hohenzollern, but a savage who scalped servants and the more indulgent members of his family. Alas, just like a Cossack, his destiny awaited him: on his twelfth birthday, he was shown the royal fleet and told that from now on he was to like sailors, not Red Men.

Once, twice as an adult—the moment with Annie Oakley, for instance—Wilhelm felt he had escaped again. Recently, with the all-but-literal weight of the planet descending upon him, he had called his advisers to canvass the newspapers and the streets in search of some entertainment to relieve him. That a Wild West show was coming seemed like a blessing. He had ordered his family to come with him, describing in no uncertain terms that they would all have fun. *Now.*

His pageboy returned, trotting down the aisle, then bowing down so that his back was horizontal to the earth. There was enough gold at the Julius *Strum* for two days of war.

"Two days!" Wilhelm exclaimed. "Two days?" Reflexively, his hand went to his head for the protection of his helmet. When it touched the wool of his civilian-style hat, he winced. Germany was completely unprepared. His people would be destroyed. An unfamiliar discomfort, beginning in his stomach, flushed quickly up his throat. Force of will prevented tears from forming. What would happen to his subjects?

The Cossacks, or at least those playing them, removed their sabers and spun them higher and higher into the air in perfect parabolas, catching the sabers each time, no matter how far forward their gallops had taken them. Their faces, which he had first taken as the weathered result of the steppes, suggested instead humid summers in the forests of the great Iroquois Nation, the Five Tribes. This was the era he liked best, the brutal life, a confederacy of warriors whose empire was the largest on the continent, whose prisoners were tortured over great fires and dishonored if they dared cry out in pain.

And now they were playing Cossacks.

"Wo ist Wild Duncan Cody?" He asked this of no one in particular, his voice the reasonable monotone of a man descending into fury.

Cody, it turned out, was preparing for his act. In the canvas tent, among the partitions of the dressing rooms, whose airless confines parlayed body heat into a fine mist, Duncan was emptying a bottle of Jack Daniel's. The poster said "Shooting While Drunk." He wasn't going to lie to the audience.

He believed the campfire adage that if you could lie on the ground without holding on, you weren't truly drunk. He reached for a three-quarters-finished bottle of Sunny Brook, but knocked the bottle off the makeup table. Its cap bounced away; its contents burbled into the dirt.

Then, remarkably, he was on the field, looking across the detritus of the melons cleaved by Cossack scimitars, which rested among the splintered sugarcanes destroyed by the *vaqueros'* horses' hooves. There was the pioneer cabin, ready to go alight; there was the Wells Fargo wagon, soon to meet its doom. All around were targets: clay pigeons awaiting their catapult, glass balls to be launched in the air, bull's-eyes and piñatas made to explode confetti when struck with a bullet.

Moments were passing, as moments were made to do. The sky was finally darkening, the clouds cooperating in such a way that the light was going from the slate gray of a German summer to a ripening orange. Duncan walked in a perfectly straight line in his Hyer boots, two-tone, stamped with sunflowers and Jayhawks, a memento of Kansas City, the elevated heels of which made to his ear a particularly noble sound as they struck the ground. There were racks of simple Winchester '73s on an oak stand beside which young Edmund and Edgar stood, ready to reload. His shadow behind him was ten feet and growing.

Duncan wore a holster slung over his right hip in which there was a Colt New Army and Navy Double Action revolver with a six-inch barrel, and under his left armpit was a .44-40 Colt Single Action Army revolver, and just below it, in a custom calfskin holster braced against his ribs, a .22 spur-trigger Suicide Special, and in his right boot was a pearl-handled, rosette-inlaid Remington over-and-under .41 rimfire-caliber Derringer with an inscription from someone named Laura to someone named Hedy.

"Ladies and gentlemen. Small children. I—am—drunk." His eyes blazed with pride. He drew his double-action Colt, aimed it, and blew a clay pigeon into cinders. Only then did he remember he had forgotten to tell Edmund to release it. The boy looked into his now empty hands with knock-kneed wonder. He made a brief chirping sound, turned tail, and ran.

There was polite applause.

Watching the boy disappear, Duncan sighed. He waved with his revolver, beckoning Edgar to come fill in for his vanished brother. Edgar shook his head no. With determination just shy of annoyance, Duncan used the barrel of the gun to indicate where he wanted Edgar to stand. Having given up all hope, Edgar obeyed. Duncan looked toward the reviewing stands. "Pull!"

Edgar hurled six blue glass balls in the air, throwing himself into the dust behind the nearest cover, a steamer trunk, as Duncan fired the double-action Colt six times.

As the report echoed across the low and level arena, all eyes swept about in search of what exactly had happened: all were broken, but had that happened in the air? Perhaps several had collided on their own—it was hard to tell.

There was a low mutter through the stands. Princes Eitel Friedrich and Adalbert shared their surprise: *Sechs? Ja, sechs. Alle Glaskugeln.* The repetition of the number six transformed it from suspicion to fact to the first footsteps of a legend: Duncan had shot and shattered all of them.

There wasn't so much applause as re-evaluation of the teetering man on the field. It was possible that Duncan wasn't actually drunk, but playing a part, no? And Duncan, though he spoke no German, was no stranger to the universal language of doubt. He made a tipping gesture with his thumb and forefinger, and Edgar trotted toward him with a new bottle of Sunny Brook. Duncan grabbed it, peeled away its cap, and emptied a third of the bottle down his throat.

When all the braves returned
The heart of Redwing yearned. . . .

There should have been more, but all he remembered was "Redwing," which he yelled, followed by "Redwing!" He tossed the bottle by its neck into the gathering dusk, the light playing on its tumbling end over end, and he drew his pistols, shattered it, and, in a cool motion, held out a shot glass as if ready to catch the resultant high-proof rain.

The result was lingering merriment. The patrons began to understand that, though the Cossacks might in fact be Indians, the drunk man was well and truly plastered. Further, there was a rare moment before them, history potentially in the making, a history on top of all the other history they were currently burdened by, and perhaps they were discovering an entertainment as yet unknown.

The next stunt involved mounting Betsy, bringing her to a gallop, tumbling out of the saddle as if out of control, and rolling upright to shoot paper targets out of Edgar's hands. He'd never exactly managed this while sober, but things had gone so well already that he felt confident.

When he was in the saddle, he told himself stories of himself. "Did you see him the first day he shot while drunk? Let me tell you the story. The forward roll he did at age fifty-eight!" After Germany, then France, and Italy, an audience with Pope Pius, the admiration of the Swiss Guard, a return Stateside.

Betsy knew how to skid to a standstill, four legs locking into place, and Duncan let the momentum carry him out of the saddle into a forward roll, and when he arose upright, hat flying away, hair leaping on the wind, pistols in hand, his eyes fell on the Kaiser.

He had in mind, finally, a witticism. It had occurred to him in a fifth of a second that he and the Kaiser were not that different—each of them dressed to hunt, each of them aware of his audience and the value of showmanship, and each shaken to the bones as a child by stories of the old and soon-to-be-extinguished Wild West. His quip was based on these facts, and samplers would be tatted with its succinct wisdom.

But there was also a difference between Duncan and the Kaiser. Duncan saw it the moment he opened his mouth: he did not matter.

It brought him to a halt. The two men were fifteen, perhaps twenty feet apart. The Kaiser shifted in his seat, passing along a silent suggestion of missed opportunities. The understanding passed between them, as chilling as an ice cube pressed to the back of Duncan's neck. Numbness shot down Duncan's shoulders and through his left arm to his fingertips. He went gray. One gun fell from his hand, and he clutched at his chest. With a small gasp, he toppled into the dirt.

There he lay, one arm under his body, the other extended. Neither hand held a gun; the pistols had tumbled, end over end, away from him. His hat lay on its brim, upside down.

An intake of breath among the crowd. Followed by laughter.

The next few minutes were vague for Duncan, involving mostly strange, grainy flashes before his eyes, his vision rendered into points of light, scratches in a negative, a hallucination of numbers counting down. He was removed via stretcher and taken back to his tent, the crowd all the while applauding and letting loose strange hoots and whistles which he could not interpret—was that the crowd's contempt, or had they, for a moment, a flash of gold, at least loved him?

Later, years later, the summer evenings of 1914 were remarked upon for the light's reluctance to leave the sky. It seemed at seven o'clock or seven-thirty to be tranquil and infinite twilight. Nimbus clouds whose bellies

were dappled with streaks of orange glowstone faded as the Wells Fargo
wagon began its circuit around the field.

The Kaiser watched in the same way he listened in church: he looked
rapt. Meanwhile, he tended to his own discontents. Just as a sermon had its
inexorable rhythms, so did the finale of the Wild West show: A Wells Fargo
stagecoach, defended by riflemen, chased by savage Indians, must have its
horses panic in harness, the lead two rearing up to show fear. A cowboy,
the Kaiser noted, must fall from the wagon as if shot, seeming to be trampled by a hundred horses, so that the crowd gasps. As the light wanes,
there must be flaming arrows that turn the body of the wagon into a candelabra. The stagecoach must collide with a pioneer cabin, it must explode
as if packed with fireworks, a family must scream for help, there must be
the threat of unspeakable violence against them, and the crackling and the
dazzle of the flames must be the backdrop for the Indians to whoop and
holler in ersatz gibberish that could as easily be Malay as Cherokee.

He had seen everything now. The form was exhausted. How can we
possibly fight without gold? he wondered. He calculated how quickly the
other securities—bonds, promissory notes, stocks, government loans—
could be converted into cash.

Then: eight mounted riders in flat-plate hats and Union Blue, yellow
piping on their trousers, armed with '73 Springfield Carbines, the first man
in line carrying the Stars and Stripes and blowing a bugle—not even holding on to his reins, the Kaiser noted with dissatisfaction. The uniforms did
not match—there were kerchiefs and caps from inappropriate campaigns,
and the holes in their clothing had been patched with white canvas. The
cavalry had arrived.

August Wilhelm surprised him by muttering that that was very accurate. He made a sweeping gesture, as if the horizon were Montana. "They
dressed as the field conditions forced them. The cavalry was adaptive to
war," he said.

"Quite unprofessional," Adalbert spat.

"But they won," August Wilhelm concluded.

The Kaiser blinked, his eyes so dry they almost clicked. Americans.
Would there be Americans in this war? He felt like a blind man groping
through a room packed with furniture. What side would they fight on?
What were their industries, their national interest, their character? All
he could touch upon was fantasy, romance, entertainment. Was Duncan
even a real colonel? And if he wasn't, did it even matter? A fake col-

onel employing real Indians to portray fake Cossacks and re-create battles that never happened, in uniforms that were correct because they were incorrect. The American character had been such a part of his daydreams, his childhood, the need to bring it down to earth and study it seemed as impossible as lassoing a cloud. Which was something Americans might try.

On the field was the final battle, cavalrymen in mortal combat with Indians. Lit from below by the dismembered, flaming wheels of the wagon, up went an Iroquois tomahawk, sharpened spike turned downward, flared brass blade gleaming against the fire, ready to impale its victim. Then—miraculously!—a soldier galloping on horseback, being strangled by another Indian, back bent over the horn of his saddle, pulled his pistol and shot the tomahawk out of the savage's hand!

The Indians' heads jerked back from punches that never really connected. They plunged into hidden hay bales when shot with blank cartridges, letting themselves be lassoed and dragged through the dust until the rescued pioneer family could be paraded on the saddles of the victorious American soldiers.

After passing the eyes once, it vanished, except for memory, and so remembered fondly.

The light was gone now. If it weren't for the dying flames, sputtering and sending up smoke, ash, the fireflies of embers, the action would be playing in darkness, hints of action, grays against blacks.

The Kaiser's joints creaked as he stood. His legs were stiff. He began a slow, rhythmic collision of his palms, which caused his family to exchange glances. Royalty did not applaud. Dona stepped on his ankle, but he paid her no mind. The piston of one arm smacking one good palm against the rotten one, until the rest of the stands joined him, all together, the city, his people, applauding in unison.

The Kaiser had learned something but, more important, felt something, something achingly lovely. There was pleasure in victory, that much he had known, but now he understood the nobility of failure. His Indians had fought magnificently against overwhelming odds.

Later, he would direct his armies to mobilize against Russia. All guilt would be on the Tsar. England would be stripped of India. Let the Americans come. He would turn Mexico against them. He would order the German borders sealed and all foreigners stripped of their assets to serve the war machine. This would begin with the show before him.

As he applauded, he counted the horses he saw, the pistols, the rifles, even the instruments, which would be good for military bands to rehearse. The Indians had survived worse.

On the field, the 7th Cavalry, the pioneer family, the Indians, they all bowed together. The applause was continuing, and, at a loss for how to react, they brought out their children, and coached them in the art of taking a bow. Even the stagehands bowed. Still it did not stop.

At the edges of the racetrack, the Onondagas caught glimpses of soldiers. Three hundred sixty degrees all around, peeking among the broken props and piles of supplies, between the tent posts, German soldiers were advancing across wisps of smoke and rising ash. Each carried a gun, bayonet forward. The uniforms were gray, with many brass buttons, and their smooth, dark helmets did not reflect light.

The crowd was beginning to sing. They were singing hymns together, voices high and almost anonymous in the night sky, syllables as strange and unknowable as anything the Wild West troupe had ever heard. It was the last war that would ever begin with a song.

6

In the first week of August 1914, as the longest fuse the world had ever known finally ignited, Americans were trapped across Europe. Even in England, the banks were closed, the pound rose overnight from $4.50 to $6.00, the stores emptied of all goods, and no officials could give assurances of what kind of war was to come.

A stream of American refugees found the Savoy: families, teachers on holiday, tourists, heirs and heiresses, adventurers, criminals. The initial queue, which looped and doubled and stretched down the Strand halfway to Embankment Park, was met at the Savoy's Thames-side entrance by a table of a half dozen "front men," shrewd junior clerks whose job was to be friendly, to ask a few leading questions, to size up the applicant's demeanor, dress, needs, and belongings, and to hand him or her a blank three-by-five-inch index card. The code was a closely held discretion, but blue cards went to the honorable destitute, white cards to those who seemed solvent, and red cards to the "doubtful cases."

Sunnyside

Lodgings were found for those who were sleeping in the parks. Loans of ten shillings a day were made. Steamer ships and freighters and tankers were located.

Weeks passed. The queues dried up. Europe seemed to be clear of stranded Americans. There were six, then just five, then one front man by the Strand entrance, and the tables and chairs where loans were arranged were mostly put back into storage.

At noon, on a day late in September, a pair of French-made transport buses, battered and mud-stained, their bonnets wired shut and windscreens spiderwebbed and shattered, halted at the Strand entrance. The back flaps pushed aside, and out spilled children, cowboys, and Onondaga Indians.

A final passenger was removed from the cargo hold of one of the buses. On a stretcher improvised from saddle blankets and wooden pikes, his shattered visage half mummified in brownish bandages, lay a ruin: Percy Bysshe Duncan.

A blue card was tucked into the folds of the stretcher. Duncan was rushed to the medical station, a converted storage closet next to the Gondoliers Room, by the ladies' coats. He lolled in and out of consciousness, speaking in low tones. At one point, he creaked, *"Er ist* nicht *Buffalo Bill."*

The Onondaga Indians explained to the front man that they'd been given a beating by the German army, had their horses conscripted, their belongings stolen, then were jailed, released, jailed again, and forgotten during a transfer between prison and the newly built detention center that had arisen, of all places, at the Ruhleben racetrack. They escaped Germany on the wrong side, and had to take a freighter to Sweden, and then another to Calais, before finding their way back to London.

In the storage closet, Duncan's bandages were changed, and his cuts and bruises cleaned, but there was nothing that could be done for him.

He was dreaming of the end of Buffalo Bill.

He'd heard rumors about what Bill was doing now. Movies were immortality, so Bill started a film company. With specificity no one else could achieve, Buffalo Bill re-created on film the entire Battle of Wounded Knee. He insisted it be shown in real time, meaning that an *hour* was devoted to watching soldiers reload and fire at flailing bodies that dropped like bruised fruit into the snow. "This is the best way to preserve not just the idea of the West, but the actual West," Bill said, incorrectly, and Duncan *could hear him.*

"Broke," Duncan Cody tried to whisper, for Bill was indeed bankrupt now. The methods whereby nickels and dimes collected from theaters accumulated and were then distributed to many people were a mystery to him. It was the end of the hunt. It hadn't been Comanches or wolves or a raging spring river that did him in; it had been the film business.

Wait, Duncan thought with the grief of a man who has caught on too late, *do you mean none of us gets out of this alive?* And there Duncan's vision began to tear free into nonsense and delusion, and Buffalo Bill vanished. After a priest administered the last rites, a nurse came to hold his hand.

At her touch, he stirred. It was a primal tunneling into his brain, some reptilian part that recognized the pleasant smell of a young woman. He looked into her face. He could not make out her features, his eyesight had faded that much, but, with some small remaining hint of caddishness, he managed a wink. She patted his hand in return.

"Can you help me write a letter?"

"Certainly," she said.

"I love your accent, miss. Where are you from?"

"London."

"Where is London?" He fell asleep. Then, with a start, his eyes opened. "I should write a letter," he said.

"I can help you," she said.

" 'Dear Emily,' " he said. But no. She had resisted him, and she might still. " 'Dear Emily,' " he insisted. He knew she no longer loathed him, but felt nothing for him, which was worse. "This is for my son," he explained. " 'Dear,' " he said. His mouth stayed open long enough that the nurse moved to take his pulse. Emily had written the name down. He remembered reading it. He remembered remembering it. Then he whispered, "Actually, fill that in later.

"Let's see. 'By the time you read this, I will have hit the last . . .' No, start over." He did not want to sound ridiculous. There was so much to say to Leonard (Leonard?), but the business of dying was so overwhelming it prevented him from thinking any of the important thoughts he knew he should say. "Okay. 'I've been a terrible dad and you don't know me.' " A pause. " 'Maybe you will find out some things, some of them will be true and many will be lies. Some of which I told.' " Another pause. Lawrence? " 'I want to tell you, there's going to be a war, and you shouldn't be in it. Don't get into the war.' "

He wasn't entirely sure he was speaking. He glanced toward his nurse, looking for signs of an audience. There were gray borders to his vision, which was already breaking. It looked like a flurry of threads raining on him, snowbanks of gray threads. He made a heroic effort to keep what he was sure was a beautiful woman in his sight.

" 'The world belongs to those who set the stage. In a war, you're a pawn, and if you're my son, you deserve better, you should have your own show, not follow someone else. Maybe later, in twenty years, when they have old soldiers going from town to town re-enacting the new war, then you can get involved, but don't do it now. I wonder what you can do, rope, ride, shoot, etc. Maybe different. I know the girls like you, Larry. Maybe, whatever you do, find a vocation and walk worthy of it.' "

Jaw slackening, eyes gone dim, he dictated only in his imagination. He was happy with himself. What he was saying was perfect.

" 'Larry, I know I am proud of you. Even if we don't know each other. I think you would like your old pappy, and can explain him to your mom, so she will do likewise.' "

There, he had opened the door closed unjustly so long ago. He had never seen his son, but he imagined him as ambitious, strong, rich enough to borrow money from, generous enough to make it a gift. And a perfect conduit back to the only woman.

Duncan lapsed into unconsciousness at the Savoy, in the converted linens-closet, gazed at by a Red Cross nurse from a good family, who closed his eyes, sat with him as long as her schedule would allow, and finally removed from her pad of paper a letter, incomplete, a letter that could not be sent. She folded it between his hands, which held it like the hilt of sword. Such was the end of Percy Duncan, showman.

☆　☆　☆

There were more casualties. In Portsmouth, Virginia, on Saturday, November 11, 1916, Buffalo Bill Cody took his last public bow. Busted flat, he was indentured to other, wiser, more savvy and heartless men, film men, who were working him in anticipation that he would soon drop dead. Now he was a featured player late in a military pageant calibrated to show the grit and determination of a country that didn't want to fight in Europe, because it did not fight other people's wars, but which would do so if it was called upon, so look out, because neutrality was just a split second from a knuckle sandwich. That was a difficult message to fit on a marquee, but people enjoyed the marching.

Bill was seventy. Kidney trouble prevented him from sitting on his horse for long. He saluted with a grimace, as if he were hanging off a cliff. Then it was over, his seven decades in the saddle. With the aid of two strong men, he dismounted from his buggy, thinking that it had all happened so fast.

But it is the essence of the sun to rise again, and here our travelogue comes to its conclusion. For the next day's sun, rising on November 12, 1916, illuminated what one might call "epanalepsis."

A curious motion was visible more or less every place that anyone cared to look. Figures moved as naturally as dust motes crossing a beam of light, or molecules rushing to fill a vacuum. The whole of America was an especially active beehive for a Sunday. It began early—off the coast of California, miles out to sea, where the searchlight of a lighthouse was in continuous rotation, a battered skiff roared up over the lip of a wave and into view, and under the stark, winking eye of the Fresnel lens, heaving up in the ocean's spray, there it was, an object in the viewfinder, a traveling idol, an answer to a question no one had even known to ask.

Two-Reel Comedy

Cupid and the Millionaire

. . . .

I say beforehand that the entire truth is not worth such a
price. . . . I don't want harmony. I don't want harmony, out
of a love for mankind. I don't want it.

—Fyodor Dostoevsky

"People write me letters and they ask me if I am as
wicked as I seem on the screen. I look at my little canary,
and I say, 'Dicky, am I so wicked?'
    "And Dicky says, 'Tweet, tweet.'
    "That may mean 'yes, yes' or 'no, no,' may it not?"

—Theda Bara, *Photoplay*, 1918

. . . .

1

In 1917, Chaplin made four excellent two-reelers, and received another raise and a new contract with a new set of financiers, and the independence to run his own studio. Intellectuals noticed him. *The New Republic* began to refer to him not as a comedian but as an artist. Not to be outdone, Edward Stone, music critic for the *Los Angeles Times*, concluded that Dukas's *L'Apprenti Sorcier* had almost the aesthetic ambition of a Chaplin film.

Sensing a groundswell, a tulipomania of appreciation, impish critic Heywood Broun suggested of *The Rink* that since Chaplin fell on his behind—but only of his own free will—he had become a Nietzschean superman. "Was it in *'Memschiches, Allzumenschliches,'*" he asked, "or in *'Also Sprach Zarathustra'* that the sage declared it was comic to kick, but never to be kicked?'" To be found ridiculous by Heywood Broun was its own kind of secret-society hazing; anyone other than Chaplin would have breathed a sigh of relief.

However—and he had a pitch-perfect ear for this music—he was also beginning to be hated.

He shot a gag reel showing himself and a magician on a sidewalk facing the orchards at the corner of De Longpre and La Brea in Hollywood. The magician—actually Albert Austin, one of his company, in a Hindu turban and beard—asks what he wants; Chaplin makes some grandiose gestures toward the orchard, describing peaks and spires and onion domes, monumental architecture fit for an emperor. Austin throws down his magic wand, there is a burst of smoke, and then time-lapse photography begins: the orchard is cleared, framing goes up, plaster, brick, and stucco, and in twenty seconds, Chaplin's new studio bursts forth from underneath the ground, and Chaplin, snapping each bill like a fresh bedsheet, hands the magician three dollars.

Actual construction took several months. Local residents were frightened when ground was broken. Studios were awful places. Mack Sennett's Edendale looked like the broken remains of a punch-drunk carnival in decline, whose farthest swampy edges percolated with rotting lumber and old food tins and Gordian knots of flammable nitrate stock atop bubbling fixative chemicals.

Laying the cornerstone of a studio caused as much talk as if it were a new castle, and the neighbors serfs anxious about the character of their new owner. The basin of Los Angeles and its outlying towns, from the mountains to the seashore, was more or less a sea of citrus groves, with small island settlements erupting among them. Since there was no sense of a single town, and since the residents were all transplants from other climes, natural allegiance went not to some phantom municipality but to each studio. To work at Metro was to bear that standard, and to tread the boards at Famous Players was to call Adolph Zukor your feudal lord, a situation that upset Adolph Zukor not at all.

The studios were developing personalities—from the gluttonous Famous Players–Lasky–Paramount combine, which gobbled up rivals like capons, to the more sultry Fox, whose stars wore real silk, so they would know the difference when acting. Inceville had the best picnics, and Triangle the closest saloons, but associating with Bluebird or Jewel came with a sense of shame, living on land owned by the duke's fourth son, the one whose parents were brother and sister.

So the neighbors around Sunset and De Longpre wondered what Chaplin's kingdom would be like. There was much relief when the new Charles Chaplin Studios began to take shape, for they resembled a quaint, well-kept English village. Chaplin's publicist, Carlyle Robinson, wrote up a handbill and paid boys to distribute it throughout the neighborhood. "Goodbye to the limp and sloppy canvas that flaps in the mildest breeze— the Chaplin Studios will have the best muslin diffusion systems in the world." And "No saloon for the employees, but a tennis court and swimming pool, to promote healthful energies."

The handbill announced an open house. Two thousand locals attended, signing the guest book with "Thank You" or "God Bless" or "You Are No Slacker." Chaplin himself did not attend. Word circulated, though no one could say from whom, that he was shy, and by the end of the day, when everyone had taken a look around the stages, peered into the wardrobe rooms to see the hat, cane, and shoes, gotten to shake hands with Edna Purviance or Albert Austin, and had a lemonade and a sandwich, the whispers of "He's shy, you know," were answered with "I know that—everyone knows he's shy." As people left, they wrote in the ledger that they were proud to have Charlie Chaplin in town.

"We're on his side," an elderly woman said cheerfully, the last person to leave. "Let him know we don't think he's a slacker." She had in hand that day's newspaper. Twice a week, the front page of every local paper listed the names of men who had been called to register for service in the army but had not come forth. The column was headed with a neologism coined by the Committee for Public Information: "Slackers."

Chaplin's name had never actually appeared there. Then again, he hadn't actually appeared simultaneously in over eight hundred different places across the country, either.

The moment the last person went home and the gate was locked for the night, Carlyle Robinson telephoned Chaplin, who, after consulting with him about how much the sandwiches and lemonade had cost (they had been donated by local businesses), told him he was brilliant. "I'm giving you a three-dollar raise. And excellent timing."

Excellent timing, for the next day, as according to plan, the dogs began to arrive.

Chaplin gathered them himself, and when the gates opened, he ushered the first shipment out of the dogcatcher's wagon and into the courtyard. Then he put his hands to his hips, regarding his playpen. His first day in his new studio. He declared that hours upon hours of playing with dogs was crucial. He'd had the idea that his next film would star a dog. Details were sketchy, but some impetus like that—an escalator, a rink, a bakery, and, why not, a dog—was how all his films began.

He went to the pound, day after day, claiming whatever dogs appealed to him. He was looking less for playful spirit, which so many dogs had, than for a sense of focus.

"Fine," he said to the clubfooted mistress of the pound, upon being handed a fluffy beige spaniel that licked his nose. "But can this one take direction?"

"Of course," she said.

"And how much is he?"

"Like all the rest. Fifty cents for the license."

"My brother negotiated a special rate, I believe."

She limped back to the front desk to consult with her trustees and returned to tell him it was three for a dollar.

So it went, until there were seven dollars' worth of dogs, twenty-one of them. They seemed to be of a thousand different breeds. At night, when the moon was full, it sounded like wolves throwing a cocaine bash for hyenas. The neighbors, the taste of lemonade fresh in their mouths, could never complain.

His crew, on the other hand, had raised their eyebrows after the first dozen dogs, and at fifteen, Alf Reeves, an old friend from the vaudeville days who had just begun to manage the shop, told him to knock it off, and then Chaplin told him to knock it off first. Since Reeves hadn't been doing anything, they both burst out laughing, and then Chaplin went and got six more dogs.

All of them were mutts. Chaplin had declared that mutts took direction better than any purebred; besides, they were intrinsically funnier. A purebred Bedlington terrier might be the butt of a joke, as he worked it out, but it would never be the joker. It was like the difference between dropping ice cream on a washerwoman (not funny) and on an empress (hilarious).

He said the dogs could have the run of the studio. The card games were disrupted by Alsatian Chow Chows chasing beagle-bulldogs under the tables, and the billyclubs in the property room were found scattered on the floor, with fresh collie-sized teethmarks. One ancient sort-of poodle, whom no one had recognized as a poodle until her fur began to grow in, took to sleeping on the canvas tarps they used in the carpentry shop when it rained, and no one could bear to move her.

"I'm worried about this," his brother, Syd, said. He was already a worrier, living life like a mouse shouldering a steamer trunk filled in its many compartments with suspicions about his livelihood and his marriage and whether something was or was not a symptom of gonorrhea. Chaplin always told him he worried too much, and Syd didn't have the strength to argue with that, because Syd was also lazy. "Why so many dogs?"

This made Chaplin bite down on his lip. He meant to count to ten, but it came out: "I'm putting you in the movie."

"What? Just because I asked—"

"I think I'll do your makeup."

On the first Monday after the pack had been established, the grub wagon showed up at noon, and the elderly Polish couple who made the sandwiches propped open their awning and displayed their assortment of dangling salamis. For several long moments, each bat of smoked meat swayed in the breeze, quietly. Then there were screams, many musical scales of excited barking, and a whirlwind of snarling fur—the awning banged shut like a screen door, and the Kowaleskis were outside of it, shaking their fists, and the dogs spilled out of the wagon, dragging their prizes through the dust, while Chaplin nodded his quiet approval.

The dogs could do anything they liked. Almost. A terrier growled at Chaplin, and that afternoon he was back at the pound. The casting process had begun.

When it was back down to seven dogs, Chaplin took them everywhere he went on the lot. When the payroll girl came to approve the raise for Carlyle Robinson ("What raise?"), Chaplin interrupted her to tell each dog to sit.

They worshipped him, and he lectured them about how that would never do, this was America, there were no kings here, one had to find one's own way, this demonstration that he was their hero was entirely embarrassing, he wasn't a martinet, he wasn't D. W. Griffith, they weren't making *Intolerance,* after all, to be a part of his crew was to be about intimacy, not spectacle, and because all were so rapt, he fed them biscuits.

A purple sort-of-Staffordshire terrier, Buttons, enjoyed biting down on a rubber inner tube, and being taken on what Alf called "an airplane ride" by being spun in the air. He could be put to use biting the Little Fellow on the behind. Mut (with one "t"), white with a brown patch over his left ear and eye, was quite docile, and might make a sweet hero. The collie mixed with Australian shepherd was a glutton, easily tempted by treats, and the two small dogs would bark at the slightest provocation. Chaplin filmed his attempts to shush them when stepping past a cop: they were inconsolable, not even cheese would silence them. The largest, a wolfhound–Great Dane, had a high-pitched bark, but that never mattered on camera, where the curl of his lip and the sudden movement of his jaws was inspired. On Tuesday, January 15, 1918, he had Alf write it in the studio log: "Ashes the wolfhound will be a good villain."

"This was a good day's work," Chaplin announced to his crew that afternoon. "Carry on," he said, and since it was four o'clock, his touring car arrived. The cry "He's leaving!" went up, and Kono, the chauffeur, opened the door for him, and the whole Chaplin Studios team—seamstresses, prop master, stagehands, carpenters, lighting crew, Rollie the cameraman, the payroll girl, the assistant director, the whole art department, the portrait painter, the several men whom Chaplin had rescued from disaster and whose jobs were now ill-defined except to be of good spirits all day long, and the entire company of actors, and Vincent Bryan and Maverick Terrell, men whom no one looked in the eye, men whose jobs were mysterious (they wrote ideas for factions on slips of paper and put them into a drawer in Chaplin's desk, where they were never seen again), and Edna—lined up on either side of the gate and waved goodbye to him, and he waved back with excitement, and his car pulled out of the studio. The elderly woman in the floral-print dress who closed the gate behind him—once, she had sung in the dance halls with his father and mother— waved goodbye, sadly.

Only when the car was a block down Sunset did he realize he had just spent two weeks playing with dogs. They had shot a few thousand feet of film, not really that much, but little of it relating to dogs. Instead, he had a faction of the Tramp trying to get a job at an employment office and being muscled out of the way by larger, rougher workers. He'd done it to a metronome. It was adequate.

There were envelopes in the car, scattered across the backseat. Fan mail. He opened the first piece at hand, a gentlemanly looking envelope of granite hue. The letter inside was of matching color, folded precisely.

Hotel Drisco
Detroit, Michigan

Charles Chaplin, Esq.
Chaplin Studios
Hollywood, California

19 January 1917

Dear Mr. Chaplin:
You will find enclosed herein a bill in the amount of $17.50 from the offices of William Delaney, M.D., for services rendered to my person after the inexcusable riot you caused in Beaumont, Texas, on Sunday, November 12, 1916. I hardly need remind you that men of integrity live up to their obligations in a timely manner.
I beg to remain
Yours very truly
Hugo Black

Had the signature, with its perfectly executed blotting, been more formal, it would have come with swags and roundels.

That morning's *Los Angeles Times* was on the seat. On the cover was news of the war, carnage domestic and foreign, and in the lower left corner the "Slackers" column, which he read through the letter "C," feeling relief, then guilt. Playing with dogs!

That evening, Chaplin skipped the gym and the book, and he sat on his bed and he hated the world. Several times he jailed the thought only to have it tiptoe back like an ambitious thief. He generally felt kindness toward the world, but that feeling was oceans away, huddled on a plank.

It began with an issue of *Motion Picture Magazine* that he kept on a plaster gargoyle by the toilet. *Motion Picture* had launched a yearlong vote among readers for the Motion Picture Hall of Fame. Their explanation was that the photoplay had come of age artistically, and now it was time to select the finest exemplars of the art form. So far, a half million votes had been cast. This was, Chaplin understood, fabulous for the movies, but even more fabulous for *Motion Picture Magazine.*

The Twelve Immortals were, as of this date: Earle Williams (No. 12), Mary Miles Minter (No. 11), Theda Bara (No. 10), Francis X. Bushman, Anita Stewart, Pearl White, Wallace Reid, William S. Hart, Harold Lockwood, Douglas Fairbanks as No. 3, and, in the No. 2 spot, Marguerite Clark. He hesitated here the way he did when approaching "C" in the "Slackers" column. At the top, with over eighty-five thousand votes, was Mary Pickford.

This did not cause Chaplin to hate her. It only suggested to him that Mary Pickford had the most luxurious golden curls in the history of the planet, and when they bounced in place, and she dug a finger into her dimple to eke out another win in the face of adversity, another five thousand people voted for her.

He looked at the list in detail. There were hundreds of names. At No. 37, in five-point type, between House Peters and Crane Wilbur, was Charlie Chaplin.

This made him laugh so hard he dashed from the bathroom, eager to share how idiotic it was. He wanted to telephone everyone he knew, and ask them all if House Peters had his own studio, or Crane Wilbur had a million dollars. Which of them had been parodied by Heywood Broun? Had House Peters been spotted in over eight hundred locations in one day? No, he hadn't.

It reminded him of all the Chaplin look-alike contests. He'd considered entering one, then heard a rumor that he had done so and had come in fifth. For some reason, for a man so much on the American mind, it was important that he should lose.

Pickford. Chaplin once mentioned in an interview that he had made his stage debut at age four. Within a month, he read Pickford saying she'd started at three. Immediately after he'd become the highest-paid person in America, at $670,000 a year, she argued to her employers that she made more films than he did, and didn't tend to shoot ten thousand feet of film for a single reaction shot. The argument was an exaggeration, but effective—she received a million dollars. She started calling Zukor, her boss, "Pops." When Chaplin negotiated his new contract, he noted that he at least wrote and directed his own films, and he had no choice but to ask for $1,025,000.

Lately, the war had sharpened things between them. Chaplin did not think war was a very good idea in general, and the more he knew of this one the worse it seemed, but it existed nonetheless, and he felt sympathy for the men in the trenches. He donated a hundred thousand boxes of chocolates to the Red Cross.

His feeling of benediction lasted until he saw the headline in the *Los Angeles Times:* Mary Pickford had become an *honorary colonel* in the Red Cross Corps. There was a photograph of her in a specially made uniform next to her brother, Jack, who had once had a terrible reputation (like all other Pickfords) as a layabout and a drunk, but who was newly handsome and forgiven, having signed up for the United States Naval Reserve.

Further, Mary had adopted her own brigade, the 143rd Field Artillery, attending their drills and sending each of them off with a locket that contained a photograph of her.

Was Pickford's idea to give the men something to fight for—her? He imagined men pulped by machine guns, piles of gassed corpses, tongues bloated, skins blistered, the battlefield as greasy as a butcher's floor, the unfazed smiling Mary Pickford on a million punctured throats.

Chaplin staged a celebrity boxing match for two thousand patrons and at the interval gave a halfhearted speech inviting men to enlist; to his dismay, twenty-five did so. At the next interval, Pickford promised an autographed photo for each new inductee, and 150 men enlisted.

One hundred fifty to his twenty-five? He was outraged. Why had she done so much better than he? Was she kept up nights, knowing that she was a siren whose song had lured 150 men to their possible deaths?

Then Pickford made a feature called *The Little American.* She played a victim of German brutalities. Her films, she declared, would now reflect the new American spirit of going Over the Top. It was a shock, because prior to this, pictures had mostly ignored the war. And yet, even before *The Little American* was released, it was acclaimed as an advance of the motion-picture art form. *The New Republic* explained: "She of the anodyne smile-and-curls, she of the banal feisty determination, she of the sleek rags-to-riches vehicles as mass-produced as any by Henry Ford, is condemned by us no longer. To repudiate this girl in haste is high treason to the national heart. She, *sui generis,* has revealed the new character of the motion picture actor: that of patriot."

Latin! The clincher of having been found worthy by *The New Republic.* So there she sat atop the gallery of immortals, place as assured as if she were Aphrodite and Hera and Artemis rolled into one. Chaplin did not stand a chance against her. In his room at the Athletic Club, he rubbed the bridge of his nose. The electric light by his bed made a mysterious hissing sound, as if it were expelling gas.

He envisioned his dogs in army fatigues. English bulldogs and French poodles fighting German dachshunds. The Little Fellow leading a charge with American mongrels in tow. It shimmered with an inherent ridiculousness. Throwing a pineapple grenade only to have a helpful dog catch and return it. Throwing it again and again, and seeing it return, bellowing smoke, with the anticipation each time of its explosion. There were dogs in combat—he'd seen pictures of them. One bulldog had been gassed, and English schoolchildren had taken up a collection, and now he had his own gas mask. Chaplin imagined the Tramp putting on his gas mask, and taking his dog, also in a gas mask, on a walk. Behaving as if it's a day in the park even through sniper fire and exploding shells. Shushing the battlefield so the dog could concentrate to do his business.

Several of his dogs in gas masks, sworn enemies from either side, trying to fight over a soup bone. Unable to get a grip on it, and it rolls along No Man's Land, coming to a halt among a larger pile of soup bones, which leads to an even larger pile of bones, some of which still wear uniforms. Then the dogs go mad with delight—enough to eat for a lifetime! The climax: racing into enemy headquarters to see who is in charge and finding— more dogs.

He saw the scenes as clearly as if he had already shot them. They rang in a way that throwing pies never would. Then he heard his brother's voice telling him the world would line up at his door to take turns killing him. Dogs as soldiers—the worst idea ever. You could never make fun of the war. There could only be praise and flowers and dignity. The war was safe for all the Mary Pickfords. He put a pillow over his face and bit down. For long minutes, he listened to his hissing electrical light and wished he had someone to talk to.

2

Chaplin awoke from a shiftless sleep and strange, half-constructed dreams, and there was some Victorian fanfare as in the music halls, the sound of trumpets, violins, and guitars.

Someone below his window was playing a *son jarocho,* with great brassy volume. There in the purple predawn, illuminated by streetlights outside the Athletic Club, among horses and eleven mariachis, standing up in his stirrups and playing the guitar with gusto, was Douglas Fairbanks. His smile was a simple one: it informed Chaplin that there was no use sleeping when someone as delightful as Douglas Fairbanks was around.

Fairbanks was a man whom film fit like a scabbard, in that you never noticed he was handsome until he moved. Then he was what Chaplin thought of as a movie star, exuding a notion that all life should be traversed by swinging from chandelier to chandelier.

And in person? There he was, smiling and singing "My Happy Heart," only now he had stolen one of the band members' hats, tossed it to the ground, and he was dancing around it in what he undoubtedly felt was a vivid Mexican hat dance.

Ten minutes later, Chaplin was on a horse next to Doug on a ride to the eastern hills. There was a wide trail with switchbacks among the chaparral that led from the edge of downtown, where the coyotes sometimes howled, up a gentle slope leading to the mouth of the Chavez Ravine. They made a wagon train of eighteen horses, for, in addition to the band, Doug had brought his cooks.

The mariachis played tunes to which Doug sang the first two or three lines, allowing the band to finish them on their own, because he could never be bothered to learn anything all the way through. He had never even read a script he had filmed; it took too much time.

They arrived in a clearing among gum trees, and camp was quickly set up. Doug and Chaplin watched the sun illuminate the downtown, the hamlets and burgs beyond it, the morning haze coming in from the sea. Doug tended to the campfire, over which a frying pan heaped with rashers of bacon sizzled. It was criminally easy to imagine him as a knight, dressed in the colors of Artcraft Studios, a blue-and-gold combination, carrying a blazon showing *himself*.

"Bacon!" Doug called out, and then "Coffee! Sowbelly! Hotcakes!"— as if each were enough to keep any rational man from committing suicide.

Chaplin thought about telling Doug of his troubles, but Doug disliked difficulties. Further, there was a complication: Douglas Fairbanks, proudly married to Beth Fairbanks, was sleeping with Mary Pickford.

Chaplin accepted a plate of food graciously. Doug was telling him a joke of some sort, but ceased. "Yes, that look."

"What?" he chirped, as if Doug might have read his mind.

"Are you all right? Are you *actually* all right?"

"Of course. Actually, has anyone ever sent you a medical bill? Someone named Black just billed me for—"

"Positively never. Aha! Did you pay your taxes?"

"Yes, I paid my taxes, Doug." Actually, he hadn't, and Syd had told him he really should, and Chaplin had told him he worried too much, and Syd told him to worry more, and then it turned into their usual discussion about whether iodine was a preventative or actually a cure.

First serving finished, Doug banged his metal plate down on a rock. "Perfect!" Patting his stomach. "This is all you need, Charlie. Never mind all that slacker business." He sucked the remains of some egg from his fingers. "You just need to get out and be reminded of the goods."

"What are the goods?"

"Us talking like this. You're twenty-seven years old—"

"Twenty-eight."

"Twenty-eight years old, young, handsome, and at the top of your game. And look at this view. God created it for a reason. He gave it to you and to me. And he put us here to see it for a reason, too."

"All right," Chaplin said slowly. "Then why does he let Jack Warner see it, too?"

Doug tossed his coffee out of his Sierra cup and handed it over to a waiter for more. He put his fists to his hips. "Now, none of *that*." Chaplin recognized this pose from one of Doug's movies, perhaps more than one, and it made him love Doug, who was now accepting a fresh cup of coffee.

"*That* might be all there is for me."

"What if you showed them all and enlisted anyway? You'd like it if you had to fight for something, Chaplin. I know it."

"You'd fight for a few pepper trees and some oranges? And to protect the liberty of Adolph Zukor?"

"You're not that cynical. You'd like to be a hero."

"My only hero is William G. McAdoo."

"Pardon my ignorance, Charlie, but—"

"Secretary of the Treasury William G. McAdoo. He signs the dollar bills. I love him."

Doug grabbed a stick, the tip of which had been burned long ago to charcoal, and poked at Chaplin, leaving soot on his dungarees. "I believe you think more of the world than that."

"I believe there are better ways to live in the world than being shot every day of it."

"No one is asking you to be shot. No army in the world would put you in the front line."

Chaplin didn't quite believe that. He stared at his plate, which was still mostly filled, since he had recently learned to eat slowly. He imagined how the men in the front lines would want to murder him for his special treatment. "All right, picture this—Corporal Douglas Fairbanks."

"At the ready. Over the top!"

"But imagine you're at the mercy of people stupider than you are. Tell me that's not your personal nightmare."

Doug worked the dirt with his stick in silence. Chaplin glanced at the design he was making. It was a crude, childish drawing of a house. Smoke came from the chimney, and a family stood outside, mother, father, baby figures, smiling. Then: "All right, Charlie. You don't want to join the army because you don't want anyone else to direct you."

"Now, that's just . . . just . . ." What it was was just *accurate*. He shook his head. "This isn't about the slacker business anyway."

Doug believed him. "Ha! Then it's about your mother?"

"What? No," Chaplin said, immediately annoyed.

"I thought she was coming from England."

"She was. Now she isn't."

"A man never outgrows his mother. She's his precious—"

"For the love of— Doug, your mother was a monster. You said so yourself."

"I should have talked to her more."

"You didn't speak to her for years."

"You shouldn't make my mistakes."

"Is the guilt you feel part of the goods, too?"

Doug looked stricken, and Chaplin was alarmed at how easily he had just sent the point of his épée directly into his friend's heart. Doug said, "Not exactly sure, old man, why you had to say that, but I have little aches and pains. Yes."

"What sort of aches and pains?"

"They don't matter," Doug said, and it was like closing a door. Doug had written a book, *Laugh and Live,* which told the rest of the world—more or less—how to be Douglas Fairbanks. It advised that happiness was a continual choice, vitality the natural state of man, that one's family was one's cornerstone, that "three squares to eat and five rounds to spar and eight hours to rest" was the essential way to contentment, or productivity, or something. Chaplin had never finished reading it and Doug hadn't, either.

He imagined Doug in the rain, hopeless and ill, repeating to himself his own advice from his chapter on matrimony: "If a man is a manly man, he should marry early and remain faithful to the bride of his youth." Douglas coughing, the rain soaking him to the marrow, as Beth, his wife, has locked him out of the house. And Doug, bellowing it again, as if trying to force a key into a lock that will not turn, "If a man is a manly man"—cough, cough, and then, weakly, "Help." Chaplin would never get to see a side of Doug like that. Perhaps Pickford got to see it. This made him want to take it away from her.

It had been quiet for an uncomfortably long amount of time. "I'm sorry," Chaplin finally said. "How's Mary?"

"She's fine," Doug said, with suspicion.

"I know we weren't talking about her."

"Well, she's worried about her brother, of course."

"I heard he was safely in the Naval Reserve."

Doug rubbed his chin. "I thought it was the Signal Corps."

"No, the uniform was definitely Naval Reserve."

"I could have sworn . . . Ah, heck, it doesn't matter. I don't know, Charlie. She worries about him."

"Why?"

"Never mind that." Then Doug said, "She's optimistic."

"Really? She is? I think it's all about chaos and homicide."

Now Doug's head was actually hanging, and he was for a rare moment not moving. He finally muttered, "Maybe you should go to a party."

"Why?"

"You'd have fun at a party."

"You'd have fun at a party."

"I'm at a party right now," Doug said. "So are you. You just won't admit it." He waved to the band, half of whom were still eating, and all of whom were discussing whether it was a good or a bad thing to bring such wealthy men up the Chavez Ravine and so close to La Loma, where they lived—for now. Quickly, the plates went down, the instruments and smiles went up, and they launched into "La Bamba," which Doug began to sing. *"Para bailar la bamba,"* he sang, repeatedly, as if there were no other lyrics.

Chaplin smiled at him, tried to breathe in the wonder of coffee, camp-fire, Los Angeles at his feet. He imagined himself exultant, a newly minted king, taking in the sights of his noble lands. He pictured the smile on his face, the pleasant brush of his ermine robe, the rush of delight, how his kingdom would be carnivals and swing sets and garden slides over which glided a thousand lithe harem girls.

But when he thought of his mother visiting, the visions of plenty vanished. He wanted more dogs. He would change the title of his film from *Charlie's Mutt* to *I Should Worry.*

Early in the war, it was unclear whether British subjects living abroad could be drafted. Then the United States signed a treaty allowing exactly that. Dozens of English actors were called home to active service. With each departure, each fare-thee-well party at Harvey's Steakhouse, or Barney Oldfield's, more pairs of eyes turned in curiosity up the filmmaking food chain.

Months before he got his own studio, early 1917, a book of comic strips called *Charlie in the Army* showed the misadventures of Chaplin in basic training. There were no similar books about Mary in the Red Cross, or

Jack in the Naval Reserve, or House Peters anywhere. The gags therein weren't witty; they reminded Chaplin of Punch and Judy shows.

It puzzled him, in that people weren't buying it because it was good, but because it reminded them of Chaplin, though—and this struck him as crucial—it was not nearly as good as *he* was. It seemed to render the unimaginable much less potent. If Charlie was in the army, then the army was not so awful. And if this was all that happened to him, if nothing unexpected befell him, the country would be safe. It sold tens of thousands of copies. No one spoke of having enjoyed it, but it was not quite disposable, because it further opened that door for speculation: indeed, why wasn't Charlie in the army?

The reason was simple: the army had requested that he *not* join. He had been told he was symbolically more valuable making movies than being in the trenches. But certain of the War Office felt that not drafting him was another kind of symbol, a wrongheaded one, and so their arrangement was never publicized. Chaplin asked for a statement Carlyle Robinson could release to the press to ease the attacks against him, and the War Office apologized, said that would be difficult, and asked whether perhaps they could do something else.

There was. He asked for it himself, over lunch with the British attaché, rather than involving Syd. It was a favor easily granted, and the details were hidden in dossiers stamped "most secret." The arrangement was meant to bring him relief.

For now, there was enough trouble: an ominous development in the fan-mail sacks. First one letter in a hundred, then two, then three contained nothing, no letter, no request for an autograph—just a single white feather. For cowardice.

Robinson, as much a master of the press as of neighborhood open houses, fought obliquely: articles appeared in syndication about the astonishing results achieved by Dr. Lewis Coleman Hall, who rehabilitated soldiers. "We set up projectors to show films on the ceilings as many of our boys are too wounded to sit up. Nothing has got through to them for weeks but when I show a Chaplin movie to a poor fellow it may arrest his mind for a second. I may say, 'Do you know Charlie?' and then begins the first ray of hope that the boy's mind can be saved."

But in October 1917, standees began to vanish. These were life-sized cutouts of the Little Fellow, distributed to theaters to promote *Easy Street* and *The Count*. They featured Chaplin in costume, tipping his hat to patrons, a befuddled but solicitous expression on his face, as if he had been hired for an important job whose duties he couldn't hope to equal. They were as familiar as cigar-store Indians, propped up at cinema entrances right next to the coming-attractions posters. And one by one, they all disappeared. By the time his last film from Mutual Studios, *The Adventurer,* was released in the winter of 1917, hardly a theater in America or Great Britain had one left.

On January 2, 1918, the 14th Battalion, Highland Light Infantry, were amassed in the trenches outside the piles of bricks and smoking tree stumps that were once the village of Sapigny, France. On the other side of No Man's Land, with its heaped-up corpses and spools of *cheveux d'ange* razor wire, was an unknown number of German soldiers, huddling in a trench system whose geographic location had remained largely unchanged in the last three years. But there were rumors of an oncoming attack; balloon observers had seen reinforcements on the Allied side, and so tensions rode high.

At dawn, the first figure appeared atop the Highlanders' trench, and it was immediately shredded by German rifle fire. Farther down the line, another figure appeared, and another, and each of them was cut down in turn before the command to cease fire was given. The *Hauptmann* in charge quietly observed, among the rising morning fog, a line of five dozen identical men atop the trenches, all of them with rectangular mustaches, all clutching canes and tipping derbies.

Chaplin's films had never been released in Germany—the Kaiser's men hadn't a clue who this was or what he represented. The order was given, and five straight minutes of machine-gun fire turned the standees into a rain of powder and paper flakes, and all that was left was a few dozen two-dimensional pairs of size-sixteen feet.

The Scots began to roar with laughter. No one could ever explain what exactly had been so funny.

There was a popular ditty the Allied men sang all over France, to that tune of "Redwing," once sung on a racetrack, long ago, by an ersatz soldier, to royalty:

> *The moon shines bright*
> *on Charlie Chaplin*
> *His boots are cracking,*
> *for want of blacking*
> *And his little baggy trousers,*
> *they want mending*

Before we send him
to the Dardanelles

That this was a popular sentiment was obvious, in that it was sung though the last line didn't even *rhyme.*

Chaplin counted up boxes of chocolate, charity events, war bonds, backroad messages from the War Office telling him to stay where he was. You could argue with committees and letters to the editor, but not with the voices of actual soldiers. Making a movie starring a dog didn't seem to be a bright thing to do. He had no idea what would happen to him.

A few days after his breakfast with Doug, Chaplin walked into the studio, tossed his cap to his valet, and announced *I Should Worry* was over; instead, they were going to make a film called *Wiggle and Son.* It was going to be extraordinarily touching. The dogs should all be returned to the pound. Edna's hair should be done in ringlets, and Chaplin would do it himself. Did Chaplin want to make another positive of *Her Friend the Bandit* for reissuance? No, he didn't—there was no time for that. The construction department should make a saloon. It should be called the Green Lantern, and there should be an orchestra pit. The property master should get tables, chairs, a full set of bottles and taps for the bartender, and instruments for a ratty jazz band. Chaplin wanted a real proscenium and real curtain, and a fire curtain and real walls, too, and the technical director needed to stop complaining and obey the property master. Syd should go into Makeup and wait there for further instruction.

With his company thus engaged, he sat Edna down and began to comb her hair. She asked him how he'd been, and he told her of story ideas he had, and she watched him in a hand mirror that she held up and turned to follow him as he moved back and forth among the makeup table, the hot comb, the lengths of false hair, and herself. He sensed she wanted to say something, and his eyes met hers in the mirror.

"Are you being good?" she asked.

"Yes," he said, hesitantly. She continued to look at him as if he hadn't said the password yet.

Her eyes were welling up. "And careful?"

"Careful? What do you mean?" When she said she thought she needed to get a tissue, he called after her, "Edna, really, what do you mean? Where are you going, Lovelock?"

And then Prince Henry of Greece arrived.

Prince Henry of Greece did not have an appointment, but had heard that one did not leave the state of California without visiting its leading avatar of culture. He signed the guestbook, about six spaces below the last prince who had visited, and he entered the courtyard of the studio with minimal retinue, for he was on vacation. Chaplin had Rollie set up his camera and filmed Prince Henry sitting at the drum kit, and the surviving footage shows the languid playboy monarch striking up a simple time signature on the snare and high hat while Chaplin dances in place. Henry asks him something, Chaplin nods and turns his toes out and walks like the Tramp until they both laugh, and then the film is over.

Afterward, it was lunch, which Chaplin took alone. There was a new stack of five books to look at, key passages underlined for him, on the topics of psychoanalysis, the Gnomonism of Sydney Hen, Milton's broadsides, the pursuit of the Anti-Life Equation, and the palaces of Alhambra.

Later, in his dressing room, there was a knock on the edge of the doorframe while Chaplin was uncorking his Max Factor. Carlyle Robinson, with a telegram. He was, like all publicity men, exceptionally well presented without actually being handsome. To be handsome would be a distraction; it was as if he had damped himself down to fit in his lovely suit. He seemed game for anything Chaplin said, although, when his memoirs were published twenty years later, they were so excoriating they only appeared in French.

"I'm sorry about this, Charlie," he said. He tapped the telegram. "I'm doing all I can for your mother."

Chaplin tidied his desk. He didn't look at Robinson for the rest of the conversation. "What's the news?"

"The authorities won't release her." There was a great, unoiled bureaucracy in England, he explained, citing names Chaplin had heard many times: immigration councils, physicians' bureaux, a hundred branches of the War Office, all of them squaring against one another in interoffice warfare that prevented one fragile lady from boarding a ship to America.

"This is frustrating," Charlie said carefully. He decided to get angry. "Why isn't she coming? Goddamn it!"

"I don't know. Every time I make headway with one welfare organization, another steps in and says, 'It is regrettable . . .'"

Chaplin smoothed out the cream on his neck. "It was a good idea. Having her come over would do wonders. Just wonders."

"Don't be too discouraged," Robinson said. "I haven't even started with the American side of things."

"What do you mean?"

"I have some muscle with the War Department over here. You've bought a lot of bonds. We can use pressure on this side of the ocean to bring her. I'm positive. Syd is very excited about this." Robinson knocked on the doorframe a couple of times, and left.

Chaplin sat in silence. He hadn't even thought about the American War Department. He considered what Robinson might be able to accomplish, until he realized he was looking at himself in the mirror, mouth soft, eyes unfocused, as if horrified by his reflection, as if expecting revelations. This was a pose he loathed. He looked away.

He tore at the label of his Rachel powder, which was well glued to its container. He absently ran his fingertip over the upper lip of the pretty girl on the label, drawing a Charlie Chaplin mustache on her.

An hour later, he came back onto the set in his street clothes. He told everyone to go home. Then he asked if the dogs were still here.

When night fell, the guard was at the gate, and Kono was waiting at the curb in the Locomobile touring car, but otherwise, Chaplin had the world to himself. He threw sticks across the courtyard, and his dogs chased them, fighting for the right to bring them back. There were Klieg lights to see by, and above that, the moon. He walked to the grass by the swimming pool, and made room in the pack to lie among them, both hands going in a frenzy of pats and scratching. He wished he were on the edge of tears. He wanted the whole world to feel that way. "I am a very bad son," he whispered to the dogs. "It's true. I am a monster. I am a bad son."

4

Two weeks later, at two o'clock on a Saturday afternoon in February, Chaplin lay flat on his back again. This time, on the floor of his bedroom at the Club. Postcards were scattered around him. He stared at the ceiling. He knew without looking that he had thirty-seven dollars on him, two tens, two fives, a two, and five ones, each brand-new and signed by William G. McAdoo, secretary of the treasury. *There is order in the universe.*

He could use his most interesting emotions for performance. Moments of desire were best, followed by fear. He called them key emotions, because, like an escape artist, he could hide them somewhere on himself and use them to unlock factions and scenes. But now he felt dread, a mélange of embarrassment and goodwill. He was awaiting the car that would take him to a party.

Chaplin was doing what he'd heard other people did: he was sharing a ride. A car would pull up, a decent-enough fellow named Eddie Sutherland would wave to him from the driver's seat, Chaplin would get in, and there would be other partygoers inside. They would drive to Santa Monica. He would have fun.

"Hullo, I'm Charles Chaplin," he said, extending his arm toward the ceiling. It sounded pretentious. "Hello, everyone. I'm Charlie." Was it more pretentious to leave the "Chaplin" off? It was a Trojan horse of informality, because it pretended he was Charlie No-One-Special, when it actually relied on those to whom he was being introduced knowing the last name themselves. He gathered up a few postcards and squared them.

The postcards were images of masterpieces of European artwork. In the spirit of improving himself, he was learning about Proto-Renaissance Florence, and to which master he could attribute what qualities. For instance, Giotto should be praised for his incisive humanity, and forgiven his inadequate perspective. His Virgin Marys were said to be especially luminous examples of the break with the antiquated Romanesque.

It was entirely possible he would not be able to work that into conversation today, for the party was at the beach.

On the other hand, it was being thrown by a man who ran a production company, and such men were legendarily insecure about what they knew. It was always good policy to frighten the men who ran production companies. Thus Chaplin had stayed up the night before, reading the most frightening party topic of them all: Bolshevik theory. Trotsky's relentlessness and sore lack of humor fascinated him, and he rather enjoyed the idea of redistribution of wealth, permanent revolution, the unity of workers. This would terrify someone like Goldwyn for two reasons, Chaplin thought: the obvious economic one, but also because it represented something more important than the motion picture. Had Mary Pickford fomented revolution? No, she had not. Had Marguerite Clark told the workers they were the means of production? Unlikely. Had House Peters . . . etc.

He wasn't sure how to express Bolshevik theory at the beach. So he had also memorized the plots of *Anna Karenina* and *Madame Bovary*, and meant to bring them into conversation as if everyone surely knew what he was talking about.

The producer's name had once been Samuel Goldfish, but his company, when incorporated, was called "Goldwyn," and so he was changing his name to match it. This strange chase after identity fascinated Chaplin, and he wondered what it would be like to be a businessman and name himself after his product. "Hullo, I'm Joe Coca-Cola." Then he thought, "Hullo, I'm Charlie Chaplin," and it depressed him all over again.

He counted out ten postcards. The writing surface of each bore, in his newly beautiful handwriting, a definition and a sample sentence. Iconoclast. Meme. Hegemony. Cynosure. Epistemology. Fungible. Cyclothymia. *Casus belli.* Trope. Atavistic.

Would there be bathing? It seemed unlikely; producers did not swim in the ocean. It couldn't be trusted to obey them.

He envisioned struggling with huge inflatable rubber starfish and sea horses, a villain puncturing his inner tube with a pin, himself propelled across the bay at high velocity while Edna was threatened by an enormous bully with designs on her virtue. Except that virtue was outdated, so perhaps a bully wants Edna to marry him so he can lay claim to a fortune. But this bothered him, too. Seeing kinetic actions first, then creating character and emotion to fill them up, like ladling sand into a sack, was too easy—everyone did it. Griffith knew how to create the most ornate spectacles, like *Intolerance*, hours of swinging braziers and slaves banging on gongs, chariots pulled by butterflies, and the audience was fooled into embracing it simply because of its size. Where was the small moment, the flirtatious smile not returned, the cuckold discovering a cuff link and saying nothing, the smile of a baby that somehow chills the bones? This was the hardest way to make things.

The car was now late, which caused him some anxiety. He had unexpectedly thought for several seconds about a scenario, and he was reminded of why he was alive in the first place, and now it seemed entirely possible to skip the party.

He gathered his ten postcards up, tucked them in his pocket, and went to the mirror. He drew in a breath and tried to inflate his love of people as if it were a balloon. It worked—he suddenly looked confident, dashing even. Small, but well presented. Dabbed—but not too much—with Mitsouko by Guerlain, from the fluted bottle that smelled like citrus with base notes of money. Black boots with spotless cloth tops, white linen trousers, silk vest, linen jacket, wristwatch, wallet, handkerchief, shirt with collar on—no, collar off—and then the face: freshly shaven, fiercely intelligent, a trove of black curls with the first flecks of premature gray connoting wisdom, and blue eyes that could bore through the most sophisticated chambers of any woman's heart, and a smile that could make a whole convent choir forget that their knees were friends. Twenty-eight years old, left-handed, the son of Gypsies and Spaniards and generations of clever forebears, an Aries with Scorpio rising and moon in Scorpio, and, according to Madame Zinka downstairs, destined and cursed to illuminate the world with how mysteriously he stood at the center of all human attention, Chaplin pointed a finger at himself and whispered, "You are a dangerously handsome man."

On the street, he leaned against a pillar in front of the Athletic Club. Saturday afternoons, foot traffic was slow, limited to locals who lived in rented rooms, actors and stagehands and others who had seen him a hundred times before. He touched his fingers to the brim of his cap for the Civil War veteran, and he raised his hands, shaking with fear, eyes trembling and shedding a bucket of tears, when a young boy pointed a wooden rifle at him. As he stood, he realized he was not actually seeing other actors. Robert Harron had moved out. So had Wallace Reid.

Syd said he no longer needed to live at the Club. Fairbanks had a house with three bedrooms. Viola Dana had three as well. Pickford had four, but lived with her mother. Chaplin could not imagine putting his books in boxes. If he had money tomorrow, he could buy a house tomorrow.

A car pulled up at the curb, honked twice, and, after a beat, honked once again. It was a long touring car, darkened windows, quite fancy at one time, the frame now dinged and pitted with mud, a society matron who did not yet know she had hit hard times. The driver popped out and loped over to Chaplin, slowing down only to run a hand through his perfectly Macassared hair. This was Eddie Sutherland, an actor whom Chaplin knew and trusted, somewhat. He wanted to direct, and he wanted a leg up, and might actually deserve it. For now, he usually played the swain who had the girl for a reel or two before losing her to the hero.

Sutherland looked over his shoulder, then back to Chaplin, and Chaplin knew there were actresses in the backseat.

"Char-lie!" Sutherland said, throwing a palm against Chaplin's as if they were two quarterbacks in a game Sutherland's team had won in a squeaker.

"Who's in the car, Eddie?" Chaplin smiled broadly.

"Two girls," he said.

"You should have brought one for yourself," he said.

"They're okay, Charlie," Sutherland said, deflating to his normal size. "You're getting in the car, right? Neither of them knew we were picking you up until now."

"Are you sure?"

Sutherland hesitated. "The girl on the left, I know her well. She doesn't care. The one on the right, her mother dropped her off at the studio this morning."

"And she said, 'Now, dear, when you meet Mr. Chaplin, don't show how awful bad we want a role for you,' or—"

"Nothing like that. But be careful with her."

"Why?"

Sutherland chewed on his lower lip, helplessly. "I don't know. Are you getting in the car? Please tell me you are." He looked over his shoulder as if the automobile might roll over the edge of a cliff.

Chaplin glared at Sutherland for about a tenth of a second. He then put his hands in his pockets and walked to the curb. He threw open the door as if entering a surprise party.

"Hullo, my name is Charlie Chaplin," he said.

There were two women in the backseat, at opposite ends of the bench. He wondered if they sat that way so he could sit between them, but then it was obvious they had left so much room not on his account as much as through a raw, primal disregard for each other. It was *atavistic*.

He extended his hand toward the girl on the right, the one whom Sutherland didn't know. She wore a good fur coat and hat, overdressing for a beach party to an extent that was delightfully wrong. She didn't strike him as dangerous. To begin with, she might have been twelve years old.

"Charlie Chaplin," he said.

She murmured in response, taking his hand limply, and looking at him out of the corner of her eye. She radiated quiet fear, as if, should she move too quickly, he might eat her.

"Pardon?" he asked.

"Mildred," she said.

"Charmed, Mildred." He turned to the woman on the left. "Charlie Chaplin," he said.

She was too plain to be an actress, though she seemed vaguely familiar. Her clothes were so expensive they looked casual: pointed button boots of imported leather, a white silk skirt, and a braided vest that Chaplin couldn't recall seeing in any shopwindow.

"I'm sorry?" she said with a hazy air, as if he had pulled her away from fantastic thoughts.

"Charlie Chaplin."

"A pleasure to meet you, Mr. Chapman."

"Chaplin," he said. She squinted at him, and he found himself continuing, "C-H-A," and his lips actually made it as far as forming the "P" before he realized he was looking at the most deadpan face he could remember seeing. It wasn't a plain face—it was decidedly handsome.

"Never mind," he said, smiling, "I forget how you spell the rest."

The car was rolling forward. He sat down on the long bench, in the center, glancing politely at Mildred before fixing the other one with a gaze. Her eyebrows lifted in challenge, by no means intimidated. Now he saw intelligence. She had a dimpled chin, a strong jaw, full lips, and a broad nose, all of which suggested an aggressive bent, and hooded eyes that prevented him from quite reading her mind. She was older than he'd realized, perhaps his age. He wanted to see her standing up, because it was hard to judge her figure, and, further, he wanted to see her walking, because he suspected the sight of her in motion would be rewarding.

For her part—as they had indeed met before—she wished to make Mr. Chaplin dance as much as she could.

"I suppose I'll have to guess how you spell the rest of your name," she said, sounding disappointed.

"I'd like to hear you guess."

"Are there exclamation points involved?"

"I'm sure there are."

"I loathe exclamation points." She looked out the window. The car pulled into the intersection and was turning left, causing a rumble over trolley tracks that made all riding within brace themselves. There were shades over the windows, and they were drawn for privacy's sake. It made traveling a bit of a mystery. Chaplin had been to Santa Monica many times but was unsure how one actually drove there, except in a very, very, very long straight line through the orchards and fields separating the many fiefdoms, and he wondered whether Sutherland knew where he was going. But he couldn't ask. There was a pane of glass between Sutherland and his passengers. Which gave Chaplin the women to himself.

"Mildred," he said. "Where have I seen you before?" He hadn't actually seen her, but it was always an excellent question to ask.

"Mother works for Ince," she said, with a slight lisp. "And before that, Triangle. She's a costumer. You've come by when you were building your studio."

"Ah. And you help her?"

"No. I act." She shrugged.

"How interesting."

"Just the sister roles, mostly"—each "s" a tender sibilant. It was impossible to tell how old she really was. Sixteen? She was one of a growing type, the ingénue, and a particularly attractive example, really. Her eyes looked ready to spill over with tears at any minute, her skin awaiting the brush of a fingertip, as if the gentlest touch would cause her to rise in goosebumps. Ingénues tended to lisp.

"Mildred was in *Intolerance*," the other woman said. "We were just talking about that before you came in."

"Lord, there isn't a single person in the telephone book who wasn't in *Intolerance*." Chaplin chuckled, regretting it instantly. "It's just that, well, Griffith's tropes have been dusty lately." There was no response, so he hurried along. "I'm sure you had quite a part, Mildred," he added, "not stuck off at the side, playing third zither during the Babylonian orgy. What part did you play?"

Mildred stared at him. Her lower lip, which was full and lovely, began to tremble. "I was in the Babylonian orgy scene. I stood in a fountain."

"She's also done other work." This was said to be helpful. He could read in the older woman's eyes the true desire to avoid the sight of an ingénue crying.

"What else have you done, Mildred?"

"I was in the *Oz* pictures. Dorothy in the first, then Button-Bright. In *The Magic Cloak of Oz*, I was Fluff. But that was several years ago," she finished, eyes rimmed with tears.

"You were quite fine in those," Chaplin said, looking sideways to invite agreement.

"I thought she was splendid."

"You see? You have two fans here, Mildred, side by side."

"And we agree on nothing else so far, except you."

"We might agree on other things," Chaplin said. "You could start by telling me how you spell your name, and I could tell you if you're doing it correctly."

"Why would you remember this time?"

This time? He *had* met her before. But he refused to feel bad about being forgetful; he met many people. "Perhaps I remember and I'm just acting."

"You're not that good an actor," she said. "Mildred, don't tell Mr. Chapman who I am."

"Do you know her name, Mildred?"

"She introduced herself when she got in."

"Hmm. Did she do it like this?" He put his head back haughtily, as if he were looking down into a courtyard filled with his vassals. He enunciated entirely through his nose, as if he were a pelican. " 'How d'ye do, Mildred? I am the Baroness X. Of the Windsor Xes.' No, I know, 'the Artcraft Xes.' Was it like that?"

Mildred laughed. "No. She's nice."

"She is?"

"She just said, "Hi, I'm Fran—""

"Ah, Mildred, no." It was Chaplin saying this. "We don't want to spoil her fun. But it's too late; I know for certain now—your name is Frank."

"It should be."

She spoke confidently, like a woman who earned her own money. Franny? She was not a Franny. He did not remember her name because now sex was involved, and this always drowned his mind like a kitten in a sack. Her name was Frances Marion, and she wrote scenarios for a living. She was also bright and egotistical enough to believe he remembered her and was just teasing her by pretending not to know who she was.

"Mildred," Frances said, "how do you know Mr. Goldwyn?"

"I don't really know him," she replied. "I have a friend who lives at his house."

At this, Frances leaned forward, truly interested for the first time. "Are you friends with Mr. Moore?"

Mildred shook her head. "Mr. Dexter."

Moore? Dexter? For Chaplin, it was like seeing the beginnings of an equation on the blackboard, and having the solution in a mad blur. "Oh, we're going to *that* house."

"Yes?" Frances asked.

"I thought we were going to Goldwyn's."

"Goldwyn is east. He rented it to them."

He had heard that four actors—Eddie Sutherland, Elliott Dexter, Owen Moore, and Jack Pickford—had taken the unusual step of all renting a house by the beach. They had united this way somewhat accidentally, to escape various Hollywood entanglements, but the result, to their surprise, was a parade of actresses who tended to visit while wearing swimming costumes. Now more clumps of handsome young men were taking to beach life in hopes of catching their spill-off.

"So Goldwyn isn't there?"

"No, I believe he sent his regrets. Or something."

Chaplin had to recalibrate his finely tuned plans to relax. The hosting chores wouldn't be courtesy of one insecure Jewish financier who had fled Poland, but instead four young men who had an eye for women. No one was going to care about Trotsky's speeches, Giotto, or memes of any sort.

"Do you think there will be bathing?" He said this to both women, and Mildred produced from her bag a bathing suit.

"Oh," he said.

"You look stricken, Mr. Chaplin," Frances said. "I doubt swimming is required."

In truth, he was heading into a sort of lions' den. Jack Pickford was of course Mary's brother (in the Naval Reserve? the Signal Corps?), Elliott Dexter had been in films with her, and Owen Moore was her estranged husband. As if asking whether there would be sandwiches, Chaplin said, "Is, by any chance, Mary going to be there?"

"Mary who?" asked Frances.

He could not tell if she was teasing. "Mary Pickford."

"Lord, I hope not," she said. "I'd like to avoid her today." Her smile was a confederate's. She looked relieved to have found a fellow traveler in her plot to escape Mary Pickford. It made him relax. He liked her.

She also liked him, but not for any reason he understood. She had written for Marguerite Clark (one of the Twelve Immortals!), she had done five or six scripts for Gail Kane and Alice Brady, but she wasn't so foolish as to think Chaplin would know about that. However, she had also written six of the last seven Mary Pickford films, among them *Rebecca of Sunnybrook Farm*, *The Little Princess*, *Stella Maris*, and *The Poor Little Rich Girl*. She had three Pickfords in production and three more in development. Pickford was shooting one now, and Frances, her best friend, was happy to be away from her for a day. She was positive Chaplin knew this. He was a decidedly handsome man, if more delicate and graceful than her normal type. She had been prepared for him to take himself seriously, to be too cordial and too distant—in short, she had been prepared to despise him. That he was teasing her so grandly made her giddy.

"Not that I dislike Mary," he was saying.

"Of course not."

"It's just that . . ." Their eyes met, and he noted they were brown and merry and ready to play all afternoon. He imagined Mildred left standing on the curb, and himself biting his mysterious sparring partner, Frank, on the neck. "Here, you be the villain. Look at me like you're going to shake me within an inch of my life."

She didn't even need to ask what he meant. Instead, she folded her arms and let one hand stroke a phantom beard while she glared menacingly.

Chaplin cowered, his eyes the size of lightbulbs; he shook his head, mouthing "no, No, NO!," arms up to protect himself, and yet, in that gesture, the hands magically framed what had become through sheer willpower an angelic face. "But wait," he said. "The hero approaches."

He turned to Mildred and, with an instructional nod of the head, invited her to be the hero. She was game, but slow to decide how to be a hero. She settled on sticking her jaw out.

Chaplin faced forward so both women could see him beam. Previously unknown dimples grew in his cheeks. He clasped his hands together and shook his head, fluffing the air around it to indicate the settling of curls. "Goodness," he declared, "is—good."

The backseat of the car rocked with laughter, and Chaplin grinned, sizing up both women to ensure that they were actually having a good time and not just being polite.

Frances cried out, "Mr. Chaplin, that does sound like her, doesn't it?"

"Goodness is good," he repeated.

"And badness?" she asked.

"Terribly bad," he declared with the same vapid intent.

"What awful scenarios she has," she laughed, wiping at the edges of her eyes.

"Oh, go ahead, blame the scenario writer," he said. "That's the easy way out. Mary knows what Mary does."

"I've read that she's changing," Mildred said.

"She's discovered patriotism." Chaplin nodded. "She's now the face of the Red Cross, which is noble. In the sense of being the kind of nobility that gets its face stamped on medals. She wants to sell the war. *Joanne Enlists.*" He rolled up his trouser leg and flexed it, winking slyly. "Yoo-hoo, if you enlist, I'll show you the other leg."

Now he could hear two types of laughter. Mildred was turning red, holding her hand over her mouth, as if shocked someone could say such a thing about Mary Pickford. Frances was tilting her head back slightly, regarding Chaplin with distant pleasure.

When all was quiet, she said, "By the by, it's *Johanna Enlists*, not *Joanne*."

"Is it?"

"Oh, yes."

Chaplin had nuances to his Pickford imitation, and had looked forward to guiding the conversation so that he could do her being determined or, when they got out of the car, dancing with joy.

"*Johanna?* Are you sure about that?" he asked.

"Reasonably sure."

"I shall make note of it when I do Mary Pickford imitations in the future, Frank."

She chuckled, satisfied they'd been playing the same game.

The idea that he might be attracted to someone who wrote for Pickford was out of the question. So, without benefit of important clues (such as having met her, knowing her name and her occupation), he tried to construct her relationship with Pickford. A friend? No, he was sure no one had successfully scurried through the maternal petticoats of that looming Argus, Charlotte Pickford. Still, he shouldn't have talked about Mary. Mildred was too well behaved to cause him trouble. If Frank was an actress, however, such a thing was like money in her pocket.

"How far away is the beach, do you think?" He asked this looking straight ahead, but only Mildred responded, pulling up the shade and looking out the window.

"I think we're in Beverly Hills," she said. "It's definitely Beverly Hills."

"Is it?"

"Do you see where the beanfield ends? They've put up a shop on the corner. Guess what? That gown in the window? It's from Paris. So is the one next to it. You can tell." She watched him in case he did anything funny (he didn't) and then returned to looking out the window.

"Frank," Chaplin finally said, turning right. "You made quite a good villain."

"Thank you."

He asked, as if it meant nothing, "Why aren't you an actress?"

"I was, for a while. I couldn't take it seriously."

This pleased him. "And what do you take seriously?"

"Many things. I'm going to France soon."

This caused Mildred to tear away from the window. She regarded her fellow woman with awe. "For the clothing?"

"No, Mildred. I'm going because of the war." This was said in kindness. "I'm very unsure of the war," she said.

Chaplin asked, "How so?"

"Well, as I recall, we voted for Mr. Wilson because he'd kept us out of the war, and then, about a week later, we were fighting it anyway. We were against it, and now we're for it."

"Ah—" said Chaplin, for he had a theory on propaganda.

"And I'm not being cynical. We're there because things genuinely changed."

"And because certain people want us there," he said.

"Yes. And it's making certain people very rich, which is a whole extra level of horror. I feel I should see France to understand why we're there, what it's doing to us, and so on."

Mildred nodded, returning to looking out the window, where a storefront beckoned.

Chaplin said, "I'm very impressed. Are you in the Red Cross, or will you be a Hello Girl, or—"

"I'm not sure. I've been meeting with Hearst's people. I might write articles for the paper about women in the war."

"Then you'll be wearing your journalist's hat?" he said, thinking of the magazines he would need Carlyle Robinson to call to suppress everything he had said about Mary Pickford.

"I write a little for the magazines, but, no, nothing you need to worry about. Advice columns, tidbits. No gossip."

"Is that how you met Mary?"

"Yes. Writing a profile of her."

Finally, that made sense to him. He concluded she was a journalist. She concluded he liked her.

The conversation had taken such an unexpected turn that the combat had drained away. He missed it. He looked past Frank, to Mildred, who had rolled down the window and was sticking out her hand to feel the breeze against it. She grinned at them both so they could see the delight her experiment was providing.

"We're going so fast," she said, leaning her face toward the breeze, closing her eyes. She held her fur cap tightly to her head.

It kept her out of the conversation. "France," Chaplin said. "That's brave," he began, thinking of spins and gloss to give the phrase a witty finish, but then he said, "It's brave."

"Thank you." She said, "I'm sorry if I was mean to you. I apologize for all the things I've said."

"That's all right."

"Then I apologize for all the things I'm going to say in the future."

He realized she was prepared to go all afternoon making him work for a kiss.

Mildred cried, "We're in Santa Monica!"

"Are we?" Frances asked. "How do you know?"

"Have you ever seen fog like this before?"

The fog went from tentative fingers to swinging fists as the car descended from Wilshire onto Coastline Drive, passing the cliffs at the edge of the park, and dropping into the elements. A stiff and insistent breeze lived down here much of the day, which generally made a life at the beach in February seem like exile.

The hosts of the party were as surprised as anyone by the popularity of their house as a destination. And to clarify the hosting duties: the four handsome actors were receiving guests, but they were by no means in charge.

In 1913, Samuel Goldfish took all he knew from having made ladies' gloves and applied it to movies. He had hired La Fontaine to design his sixteen-button kidskin gloves, and the forty most skilled seamstresses in New York to sew them. "You have to see the quality, and *then* be *told* that it's quality," he explained.

When he was making movies, this translated in his mind to the following: you could not have culture unless it had an explicit, *quality* moral. "Love conquers all," for instance, or "Obey your elders." But not both together. It was best not to confuse the audience. He spent the most productive fifteen minutes of his life sorting through photographs of his stable of actors and assigning single adjectives to each one of them. Geraldine Farrar, for instance was "glamorous." Rachel Bryer was "adorable." Butch Cliff "rugged." Alan Germaine "sophisticated." He was startled to see that in his frenzy to hire the best, he had both a Simone St. James and a Simone St. Michel. He fired the latter and declared the former "unique."

All publicity and interviews from then on hinged on these single qualities' being repeated, so that there was no mistake. His films reflected his belief that what America most wanted was equally clear-cut: three and a half reels of sorrows, resolved by five minutes of happiness.

His success led him to believe he was correct in all decisions, which caused him to snap facts and other people's opinions like twigs. He felt his employees were his family, a curse that his actual family would wish on no one. That the actors—his children—would have a party without supervision struck him as a terrible idea, so, two days beforehand, a cavalcade of trucks had pulled up in the driveway. In their beds were dead trees. Most of them were coastal oaks, whose corpses were gnarled and mighty, and they carried with them the winter atmosphere of giants struck down in their prime.

A crew of fifteen men set to work planting them around the house and along the beach. Anchoring them into sand was difficult work, involving buried concrete beams and leather straps for balance. But Goldwyn deemed the work necessary, for, just as an actor's appeal had to be simplified, and culture needed a moral, and a movie's emotional twists needed to be set by the stopwatch, a party needed a purpose. And there wasn't going to be a party at his house unless it made all present better people. This party was going to be *about* something.

The house was Cape Cod clapboard, shaped like the letter "F," its horizontal strokes flanking a large patio that opened onto the beach. It was set back from the road by a good thirty feet, and the meandering driveway was already an ersatz parking lot, with roadsters and sedans and even a pair of motorcycles angled along the pavers.

Sutherland parked, and his guests disembarked, and there was some stretching and joking about the difference in weather, curiosity about who had arrived already, and then steps were taken toward the party. Except by Chaplin.

"I'll be there in a moment," he said.

Sutherland walked between the women, glancing behind to make sure

Chaplin wasn't about to bolt, and they walked down the driveway, Suther-land telling a story about a friend of his, a cowboy who worked for DeMille, who had actually fired an arrow at him, piercing his bullhorn, and the women were laughing, making teasing sorts of replies, questioning how on earth someone could fire an arrow with such accuracy. "William Tell him-self" was as much as Chaplin heard, their voices and forms consumed by fog long before they reached the front door, wherever it was.

In the winters, people asked him a hundred times a day if the fog wasn't just like London, and he had finally learned to assent rather than explain that, no, it wasn't. He had read in a book on neurology that you cannot remember pain, only that something was painful. Likewise, he couldn't really remember London fog, except that it smelled like onions and fish and soot, and its sheer weight promised that walking through it would crush you.

It was three-thirty in the afternoon, by his watch. The weather on a Cal-ifornia beach on a winter afternoon produced fog that was playful. The wind blew it in banks, ghosts chasing one another over the beach, and in between them, shafts of light that made the sands shimmer like piles of gold dust.

There was no one else who felt as he did right now. There was no way to communicate this feeling. He could not pin it down as a key emotion. What arose from it was yearning, the urge to go to Lambeth again, happi-ness that he was rich now, contentment, restlessness. He hated it when actors complained about their childhoods. The only part of his childhood that he remembered as terrible was hunger. "But isn't that what America is about," he said in company, often, "hungry young men who pull them-selves up by their bootstraps? Then eat them?" Laughter.

He listened for gulls and buoys and imagined he heard the wail of vio-lin music.

Except: there *was* violin music.

He walked toward it. The sound of his footsteps was absorbed by the fog. He clutched his jacket tighter. He thought it was a transcription of something bleak by Schumann, a sonata whose weariness reminded him of crows circling endlessly on the wind.

Chaplin spotted a boy standing at the edge of the pavers, by the entrance to the house. He was barefoot, dressed in a toga cinched with a single golden rope, and he wore a wreath that was supposed to be laurel, but was actually sage. His face had been painted white.

He nodded at the boy on his way into the house. He heard the cacophony inside. Owen Moore, Mary's husband, was greeting guests in the entryway. Chaplin turned on his heel and then he was outside again.

"Pardon," Chaplin said to the boy in toga. "Were you hired to play for the party?"

He nodded carefully, managing to do so without dislodging his violin, which he continued to play.

"Of course you were."

Chaplin rubbed his hands together and grimaced. "Aren't you cold?"

The boy looked left and right, nervous he was being spied upon. He nodded.

"You are cold? I'm sure they have some tea inside. Wait here. Oh, yes, of course, you have to wait here. But—yes."

Chaplin returned to the house. There was a small foyer currently lined by banks of coatracks, and the passage between them was narrow. Owen Moore was still there, shaking hands as if this were his own circle of hell—helping guests with their coats left him with no hands free for a drink.

He and Chaplin gave each other the nod of professional dislike, on one side indicating, "Yes, I know your best friend is sleeping with my wife," and on the other, "You're a mean drunk living off your wife's money," and then they shook hands.

When Chaplin emerged on the far side of the coatracks, there was a living room in which a dozen people stood with drinks, in clutches of three or four. The outfits on men with excellent physiques varied from casual linen to bathing suits that would shame a lifeguard. He did not see any women dressed for swimming, which was a little disappointing. But there were several men in uniform. Jack Pickford was not among them. It was hard to tell if any were bound for overseas duty, or if they were in the mysterious local corps that provided army officers with important morale-boosting visits to film sets. He heard laughter and murmurs, colliding conversations that made up the strange music of parties: boasts, secrets told, lies, exaggerations, all cloaking the humbling, frightened desire to be found interesting.

The setting was less a beach house than the idea of a beach house lifted from the Atlantic states and dropped in Santa Monica, with fireplaces in every room and overwrought shutters and storm doors for nor'easters that would never come. The current residents had stolen what they could from studio property rooms and thrown haphazard couches and tables wherever they now sat. But original to the house were, Chaplin guessed, the scissored crew-boat oars, the life preservers, the shellacked grouper, and the sign over the bay window that read "Nantucket 5 Mi." He wasn't sure who was supposed to be reassured—guests from the East? the house itself?—but the display suggested that even though the house was in California, it was still a legitimate child of the ocean life.

He was sure there would be tea in the kitchen, wherever it was. He walked down the hall, nodding and smiling vaguely as people met his—

Ack! It was Pickford! He blinked. No, it was just a girl with the same perfect curls. She darted from one of the bedrooms, nearly bumping into him, her drink splashing over the rim of her glass. She was short, her hair a highly organized simulacrum of Pickford's, and her mouth hung open so fully he imagined he could hang a bucket of water from her jaw.

"Hullo," he said, "I'm Charlie Chaplin."

"Yes," she said. "Yes. You are. Oh!"

He could find nothing attractive about her in a glance, and so he stayed. "Is it a good party?"

"Yes. Good."

"I just arrived," he said, brimming with love of all humanity, even the plain, speechless girls. "I'm hoping you can tell me where to get a cup of tea."

"I don't know." Her hand clenched around her drink, and the other reached behind her, finding the wall. "I'm sorry," she said, and walked past him, back toward the living room. He sighed, and proceeded down the hall. He shouldered past more people, nodding at them and smiling, until, aghast, he saw Pickford! No, it was Mae Murray, whose hair was also professionally and slavishly done like Pickford's, so Chaplin slumped backward, directly into the path of a waiter with a tray of food. They barely missed each other.

He was face to face with Mildred.

"Oh," he said, for she had changed into her bathing costume. It was black mohair, and belted, with a modest skirt that ended far below the hips. His grandmother could have worn it. "You look lovely," he said.

She played absently with the strap of her bathing cap, which was red. "I think I'm going to swim, but I might be too cold. I don't like cold."

"Neither do I. How can you trust someone who says he likes to be cold?"

"You can't," she said, shaking her head. "Goodbye, Mr. Chaplin." She trotted out the door, onto the patio, where she found a towel to wrap around her waist. She slowed and stopped, joining the crowd. Her curiosity was intense enough that Chaplin strolled outside, too.

Sunnyside

The fog absorbed the edges of the scene, making him feel as if he were on an island. The crowd was of perhaps twenty people, more of them in swimming costumes than not, and all of the women, like Mildred, draping their thighs and legs with knotted towels.

Beside the dead oak tree was a short marble pillar, and on it stood a balding man with tufts of black hair above his ears and a crêpe ring-beard glued to his face. He was dressed in velvet breeches, like a courtier in Shakespeare, and he was reading aloud "Thanatopsis."

> Thou go not, like the quarry-slave at night,
> Scourged to his dungeon, but, sustained and soothed
> By an unfaltering trust, approach thy grave
> Like one who wraps the drapery of his couch
> About him, and lies down to pleasant dreams.

He closed the book, and regarded the crowd like a displeased schoolmaster. Finally, someone—it was Mildred—clapped enthusiastically, and many others did so, quickly disbanding, threatened that he might open his book and read more.

"Charlie!"

He was already smiling when he turned to see a face he half recognized. He thought of boats when he saw her.

"It's Katie O'Dell!"

"Yes, *hello*, Katie." He still didn't remember her. She stood with a tall, rawboned, silenced girl, whom she introduced, but whose name he did not catch.

"Charlie directed me in *The Immigrant*," Katie was saying.

He recalled. She had been in the dock scene, just to the left of him when the immigration officials tied the lasso around the huddled masses. She had taken direction well, the camera treated her exactly right, and during the lunch breaks she had talked so much he had taken his sandwiches to the car.

"Charlie is *such* a *good director*!" Katie made chopping motions with her hand as she said it. Her friend excused herself to find more to drink, and Katie said, "She's nervous."

"I understand. Do you know where I might find tea?"

"There's a bar on the beach, and they have coffee, which is fantastic. Just fantastic," she repeated. "Charlie!"

"Katie?"

"What are you working on now, Charlie?"

"Oh—dogs."

"No, what are you working on? What film?"

Her voice was like a trumpet. He was aware that he was standing in the midst of a group, that there should be overlapping conversations, music, the rhythm of the ocean and the breeze, perhaps the actor beginning to declaim again. In fact, it was cold enough that the whole patio should be empty. But it felt as if the question of what he was working on had brought a dead silence, that the brass of the trumpet had belonged to Gabriel, and the world was awaiting the voice of judgment.

"It's about dogs. It's called *I Should Worry*."

Her face fell. "It only has dogs in it?"

He could kiss her. "Yes. No humans. It's an experiment. I believe it will be a smashing success."

"Okay. Sure." Her friend chose that moment to return, which prolonged an awkward silence that Chaplin enjoyed. Katie had given him a wonderful excuse to keep actors and actresses at bay, and he wanted to thank her. "And," he said, "not that you asked, but of course I will always keep you in mind. For other kinds of parts." He touched her lightly on the elbow, and from his eyes projected a pure, happy, open, avuncular concern.

"Excuse me?" she said. She cocked her head, shifted her glance to her friend, and then to the fingertips on her elbow. "What exactly does *that* mean?"

"It means . . . just . . ." He couldn't for the life of him explain it in words different from those he had used. What else *could* it mean?

She cast upon him the look she would give a charmless milliner, and then, taking her friend by the arm, left.

Chaplin watched them go. He found the bar and asked for tea. He was rewarded with a squint, and then, when it became apparent he hadn't been asking for anything in code, the barkeep pointed him toward the kitchen.

He passed Mildred, who, though still clad in her red swim cap and towel, hadn't yet made it to the waves. She was engaged in conversation with Elliott Dexter, a criminally handsome man slightly older and much taller than Chaplin, and she was hiding her smile behind her hand in a way she hadn't quite done for him.

Dexter spoke with the mid-Atlantic enunciation of a stage performer, which he had been for years before motion pictures created an unexpected second career. He had the jaded affect of one who realized that the party, the business, the ambition, were all just a bit silly. Chaplin would have liked him had Dexter not been impressing a girl whom, he had to remind himself, he didn't want.

"I was telling Mildred," Dexter said, "I'm not sure I understood that the party needed a theme."

"There's a theme," Mildred repeated.

"Mr. Goldwyn insisted on the theme of 'All is vanity,' " Dexter said, taking a slow drink and smiling halfway.

"Oh, Lord, is that why the poetry—"

"And the trees, and the statues—"

"I haven't seen statues."

"They aren't here yet. I believe that's the climax. Parties apparently need climaxes now." Dexter sighed as if he were stranded among well-meaning savages who worshipped the most charming idols.

"What would the point be of all this?" Chaplin asked.

"I wish Goldwyn were a nihilist. It would spare us all." Which made Chaplin laugh, which made him angry. Another sip of his drink, then Dexter said, "Not that a crowd like this couldn't stand a little moral education."

This felt like a challenge. "When it comes down to it, half of Hollywood is Emma Bovary, when you think about it," Chaplin said. "We are all terribly bourgeois, actually."

Dexter gave a pleased nod. "I hadn't thought about it that way." Meaning also he hadn't realized the clown Chaplin could think of such a thing.

"Of course, we haven't a hardworking doctor of a husband to bankrupt along the way. All we have is Goldwyn and Zukor."

Dexter laughed, but, more important, Chaplin saw new credit in his eyes.

He continued: "All that's left is for each and every one of us to throw ourselves under the wheels of a train."

Dexter swallowed. "I suppose so," he said, betraying the tiniest confusion, and Chaplin knew the man had never cracked a word of Flaubert. Ha!

Chaplin turned on his heel, happy to have scored a point, trying to remember where he had seen a bathroom, for he wished to freshen up his vocabulary words and then talk some more to Dexter, who could stand a few belts of meme, hegemony, and Giotto. But as he stuck his hands in his pockets, he realized they were empty. His cards were gone.

Had he left them in the car? In the street beforehand? Were they scattering on the beach somewhere? Patting his pockets (and why did people pat their pockets when they knew they were empty?), he felt eyes upon him. He saw, reflected in a window, that a man was staring at him.

He calmed down, pretended to push back his unruly hair, as if he'd been using the reflection as a mirror, and he turned back toward the patio.

Standing distinctly away from those who had come to the party for fun was a single man. He was holding a glass of water. Older, with a potbelly over which hung a limp blue tie, he stood in his shirtsleeves as awkwardly as if awaiting a doctor's examination. He had thin salt-and-pepper hair parted in the middle, watery blue eyes behind spectacles, and yellowing teeth, which he was now snarling with—no, he was smiling.

Chaplin nodded once, and the other man gave him a single wave in return. This man had nothing to do with films. He was not a banker or a businessman who wanted to invest. Those with keys to the vault were like bull's-eyes to every pretty girl at every party, and this man had no brand-new friends. Chaplin's immediate feeling was that he worked for the government and was there to arrest him.

In fact, the man took a step toward him, and so Chaplin turned and went inside, back into the house. By the time he'd found a nice, tall over-stuffed chair in the living room, one that he could get lost in, he felt silly.

The chair was comfortable, and it gave him a view of the patio. He took a pleasant moment to consider the figures of the women outside, and felt that if they truly wanted to be considerate, they all needed to lose their towels.

"Oh—my—God, but he's terrible!"

He recognized the voice, which was from the brass family: Katie O'Dell.

"I know. I wasn't doing anything."

"Neither was I!"

The voices were coming from directly behind his wing chair. He tucked his legs up under himself, folded his arms, shrank in place, and waited for more.

"I was *just* asking him what his new project was, and he took me by the hand and said he wanted to keep me in mind, and then he said it exactly like this." She paused. " 'For *other kinds* of parts.' "

Chaplin wished he could see her, if only to see how she'd imitated him. No one ever got it right.

"He told me he'd just arrived," the other woman said, "and he asked where to get a cup of tea," she said. When there was no response, she continued, "But it was the *way* he said it. It was *obvious* what he actually meant."

There was more general agreement about what a toad he was. Chaplin considered rising in the chair slowly, as if he were a periscope breaking the waters. The women wandered off, and he put his hand over his brow.

When he took his hand away, sitting on the coffee table as quietly as if she had floated there was Frank.

"How are you?" She had a drink in her hand, and there was lipstick on the glass.

"I want to leave," he said.

"We just got here."

"And yet I've been here a very long time."

"I suppose I have, too. There are many seventeen-year-old girls in swimsuits, hoping to be given screen tests. I wish we all did something more honest, like white slavery."

"Do you have a pen and a piece of paper?"

She shuffled through her purse. "I thought gentlemen of your stature carried things to write on."

"I do; they just seem to have vanished. Heh. Heh-heh."

His public laugh was always more demonstration that he was having a good time than actual pleasure. This, however, came from private stock: *Heh. Heh-heh.* Much darker.

"Mr. Chaplin?"

"I had an idea. A fan asks for an autograph. I obligingly search for a pen, but can't find one—no, I get an old deaf-mute to give me it, someone truly decrepit, Loyal Underwood, only he thinks I want a pen-*knife*. I return to the fan gaily, but I carve right through the scrapbook, and then cut through a photograph of myself. I realize I can't sign anything with a pen-knife. By accident, I draw the blade across the tip of my finger and open a vein; then there's some business with that, but after the first geyser, I am still accommodating. I sign the fan's paper in blood. He's thrilled. All of his friends come around. They have increasingly difficult requests. Can I sign their shirts? Can I inscribe photographs for each member of Congress? There's a child who won't take his bottle—do I mind if he uses my finger? Can I write out the Song of Solomon in my blood? And I pass out and die. The end."

"No, not the end."

He regarded her with irritation, but she continued anyway.

"You pass out after your fan announces that you were adequate, but

Mary Pickford did both the Old and New Testaments in blood, and that she's going to be nursing you back to health from her new post at the Red Cross. That's the end, the close-up on your face with your mouth an exact little 'O' of horror."

He sighed, "I should give you a raise."

"I don't work for you, though."

"Even better. I can just use it, and if you ask for money, I can turn you over my knee and spank you."

He could hardly believe he'd said it. But she hadn't run away. She hadn't even blushed. Instead, she took a dainty sip of her drink. "You could try to spank me. If you're good, I'll show you the closet in which I keep the larger, faster, more skillful men who tried before you."

The party seemed much noisier than it had a moment before. Could people talk like this? What would happen if they did?

"Oh," she whispered, "those blue eyes a poor girl could drown in. Who would ever save me? May I tell you a secret?"

He nodded. They were as hushed as conspirators.

"You look like Donatello's *David*."

He felt confused excitement, pleasure at a compliment, but mostly he wanted to correct her. "Michelangelo."

"No, you don't look like Michelangelo's *David*. You look like Dona- tello's. That one is smaller and more graceful and sensual, not the slab of masculinity dropped from the heavens. I like Donatello's *David*. He has a soft hat, and his hips are cocked to the side like a girl's. He would like to be worshipped but would also be grateful for a kind word."

"Frances?"

"Speaking."

"Not Francesca or Frangipani or—"

"Not unless something drastic changes."

"Now, was that so hard?"

"It took you many, many hours to say my name, so apparently yes." She took a sip of her drink.

"Will the next phase involve flaming hoops, Frances?"

"I'm not generally this mean to people."

"You have a wit about you."

"But generally I use it constructively. With you, I just want to be *so mean*." She looked about to see if they were unobserved, and she whis- pered, "But there was a turning point for me. Finding out you were an iconoclastic cynosure."

"I'm—" Apparently, he could still go red.

"A fungible cyclothymiac who believes in hegemony as a *casus belli*." She shook her head. "That is so . . ."

She not only had his words, which was awful enough, but knew how to turn them into adjectives if necessary. She was terrifying. They were both quietly aware of what was going to happen next.

"Charlie, I still have your pen here. I think I also have something to write on."

"That's all right."

"Little postcards. We could try to find a pen-knife. Maybe I could hurt you."

"Where do you think we might find a pen-knife?"

They stood together. How simple it was. He walked as if destiny had taken over his muscles and he was riding along. The crowds had thinned, many more people outside now; the instinct of actors had taken over, and they sensed the onset of a buffet. The food, courtesy of Goldwyn, looked magnificent, and players dressed as preening French chefs were in line to serve minuscule portions while intoning to each customer exactly how thankful he or she should be to receive them. Plates and napkins were in hand. No one was eager to be first, but perhaps fifty were willing to be second.

"Wait," Frances said. They were at the edge of the living room. "Do you know the layout of the house?"

"A little."

"It's like the letter 'F.' "

"Just like everything," he said.

"If you go all the way down the hall, there's a wing that doesn't face the patio."

"I like how you think."

"The farthest bedroom? At the very end of the hall."

"I'm going to make myself known on the patio," Chaplin said. "Five minutes."

They split off in perpendicular directions, Frances strolling down the length of hallway, and Chaplin ambling outside and grabbing a dinner plate and getting in line. He made much of the discovery that brownies were for dessert, and declared them the opiate of the masses, which caused some laughter. He noted the government man, who sat on the edge of an Adirondack chair, plate in hand, staring at the queue of diners as if intimidated.

As the line progressed, Chaplin demonstrably remembered, shooting his cuffs and examining his nailbeds, that he needed to wash up before dinner. He excused himself and headed back into the house. He went through the living room and the game room, and as he passed the kitchen, the swinging door blasted open, slamming to the wall. An apologetic waiter burdened with a platter of coq au vin squeezed by.

Farther down the hall was a pair of French doors, closed, which he slipped through and quietly closed again. Before him was a corridor that was dark except for the dim illumination of electric lightbulbs. He counted eight doors, four on each side, as carefully laid out as an urban hotel's. In the distance was the sound of the party—laughter, the clatter of utensils, and a small orchestra falling in tune, some kind of chamber octet tuning up to play, no doubt, sepulchral music to remind everyone that all was vanity, everyone would die, etc.

Technically, two rooms were the last on the hall: one door to the right, one left. He chose the door that did not face the beach. Easing it open, he saw Frances immediately. She was half propped up against the window seat, somewhere between sitting and standing, her arms folded, her legs extending into the room. She was in a new mood.

The bed was taken. The sheets were a filthy tangle, as if, for several weeks, they had been washed in alcohol, then dried in the sun. There were heaps of clothing at the foot, lingerie and the uniform of—yes—the Naval Reserve. Along the nightstand were empty bottles and, in surprisingly well-organized symmetry, a series of syringes topped with medicinal needles. Lying in the bed were Jack Pickford and Olive Thomas, newly-weds. She was a lovely young girl, prone to good times, and what compromised the pleasure of regarding her slender body was its condition: she was gray. Jack's skin was the color of earwax, and Chaplin wasn't sure if they were dead.

"They're alive," Frances whispered. "I checked. Oh, the weary hero of his country."

"What should we do?"

She stood and arched her back in a stretch. Humming Mendelssohn's "Wedding March," she gathered up the syringes and wrapped them in a towel. "There's probably a better room for us."

The two of them left together. The room directly across the hall was empty. Frances dumped her towel and its contents into a wastepaper basket, and then sat on the bed. Chaplin locked the door. There were two ways this could go, and one of them involved ignoring what they had just seen.

Frances bit at her thumbnail. "I feel very sorry for her."

"Not for him?" This would be going the other way, he realized. So he pulled up a chair.

"He loves his pain. And he's spoiled. She goes which way the wind blows. It's more of a tragedy in her case. Or perhaps I just feel more sympathy for women."

"As do I," he said, eyes brimming over with sympathy. She looked up, her thumb still at the edge of her lip, and she began a low, chortling laugh. It was so sure of itself that it made Chaplin slightly nervous.

"Of course you do," she said, closing her eyes and opening them as if for the first time. It was a beautiful motion. "So," she said.

He stood, and with the heel of his shoe kicked the chair up, tumbling it over his head, back into his hand, now extended forward, and setting the chair on the floor, next to the bed, where he sat again.

"That was clever." She laughed.

He whispered, all in a pleased rush, "It both got me closer to you and made you laugh, which is a highly efficient outcome: two benefits to a single action, one of the laws of the conservation of comedy."

"Oh," she said, patting away a grotesque yawn. "Comedy."

"Have you studied Dr. Freud? He believes everything is based on repressing our sexual natures."

"Dr. Freud was almost like an uncle around our house." She settled back on the bed, kicking off her boots, and putting an arm behind her head. "My mother has been in therapy since the hot summer of 1898, I think."

"Oh?" Was there nothing he knew more of than she did?

"Our neighbors in Pacific Heights had all done it, and Mother was highly competitive."

Chaplin, in his chair, crossed his legs, and opened an imaginary notepad. "I zee. And vat is your relationship mit your mutter?"

Frances shook her head no—she wouldn't be answering that. She asked, "Do you know what one of the tenets of comedy is?"

"It could be—"

"Aggression." She grabbed him by the vest, pulling him on top of her. Her mouth was on his, and one hand behind his head. She knew how to kiss not just with her mouth but with her full body, calves wrapping around him, hips rocking as if they were pressed against a saddle. Her hand slid down to cup him between his legs. "You'll make me happy," she murmured. "This is going to be much better than comedy."

"Comedy is highly sexual," he said in quick breaths between kisses. "It's all about one character dominating another."

"I agree. Now hold still."

He felt a pang of fear. Her vest and shirt were off, and he had worked her skirt up, and his coat, cap, vest, and shirt were already in an attractive heap on the floor. Her self-confidence was avaricious, as if she had never been sated and might consume him, then skulk about the party, looking for more.

"Comedy is about conflict," he said, "about resolving one conflict by creating another." It annoyed her to hear him talk—he knew it. She was kissing him after every word, almost after every syllable. His trousers had unbuttoned themselves; where had his undershirt gone?; the shoes were too complicated to untie. He felt that if he stopped talking he might die. "Say I'm pursued by the cops—"

"I hate you," she whispered.

He threw her skirt across the room, where its buttons hit the mirror with a sound like pebbles against a window. She was in her crêpe de chine combination, lace and decorative bows at the bust, and then she pulled this off over her head, leaving her in silk stockings, and only then did she relax. Her eyes seemed to dim, and she smiled languidly. The reason for her ease: nude, she won all arguments. She was all curves, and that a girl with such a wicked tongue and rapid mind also had the lush body of a Pre-Raphaelite struck him as colossally unfair. He decided he no longer believed in God.

Luckily, that meant the next hour would not cause him to go to hell. He kissed her excellent mouth, feeling her mean-spirited tongue fencing with his, but now distracted, now aimless. It was not his imagination; the track had skidded out from under them, and they had drifted.

He could feel her trying to reignite the moment, but it was no good. "I'm sorry. I'm trying," she said, "not to think about Jack and Olive."

"Just imitate me," he whispered.

"I will, in a minute." She draped her arms about his shoulders. "I know this is frustrating, but, just for a minute . . ." She ran her finger along Chaplin's arm, tracing a vein she'd found. "You see, I saw him in uniform and I thought he was cured. Why would I be fooled by something like that? Me."

"I admire . . ." What exactly did he admire? He sensed he needed to say something sweet, though not cloying. "You genuinely care. You play mean, but you have a tender side."

She kissed him. "Maybe that's why I write the way I do."

"I suppose. Pardon?"

"When I sit down to write, I always think of problems women and girls suffer through." She absently rubbed at a bug bite on her side. "But that has nothing to do with seducing you, and we were so close to that."

"Where were we?"

"Your mouth was just about to go . . . here." And she indicated an excellent place to begin. He was as happy as he had ever been, and, in fact, happier than he would be for the rest of the day. Her eyes were closed, and she made small sounds of pleasure. Was it the rush of blood away from his brain that suggested this was a good time to know her better, or just the desire to pause? It was pauses that made anticipation. You built to a plateau, the moments of silence between drumbeats. They shared a look, and both laughed for what would be the last time. Absently, Charlie said, "So—what do you write?"

She appeared not to have heard the question.

"You write articles, but what else besides?"

She lifted herself onto an elbow, her back going from liquid to solid. With a rush of fear, he realized he had never seen her angry.

"You don't know."

"Which is why I'm asking."

"You genuinely don't know."

"Know what?"

"Oh. My. God." She ripped a sheet away from the bed, and draped it over herself. She said, "Idiot, idiot, idiot," obviously not referring to Chaplin, who was bewildered. "All that time in the car," she murmured. "The whole time . . ."

"What?"

"Charlie, I'm Frances Marion."

The name meant something, but he couldn't make his brain do the work to explain it. He felt like a child being scolded for ill behavior he could never hope to understand. He was trying to connect his vaguely ill feelings about the name Frances Marion with the woman in bed with him. Had she insisted she was an arsonist, he could have understood that more easily. Why was she insisting she was Frances Marion? And who was that, anyway?

She looked up. "I write all of Mary Pickford's scenarios. All the ones you hate."

He stumbled. She was joking. She was not joking. He had been kissing Frances Marion.

"It's okay, Charlie," she sighed. "She hates your pictures, too."

"It's not her films so much as her persona. Now, now, you see, she's made herself a cynosure." He hesitated. He hadn't meant to use that word. He had kissed Frances Marion. "See, see, there's the person, right, and then there's the idea of the person, which is backed up by, but not entirely generated by, the pictures, and— She hates my pictures?"

"Please." She drew her knees up and buried her face against them. "You hate her films and her image and you hate her. Which is fine, because she hates you, too. And you know why? Because you two are the same *fucking* person."

She threw her head back so that it tapped the wall. She tapped it again, more purposefully. The sheet fell to reveal her breasts, so she re-covered them, tucking them in so that the bed linen might as well have been whalebone.

"Idiot," she whispered.

The terrible thing was, he wanted her more than ever. He tried to be reasonable. "Frances, we hate each other, we agree on that. That doesn't have to mean we can't sleep together."

The laugh started low, from the gut, and built until it was a bird in flight. She pounded the frame of the bed with her hand, and then slapped her own knee. Then she said, "You need to get me my clothing."

He pulled his trousers into place. He found all her several layers and brought them meekly to the bed. He thought he might yell at her. "You know," he finally said, "I do genuinely like you."

"Charlie. Have you seen one of Mary's pictures?"

"Of course I have."

"You lost your 'h,' " she whispered. " 'Have' has an 'h.' "

The observation had been expert, the stab of a stiletto.

"All right. What have you seen?"

He might yell, triumphantly, "All of them," but that was a pose. "The one—I've seen *Rebecca of Sunnybrook Farm,* and, and I've seen thousands of them. What's that one? *The Poor Little Rich Girl,*" he said, naming the vegetables left on his plate. "I've seen the premiere of every damned—"

"You're jealous." She pulled on her crêpe de chine.

He set to getting his shirt on over his head. Backward. Then he shuffled it the right way. Not only were his boots unlaced, but they were across the room. He had thrown them there.

"You haven't made a film as good as you are, Chaplin."

He shrugged. His back was to her, but he could hear the rustling of linens as she spoke.

"You know what your curse is?"

"No, thank you." A shoelace had snapped.

"You liked how I talked before. One day people will no longer just say that you're funny."

"Ah, they aren't going to think I'm funny."

"Did I say that? Mary makes people laugh but also cry and feel frightened and feel triumphant, and no one will ever ask why or how. That's because she's just a person. The people that write about her ignore the parts which can be ignored, like the mystery of it, and instead they see the curls and the spunk and the parts that can be dismissed. And she's not the only one—Fairbanks and Mary Miles Minter and Theda Bara and—"

"Yes, I get the—"

"No, you don't," she said, as righteous as the smartest girl in class. "Look at me and listen for just one moment. You haven't made a film as good as you are."

"Is this the part of you that's mean or smart?"

"I've been thinking about it longer than just today. Your films are good. They're funny. You have little flashes of something else, moments of greatness, but you haven't managed to tap into it."

"*The New Republic* doesn't agree with you."

"It's only going to get harder." She was just warming up, and the more she articulated, the better she seemed to feel. "You're a genius, which means you're going to be put under glass. People will still go to your pictures, and because you're good, they'll still laugh, but there will always be a windowpane between you and them, because even the most ignorant foreigner will know you're supposed to be a genius. And even if you stop making movies that are funny, but engage all the known emotions from A to Z, even if you create new emotions that people have never felt, and play them like a harpsichord, you'll be playing on the other side of a wall that no one will ever climb." She sounded pleased with herself as she theatrically examined some blemish on her wrist. "You're twenty-eight years old—I know because Mary talks about her age nonstop. You're only twenty-eight, but—"

"I know, I know, all my work is awful."

"—maybe your chance is over."

"Of course." He frowned. "What chance?"

She nodded, dreamily. She had put on all of her clothes, and was sitting on the edge of her chair, bright-eyed, as spent as if they'd tangled up the sheets successfully.

Chaplin had nothing to say. After such a vigorous crucifixion, he should be the one sitting down, and yet he felt nothing whatsoever. He regarded himself in the mirror, snapped his cuffs just so, pulled his vest and shirt into place. Finally, he threw open the curtains, which faced the beach. He hadn't particularly used force, but nonetheless they had come off their rack, with a clatter, and he held them in his hands.

He tossed them to the bed, and left the room.

6

By the time Chaplin returned to the patio, dinner had ended. Five tableaux under the twisted limbs of the giant oak had been illuminated with lipstick lights. He stared at the entertainment without feeling a single damned thing.

The oak, massive, towering, and dead, made the backdrop to actors in white powder posed as famous tableaux: Laocoön and his sons beset by serpents; Rodin's *The Thinker;* the *Winged Victory;* the suicide of David in his bath; and last, to his displeasure, was a slight youth in foppish hat and palm-frond-sized saber, labeled "Donatello's David."

"Behold," a voice declaiming like a carnival barker with the pretensions of a college professor. It belonged to the actor who had read "Thanatopsis," with his bald head and crêpe beard. "All is vanity," he said. "The pride of Icarus leads to the fall of Icarus. The temptations of Laocoön lead to the tortures of Laocoön. The grandeur that was Greece and the glory that was Rome, reduced to rubble, their marble burned by savage races. Such is as it shall ever be."

There was nodding in the crowd, muffled acquiescence, as if no one had really considered this before.

"What about David? The one by Donatello?" Chaplin yelled this, for he was suddenly suspicious. Heads turned, first to locate the voice, and then back to the stage, where the orator was looking with confusion at the actors portraying statues. Chaplin mimed spinning a rock in a slingshot, and then mimed it colliding with his own noggin. "As I recall, he wins. What's the vanity there?"

Unfortunately, the orator's notes did not explain how this statue oozed vanity, but Mr. Goldwyn had been very precise: all had better be vanity.

Chaplin continued, "Ladies and gentlemen, since all is vanity, don't bother asking Goldwyn for a raise." Which put his finger on it nicely. A few young executives in the Goldwyn company exchanged frightened glances: Chaplin had figured it out. Goldwyn, who, it should be remembered, was somewhat insane, *did* hope the moral was going to save him when it was time to renegotiate. Chaplin's uncovering it had been a kind of genius of wrong turns, from hating the statues, hating Frances, hating himself, hating all that Goldwyn stood for. It was like discovering the source of the Nile by way of Neptune.

Chaplin searched quickly for Mildred (didn't find her) and Dexter (clutching a drink with a weak smile) and Frances (not there), and he also caught sight of his blue-eyed government agent, who was staring at him with blank assessment, his wide face a carbon-copy form that had not yet been filled out.

"You there, Dah-veed in the bath, how much are they paying you to sit in this bath all night? Not nearly as much as that Chaplin makes in the time he takes to twitch that mustache." This caused some laughter, and Chaplin realized he had just taken on a character. He thought quickly, attacking that which he feared most: he dashed to the government agent, whispered "Pardon me," and took his round spectacles off his face.

The man's hands leapt too late to protect himself, his eyes sent into a squint that his neighbors found comic. Chaplin found the orator, said, "Pardon me" again, and tore off his beard. The actor, taking the temperature of the crowd, quickly turned his open mouth into a smile, as if he were in on the joke.

Chaplin huddled near the tree to slap on the beard, the spirit gum only half sticky, to adjust the glasses, and to work up a head of social outrage, and when he strode through the statues to the crowd, he was ready. "Comrades!" His back was stiff, he had planted a fist at the base of his spine, and his other hand extended, sweeping across the crowd as if they all belonged to him. He had become Leon Trotsky.

"You see, comrades, that we need not divide ourselves into financiers, actors with their own production companies, actors without production companies, extras, actors who need to wait in the bath for four dollars a night. Comrade, tell Trotsky the truth—is it four dollars?"

The young man, spellbound, nodded.

"Four dollars! When a buffoon like Chaplin makes one million twenty-five thousand. That is the thing that divides us. For there are perhaps, what, twelve immortals who are showered with money. And the rest? Showered with broken dreams and promises, chaos and homicide in the streets!"

Someone shouted "Yes," and there was nervous laughter, for, though there wasn't much homicide in the streets, now that it had been said aloud it could happen at any minute. "And in this issue I am starting not from the angle of any faction or party, but from a broader view. What are revolutionaries but actors? What are actors but revolutionaries? And, representing my fellow actors, I choose to address you, the Hollywood bourgeois moneymakers, as equals. Even though in Hollywood no one is equal." The dialectic was perfect, the enunciation perfect, the accent perfect, the grammar startlingly true. Though no one here had heard Trotsky, they knew he would sound exactly like Chaplin. Who wanted to tear the system down.

"Comrades, I am not hoping to convince you this evening to overthrow this corrupt system, for that would be too bold a hope. Instead, just acknowledge that you and ourselves, together, we are suffering all the pangs and agonies of the revolution. You, comrade, say you work for Goldwyn. And you, Mademoiselle Comrade, you say you work for Ince. But it is not so—you work for yourselves, and Goldwyn and Ince, parasites lacking the means of production, live off of you. And yet they ask for your loyalty. But does the financier or the production company sweat in the field? Especially when you need to do thirty-seven takes because of the wind? Does the doorkeeper of the barracks filled with gold know the agonies of threshing wheat before the camera, when the Klieg lights have snapped? Who knows the agony of falling from a horse day after day? The actor! Who needs to apply tincture of castor oil after a day under the lights? The actor! Our principle is—all power to the actors." He underlined this with a thrust of his fist into his palm, and to his surprise there was no laughter, but instead some applause. "All power to the actors!" he said again, and there was more applause. "Comrades, say it all together, 'All power to the actors!'"

The crowd roared it with passion that could have blown him backward.

Even the human statues had broken ranks, squatting on their pillars, chanting, All power to the actors! Why had no one noticed before the disparity of power in Hollywood? All power to the actors! The glasses rendered his eyesight impossible, and his beard was in danger of falling off, but he had memorized the sway and the sense of Bolshevik speeches.

"Whether this will lead to an insurrection depends not only and not so much on the actors as on those who, in defiance of the people's unanimous will, still hold the studios' power. Is this an insurrection?" He cupped his hand to his ear. "Is this an insurrection?" No one knew how to respond. He had on his lips the next line of a Trotsky speech, "This only awaits the sweep of history's broom," but he could not make himself say it. He throbbed with a kind of power he did not normally feel except in character. He faltered. For he was not just an actor, but a man in charge of hiring actors. He was labor and management, one extremely large shoe in each camp. There was a group waiting to, upon his word, strike, loot, and break windows in the streets of Santa Monica. "No, this is not an insurrection," he finally said. "Comrade in the bath, they are paying you four dollars? And you deserve that four dollars? And you work for that four dollars?"

The man slowly nodded, and Chaplin nodded with him. But then Chaplin turned the nodding into shaking his head no, which the man followed, also shaking his head no.

"That's right. For you are not a wage slave. The four dollars is all they know how to reward you with. But your actual reward is—to make art. Comrades, so it is with all of us. 'All is vanity'? Nonsense! The world is not ruled by chaos and homicide—such a worldview is despicable. Take their money! But art gives shape to the incompassionate and frigid world! Nothing is vanity! All for art!"

So ended Chaplin's first political speech, a mélange of beliefs both real and imagined that took a hairpin turn. His head was throbbing. He crossed his arms and leaned against the oak tree behind him. He was thinking, "I have saved myself, I have saved myself," the repetition like a pulse beat. He felt every ounce taken out of him, his entire weight given over to the lean. He was unprepared for a seismic shift, the feeling of tumbling across a ship's deck, as the tree groaned, uprooted, its anchor chains dancing like startled arms, and, with a crash of branches, fell over.

Which was the full-stop punctuation his speech had lacked beforehand. He righted himself, dusted his linen jacket, tossed away the beard, carefully peeled away the glasses, and tried to smile as he checked his knees for permanent damage. No one was wondering about his values anymore—men were holding their sides and women were reduced to weeping. He nodded at them, assessing the effect of a routine. The fact was, at this moment, he wanted the world to love him forever so he could tell them, forever, what idiots they were for doing so.

7

It was later in the evening. Chaplin had taken off his shoes and his socks, and rolled his trousers. He had no idea what time it was. The sun had set. There was a scattering of those recently planted dead trees to walk through, a weak forest that begged to be mighty enough for a trail of breadcrumbs. He walked toward the sound of waves.

He was still thinking, "I saved myself," but with less insistence. He had to get away from the feeling of people, but he didn't want to go home.

On the other side of the trees was the open stretch of sand. At his feet, driftwood, knobs of kelp, flecks of tar, tiny seashells, and all around him, now that he was twenty or thirty yards from the house, was a bubble in the fog, as if he were traveling with his own dome of solitude.

In a way, the party had only caused his thoughts to make a loop, from standing alone in the fog and musing on emotions he could not name, to the same fog, perhaps the same emotions. He couldn't exactly remember the details of how he had felt those hours before. Feelings were like that—you were never sure if you had actually recaptured them.

It turned out that, the farther he went toward the waves, the more the sands sloped down, as if curving with the horizon. The beach was damp, then wet and packed, and the fog was no longer dense but more like a distant envelope. There were lights on a dock to the south, and one or two pulsing from a fishing boat. He saw a woman swimming. She was striding out of the breakers, then, as she found her legs, trotting until she was free from even the touch of seafoam. It was as if she had swum from across the ocean and he had discovered her.

She waved at him. It was Mildred. In her red swim cap.

She found her towel, and began to dry the black mohair bathing suit he had found so modest.

"Hello, Mildred," he said, approaching.

"Hello, Mr. Chaplin."

"You really can call me Charlie. I even prefer it."

"Okay." She dried her shoulders and legs in silence.

"Did you enjoy your swim?"

"Oh, yes. The ocean isn't so cold when you bear up to it."

"Unlike people," he said. She cocked her head, a smile on her lips waiting for the moment when she understood. "Nothing," he said. "I'm being stupid."

"No, you aren't. Are you enjoying the party?"

"Yes," he said. "How long have you been swimming?"

"I took a long walk first, then . . . I don't know."

"I prefer it down here, too. I like places that are on the edge of things, like the map, or the last building in a neighborhood. Sometimes I stand on the beach like it's the bow of a ship."

"When I'm swimming, I don't know why I like it so much. It might be that there are so many fish beneath me."

Charlie laughed his rare, honest laugh: Heh. Heh-heh.

"What?"

"No, do go on."

"I'm up at the top and there must be miles and miles beneath me with seals and dolphins and then at the bottom are little things like spiders and snails and crabs that live in coral."

It was endearing and genuinely childlike. "You know what Dr. Freud says about swimming?"

She shook her head. "Can we walk while we talk? It's getting late."

They walked up the slope. "It suspends you gently, but also there's a little bit of fear and excitement, because of the way the waves can suddenly take you."

"Hmm. Yes, I think that's right."

"Freud would say that's like sex," he said.

"Oh." She didn't look at him, but continued toward the house. He couldn't tell if such talk had made her redden.

"Freud says sex is at the root of comedy, too."

"Hmm." Her legs, striding across the sand.

"What do you think of that?"

"I don't know," she said. She stopped. Then she said, "I don't know," again, as if she had considered it long and hard. They were still some distance from the patio, and the ocean had also vanished. It was dark enough for them to see lights from the living room make haloes through the silhouettes of dead trees. He had the urge to crush her. And then rescue her.

"Don't you like talking to me?" he asked.

"I do. But it's after dark, and I have to telephone Mother."

"I'm not telephoning my mother," he said.

"Why not?"

The exchange had happened so quickly, it only now caught up with him. She was young enough to be calling her mother. And now, in her innocence, she had asked him a question he hadn't thought of answering.

"Well, she's in England," he said, slowly, and he had a vision of an elephant backing up into a doorway, tail-first. A man reaches for the tail, thinking he's going to pull a garden hose through, and, no, it's an elephant, three-story haunches pressed all about the frame.

"I bet you can call England. Can you?"

"I can."

"Why don't you talk to your mother? Is she one of those awful mothers?"

"No, she's wonderful," he said automatically. Then, thinking about it, he added, "She's quite nice. Everyone loves her. What's your mother like?"

"She likes sewing. She's very clever about that."

"No, I mean—"

"She also likes to sing, and she's fond of reading the paper aloud over breakfast so we'll all know what's going on in the world. She's good."

"That's very nice," he said. They took a few more steps toward the beach house. There were pairs of lights turning together, automobiles leaving the parking lot, and the motion fluttered among the branches of the dead trees.

"Do you think they'll let me use the telephone?"

"I don't see why not."

"It can be expensive to call from some places."

"Mr. Goldwyn should pay for whatever you desire."

"You're nice, Charlie." In a few more steps, they would be in sight of the house. Mildred seemed to drag her feet in the dunes. "I have something to tell you. It's embarrassing."

"Please tell me."

"It's embarrassing."

"I'm nice, remember?" Was she flushed?

"I once entered a Charlie Chaplin look-alike contest," she whispered. She covered her grin.

"Did you? Did you win?"

"I came in fourth."

"Show me your Charlie Chaplin."

Mildred asked if he was serious, and when it became apparent he was, she looked at the lights coming from the house, worried about being seen. "Okay," she finally said. She put her towel to the ground.

She walked ten paces away and turned, but Chaplin halted her. "No, I'll announce you. Here we go. 'Now, for your pleasure, Contestant Number One, Mildred—'"

"Harris!"

" 'Mildred Harris, star of *Intolerance* and the *Oz* films, as the wicked slacker Charlie Chaplin.' Go!"

She walked toward him with her toes turned out, twirling an imaginary cane, and bothering her upper lip as if it itched. She raised her red swim cap and let it snap back into place. "Now, wait, here, wait, wait," she said. She raced away. When she'd achieved the necessary distance, she called to him, "The cops are after me now."

"All right."

"There's a corner. Oh, we'll pretend this tree is a corner." She hustled toward him, arms pumping well out of proportion, then, hopping on one foot the requisite three times, rounded the corner of the tree. She bowed.

He applauded for her. "Very good. Nicely done on sand. Well worth fourth place. Now I'll do Chaplin."

"You do a Charlie Chaplin impersonation?"

"I do an impersonation of a Charlie Chaplin impersonator." He warmed up: shaking out his shoulders, three steps with the toes-out walk, the wriggle of the mustache, the pivot, and three steps the other way, the imaginary cane, whose tip poked him in the eye. Then he ran in place, and performed the turn around the corner, but all the time ruining it with his facial expression, a fearful grimace, eyes darting and mouth moving in silent calculation. He bumped into someone on his left, tipped his hat to him, and, while bowing, accidentally bumped into someone on his right, requiring him to turn and give a second bow, which caused yet another bump and apology, until he was caught in a thicket of anxious attempts to set things right.

Then he clutched at his heart, seized up, and fell over, dead. His legs kicked.

Mildred applauded for him, and helped him back up. He had just ruined his jacket in the sand, but he didn't mind. She had an odd laugh, as if many separate, distinct, funny thoughts came to her while she sized up the situation, with several seconds' space in between them.

"What?" he asked.

"Do you read the funnies?"

"No."

"Do you read *Krazy Kat*?"

"No, I don't. Why?"

"Because you're just like him. Or her." She was holding her hand before her smile again, and because Chaplin didn't understand her, she tried to explain, with bursts of giggling in between: there was a cat who was a boy sometimes and a girl sometimes, but was more like a sprite, not quite real, but ever so hilarious. "The cat is a pooka," she explained. "Not really a boy or a girl, but a sprite," which was the second time she'd said this, and it annoyed Chaplin to hear it again.

She was waiting for a response. He asked, "Does anyone love the cat?"

"No," she said. "Oh, wait, the dog loves the cat."

"Yes, of course. And the cat loves the dog?"

"No, the cat loves the mouse."

"Does the mouse love the cat?"

"No, the mouse hates the cat. And the dog. And everyone. He even throws bricks at him. Or her. You know?"

"Now it sounds realistic." When she continued to giggle, he said, "No, truly, that's how love works."

"It's not," she declared. "Love doesn't work that way at all."

"How old are you?"

"I'm"—she swallowed—"seventeen." It was ingrained, the shift between the first word and the second. She had gone from girl-on-the-beach to actress. "Seventeen" went with the right clothing and the photograph for the casting agents. It was a good age for any girl's career. "No, I'm sixteen," she said.

"Oh."

Her posture was contrite, and she looked at him from the corner of her eye, as she often did, but this time chewing on her lip. There was a car horn in the parking lot, someone honking for attention, a couple of short and simple beats upon the steering wheel. "I'm sorry," she said.

He didn't know what she was apologizing for—being sixteen? lying? needing to go call her mother, which she hadn't? He liked having her be sorry. He wanted her to act polite, to walk carefully, looking for approval, and he wanted never to grant it. He had in mind offering her the thing no one else had gotten today. "Mildred," he said. He was going to offer her a screen test.

"Can your mother ever come here?"

The screen test evaporated. He said, "She can. She's been trying to."

"It must be dangerous. How would she travel? By boat?"

A great deal of time passed. "She'll travel . . . by soap bubble."

Mildred cocked her head. She reminded him of someone. She regarded Charlie with curiosity, a simple gaze that could never understand him. She reminded him of Mut. "My mother—her name is Hannah—she's always had a great sense of fun," he said. He left this here as if sizing up how exactly to get the elephant through the doorway. "Here's an example. When we needed to go somewhere, let's say she needed to bring her mending to a customer, she would make me guess how we were going to get there. And I would guess the underground first, because the tube frightened me and I loved it so much, and she would say, 'No, not the tube.' " He paused. "Is this boring?"

"No," Mildred said.

"And I would guess the bus, and Hannah would say, 'No, not the bus,' and we would go on like that, taxi, on foot, cart, phaeton, carriage, and it would get sillier and sillier, and she would say, 'You haven't asked if we're going by riverboat yet,' and I would ask, 'Are we going by riverboat?,' and she would say, 'No, of *course* not, we're not going by *riverboat*,' as if that was the most ridiculous thing she'd heard, and I'd ask about sedan chairs and bicycles, and finally, when I was laughing so hard I couldn't stand it, she would say, 'Charlie, I'm going to blow a soap bubble, and we'll step inside it, and we'll travel to Covent Garden by soap bubble.' " This had been a long story. He didn't know if it was a good one. So his eyes flicked to Mildred, who was watching him with her fingertips over her mouth, the way she might watch someone juggling on a highwire.

He used his hand to brush her fingertips from her face. Since she allowed him, he positioned her hands at her side.

"Did she ever do it?"

"Pardon?"

"Did you and she ever travel by soap bubble?"

He wished for a bright light to examine her by. It was the question of a child who has grown out of believing in fairies, but who nonetheless suspects that on certain occasions, when the disappointments of the adult world are somehow suspended, perhaps a man in a foreign city, a pooka, long ago, just once, by means that could be explained if only she knew more about the universe, might have traveled by soap bubble.

He continued to move her arms about, waiting for the moment when she would resist. He placed her hands on her hips, elbows out. His voice was raspy, as if he had been talking for days. "My mother is in a hospital," he said. Which was just like saying, "I'm seventeen," and so he said, "It's more of a clinic, it's a resting place for the insane. She's actually quite mad. Put your hands behind your head."

Mildred obeyed. She threaded her fingers together and brought her arms down so that her hands rested on the back of her swim cap. "She's insane?"

"She'll never recover. She has fits, and sometimes they need to confine her so she doesn't hurt anyone. I want you to adjust your legs like so." He tapped her on the insides of the knees so that she shuffled them apart. "Arch your back slightly."

She made a pretty picture, legs spread, elbows pointing skyward, the only color on her whole body the red swim cap, his whole sight of her set against shafts of light threading through the skeletal trees that were her uncanny backdrop. There was no reason for her to let him do this to her; they had gone beyond any sort of decent conversation, left polite social behavior miles behind. He looked carefully at her face, which was going into places where the villagers and the outcomes were less sure.

"How long will I stand like this?"

"I'll tell you," he murmured. "I love my mother's madness. I think it made me what I am. Does that frighten you?"

"No," she said.

"Really?"

"A little," she said.

"Are you really sixteen?"

"Yes. I will be."

"Keep your back arched. You're doing well." He brought his hands up. Because she was on the slope, she stood slightly taller than he did. This gave him excellent access. He traced the air over her body, his fingertips just an inch, sometimes less than an inch, from actually touching her. It was a kind of pantomime. "My mother frightens me sometimes. I love her, but I just don't know what to do about her. You're very beautiful. I like very much that you're being such a good girl. My mother has been trying to come over here, but I've been stopping her. No one knows that, Mildred.

Look." With his eyes, he directed her to look at his hands. They were suspended above the surface of her bathing suit, just at the level of her chest. He could touch her breasts if he wanted. "You're trembling."

She nodded.

"You're being very good," he said. He took a deep breath to remember this moment when he could do anything he wanted. Then he took a few steps away, brought her the towel, shaking the sand from it, and dropped it around her shoulders. "You can relax now."

Her hands went down. He straightened the towel, which she clutched at, and he asked, "Would you like to see me again?"

She nodded.

"Off to call your mother, then," he said. "Goodbye."

Mildred hesitated. Perhaps she expected something less abrupt, but there was nothing in Chaplin's face to argue with.

"Charlie?"

"I said goodbye."

She held on to her towel and ran through the trees until she disappeared from view.

Chaplin's eyes flashed. He had tears in the corners of his eyes. He felt magnificent.

☆　☆　☆

He walked back to the party. There was some disturbance on the patio—a few of the waiters were gathered around someone lying down. There were cries for blankets.

When he was close enough, he saw what had happened: the boy in the toga who had been playing violin in front was sprawled on a makeshift stretcher. Chaplin had forgotten him. His limbs were blue from cold. "Someone get this boy hot tea!" one waiter cried.

This caused Chaplin to walk in a different direction, with his collar up against his cheek.

The new route took Chaplin past the entrance of the house. Where was Eddie Sutherland? The car was still in the parking lot. He walked along the flagstones that surrounded the house, peeking into the kitchen, whose windows were steaming, and then along the farthest wing. Someone had planted rosemary, which was struggling in the salty winds, but there were also young scrub pepper trees and sage and lavender on the leeward side.

Since his overthrow of the "All is vanity" theme, instruments had been located, and amateurish jazz chords were beginning to issue into the night sky. He recognized the insistent beat of the "Calico Stomp," which anyone who could rub two notes together might play. He, for instance, could play it if anyone asked.

He completed a circuit of the house until he was on the beach again, by the patio, where he saw the band and its dozen or so admirers. There was a dashing fellow he'd never seen before, with a guitar, and another such fellow on clarinet, and Eddie Sutherland was playing the banjo. Chaplin took a step forward—it would be fun to conduct such a band—but then he saw that Frances Marion had a cowbell, and was saying something—he was too far away to hear what—that caused the rest to slap the benches with their palms. She banged on her cowbell, and soon they were back into the "Stomp," and they even had a singer, in the form of Elliott Dexter.

And Dexter had his own audience. Mildred. She was sitting on a brick-work part of the patio, legs drawn up under her towel. She rubbed her nose—an itch from drying salt water—and then her face returned to a rapturous trance. She had come to the party for Dexter, and now she was in her rightful place, as if nothing had happened with Chaplin in the makeshift forest.

Here it was, the tease of company that is doing well without you. He clasped his hands behind his back, and walked the way he'd come, poking at odd driftwood with the points of his expensive shoes. Rest tomorrow, back to work on Monday.

Ten minutes later found him sitting on a slab of sandstone rock, to the north. He was putting the Little Fellow through a whole range of emotions. The dog loves him. He loves the dog. The dog might as well be Mut. Together, they would have many adventures. He would rescue Mut from Ashes the wolfhound. Mut would rescue him back, somehow. He imagined training the dog to break windows so that the Tramp could come by seconds later and get work, fixing them. A film easily as good as he was.

"Mr. Chaplin?"

A stocky figure was approaching in the darkness. It was apparent he had never walked on a beach before, and found the presence of sand in his shoes unwieldy. It was the government man whose round glasses Chaplin had stolen and returned earlier.

"Hullo," Chaplin said.

"I'm sorry to bother you."

"Yes. I'm sure you are," Chaplin said. His throat choked up. What had he done that was coming back to kill him? It was always like this in his idle musings when he was trying to sleep, a bureaucrat tracking him down and delivering him a sheaf of papers that condemned him to smash piles of rocks with the edge of his fist for the rest of his life.

"Oh," the man said. "Apologies." These were not the words of a gadfly in hot pursuit. Instead, he seemed homely, the pudgy sort who always wanted to be helpful and for everyone to get along peaceably. He was *pleasant*. "And to tell the truth, I hadn't been to a party before. I mean, I thought I'd been to parties. But this one was eye-opening." He had an easy laugh, a *pleasant* laugh, which made Chaplin distrust him even more.

Then he had a sheaf of papers in his hand. He was extending them toward Chaplin. Chaplin took them. He couldn't see what they said. It was too dark. "Maybe we should walk back together," Chaplin said. He barely glanced at his new companion, who toddled alongside.

"I understand you've become your own producer, in a sense," he said. "That must give you tremendous freedom."

"Which I value highly."

"As would I. I was just curious—and if I'm being too nosy, let me know—who owns your negatives?"

"Pardon?"

"I mean, I'm sure your financiers do at first, but after they're withdrawn from circulation, what happens to them?"

What an odd question. "They own them for seven years, then I—" He had a terrible thought. "Is this about taxes?"

"What?"

"I'm curious in return about the source of your curiosity."

"Oh. Ha! That's pretty funny. Too nosy for my own good."

Chaplin stepped up his pace. They were closing in on the north side of the house, the familiar, less used wing of bedrooms coming into view. It forced the other man actually to trot after him.

"I'm sorry, Mr. Chaplin, I just thought that since we had friends in common, and since you've spoken so highly about my little endeavors . . ."

He stopped. "I don't know you."

The man's face went keen with embarrassment. "I thought someone might have pointed me out to you. Gee." It was odd to hear a grown man say "gee," but not as odd as what he said next. "My name is Bill McAdoo. I'm the secretary of the treasury. I sign the dollar bills."

His hand went out, so Chaplin could shake it. Which he did.

"You're William McAdoo?"

"Speaking."

Chaplin felt lightheaded, as if the ocean air had thinned and he were standing on a mountaintop. "I'm . . . I'm a fan of yours," he said with trepidation.

"I was in my office last week, and the darnedest thing happened. My phone rang, and it was Douglas Fairbanks. I mean, well, anyone can say he's Douglas Fairbanks, how are you going to know, right? After we cleared that up, he said I was a hero of yours, and that was my second moment where I told him to stop it right there and let's he and I straighten it out. I mean, why would I be a hero of yours? When Mr. Fairbanks explained the context, I realized you were being a little facetious. I mean, is that right? Just a little bit?"

Chaplin nodded, reconsidered, and then nodded again. "I have a sincere respect for money," he said, as if he were testifying in court; he still had no idea where this was going.

"Me, too. Well, anyway, your friend seems to like to josh as much as the next guy, and maybe he wanted me to surprise you and whatnot. But then he asked me what I actually did for a living, and we fell to talking, and it turns out we might all have more in common than you know. Are you okay?"

Chaplin and McAdoo had halted twenty feet from the house, and McAdoo was facing east, toward the bluffs of Santa Monica proper. The darkened wing of bedrooms was in Chaplin's immediate field of vision. As McAdoo talked, Chaplin noticed a light flick on in the bedroom closest to them, which was, if his sense of geography was correct, the same room in which he had almost bedded Frances.

"Mr. Fairbanks said you and he were discussing the war effort, and he said that you thought doing something outside of your normal activities might cheer you up, and—are you sure you're okay?"

"I'm very fine, yes. I'm just chuckling because Douglas has a way of putting things very boldly."

McAdoo straightened his glasses. "Do I have it wrong?"

"Do you . . ." It was a brilliant question. Chaplin was utterly trapped. He was not visibly squirming only because of sheer force of will. Also, there was movement in the bedroom he was facing. "Please, tell me more."

"I wanted to put an opportunity your way that is fairly unusual. We need to pay for the war. I've been in Washington long enough to know I can't just appeal to patriotism."

"You can't?"

McAdoo chortled. "No one wants to buy that. They just don't want to *not* buy it. Especially when their neighbors are around. Appealing to patriotism is a bit of a stalemate unless you've got something else you're selling with it."

This man was more complex than Chaplin had given him credit for. And what was going on in the bedroom? There were shadows falling on the window.

"Part of my job is keeping an eye on the country's money. And a fantastic amount of money has to pay for the war. More than anyone can imagine. Fantastic. We've had a couple of loan drives, and they've done well, but . . ."

Chaplin sensed where this was going. "I've bought over a hundred thousand dollars' worth of bonds myself."

"I know." He put his hands out as if to calm him. "We all know. That's good."

It was Mildred. She was in the bedroom. She was alone, and had shut the door behind her, and then crossed back again to lock it. She was still in her bathing suit, with her towel around her shoulders.

McAdoo said, "But people still think you're a slacker."

"I'm not!"

"I know," he said again, this time less to calm him than in shared amazement. "But there it is. The idea of you being a slacker is more powerful than the reality of your situation."

She was laying out her clothes on the bed.

"I think we can change that idea. I've noticed—heck, anyone who subscribes to *The Wall Street Journal* has noticed—that you've sold quite a few movie tickets in the last few years. We've never really harnessed that before. And I understand—heck, I was there when you were speaking there before—brilliant performance, truly humorous, and I liked that little one-hundred-eighty-degree"—he made a half circle in the air with his fingertip—"anyway, listen—I get the point."

Chaplin smiled at him, to show they were confederates, but also staring through him to Mildred, who had maddeningly paused to rub some kind of lotion on her bare arms.

McAdoo didn't notice the distance in Chaplin's gaze. He was instead carried by momentum. "I'm wondering if you might put that same effort you just showed, with your Trotsky and whatnot, into selling the Liberty Loan."

"What? Ask Pickford?"

"I know Mary Pickford will say yes. That's why I'm asking you."

Mildred freed her hair from her swim cap and shook her head. Her hair was a honey blond, in loose waves. She ran her hands through it and shook it again. "All right," Chaplin said.

As McAdoo cleared his throat, Chaplin realized Mildred couldn't see him. She wasn't posing or performing. She moved her fur coat and her dress to the bed, and then, with her back to the window, peeled her swimsuit off one shoulder, then the other. She drew her towel across her shoulders, wiping away sand, and then tossed the towel to the floor.

McAdoo outlined a plan, a coast-to-coast Liberty Loan Drive of Hollywood stars appearing in city squares—Wall Street! LaSalle! the French Quarter! on the steps of the Capitol!—envisioning unparalleled crowds of millions met by marching bands, soldiers, and the new royalty of cinema. They began to fade into insubstantial promises that Chaplin nonetheless begged to continue, sounds of seduction and love. He could see Mildred so clearly, with such focus, it was as if an iris had opened up around her. She put her hands behind her head. She arched her back. He could hardly breathe when he realized what she was doing. She parted her knees, settling the weight, heel to heel. She was remembering, like a child, and, like a child, playing it through again, and how exactly was that distinguishable from acting? It was, it wasn't.

In a moment, she would turn around. She would have to, for her dress was on the bed, and when she turned, Chaplin would see all of her, nude. A gift she didn't know she was giving. McAdoo was no longer speaking. He had finished his proposal a few seconds before, and was awaiting Chaplin's response. McAdoo's eyes were excited, dangerous with ambition. And, not so far away, Mildred was lowering her arms. She began to turn, the electric illumination of the room lending the leading edge of her skin a brilliant glow.

Serial

The Winking Idol

. . . .

In a word, the whole of humanity seen from the angles of
the cosmic imagination are Charlie Chaplins.

—Charlie Chaplin

. . . .

1

How to pay for a war?

Secretary McAdoo was mild, dreamy, curious, polite, patient, and, as Chaplin had decided, pleasant. His exclamations to Chaplin—"Gee" and "Gosh"—were as controversial speech as he allowed himself. He loved to dance, even when there was a war on, for which he was criticized not one whit, for he danced only with his wife, and his wife was Eleanor Wilson, the president's daughter. And who but a cautious, polite, political man would marry the president's daughter?

He loved her, but with expedience rather than passion. Passion he saved for something else: money. Loved not with avarice, but with sincere appreciation.

For years, he had had a daydream, an *idée fixe*. It had started early in his marriage, when he and his wife had walked one afternoon in the park, and she spoke of the children and their various needs, and he made the small noises of assent he'd learned to make. His eye fell on one man feeding the birds and another feeding the squirrels, and his mind launched a general theory of the costs of pleasure. Three cents for a bag of peanuts that attracted four squirrels, versus stale bread that had come from a five-cent loaf, which produced a careless flock of pigeons ever changing in number. It seemed that the pigeon fancier won, but it wasn't that simple: each squirrel had more of a personality than each pigeon, and domestic gain had come of that five-cent loaf before the excess was committed to its secondary use. So a formula would have to take that into account. Multiply by how long each kind of creature stayed, but subtract the relative costs of cleaning up after them. Might someone actually anticipate needing stale bread and thus purchase day-old loaves, and might another person with a mind for the same formula purchase metric tons of peanuts to beat any pigeon feeder at this market? Only then to be undone by the costs of storage? What if you loved pigeons and purchased your own park, and kept the squirrel feeder—your rival—out? If the squirrel feeder moved to a new location, how would he travel to the next park (bus? taxi? at what fare?), and how long would it take to begin attracting squirrels in a new location? Settling in a new park might actually cause its own spiking pleasure, though the melancholy of having been exiled might outweigh it.

Each man might get married, if only the better to distribute, with his new spouse, peanuts or stale bread, and somehow to multiply the pleasure thereby gained. But if the marriage went sour, perhaps no amount of bread or peanuts could actually give any pleasure, and there had to be some variables to measure the heart's capacity to be fulfilled by the intangible reward that money could buy. His children grew, McAdoo's marriage continued, and it became automatic upon entering any park, even when his wife was no longer speaking to him: an ever-expanding metric to compute costs and benefits, squirrels and birds in eternal competition.

Until war was declared. Now he had a very simple question with infinite variables: how to pay for a war.

McAdoo looked with envy at the work of Enoch Crowder, the genuinely unpleasant bureaucrat who had determined that American psychology would not tolerate an outright draft, but would sprint to the army physicals by making the examiners their local aldermen and druggists. Call it "volunteering." This had worked.

McAdoo found Crowder's work brilliant. For it reflected his discovery that, when one was considering complex events, almost everything was equally true. It turned out that it was a matter of who phrased the argument first.

He wrote on his letterhead that to pay for the war was patriotic. America was the humble servant of its people, asking them to lend two hundred million dollars at 3.5 percent interest. The interest rate was abominable, but McAdoo explained to the country that this would keep down the cost of the war. He called it not a "War Bond" but a "Liberty Loan." Then he folded his arms and sat back and waited without challenge for someone to have the gall to argue against buying a Liberty Loan.

When it turned out the war cost more than he'd thought, and the subscriptions to the loans were inadequate, there was a second round of Liberty Loans, which also didn't pay for the war. A lesser man would have changed his ways, but McAdoo read the landmark studies *Psychology and the American Business Model* and *Industrial Psychology: The American*

Crucible by Dr. T. H. Münsterberg to demolish what stood in his way: psychology.

Reading the books was like being bathed in light. He had never before felt he understood the worker. He wrote in the margins, "Aspires to greatness, and when that fails, goodness." "Does not see self as cog but as essential." Finally, "Optimistic—things will get better, even if he doesn't understand how." This was when he determined that patriotism couldn't actually be sold, that people, to use his phrase, "only wouldn't not buy it." Then, like a wish granted before he'd known to make it, he received the call from Douglas Fairbanks. Actors. Hold them up side by side with the war effort, and the mind would draw a straight line between them.

That author T. H. Münsterberg had given him new ideas caused him to get out his letterhead to write him a letter of appreciation. But his secretary looked at him in disbelief.

"Münsterberg?" His secretary had graduated from Princeton, read *The New Republic,* and was still flush with the idea that wherever he stood was the fixed magnetic center of the nation. This annoyed McAdoo, but, on the other hand, his young charge *did* keep abreast of gossip. "The photoplay writer?"

McAdoo felt confused. He had been thinking of the picture houses, of course, but they had no relation to Münsterberg. Or so he thought. "No, the industrial psychologist."

"He writes on motion pictures also. Sir."

It was a "sir" that meant a certain young man would be at his club tonight, telling his friends about his employer's ignorance. McAdoo let himself be a fool. "And?"

"You aren't actually writing him a letter, sir?"

McAdoo asked him to say what was on his mind, and his secretary, in hushed tones, told him all that he'd heard. This was how McAdoo learned the shameful story of T. H. Münsterberg.

The letter went unsent. McAdoo turned to other matters, for he was ambitious and there was a war on.

Shortly after meeting Chaplin at the beach house, he started to plan the largest public event in American history: the Third Liberty Loan Drive. He had a corkboard to which he affixed cards with new ideas: contests, sales of pies and flags, and, as he grew bolder, after a walk past 1600 Pennsylvania Avenue, where sheep now grazed in the spirit of wartime responsibility, a new card went up, "Shear the sheep. Auction their wool." And

Hollywood movie stars touring from town to town, with a display of military hardware to greet them. One of the last cards read, simply, "publicity," for he thought it was a good idea but he wasn't sure how it worked. No one was—yet.

He stared at his corkboard, trying to make it all cohere into one idea. Then it did. Patriotism no longer conflicted with pleasure. They were now transitive. This was not a series of parades, but a drive from one shore to the other, manifest destiny, and had to be planned for as if it were as inevitable as the swell and crest of an awesome wave.

His secretary saw him staring one morning, and stepped toward the corkboard with confusion. For it was now empty except for two cards. "Why have you written 'squirrels' and 'pigeons' on the board?"

"Because we're going to attract them all."

2

On the evening of Wednesday, April 17, 1918, two hours after the last scheduled arrival, the San Francisco train station contained but one patron: author and Harvard School of Psychology Professor Timofy H. Münsterberg.

A broken man, he planned to spend the night on a bench, his overcoat rolled into a pillow, and a pair of film canisters propping up his feet, which he had to elevate while he slept, a new requirement for his rapidly fading health. Alone and periodically confused, he recognized that his spirit was softening like tallow and his flame was at its end. He was about to make the last scheduled appearance of his public career, at an event where he would not be the star, or even a supporting player, at one of those strange moments when the threads of the known universe tied into a many-stringed knot through which all destinies seemed to pass at the same time.

Born in Danzig fifty-three years before, Münsterberg had been for most of his life a rosy-cheeked man of great extemporaneous passion, whose erudite pen could make the consumption of a grilled-cheese sandwich sound like all that Olympus would a mere mortal allow. Harvard had drafted him in 1892, bringing his light to America, the cultural hinterlands, where he applied psychology to the American industrial model. "Applied psychology" sounded enough like "how to make workers happy to tighten bolts more quickly" that corporations invited him to lecture, and they found his enthusiasm for capitalism so delightful that he counted among his patrons Henry Ford, Andrew Carnegie, Theodore Roosevelt. *Les bons temps.*

He found his higher calling one afternoon in the spring of 1915, when, trying to shake his mind from his homeland (the Second Battle of Ypres had caused him to wonder if there would be a third, a fourth, a fifth, and what terrible weapons each iteration would make credible), he went into a motion-picture house for the first time. He was transfixed by the film: *Neptune's Daughter.* It starred a woman he had never heard of, Annette Kellerman, whom later investigation revealed to be the world's favorite diving beauty.

Neptune's Daughter was a fable about a mermaid and her romance with a human king whose fishing nets had caught and killed her sister. After wicked intercession—a villainous adviser to the throne convinces the king that the mermaid should be put to death, a reel during which Münsterberg pulled at his beard in worry—the lovers were united in a happy marriage of earth and sea, and he sighed in relief.

Seeing the motion picture, his first, overwhelmed him in ways he couldn't immediately analyze, so powerful was the sense of sheer delight. In ways no book, no painting, no musical performance managed, he was *absorbed* into the narrative, a welcome exchange for worries about phosgene gases and machine guns. There were settings of sumptuous Mediterranean palaces and undersea kingdoms, and at one moment, a score of courtesans took to the beach in very little swimwear, as was, according to the production credits, true to the period. It was possible that in one or two scenes the women were wearing nothing at all, but Münsterberg was unsure. He saw it sixteen times.

He became consumed by the idea of diegetic effect, the process by which a work of art ceases to be brushstrokes, or notes of music, or words on the page, or, in this case, a series of changing camera angles, and begins instead to pull the viewer, the reader, the listener into experiencing it as reality, or, more specifically, a mass-audience reflection of their singular and personal perception of reality. Because he had never thought about movies, he did not know the vocabulary and he made up his own. He called close-ups "bust-shots," and these were, he felt, what set film apart from all other media. For the first time in history, the audience for a drama could break ranks and be brought onstage. This technique forced the viewers into its emotional interchanges, expanding their relationship with art in unexplored ways.

He sought out the few cinematic palaces of Boston, and the tiny rented halls in bad neighborhoods, and the lowest nickel-dumps, where the proprietors nursed babies and accepted eggs or cans of heating oil in lieu of coin, showing films three and five years old, scratched and spliced and projected onto bedsheets, playing to an audience of tramps and criminals and chatting domestic servants and fallen women cradling other nursing babies who wailed against the accompaniment of drunken and inappropriate piano rags.

He somewhat enjoyed the lowbrow comedies and melodramas and westerns. He tolerated the travelogues (the lack of a single protagonist bothered him). The serials engaged him the most. He missed *The Perils of Pauline*, but managed to see *The Exploits of Elaine, The Hazards of Helen, The Purple Mask, The Broken Coin,* and *The New Exploits of Elaine* (except the sixth episode, so he was confused about how she had managed to escape from the exploding cabin after the flaming birch tree fell on it).

Melodrama reminded him of philosophical inquiry in a way he found embarrassing. In his cramped office at the top of the library, where there were no windows on the courtyard but only a transom that faced the stacks, Münsterberg wrote every night at midnight about the pictograph, imagining himself shackled by masked Serbs, tossed in a gunny sack down a staircase, landing in an eight-cylinder automobile he would race at tremendous speed down country lanes while evil Nieuport 17 aircraft fired Vickers machine guns down upon him, and kerchiefed cowboys on horseback thundered behind, shooting Winchesters and Colts, hot lead whizzing past his motoring goggles and smart leather cap and matching fingerless gloves as he kept pace with the express mail-train, and there was a conductor shooing him away, telling him to slow down, the road was about to cross the train tracks, slow down, but Münsterberg jammed down the accelerator with a flattened stick and prepared to make an impossible leap from automobile to railroad car, for in the caboose, gagged and panicked and surrounded by ill-intentioned, apelike Bolsheviks, lay his idea.

His idea often looked like Annette Kellerman.

The concept of alter ego was made visual. It turned out that actors sometimes had people who performed stunts for them, unnoticed *stand-ins,* which meant the audiences identified so strongly with the idea of the object being watched that they accepted its fungibility as long as the substitution was graceful. Which was why the actors were so important—they were the audience's *stand-ins*.

He wrote asides onto the backs of envelopes and across the margins and gutters of newspapers. "In every kind of story," he wrote, on a front page with headlines telling the latest news from the village of Sapigny, "we admire a change in circumstance, particularly one brought about by a character's most vivid personality traits. But that is not realistic. We are rarely the custodians of our own fate. Once, when there were kings and queens, yes, once, up to three years ago, yes, some small, royal percentage of people had control over destinies. But film, more than any other medium, calls not just for a protagonist but for a hero. Therefore film is unrealistic." But this was exactly the opposite of how he felt. Why?

The question, unanswered, sent his idea onto an ice floe, which, broken from its pack, drifted into a river, and he was on the bank, sprinting beside, calling out to it.

Perhaps the answer lay in the American industrial model. Americans thought they were more in charge of their destinies than had any society of the last fifty centuries. Americans were people upon whom the inevitability of death was wasted. This attitude might be why Americans made movies, and why those movies had heroes who were the centers of their own universes, who actually prevailed in unlikely circumstances, which caused continental folk such as himself to admire them. Which meant that the actual hero of all American films wasn't a single person, but an idea.

What if there were a pure moment where diegesis was cast aside, and a step was taken outside the bounds of narrative, and pure *critique* was expressed instead? To utterly suspend all momentum of story, not as an act of supreme egotism (were filmmakers egotistical? he would have to investigate) but as a celebration of the form—this could be a moment of transgression, but, contrary to instinct, might it not also be a moment of pure communion? He felt gooseflesh—what if it were the sheer *unreality* of the film that made it feel so vivid and consuming? Perhaps the real hero was not a fictional character, or the actor onscreen, or the creator of the pictograph for unleashing him onto the world, but the *audience itself, for feeling uplifted*?

The evening he wrote all this down, he was so excited he drummed his fingers. He tugged on his beard. He stood and sat down. The lights burned late in his office. He was not a pacer; instead, he stood up on his captain's chair and looked out over his transom, at the stacks, imagining hooded figures slipping between them, an opalescent crown-coffin jar marked "chloroform," the slow turn of his doorknob in a gloved hand.

He wrote a letter to Annette Kellerman.

He did not want to seem like a fool, so he was carefully withholding of both his analysis and his praise. "I have seen *Neptune's Daughter*. Having consulted Vergil, Ovid, and Livy, I conclude that Neptune did not have a daughter. Perhaps your photoplay was illustrative of an incident from Poseidon's daughters, Rhode and Benthesicyme, which would be understandable, for people are frequently confused. Did your scenario describe the bathing customs at Peloponnesus? Please advise." After considering whether such a supplement might make him seem swell-headed, he enclosed a monograph he had composed on the cinematic art. It was called *The Photoplay: A Psychological Study.*

A month later, he received an envelope with a New Jersey postmark. Inside was an inscribed photograph of Miss Kellerman in her one-piece bathing suit, along with a folded single piece of pale-violet stationery on which was written a note in purple ink, with letters so small and finely composed they might have been etched by a needle. Miss Kellerman had never before received a letter from Harvard about her film, and she expressed pleasure at Münsterberg's attention. She didn't know about Poseidon, but she was planning on making more movies in Hollywood, California. If he was ever in Hollywood, California, he should come to the studio and say hello.

Münsterberg carried the letter to class, placed the photograph on his shelf, watched *Neptune's Daughter* again as if visiting with a friend at teatime. After consulting colleagues, he was horrified to learn that Hollywood was a cauldron of vices unknown since the days of Pliny's Villa Comedia. What was Annette Kellerman doing there? Perhaps it was his duty to rescue her, but perhaps she had already succumbed. He watched *Neptune's Daughter* again, searching her eyes for shiftiness and opium, decadence and kohl makeup, but came away realizing something far more disturbing instead: there had been a camera, a scenario, painted sets, flats and scrim, canvas rigging that sometimes actually waved in the background. He had known this. And yet there was a whole new set of illusions whose depths he had not plumbed. He looked at the opening titles and realized with a thud that, according to copyright, the film had been made in Fort Lee, New Jersey. He had been so sure it was made in Bermuda.

Miss Kellerman was *acting*. She was not an actual mermaid (he had already known this), but he had also mistakenly credited her with scholarship in Greek mythology just because she had appeared in a photoplay dramatizing an alleged classic event. Further: just because he had seen her face reflecting emotions, it did not mean she actually felt them. All the perceptions were in the mind of the beholder, who, besieged by the movement of celluloid illuminated in a darkened room, was searching to complete an emotional circuit, a child searching for a breast.

Or she felt them.

Meeting Annette Kellerman would not illuminate him, for he would bring his own unmet needs. In other words, it was impossible to ever finally rescue his idea, to marry it, and to live happily ever after with it.

It took him long nights at the library to think of the oxymoronic name of the medium itself, the moving picture, and he asked himself: what if the motion was essential, meaning the pursuit was eternal? His way would always be blocked by unshaven rascals in striped shirts and black domino masks, carrying blackjacks and speaking in rude slang, and the life of an idea was always one best lived screaming its lungs out at the railroad tracks, the sawmill, the limestone rapids, eternal peril. This, perhaps, was the lesson of the moving picture, the satisfaction of eternally unspooling mystery.

He decided Annette Kellerman was genuinely sweet and did not live in Hollywood, but must visit from a seaside town, where she no doubt lived with a suitable chaperone.

Kellerman actually did lead a clean life, that of an athlete, an early convert to the cult of the temple of the body. She had caused scandal by wearing the first one-piece bathing suit at Ocean Beach in Boston. That she was now bathing in nothing at all, on film, which millions of people could see, was horrifying to clergy and state censors. They wrote letters to editors: Miss Kellerman was nude! William Fox, her new producer, was unable to argue the point, for he had noticed that motion pictures featuring nude women tended to draw large audiences. He had planned to show nude women in as many features as he possibly could. In fact, Kellerman's new movie, *A Daughter of the Gods,* had over *two hundred* "mermaids" in it, a coded suggestion as to what span of flesh would be shown. More editorials appeared, condemning movies as cesspools where wholesome narrative went to die.

Fox told Annette Kellerman they were in trouble, not just their million-dollar production, but the entire film industry. How could they fight the argument that film was essentially a corrupt venture? Especially when *they* believed it?

Münsterberg received a baffling letter from someone named Adolph Zukor. Apparently, he was in the throne at a place called Paramount, and he was an ally of Fox. Zukor wrote that Münsterberg's erudition (he used this word) impressed him. He loved *The Photoplay: A Psychological Study*. Would the esteemed professor be interested in scribing a monthly column for *Paramount Pictograph*, a magazine celebrating the achievements of motion pictures? It would be distributed widely, and appeal chiefly to intellectual analysis, Zukor said, in the spirit of promoting the pictograph as an art form.

Münsterberg, delighted, complied. He was pleased to see that the debut issue featured actual photographs of Annette Kellerman in Bermuda (he had been wrong about being wrong about *Neptune's Daughter* being filmed there). In his second editorial, he wrote an essay analyzing the Paramount pictograph itself, an almost impenetrable discussion of diegetic effect applied to an entirely new medium. Never before had there been a profession so compelling that a magazine celebrated it. He concluded that film was a perfect tool for *rapprochement* with Germany: "No one wants war. Looking to aggression as a *casus belli* is only fruitful when we recognize our own aggressions as *prophases*. Settling with Germany is in our best interests."

The bastions of morality were struck dumb—an intellectual was proving that the photoplay throbbed with the best of the human spirit. Soon enough, he received a request from Universal: would he consider taking his lecture on *Neptune's Daughter*, the heart and soul of *The Photoplay: A Psychological Study*, from theater to theater? The chance to play lecturer, intermediary, and interlocutor—stand-in!—was too important to pass up. He accepted.

For the first several weeks on the Redpath Chautauqua circuit, after a mother-daughter team of tragedians performed bowdlerized selections of Shakespeare, Münsterberg had shown *Neptune's Daughter* and spoken on the film's use of bust-shots or scene cards or lighting. "Look! Look how the sneer of the concubine forces our focus hither, to, yes, this bust-shot of the mermaid, her maidenhood in flower, her conflict when sacrificing herself for the honor of her people! See the intercutting among herself and her beloved and her rival, how it forces us to wonder if we have the same fortitude ourselves? It en-nobles us to answer that yes, we do!"

He freely explained what the *audience* was feeling rather than the characters, and who was the audience to disagree with a man from Harvard! When he spoke at the edge of the screen, he himself was transported, along with his audience, into a sunny realm where the citizens were all smarter, happier, and bursting with the fruit of knowledge. If we were mermaids, of course we would make the right sacrifices, for we are all as good as our heroes, if only for as long as we are watching them. There was hearty applause in every audience, both for his passion, and for themselves, because he had made them feel intelligent for having already enjoyed Annette Kellerman. At first, this was enough.

Six weeks into his tour, in the San Francisco train station, the coat under his head, the canisters of his beloved movie under his heels, Münsterberg was a shambles. He tried to make himself comfortable as night fell. But at nine o'clock, long after the last scheduled train was supposed to pull in, the middle platform came to life with the arrival of a ten-car train from Stockton. When it nosed into the station, the doors flew open, and out spilled a party. Two hundred people jumped, skipped, and sprinted off the train, waving their arms and singing with off-key enthusiasm.

This was jarring enough to Münsterberg. But then, two platforms over, a second train arrived. Ten minutes later, there was a third train, and a fourth. All night long, trains arrived from San Jose, from Santa Cruz, the mountains and the valleys around the Bay, and farther: Sacramento, Eureka, the mining towns of the Sierra. One of them came from Reno, Nevada, and another from Eugene, Oregon.

Münsterberg pretended to sleep, his spine to the platform. Some of the revelers began to nail up bunting, and the sound of hammering finally uprighted him. He rubbed his eyes—the bunting fell in patriotic semicircles of red, white, and blue. The people who had gotten off the trains had made their own signs and placards to identify themselves, and they were beginning to gather together in various groups, farmers here, lumberjacks there, and in various other stations were Knights of Pythias, Sons of the

Serpent, honor guards, ladies' auxiliaries, and Gymnasium Girls, the last of these practicing forward cartwheels and shrieking in happiness.

Münsterberg stood, his weak heart thumping with dismay. He hoped this carnival was but a nightmare, but, no, he was fully awake and becoming alive with bedazzled horror. He understood what the crowds and the practicing and the bunting meant.

The Third Liberty Loan tour had arrived in San Francisco.

The loan drive had begun on April 6, 1918, the anniversary of the United States' entry into the war. The first rallies had been staged in New York, with special guests Charlie Chaplin, Mary Pickford, Douglas Fairbanks, and cowboy idol William S. Hart. On Wall Street, Chaplin spoke through a megaphone to twenty thousand people while Fairbanks lifted him high into the air.

Then it was Philadelphia, then Washington; then they split up. Fairbanks and Pickford headed to the Midwest. Hart took the West and Southwest, and Chaplin went south, speaking in Charlotte, Columbia, Augusta, New Orleans, and Memphis, where his nerves began to fray.

He had finished work on his new film, *A Dog's Life,* only the night before leaving for the loan tour. It could well have been a disaster, for he had taken certain risks in tone that he couldn't defend now.

In a telegram from Memphis, Chaplin told McAdoo that he had never seen so many people in his life. He wasn't sure he could speak again in public. "I like to go among people and get intimately acquainted with their loves, their hates, their politics. So, when, in a great bunch of human beings, I see on every face only one emotion, curiosity, I want to get away as fast as I can." He dreamed at night of rabbits that ate people.

McAdoo shuttled to Memphis to see Chaplin. On the evening train out of the city, he listened to Chaplin's complaints and tutted sympathetically, "Of course you can sit the rest of the tour out," and then, changing the subject, smiled and slapped his knee and told Chaplin he had the most foolish thing to report: *Motion Picture Magazine* had sent Syd a wire saying Chaplin was now No. 14 on their list of immortals. Up from 36 or something. What a ridiculous thing! How silly people were to vote in such a contest! McAdoo laughed, and Chaplin, eyes unfocused as if seasick, laughed. And later asked McAdoo if it was possible he might speak in just one or two more cities.

The plan was to reunite the four stars in San Francisco on Thursday, April 18, 1918, twelve years after the Earthquake. Hence the forty-eight-point predictive headline in the *Chronicle:* GREAT THRONGS WILL CHEER LIBERTY PAGEANT, with the equally directive twenty-four-point subline: OUR SAN FRANCISCO TO BE SHAKEN BY PATRIOTISM.

San Franciscans laughed at the *Chronicle* the way they always would. This laugh was particularly rich: they would not be sold their emotions in advance, particularly by such an old shell game as patriotic fervor. It was as if the government and the de Youngs thought the City That Knew How was populated by chaw-dipping men, and children running wild in stained gunny sacks, and toothless women struck dumb by the glow of electric lights.

Below the headline was a narrow photograph: behind Lotta's Fountain, once the gathering place of Earthquake survivors, was a sixty-foot turret, a crimson "Liberty Tower," upon which was written in words a full story tall:

CRUSH

THE

KAISER

WITH

CASH!

At the top was a clock face that, instead of telling time, showed how many millions had been collected. High noon was the San Francisco quota of $210 million.

But the light of the bacchanalia was now bent by a lens that no one much noticed. The remainder of the *Chronicle*'s page one consisted of the weather (high of sixty-two degrees); advertisements for Hart, Schaffner & Marx (specializing in officers' wear); a notification of the latest Chaplin film, *A Dog's Life,* opening at the New California on Market; a list of slackers; and two articles.

One article was just a sentence long: John Cowper Powys, critic and orator, had changed his evening's lecture on "Shaw and Swinburne" to "Wicked German Kultur."

The other article was several capital inches, dead center of the page, running above and below the fold lines. It explained why a tired old academic was now cowering in the train station, uncertain of who was watching him, or where his enemies might be. The article's diction and shorthand suggested it was the latest development in a case with which even the casual reader was familiar. In the smooth, authoritarian font that suggested avuncular calm, it read: MUNSTERBERG PAID AS SPY MASTER WHILE AT HARVARD. The subtitle read "Noted psychologist advised *rapprochement* at Kaiser's pleasure."

This was a lie, unbelievable—*if one thought it through*. But careful thought was hardly the background tone of today. Energetic newsboys were handing out the *Chronicle* for free. It was being read with high spirits.

4

Münsterberg was not the only man whose story was going far and wide. As mentioned, the *Chronicle*'s front page listed the slackers, men who had chosen the worst week to sprint from registration, their names distributed on the day when San Francisco's population had doubled. In the final column, his name near enough the end to stand out from the pack, was a man turned from lighthouse assistant to fugitive: Leland Wheeler.

He was at the prow of the midnight ferry, cap pulled down over his blue eyes, lapels turned up to hide his distinctive jaw, weathered fist clutching together the front of his coat, slab of torso leaning into the mists spilling up from the Bay. He looked exactly like someone who had broken the law.

This appealed to approximately three-quarters of the women who were also on board. For instance: Miss Andrea Pike, a San Franciscan returning from a visit to her maiden aunt in Oakland. Pike, who went by "Andy" when she was with her set, wore a blue georgette-crêpe beaded dress— something Lee wasn't sure he'd seen before—and a man's bowler hat, which he had certainly never seen a woman wear.

Andy rocked on her heels, amused by the handsome man who was try- ing not to look at her. She tore her ferry ticket into pieces, crumpled them up, and, with careful flicks of her finger, fired them at the back of Lee's head. The last one connected, and he glared at everyone until he found Andy, who burst into laughter.

Then she was standing beside him. She pointed her white leather boots through the railing, angling them as if to show off the approximately four thousand eyelets each had. She waited for him to speak to her, and when he didn't, she said, "Might I have your ticket? I'd like to throw it at you."

"Listen," he said, carefully. "You shouldn't talk to me."

It was not a reply she had expected. She could not tell if it was sincere, or the best conversational gambit she had ever tripped across. But either one was fine. She faced him, lips parted, mouth slightly upturned in a smile of astonishment.

Approximately one hour later, they were six stories above Sutter Street, in her flat, on her bed, with half their clothing on the floor. There were buttons everywhere, and he had actually used a knife to cut the laces of her boots.

Lee was aware every moment that he was a hick and a rube and just an amusement to her, but he proceeded with fatalistic abandon. Tomorrow he might be in jail, nothing much mattered except tonight, etc. Andy, for her part, enjoyed the fatalistic abandon. The combination of this, and how hard his biceps had felt through his coat, had propelled her as far as inviting him up for a drink; the rest of the momentum came from Lee himself. She had never heard of St. George Reef, but by the time her clock read two, she wanted every man she met from now on to have come from there.

By four, when they had finished, again, she was so exhausted that she did not want to believe that he was now adjusting all the lamps in her room and asking her sincerely if by this particular light he looked much like Wallace Reid.

When it became apparent he was not coming to bed until she admitted that, yes, he did look like Wallace Reid, Andy's heart broke a little. This was followed by a half hour in which they lay together like spoons, Lee explaining to the nape of her neck that he was meant for bigger things, he hoped to escape registration—he had a plan—and he had once taken a screen test given by the famous Hollywood cameraman George Barnes, of *Betsy's Fatal Slip*, and he had saved his half of an eight of diamonds, and would she like to see it? Here it was. See?

They drifted into a vague sleep, Andy having repeated anxious half dreams in which she actually had to eat breakfast with this sincere man. When the sun was coming up, he surprised her by making love to her once more, slowly and, better, silently. Afterward, she was spent. She had a cramp in her calf muscle, but could not even massage it.

Lee made coffee while Andy bathed, and after he finished in the bathroom, she scrambled some eggs and made toast. Both of them felt the sense of acceleration that comes from an hour of sleep, the sensation that if a pin dropped, not only would you hear it, but you could probably catch it on its way down.

"Do you want to know the dream I had?" he asked.

She considered.

"I found some mice in a field, and they were all injured."

"Mice," Andy said.

"Or otters or . . . Anyway, they were hurt. So I bandaged their heads and I bought them magazines to read while they recuperated."

She did not say anything, and so he tried again.

"There's a great deal of cruelty, and sometimes . . ." He changed course. In *Photoplay* one did not discuss rescuing mice. "Sometimes I can be cruel myself," which he hoped saved it.

They ate the last few bites of breakfast. The windows were open, and there was a continuous dull commotion outside, a distant, unfocused rumbling, as if crews were dragging lumber to construction sites, and there were shouts on the street that echoed up the sides of buildings.

"I have to go," Lee said.

"Oh, are you sure?"

He stood, and she realized he was going to leave now, so she wiped the corners of her mouth. "Farewell," she whispered.

"This is going to work," he said. "It's going to be tricky, though."

"Good luck." Which she found herself meaning. She had seen women sending their men off to war, perhaps, or maybe she had only thought she'd seen it. She wasn't sure how to say goodbye to a man trying to avoid going to war.

"I will come back," he said.

"Oh. Good."

"I hope I didn't make you late for work."

"It's okay, Lee."

"I can walk you."

"Goodbye, Lee. Good luck. Really."

When he had left, she smiled to herself—she was liking him better already—and checked her hair in the mirror in preparation for walking to her job at a jewelry store at Post and Grant that was going to be robbed.

5

When Lee stepped onto the street, he remembered he had meant to tell Andy his name was Leland Wallace or Lee Reid or Wallace Wheeler, but telling her his real situation had made her his accomplice, which was less lonely. He had thirty-five cents and no safe place to stay, and he was beginning to feel guilty for having left without telling his mother what he was doing. Still, he walked as if San Francisco were his home. A confident gait struck him as a fine disguise.

He imagined himself a running stream. He was dappled with sunlight, and trouble passed through him, leaving him clear, cool, intact, and, best of all, shallow. He had read the Fairbanks book *Laugh and Live,* and had realized that such had to be the root of Fairbanks's personal philosophy, for surely one had to decide *aggressively* to be so shallow. He hoped he had been shallow enough with Andy.

He was now hip-deep in Boy Scouts. He tipped his cap, and they waved Liberty Bell door hangers at him.

Every Boy Scout in the city was similarly employed, fanning out from encampments in North Beach, Golden Gate Park, the Fillmore, and Union Square to canvass the city with reminders. Their secret orders, given over campfires in the predawn darkness, were to ring doorbells and then run, as quickly and quietly as if tracking a white-tailed deer, to the next residence. When they were done, and business hours had begun, they would ask every storekeeper if he had bought a Liberty Bond today. Boy Scouts—trustworthy, loyal, clean, and so on—were irresistible forces.

But the financial district of downtown San Francisco was a tougher nut to crack. Although corporations subscribed in force, junior clerks and auditors, secretaries and copyists tended to hide under their employers' wings. Surely, if the New York Life Insurance Company had pledged $450,000, its employees who owned but a suitcase, a few drinking glasses, and two pairs of shoes needn't contribute personally?

The Liberty Loan Committee determined to deploy here their most devastating resource: Girl Scouts.

Rebecca Golod made an excellent Girl Scout.

Her parents and her aunt and uncle had left East Texas soon after the train-station riot (too many Golods in Beaumont), moving steadily west, month by month. They tended to stay in a town until the locals realized the hardworking family with the boisterous arguments might actually be lying when they said they didn't know where their neighbors' horses had gone.

Then they reached San Francisco. This city had a fluid relationship with crime and truth. As long as you had a sense of humor about the crimes you planned, someone somewhere would find a place for you at the table.

Harvey the Horse Thief Golod, whose specialty was stolen and swapped meats (hence the nickname), made immediate friends at the abattoir and within weeks was earning rent for the whole family. His brother—Mordecai, Rebecca's father—thought more conceptually, and slowly. Mordecai tended to walk the streets with his hands at the base of his back, woolgathering, and at the family home, during the raucous banging and shouting of dinnertime, the notepad came out.

Mordecai noticed two things upon moving to San Francisco: First, the police here were the best in the world—airtight and right and square as a billiard ball; in other words, many of them could be bought. He had never bought a cop before, but he liked the idea. Second, Rebecca, now thirteen years old, had grown to be a great beauty. Mordecai told her so, but the compliments were like pebbles bouncing off a window. He also told her that, with a mind like hers, she could be a scholar of the Talmud. This she listened to more carefully, for it would be about studying goodness. But she quickly figured out that roles for women as Talmudic scholars were slim pickings.

Ah, but to be a Girl Scout—that was the personification of goodness. When the leaders of Troop 14 came to her eighth-grade classroom to show off the sash and kerchief and khaki uniform, she appraised them like dull birds with hopeless plumage. But then they left their book behind, *How a Girl Can Serve Her Country,* which described in its first chapter (after the introduction, which was about virtues or something) how to track animals in the snow. Rebecca remembered Chicago—how useful this would have been for her uncle Reuben when Ivor Overholt had run off with a pallet of furs.

Every chapter had something helpful like that. She was especially impressed with the sections on tying knots, signaling with Morse code, and using a magnifying glass to start fires. This was her own Talmud. She accrued badges like summonses, flimsy tin disks celebrating her achievements as Interpreter, Laundress, Farmer, Child Nurse, Artist, Needle-woman, and so on, until her uniform was blinding with them.

She coveted the ultimate award, the Silver Fish, which required "skills beyond imagination."

By the time the Liberty Loan Drive occurred, Rebecca was so success-ful she was put in the lead of collecting money between Pine and Califor-nia Streets. When her duties were described to her, she made the troop den mother explain them four times, which surprised everyone, because Rebecca was usually so intelligent: Rebecca was supposed to walk into a business and, while three girls of her choosing sang the "Buy or Die" song (to the tune of "Over There") a cappella, she was to accept pledges to buy twenty-, fifty-, or hundred-dollar bonds. She was to put these IOUs in a special envelope and hand the envelope in at the end of the day. Further, if anyone actually handed her money, as some well-meaning souls did, she was to hand it back and explain that there was no way to account for cash.

"Just hand it back?" she asked, more than once.

"Yes. Otherwise it will get lost and no one will know—not the person who donated it, not the government, not us—it will vanish without a trace."

"Oh. So just give it back, then. Oh."

On the fourth iteration, she understood that this wasn't a trap. The Girl Scouts were just unprepared to have a Golod in their midst. The morning of the Third Liberty Loan Drive, Troop 14 raised twenty-three thousand dollars from local employees, and Rebecca pocketed $183 in untraceable loot. When the troop met up at Union Square for lunch, she ate her hot dog with tears in her eyes, which her elders ascribed to patriotism, and they were right.

The girls were given an hour off to spend with their families. Rebecca's did not come, which might have bothered her but she was feeling full of beans. She looked in the store windows on Geary. Every moment, the $183 in the grouch bag around her neck seemed to be giving off heat. She con-sidered how humbly she would wear her Silver Fish badge.

"Gum!"

The street was swarming with girls, smaller than Rebecca, perhaps nine years old. The Adams Gum Company of Oakland had engaged doz-ens of them, dressing them in Red Cross uniforms, and instructed them to hand out gum. She watched, the idea of adorable girls being a com-modity crossing her mind for the first time. Now there was a small, dimpled blonde, her Red Cross wimple starched to perfection, smiling up at Rebecca, tray of gum hanging from a canvas harness around her shoulders.

"Gum?"

Rebecca considered it. She reached out for a sample, but somehow, accidentally, hit the tray as hard as she could, sending packs raining upon the sidewalk.

"Sorry," she said.

She helped the little girl put all the gum back, a vision of cooperation to all passersby—two lovely girls in two patriotic uniforms!

Across the street, until recently gazing in shopwindows—for he was stony broke—Lee Wheeler watched in amazement as an oblivious and angelic girl fumbled in the gutter while a Girl Scout pocketed her weight in stolen gum.

Lee took a step forward—he knew exactly what he had seen, and setting this right appealed to him. But he halted. The Girl Scout looked directly at him, her dark eyes piercing the bustle of the parade-bound crowd like a fire burning through silk. And then a patrolman descended upon the girls with a friendly sigh, patting each on the head, and Lee decided it was in his best interests to move along.

Rebecca Golod's eyes followed him, which caused her to lose track of her loot, which flustered her. As she was thanking the copper, she could see from the corner of her eye the straight and powerful back of Lee Wheeler. She told herself she had to remember him, because he had almost goofed her racket, but that did not really explain it.

Down the block, he slowed at a construction site upon which posters had been glued. The Liberty Loan Committee, noting the success of posters by Flagg and Christy, had run a contest, and the winner, Miss Katherine Moody of Santa Barbara, was judged to be exquisitely guilt-inducing. The flames of Belgium, ruins before which sat an Alsatian shepherd wearing the Red Cross markings of a service animal. The text read, "Even a DOG enlists—*why not you?*"

Which gave Lee pause. He saw his mother shaking her head.

I *am* joining the war effort, he thought. Just *differently.*

On the corner of Market and 4th was the neck-craning New California Theatre, a vast Gothic structure not yet six months old, its roofline jumping with flamboyant spires, its concrete face etched with biblical scenes, Old Testament toward the entrance, New Testament toward the exit, as if movies themselves were the bridge between them. It had been designed to overwhelm, and in the case of Lee—who had never been to a theater grander than the Bijou in Eureka—it worked.

There were six posters far above the street, each the same massive image, twenty-four sheets in size, Charlie Chaplin against a turquoise background, slumped in a doorway, crestfallen, a crestfallen mutt leaning against him. "*A Dog's Life*," it read. "His first million dollar picture."

The posters hung from dowels, waving in the breeze like the flags of nations. When the dowels hit the side of the building, they sounded as martial as drumsticks.

Many stories below, Lee approached the ticket office. He asked for a ticket to the show.

"Fifty cents."

Lee stared at the quarter and the dime in his palm. It took him a moment to understand what the girl had said. He looked at the menu of prices overhead, then back at her. "Fifty cents?" he asked. Before he could stop himself, he was saying, "Isn't that a lot?"

"There's a special." Every box-office girl he'd seen spoke as if it were a chore; this one, on the other hand, was an excitable cup of coffee. "Look, right there," she said.

A sandwich board told the story:

TODAY! ONLY!
FEATURE PRESENTATION: A DOG'S LIFE! (CHAPLIN'S FIRST
MILLION DOLLAR PICTURE) NEW NEW NEW
CHAPLIN CHAPLIN CHAPLIN!!!
~~TRAVELOGUE: IN NEW ZEALAND WITH COLIN McKENZIE (IN
THREE-DIMENSIONAL STEREOGRAPH)!~~ (CANCELLED)
NEWSREEL: REAL ACTION FROM FRANCE!
THE BEST FOUR MINUTE MEN!
TWO-REELER: THE BARON OF THE PINES!
SING-ALONG!
THE NEW CALIFORNIA 40-PIECE ORCHESTRA!
SURPRISES! SURPRISES! SURPRISES!

"That's fifty cents?"

"There's surprises," she said.

He wanted to ask if he could pay thirty-five cents and skip the surprises, but he didn't want to seem sarcastic. "Is it the Four Minute Men?"

"That's not the surprise. And it's not Chaplin. He'll be at the parade, but—"

"I've got it," he said.

"But not here," she finished. "People hear 'surprise,' and they get too excited." She looked around as if the police might hear her. "That travelogue from New Zealand?" She leaned forward, sharing a secret. "The special projector caught fire. Our manager? Wearing these weird goggles? Almost blind." She nodded, sounding delighted at this misfortune. Her voice dropped to a whisper. "And the surprise thing? It's not that great. It's sort of a lecture."

The show started in thirty minutes. He had to get in.

He was facing Market Street, rubbing his chin, and sighing. Women walking in pairs regarded his pensive gaze, and if his eyes fell upon one of them, she straightened.

Lee needed fifteen cents. There was a possibility that frightened him. It seemed to him as impossible and as fraught with danger as a trip to the canals on Mars: the Department of Commerce, Bureau of Lighthouses.

The Department of Commerce, Bureau of Lighthouses, was a tangible place, an office in a building, but for Lee it was like the house of a cast-bronze god. Since he was seven years old, he had bicycled invoices and reports to the Crescent City Post Office, addressed to Bureau of Lighthouses in his mother's handwriting. Paychecks came from there. In his imagination, the Bureau of Lighthouses looked like the Parthenon.

In reality, it was on the fifth floor of a narrow building on O'Farrell, just off of Market. Among many duties tending to the welfare of lighthouse keepers, in times of emergency they could make loans of up to ten dollars each.

He did not go up right away. Instead, he stood on the street and counted the floors, imagining which windows were theirs. If his mother was searching for him, the Bureau would be the first place to notify.

The street before him was filling with spectators lining up for the parade. O'Farrell was the staging area for Allies of the United States. In the last few weeks, war on Germany had been declared by Guatemala, Nicaragua, and several other coffee-producing nations outraged at German U-boat warfare. So there were groups of foreigners in tropical costumes, fitting their mules with colorful saddle blankets and woven sacks stenciled COFFEE for the march up Market Street.

Also, the Onondaga Nation had declared war on Germany. Under a treaty negotiated in the eighteenth century with George Washington, the nations under the Iroquois Confederacy had the power to declare war separately from the United States, and the Onondagas had done so because of a specific insult against them in Berlin, after a Wild West show.

So O'Farrell Street, already hosting men in serapes, was now the site for a half dozen Indians who were preparing to reprise some of the very act that had so enraged the Kaiser.

Lee walked past them. He needed to give the Bureau his name so they could confirm he was on the payroll. He worked up the courage to approach the Commerce building, found the lobby, and then, after the doors swung shut behind him, took the stairs two at a time to the fifth floor.

The Bureau of Lighthouses was the last door at the end of the hallway, gold letters on frosted glass, with the familiar seal below, the Pharos of Alexandria. He was unsure if he should knock. He remembered his badge, and fumbled in his pocket to put it on his lapel: a red enamel star showing he had been the best Assistant Keeper of the winter of 1916. He threw open the door and immediately waved, as if he already knew and loved what he would find within.

"Hello," he said.

There was a small anteroom inside. At the end was a short white counter with a teller's cage, as if it were a bank window. Sitting on a stool, smiling, wearing a green auditor's visor, was a German—Alsatian—shepherd.

The room was silent except for the dog's panting. Lee looked left and right. They were alone. He took a couple of steps closer, and let the door close behind him.

As Lee approached, the dog's eyebrows moved to register all sorts of momentary emotions: pleasure, playfulness, and, as he got closer, suspicion.

Lee put his hands on his hips and said, with only a trace of fear, "Hello, boy."

The dog let out a thunderous series of barks that echoed in the anteroom, causing Lee to flinch.

"Oh, I'm sorry!" It was a man's voice. "Barney! Get down, now! Bad dog!"

Barney licked his lips. One second later, he was off of the stool, and a languid, puffy man of fifty was in his place. He was wearing a sporty hat made from the American flag. He apologetically dabbed at his mouth with a napkin.

"Whenever I leave the counter— May I help you?"

"I'm from St. George Reef," he said, tapping his lapel.

"Ah." The man raised his eyebrows. "A far-flung correspondent." He said this with a cosmopolitan air, as if making fun not of Lee but of the phrase "far-flung correspondent."

"Yes. Well, anyway, I need a Clayton loan."

"Oh." He bit his lower lip. "Actually, we've changed the forms. They're now called advances. But I can get you set up over here to fill them out. Here for the big war drive?"

"Yes."

"Mmm." The man took his time digging through a drawer. Lee heard the sound of toenails on floorboards, and craned his neck to see the dog walking in circles, settling down on a neatly folded blanket by the window. "Fill out all the information here, here, here, and here. Skip this part here. And sign here with your full name."

Lee accepted the forms. Eleven minutes. The man left his stool, and sat down at his desk. The man's hand dipped into a bag of cookies, and he began methodically chewing again. "Would you like some shortbread?" he called over his shoulder.

"No, thank you."

"The Girl Scouts were nearby. Turns out that if you give twenty dollars directly to them, you get free shortbread."

"That's okay."

"I gave thirty. She gave me some gum, too."

Lee could not listen. The first question was "Name." He considered writing he was one of the Field brothers. He began filling in his address, his shift, his reasons for the advance ("travel"), skipping over each place where he could insert his name. Max Field. His name was Max Field. Maybe.

The man suddenly banged on his desk. "Oh, right," he said, as if startled back from a daydream. He ambled to a shelf of tall black scrapbooks, each one of them the size of a world atlas. "It's been so long since I've done this. St. George Reef, you say?" He hefted down a volume with the name of the lighthouse etched upon the spine. He brought it to the teller's window and struggled to page through it. Here were photographs, each with corners tucked into black paper backing. The first pages showed various angles of the lighthouse, and the remainder showed each person who worked there.

With a feeling of shame that spread across his face, Lee thought, "Oh, that's why they took those pictures."

"What did you say your name was?"

Lee didn't answer. He didn't need to. The book seemed to open of its own volition, something bulging between the pages. "Oh, look at this," his interrogator said.

It was a stack of photographs of Lee. Him as a cowboy. Him as a ladies' man. Holding an épée. Gazing toward the horizon. And more. All brilliantly lit, they spilled onto the counter like rhinestones. The man picked one up.

"This would be you?"

"Yes, sir."

"Leland Wheeler." The frown continued. Eyes danced from portrait to Lee and back several times, and judgments were tabulated. "Where did you get the gaucho's costume?"

"Well, it was . . ."

"And why did you send these photographs here?"

"I was just . . . I mean . . . opportunity." Lee burned with humiliation.

"Handsome man," he said, almost a murmur. "You should be in the picture show, Mr. Wheeler."

"Really?"

"Let's see. Five dollars . . . to . . . Mr. . . . Leland . . . Wheeler. I'll go to the safe."

So there it was: the Bureau had his real name. If he stayed, at least there was five dollars in it for him, as long as he wasn't arrested. The man hummed to himself when opening the safe. It made Lee want to jump out of his skin.

"Okay, here you are." The man was back again, counting out dollar bills onto the countertop. "We'll take a dollar from each paycheck until we get it back."

Lee took the money. He counted it. He put it in his pocket. He checked his watch. Six minutes. He should leave.

The man sighed. "Well, don't spend it all in one place."

Lee turned. He walked toward the exit door. Then he realized what was bothering him. He turned back. "Excuse me. Were there any—I don't suppose—" This was a terrible idea.

"I'm sorry?"

There was no reason to do this. "Was, well, was my mother looking for me by any chance?"

"Beg pardon?"

Lee wasn't about to ask if there was a bulletin issued announcing his absence. But that his mother hadn't even tried to find him made him feel off balance.

The man put a finger to his lips. "Don't go anywhere." He made a brief trip to his desk and back. In his hand was now a small envelope. "I haven't really been sure what to do with this. It's sensitive," he said. His eyes now tried to size Lee up. "How many other young men are there at your station?"

"Just the Field brothers."

"Does their father work there, too?"

"Yes."

"And you're the only other man there, roughly your age?"

"Well—listen, I have an appointment—"

"Ah! Your mother is Emily Wheeler." The man said this suddenly, a house on fire, propriety leaping out the window.

"Yes, she is."

"Emily Wheeler," he said to himself. "That was all anyone talked about."

"Pardon?"

He cleared his throat. "In any case, I believe this is for you. It was delivered this morning by the Onondaga Nation."

There was less than five minutes to go, surely. Four? Three? And yet Lee was frozen to the spot. "Excuse me?"

The man held up the envelope by its corner and said, slowly, for there were few times in his life he would get to say this, "The Onondaga Nation asked me to give this to you."

There were thumbprints across the back, and the whole affair was wrinkled and creased as if it had ridden over many waterfalls in a barrel. The envelope read: "To the 25-year-old child at St. George Reef Light-house." The age had been crossed out and rewritten several times—22, 23, and finally 25.

The picture show might have started. He could read this on the way. Still, he opened it while standing in the Bureau anteroom, with the odd man wearing the star-spangled hat sitting on his stool.

Inside was a letter wrapped around a second envelope. The hand was careful, like that of a person copying out Bible verses. There wasn't a smudge, and each letter seemed to have been written individually, a separate continent.

> My name is Nellie Hill. I knew a man named Percy Duncan. For years, he told about a woman lighthouse keeper and how they had a child. This equals he is your father. He died because of the Kaiser (long story). He wrote you this note. I have carried it on every trip west since. Now I know about the Bureau of Lighthouses, I am giving it to you. I have not read it. It is not my business. I hope it answers your questions and tells you where you came from.
>   Sincerely yours
>   Nellie Hill
>   (Onondaga, Syracuse, NY, USA)
>
> P.S. Your father toured in a Wild West show, played for famous people, saw the world, etc., etc.

Lee read the letter through, and it dropped to the floor. He picked it up, but it almost slid through his fingers again. The man who had helped him had returned to the window, where Barney was parked, watching Lee's every move with interest. Lee wanted to ask questions, but couldn't for the life of him determine what they were.

He reread the letter, which went blurry on him. His father had a name. It was Percy Duncan. The many nights of slow drifting into sleep, when he had imagined he had been created from mud. He felt in his stomach as if he was going to be sick. The man who had left. Or? The man who had an excellent explanation for leaving. Or? That distant feeling, *If only I am good enough, he'll be here when I wake up.*

He saw himself, in silver nitrate, reading the letter and blinking away tears. There was musical accompaniment. Deep in his heart he knew he was the type of person who had things like this happen: shouts from the grave, long-secret parents, reprieves from the governor, maps tattooed on convicts' hands.

Next was a cream-colored envelope with the return address of the Savoy, London, in raised silver letters. He envisioned half an amulet, a treasure map, a sinister warning, a photograph.

The letter was written in a firm hand.

Dear _____

I've been a terrible

Lee turned the letter over. He looked for a second page. He opened his mouth to ask the clerk for more direction.

He wondered why his name was missing. "I've been a terrible" what? Father? "I've been a terrible long time in writing . . ." But there was nothing, not even enough to build a fantasy. He shook both Nellie Hill's envelope and the Savoy's, as if mysteries might break free, but they didn't. A feeling of disappointment crawled up. Why had no one let him know that death ended stories before they were supposed to end?

"Excuse me," he said, in as quiet a voice as he had ever found. The clerk looked up from his gaze out the window. Lee realized he had nothing to say. "Thank you." He shoved the letter into his pocket. The show was starting.

Two steps at a time down the staircase, and then into the street. He was so late he had to run, which was made harder by the crowds, and harder still by tears. Of course, he ran past the Onondagas, but he was not even looking.

A few seconds later, Lee's flight back to the theater was interrupted, for there was an most ungodly mechanical roar. San Francisco had never heard a noise like this. Necks craned, small boys were hoisted up on their fathers' shoulders, and on the second and third floors of office buildings, workers ceased to work and pushed toward the windows, the better to see what guttural explosions had just announced the opening of the Third Liberty Loan Drive.

Men were not the only ones going overseas. There would be women serving as nurses and drivers and telephone receptionists. When the girls of Mills College learned of the courier service, en masse they volunteered, and eight were debuting today to lead the parade. Each of them was mounted on a new olive-drab Harley-Davidson Model J horizontally opposed twin. Each of them had started her machine with a single down-thrust of the kick-starter, causing the windowpanes of Market Street to shake, and little girls to put their fingers into their ears, and the parade to begin.

They rode slowly, a walking pace, with their hair trimmed short enough to fit their helmets, and their goggles lowered around their necks, hands waving and occasionally scooped down to rev their engines again, which sent pockets of the crowds into displays of cheering.

Behind them strolled powerful wives of industry and culture. They had determined exactly how many feet to keep between themselves and the exhaust pipes before them, and behind them were women driving motor trucks, and in each truck bed was a different tableau: a woman canning vegetables in her home's kitchen; women holding jars of preserves marked "jam"; a field where women farmers threshed wheat and held up stalks of corn, urging conservation of the first and consumption of the latter.

Next was a careful display: the Daughters of Israel marching next to the Daughters of Arabia Petraea. Behind them were the Daughters of the Confederacy, marching with the Colored Women's Red Cross Circle. The sight of these groups together caused, along the entire parade route, exactly the same four stages of reaction: silence, amazement, understanding of the urgency of this war, then lusty applause. Perhaps the emotions *should* be shaken, the spirit *should* allow itself to surge. When the Girl Scouts of San Francisco scattered red and white rose petals from handmade berry baskets, singing with their ragged little voices "America the Beautiful," San Francisco was becoming convinced.

Rebecca Golod was not among the Girl Scout singers, for she had another appointment.

As for Lee, he had enough money now for an orchestra seat (seventy-five cents), and the show had begun, and he shot through the doors and past the Old Testament panels, his coat flapping behind him, and he was in the lobby of the California, wildly out of breath. He could hear the subsonic distant pipe organ, which rattled the bones of the theater.

He approached a bright-looking usher whose cap tilted jauntily. "Have the Four Minute Men gone on yet?"

"No. They're showing the newsreel."

Sunnyside

The usher checked his ticket and opened the door for him. The pipe organ reached a crescendo. Onscreen, two men were duking it out, bare-knuckles-style. Their punches intercut with a woman, who had her nails to her teeth, eyes wide, as if someone had stepped on her foot. Finally, an uppercut knocked one man clear across the alley, and the woman covered her face with both hands. Lee remembered the name Percy Duncan. The blank space where his own name should have been. He felt a slender gray crack begin in some marble façade deep in his mind.

This was unusual newsreel footage—something struck him as wrong. As Lee found a seat on the aisle, he saw a close-up of one fighter, looking deranged, smeared with dirt, eyes bulging as if he were going to explode. He snarled, and the card "I'll kill you, McShane!" came up, and Lee realized he was watching a melodrama. Not a newsreel. That was what he had known was wrong. It had been a disconcerting sensation until then, like fumbling in the dark and forcing his shoes onto the wrong feet.

Even though he'd missed most of it, he quickly had the plot in hand: it had to be a two-reeler, and hardy Frank McShane and his rival, the foul Dusty, were loggers desperate for the affections of pretty Monica Beale (May Allison). Dusty had tried to rob the main office, pinning it on McShane. At any minute, for time was running short in this final reel, forgotten evidence would have to be found, exonerating McShane and sending Dusty to jail. Lee could feel this as a definitive fact, the laws of melodrama rooted as strongly within him as his molars.

And yet he was drifting away from it, as if it did not matter. An old feeling, like the "why"s he had asked as a child—why was this story even happening?

The organ played an Oriental theme. And Aktu, the trusty Inuit, to whom no one would listen before, appeared. He had a map to the office drawn in Dusty's hand, and in large letters were the words "We'll rob it tonight!" and it was signed "Dusty." Which was highly incriminating.

This set off a fresh round of fighting, Dusty now thrashing like a fish on a hook, strength ebbing. And now the just deserts, thought Lee. And yet, instead, a messenger boy raced up, shouting. The fighters paused. The organ played a series of suspended notes, a voice asking, "And then? And then?" The crowd onscreen milled around the boy, begging him to tell them what was wrong. He held up a newspaper. The headlines were a mile high: GERMANS SINK LUSITANIA!

Lee had not seen this coming. Dusty and McShane were no longer at each other's throats. McShane stepped forward, into a shining light not previously seen. McShane declared that if his country was at war he was needed. He grabbed Monica by the shoulders, gave her a perfunctory kiss. "I'll enlist today!" the card read. "Will you wait for me?"

There was a swell from the pipe organ, a rising insistence that the climax had come. A policeman hauled up Dusty by the collar. He gesticulated with his baton, jabbing for emphasis.

A card came up. "I could run you in, Dusty. But you can make it right by enlisting instead."

Dusty's hooked-fish face fell away, and a spirit of enlightenment rose in its place. Didn't his face, once greasy with sweat and shining with untrustworthiness, now take on a handsome glint?

"I'll do it!" he exclaimed. The organ was now at full volume, each note its own shaft of light and revelation, and McShane and Dusty shook hands, and at their sides were now a marine, a naval ensign, a doughboy, and a flyboy in a leather cap. They all put their hands into the handshake, and THE END was on the screen as the organ went up and over and out with a final flourish on the keys.

There was applause that struck Lee as curious: it was scattered, but those who clapped did so with a rapturous lust. He applauded, too, but only because he didn't want not to applaud. The house lights went up. He saw he was in a theater no more than half filled, but it was of epic size, seating perhaps two thousand people.

Then Lee thought, again, that his father's name was Percy Duncan. It made him anxious. It felt like deflation, learning how a magic trick was done. Which war had he died in? This one? But it seemed so long ago, the Wild West showman. It made him sad for his father.

A spotlight found the lip of the stage. Stepping down were several men in evening clothes. They found chairs, and sheet music, and then hoisted brass instruments, and began a fanfare as the lights sank again, and the flicker of film illuminated the broad screen.

NEWS FROM FRANCE!

The quartet played a few bars of "Over There," and then "It's a Long Way to Tipperary." There was an attack of some sort, puffs of smoke over a grayish mass of land, then some vague movement at the upper left-hand corner of the screen, followed by a reaction, then soldiers in the trench listening to the wireless, and showing joy, as something mysterious had been accomplished. To pin your talents on something so exhausted as a Wild West show . . .

While the quartet played a few staccato stings, a card came up: "The following is the most remarkable footage of the war, the French attack of February 2. The realism is unparalleled."

Lee leaned forward, putting his elbows on his knees and his chin against his palms. In the trench, a company of *poilus* assembled before their lieutenant, who, with a series of short, sharp nods and gestures to the sky, explained they would be going Over the Top. There were exchanges of hugs and the extended kissing of crosses, which were carefully left behind on posts mounted for this very purpose.

As they were assembling by the ladders, a nurse ran into the huddle of men. One was her sweetheart. She removed something from around her neck and put it around his with a kiss—it was not a cross or a medallion, but a pair of child's puppets, a boy and a girl made of yarn. Lee did not know what they represented, but the men in the trench all nodded.

The next card read "The Moment," and then the music was very soft, a heartbeat. It took Lee time to understand what he was seeing. The bottom half of the screen was a crude dirt wall, and the top half was sky. It was the view if one was standing at the bottom of the trench and looking upward. Suddenly packs of soldiers scrambled vertically, dozens of them ascending ladders, ants pouring out of a nest, and then the nest was empty.

The shot continued: several seconds that showed the edge of the trench, the tips of the ladders, the gray sky. At first, there was anticipation: what would happen next? But then it was apparent there was no "next," just the pitiless clouds, the emotionless dirt. It was quiet as a poem.

Then—a dissolve. There was a shot of the nurse, sitting in a chair, head down, her ringlets of blond hair covering her face. A major of the French army was handing her a necklace: the finger puppets! She took it meekly; he looked embarrassed, waved his hand abruptly, and left the frame. The music dropped down, faded until it was not even a whisper. You could hear the sounds of sobs being stifled. All was vanity.

The words THE END came up. Lee quickly wiped away tears. He was thinking that he had to remember what had caused him to weep, how he could try to recall it and use it when asked, how he would weep when jilted by his bonnie belle, or kneeling by his father's grave: here was exactly the emotion to feel. And then he remembered that he had just trod across his father's grave, and he tried to feel sad about that, but it was like trying to carry water cupped between his hands. He could not think of a single reason to live. Every ambition was swallowed by the grave.

As the newsreel ended, all through the audience people were shaking their heads, an air of depression having settled upon them. But then the spotlight found the huge clock face that stood by the apron. There was a drumroll from the orchestra pit, and the hands of the clock, of their own volition, sprang forward exactly one minute. The clock went forward another minute, and the audience caught on, yelling in a cacophony of voices, "Two!" Another minute forward, and there was more agreement, "Three!" Then, finally, the fourth minute, and the whole audience to a person yelled out, knowing it was the conclusion, "Four!"

Out came the men. In their suits of fine blue wool, in their white-and-red pinstriped shirts and their blue silk ties, the Four Minute Men. There were four of them today.

Lee eyed them, and he cracked his knuckles one by one.

They had started in 1916 in Chicago, where a local man with strong opinions had fumed at how it took four long minutes to change reels. So he was inspired to get up from the crowd and declare that he would speak on the need for fighting Germany. Given that the United States was not yet at war, and Chicago was shoulder to shoulder with Germans, his remarks were controversial, but his style was grand, and there was applause.

Within a month, he had moved to larger theaters, and so many owners asked him to visit their houses during the four-minute breaks between movies (but not between reels of the same movie; that interruption had proved disastrous) that he recruited his friends to fill in. The idea quickly spread to other cities, and Washington realized it should, in its way, federalize the program. Peer-review boards judged performances on projection, poise, demeanor, dress, clarity, forcefulness, and grammar. They swarmed to every movie theater, church, and picnic in America. Biweekly bulletins contained helpful reminders like "Consider the words of Jesus Christ, Master Four Minute Man."

There had just been a photo spread of ten good Four Minute Men in *Motion Picture Classic* magazine, with accompanying discussion of how they could well become motion-picture stars. And now the best in the country were touring together in the Liberty Loan Drive.

Four Minute Men were exempt from military registration.

Further, there were auditions later this very afternoon. A limited number of slots were open, but one had been booked in advance, via ship-to-shore telephone call. From 4:08 to 4:12, the slot was held by Mr. Lee Reid, who by a very similar name was sitting in this very theater, watching his competition, and realizing that his name would not be Lee Reid but Lee Duncan. His ambition had reignited.

Onstage, one of the Four Minute Men had dug his hands into his pockets, and strolled to the center of the stage. He kicked his heel downward a few times, modestly. He was saying, "The topic, my friends, the topic today is 'The Fruits of Your Labor.' "

Another man walked past him, downstage, saying, as if it had just occurred to him, "Have you ever stopped to think that, every moment of your life, the vigilant eye of Uncle Sam is watching over you? How he is the master of the biggest business in the world? And how it is all *your* business?"

A third man, standing still, continued, "He has more might and majesty than all the kingdoms of history—and all this might and majesty is *yours*. Have you ever stopped to think about that?" He paused, folded his arms, and looked directly into the crowd. "Have you, San Francisco?"

Upon hearing itself mentioned, the crowd was helpless but to applaud, though what precisely they were applauding was unclear and unimportant, for the final man was already speaking rapidly, like a preacher awed by his topic: "He makes safe the ocean lanes for the way of the mariner. He measures the heat of the stars. He fixes the standards of weights and measures." His voice went deeper, it echoed, it had friction as it carried him into excited realms. "He speeds the sure, swift flight of the three-cent letter!" (There was applause.) "He smites the rock, and the dead waste of the desert teems with life!" (More applause, mixed with cheers.) "He makes two stalks of grain grow where only one grew before," and then, squeezing in more before the rhythm of the applause took over, he added, "and some of that is hops, barley, and malt, thank you, San Francisco!"

Lee watched as the first man, the one who seemed most reasonable, lowered the boom. In his quiet but firm tone, he said, "But now Sam has turned warrior. He has grappled with the mad power that has transgressed the rights of mankind."

The second shook hands with him, a finger-and-palm-tapping affair suggesting Masonic intensity. "He wants to borrow your money. And you want to lend it. Don't you, San Francisco?"

Throaty calls and cries, demands to be taken seriously. Yes, San Francisco wanted to pledge money.

"You wish to buy bandages for the wounded, San Francisco?"
They did.
"To buy bullets for your children's guns, San Francisco?"
Oh, how they did.
"You want your boy to have anesthetic and bandages when they take

out that bullet"—tying it all together. "San Francisco? Are you with America? I can't hear you."

By the end of the speech, the four men were side by side, waving to the audience, which was on its feet with admiration. Lee stood carefully, eyes sweeping the aisles, assessing the reaction. Girls fifteen and sixteen years old rushed to the lip of the stage, holding photographs and fountain pens. Simultaneously, the aisles flooded with Boy Scouts running toward the audience, and the promissory chits ran across the rows of seats and toward the patrons, and then, signed and pledged, back to the Scouts, as efficient a motion as the full-moon tide. Lee whistled. Nothing he had seen had impressed him.

Someone tripped against him. A rumpled older man, dressed as if he'd slept on the ground in his tweed jacket.

"I'm sorry," Lee said.

The man did not respond. For a moment, in the half-light, they exchanged a glance. The older man was clearly in tears. He was carrying canisters of film, which struck Lee as odd. Then he was gone.

7

Münsterberg fled into the daylight. His glasses were sticky with tears. He walked one way on the sidewalk, then another, confused by the noise and distraction; that he was in the thick of parade watchers made him sick.

He found the alleyway behind the New California Theatre, and sat down on the first steps of the metal staircase that ascended three stories to the projectionist's booth. Finally, he collapsed, cradling his print of *Neptune's Daughter*.

He was to have been the surprise. Management felt that, with the rumors, they would rather he speak without being billed, to prevent the wrong element from causing problems. After several weeks of harassment on the vaudeville circuit, he had felt so grateful to be allowed his lecture that he had sat in the darkened movie house with the obedience of a child.

He had sat through the absurd, ridiculous, wonderful two-reeler, mood actually lifting for the first eighteen minutes or so, as he wondered how McShane could win Monica's heart when the evidence was so stacked against him. But then! The *Lusitania*? The enlistment for criminals? The American Expeditionary Force appearing in a logging camp in the lost million acres of British Columbia? The applause felt like a reward for the crushing of the rules of narrative like dried leaves under the foot of an enraged baby.

The newsreel truly confounded him. For the single poetic shot showing the men leaving the trenches, the open sky, the deadly block of land below, was indeed real. But the nurse, finger puppets, the weeping widow—this was from Gaston Leprieur's 1916 melodrama *La Chanson de Nanette, Infirmière d'Armée*. The nurse wasn't a nurse—she was Cécile Guyon and she was kissing not a soldier, but Henri Bosc.

Münsterberg had watched this development with his mouth hanging open. The film stock was different. The light did not match. Even if the patrons had never seen *La Chanson de Nanette, Infirmière d'Armée*, surely they had to perceive that this drama was entirely manufactured. And yet, instead of holding the manager at knifepoint, the audience had wept. Wept!

When the Four Minute Men took the stage, Münsterberg was at the edge of a cliff, and there was no friendly lieutenant in a canvas-winged RE 8 to swoop by at an opportune moment. Instead, a high wind was blowing, a crop-killing frost was in the air, and no one was coming after him. For four minutes, Münsterberg felt his death approaching. Stand-ins, diegetic effect, a roof collapsing because the piers had never been properly shored. He had made a foolish assumption, a basic one about art being a mirror held up to nature. It turned out film was about ideas, and an idea could be enthralling when it was a *lie*.

The rumor about him had no source. It was a quality of the air, a gas whose existence wasn't noticed until it ignited. He was not an agent of the Kaiser. He just didn't want his lovely northern countryside, where his family had a sugar-beet plantation, where he had spent summers at the natatorium, writing letters to a lonely cross-eyed girl who played the cello, destroyed. But audiences no longer saw a Harvard professor of applied psychology telling them how wonderful they were for loving the movies. They saw a German spy.

He could hear throbbing through the wall against which he sat—the opening notes of the recently seated forty-piece New California Orchestra playing the overture for the new Chaplin film. He had so been looking forward to Chaplin. Lonely Münsterberg, sighing that no one else could understand what it was like to have such ideas fly about the atmosphere until the person himself was replaced.

There was a startling *Bang!* above him, at the top of the stairs, the projectionist's door slamming open against the ironwork stair rail. Münsterberg glanced upward. A small, dapper young man holding a derby hat was cringing at the top of the stairs. Obviously embarrassed to have caused such a noise, he held a finger to his lips, and daintily, with caution fully out of proportion, he edged the door closed.

His suit was pure bespoke tailoring, his pocket silk alone a week's salary. He had black curly hair that was waxed into place, and for a moment, when his fingertip was under his nose, Münsterberg had thought, just a little bit, that he looked like . . . But, no, that wasn't likely.

The young man floated down the stairs, each step of his shoes making no sound, really quite an accomplishment on such open metal grates. He clutched at his hat as if it were a baby, and maneuvered around Münsterberg on the last stair, finger still to his mouth.

Muffled by the thick stone walls, the orchestra continued playing its overture, plaintive and sentimental, with small leaps of humor among the horns. The young man nodded vaguely, and looked back toward the theater, craning his neck and shading his eyes the better to see where the vast *A Dog's Life* posters were resting. He shrugged, red with embarrassment, as if Münsterberg had caught him having himself paged.

If Chaplin were not in costume—that is to say, if the real Chaplin descended from the screen—this was Münsterberg's idea of how he would dress. "Are you . . ."

The young man fitted his derby on and spun on his heel. A second later, he was at the mouth of the alley, and then he was gone in the crowd.

The sounds of the crowd returned, the parade noises, the children's shouts, and the echoing of many horse hooves on asphalt. Münsterberg felt as he did when he tried to read a book in a dream, a maze of codes and words that made brief sense and came apart when he tried to consider them. He stood up, clutching his reels of film, and followed in his pooka's path.

Several blocks away, at the corner of Post and Grant, stood Shreve & Co., the finest jewelry store in San Francisco. Founded when armed and unshaven customers still wearing chaps paid for their bawdy sweethearts' diamond rings with gold nuggets they had mined themselves, Shreve had become, through the gentle softening motion of time, the store where anniversary rings were dutifully purchased for wives. It was a notoriously difficult place to rob; the first looter after the Earthquake had chosen Shreve as his target, and he was consequently the first person shot by army troops, his body left in the street with an exquisitely lettered gold-leaf sign around his neck—"He tried to rob Shreve & Co."—until the raging city fire consumed him.

Andy Pike, feeling bleary and in need of coffee, stood at Shreve's counter this very moment, soon to experience a run of very bad luck. Shreve was the only establishment in several blocks that could change a thousand-dollar bill. So Andy had come from Pike's, the jewelry store at which she worked across the street, to get ten one-hundred-dollar bills for the handsome rabbi now at her own counter.

Pike & Sons had not been blessed, as had Shreve, with sixty years of history and reputation. Still, mistresses needed ornaments, too. Married men rarely went to Pike's Place, as it was best known, but instead sent a confederate or an attorney or, as Andy surmised had happened today, a rabbi.

The intersection of Post and Grant was so heavy with traffic diverted from Market that it required a policeman's whistle to sort out the entrances and egresses. Andy stopped on the corner, was waved on with a wink (she had that effect on policemen), and then returned to her store, where her father was continuing negotiations for a pair of pearl earrings and a matching brocade necklace.

Inside, the bell over the door rang when she entered, and the rabbi turned around from the black velvet upon which his future purchases were draped and gave her a nod that was polite. For pretty girls, Mordecai Golod was always polite.

In the meantime, the main part of the parade was surging up Market. The Signal Corps of Camp Fremont marched with their squadron of trained homing pigeons. Then a float drawn by Esquimeaux dogs wearing special harnesses. Upon it was a dachshund fitted with a tiny helmet who was barking incessantly at a goat that had been tethered next to it, and written in festive yarn was the phrase "Get the Kaiser's Goat." Then doughboys from Camp Kearney in their field uniforms performed a relay race with hand grenades. This made the crowds slightly nervous, worried about their boys, proud of them, and anxious to kill things themselves. Then: the tank division.

No civilian had seen a tank. For years, no one had been allowed to *film* a tank. The device hadn't even had a name, until it was decided that, to confuse the enemy, "tank" could describe a device to carry water. Recently, their existence had been revealed, but they were more discussed than understood.

There were six of them, in rows of two, and the *Chronicle* photographer scurried up a lamppost so Miss Kathryne Booth, retired from the float where she had been Liberty Leading the People, could hold aloft the Stars and Stripes. The next day's front page: from the gutter to the margin, the fresh face of democracy, and behind her the line of six tanks followed by its proud (and burdened) marine guard.

The tanks were gray and sturdy and slow as elephants, each with gigantic pairs of all-around tracks that flanked sheltered cabins which bulged with huge brow ridges, like brooding insect gods. Their sides were walls of metal and rivets interrupted by machine-gun housings that swept back and forth like inquisitive and deadly antennae.

It was like watching the winning horses be led to the starting gate. There were no longer questions about supporting the war, for not only was it justified, but the tanks were the means of ending it. More Liberty Loans were sold when they passed than with the transit of any other floats; fitting, for the parade was now winding down.

Just as the tanks were passing, Lee left the theater, for *A Dog's Life* had ended. He was feeling jaunty among the rush of fellow patrons. The theater had filled to capacity just before the Chaplin had started. There was a good deal of laughter now, even when they were exiting, and a man with a thick mustache and a full belly was saying to his friend, "That scene with the dog's tail beating the bass drum!" His friend, a tall drink of water, laughed and replied, "And what about when he had knocked the crook unconscious and was pretending to be his hands?"

Sunnyside

"And the dog's tail and the bass drum," his friend said.

Lee found himself walking like Chaplin. It was contagious. The crowd was thick but separating, the end-of-parade noises winding down, the streets littered with streamers and trash and sawhorses, automobiles parked half on the sidewalk, and with every obstacle, Lee had the urge to doff his hat, politely spin around pedestrians, step onto a roller skate, backflip over a man pouring concrete, and tumble into a trough of bluing.

He faced the crush of people with supreme confidence, as if for a moment he understood it. The world was at war, but the world also seemed like a Charlie Chaplin movie, full of scowling society matrons, mountainous mustachioed toughs, pretty girls who hadn't enough to eat, and pies left at dangerous angles at the edges of tables.

There had been something extra in the movie that he'd never seen before in a Chaplin, and it began with the dog. It was an extension of sympathy, and even now, thinking of the single, small moment of Chaplin offering the dog milk from a bottle, Lee was again at the edge of tears.

He thought of his father again, quickly, and his heart fell as if down a lonely well. He wanted to be away from the crowd. There was a newsstand inside the lobby of a hotel, so he went through the revolving door.

The newsstand was a blaze of primary colors and pastel cover models, and Lee's eye spotted the bright-red May issue of *Motion Picture*. The image, painted by Leyendecker, was the face of Mr. Charlie Chaplin, as the Tramp, forlorn and with a single smudge of soot on his weary cheek. The text read, "A Dog's Life for Charlie? Or an Immortal's?"

The lobby was all dark oak, marbled floors with brass fittings and tall fluted columns, rather smart. The wealthy stayed here, the type with matching, monogrammed, leather-bound, silk-lined portmanteaux, which made Lee feel inadequate. He would make this quick: he did have the ten cents for the magazine, which he wanted to reach for, but there was someone in the way.

It was a small, dapper man with unruly black hair smartly parted to the side. He smelled, almost too much, of Mitsouko by Guerlain, which made Lee assume he was rich. He was admiring the magazine rack, it seemed, the whole thing, top to bottom, as if everything interested him equally. And his hand stole toward the *Motion Picture* number, then withdrew.

Lee was thinking about how he would answer questionnaires in the future. "Name: Lee Duncan. Hobbies: Lee Duncan."

"It's all right, go on, get it," Lee said.

The man glanced up, slightly red. "Get—which?"

"The *Motion Picture* magazine. It's all right." Men tended to be shy about admitting they read about movies, particularly when Chaplin and not a pretty girl was on the cover.

"Well," Chaplin said, for it was of course Chaplin, "I know, it's embarrassing, but I have reasons. . . ." Which was true: he wanted to see whether he had made the list of Twelve Immortals.

"You don't need other reasons," Lee said. "In spite of the gent on the cover, it's a good magazine."

Chaplin performed, overriding a personal aversion to such things, a perfect double take. He wasn't being recognized—he was being *insulted*. He had been hiding in his hotel room most of the day, and here was the first conversation he'd had. He rolled the magazine up in his fist, and his voice came out Plains-state flat American. "Have you heard terrible things about Chaplin?"

"Only what everyone else has." Lee paid his dime and took his magazine.

"I've heard he's a slacker," Chaplin said.

"He's too important to draft," Lee responded. He had become quite firm about this. "Some men are gifted that way."

"I hear he gets paid for doing nothing."

"I just saw the new Chaplin. If that's doing nothing, sign me up."

Chaplin had, rising in him, a list of accusations. He so wanted to spell out all his shortcomings that they burbled on the tongue. I hear he didn't pay his taxes. I hear he agreed to sell the war. He travels by solid-gold motorcar from town to town, stealing other men's ideas and leaving them gravel in their place, and when he's hungry he reaches into a sack of half-digested children that he drags behind him. Instead, he asked, "The new Chaplin? And you liked it?"

"Yes."

"How so?"

It dawned on Lee that he had never been asked his opinion before. When he had talked about movies, no one had drawn him out. He didn't want to be an idiot in his first conversation with a stranger in San Francisco, particularly one who so smelled of success. "Well, it's fuller than most. Have you seen the last Chaplins?"

"I've seen a few."

"This one feels fuller."

Chaplin waited, arms folded, for more analysis. "Fuller."

"That's exactly it." Lee smiled. "It appeals to every emotion. It's very sentimental."

Chaplin wanted to take this tall, handsome man (he hadn't noticed before how handsome he was) out for dinner and to divine his thoughts on all things, not just himself, but politics and industry and the mysteries of creativity. "When you consider it as a whole, is it as good as *he* is, or just good parts that—"

"Oh, I know," Lee said with the snap of inspiration. "He's almost as good as Pickford like that. Suddenly."

"Excuse me?"

"It's like he's been watching Pickford films and has taken something of that mysterious way she has."

"Pickford?"

"She always does something to put you on her side, like— Oh! Say, didn't she have a dog in *Stella Maris*?"

"I don't know," Chaplin said immediately.

"Isn't that the one where she fed him from a milk bottle?"

"No," he declared, hands on his hips, but now unsure.

"Maybe that was *Poor Little Peppina*."

How many films had she had dogs in? "I don't think so. No. No."

Lee shrugged. Very few people knew as much about the movies as he did. He didn't want to show off, but: "She did," he said. He had to get to his Four Minute Man audition. "Anyway, enjoy your magazine," he said. He saluted the smaller man with his own rolled-up copy, winked (it was becoming a habit), and walked across the lobby, vanishing through the revolving doors.

Chaplin wanted the oaf to return, to insult him more, to enrage him thoroughly, to the point where they would come to blows. Instead, finding a chair in the corner of the lobby, he licked his finger and began to page through the magazine.

Beth Fairbanks had announced her intention to sue for divorce. She told the press that her husband had been seeing another woman, whom she would not identify.

And there it would have rested quietly had not Owen Moore, Mary's husband, decided to defend her honor. "The other woman is now ill," he told the press, "and under great nervous strain. So I feel it obligatory upon myself to make a statement to save her from humiliation."

Since no one had identified Mary Pickford as the other woman, his comments were far from helpful. They were reported without the dotted lines being connected, since newspaper reporters were still not quite sure what one was allowed to say about movie stars. Besides, this was Doug and Mary, and so each paper waited for someone else to make the first clarifying move.

Chaplin, trapped on a train going across the South, had sent inquisitive cables to Doug. Doug was Catholic. Mary was Catholic. The public might destroy them for their happiness. If Doug wanted to phone him, he was available, and here was the hotel he was staying at. If Doug wanted to send a telegram, Chaplin had left word that it was to be delivered to him at any hour. As he went from Atlanta to New Orleans, he grew more fond of the clandestine lovers.

But by the time he reached Memphis, he realized that his friend was not going to talk to him. The trip to San Francisco was a melancholy one: Chaplin sat by the window of the train, every passing mile imagining Doug crying in Mary's arms.

There was more. It was small but substantial enough for Chaplin: his own secret romance. No one could know about it, it was entirely unlikely and unsuitable, but over the last weeks he had quietly arranged for her to meet him in San Francisco. He imagined Mary Pickford finding out, and he shuddered.

Someone struck a blow across his back. He was in the hotel lobby. The magazine shot out of his lap and onto the floor.

"Doug."

"Cheers, old sport."

"How long have you been here?"

"Say, that's a fine-looking fellow." Doug carefully scooped up the magazine from the floor. He placed the cover in front of his face, and did a determined shuffle-step walk.

"Just give that back. Please."

Which was exactly the wrong thing to say, for it caused Doug to leap from the floor to the arm of the chair, magazine held before his face. He pretended, as if the smiling mug on the magazine were his, to pick his teeth. Chaplin was ready to be truly annoyed—how could you ask a man how he was faring when he was holding a magazine cover bearing your picture over his own face?

But then he saw that the man who had just insulted him had returned, and was standing in the lobby, staring.

Sensing that he was not the center of attention for some terrible reason,

Doug lowered the magazine. He glanced from Chaplin to the silent, staring Lee Duncan. Slowly, the corners of Chaplin's mouth turned upward. He angled his head, an acknowledgment to Lee, who had only made it fifteen feet down Market before a dark thought—who exactly had he just been speaking to?—hobbled him.

And then Chaplin smiled at Doug, as refreshed as if he'd just gotten a massage. Some kind of curtain dropped down between the movie stars and Lee, who of course recognized Fairbanks, and who understood he was welcome to leave.

Lee walked away with his face aflame. Tossing his magazine in the trash, he felt as if the sidewalk were cracking open and hands were waving through, ready to pull him into the earth. Lee thought of all the times he had forgotten to tie the station boat with the pinnacle knot. He thought of how he had punched both Field brothers for no better reason than that they had a father. And how they had both pummeled him, for he was a terrible fighter.

He would serially let down everyone who had ever known him. In a punishing moment, he found his reflection in the window.

He would visit Andy.

9

At that moment, Andy was being robbed.

It was late enough in the afternoon that the hour of sleep—rather, the seven hours of not sleeping—had caught up with her, and she couldn't follow simple discussions. For instance, her father and the Rabbi Golod had been speaking for a very long time—negotiations were protracted over what exactly he was buying, and for whom—and she had been sent out twice now, once to change the thousand-dollar bill, and a second time to bring back egg-salad sandwiches.

Mr. Pike negotiated the way a bull negotiated with the rider on his back. Normally, this resulted in a quick sale, but Rabbi Golod seemed built of different stuff. The two men were insulting each other's thievery, ill-suited knowledge of the diamond industry, and amateurish misunderstandings of the Henry Wade school of cutting, and then Pike decided Golod was all right, and it was time for egg salads all around.

That was an hour ago, and the sale had yet to be made. Resting on a black velvet pad before Golod were the pearl necklace and two matching pearl earrings; a ring with a reasonably transparent, reasonably large-girdled sapphire on a chain; a cabochon-cut, rich and vivid ruby with no inclusions or blemishes, about which there was disagreement as to whether it had been heat-treated. But the discussion had been abandoned, and Golod had eaten only a bite of his sandwich before sketching with his Waterman pen a round diamond. He asked if Pike had seen one like this before. Pike glanced at it cautiously.

Golod described it. "It has different culets than what you normally see. And smaller tables and crown angles."

Pike shook his head. But something familiar was peeking up from the sketch, something to his mind potentially wonderful. "That's not a European design," he said.

"For a merchant, you're very perceptive." Golod chuckled. "It's American. Done with a bruting machine."

There had been rumors. American diamonds had thus far either slavishly imitated the cushion cuts, the rose cuts, the European models. Or they had been disasters. But now? Pike wiped mayonnaise off of his lip. He said, quietly, "So are you saying Tolkowsky's theories—"

"What they can do now is an ideal, round, brilliant design with a mathematical foundation based in optics—"

"To maximize the fire?"

"Are you ready?" Golod's eyes twinkled. "Forty-point-seventy-five degrees."

Pike knew he was being teased, but could not resist asking, "Which is?"

"The correct pavilion angle for that balance is exactly forty-point-seventy-five degrees, my friend Pike."

"But what about bezel angles? If light comes in from an oblique angle, aren't you worried about how bezel angles—"

"Ask them at Shreve," Golod said dismissively.

"I will, but . . . Excuse me?"

"They have one over at Shreve."

"No, they don't."

"You can ask them about the crown angle, too. I can't remember what they told me."

"I haven't heard about it."

"They're torn about whether to call it an 'ideal cut' or a 'perfect cut.' Personally, I think calling it 'perfect' is asking for trouble." Golod rolled his eyes upward. Since Pike was still regarding him with suspicion, Golod continued. "You're telling me it strikes you as unusual that your competitor didn't happen to mention their innovation to you? That's actually positive—it suggests you're actually a competitor, take it as a compliment, Mr. Pike."

Pike folded his arms. He looked over Golod's shoulder, toward Shreve. Which was closing in ten minutes, so the staff could see the movie stars. Now he looked at the gems spread out on the velvet pad on the counter. "Where's our deal?"

"It's going well." Golod reached for his sandwich. "Go see your diamond. You have to ask Mr. Lewis, in back. I can eat."

Pike didn't move. Golod made a small noise, a clearing of his throat, and fished into his pocket.

"Here," he said, taking his ten one-hundred-dollar bills. "Do you have an envelope, perhaps?"

"Andy?" Pike called to his daughter, who bolted from her stool as if her father had delivered her an electric shock.

She said, "Yes?"

"Envelope, please?"

While Pike shrugged on his jacket, Golod opened the envelope, dropped the ten one-hundred-dollar bills inside, and then tapped them against his lap, lost in thought.

"Yes?"

"Do you have a sponge? I'm not fond of licking envelopes."

"Andy?"

This time, she was ready. Her father stepped toward the window, looking anxiously through the crowds to Shreve's window, while Golod slowly used the sponge to dampen the adhesive of the envelope. He said, "There we go." With a flourish, he sealed the envelope and handed it to Pike. "Hold on to this, Pike, and come back, and I will finish my sandwich and perhaps talk to your lovely daughter about school."

"I'm not in school anymore," she said.

"And a thousand schoolboys wail." He smiled.

Pike took the envelope (it was suitably thick and full, since Golod had cut the enclosed pieces of newspaper perfectly) and left his shop. The bell tinkled on his way out.

Andy watched her father. The traffic was apparently still heavy enough to demand that the patrolman assist at the intersection, even now, as the parade was breaking up. The rabbi took several bites of his sandwich. He smiled at her, and dabbed at the corners of his mouth.

"So, Miss Pike, if you aren't in school," he said, upending the pad, and sending the ruby, the sapphire, and the pearls into a sack, "what holds your interest?"

He had dark-brown eyes, and his beard, though exotic to Andy, struck her as probably soft rather than scratchy. "I've been going to dances," she said. The rabbi tightened the silk drawstring around the sack, and pocketed it, continuing to regard her as if awaiting more conversation.

"My wife loves to dance," he said. "I've been meaning to learn more of the new ones. What is that fast one called? The Turkey Trot?" He took another bite of sandwich.

"Well, that's not new, really," she said. Her brain was having trouble measuring and comparing several facts: he was being entirely reasonable and friendly; he had just pocketed a small pile of gems; he was still enjoying his egg salad. "Excuse me? I—do you—"

"Yes? You're being a very good daughter, Miss Pike." He stood from his stool, sighing, and then touched his fingers to the brim of his hat. And with two strides, he was out the door.

Andy shrieked. She shrieked at the top of her lungs, which did her little good, since the atmosphere outside was still overrun with the dissassembling parade. She dashed from the store, and shrieked again, "Thief!" But at that moment, the Miss Hamlin's School for Girls Marching Band was passing by, part of the rush to Lotta's Fountain and the speeches by Hollywood actors.

"Thief!" Andy cried, her eyes fixed on Rabbi Golod's receding form— he was walking slowly across the intersection, head down, hands clutched together as if lost in a conversation with God (which, although he wasn't actually a rabbi, was not a pose). In seconds he would surely be lost— Andy's eyes were watering with blind panic, and then, looming over her, was six feet four inches of Lee, who was feeling melancholy.

"Hello, Andy," he murmured.

"Oh, God—Lee!"

"I've just been thinking how meaningless—"

"I was just robbed! He's over there!" She pointed.

"Robbed," he said.

"The rabbi."

As if he were jumping into one of the station boats, Lee was already dodging through pedestrians, a broken field of obstacles, shoving them out of the way, crying "Excuse me," until he was at the curb. Rabbi Golod was in the crosswalk. Lee broke from the tight bands of foot traffic and darted into the road itself. The patrolman blew his whistle at him just as Lee grabbed Golod by the overcoat and spun him out of the crowd.

Golod didn't struggle. He put out his hands in supplication and looked at Lee like a kitten with a wounded paw.

"Hey!" The patrolman had brought out his club, and put his hands to his hips. It was unclear upon whom he most wanted to use his weapon.

"Officer," Lee said, swallowing hard, "this man robbed that jewelry store."

The patrolman used the baton to push back his cap. "The rabbi? The rabbi robbed a jewelry store?"

"Yes," Lee said, not quite sounding sure of himself. Where was Andy?

"I see." The cop, whose badge said McKinney, was now regarding Lee as if he might want to beat him like a carpet.

"I just—" Lee caught his breath. "I'm a little—I just saw Chaplin," he said, as if that might help.

McKinney looked interested. "Really? Huh. Is he smaller than you'd think?"

"He looks delicate."

Andy arrived now, out of breath. She began to tell her tale: Rabbi Golod coming in, the long negotiations, the thousand-dollar bill and the change she'd made, her going out for egg-salad sandwiches, how her father had been sent to Shreve, the dumping of the jewels into a sack, and so on.

Lee listened with a kind of mild pride. He had chosen a whirlwind of a girl. When she pointed across the street to Pike's Place, he saw a bruise on her arm that matched his fingertips.

"Is this true?" Officer McKinney glared at Golod, who did not answer but instead looked to Lee and Andy, as if perhaps they were being addressed. "No," said McKinney, "I'm talking to you . . . Father." The last word was a guess of sorts, but Golod accepted it with a shrug. "So—is it true?" McKinney continued.

"I would take issue with it."

"What does that *mean*?" Andy cried. "What does that even *mean*?"

"It means it's an unreasonable interpretation of what happened. I'm willing to discuss it, though."

"Then what's your story?" McKinney had flaming red hair that spilled out from under his tall cap, and yet he wasn't a hothead, to the dismay of his fellow officers, who had wanted to nickname him "Hothead."

Golod frowned. "I'd like to know what his story is, the fellow who grabbed me."

"Okay, all right, let's get the names straight." McKinney brought out a pad of paper. "What's your name, pal?"

Andy said, "It's Lee Wheeler." Upon seeing his reaction, she said, "I mean Reid. Wheeler Reid." Which might have been fine had he not said "Lee Duncan" at the same time.

"What?" McKinney barked.

"That's suspicious," Golod said helpfully.

"No, it's not," Lee said, but he was turning red.

Andy said, "It doesn't matter, I just want my father's things back or he'll kill me."

"Settle down, miss, one thing at a time. Now"—McKinney poked a finger at Lee—"what's your name?"

"Lee Duncan." He swallowed. He tried to look humble.

"Then why did she call you the other name?"

"Lee Wheeler is," he said, "my stage name."

The cop's eyes narrowed. An actor. Lee had escaped one kind of suspicion only to be straitjacketed by another. "Okay. And how do you know the girl here?"

Andy said, "It doesn't matter," which stung, because he had wished to hear her say, "We are sweethearts." "Just get the bag," she said. "Make him turn his pockets out."

"All right, Father, you heard the girl. Turn out the pockets, pronto."

Golod silently, and slowly, as if a great burden were upon him, turned the pockets of his great wool coat inside out. There was nothing in them. It made him look penniless.

"Keep going," Andy said. Golod opened his watch pocket, removed his wallet, handed over change for the bus, small bits of notebook paper, a pencil stub, going pocket by pocket with great thoroughness. Andy had a glare on her that held Lee in thrall. Passersby saw the cop, the rabbi, the beautiful girl, the handsome man, and they tended to hesitate at the crosswalk, as if such a gathering had to result in drama.

"Hey!" Andy's eyes flashed. "Right there. What's in there?"

Under his coat, Golod wore a sweater, and Andy had seen it several times now as he sorted through all of his possible hiding places. There was a suspicious lump at the bottom. She grabbed at it, Golod feigning ticklishness, and she quickly found a secret zipper, and then she found the bag of jewels.

"Look! He stole this!" She held it up less in triumph than in outrage, for she could still not believe how shameless the theft had been. There were bystanders already, and her cry made people break off from their destinations to try and see what was happening. A dozen, two dozen, like catching flies with honey.

"Well, now," said Officer McKinney, and his hand landed on Golod's shoulder, his baton jabbing in punctuation. "Thought you'd steal from Pike's Place, did you? Thought you could steal from a pretty young girl and get away with it, did you?" When faced with outrageous behavior, the cops of San Francisco, even those who weren't hotheads, tended to become operatic. "We'll just see about that, Father. The jails might not be overflowing with rabbis, but I'm sure you can put your learning to use in the prison laundry."

Golod said, "May I speak?"

"No, you may not," McKinney said.

"I did steal the jewelry," he said. "I'm very sorry."

"Sorry isn't good enough," Andy said.

"Well, you're right, Miss Pike," Golod said. "But you shouldn't compromise yourself with actors."

"I'm going to be a Four Minute Man," Lee explained.

"I want the rabbi arrested," she hissed. She shook the contents of the bag out, to make sure all the stolen merchandise was there (it was), and then she continued to stare hot needles at Golod while McKinney, in full lather, repeated vital points about common decency.

Lee was, to his consternation, falling in love. Each time she pointed or jabbed, he saw the bruise on her arm and he wanted to hold her again and tell her how confused he was about his father. He didn't want to go to his audition. He wanted to make Andy happy. How did you will a girl to kiss you, especially when she was clearly not in a kissing mood? Wanting a kiss made him feel childish, presenting a scraped elbow to be bussed. He took a thoughtless glance toward Pike's Place.

The door was just swinging closed.

Exiting was a Girl Scout.

Lee blinked. There had been Girl Scouts everywhere today. They had been soliciting Liberty Loans in thousands of businesses. He might have just looked away, and back to the situation at hand, but for the amazing fact that, regardless of the hundred yards between them—the swarming crowds, the belly-to-bumper automobile traffic—the Girl Scout was *looking right at him.* Again. He had no doubt he was looking at the girl he'd seen before, the one stealing gum, and as this thought crossed his mind, she flinched. Then she was gone.

"Say," Lee said. "Officer—"

"We're going to make an example of you, Golod!" Now the crowd was thick and tight around them, people butting up against one another and trying to see, as if this were an extension of the parade. Officer McKinney held Golod by the sleeve, and the latter wore a truant disposition, head hanging so that his hat obscured his face. The patrolman addressed the new audience. "Folks, this man is going to the pokey for a long, long time."

"I deserve it," Golod murmured.

"Thousands of citizens did their duties today, they were proud to be American supporting the war in the best way they could. But you! But wait a minute." McKinney rubbed at his broad chin with a beefy palm.

"But what?" Golod looked up.

McKinney glared at him. "I could run you in. Or—you can do the better thing. You could *enlist.*"

"What?" Andy took a step forward, ready to swing her fist at Golod as Lee held her back. The crowd voted with wild assent.

"I think you're going to enlist, pal."

Golod looked around, baffled, as the citizens of San Francisco agreed, with calls of "Enlist!" coming from all points of the compass.

"He can't enlist," Andy said. "He's a jewel thief."

"Calm down, Andy," Lee whispered.

"Now, miss," McKinney said, "the jewels were recovered, and in the spirit of the day—"

"Enlist! Enlist! Enlist!" the crowd chanted. It is difficult to say who was most surprised by this: Andy, who was also infuriated; Lee, who had been annoyed enough when he'd seen this in the movies; Golod himself, who looked at McKinney, who, with a flick of his shoulders, the smallest telegraphing of concern, grabbed him by the collar and started to walk him away.

The small crowd dispersed. Lee started to tell Andy he was putting aside his audition for her, and he reiterated that he had a story to tell—father, Chaplin, remember their late night together—but she could not listen, for she saw her own father leaving Shreve & Co., and needed to intercept him.

So Lee was left alone. He brought his arms down behind his head and made a cradle of his fingers. "Nuts," he whispered: Andy had found him uninteresting.

Lee was walking, then trotting toward the Curran Theater, feeling an unmet, sickening, growing *need* in his chest, the type of crushing emotion found only in men condemned to having depth. With every step, he recounted ways he should have ignored Andy, asserted his life of ease and disdain, and then he was carried far enough away that the marquee of the Curran loomed ahead.

Andy and her father talked (he had repeatedly been rebuffed by George Lewis about the ideal-cut diamond, but he had persisted, and persisted, and finally had been thrown out of the store for shouting). Andy held the sack of jewels, feeling as if the day had tossed her around like an ocean wave. She was considering how to break the news to her father—robbed, saved, how she had behaved perfectly the whole time—as they walked back to their own store.

Which they found had been robbed a second time.

As for Golod, McKinney took him up Grant and through the entry into Chinatown, where, turning a corner, he let go of his sleeve. On the second floor of a safe restaurant, the two of them met with Rebecca.

She was still in her uniform—McKinney pronounced her "adorable" and "a real heartbreaker." McKinney lingered, and Golod wasn't sure if he was going to be asked to be paid again, but the fact was, he was delighted to be part of the caper and didn't particularly want to see it end.

"We're really done?"

"It's all over."

"You plan well."

"Thank you."

Overhead, songbirds were singing in their elaborate cages. McKinney had a kind of starlight in his eyes. When Golod saw this was so, to sew up the idea of future mutual endeavors, he gave McKinney a tip: an earring.

McKinney was touched. He tried to give it to Rebecca, but she announced she was only thirteen, wasn't allowed to wear jewelry yet, but thank you very much, sir.

"When I earn the Silver Fish from the local Girl Scout committee, Papa will let me wear that, sir."

McKinney clicked his tongue, what a polite young girl, pocketed the earring, thanked everyone all around again, and left, whistling to himself.

Immediately thereafter, Rebecca opened her knapsack, to show her father the haul she had managed to liberate from Pike's Place. It was a glorious moment for Mordecai Golod, an early supper with his beautiful, intelligent daughter. They toasted with small blue porcelain cups of tea. *L'Chaim!*

10

Lotta's Fountain burbled compliantly at the triangle where Market decapitated Kearny and Geary. It was an ugly cast-iron drinking trough with a strange lopsided pillar featuring scrollwork that might or might not have included lions' heads (they were animals of some sort), but it had had the fortune to survive the Earthquake, pipes intact, and so it had become a symbol of resourcefulness, manna, and all the off-kilter pleasures San Francisco had to offer.

A platform stage five feet high was built flush to the Liberty Tower, and at its distant edge was something odd: a wooden tub about ten feet tall. Draped in roses and filled with water.

From the audience, the sight was promising: an empty stage always had potential, but then there was the curious bathlike tub (perhaps Chaplin would fall into it?). Then the Liberty Tower itself, six stories tall, "CRUSH THE KAISER WITH CASH!" and since it was late afternoon and the shadows were lengthening, the tower's crimson walls seemed to glow with heat. The clock face at the top showed the loan was 90 percent subscribed, by a complex formula that estimated pledges, constantly updated and approved by McAdoo every several minutes.

Reverse the angle, and gaze from the platform and into the audience. A newsreel photographer was there to capture it, a vision too broad for that camera's small, dull eye: a sea of black wool, upon which seemed to bob many bright faces, the uniform of straw boater or tweed cap making it seem like a shoreline upon which shivered an infinite rookery of seagulls and terns. The atmosphere—odd in such a broad outdoor space—was claustrophobic. People were hanging from the lampposts, and they jammed the windows of the *Chronicle,* the *Examiner,* the *Call,* the Palace Hotel, and when the camera had swung as far south as it could, there was still no letup, the crowd seemingly stretched around the world to meet itself. And they waved as if they were not merely there to see the actors, but to make their own mark on the day with a kind "hello."

The camera could not capture the noise, a Babel of voices, some singing, some shouting for friends. It was like hearing all the known songs of the world at once.

Crushed to the edge of the stage was Münsterberg. He had followed what he was sure was Chaplin and somehow ended up pressed against the platform. He found that if he stacked his reels of film on the ground and stood on them, he could see a little better. There was movement behind the platform, serious, gray-faced men with their collars turned up, consulting on business that, from their demeanor, seemed to involve important machines that required scores of straining, shirtless workers to turn a single squealing valve. He still didn't know what he'd stumbled into; he wondered if he could ask someone behind him.

"Owen Moore was no good for her. He takes drugs," said an older man. He folded his arms, as if to protect himself from a volley of facts. Münsterberg realized he'd been hearing the conversation for several minutes, but only now had his mind acknowledged it.

A woman in a cardigan was saying, "Mary's the best one in her family, by far. Her mother is controlling, and her sister married a lush, too, and Jack—"

"He enlisted. Jack is in the navy."

"He's a drug addict," said the man who'd claimed the same thing about Owen Moore. "Jack and Olive Thomas are vipers. They do cocaine, and sometimes they do it with Owen Moore."

So many people volunteered what they knew that Münsterberg couldn't keep track of where the information was coming from. But he kept hearing a puzzling fact, a romantic connection between Mary Pickford and Douglas Fairbanks, something he hadn't read anywhere. And yet everyone seemed to know it.

"Beth is a wet blanket."

"She seems nice to me."

"Doug doesn't need nice."

Münsterberg tried to imagine Doug with Mary. They seemed like a profoundly well-suited pair, and the emotion it engendered was so simple it startled him. He was happy.

He puzzled over what pairing of lovers Doug and Mary best resembled. But of the first dozen that came to mind (Dido and Aeneas, Helen and Paris, Abélard and Héloise, Antony and Cleopatra, Romeo and Juliet, etc.), none had ended well. Why did he have faith that this couple would be different?

In fact, what did he or anyone around him know about Doug and Mary? Only what they had all seen onscreen, *acting,* and what they had read in the magazines and newspapers, which had also insisted he himself was a German spy. He knew nothing about Doug and Mary. His happiness depressed him.

It dawned on Münsterberg that he was about to see Pickford and Fairbanks and Chaplin and Hart speak on behalf of the war. He wanted to leave. Between him and the street corner were several hundred thousand people. Bitterly, he returned to looking at the stage. The tub of water, near the far corner of the stage, gurgled and spat as the wind whipped across it.

He saw one plain-faced and well-fed man in his fifties ascend to the corner of the stage platform and adjust his glasses to stare outward.

This was Secretary McAdoo. McAdoo was motionless, gazing at the populace in what he did not know—for he was unfamiliar with show business—was the time-honored tradition of the manager gauging the house.

They had not yet made enough money. Also: he could not find Chaplin.

Fairbanks volunteered that Chaplin was probably sulking, but he only rolled his eyes when asked what was causing it.

"Do you know where he is?" McAdoo asked.

"Pardon me," Fairbanks said, for he had stood still for several minutes now. With a quick running jump, he hurtled himself to the top of the sawhorses between himself and the crowds. He waved. "Hello!" And the crowd roared, so he waved again, and then dropped to the ground, and stepped back to Pickford and Hart. "What was the question?" he asked.

McAdoo sighed. He checked his watch. "And are you all right, Mary?"

"I'm well, thank you." She gave a beautiful smile. Her famous curls were tucked under a mink cap. She was a tiny woman, five feet tall, and she wore a coat draped so long it looked as if a sable had eaten her. She gave no outward appearance of anything. McAdoo knew she was troubled only because he'd seen her in New York, before the gossip had begun. Then she had been energetic and inquisitive about every detail; now she was behaving professionally. Her smile was a weapon he'd never encountered before—it made her seem approachable and human without actually giving anyone a foothold within a thousand yards of her. She cleared her throat. "Is . . ."

This single syllable, a question mark implied at its end, sent Fairbanks skipping to obey. "I don't see her."

McAdoo asked, "Who are you looking for?"

"Someone was coming to help watch Mary's back, as it were," Fairbanks said.

"I don't mean to be a bother," Mary continued, with a new smile that radiated utter relaxation.

"We'll find her for you, Mary. Who is it?" McAdoo asked.

"It's all right, truly. Genuinely," Mary said, which had the magical effect of making the rest of the world certain it wasn't all right. McAdoo, who had more details to attend to than God at the creation, and was still missing one of his stars, now wanted nothing more than to set Mary's mind at ease.

"Ah. She's right there." Fairbanks pointed as she was escorted between two sawhorses. "Hello, Frances."

Frances said, "I'm so late, Bug," and reached for her hand.

Mary looked her over, a parent examining her child for dirt under the fingernails. "Where have you been, Scruffy?"

"I couldn't get through the crowd."

"You washed your hair."

"I did."

"Still wet," Mary said, raising an eyebrow. "So what kept you?"

"I said the crowd, didn't I?"

Mary smiled as if the issue were resolved. But her eyes flicked to Frances's hair as if it might be a murder weapon.

"What?" Frances asked.

"Hello, Charlie," Fairbanks said.

For Chaplin had appeared from the opposite direction.

11

Less than mile away, the Curran Theater was closed for renovations, its façade covered in scaffolding, its entryway dark and draped in canvas netting, its lobby-length aquarium drained and empty save for the rock model of the Golden Gate passage through which, in better days, exotic fish swam past undersea spotlighting.

There were tables in the lobby, the closest being a military recruiter's. He wore a broad campaign hat and sergeant's stripes, and he stood with hands on hips, ready for action. Lee stepped past as if the table were manned by asps.

At the next table was a happy-looking woman with wild gray hair tucked into a conical paper hat of American flags. Lee gave his assumed name, explaining that he was now Lee Duncan, not Leland Reid. He'd worried for several blocks about how to explain this, but she just crossed out the old name and wrote in the new, and gestured that Lee should quietly enter the house.

Inside, the lights were low on the theater seats, and bright onstage. Lee wondered how he could pretend this meant something. A forthright young man who had thought to dress in blue wool coat and red-and-white pinstriped shirt and blue tie—just like a Four Minute Man!—was hectoring his nearly invisible audience.

> Some say that from this conflict
> Our Nation should keep out.
> That sounds to me like sacrilege
> And smells like sauerkraut.

Lee's eyes narrowed. Four Minute Poetry. He had heard rumors that there were Four Minute Poets. This one prowled from stage left to right like a big cat, gesturing into the lights as if he were flinging scoops of water into the audience.

Sunnyside

Kaiser Bill, he'll grab and steal
Most everything he can haul.
He'll take your farm, your factory,
Your wife and babies all.

Now a reverse flinging motion, as if taking things back and stuffing them into a sack.

He'll make you work, he'll make you sweat,
He'll squeeze you till you groan.
So be a man and come across,
Let Uncle have that loan!

"Thank you."

This came from the middle of the orchestra seats, where a row of five people sat. Lee, eyes adjusted, could see their silhouettes from behind. These would be the judges, grading each performer on that famed rubric of projection, poise, demeanor, dress, clarity, forcefulness, and grammar.

Most of those who auditioned, Lee knew, hadn't a clue what the judges wanted. But he was a leg up, for he had purchased a pamphlet from an advertisement in the back of *Photoplay*, "240 Seconds to Glory: A Guide to Learning the Four Minute Ropes." Here he learned that most speakers wear their trousers too long. Onstage, your trousers should be hitched higher than normal. Do not try rhetorical flights of fancy, because your audience will hate you. A speech should have fifteen seconds of opening words, forty-five seconds to describe the campaign, two minutes forty-five seconds to heart of appeal, fifteen seconds to seal the deal.

The pamphlet cautioned that to attempt poetry or singing without the requisite knowledge of poetry or singing was a sure recipe for failure.

All it really took was competitors. Discounting his doubts as those of a wartime saboteur, Lee felt emboldened by his original plans. He wasn't going to say a word. Making a leap that is perhaps faintly familiar, one equating passion with ability, as if staging his own battle with enormous rocks, Lee Duncan was going to be the first Four Minute Actor.

At Pike & Sons, policemen and a detective crowded the small store. They had all eaten lunch together, and the smell of onions and sausage was overwhelming. Their embarrassment led them to be highly courteous to Andy, who had dissolved into tears. It was as if her spine had melted. She was flopped forward on a now empty jewelry case, silently shaking with horror that didn't seem to be ending.

"Just, just, just calm down," her father was saying. And then, not helpfully, "I told you to calm down!"

"Miss Pike," Detective Collins said, speaking into his sleeve (he found his own breath abominable), "if you can take a slow breath, just one slow breath for me. Good. Thank you. Now, I need to know, did anything unusual happen to you today, before the robbery?"

She sniffled. "Like what?"

"Well, did anyone unusual come into the store? Was anything out of place when you came in to work?"

She shook her head.

"Then this might be a little more sophisticated than we knew. So don't blame yourself. But just think for me. Outside the store—forget the store for a moment—have any strangers spoken to you recently? Done anything to ingratiate themselves into your life?"

She blinked, and dabbed at her eyes. "A stranger?"

"Lee Duncan, next!" He bounded onto the stage.

The house lights went up momentarily, for the judges to introduce themselves. Each in turn stood up, announced his or her associations, then sat. Mrs. Franklin Geary, head of the Liberty Loan Committee. Christopher Sims of the Institute for Speech Benevolence. Charles Wollbert, associate editor of the *Quarterly Journal of Speech Education*. Andrew Mellon Tonkovich from the Creel Committee on Public Information. Then, standing last, Mr. George Barnes.

Barnes's self-effacement when speaking was just slightly more overt than the rest. "George Barnes, of Hollywood, California. Motion-picture director and producer. *Betsy and the Burglar, Traditions of the Tartans, The Woodsman and the Fall,* and so on."

Lee straightened. "I'm sorry," he said. "George Barnes?"

"Yes, sir. We look forward to—"

"*Betsy's Fatal Slip?*"

Barnes grinned. "Oh, you know my work?"

"On *Betsy's Fatal Slip,* you were the cameraman."

Barnes made a sort of a clucking deep in his throat. It was the sound of a fish being caught on a hook. With his cheeks burning, with a sense of righteousness, Lee reached into the pocket of his trousers. He withdrew something tattered and folded and yet still highly recognizable: one half of an eight of diamonds.

By all reason, Barnes should have sat then, but he did not. This was an entirely new job for him, one with a measure of respectability that, when drunk, he claimed he would kill to keep. He seemed to have both something to say and no way to say it.

Lee said, "I'm a fan of yours. Your work taught me the spirit of fair play. If that sounds reasonable."

Barnes laughed, "Ha-ha," as unnaturally as if it were Morse code.

"Mr. Barnes?" Mrs. Franklin Geary leaned forward so far that the feather on her hat almost poked Barnes in the eye.

The house lights went down. Lee Duncan began his audition.

☆　☆　☆

By Lotta's Fountain, there were bursts of applause from the audience that came with the insistence of a rain dance—if only they clapped long enough, surely the actors would appear. The afternoon shadows had lengthened, and with them came the famous wind that gave the herringbone delta its nickname of Cape Horn.

Hart was restlessly bending and flexing his roping arm, because he had recently taken a fall from his beloved pinto, Fritz. Fairbanks looked impatient and Chaplin deathly ill, though it was hard to guess whether he was more afraid of the crowd or of Mary Pickford. Who was staring at her best friend.

"Frances, have you met Charlie?" she asked, in a way that was remotely singsong.

"We've met," she said.

"Charlie, you've met Frances, haven't you?"

"Why do I call you 'Bug,' Bug?" Frances disengaged from her friend and walked away. Mary gazed about as if she had no idea what had just happened.

"Are you all right, Doug?" Chaplin asked.

"I'm the pepper on life's steak."

Chaplin smiled at Mary, a smile so tight you could play snare drum across it. "With everything that's happened, I wanted to know how you are, you and Mary."

"We don't need to talk about that," Doug said. *Why not?* Charlie wanted to ask. Doug narrowed his eyes. "Say, is there something going on with you and Frances?"

"Doug." Mary spoke that syllable, and Douglas was struck silent.

"Could I have a last word with you?" McAdoo strolled up. He intended simply to explain the order in which they would appear. He did not mean to burden them with a terrible fact, that the Loan Drive today was not a success. They still needed to raise a great deal of money.

There was sunlight behind him, so it caused them to squint. In a huddle, from noon: Hart, then Chaplin, then Fairbanks at six o'clock, then Pickford, then, with a slight gap, McAdoo. All he could think, as he looked from face to famous face, was "I am taller than all of them."

"I have some numbers here," he muttered.

"Are they excellent?" asked Mary.

"We're at ninety-two percent of two hundred ten million."

"Well, that's excellent," Fairbanks said.

"No, not quite. We should have gone over the top already."

"I don't see the problem," Chaplin said. "This is largely ceremonial, us appearing, isn't it? What's the problem if we sell only two hundred million instead of two hundred ten?"

"Jeez," sighed McAdoo. "It means we can't pay for the war. Which— I mean, you're all educated. It doesn't mean the Kaiser will be driving a chariot down Wilshire, but, well, I can't think of a worse tragedy, really."

Mary said, "You might have missed the speeches, Charlie, but if you buy a bond, it helps clothe and shelter the troops."

"I know that."

"I can genuinely think," said McAdoo, "of no worse consequence than San Francisco not going over the top. That sends a terrible message."

"We'll do the best we can," said Pickford. A small part of the crowd had started chanting her name, and she looked at her wristwatch. "Perhaps *I* should go last," she said.

"Mary," cautioned Chaplin.

Bill Hart would go first. Hart, who had a face chiseled from a stone mesa, was fifty-three years old. He wore a tweed suit and a tan silk Stetson Careyhurst hat the width of a serving platter, and he was toying with a thirty-five-foot length of No. 4 silk rope. He was a former cowboy who enjoyed the prairie, the desert, his horse, his bulldog, thinking of new stunts, and making films. He was frightened of attention, women, and seeming swell-headed. *Photoplay* voted him the man you would most want at your side during a stampede.

After Hart dodged around the tank of water and strode to center stage, he performed the same roping tricks he had done in New York, Philadelphia, Denver, Houston, and Los Angeles, while delivering the same somewhat stirring speech that lasted exactly four minutes (he did not believe his fame bought him even an extra few seconds onstage).

At the end, an actor dressed as the Kaiser began to sneak up on him from behind, stepping high, in full military regalia, his arms drawn back like vulture wings, and fingers pointing down like claws. The crowd pointed and called, "Bill! Bill!" and Hart turned and flung his lasso over the Kaiser.

Fairbanks skipped onstage with a giant mallet. Its dowel was six feet long, and its barrel the height of a man. Written on its side, in letters the farthest spectator could see, was the phrase "Liberty Loans." While the Kaiser thrashed in the ropes, Fairbanks wound up, whistled through his teeth to get the Kaiser's attention (after all, it was not fair play to hit him from behind), and then walloped him with such force that he, Fairbanks, was lifted off the ground.

The Kaiser stumbled, weak in the knees; the crowd cheered; Fairbanks gestured toward him as if asking whether he should finish him off; and so Fairbanks took a second swing, and a third, which knocked the Kaiser flat to the ground.

Stepping on him with one foot and then raising his arms in victory, Fairbanks grabbed a megaphone and led a rousing chorus of "Over There" (even he knew all the words). As Fairbanks and Hart stood onstage considering whether to ad-lib and toss the Kaiser into the water tank behind him (they decided not to), McAdoo was watching them, feeling nostalgia for an event that had not yet even finished.

This left Pickford and Chaplin together, alone.

"No," Chaplin was saying. "Stop speaking to me like that."

Pickford narrowed her eyes. "The timing was amazing."

"I can't help that. I was taking a walk. I didn't even know she was here."

"Where did you walk?"

"I didn't— Oh, all right. The box office. I wanted to see how the new one is doing."

"Oh." Mary glared at him. She was not going to be distracted.

"It's breaking records, apparently," he said.

"I know you two have a history," she said. But that was roughly all she knew.

"Mary, have they assigned you one of those assistants?"

"An assistant?"

"A person who gets you things? If not, you can borrow mine and have him buy you a coffee can full of worms and a nice rod and reel, and have yourself a nice fishing trip."

"Bill McAdoo said you were taking a nap."

"Well, he doesn't know where I go any more than Owen knows where you are. Mary."

She glowed red, which showed exactly how hard Chaplin had slapped. When she broke their eye contact and looked to the ground, he began to feel a creeping sense of guilt. "Mary." The words "I apologize" almost came to his lips. "Oh, look, nothing has happened." And then, with full steam, "There's nothing I'd like better than to say I was banging your best friend, if only because of how much that would annoy you."

This succeeded in getting her attention. He felt better for having said it. He felt as if the animosity between them might be on its way to melting, a puddle and pool of warm feeling. Was she about to blaze with a smile?

"Charlie," she said, carefully, "you are the most miserable little son of a bitch I've ever met. If it weren't worth fifty thousand dollars every time I spit, I'd spit on you."

He stammered, "I—I wouldn't let you spit on me if I were on fire."

"I hope you catch fire. And syphilis."

"Then I'd be one of the Pickfords."

"Oh, you could still be a Chaplin."

"Miss Pickford, you're on." It was a page from the Loan Committee, voice cracking and eyes blinking with excitement. Mary doffed her sable, carefully handing it to her assistant (she did have an assistant, but didn't like to discuss it), and took off her mink hat, and shook down her jaw-dropping array of golden curls. The sight was so rich, it shut even Chaplin up. She straightened her simple plaid dress, and walked toward the stage. All the while, no matter which direction her body pointed, she was glaring at Chaplin.

The moment her tiny form hit the stage, there was a roar, and if the ignition of motorcycle engines had been enough to startle the city, this was, finally, the city making its own overwhelming noise. San Francisco, when aroused, provided the best mirth and enthusiasm in the world, and upon their first sight of Mary Pickford, all of Market Street issued a warm, wordless welcome, and a demand to be well received in turn.

It hardly mattered that Hart and Fairbanks were still on the stage, standing to the side, their captive Kaiser lying on his stomach. Small Mary walked before the water tank, to the front of the stage, her hands clasped before her, not yet smiling, but seeming instead, head cocked, just to listen, as if she wasn't quite sure yet whether the reception was heartfelt. In turn, the audience roared harder, with lusty abandon, full assent: Yes, really, truly, genuinely, we're here, we love you.

"Hello," she said.

A tidal wave in response, then a wriggle through the crowd, as person after person, attempting to applaud, realized that, with the crush of humanity from side to side, the only way to do it was to raise one's hands over one's head, and so the air was filled with palms.

"I'm Mary Pickford," she said, perhaps the least necessary introduction in fifty-five centuries of recorded civilization.

Smashed to the stage, glancing behind himself at the seeming millions hammering on his back, Münsterberg was unimpressed. Mary Pickford was a small woman, plain if expressive—and how many small women with expressive faces were there in the world? Why care for her opinion over the police, or the teachers, or the physicians, or the men who dug oil wells? He began to loathe himself for having devoted his energies to Miss Annette Kellerman, another siren whose song was not objectively that interesting. He doubted that the *Argo* sailors, dashed upon the rocks, thought it had been worthwhile. He imagined a small community of them, bruised, shaking their heads, looking from face to confused face, and asking, "You, too?" Mary Pickford was nothing.

In this, he agreed with Charlie Chaplin. Chaplin was unimpressed. How much did the audience really love her, and how much did they love the idea of loving the idea of her? Give any one of them four minutes alone with her, and he would have the answer and three minutes thirty seconds to spare.

McAdoo was approaching. He sorted through scraps of paper. "Hello, Charlie," he said absently.

"Is something wrong?"

McAdoo looked at the clock on the Liberty Tower. "We are ninety-four, almost ninety-five percent of the way to our goal."

"Good?"

McAdoo said, "Not really. We're not going to make it."

"I see the bond salesmen all over the crowd—there are booths up and down the street. Surely that's fine."

"No one is buying bonds. They're watching Pickford."

"They seem to be watching me, too. My movie."

McAdoo gazed at him. "Pardon?"

"It's, well, I'm embarrassed, but . . . I was worried that people wouldn't go see it, but it seems that for some reason all the shows are selling out."

McAdoo's eyes performed a strange, jerky dance about the landscape, Chaplin's face, and then behind him, the barricades. "How much has it made?"

"I'm not sure. More than anything I've done."

"I hadn't thought how all this would also help you, if you had something new to sell." Then he was back at his calculations. Chaplin tried to dismiss that with a shrug.

In the meantime, Pickford was saying, "Forget I'm Mary Pickford. Put it out of your minds. I could be any American woman. We all have the common goal of protecting our allies and spreading freedom," she cried. The phrases carried farther than had Hart's, or Fairbanks's, her voice seemed to be one with the winds blowing down the street, but McAdoo was right—no one was opening a wallet. In each city, when it had reached its quota, there had been celebration of going "Over the Top." The headlines always cheered completion that way, as if raising money were exactly the same as sprinting out of a trench and onto the battlefield.

McAdoo couldn't let the whole campaign end with such a thud. It frustrated him to know that there was a sizable amount of cash within the country's reach, and yet that there was some final piece missing. He saw white-and-grayish blurs pass overhead, a flock of pigeons escaping the cooling streets for better, sunnier climes.

"I have an idea," Chaplin said. "A piece of paper, please?"

It was a mean-spirited idea.

"Dear Mary," he wrote, and then elaborated. It was simple. He handed it to McAdoo, who frowned while reading it.

"Are you sure?"

"How badly do you want to go over the top?"

McAdoo chewed on his lip. "It could work."

12

The Curran Theater stage was twenty yards wide, a distance few actors could command. Lee asked for a lipstick spot, and a baby spot, just so, with a red gel, commands that amused the lighting crew.

"Go," said the prompter.

He ran through an internal checklist: Am I breathing? Am I positioned correctly? Are my trousers hitched?

He began his four minutes.

Here he was, hoeing in a field, wiping his brow from the simple exertion. He hadn't a single prop with him except his imagination, and yet the action, hoeing, was as vivid as if he had brought his own beanfield on stage. Then! He was tapped on the shoulder by someone much taller than he. Lee shook a mighty hand, threw down the tools, picked up a rifle (again, there was no rifle, but he acted), and marched.

He marched as far as the door of his best girl's house, where he said a tearful goodbye, and promised that one day he would return. Straightening his hat, he prepared again to march, but was stopped short. He mouthed the word "Mom," and then was sharing one last embrace with a woman who had been thoughtful enough to bring a pie, which he carefully carried to the troop train; he waved goodbye from the platform.

A minute and thirty seconds had passed. Now was the big action scene. He was in the trenches, grinning as bullets and mortar fire sang overhead. It was his time! Over the Top! Lee crawled on his belly, raced through the razor wire, and found himself in No Man's Land. He raised his rifle to his shoulder, put his finger to the trigger, and squeezed. Then, in confusion, he looked at his rifle as if something was terribly wrong. Carefully, slowly, he looked into the pouch where his bullets should be.

The tension, he had determined, would arise from whether in fact he had any bullets.

He strode across the stage, setting up another place and time, bringing himself Stateside, where he was a swain drinking champagne with a girl on each arm. He was just about to drop a wad of bills for a new bottle of champagne. Then he, like Farmer Lee, felt a tap on the shoulder.

He looked up, and from his reaction, he was seeing the noblest, kindest, most influential face in all the known world. Soon he was nodding, pounding his fist into his open palm, and mouthing, "I'll do it!" He scooped all the money off the table, dismissed the oncoming bucket of Dom Pérignon, and handed over the greenbacks to Uncle Sam.

Then, with six mighty strides (three minutes twenty seconds had elapsed—forty seconds was left), Lee was back on the battlefield, looking into his pouch. There were bullets! Courtesy of the Liberty Loan extended by the handsome man-about-town. All it took was a few shots from his rifle, some quick work with the bayonet, and Lee had surrounded a whole platoon of Boche soldiers and was awaiting his medal.

His mission accomplished, he furloughed in Paris, where he sat in a café, toasting his comrades, and then the big surprise ending like a dream: who should run to his side but his mother, who was so worried about him that she had actually shipped herself to Europe. The end.

"Four minutes!" cried the prompter, and then it was over.

Lee stood alone onstage. He had an uncontainable feeling of joy. Toward the end, he had forgotten himself and had become everyone, all those sacrificing, all those fighting, everyone in the audience. It was as if he were an empty vessel and the rest of the world could imagine themselves being him. He hadn't known it would feel so rich.

There was silence. He was trying to control his breathing, which had gotten out of hand with all his exertions. The ending, in particular, had almost made him cry real tears.

He heard clapping. It was one pair of hands. George Barnes had stood, and was giving Lee a solo ovation. The others stared at him. But Barnes would not be dissuaded. He began a whispered consultation with his peers: Lee Duncan was just what they were looking for.

"We didn't understand half of what he was doing. Mr. Sims, did you understand what he was doing?"

"I liked the kick to the face."

Mrs. Geary frowned. "I thought he was swimming."

"It doesn't matter if we understand it," Barnes said firmly. "The camera will."

"I thought gestures on camera were supposed to be smaller than those onstage," Tonkovich said, hesitating.

"No," said Barnes.

"He's meant to be onstage," Mrs. Geary said.

"Exactly. Do you want to be the one who tells Mr. McAdoo we could have had Lee Duncan for our cause, but Famous Players–Lasky got him instead?"

This was logic no one could argue with. Unless Lee Duncan was nabbed now, he would be chloroformed and kidnapped off the streets by ruthless talent scouts who would deliver him to Adolph Zukor, posthaste.

"Mr. Duncan," said Mrs. Geary, "the board has made its decision. And you need to know this is highly unusual, but we want you to know right now that you have been accepted as a Four Minute Man."

His eyes lit up. "Are you serious? Really? Seriously?"

"We're most serious. Mr. Tonkovich will administer the oath, and . . ." She had more to say, but Lee hardly heard. At first, this was because he was almost drowning, swamped by the uncommon feeling of having all of his dreams come true.

That was at first.

A single figure had stood up in the back of the house, and walked down the center aisle. Her hands clutched at the throat of her wool cape, which was thrown over a simple uniform of blue with gold braid, a smart cap atop her gray hair. And as she came into the light, she seemed to glow under the spots, as if tiny beads of water, a mist, clung to her. Though she was silent at first, all eyes were upon her, for she radiated a kind of quiet authority. "Oh," she said, whispering it. "Oh, Leland."

"Mom!"

Pickford was onstage when she became aware that McAdoo had sidled up to her. He whispered in her ear, and waited for her reaction. She nodded. He whispered again, pointing toward the clock tower, the 95-percent subscription, how it had stalled there. She nodded. And then he handed her Chaplin's note.

She read it. This took almost no time, for it was just a sentence long.

Dear Mary:
   Why don't you auction off a curl?
   XOXO
   Charlie

Her tongue went deep into her cheek, as if she was biting down on an insult. Chaplin watched her pace across the stage. He wished he had written, "Dear Mary: Why not just BE a whore?" He felt as pleased as a spring lamb rolling in zests of clover.

Of course, Chaplin had never actually gone toe-to-toe with Mary Pickford before. She regarded him in a way he did not understand: her eyes went fathomless on him. It was a look studio heads had learned meant their days were going to be painful.

"Say," Mary said, to the world. She approached the edge of the stage, appearing now quite ragged. She had done nothing to her dress or her hair or her makeup, but the smallest clench of her shoulders, the subtle draw to her mouth, a wince as if from the impact of many unseen blows, had turned her into an orphan.

"San Francisco. My beloved San Francisco. We have not yet gone Over the Top. I cannot believe it, but Mr. McAdoo has seen the numbers, and he tells me that it is so." She spoke as if this were their last moment together before they were to be taken to the coal mines.

Who among us will go just a little further and actually give—not just what we can—but *more* than we can?"

She paused. The crowd was chastened. She put her right hand into her hair and extended it, stretching out a fistful of the mane that had made her famous.

"Does anyone have scissors? I'll give them back."

What she proposed was not immediately obvious, but there were sudden screams from directly across the street, on the second floor, the Knightly Barber College, where a row of a dozen young men in white smocks now extended their shears and cried out for the right to cut Mary Pickford's hair.

Oddly—or not, for who can say of San Francisco?—there were fifty pairs of scissors in the crowd, all being ferried forward, hand over hand, above people's heads, until they began to clump and clatter onto the stage in a pile. Pickford looked back toward her small group to see who would do the honors. Fairbanks shook his head—first, he wasn't sure about touching her in public, and, more so, the act itself made him queasy. Hart, McAdoo, and all the staff also hesitated, for *no one* had cut Mary Pickford's hair. D. W. Griffith's irascible cameraman Billy Bitzer had said film was created only to show horses in gallop, the Bible in motion, and the tender fall of Mary Pickford's curls. Her hair had caused five thousand women to come to Hollywood, to see if their hair was as perfect, and five thousand women had gone home humbled.

Even Chaplin hesitated. A figure brushed past him and stepped up the stairs to the platform. It was Frances Marion.

Mary handed her a pair of scissors.

"Can you take one good hank?"

"I'm going to shave you bald, Bug."

It was an odd thing, being able to talk in front of what looked like the entire planet's supply of people, but no one could hear them as long as they talked quietly.

"Don't hate me, Scruffy."

"I don't. And I wasn't with Charlie."

"I believe you. Take a good, long piece from the real part, there."

The scissors hesitated. "Are you sure about this?"

"No."

The wind shifted; whitecaps appeared on the surface of the water tank behind them. A moment later, Frances had sheared off about eighteen inches, curly and heavy. Mary thanked her, and then held the braid up above the audience. There was the kind of confused wonder that would greet an auction of pieces of the Constitution.

"It's time to go Over the Top. What am I bid for this?"

A hand went up in the crowd. "Five thousand dollars!"

"Six thousand!"

"Eight thousand!"

"Nine—no, ten thousand dollars!"

From far in the distance, across the street, the windows of the Knightly Barber College, where quick consultation among the master barbers had decided the braid would bring them priceless publicity, there was a shout: "Thirteen thousand!"

Pickford's eyes found, to the left of the stage, a quiet gallery of dignitaries who wore beaver coats, and their wives, who had led the parade down Market Street. They had as of yet been unmolested. She said, "Gentlemen, *I* could buy this for thirteen thousand—surely you could pay more?"

Which is how Mary Pickford ended up auctioning off a curl of her hair for thirty-three thousand dollars. At the end, the locks went to the de Youngs, who mostly wanted to keep it away from the Spreckels family. It was later photographed, and then went into a jeweled window in the *Chronicle* lobby, where for the next ten years drunken newsmen attempted to stroke it through the plate-glass display case.

The addition of thirty-three thousand dollars was welcome, but still

McAdoo checked incoming receipts against some projections he had in folders. They still weren't Over the Top.

"Charlie, there's a lot riding on you."

"How so?"

"We need to raise more money."

"How much?"

"About two million."

"Two—but she only raised thirty-three thousand. I have to raise two million?"

"No, no, you just have to raise . . ." McAdoo ran his finger down a column of numbers scrawled on the back of a legal tablet. He turned it back over several times, showing off what looked like a handwritten musical score turned inside out by a lunatic. There were function and derivative signs, and several side-formulae that relied on further Greek symbols.

"What is that?" Charlie asked.

"Oh, it's just a formula," McAdoo murmured. "It's still in process. For every thousand dollars you raise yourself, another amount, something between ten times and a hundred times, depending, comes in at the Liberty Loan booths throughout the city. So, when Mary sold her braid, it motivated, I estimate, another one million two hundred thousand in pledges."

Chaplin stared. He was torn, feeling the dreaded tug to go onstage, but also fascinated by what he was hearing. "Between ten and a hundred?"

"It's much more precise than that, but there are many variables. We're at ninety-seven-point—what?—eight percent. I based it on a pet project of mine, an attempt to put real value on the more intangible desires."

"Why does part of that formula say 'squirrels'?"

McAdoo reddened. "Never mind. Can you outdo Pickford? You need to raise fifty thousand."

"Of course I can," he said.

"Well . . . Go on and give it your best," McAdoo said.

☆　☆　☆

"Mom," Lee said again. She kissed him, and he could smell the wet wool of her uniform, the salt air about her, her Lady Pompeii shampoo, her Duveen's face powder, which made him realize how much he had missed her. "You found me."

"Leland," she said, "of course I found you." She explained that after he'd been gone for about an hour, she'd been puzzled until the postman arrived with a delivery of a parcel of books on how to be a Four Minute Poet or Four Minute Singer. She had been in San Francisco almost as long as he had.

Lee introduced her to the judges, who were looking at their watches, and muttering to themselves about the schedule being thrown completely off. He took his mother by the arm and shuffled with her up the aisle. "Did you see me acting?"

"I did. I liked the part about the mother. And the horse."

"Are you proud of your son?" George Barnes asked. Barnes had followed them, for he had a cameraman's eye for mother-and-son reunions.

"Mom," Lee said, "I found out—Percy Duncan," he said, and looked for a reaction. "My father?"

"Oh," she said, with an exhalation as if she'd been shoved.

"He toured the world, didn't he?"

"Oh," she said again. She had been preparing for one crisis, and a different one had blown to shore. "Yes, he did."

"He's dead. Did you know that?"

"No," she said. "Dead?" It seemed to throw the next five things she'd planned to say out the window. "Dead?"

"It was the Kaiser who killed him."

Emily squinted, exactly as if someone had been cooking a radish. "Did he, now? Who exactly told you this?"

"The Kaiser killed your father," Barnes said.

"I saw Chaplin," he added. "I also stopped a jewel robbery," he said. "You would have liked seeing that."

"That sounds very nice," Emily said. "But I'm not sure about this Kaiser business."

"You—you stopped a jewel robbery?" Barnes said. His idea for a newsreel was too small for this man. Luck had delivered something truly wonderful his way.

Self-conscious, Lee added, "Of course, this is the most important thing to happen."

Emily nodded, wits returning. "I came to stop you."

"Mother," Lee said, tears back in his eyes. For he was about to discuss his father. Then he heard what she'd whispered. "What?"

"You can't go onstage. You promised me." She touched the stripes on her cap. "The uniform, Lee."

He took a step backward from her. "Mom . . . you're not even a real sergeant."

"But this is your chance to be real. You'd be the first in the family to serve."

He sensed that pointing out that his father had been a showman would not sway her in the least, and then he was going to say something about defending his death at the hands of the Kaiser, which also might go to her point about the uniform, so instead he whispered, "I'm going to serve my country."

"Not really," she said meekly. "This isn't really serving your country."

Which made Barnes speak up in Lee's defense. It began automatically, because the idea that he might sign up a man whose father had been killed by the Kaiser, who had foiled a jewel robbery, whose mother had come to see him off (this part was difficult, but promising), was like being dealt a royal flush. Further, he noticed how Lee resembled Wallace Reid, which was no tragedy. Barnes spoke passionately for over a minute, with the conviction of a man who knows he is entirely wrong—like a movie producer, in other words. It was an elliptical track, only within speaking distance of the truth toward its abrupt end: ". . . and perhaps none of this matters, but the country seems to think it matters, so who are we to argue with their will?"

He would have had more to say but for a final interruption. From the entrance came a rush of blue and brass, a mass of motion, arms holding batons, whistles held to pursed lips, something fanning out among the orchestra, going from blackness and into a glowing brilliance as the lighting crew moved their spots the better to illuminate them: the police had arrived.

"Leland Wheeler, aka Leland Duncan, aka Leland Reid—you're under arrest."

☆　☆　☆

Before he went onstage, Chaplin removed his rings and handed them to his assistant. He boxed and dodged, then cracked his knuckles, removed his hat, touched carefully to make sure his every hair was in place, then replaced his hat at a slight angle. He walked up the steps as slowly as a gunfighter. He had with him a bullhorn.

Behind him was the odd, deep barrel of water over which the restless wind played and made temporary waves that sloshed against its wooden sides. Before him, the crowd.

"Ladies and gentleman of San Francisco," he said, into the bullhorn, "I'm Charlie Chaplin." To which, again, the city responded with great acclaim. "You all know that we're going to France and giving that old devil the Kaiser what-for," he said. "With every citizen doing his duty, well, we can each make every dollar work for the betterment of the world. We are all here today because the mere act of being here is equitable with the best of all citizenship." This hadn't come out as he intended. "A man can enlist, and those who do not enlist can come forth with portions of their wages and support the man who has enlisted." Chaplin swallowed. "If we make no further impact today than to convince you of the importance of our cause"—he hesitated—"then our job is not even half done. For our men overseas." He changed course. "Let us say that you grow potatoes. If you grow several more potatoes than you are used to, then, by all means"—he forced his voice to a shout, and hit his fist into his palm—"*donate the extra potatoes!*"

Münsterberg was enraptured. He was looking almost directly upward. Chaplin rocked from foot to foot, his fingers in a death grip around his bullhorn, and his shoulders tight and as narrow as chicken wings. This was nothing like the self-possessed character who had winked at him in the alley. Münsterberg could feel the mood of the crowd shifting along with his own. "You tell 'em, Charlie," and "That's the spirit, Charlie," interrupted his comments at odd moments.

"For it is in our nature to be generous," Chaplin was saying. He felt abandoned. He hated the war. He hated that the country was in it, that there was no place to go but forward, that more atrocities were to come. He felt people were never intentionally beastly or malicious, but they were pompous and foolish; awful decisions were made by men divorced from their own humanity. He thought that universal peace was within reach if only people ceased to be stupid.

When he had pretended to be Trotsky, he had spoken well. But now that he was trying to be both himself and a servant of the world, he was failing. He persevered, believing that the simple act of faith, the spirit of talking with the audience, would lead to a kind of communion.

"Do the walk, Charlie."

A voice from the crowd said this helpfully. It was like suggesting he duck an oncoming pie, or turn around when Eric Campbell was about to squeeze him to death. Chaplin didn't hear it at first—his own voice was droning on and on—but then someone else yelled it—"Do the walk"—and then several people—"Do the walk, do the walk." There was nothing unkind in it.

Chaplin's eyes swept across the hundreds and thousands and hundreds of thousands of upturned faces. His gaze fell toward the stage platform, and, for the briefest electric shock of a moment, he and Münsterberg locked eyes, and Münsterberg saw, in slow motion, a human heart breaking.

Chaplin turned his toes out. He stiffened his quadriceps. He shot out his knees, and ambled as if on a Sunday promenade, twirling the empty air as if he had a cane. He went to all four corners of the stage, each time bouncing on one leg, three times, and when he was finished, he had a brilliant smile on his face that came, Münsterberg knew, from elsewhere.

As Chaplin bounded in place, his thoughts weighed more than he did. He realized he should have charged the crowd: "For every step of the walk, you need to pay a thousand dollars."

He couldn't remember how old he had been—seven? eight?—when he had found a discarded newspaper and made a paper hat from it. He had walked the streets for hours, trying to sell it for food. Something had happened—someone had hit him from behind, or he had stumbled—and the hat had dropped into the gutter, and even though he picked it up quickly, it was filthy and wet and it smelled of the sewers. Until nightfall, he still walked and held it aloft, calling out, "Paper hat, paper hat," and no one bought it, and finally, exhausted and hungry, he had taken a bite from it, and that night he had slept in the park.

On the Liberty Loan stage, he fell on his behind, he righted himself, he went into his inebriate routine, mindlessly, the way a singer went through scales or an insane person counted buttons. He stumbled, feigned dignity, and then became as limber as a dishrag while his mind was elsewhere.

Münsterberg found his hands gripping into fists. He wished he had a pen. Something strange was happening to him. Chaplin films had always inspired sympathy; the Tramp was a perfect character for such a thing. But now he was feeling sympathy for Charlie Chaplin himself, and it was like having the transept and nave of a cathedral explode, to show the blue skies and great wonder of God's creation all beyond it. His mind was racing in a way it hadn't in months, and with it the smallest possibility, just a tickle in his brain, that perhaps the movies hadn't betrayed him after all. Chaplin was a real man embracing the war, buying into the real world's illogic and lies the same way Münsterberg had bought the illusions promised by film.

To support the war, he was now resorting not to his own self but to an act, a pas de deux of himself and inauthenticity, sending to work his *stunt double* for his actual feelings.

In a better world, Chaplin might have taken from his glance with Münsterberg something of the professor's passions. Instead, he fell face-first with a convincing slam that made the whole platform jolt. He twitched his legs in hilarious spasms.

He was face-to-face with a soldier.

He had not seen an actual soldier all day, or if he had, he had been part of a formation, something subsumed into a machine. But this private was alone, he had a scar slicing his eyebrow, he somehow had fought his way to be near the stage, and now was gazing directly into Chaplin's eyes. He might have been eighteen. There was no color to his face. He wore his overseas cap and olive-drab uniform, and his fingertips clutched at the edge of the stage as if he might otherwise be pulled away. Unlike most of the crowd, he was not laughing. And yet he was not critical. The gaze did not tell Chaplin that he didn't matter, or that only one of them was real. The emotion in the young man's eyes was pure fear.

Chaplin thought, with a falling-away of his own frayed nerves, *I forgot.*

He felt a tap on his heel. It was Pickford. He looked again for the soldier. Gone. Pickford scrambled onstage.

"Finish up," she said. "I have an idea."

The idea was not hers. It was McAdoo's. He had suggested it offhandedly, perhaps because it seemed innocuous to him.

The audience roared as she took the platform alone. She looked up, past the sloshing moat of water, at the Liberty Tower. "People of San Francisco, the Liberty Loan clock stands at two minutes to noon. We need to make a final push, one last surge, to go Over the Top. I have but one thing left to offer."

She folded her hands before herself, looking every bit the model of supplication.

"A kiss."

Chaplin was in the backstage area, brooding over what he had seen on that soldier's face. Then he heard. What sort of kiss could Mary Pickford provide? It would be something between kissing your sister and kissing your sister's frying pan. He wanted her to look into that boy soldier's gaze and tell him that her kiss would save him.

There was a strange, tidal motion forward as hand after hand shot up, spring-loaded. A hundred men called out their opening bids—one thousand, five thousand, eight, ten, twelve, fourteen, eighteen—and there was confusion as Pickford listened, putting a hand to her ear and leaning over precariously. Twenty-two? There was a bid for twenty-five.

At twenty-eight thousand, it stalled. "Going once," she said, cautiously.

They would not go Over the Top. Twenty-eight thousand wasn't enough; it was less than the curl had gone for. People did not want to kiss Mary Pickford as much as she had thought. "I will kiss the first girl who buys a thousand-dollar bond," Chaplin thought. "I will bend over the nearest sofa the first girl who buys a ten-thousand-dollar bond. And, just for the hell of it, I'll roger the rear of the first woman who buys a million dollars' worth." All the things he could have said.

"Going twice?" A look of genuine dismay swept her face. She was worried about not delivering money as promised, about not being a good girl that way, and perhaps she worried that she was not that attractive. This touched Chaplin unexpectedly. Every day Chaplin awoke ready to hear he was no longer needed. It was a nightmare to have the crowd tepid to your charms.

"Thirty thousand!"

It was difficult to find the source of this shout. The bidder was highly unlikely: Chaplin.

Pickford herself underwent a quick transformation—the pleasure at a new bid was quickly drawn, quartered, and burned at the stake as she realized whom she might have to kiss.

"Thirty-one," someone cried from nearby.

"Thirty-three," Chaplin returned.

The same voice seemed to swallow, then: "Thirty-five!"

"Forty," Chaplin said, looking at his nails. Suddenly the world made sense. He was going to enjoy this kiss more than all the oysters in heaven.

"Fifty, *Charlie.*"

Chaplin had not been paying attention until now. But the combination of the jump in price and the use of his name caused him to look to the stage, where now stood his competitor, an annoyed-looking Douglas Fairbanks.

For a moment, he was equally annoyed, and then, as the ramifications of Douglas bidding on a kiss from Mary started to rain down on him, he felt a chill, the rising of goosebumps, a stew of awe and wonder and even the slightest bit of horror.

13

The interior of the Curran Theater was filled with auditioning men arguing with staff members over why their allotted times had come and gone (punctuality was, after all, the hallmark of the Four Minute Man). There were police, Liberty Loan volunteers, the judges, the army recruiter (despairing of making a single new soldier today), and Lee and his mother, who were at the heart of a double half-hitch, half-Carrick-bend knot of cops. That the scene did not descend into fistfights was a credit to the temperament of Emily Wheeler, who found her head clearing by the minute. She excused herself and Lee and found a manager's office in which an interview could be held, and Lee (she thought) quickly acquitted.

Once in the office, and seated, Lee looked about himself for allies, and noted only then that George Barnes seemed to have melted into the walls of the theater simultaneously with the appearance of the cops.

The manager's office was dismal, with torn leather chairs and a single waffle-wired window smudged over with soot. Lee and Emily were alone. "Tell me about my father," he said.

"I don't know what to say about him."

"Anything."

"Oh, Lord," she whispered. "I am drawing a blank, Lee. All the things I could tell you about him are disappointing." When she saw his eyes, she shook his head. "I didn't want to disappoint you."

"Like he was on a submarine? Like he stole a loaf of bread?"

"I wanted to stimulate your imagination."

"You what?"

"I don't know," she snapped. "There aren't rules for this kind of thing. I was trying the best I could under very trying circumstances. You try being a mother."

"All right, I will," he said. He crossed his arms and gave her a look so serenely confident that she was, for the thousandth time in her life, chilled by the resemblance. Here was a young man whose ideas were good because they were his own, tempered, God help her, by a dash of her own stubbornness.

There was a familiar form peering around the open door. It was Andy Pike, her hands tight on the doorframe. Lee inclined his head in pleasure.

"Mom, this is—"

"You bastard!" Andy cried, throwing herself at Lee, all fingernails and then, as he protected himself, surprisingly able fists. It took two beat cops to pull her away.

Then the doorway was empty again. Lee was standing amazed and speechless. Emily was, again, shaking her head.

"I tell you, Leland, I know what you inherited from him."

A red-haired detective entered, introducing himself as Collins, followed by Officer McKinney, whom Lee recognized immediately from outside the jewelry store. Both of the policemen shook Emily's hand, but not Lee's.

The interview was recorded by a young, fastidiously groomed subaltern who used a red pen on long, ruled paper whose every line was numbered. The detective adjusted his already excellently knotted heritage-silk tie, smoothed his Irish-wool jacket, and laid out the case against Lee, sentence by sentence, beginning with his seduction of Andy, continuing with the feint by his associate the rabbi, his deceptive distraction of Officer McKinney, and ending with the robbery of Pike & Sons by person or persons unknown.

"That's not—that's not—no," Lee sputtered.

"Are you disputing the facts in the case?" The detective looked at his thumbnail, turning it so the light carried across its well-buffed surface.

"Yes!"

"Did you or did you not spend the evening and early morning with Andrea Pike of 522 Sutter Street?"

"Well . . . yes," he said, attempting to avoid seeing his mother put her hand over her eyes.

"Lee," she said.

"Sergeant Wheeler." This was not just glad-handing. "You can wait in the lobby, if you'd like."

"No, thank you," she said.

Detective Collins swallowed. "Officer McKinney, would you escort Sergeant Wheeler outside?"

McKinney hesitated. He had planned to be present at a key moment. "Maybe she should stay. She's his mother."

Collins nodded. He had a photograph of his mother in his wallet, and one on his desk, and another which he kept in the glove box of his automobile, in which, on Sundays, he and his mother would take rides. "All right. Mr. Wheeler—"

"Duncan."

"Did you or did you not talk to Officer McKinney for the same five minutes in which Pike & Sons was robbed?"

This line of questioning struck him as a trick, and as he considered how to respond, McKinney interrupted. "I should frisk him. He could offload the goods, sir."

"In a moment."

McKinney was in truth feeling rather excited about how Leland would soon go to jail.

"How do you account for what happened?" Collins asked.

Lee considered this. He looked to the desk, to the floor. "Hey," he finally said. "There was a Girl Scout."

"Pardon?" Collins said.

"Yeah. I saw a Girl Scout leaving the store."

"You're blaming the jewel robbery . . . on a Girl Scout?" Officer McKinney said this. Collins's eyes flicked from Lee to Emily, to size up her reaction, which wasn't approving.

Lee said, "I saw her stealing gum earlier."

"The same Girl Scout?"

"Definitely. I can describe her."

"You can describe the Girl Scout?"

"If that would be helpful," he said, diminishing as the words came out. He understood no one would be pursuing that part of the story.

"Sergeant Wheeler," Collins said carefully, "can you account for your son's whereabouts?"

Emily let out a sigh, and then, losing a struggle with the fates, shook her head. Which was the end of the line.

"Officer McKinney? Frisk him."

McKinney was on him, quick as a grease fire, and after he had shuffled through the first pocket, there it was, in his flat, broad palm: a single diamond earring.

"But," said Lee, "but . . ." Alas, handcuffs were slapped on his wrists, heavy plug-eights, and they shut with the weight of a curtain dropping.

☆　☆　☆

The winds had picked up near Lotta's Fountain. Men in the crowd had to hold on to their hats.

"Going twice."

Mary Pickford said this almost to herself, but she mechanically put up two fingers so the world could see the status of the bid. It was still fifty thousand dollars, to Doug, and this made her doubt the Lord God's kindness in a way she rarely had. She felt like a fool, as if she had leapt out of a window on a dare, reasoning that there had always been an awning to break her fall. And yet never had she been as frightened as she was now, all because of the possibility that she would have to kiss Douglas Fairbanks in front of the largest crowd anyone had ever seen.

She knew there were rumors, yet also knew that as long as all was kept private and discreet, a certain amount of "behavior," as her mother called it, would be tolerated. But not this. They could, in one embrace, extinguish both their careers, topple Hollywood with the moral scandal, and find themselves torn limb from limb.

That was not the full reason she was terrified. Pickford had a recurring nightmare: She was back in vaudeville, shoved onto stage, naked. She had nothing to cover up with, and the sightlines brought all of her into the pitiless judgment of the lights. And the end of the nightmare was always the same, and always a surprise that made her awaken with a scream in her throat: there was no one in the audience.

To appear onstage supporting the war was not a nightmare for her, because she knew the world never saw her. But this moment, Doug, was an incursion that swiped right at her heart.

They had met at a party three years ago, at an estate near Tarrytown, New York. It was what Mary called a vine party, because it was for climbers. But she owed the hostess a favor, and she and Owen came. Doug was there, with Beth. It wasn't love at first sight. Mary rarely even looked at anyone anymore.

But in the afternoon, a walk was proposed in the countryside. The estate touched Washington Irving's old homestead, and the view just across the property line was said to be astonishing. Mary went because she didn't want people to say after she left that Mary hadn't even gone for a walk with them. There must have been two dozen people who decided to come. Beth came along, and so did Doug, and because Beth had a martyr's set of heels on, and because Doug was Doug, they were soon separated. Owen went, to prove he could leave the liquor cabinet, but he didn't really want to walk with Mary.

Mary walked with Doug at the head of everyone. She had always been a determined walker, and had always been the first in a new town, on a new set, or to find a new apartment, towing her family behind her like rafts behind a barge. She could never remember what she and Doug talked about, just that he was courteous, and knew who she was, and did not care that much. He pretended that, the closer and closer to Washington Irving's they went, the more likely he was to fall asleep and grow an extravagant beard, which he proceeded to pretend to trip over, even long after it had ceased to be funny. Which made Mary laugh even harder. But that hadn't swayed her. Men made her laugh all the time.

There was a soft earthen bank, and a clear, cold stream running over smooth river rocks. Irving's estate was on the other bank. Mary was first into the river, only realizing that it was deep by the time she was six feet across. The freezing water rushed over her shoes and stockings. The rocks were slippery—if she went forward or retreated, she would fall. Her husband was a distant speck on the path, although not so distant he couldn't see her if he wanted to. She was aware that, at some point in her marriage, she had started to make excuses for him, and here was a new one: he didn't have to rescue her.

She was freezing, off balance, ready to tumble, and she said, quietly, the word "help." She couldn't remember having said it in real life *ever*. And now the word brought tears to her eyes.

Then there was a splash, and before she knew what was happening, she was swept up into the air. Doug cradled her in his arms, and walked with her as if he were carrying a kitten. Four steps, five, and then he deposited her on the far riverbank, where Washington Irving's estate began.

There was a bend here in the pathway; no one could see them. Doug had carried her, and from one side of the river to the other, everything had changed.

Later, even in her elder years, when Doug was all she spoke of, and she had many memories, this was the most vivid, this first moment in a new land. She looked again at the bend in the road: yes, she was hidden from the rest of the party. Then she looked at the view, which was more magnificent than any she had ever seen. Hundred-foot white pines, wind shaking their branches so that needles came down like a new kind of weather. In the distance, valleys thrown into shadow by passing storm clouds. It wasn't like a dream. It was as if the rest of her life had been a dream, and this was a glorious kind of wakefulness. Birds were calling; she wanted to know all their names. There were animals somewhere far away, among the farthest pine trees, and Mary wanted all the time in the world to go and see what they were. Nearby was a cobbled-together house, with a chimney, with smoke coming out of it. It was Irving's old Dutch-style house, and it was where Mary wanted to spend the rest of her life.

"What do they call his estate?" Doug asked.

Mary had been wondering the same thing. She couldn't remember at first. And then she did. "Oh! Sunnyside."

It depressed her that soon the place would be swarming with people. "I don't want to tell anybody," she whispered. "It's a secret."

"It's our secret," he said.

Something in his tone made her sure that they were speaking of different matters. She had spoken like a girl—it was impossible to keep Sunnyside secret; everyone knew they were going to Sunnyside, everyone knew Sunnyside was there. She wanted to keep secret how it made her feel. What Doug meant confused her until he indicated it with a discreet nod.

Then she abruptly stopped holding his hand.

So now, onstage, was the culmination of all her fears, some so wretched she didn't know she had them: a kiss from Douglas, in front of the world, a single gesture that could destroy all her private moments, raze the kind of Sunnyside that traveled with her, a snow globe in a purse, smash it with a tack hammer. Couldn't it be a small kiss, on the cheek, a comrade's blessing? No. It wouldn't be. For here he was, he was coming at her, determined, as if this were as simple as surfing on a wave, jumping from a moving train, boxing with eight armed men.

"Going, going," she said, in a trance.

All of Market Street, from those smashed against the stage, like Münsterberg, to those watching from behind the barricades—Chaplin, Hart, Frances Marion—to the wealthy who stood at the open windows of their Palace Hotel suites, to the farthest, tiniest dots by the Ferry Building, who needed opera glasses to see, had stopped breathing. The crowd was a mosaic of men in black wool, women with feathered hats, khaki or olive-drab uniforms pressed up against Red Cross nurses, motorcycle messengers in leather helmets clutching at each other with the unbearable tension, the Knights of Pythias holding their elaborate headgear to their hearts, Onondaga Indians straining to see over taller heads, newsreel cameramen whose film had long ago run out holding their useless machines to their hips, members of a dozen different marching bands whose uniforms clashed and tangled, red against orange against purple, the man from the Bureau of Lighthouses kneeling by Barney the dog, and tiny girls who no longer had gum to give away held atop their fathers' shoulders and biting their fingernails.

There was at this particular moment no more important place on earth to be. "Gone," said Mary Pickford, for she had surrendered all sense. She did not care about her future or the war, she had surrendered. She had forgotten she was Mary Pickford. She closed her eyes.

Douglas kissed Mary in San Francisco, California, at Lotta's Fountain, on the last day of the Third Liberty Loan campaign, before the entire city and much of its surrounding populace. He bent her backward, off her heels, his arms enwrapping her so that she went limp. His lips touched hers, which parted.

A dozen feet away, looking upward at them, both hands to his mouth, Professor Münsterberg felt what the Italians called *un tiro all'anima,* a tug at the soul. He had seen, up close, that they were not actors. They were human beings, only more so. They were just as noble and worthy as all the fabled lovers of the past, and seeing their passion like this lit up the uncertain future.

Then Fairbanks broke away, the grin of highway robbery on his face. And with this, the trance broke, and the whole world knew: Doug and Mary. Doug and Mary had collided, as streams running into rivers, and then rivers making a new ocean. And before there could be more to think—marriages lost, the word "infidelity," and also the alcoholism, the drugs, the beatings, the misfit families, and the possibility that America should not stand for such behavior—

"Over the Top!"

The bell on the Liberty Tower chimed. McAdoo had given the signal, and the hands raised to high noon. San Francisco had raised its $210 million. The clock chimed again, a mighty basso peal, one loud, slow, echoing chime that shook you by the shoulders, the viscera, the knees.

"Over the Top!"

And so it went, slowly, growing, the call of the bell and the response of "Over the Top." There were flashes of fireworks that launched into the air, pillowcases of confetti fell from the roofs of buildings, banners on the sides of buildings rolled down, the band by the stage struck up more Sousa, and ever so slightly the face of the clock on the Liberty Tower trembled.

The crowd commenced dancing, a happy bobbing up and down like corks, hugs exchanged, vouchers passed hand over hand toward the distant Liberty Loan booths, where men in green eyeshades tallied up the pledges.

"Over the Top!"

The sounds of cheering and the mighty toll of the bell reached as far as the Curran, where the line of applicants for the Four Minute Men stretched out down the sidewalk. Lee stood with Detective Collins.

"Mom?" Lee asked. He was asking her, with that name, to believe in him. She responded by putting her hand on his arm. She did not believe in him.

There was a story he had read in a book of dark fairy tales, its etchings as grim as if executed by prisoners. A balloon is floating, and it boasts, "I am up because I want it so," and what it doesn't realize is that its string is in a girl's fist. She loses interest, her fingertips separate, and the balloon, unmoored, goes alone into the air, subject to something it has never known before: the winds.

A young boy holding a fistful of newspapers raced into the lobby, crying out, "We've gone Over the Top! And Pickford kissed Fairbanks!"

There were cheers. No one knew which part he was cheering for: the two facts were inseparable now, as if both were patriotic and romantic, pride and pomp, Doug and Mary, Stars and Stripes.

Detective Collins wiped at his eyes. He looked at Emily, who had linked her arms around Lee's elbow, and he could not further harm this lady. He inserted the key into Lee's wrist cuff.

Lee looked at his freedom with amazement.

"Not so fast," Collins said. "I know you're just an accomplice." He sighed, and his gaze went wide. "You could go to jail, Duncan. I could send you right there, right now." Then he nodded at the empty recruitment table. "But you can make it right. And you know how. By enlisting instead."

"Oh, yes," Emily said.

"I can't enlist. I'm a Four Minute Man."

Actually, he wasn't. The morals clause had been invoked. It was as if he had gotten on the wrong boat and was now sailing to the Dry Tortugas. Helplessly, he looked toward his mother, and their eyes met, and she burst into laughter.

Her laughter was high and wicked, a trembling at the top notes that then descended into dark, heaving gusto. It was as if she had broken some compact with herself, for both hands went to her mouth, and then she was red-faced and laughing again, contorting with the effort of trying to contain it.

"Over the Top!"

Münsterberg was weary. He had slipped off of his film canisters long ago. His eyes were weakening, though not in despair, but in prolonged excitement. The triumph of Doug and Mary had mangled him through an emotional clothes wringer. Mary Pickford had stood up against the world, and declared her desire, and the world was won to her side.

He saw assistants escorting Mary and Doug away quickly, and the stage was empty from its forward edge to the water tank at its rear. Münsterberg's grin slowly faded, and the cheering continued in his ears, and it occurred to him that the kiss had bought America new months in the war. It had paid for bullets and tanks and bandages and tinned bully beef and bedrolls and puttees and troop trains and sailing vessels and research into new bullets, new gases, new ways of scorching the earth.

It was not entirely fair, but he saw an image of his family's sugar-beet farm, high stalks trembling in the sweet southern breeze, the small high-timbered Dutch house with the chimney that always backed up, and then this fading into a Golgotha of debris and mud, tens of thousands of fresh boots crossing over razor wire. All predicated on a kiss.

The serial was over. There was no heroine, no jeopardy, no enemy, no hero, no fight. Instead, there was only an eternal machine whose wheels turned with the same merciless precision as reels on a projector. America had the first successful perpetual motion ever seen, eternally extending a promise with one hand and taking it back with the other.

"Over the Top!"

Then the circular face at the top of the Liberty Tower lifted entirely, on a slow, oiled hinge, showing off its simple, faux clockworks.

When the clock face was parallel to the ground, it wobbled in the breeze, and then a plank extended from deep inside the tower's housing, broad and curved at the end, like a tongue. Münsterberg watched with mild interest. No one but himself seemed to notice.

At the top of the tower, a healthy-looking figure stood in bathing gear. Smiling, she walked the plank to its forward edge. Turning backward, pointing her fingertips into the air, she flexed her proud thighs, bouncing once to give herself loft. Then she, Annette Kellerman, dove.

She hit the water tank perfectly. There was a splash of water that swamped the stage, a spray across Münsterberg, who cried, neither loudly nor fiercely, but with the dismal low sound of an animal at the end of a hunt. He toppled to the ground, where he disappeared among the buffalo-like stampede of the crowd, and hands went down to rescue him, which was impossible because of the many bodies jostling up and down with excitement. He was gone. What they came up with instead was the film canisters. There were attempts to keep them steady, but they were impossible to balance, and they passed over the crowd, floating to the center of Market Street, where, inevitably, the lids popped open.

Then blue and green and red and yellow fireworks that slide-whistled and popped in the air, and the last confetti and ticker tape fell upon the crowd, where it clung to lapels and hats and uniforms and musical instruments, and with the winds off the Bay, reels of film unspooled into the atmosphere, caught on updrafts between the buildings. People began to fling it with abandon, yards of heather-gray film stock with its tiny rectangles of images from far-off lands, Bermuda beaches, Atlantic City film sets, the surrounding sprocket holes tattered from years of use, a story unraveling across the city. There were frozen images, one by one, of Annette Kellerman, mermaid, held in a fixed sequence, and they were also moving, pitched by hands, transparent for a moment in the light, then falling again for the next set of hands to throw them aloft, and no one could now know how far they would travel until gravity would finally pull them down at some unknown time in the future.

McAdoo had gone to look for his stars, to thank them, and to ask if they would be available for the Fourth Liberty Loan campaign, which he projected would be necessary in November. But he could not find Chaplin.

This was because, the moment his feet left the platform, Chaplin kept walking. He had spotted an alleyway that led to Mission Street, where he turned left and walked, hat pulled down, for several long blocks. He was charged with the kind of energy he always felt when leaving the stage, a clotted feeling, a combatant escalation and detumescence.

He remembered the face of the young soldier. He wished he could have done it all differently. He wanted not to sell anything but to make that nameless boy feel better. He wanted to volunteer to join the infantry. He imagined close-order drills with a Springfield, camouflage training, standing in a trench and firing off rounds. He wanted to protect this young man. "You only need your gas mask when someone sends you Limburger," he thought. "Just follow me."

He halted in his tracks, and realized he needed to lean against the nearest building to keep from falling over. He felt sick. He wasn't going to join the army. Nothing he could do would make anyone feel better, ever.

The rendezvous spot was six blocks away, at an apartment he knew from his days at Niles Canyon. He had met Edna here, the day he'd made her his leading lady. As he approached, he paused to tie his shoes—they didn't need it—to look around and see if he was being followed. Mary Pickford must not know, and the thought of her judging him gave him a feeling of ill joy.

It was one floor up, in a clapboard place built before the Earthquake, whitewashed and sturdy. Inside was a sitting room, furnished anonymously, with care and thrift, and a large brass bed that was the flat's only indulgence. He had arranged this meeting so carefully, after weeks of slow motions, that he was afraid it would slip away.

Outside the door, tacked to the wall, there was a single poppy, the sign that she was there. Knowing her had changed his work already, and knowing him had, she told him, made her a finer person. She was a challenge to his autonomy, and when he could bear to touch her (knowing he was going to touch her was almost painful, an ache at the base of the throat), he was seized by her essential decency and sweetness. She was infinitely worth knowing, and she would make him walk taller.

They hadn't yet made love. Today would be the first time.

He knocked, twice, then knocked again, twice.

She was standing at the end of the bed. Her face was flushed with excitement. She wore patent-leather shoes, white stockings, a kilt, a starched white blouse. Her book kit was lying on a chair, schoolbooks, texts in history and biology and grammar, still bound together with a simple strap. She had left home that morning as if going to school, and instead Kono had driven her to the train.

He could hear her breathing. "Hello, Charlie," she whispered.

"Mildred," he said. "Have you been good?"

She nodded.

He closed his eyes. She smelled of soap. He opened his eyes and there she was again, his. He walked toward her slowly, enjoying each step. "Put your hands behind your head."

It was hours later. The evening was clear and cool, not a lick of fog, the stars brilliant, and the lights of the city twinkling, a dome over the continuing carnival below.

Telegraph Hill provided an excellent view for Rebecca Golod, who stood alone in a patch of grass, under a tall oak tree, smoking a cigarette. Two bus rides away, in the Fillmore, her family was celebrating its payout. She had slipped away.

She was a hero at home. She had $180 of her own on her. But what had her attention was a mystery: the tall, handsome man she had seen twice, once when she was stealing gum, once when she was leaving Pike & Sons. She now had a faint memory of eighteen months before, in Texas, the train station, the man who had tried to steal her spyglass (at least, that's how she remembered it). Then she had noticed Hugo Black, and he had disappointed her. She felt the man she'd seen today would not be disappointing. But details were translucent and hard to catch—what did she mean by "disappointing"? Part of her wanted the tall man from today to walk up to where she stood, and then to . . . The rest went all foggy. How did one go about kissing, anyway? It seemed to her that your noses would get in the way.

She took her money out of her bag, put it on the ground, weighed it down with rocks, each pile a separate denomination. She counted and recounted. She looked at the stately twenty-dollar bill. Series 1916 A, from San Francisco, Bank "L," a Federal Reserve note signed by William G. McAdoo.

She heard a strange metallic sound, the yawning of rivets torn from lumber. She scooped up her money.

She followed the sound, carefully avoiding the vegetable patches and the spools of wire around them that kept the deer away. Directly below her was a large lot surrounded by warehouses. It was lit with arc lamps, and there were a dozen men hard at work. There was no way to see into the lot from the street, but she was of course overhead, alone among the small bits of plowed earth.

Even she, who was used to prying up the edges of things and looking for creaking beams and supports, was taken aback. She saw the six tanks that had rumbled down Market Street.

Years later, at picnics or in overheated living rooms, at rest homes or late at night, when the scrapbooks came out, San Franciscans remembered that day as the turning point. There was the kiss between Fairbanks and Pickford, of course, but the moment of determination, when everyone knew that it wasn't just pluck and spirit and can-do, but sheer, cold, hard industry that would turn the tide: that was the sight of the tanks.

This was when historians turned off their tape recorders. Because America had produced no tanks during the war. Not a single American tank had been built.

What Rebecca saw that night was the importance of an idea, dismantled. She was staring down into the lot of the Kissel Car Company. As men stood guard at every entrance to prevent passersby from seeing into their yard, the tanks were pulled apart. First the papier-mâché machine guns were cut into pieces. Then off came the plywood that had been painted to look like metal. Then the tractor treads were loosened and set in a pile, to be returned to the actual tractors that used them. Finally, the Ford flatbed trucks that had provided the chassis were restored: sheet metal returned to their bodies, doors refitted, windshields bolted back into place.

There was a bonfire that night for the ersatz tank bodies. Rebecca stood and watched, and when she got tired of standing, she sat on the ground, knees up, unable to see the fire, but witnessing the smoke, the illusionary way the heat made the air seem to curve, the way the cinders glowed and went to ash.

She knew that the flames would have to decay at some point. But for now, they were spreading as if they could ignite the entire map. Deep inside her, she began to feel there was more to this life than $180 and her family's love. There might even be more than the Silver Fish badge, though she knew it was rightfully hers. Somewhere there were greater opportunities.

"I love," she murmured. This was a phrase she had sometimes whispered, when no one else was around. "I love."

She thought of the man in the train station from months ago, and she shook her head no, and then she said, "I love," and thought of her handsome man from today, and then, no, that was not what she loved, either.

"I love . . ."

Before her, finally, the flames were peaking, she could see their orange tips jumping in and out of sight. It was a very large world. She knew there was be a place for her somewhere, and she knew she hadn't found it yet. Gazing over the burning pyre, listening to the celebrations beyond, she knew she would find it and it would welcome her.

Our Feature Presentation

Three Blue Lights

. . . .

Comedy effects are always to be derived when actors place large and powerful creatures in ridiculous situations. Audiences like to see power defied. Here the comedian swinging on the ostrich's tail is supported by an invisible wire from an overhead trusswork which, fastened on an auto, moves along with a speed equal to that of the bird.

—Homer Croy, caption for photograph in
How Motion Pictures Are Made, 1918

A turnip once said: "I taste very good with honey."
"Keep talking, you braggart," replied the honey, "I taste good without you."

—traditional Russian folktale in its entirety

If bad dogs only had been in the world, the word "dog" would hardly have degenerated into an insult, for our delightful human race has a most tremendous respect for teeth which are ever ready to bite.

—Max von Stephanitz, *The German Shepherd Dog
in Words and Pictures,* 1925

. . . .

1

Illuminated numbers that were achromatic as soot counted down within a target-shaped medallion, crosshairs that now rippled back and forth, for someone had opened a door, and the bedsheet had begun to shake in the wind as if filled by a ghost.

"Sorry," whispered McAdoo. "Sorry about that."

The countdown indicated that the upcoming film would be military in nature, for the War Department required all training films to begin with a focusing mechanism that would cause the audience to pay strict attention. Hence the development of the *leader*, which was the prefix today for a different kind of film.

McAdoo took a seat in the back of the room, the basement of the White House, where films were shown. It was a cold place, with tiny smeared windows at street level and exposed pipes in the ceiling, some of which had cloths knotted around them to indicate where ancient leaks still needed to be fixed. The seats were a dozen caneback chairs from the second Cleveland administration, squeezed among the towers of stored furniture and linens and artwork and dinnerware.

The audience consisted of McAdoo, some representatives of the War Department, and a young man from the Department of Public Information, who asked if the projectionist should start over.

"Keep it rolling," McAdoo said.

It was Reel No. 2 of Mack Sennett's comedy *My Official Wife*, which had played in theaters about four years before. McAdoo watched as immigrants from a Lower East Side tenement concocted a scheme to bring their sweethearts into the country so they could marry them. At least, that could have been the plot. Mostly, it involved a tub of water in the living area into which people stepped, fell, dropped pets, pretended to swim, chopped vegetables, and dumped upon passing policemen. The action shifted outside, and one of the men from the War Department—McAdoo didn't know his name—called: "This is it. This right here. Good." There were anarchists on the screen now. You could tell they were anarchists because they had peaked caps, crazed eyes, and triangular beards with points that could stab through a bird's-eye maple plank.

One of them was standing on a milk crate outside the tenement, bewitching a streetside audience. He wore small round glasses, and as he spoke, he rubbed his hands like a rodent washing food.

When he was gone, a vigorous pie fight began.

"Was that it?" asked McAdoo.

"That was it," answered the man from the War Department. "Later, he comes back with pie on his face."

"Umm-hmm—a stand-in, maybe?" McAdoo nodded.

The War Department man hesitated. "What's a stand-in?"

"Apparently, when you can't see an actor's face—say he's doing a stunt—" McAdoo was impatient. "Forget it. Let's watch the war films now. Show me what else you have there."

The reels of film were being changed with a clatter. Someone made a joke about having four minutes free, in case anyone wanted to say anything. McAdoo didn't laugh. For the first time, the United States government was making moving pictures.

Not until Germany protested the footage shot of their invasion of Belgium had it occurred to the Allies that the picture-show newsreels were less an intrusion than a way to shed light on the battlefield. Thanks to the serendipitous rise of motion pictures, this war was the first one civilians had ever *seen*. And then, because of the war, portable cameras were invented, with better mounts and pans. Before the war, the picture show had been for the working classes, but newsreels made it seem as if attending the theaters was a civic duty. As the educated showed up, dramatic features became more complex, though McAdoo would need serious integers to understand the chicken-and-egg of that phenomenon.

Zukor and Goldwyn and Fox and First National wanted fresh war footage every week, and since the footage could increase patriotism, of course the military was willing to provide it.

But where might it come from? Photographers were like masterless samurai, with fuzzy allegiances, drinking problems, and psychological disorders that allowed them to toss their tripods on their shoulders and chase battling units through exploded submarine terminals. They were not to be trusted.

The United States assigned photographic duties to the Signal Corps. The Red Cross, charged with distribution and unclear on the notion of profit, allowed the four major news distributors—Pathé, Universal, Mutual, and Gaumont—to compete for the footage via games of ro-sham-bo, and from there the accounting system broke down.

Which is where McAdoo came in. Fresh from the Liberty Loan tour, he was President Wilson's point man in the picture show. America would get into the film business itself. The first film produced by the Signal Corps was *Pershing's Crusaders,* and this was the footage now showing in the White House basement.

The country's first film was indistinguishable from the earlier newsreels—here were soldiers in basic training, then men on the decks of ships, waving, then horses being curry-combed, soldiers oiling their rifles. McAdoo thought that after a while all shots of battle seemed the same. And you never saw the human pulp that followed an explosion. Not that anyone needed to see that. He struggled to right himself against the chair, his calves aching, his shoulders throbbing, wondering how Grover Cleveland's Cabinet had stood the discomforts of a caneback chair, no pillows.

When the lights were up, he was shocked to see the young men of the War Department, several of them, wiping away tears. "I never understood before," one of them said, pausing, for he was suddenly in unfamiliar waters. He had blond hair with a messy parting, and the makings of a second chin. "This is not the war described. It's the war."

"You know, uh—I'm sorry, is it Jim?" said McAdoo.

"John."

"Sure. Sorry. But it's not the war. It's mediated by—"

"Mediated?"

"Well, are you familiar with the term 'diegetic'— Oh, never mind. Listen, we have other business to talk about."

"It's just that"—John could not quite let it go; he sniffled—"it has no editorial slant. It's objective. I've never seen that before."

"Oh, gosh, look." McAdoo considered, and reconsidered. If this was how an audience of intelligent men felt, then perhaps the war films were an excellent tool. Plus, he didn't want to make Jim feel like an idiot. "All right," he said. "Let's just finish the war soon, okay?"

Sunnyside

Such was the atmosphere in the White House lately. As McAdoo dismissed the younger bureaucrats, they were discussing how, after the war, the energy and commerce and power marshaled against the forces of evil could be redirected. A mighty body of nations using diplomacy to solve disputes, end poverty, raise standards of living. With the application of "sanity and intelligence and morality," Wilson's three graces, America would establish on the world stage something close to paradise.

It was damp in the basement. The door closed. Now it was just McAdoo and the projectionist. "Show me again, if that's all right."

"The war footage?" asked the projectionist.

"No, the other." McAdoo, curious as ever, asked what film was actually made out of (guncotton, it turned out), and why it glowed the way it did (silver nitrate), and how long it took to develop (the projectionist didn't know), and what all those processes cost (again, he didn't know).

"Oh, shoot," said the projectionist, which made McAdoo like him. He was homely, balding, with tufts of hair that stood like juniper bushes. "It's all tore up. I have to splice it."

"Take your time. Oh, and what's 'splicing,' anyway?"

As the projectionist explained what he was doing, McAdoo thought about the phrase "the world stage." If the world was a stage and America newly in the business of making pictures, then imagine the concept of the stand-in writ by lightning: America turning the future into its own motion picture. The country was now powerful enough to structure the peace that would surely arise after the war ended. And that, Münsterberg would have said, meant imposing narrative upon what was essentially chaos.

4 . . .

3 . . .

2 . . .

Back to *My Official Wife.* The tenement. The immigrants. Then, outside—the anarchists!

"Can we hold the image still?" McAdoo asked.

"It's a risk. The film might catch fire."

"Oh dear. Well, let's not do that." McAdoo stood, walked toward the screen, and looked at the anarchist carefully. "Are we sure it's him?"

The director of *My Official Wife,* Mack Sennett, was never much of a stickler for realism. But he announced to his competitors that, by an awesome stroke of luck, he had combed the Brooklyn neighborhoods around the Vitagraph Studios during the ten-week period when a certain anarchist was in exile in New York. And eager for five dollars' salary. The logs for the players at Vitagraph were clear: that man on screen had signed in, or someone signed for him, "Bronstein, L." In Cyrillic.

"Mr. McAdoo, the stock is flammable. I should—" Suddenly a sound like a whip, a screen gone white.

"Broke again?"

The projectionist worked with a razor and film cement, and then he had the reel back on the projector. "They just standardized this," the projectionist said. "It's three perforations per— Oh, shoot."

"That's all right."

"To get it out, I have to go forward. Sometimes there's a problem and you can't back up. Sorry."

The cut was rough; the perforations missed the uptake tracks before lining up, and then the image was clear: the anarchist. He was on his milk crate, earning his five dollars, Lev Davidovich Bronstein, now known as Leon Trotsky. When the war was over and the peace began, there were many annoyances that needed to be dealt with, and the man onscreen was one of them. McAdoo had been as curious as anyone to see footage of his face, since he tended to avoid newsreel photographers as if they were snipers.

Then his face was gone, and the projectionist said, "Oops," for he had put the leader in the wrong place, and the countdown was now beginning. "What a mess."

McAdoo thought he should leave, he should pack, he'd seen this part before, it was just numbers now, but he could never bring himself to leave the picture show, so here he stayed, imagining the coming world, America's movie, and, dreaming of peace and relief—always found in the last reel, not the first—he put his chin down on the chair in front of him.

4 . . .

3 . . .

2 . . .

2

In July 1918, the U.S.S. *Olympia*, a frequently patched-and-welded cruiser, plugged across the North Sea, zigzagging among decoy ships to avoid sudden death by torpedo, or the remorseless sway of a plum-colored mine. Aboard were thirteen hundred Allied soldiers, a polynational force under British command: French, Italian, Canadian, and men of the Royal Scots Regiment. Also belowdecks were Company K, of twenty-five forward troops from the 339th of Detroit. They assumed with heartbreaking naïveté that they were heading to France.

Almost to a man, they throbbed with superstition and trust. The *Olympia* was obviously a lucky vessel to travel on, for it had seen famous service in the Spanish-American War—each doughboy had his photograph taken in front of the polished brass plaque that marked the location where Commodore Dewey had intoned, "You may fire when you are ready, Gridley," twenty years before. In truth, the men of the 339th of Detroit were anxious to have their own famous phrases coined, to go Over the Top, even if by 1918 most of them were aware that war was no longer a guaranteed jolly rite of passage. It had turned out that war could be tremendously positive or tremendously awful, sometimes both at once. But at least it was *tremendous*. And when faced with the opportunity to have stories to tell for a lifetime, none of the 339th, Company K, was really going to ask troubling questions, such as "If we're going to France, why has the quartermaster outfitted us with ham-handed mittens and fur-lined hats?"

Private First Class Hugo Black was an exception. His diaries, among rhapsodies to his last Stateside glass of Sémillon, his last bite of *boeuf à la Bourguignonne aux chanterelles*, reveal a man troubled by where exactly he was going, and *why*. Hugo, who had shunned human company since the disastrous East Texas riots, was now in the 339th.

Hugo was officer material, but he had volunteered for the infantry in a burst of feeling for the common man after a drunken evening—immediately regretted—of reading aloud the poetry of Walt Whitman. He had disappointed his father (he of the "I am an engineer of engineers!")

by not becoming an engineer. And soon the realities of his situation became apparent. He was disappointed by performing KP ("What black sun and scorched earth conspired to grow these limp and tortured carrots?"), by the medical staff (the only medication aboard the *Olympia* was the ghastly cathartic Number Nine Bullets), by the weaponry (their Springfields had been replaced with the somewhat mysterious choice of Russian Mosin-Nagant rifles, which were said to be most accurate when firing around corners).

But, most profoundly, he was disappointed by his fellow soldiers. How had the AEF found twenty-four men from Detroit with whom he had so little in common? The rest of them, for instance, discussed baseball as if arid Navin Field were 1918's *agora*.

Outnumbered by a thousand foreign soldiers who had the benefit of European education, Hugo had been horrified by how the 339th, Company K, manifested civic pride. They didn't brag about Stokowski conducting the Detroit Symphony Orchestra, or ballet nights at Ann Arbor directed by Ossip Gabrilowitsch. Instead, one evening at the mess, over sloppy buckets of M&V dribbled across unbreakable biscuit rations, a horrible little rat of a man, Pfc. Wodziczko, bragged to the British, the French, the Italians, that Detroit, Michigan, was proud home to not only the Tigers, but also—he paused to savor it—the world's largest stove.

There was a kind of babble after that, with one side of the table—the American side—agreeing that you could keep your Westminster Abbey, your Louvre, but the world's largest stove was something to behold; the other side, the European, was translating this late proof that their new allies were in fact a befuddled gaggle of swamp geese barely fit for the stewpot.

"Stokowski," Hugo announced, weakly. "Have they told you about Stokowski?"

He was drowned out by Wodziczko, who cried out that it was rumored that soon they would eclipse Dayton and secure the world's largest cash register. Detroit was a city on the move!

Hugo had been given charge of several two-reel melodramas and comedies, including *Johanna Enlists*, featuring Miss Mary Pickford. Her popularity had swollen yet again; she was unstoppable now that she was arm in arm with Douglas Fairbanks. If she broadened his appeal, he lent her a certain *joie de vivre* that hadn't yet been suspected. To watch her laugh, it was said, was to remember the springtime hills of home. Alas, Hugo swapped away his canisters of *Johanna Enlists* to British officers, who gave him a pint of rum and a one-reeler starring Freckles the Educated Chimp. He attempted to show the chimp film to the *Olympia* sailors, ending up barricaded in a supply closet after the audience had knocked over the projector and set fire to the screen.

Two weeks out of the port of Newcastle-on-Tyne, with still not a speck of land in sight, Hugo remained with the linens. He slept on a bed of absurdly warm overcoats that had been stiffened with layers of grease, and listened from the cozy company of brooms, mops, ammonia, and dustpans for the ship's F-sharp bells indicating a shore landing was nigh. He had expected savage behavior from his countrymen, but that the deprivation of Mary Pickford had caused riots by the Italians (scions of Dante!) and the French (who could gaze daily upon the *Winged Victory of Samothrace*) dismayed him.

On his last night in exile, he broke open a crate to find mustard-colored English-Russian phrase books, which he read by candlelight.

How many versts (⅔rds of a mile) to headquarters?
Skol 'ko vyorst do shtaba?

Drop your weapons—we are soldiers!
Pozhaluysta, nie streliayte—my devstvennitsy!

He had placed his destiny in the hands of a bureaucracy that expected soldiers in the Belleau Wood to bark orders in Russian. "I am doomed," he wrote. "I belong nowhere. Why am I here? Where am I? And why do we have overcoats? I am depressed."

Hugo's destination was a secret. Having the boots of two million fresh American troops ready to lay siege to the Hindenburg Line had lent a heady kind of momentum to the United States of America. President Wilson ordered the 339th Infantry Regiment of Detroit, Michigan, to invade Russia.

There were twenty thousand tons of Allied matériel stored in North Russia that could fall into German or Red Army hands. And an invasion of Russia could open a new front against Germany. And the White Russians could use help against the Bolsheviks. And so on. These were reasonable *casus belli,* but they were largely irrelevant. Wilson had given the subject far less public consideration than, say, sending troops to Europe in the first place. Once war had been declared, a little more war was barely something to fret about.

But in his private *aide-mémoire,* written with one of the legendary green Ticonderoga pencils crushed from stem to stern by his anxious molars, Wilson confessed a secret, one that gave him cluster headaches until he awoke his wife to discuss it by the bedroom fireplace, which was kept cold year-round in the spirit of wartime sacrifice. Wilson had a moral compass that pursued "north" with the strength of a Presbyterian minister—and his idea was a deeply moral one.

The Allies weren't engaging the *real* Russian populace in battle, just the Leninist criminals, the gullible, and the easily led. The Bolsheviks were wild-eyed, frothing men who shouted more than they made sense, but they were men with passion, and as Wilson gently explained to Edith, he had seen footage of Trotsky, he understood his primal appeal, the crowds had no one better to follow. And in this sympathy was President Wilson's secret hope, tucked deep within the *aide-mémoire,* swaddled among qualifying clauses as if nestled in baby blankets: that the mere fact of Western boots plowing the snow would leave seeds behind, causing democracy to erupt and flower spontaneously.

Joining the 339th would be the 310th Engineers and hospital units to stand alongside Canadians and Europeans until a solid mass, an unstoppable wave of fresh men, was ready to swoop down from the north. Almost eight thousand men in total! But that would take time, and preparation, which is why U.S.S. *Olympia* had been sent in advance.

Pfc. Hugo Black stumbled deckside to fall into formation with his company (who still hated him) just as the *Olympia* passed the harbor breakwater of Archangel, Russia, twenty miles up the flinty and sulfurous Dvina River. Russia? There was no longer time to despise Hugo, for there was a wholly new and unexpected country to begin despising.

Archangel was a shoddy place. Three degrees above the Arctic Circle, cloaked under darkness six months of the year and under clouds the color of a soiled tunic for the rest, it had been discovered and dismissed by Peter the Great as a tedious disappointment. Fifty thousand tired souls lived in borrowed rags, their importance extinguished the moment Russia found a warm-water port. There were open sewers, and frightening-looking prostitutes who stood by them. Every structure from the waterfront to the factories to the lean-to government buildings looked as if it could be folded up and run off with in the middle of the Arctic night.

Muddy-looking citizens lined the wharves, and though the European troops ignored them, the men of Company K rushed to the rails. There were no guns pointing at them, but, on the other hand, Hugo couldn't quite hear, say, howls of pleasure.

The atmosphere was tense, the city unsure if a sigh of relief was in order. A bloodless counterrevolution had just been executed. The aristocracy and the peasants had never embraced the Bolsheviks here. Further, the working class was impressed by the Allies' promise of cigarettes, which they'd been running low on under Lenin's brief tenure.

The landing would be relatively safe, but for one small detail: because a thorough looting of a city always took longer than expected, one last train of Bolshevik soldiers had yet to depart. It waited, black as soot, on the tracks between the dock and the warehouses, not fifty yards from where the *Olympia* was about to land. Cross-gates were open, and men tugged toward the cars mules and horses, wheels of cheese, tungsten blocks, spools of copper wire, and whatever antique carvings of saints weren't nailed down. The train engineer, an Uzbek whose tertiary syphilis made him occasionally a tad grouchy, was tinkering with its wood burner.

The *Olympia* dropped anchor at half past eight on the fair but hazy morning of August 2. The two bluecoat sailors who jumped upon the docks to tie the pug-nosed ship's lines were the first Allied soldiers whose heels touched Russian soil. A gangplank appeared on deck, and Hugo's company was among those drilled in the art of the gangplank march, so they could disembark in haste without falling into the water.

On principle, the 339th resisted taking orders from the British, but they followed their drill with accuracy. *Step, shuffle, step, shuffle, step, and POUNCE to dry land.* Hugo, who remembered childhood breakfast-nook conversations with his mother, an Anglophile, looked carefully toward the mission commander, Major General Frederick C. Poole, for the upcoming moral lecture that would explain why they were in Russia. Currently, Poole was speaking through a bullhorn about how the Allies should react with tact and decorum when greeted with "embarrassing enthusiasm" by the oppressed populace.

And yet the overwhelming murmur among the Russians squinting toward the gangplank to watch wave after wave of soldiers who disembarked in bowlegged but proud formation, was that of an audience in a puppet theater whose eyes were drawn upward along the strings. They were asking one another, "And where are the Jews?"

Soon the Americans stood in formation dockside, sandwiched among dozens of careful rows of Allied troops posed as if starched before the industrial blight of sawmills, their field hats, bedrolls, and wickedly ill-tempered new rifles piercing the air that curdled over smokestacks. There was a tang of marine waste and metal slurry, a hint of old sawdust. It reminded Hugo of the ghostliness of the hoop-and-stave works, which he and his father, the engineer of engineers, visited on Sundays. Poole stood on a platform with his bullhorn.

When, in 1907, Viscount Haldane shook the British Army by its bootstraps to eliminate the shirkers, buffoons, and muttonheads, he meant to leave only "a sharp point of finely tempered steel," and yet, with the grip of an eighteen-stone stoat on a rooster's neck, General Poole survived. A fan of amateur theatrics, the first to volunteer to declaim *The Faerie Queene,* and ill-poised, as if his body were made of sagging dirigibles, Poole felt the hand of God had blessed him with the gift of harangue.

So there were windy opening remarks about the making of history and aiding of empires, during which Hugo, as if counting his own teeth, remembered those breakfast discussions with his mother, and how disappointing his letters home were going to be. He noticed that there was a rail track between the warehouses and the docks, and on it, a train of a bizarre 0-6-2 wheel pattern, and a black iron cab tower that looked Gothic, as if it should be flanked by gargoyles. Why were the men tending to its hotbox looking at the assembled troops so nervously?

The meat of Poole's speech made as much sense to the average Russian as any other political speech of the last several years. But this one was special, in that Poole had delivered it in English, without translation. However, the weather was warm, and everyone enjoyed being outside without anyone pointing bayonets at them.

On the other hand, a train full of armed men showing off wrecked teeth, smiles looking unfamiliar on sallow, unshaven faces . . . Hugo considered this: hadn't the adjutant aboard the *Olympia* detailed how to spot the enemy? They were said to wear no single uniform, but instead to have coarse and addled features ringed by mops of unkempt hair, and clothing made of burlap or flour sacking. Further, they would sprint like bunny rabbits at the first shot fired.

The wheels of the train started to groan and turn as if breaking off a decade of rust. The departing fighters seized this final opportunity to blow kisses toward the Allies. A voice cut through the crowd, a British soldier's, anonymous in the ranks, but a voice with a permanent impact upon the campaign in North Russia: "I say! Those men on the train! They are positive Bolos!"

Poole returned to his notes, setting a precedent against common sense, chugging toward a distant rhetorical triumph, as the Bolsheviks waved dirty handkerchiefs and the train, swaying like a drunken dowager, departed.

When the speech was over, the Royal Scots were cued, and they upended the gunnysacks of cigarettes, which caused actual Russian applause. There was a riot—momentary and polite, by current standards—and the cigarettes were gone.

The troops chattered with excitement at the introduction of "Bolo" into the fighting man's vocabulary. As they disbanded, told to find lodging, their yells echoed up and down the emptying wharves. Bolos!

The matter of epithets was crucial, for each entrant to the European War, save one, had monikers crafted by another player. So, courtesy of the English, the French were *poilus*, because they were very hairy. And the French called the British "Tommies," and the Australians named the Turks "Abdul," and the Australians were "diggers." When the first Americans landed at Brest, the crowds, with equal measures of derision and romantic longing, called them "cowboys." But the Americans, who were not actually Allies but Associates, disavowed the name and instead went by the mysterious, self-generated nickname of "doughboys."

The twenty-five Americans followed Lieutenant Gordon along the railroad tracks, ignoring the calls by other units to join them. As their land legs returned, they walked with the swagger of city boys whose reputations were growing. They followed Gordon, tromping as if each step pounded in their point: Detroit made cars, tanks, ammo, stoves, and, best of all, Americans.

Gordon, with a rainwater smile, frequently plastered into sweet agreeability, was well liked by his men. He and Hugo had gone to the University of Michigan together. Hugo had taken more difficult classes and scored higher grades than Gordon. But Gordon had dressed *à la mode,* and was frequently covered in girls. Hugo sniffed that the only heroism he'd shown then was having mashie-nibbed out of a double-bunkered trap on the Grosse Pointe Country Club golf course. Further, Gordon had success-fully grown both a mustache and a faint British accent since becoming an officer.

There was an abandoned steam shop on the second story of a rattrap quayside sawmill. The windows hadn't been shattered, so the mosquitoes were kept out. But the platoons had hardly dropped their bedrolls and cracked open their mustard-colored phrase books before sharing a feeling that something had just been snatched from their grasp.

It was admitted the Bolos hadn't left that fast. They didn't expect any-one to chase them. From the steam shop, the doughboys could look out the smeared windows and see other locomotives and trains just *standing* there. Hugo, in exasperation at this point, reminded them that their charter was to protect Allied matériel, not to chase anyone. There was some debate as to what exactly matériel was, and if, it was surmised, with rising excite-ment, it was possible that matériel might be *spools of copper wire.*

"Then," said Private Wodziczko, who Hugo had noted was helpful, "to safeguard it, we have to get it back."

"No, we don't," Hugo responded, and was ignored. There was a discus-sion: what was stopping them from taking a train and hunting the Bolos down like yammering whelps?

Of course, the only thing stopping them was that none of them knew how to operate a locomotive.

Hugo, with no small reluctance, said, "My father designed locomo-tives." And then, before he could stop himself, he added, "He was an engi-neer of engineers." He grimaced, but then there were many calls as to how clever that phrase was, and Hugo was grabbed by the shoulders and arms and ordered by Lieutenant Gordon toward the railway yard to find a suit-able locomotive to steal.

3

Hugo protested that he was behind on the new technology, that diesel had displaced steam. He was unfamiliar with the type of coal they used in Russia, Lord only knew what kind of electricity was necessary, and he'd really only worked on the tiniest shunters, shays, and switchers. But when he reached the train yard, his protests died in his throat.

There were a dozen locomotives in various stages of decay, all of them the most rudimentary design. After a moment spent in each cab, he found one that was in working order. He felt a protective tenderness toward it. It had been copied in a hardscrabble way from an 1870s American articulated-compound tender engine and reduced in scale for the three-foot-six-inch local rails. The result looked like a child's drawing of a train, with an endearingly clumsy cowcatcher and a blunderbuss of a smokestack that flared out like an ice-cream cone. The twin domes were as dainty as a lady's wrists, and the boiler couldn't have held fifty gallons of water. The train was adorable.

"It burns *wood*," he murmured, standing by the half-filled and rusty tender as if it contained a litter of mewling kittens. For once, he wished his father were with him.

He exclaimed that a child of nine could operate this train. Delighted that he, not Gordon, had to be in charge, Hugo directed his fellow men to examine the couplings, frail as hairpins. While the gunnery bolted a Lewis machine gun to the single flatcar, Hugo considered for a long moment whom he hated the most: Private Wodziczko. Wodziczko annoyed Hugo courtesy of his unwavering love for, in ascending order, God, his mother, the flag, the world's largest stove, Lieutenant Gordon, his mother, and perhaps Lieutenant Gordon again. Hugo almost skipped like a schoolchild across the engineer's duct, grabbing Wodziczko by the shoulders and forcing him to squat unblinkingly before the steam gauge in the cab, where it would be dirty, hot, and if fortune reigned, dangerous.

There were many other jobs up and down the train—tender handler, rail guard, splitter, brakeman, and so on—which Hugo, dizzy with pleasure, assigned targets for revenge. (There were Finch and Bryzinski, who'd stolen his chocolate rations; Gaulfeld, who had talked about jazz as if it were music; Wassily, who had asked him which breweries made champagne; Parker and Lyons, of disparate heights, who had shamelessly tried to nickname themselves Mutt and Jeff; the list was infinite.)

The train cab was capped tightly, enclosed and stuffy. As the engine heated up, Hugo and his companions—Lieutenant Gordon, Private Wodziczko, and the others crawling past the tender—began to feel adventurous camaraderie. That Gordon had located the previous engineers' tot of vodka stashed above the cab's forward window helped immeasurably.

The train rolled out of the yards and down the only set of tracks that led from town. Which was fortuitous, because the Americans had no idea where they were going. The city quickly fell away, lumber yards and train maintenance pits replaced by tumbledown peasant shacks, and then trees. Hugo felt like an expert, however, as the first distance marker, and then the second, flew past. "Those are versts," he said with pride. "Two-thirds of a mile."

"I know that," said the tiny Wodziczko, whose admiration for Lieutenant Gordon admitted no light to shine on anyone else. "Everyone knows that."

Hugo put his hands on his hips. "You keep watching the pressure gauge, Wodziczko."

"Don't show off, Hugo," said Lieutenant Gordon, rocking on his heels. "And don't give orders, either." Then there was agreement between Gordon and Wodziczko that everyone knew how long a verst was, and to pass the vodka.

The tender was full of stone pine, which burned with fierce heat yet took ages to consume. Hugo's anger at Gordon's lordly ways and Wodziczko's desire to caddy for officers was eclipsed by the excitement of pursuit, even at such a slow pace, across the foreign territory. Hugo—who didn't drink—was bouncing on his engineer's chair, making noises with his cheeks that echoed the sound of the driving wheels. The trees—for that was the entirety of the view—did not whistle by in a blur, but their passage was intoxicating. Hugo pulled the whistle chain, hoping for a basso announcement to the Bolos that the United States was on their tail. Instead, the sound was swallowed as if some vast biblical sea creature had already opened its awesome and awaiting mouth.

The train was rolling through the forest, with tall and dark spruce, alders, and endless pine trees, massive, shoulder to shoulder, frowning giants whose roots clutched at trackless miles of swamp. Hugo wanted to see something else, something other than forest, and yet there was no escape. The tracks curved gently left, or gently right, but still there was no view other than what was quickly becoming unbearable. As the twentieth and twenty-fifth verst markers rumbled by, the forest had begun to work a strange and malicious magic upon the train crew. Without a word on the subject passing from man to man, they realized where the forests of fairy tales had come from.

"Hugo?" Gordon leaned against the engineer's cab with folded arms. "Just for the sake of asking, how do we turn this thing around?"

Hugo swallowed. He fixed his eyes forward, as if the answer were currently eclipsed among the continuously parting curtains of pine trees. "Umm."

"Oh God."

Several versts ahead, the Bolsheviks were having a picnic. There had been a percussive series of explosions in their locomotive's hotbox; then the boiler had slowed to a stop, and disagreements among them percolated about what to do. They could agree only that they were hungry. So out came the cooked chickens, and soon the men who'd taken on the engineering chores were lying shirtless in the sunlight.

The men in the cattle cars were in no mood to fix the train, either. They rolled open the cross-gates and spoke with some villagers from nearby Tundra, who began to file out of the forest burdened with trinkets and good-luck charms that they'd taken to selling to soldiers who occasionally stopped here. Further, flirtation occurred: there were plump farm girls who still had all their teeth, for whom the sight of a man with his own rifle was the height of sophistication.

A strawberry-nosed lieutenant, intoxicated by the promise of attention from one fresh-faced beauty, became bossy, and ordered four of his most handsome brethren to trot back and burn down the bridge they'd just crossed, just in case.

So it was that the doomed train carrying the 339th, Company K, underwent several reversals of fortune. They were at first on the verge of panic, brought on by the unchanging landscape, sunlight flickering through the looming trees, which hugged them as if squeezing out their very breath.

And then—relief! The track ran straight, but the trees fell away—ahead was a canyon, and at its bottom a lovely, sinuous river, and crossing it a trestle bridge perhaps two hundred feet long. Hugo slowed the train, the better to enjoy the change in scenery. He opined, and Lieutenant Gordon agreed, that it would be good to halt here and determine how to get home.

The train eased to a gentle stop. It was a hundred feet over the riverbed, where the waters rushed around blue granite, which came up in tufts and spikes. Hugo looked hopelessly for a reverse driveshaft, examined the bizarre lettering on the dials and switches, and thumbed through his phrase book to see if it contained the words "reverse" or "backward," which it did not.

Meanwhile, the men of Company K took their ease. They smoked on the flatcars, missing Detroit, where eternal summer was to be spent playing stickball, chatting up girls, listening to their fathers plan on Fridays for the end-of-the-shift chimes of the Moskowitz Brewery, which meant one free barrel of beer for the neighborhood. Hugo fussed with his gauges, wiping them down with his kerchief as if that gentle care would cause them to whisper their secrets to him. But he was stalling. The train would not go backward. He listened to the breeze (according to the phrase book, it was a *sirokko*), which was so different from the breeze off the Great Lakes. This one made him perspire. In this his reaction matched his mates'—the alien forest landscape to which summer had come with such violent joy made them all anxious.

At the other end of the bridge, four grizzled men appeared, carrying bales of hay on their backs. They wore derbies, tight woolen jackets with tears at the seams, enormous trousers stolen off more prosperous men, and huge, soft felt shoes. When Hugo saw them, he waved a wobbly, nervous greeting. Hesitantly, they waved back. Then they seemed to consult one another. As if reaching consensus, they suddenly dumped their hay to the tracks and, fast as horses, ran off the way they'd come.

"That's a queer kind of greeting," Hugo said.

"Were those Bolos?" Wodziczko asked.

"You see Bolos everywhere," Hugo sneered. "Why would Bolos be carrying bales of hay? Obviously, they're peasants."

"They were Bolos," Wodziczko insisted.

"Your mother's a Bolo, you toad!" Hugo turned his back on Wodziczko, who was looking in vain for someone to hold him back from attacking. "If you punch me, tiny man," Hugo said calmly, "I'll throw you into the river and you'll hardly make a splash."

Gordon looked for a moment beyond it all, lordly and noble, until, focusing his field glasses, he toppled over. "I'm fine," he murmured, closing his eyes. The empty vodka bottle rolled from the cab and hit the tracks with a sturdy clang before dropping silently into the foaming river.

Hugo stole the field glasses away from the peaceful-looking lieutenant and left the cab. With the rapids so far below him, his head swimming with the height, he gingerly hiked along the footplate, one hand on the boiler, the other on a handrail, until he was smack atop the cowcatcher. He was glad he was not a drinker.

Wodziczko joined him, and for long moments they argued over what exactly was ahead of them. Finally, Hugo declared, "It's a village, definitely. There's a sawmill smokestack. You see?"

Indeed, there was now a thick black column standing at the edge of the field—it was visible even without the field glasses—but why hadn't they seen it before?

It wasn't a sawmill smokestack but a piece of equipment the Bolsheviks had been storing in the village grain house for several weeks: a 4.5-inch howitzer that lobbed sixty-pound shells with reasonable accuracy. They had dragged it on a donkey cart to its present location, had successfully loaded it, and were currently consulting the tattered field manual on how to aim it.

Hugo saw through the field glasses a flash at its tip no brighter than the lighting of a match, then heard a sound like wind rushing over a deep jug. He yelled, "Incoming!" just as the shell shrieked overhead and passed beyond them. It landed in the river with a muffled explosion that sent a spray of shattered rock in all directions.

"Bolos!"

They were under full attack: the hills ahead bubbling over with men pointing guns at them, men of no particular uniform but united by wild aggression, shouting "*Hourra, hourra!*" as they charged.

The men of Company K flailed around the body of the train, looking for shelter, as the first bullets whizzed by them. Gordon arose from his swoon, vomited with some efficiency, and ushered his men as best he could. Within moments, all were safely behind the locomotive, which provided several tons of protection. "To the Lewis!" Gordon cried, and two men immediately fell to the flatbed on which the Lewis was mounted, one to fire and the other to feed the bullets through. Alas, their first volley was also their last, for there was a horrible sound of riveting and ricochets: the same locomotive that shielded them from the Bolsheviks was also directly in the line of their own fire. "Stop! Cease! Stop!"

In the silence, Hugo found his voice, and cried, as if someone might hear him and obey, *"Pozhaluysta, nie streliayte—my devstvennitsy!,"* which wasn't actually effective. Instead, another deep sound, a wheeze, almost musical, and then the screech of another sixty-pound shell, which fell long again, bringing relief, but only for a moment: it had landed on the riverbank behind them. The result was a smoking crater six feet deep, and surrounding it, twisted metal still glowing with heat, the now ruined railroad tracks home.

This was when the Bolsheviks returned to their original plan of burning down the bridge entirely. The hay bales were to be distributed among the wooden beams of the scaffolding, and shouts went up for more paraffin wax with which to ignite them.

To their credit, the 339th had recovered their wits, and had begun to return fire. They were flat against the top of the engineer's cab, and on the narrow gallery by the boiler, in excellent adaptation to the landscape. The Mosin-Nagant rifles, however, were not the weapons of choice at such distant range. As soon as the Bolos realized what was being fired, they shared a hearty laugh and went back to work without worry.

With the way to retreat a mass of smoldering ruins and the way ahead just about to be set afire, and their own arms roughly useless, the Americans fell to bickering. Eventually, it was settled that Hugo was to blame for their situation, because he hadn't known how to make the train go backward. He wiped his brow with his kerchief, and it came away red. He'd been grazed—by rock debris, by a bullet, it was hard to tell—and when he stared at the blood with some disbelief, that, too, caused grousing. Wodziczko rolled his eyes.

"I'm wounded!"

"You were just *pipped*. We're going to die. We hate you."

The normal soldier's lament struck at a man's odor or ancestry; a simple declaration of hatred was startlingly direct. As much as he felt guilty (Wodziczko's accusations stung worse than the wound to his forehead), Hugo also hated everyone on the train. He reached a terrible conclusion. If he was going to his death, he would take them along. He released the horseshoe brakes, teased the throttle open, and felt the pleasant shudder of the wheels unlocking.

The doughboys were startled, of course—and as a bleeding Hugo smiled at them all, he pointed straight ahead. His face, darkened with dust and blood, looked as if it belonged to some minor bureaucratic demon, a Malebranchist devoted to stirring a shallow pond of fire with a short stick. "We're going *that* way," he hissed.

"Hello!" Lieutenant Gordon cried. "Yes. Yes indeed!"

Hugo looked toward him with confusion—he'd hoped for some recriminations before they died—but even Private Wodziczko was now pumping his rifle in the air.

"Over the Top!" Wodziczko yelled back to the men on the flatcars. "We're going Over the Top!"

They had no specific war cry, so all they did was bellow whatever guttural noise came first and best, a few of them crying the marines' E-EE-YAH-YIP! Hugo, surrendering to the madness, managed to yell his single aggressive phrase, *"Pozhaluysta, nie streliayte—my devstvennitsy!"*

The Bolsheviks, for their part, pricked up their ears. Then they had trouble believing their eyes. The train was coming *toward* them? Toward the burning hay bales? Toward two hundred troops and heavy artillery? For the first time, they began to wonder who exactly was running this train. Not the French. Perhaps the British? Impossible.

With no concern for the steam-valve pressure, Hugo brought the train to a full and majestic roar. As it passed over the bridge, Bolsheviks were flying outward like ripples across a pond. Several clung to the bridge's superstructure, and the men of the 339th fired their rifles through the smoke, perhaps in some cases actually hitting Bolos, for there were sudden cries and hard-to-place clattering sounds.

Around the bend was the other train, Bolos above and below it on the hillside. The Lewis team fired into them like a rough-house gang, mowing down armed men without even needing to aim. It was a blur, bodies scattering with the chaos of billiard balls, the train chuffing along for a glorious several seconds, the whole of the 339th concerned with killing as many of the enemy as possible, until Hugo happened to look straight ahead, with a gasp, as they rammed directly into the last cattle car of the train parked ahead of them.

They were going no faster than a brisk stroll. Still, the impact lifted the Bolos' last car off its axle boots, and sent the Americans' locomotive aslant, where it ran senselessly until Hugo fumbled with the emergency full-stop.

The Bolsheviks fell into a nonstrategic retreat. Their train cars emptied, and the men ran as fast as their secondhand boots could carry them. Within minutes, the Americans faced no enemies except the dead who were lying across the hillside. There were also two villagers who'd been machine-gunned to death by Company K.

The Americans felt terrible about this, but at the same time were so happy to be alive, and so excited to have driven back the Bolos, and, further, they were brimming with such confusion about the propriety of meeting villagers, and so nervous about speaking the Russian from their dirty yellow phrase books, that a round of apologies was never quite delivered.

Instead, it was noticed that the village of Tundra was next to a verst marker, number thirty-eight. Out came the Brownie cameras, and then, in groups of five, the men posed around it, holding aloft captured Bolo rifles, cat-fur hats, broken-backed novels in Cyrillic. The enemy ammunition for the Howitzer that had been fired at the 339th caused some consternation—each shell was stamped MADE IN USA. At first, this seemed like some sort of trick. Then it was remembered that the United States had indeed outfitted Russian troops, before the disintegration of the country and the rise of its latest ruling tide.

The men of Detroit remained in the village nervously, eyeing the bodies, waiting for recriminations that never came. Finally, Hugo, in the same bold spirit that once caused him to stride manfully across the parquet floors of the Grosse Ile debutante ball to ask the exquisite Missy Farmer to dance, approached a small knot of elders. His phrase book was gone. So he was left with his two lines of Russian, one about headquarters. He considered the other phrase for a moment, the one about being soldiers, drop your weapons, and he realized he could bisect it, and then patted his chest. He swept his hand behind him to include the rest of Company K. *"My devstvennitsy,"* he said, and then modified it, *"My devstvennitsy ameri-kanski,"* as if announcing that they had an official designation, a respectable nationality, a job description, might explain that they would do no further harm.

In response, a startled silence, as if Hugo had paraded a bright-red calf before them. The village *burmistr* puffed through his whiskers and tried to catch his constables' eyes without letting his surprise be seen. It was a very private admission for these foreigners. Then one ancient *starosta* and another whispered through cracked teeth, hiding mouths behind twisted hands, the *babay* veiling their words behind their stained summer scarves, that perhaps in America such a thing was discussed openly, as a sign of innocence. Weren't the *starosty* proud that their own children were also virgins?

Soon there seemed to be a thaw in relations. The soldiers' guns were nonetheless stared at, so they couldn't quite put them down with their packs. Eventually, some of the village girls began to dance with each other, looking over their shoulders to make sure their gaiety was being noticed. A head functionary of the village tentatively asked for permission to salvage the cattle cars, and when he and his friends found food and drink and horses, they were happy enough that they even claimed that, yes indeed, they could use the antiques and spools of copper wire. For the most part, they seemed not to mind their casualties (through a combination of pidgin Russian, Polish, and hand gestures, they indicated that the dead men— two brothers—had been drunks and no one much liked them anyway), and they invited the Americans to help them feast on the remaining roast chicken.

Here ended the first battle between the United States and Russia. Of course, the 339th had to find a way home (they would walk the thirty-eight versts over the course of two days). And eventually they would lay a whole host of curses upon the Russian peasantry, but for now, there was a tentative celebration between two unlikely groups, from Detroit and Tundra. It did not last into the evening, and no one passed a jug of *samogon* or flung open the doors of a blockhouse to the Americans.

Hugo, among others, noted that on the outskirts was a small group of men with the blackest beards. They did not smile, they did not participate. Instead, they laid heavy cotton blankets atop the dead bodies and weighted them with small stones, in a cross formation. They kissed each rock before allowing it to join the pattern. And when they looked back up, it was to stare at the men of Company K with utterly unreadable faces.

But they were among the few, and were mostly ignored. Instead, Hugo's diary for this day ends with a description of cheer and greetings. He mentions how stocky and underwashed, yet strong and friendly were the peasant girls ("They are as dirty and rough-skinned as potatoes, and such is their shape as well"). The entry ends with a fastidiously written and extremely bad poem on the Northern Lights ("One cannot bear malice / Under such enlightened borealis," etc.), and then, in a final nighttime scrawl, a note that the remainder of the 339th was on its way, with the 310th Engineers, an overwhelming force of five thousand nine hundred men to overthrow the Red Menace. "This will be so easy!" he wrote, and "Moscow by the spring!," before falling to his bedroll on this cool, refreshing Russian evening, a month before the first spidery touch of winter.

4

Corporal Lee Duncan was a man of no newly erupted talents since his audition in San Francisco, unless one counted lying. Throughout basic training, when he was asked where he was from, he murmured that he was an orphan, and though it wasn't an answer, it was a kind of answer, and his fellow enlisted men tended to leave him alone.

He smiled sometimes, to keep people from talking about him, but he was now aware that to dream did not mean to conquer. To succeed—for instance, to be for a few seconds a Four Minute Man—did not mean it would stick, the love of a mother for a son could be like turpentine, ambition was for chumps, there was no actual value to the universe, etc.

His glowering, along with his mournful guitar ballads ("Greensleeves," and many tunes that sounded like dirges for funerals held at sea), the commanding jawline, the cheekbones, the newly serious eyes, made men and women alike think he must harbor awesome secrets.

In San Francisco, he had signed up for the Air Service, since a reptilian part of his brain still recognized that at least the uniforms were vivid. He enlisted under the name Leland Duncan to honor his father and anger his mother. He was sent to Kelly Field in Texas for basic training, and then the School of Fire in Oklahoma, where he was put in a motorboat and told to shoot a Vickers at untethered balloons while the boat made tight figure-eights. He did not hit a target even once.

On the train to Mineola Field, Long Island, he sat with his nose to the window. The train was delayed because an ammunition explosion had blown the previous train off the tracks and into a lake. Those shattered railway cars each contained eight horses, and they were slowly sinking. There was apparently nothing to be done for them, but for six hours, from the late afternoon, through sunset, and into the night, Lee heard the horses crying out. At first there were many different types of whinnies and moans, and by the end, just one final horse, voice torn, making a braying sound of terror as the waters rose up and percolated over the carriages.

Lee did not know why it had once seemed important to be in the movies.

When it was safe to move on, the train rumbled ahead. But he heard the horses every day for a month.

In Aldershot, England, a man asked him if he knew he looked rather like Wallace Reid, and he felt both devastated and proud.

He learned about airplane maintenance, how to take apart motors and machine guns, all the signals for *réglage,* and then, on the last day, it was arranged that he be attacked by a dog.

The dog was a captured German shepherd named Goose, and he had been trained as a killing machine. It was unlikely that any of the men would encounter such a dog in the field, or so they were told, but it was important to know how to survive their ferocious attack.

Goose was black and tan, barrel-chested, with tall black ears, one of which had been perforated by a bullet. The enlisted men stood in the center of a field, with protective padding on their hands and groins and around their throats, and they were told to go limp when Goose attacked. "Drop facedown," screamed the sergeant major, "fingers laced behind the neck. Thus, if a Boche dog goes for your jugular, he will only bite off your fingers."

Lee was the twelfth in line. He watched as the eleven previous men were lined up, as they decided either to stand their ground (and were attacked and knocked down) or to run as fast as they could (and were attacked and knocked down). Goose didn't make a single sound. He behaved as if he neither enjoyed nor hated his duty, but saw it as a necessity.

At first, being knocked to the ground appealed to Lee. It would feel like something.

But then he thought it couldn't be much of a life, could it, knocking people down? By this date, hadn't everyone had enough of cruelty? Further, he remembered he had saved his biscuit ration from that morning, and still had it in his pocket.

"Duncan!"

Lee strapped on the protective pads, palming the biscuit in one glove, and then stood his ground. Goose was led back into place, fifteen yards away. Lee looked into the dog's eyes. They were black, absorbing all light and emanating nothing in return. Lee inclined his head. He gave a small half smile. He could not be the only creature in the universe who wanted things softer than himself not to suffer. Was it possible, maybe, to flirt with this dog?

"Good boy," he said.

Three seconds later, Goose had knocked him to the ground and was barking savagely, an overwhelming and terrifying racket that caused his handler to break form and race for him. Lee submissively got into position, facedown, hands behind his head. His biscuit slid out of his glove, and Goose picked it up between his teeth, and gingerly, as if carrying a fresh egg, brought it to his trainer's feet. Then he sat down and looked toward Lee, with a clear look of *j'accuse.*

Lee drew extra latrine duty that night.

He went to Paris. He was in the City of Light for a grand total of twelve hours. He spent two of them walking in unexpected humidity (every other day it had rained), thirty minutes sitting in a park, fifteen minutes flirting with a woman, and the remaining time pressed against her in an apartment with open windows, high ceilings, white plaster walls displaying lithographs of Italian villas, and bunches of dried flowers that were hung upside down over the great sleigh bed. She had a half dozen easels with half-finished egg-tempera still lifes, gesso stains on the tables, unstretched canvases in stacks, and when he'd undressed her, she told him to mind the razor blades she'd dropped on the carpet.

Since she never finished her paintings, she made love with great passion (she said that explained it, but she said many things).

He tried to tell her his name approximately sixteen times. Touching her finger to his lips, shaking her head, she said, *"C'est la guerre,"* as if this also were an explanation, rather than just a phrase that amused her.

Afterward, she pushed back the bangs of her short hair and evaluated him. She told him she had picked him up because he was plainly so sad, and she planned to leave him happier than when she had found him.

"That," she said, pointing to the place their bodies still touched, "was like this." She displayed her hand, tucked into a fist. "What's going through your heart?"

"I don't think I have one. I wish I did."

Her cheeks pulsed, for she was going to burst out laughing. "Oh, but you do," she said, and she pointed to her own. It was said for the sound of it.

"How did that happen?" he whispered. The more serious he was, the more serious she looked in response. "You shouldn't do that," he said.

"And you shouldn't be sad," she said. She pushed away and walked across the room, shift trembling about her hips, and she opened a dresser drawer. She withdrew something, and she looked at herself in the mirror as if wanting to catch herself in the act of going a step too far.

She returned to the bed. She gazed at the pair of finger puppets mournfully, and passed them to him, resigned as if she were handing him a revolver with one bullet in it. The French, with their wellspring of such things, had a name for gifts like hers: *les jouets pour les jouets,* toys for the toyed-with. Because, for the most part, if you weren't an amused woman of Paris, they truly had tremendous sentimental value.

They looked tiny and soft in his palm. "What are these?"

She cuddled against him and explained that the provenance of the dolls was crucial: they had to be given, never purchased. They proved that somewhere a girl loved you. Not of course in this case, she said, for she and he were beyond such things—she looked to see if he understood the twinkle in her eye—but look at the puppets again, she continued. Made of cotton batting wrapped in cloth, worn around the neck like a religious medallion, they came in a pair, a boy and a girl, attached by a single frail-looking string.

The dolls were French, and, as with all things French, the parable behind them was about love. There had been an air raid, a crowd had fled to the shelter, only two survived: *these two lovers.* Or, when a different message was being sent: an air raid, and these two *died hand in hand.* In either case, the story was about the melancholy, redemptive power of *l'amour.*

Lee heard all this delivered in her dry tone, which reminded him faintly of the film magazines he'd read so long ago. Every word she spoke suggested a different, entirely opposite meaning, but she was being neither ironic nor diplomatic, yet something entirely beyond his experience: jaded.

"And what do you think?" she finally asked.

The posture of the dolls was perplexing to him—given that there was a war on, and the dolls were meant to reassure men that their girls would always be true, shouldn't the boy and the girl look *equally* in love? Shouldn't the girl—her name was Nanette—not be so evasive-looking, so ready to prance out of town at the slightest breeze? Shouldn't the boy have a less ready-to-be-disappointed look on his face? How soothing was that for a man going to the front?

"Really, Corporal, what do you think?" she whispered, eyes drifting closed.

One boy, one girl, a string between them. How frail it felt to attempt one small gesture encapsulating a commotion of feelings: faith and hope, and perhaps some small amount of love, made featherlight. He felt an unfamiliar blossoming in his throat. He whispered to her, "Anyone who has faith in me is a sucker." He tossed the puppets at her. They landed on her shoulder.

Which made the laughter she had been holding in finally burst out. Lee kept turning his head and twisting around in the bed, attempting to look sincere enough that she might stop laughing.

An hour later, he was in uniform and on the street, foot-slogging to the train station.

And the puppets? They were there, around his neck, and occasionally he fingered them, looking as puzzled as if he'd found seashells on a mountaintop.

The American Expeditionary Force shipped him to Le Havre, then Amanty, then Ourches, France, where he served in the gunnery of the 135th Aero Squadron. No matter how get-along he acted, the men were frequently irritable in response, and not because *c'est la guerre.*

The 135th was an observer squadron, a designation that made its members insecure. They were known as the Statue of Liberty Squadron, which irked them, in that it was accurate: a statue stood still and watched life pass it by. Unlike the famous 94th Hat in the Ring Squadron, which was designated for pursuit—and dogfights, and the making of aces, the 135th did not tend to kill Germans. The 135th was to take photographs, count troops, direct artillery—in short, its work was painfully short of glory.

Lee overheard officers complaining about the very brass on their lapels: a *pursuit*-squadron officer wore a badge with two wings; an *observer* squadron's badge had one wing. As if the pilots would just fly in circles. Maddening!

Though there were manuals to teach them French, and classes in assembling every knob and sprocket of the Croisset bombsight, and training missions in SPADS culminating in whip stalls and sideslips, and enough engine failures to make every mission dangerous, there was something missing. There was no formal instruction in how to look like a hero.

They tended to lean on measures of ferocity—their mascots. The late

Sunnyside

Baron von Richthofen had had a huge dog, Moritz, and so the 135th found themselves a dog. Her name was Banjo, and she was by nature timid rather than fierce. She did not like beer, and when presented with an effigy of the Kaiser, she tried to run away instead of attacking it. This barely mattered—they poked her with sticks a few times, and she snarled, and that was enough.

Mostly, Banjo hid in a packing crate outside the mess tent. When a leather-coated ace from the 27th or the 94th or the 213th—pursuit squadrons—visited, the officers showed him Banjo, and his habits were meanwhile studied as if he were a little-known species of gazelle.

Upon the aces' departure, the officers of the 135th shunned the chocolate bars they'd been issued and sought out white chocolate with almonds (Eddie Rickenbacker's favorite), and they played galloping dominoes (favored by Frank Luke). They wore wristwatches with radium detailing (as did William A. Bishop), but also bandaged their dials at night to show they were wise to air raids, a suggestion during a visit from Lufbery. The cook went on drunken lemon-extract binges, claiming antecedent in the life of some ace or another, but then he was doubted and sacked.

One morning, Banjo disappeared. Mascots were sometimes kidnapped by other companies, or they died. Lee asked where she had gone, and there were shrugs all around, and so he shrugged, too. Life came with detours and body blows. He had wanted to be in Hollywood; he was in France; he could say *c'est la guerre* as needed. He played cards with the right kind of fatalism, he drank and passed the bottle quickly.

With many quiet hours to himself (his duties, as we will see, were to maintain the guns of one particular DH 4) he began to realize that his ambition had been a friend to him. Without it, he was rather lonely.

He courted officers. They reminded him of movie stars. In his early weeks, he sat in on their discussions at the Grass Shack, a hut with an upright piano and several card tables. He rarely seemed to volunteer anything, but somehow made known, as if by osmosis, how to slick back one's hair, how to have one's collar stand upright, how the cheekbones could be made to pop. Since the boundaries between enlisted men and officers were but vaguely enforced, Leland was seen at first as an interesting natural resource. His downfall was swift; it involved women.

Frenchwomen were terrifying. Everyone knew *one* particular thing about Frenchwomen. There was a song about it. Someone in the Grass Hut began to sing it one night, and the rest joined in:

That's the wrong way to tickle Marie
That's the wrong way to kiss
That was the right way back in the USA
But Marie expects bliss

It ended with shocking news:

Good bye to your Aunt Tilly
Hello, savoir faire
If you want to know the right way to tickle Marie
You've got to kiss her down there

The men of the 135th were as disturbed by the prospect of kissing Marie as they were fighting a skyful of Fokkers, but they sang as if the power of their voices might render them skillful. It was roundly agreed that Marie and her kin were impossible to please, that no man alive could really win any woman's heart, love was a game of chance best played by the incredulous or the suicidal, it was bridge with traitorous partners, scoring kept by an idiot, a marked deck.

Capping the subject, one reedy lieutenant said, "The Hindenburg Line, I say, is *only* impenetrable."

Throughout, eyes began to flick toward Leland, who said nothing, simply sipping at his thin beer like anyone else.

Yes, it was roundly agreed, any man, Allied or otherwise, with the Norse god–like requirements to ignite a woman's fancy would be fêted into the night, made an honorary colonel, celebrated in madrigals, and within his own lifetime, all legal tender would feature studious engravings of the many angles of his heroic face.

A captain with jug ears and a shoelace mustache was the first to see the things Leland sported as if they were regulation issue: the finger puppets.

There they were, Nanette and her boy, as if they had grown there, as if they were appendages, and the captain knew, as did all the other men who fell silent upon gazing at Leland, that this enlisted man, the one with the sad eyes and endless cheekbones, had walked into the aerodrome with a better story than anyone had as yet accumulated, after many months in the war. No one asked if he had really gotten the puppets from a girl, no one teased him about buying them himself, no one quizzed him for details, because the response would be too painful. There was no doubt that

Leland knew the right way to tickle Marie. Conversation drifted, throats cleared, the late time noted, and the room emptied.

And so, for a while at least, he continued to be lonely, until he pursued the friendship that almost killed him and brought him the love of his life.

5

The film business was pioneered by salesmen, dry goods, men with a single suit and shoes they had to share with younger brothers, men who had come from the wind-blown steppes of Eastern Europe during lulls between pogroms. They believed in fortune as if she were a statue, like justice, say, or a goddess of the harvest. As they acclimated to American ways, they determined that fortune was as fickle as opinion, and as easily offended as a chorus girl.

Not one of them believed in the sustainability of the motion picture, just that it was a commodity whose popularity was expanding. When it, like all commodities, was in its sunset, in a year or in ten, there would be hammers or stucco or ten-ton blocks of granite to sell next.

But the numbers in 1917 were unexpected: box office was up. Even though everyone in the country had seen movies, they all wanted to see more of them. At Paramount Studios, Adolph Zukor, who had owned Mary Pickford at one point, let loose a trial balloon, charging exhibitors a percentage of the box-office profits, *and they let him.* He was puzzled by this, because he had thought there was too much competition out of his control. But then an inspiration: he asked for a complete list of films from overseas distributed in the United States that month. The number? Zero. A couple of years beforehand, perhaps half the films had come from Europe. But Europe was otherwise engaged, and so now America was the center of this particular universe. Which fascinated Zukor. People would pay more to see movies, and see them more often if the studios provided them. Studios could continually adjust terms to their advantage, and there was still plenty of money to go around.

Zukor did not live in Hollywood much—he was suspicious of the weather, and preferred New York. But he was at the Paramount studios in the summer of 1918, because he sensed yet another change in the market-place—in other words, *fortune*—and he wanted to lay his finger on her pulse.

Only forty-five years old, Zukor nonetheless was stooped like a buzzard, as if youth were a folly he had defeated. He wore Victorian high-collar suits, and walked through the lot so quietly, his presence striking such panic, that his nickname was "the Creeping Jesus."

When he was driven from his office to the flats of Hollywood, he saw the first peacock displays of wealth, houses put flush to the road, each of them a tribute to an individual's dream of trumping his forefathers. "I want Monticello, only better," Julian Eltinge had said, and it was made so, high over Silver Lake. All around Sunset there were construction sites and exotic gardens springing up around them, reminders of the Taj Mahal, Versailles, Sunnyside, Windsor Castle, Schloss Neuschwanstein, each seeming to have over its roof, over the scaffolding and armies of Portuguese construction workers, hanging in the blue and pleasant sky itself, a single broad question mark following: "Will we get away with this?" Zukor imagined the almost unspeakable pleasures, as a Hungarian Jew, of building a house exactly like Buda Castle, *only better.*

He would not actually do this—he had little feeling for architecture—but he enjoyed the feeling of success, and he was troubled only by one problem: actors. Actors were paid entirely too much money.

One afternoon, William McAdoo visited Zukor at the Famous Players–Lasky lot near the top of Vine Street, where Hollywood started to rise into the wild foothills. McAdoo had been visiting Los Angeles with some frequency since the Liberty Loan Drive in part to drum up support for the Fourth and Fifth Liberty Loan tours (scheduled for November and January), but also because of the United States government's production of *Pershing's Crusaders* and its sequels.

Zukor had spent the previous day determining, via his web of informants, that McAdoo had never been to a studio before. So he arranged a tour. It was as devious as any of Zukor's arrangements. By the time McAdoo was led to Zukor's office, he had passed through sixteenth-century Venice and a seraglio in which harem girls sprawled and read *Photoplay* while the focus pullers attempted to keep them in frame. He had also seen a barroom brawl in which Hobart Kintey was thrown through a window (it was spun sugar, McAdoo learned), threaded his way through a crowd wearing togas, run into the dizzying Billie Burke (who had kissed him on the cheek), and thoroughly lost his balance.

Zukor's office was a sixty-by-forty-foot room with twenty-foot beamed ceilings, and walls painted with gold flake. There were late-Baroque paintings, copies of Titian, on each wall, and at both ends was a fireplace that a man could stand up in. His desk was as far from the entry door as possible, which meant that McAdoo was in the awkward position of saying hello first upon arrival, then having to walk approximately fifty-five feet across a single Lavar Kerman rug that had taken an entire Anatolian village sixteen years to weave, before he could shake Zukor's hand.

McAdoo sat down in a chair before Zukor's desk—his next mistake, because Zukor had designed the furniture so that no guest could sit back and still see his host over the rise of his Brobdingnagian desk.

America, via the Committee for Public Information, had produced three films, which Zukor had arranged to have distributed, gratis, as a show of patriotism. This led McAdoo to his uncomfortable slant before Zukor. McAdoo took out a piece of paper, which he smoothed out on his knee. He could barely see it at first, with his eyes still pinging from the dazzle of radium lights, and he twitched his nose, recently treated to the ozone smell of bolting electricity. He adjusted his glasses.

"Let's see here. *Under Four Flags:* $63,946.48. *Pershing's Crusaders:* $181,741.69. And then there's *America's Answer.* That one has grossed, as of a week ago, $185,144.30." He looked up and raised his eyebrows.

Zukor nodded. "Yes?"

"So where is it?"

"Where is what?"

"The $430,832.47."

Every smile cost Zukor's face five dollars, it was said. He produced the sympathetic look one would give the good-hearted simpleton whose father was the town drunk. "The exhibitors keep most of that."

"Sixty-five percent. I've read the contract. The distributor gets the rest. That would be us."

"That would be Paramount."

"No, that would be us," McAdoo said, pleasantly. "You've donated your company's services to the war effort, as per your terms of contract with the Division of Film. I'm sure you wouldn't be violating those terms."

"Certainly not," Zukor said. "Are you questioning my patriotism, sir?"

"Do I sound like it? Gosh, I hope not." McAdoo clapped his hands together, a man who knew things could be worked out. "Because withholding what belongs to the government during wartime would be treasonous, of course."

Zukor pushed a button on a desk and called into his intercom, "Send in Miss Zoe Chambers." The far door opened. McAdoo heard the sound of heels shuffling across the carpet, and then there appeared one of the ten most beautiful women he had ever seen, blushing with fear, and smoothing out her skirt upon her arrival at Zukor's desk.

"Miss Chambers. Please fetch us the books relating to the Creel Committee films."

She hesitated. "Which volumes, Mr. Zukor?"

"All of them. Of course."

Miss Chambers's eyes widened in anticipation that the slightest delay would have unspeakable repercussions. She was relieved that Zukor had not called her into the mauve room.

When she was gone, Zukor said, distractedly, "The Creel pictures haven't earned a cent."

"Excuse me?"

"They've been disasters."

"They've earned hundreds of thousands, Mr. Zukor."

"I'm afraid they haven't," he sighed. "When you strike the exhibitor's cut, that leaves you with a much smaller percentage. After the studio expenses that are nonspecific to the films, we actually took a loss—a very small, to be sure, but a highly patriotic loss—on your films."

McAdoo looked as if Zukor had slipped him a rubber penny. "I find that hard to believe."

"It's a complex business."

"I'm paying for a war right now. That's complex business."

"That might not be as complex as making movies."

McAdoo leaned back in his chair. The chair back was more distant than he had judged, and the angle he was sitting in an obtuse slouch, so he returned to hovering at the edge of his seat. "All right, then, Mr. Zukor. Explain how our handing you three free films, which brought in almost half a million dollars—and did I mention they were free?—cost you money."

Zukor talked. He steepled his fingers, tapping them against one another when making an especially important point. He explained that, though the negative had been gratis, the cost of producing positives, coupled with trade-press advertising, could not be separated from the normal business of running Paramount. When 70 percent of the drying racks were running, say, the latest Arbuckle, and the other 30 percent reels of *America's Answer,* they could not ask their technicians to forgo 30 percent of their pay. There were volatile chemicals whose price had risen, not that

Zukor was complaining about such a thing, since the start of the war. The cost of a foot of orthochromatic negative film was now a halfpenny more. The electricity that spun the drums did not differentiate between commercial and patriotic pursuits. There were loans against perceived box-office profits, which were used to pay salaries, which were up.

"Then there's distribution," he sighed, as if it were an impolite cousin who he wished would cease coming to dinner. "Say I have the wagon taking two reels of the new Arbuckle, two of the Geraldine Farrar—we distribute her, even though we don't produce her, so that's an entirely different system of accounting—and also one reel of *Pershing's Crusaders* across town." And from there he was off on incidental and incremental costs, recoverable expenditures, single and multiple outlays, technological development monies, splendid schedules that made accounting of the distance between "net" and "gross" rather an all-night party with silly hats on.

It is safe to say that Zukor's explanation was accurate, but not quite complete. Instead, as he spoke, he was constructing dreams from the ground up—the way workers in Hancock Park were erecting ersatz Xanadus—capped with a giant question mark: "Will the government actually let me get away with this?"

Miss Chambers returned, pushing a library cart heaped with leather-jacketed accounting ledgers. She rolled it across the fifty-five feet of rug, cart wheels squeaking like, McAdoo observed, a rat.

Zukor, meanwhile, felt expansive. "I do know why the films failed," he said.

"Oh, do you?"

"Honestly, yes. They had no hero."

"What! The United States is the hero."

"That's abstract. The audience wants an adventure."

"Adventure?" McAdoo blinked. "The largest war in human history strikes me as adventurous, Mr. Zukor."

"It's abstract. Does the boy get the girl?"

"What boy?"

"The boy. Does he get the girl? Do they get married?"

McAdoo looked at him blankly.

"Does the wayward son succeed? Are mother and child reunited? Does the snob get his comeuppance?"

"That's not what these films were ever about, not when you agreed to distribute them, and not now."

"Does the princess get rescued?" The hoods of Zukor's gin-colored eyes lowered. "Is evil punished?"

"Of course evil is punished!"

"I'll grant you that. But it's not on the screen yet, and you can't see it, so no one cares."

"You're a clever man, Mr. Zukor." Somehow, they were no longer discussing where the money had gone. "You're describing what makes people go to your films, not ours."

"My films make money."

"Ours did, too. I think the story is in those ledgers."

"Which you're welcome to audit, as per the contract."

McAdoo nodded. "I'll have my men come by tomorrow."

"The books will be here for them." Zukor stretched out his limp hand for McAdoo to shake. "I'll be sure to let them tour the studio first."

Standing, McAdoo made a note to himself: try to find some auditors who didn't care about the film business. One hug from Billie Burke had thrown him off course. Lord only knew what Zukor could throw in the path of a pair of twenty-two-year-old junior clerks from Bethesda.

Zukor watched McAdoo go. Finally, Miss Chambers spoke.

"Will that be all, sir?"

But she had barely managed the entire sentence before Zukor had pushed the button under his desk. A bookshelf swung open. Behind it was the mauve room. His eyes swept inexorably from the hidden chamber to Miss Chambers with a kind of parched joy. "There's one more thing," he said, and then opened and closed his mouth, taking in her expression with delight.

Outside, McAdoo walked to the front gate slowly. He was furious, and had no place for the anger to go. Hanging over the gate was the enlistment flag that every studio displayed, with one star for every employee now serving. Paramount's flag had 220 stars, and McAdoo watched a man in overalls standing on a ladder to pin another star up.

He had no other destination in mind. Yet. But a car waited for him, courtesy of Zukor. He considered taking a taxi, but then thought that being spied on wouldn't be that bad.

He climbed into the Cadillac's backseat and asked to be taken to La Brea, the Chaplin Studios.

6

In Russia, the scaffolding of democracy was being erected. First, General Poole sent a message to the War Office. It read: "I occupied Archangel today." He added, "The people simply went wild with joy to an extent almost beyond imagination."

Then he ordered the reopening of the factories, which caused sighs of relief among the populace, until they realized he was concerned with one specific job. Three local carpenters were called up, and the remaining eight thousand workers were sent back home for another day.

A sawmill was set to work, two dozen boards were planed, and then the doors of the metals warehouse were thrown open and, under the watch of Royal Scots, a ten-pound box of nails was signed out, along with four hammers and four saws; then the warehouse was bolted shut again, and British troops took their materials to the public square.

The public square, such as it was, faced the cathedral. There were no trees or fountains (impossible in the winter months) or benches or public monuments, just a dirty patch of earth surrounded by empty flagpoles and a scruffy assortment of market vendors' pushcarts. Over that long afternoon, Poole's men put together a kiosk. A Tommy known to be a fastidious calligrapher printed in Cyrillic the exciting invitation that was finally nailed to the top: JOIN THE SLAVO-BRITISH LEGION!

This would be the first sign of a new society congealing: an army to promote its self-defense. The only Allied dissenter to this scheme had been France. Approximately fifteen minutes after Poole's Slavo-British Legion recruitment desk had been started, a platoon of *poilus* assembled a much sturdier and better-painted platform. Surmounting it was an eight-color stone-lithographed poster of impressive size, declaring, in French, "Perhaps the French Foreign Legion Will Have You." The illustration was of a legionnaire standing by a sand dune. This concept—a desert—was so alien to the locals, and the appeal so disdainful—the French deigning to let Russians into their army—that the recruiter ran out of applications by sunset.

The Slavo-British Legion, within a single day, had five thousand volunteers who could all read and write, they said, who swore allegiance to the new government, and who had to pass but a simple medical exam before their training could begin. It was such a rudimentary exam (open mouth, count teeth, open shirt, tap chest, open trousers, check for syphilis) that—fatally—no one thought to simplify it a touch further.

"This afternoon, we inaugurated the Slavo-British Legion," Poole wrote in his next telegram. "It is imperative that we push on to Moscow. Next I will begin the government."

The reaction among the Imperial General Staff was bemused, for they were wondering if he would next bridge the Azores and cure typhoid.

Still later that afternoon, around seven o'clock, General Poole, who did not sense his time was running short, introduced the town council to their new leaders. This was not an invasion, he explained, but a restoration of ideals. The new president of North Russia and supreme commander of Archangel was now Mr. Nicholas Chaikovsky, whom no one had heard of.

Poole stepped aside at this point ("Please cable Headquarters and tell them the government has been started, and re-emphasize the importance of Moscow by spring"), and exited with his men, for he was going to reopen the opera house. He understood that there had never been a production of Gilbert and Sullivan in North Russia—not *The Mikado*, not *Penzance*, not *Pinafore*—and he aimed to plant that particular flag himself.

This left the administrators and bureau chiefs to meet their new leader. Nicholas Chaikovsky came out from behind a curtain and bowed before the council. He had the white mane of an aged Viking, and blue eyes that flashed with confidence. Apparently, he had been a member of the Constituent Assembly in tsarist Russia, or he was a religious leader—his credentials, if pressed upon, tended to splay. He had spent twenty-five years in exile. He spoke English, believed in God, and was able to produce testimonials from a couple of Russians who had pined for his return. Further, he spoke well of capitalism, so the United States sent him into Archangel.

Which needed him. Sallow-faced ministers explained: in the wake of counterrevolutions, the town had been sacked as effectively as if worked over by second-story men. There was no money. The influx of soldiers overburdened the poor sewage system, the ground all over town was covered with excrement and effluvia, and the townspeople tended to throw dead farm animals into the streets, where packs of wild dogs fought over them.

Chaikovsky invited every minister in the room to dinner at his palace. The delight at this invitation was somewhat undercut by the discovery that

Chaikovsky had given himself a palace, but he was an excellent host, his speeches were persuasive, he insinuated there was a great deal of power to be shared, he loved the people of Russia, things hadn't been the same since 1873, but soon they would be.

Two mornings later, the streetcar conductors vanished.

Rather, they elected as a unit to be sick. All being sick together struck them as the most genteel way to be noticed, and perhaps there would be soup.

Chaikovsky ordered the conductors back to work at the same time that Poole ordered Allied soldiers to duty. The soldiers made it to the electric-trolley station first, and the workers who appeared soon after stared in disbelief as their jobs were apparently taken from them by occupying forces.

One of the men so drafted was Pfc. Hugo Black, who had spent the previous several days walking back from Verst 38. He was in a mood. His protests that he knew nothing about streetcars weren't believed, since it was quite obvious he had already operated an entire *train*. Grudgingly, he studied the schematics of the trolley car, which had been copied from a Key Route design in America, with overhead single-phase electricity—a fundamental system, just what the DUR was running in Detroit.

Hugo noticed screw holes by the gearbox where a familiar faceplate had been removed: the driving turbine had been built by Westinghouse. This discovery was like meeting an old friend who had been robbed and beaten by hooligans. He was reminded of home, his enlistment, and how much he already hated Russia.

Within the hour, he'd taken the car for an angry little spin down to the Smolny sawmills, and back to the yards. The ride was jumpy, the car smelled as if someone had coughed into a sardine bucket, and every surface was slick and tacky with fish oil. He could not imagine a more disgusting place. When asked whom he wanted to assist him, he whispered, "Wodziczko."

Then he took his first passenger run. Wodziczko stood at the front to take tickets. But at the very first stop, when three heavily bundled workers stepped into the car to be taken to the herring cannery, Wodziczko didn't know how to make change. This led to exchanges of coins and paper money between the soldier and the woolen-capped-and-coated passengers that looked like khaki starfish arguing over a catch of sand dollars.

Hugo didn't know the names or locations of any of the stops. No matter where he jerked the trolley to a halt, someone would yell at him and gesture either backward or forward with rude, red hands. Hugo began to imagine they were saying, "Don't you understand? I have to walk on these hands back to the stop you missed." Which started to amuse him. Especially when he discovered that if he hit the clutch and played the handbrake just right, he could cause boarding passengers to spin down the aisle like children's tops.

The squawking from the pinched little passengers bounced off him like flecks of birdseed. It occurred to him that it made no difference what he said or did. "Next stop, Michigan Avenue," he called. "Changing lines here for the Gratiot Corridor and Port Huron."

Which made Private Wodziczko laugh and cry out, "Jefferson Avenue. Grosse Pointe Park next stop."

"Hello!" Hugo yelled, for his ideas were being stolen.

By the time the sun set, and Hugo was off duty, he had heard not a single word of gratitude aboard the trolley except, he thought, for one. Quite a few Russians, upon seeing him, nodded and quickly said, *"Brekher,"* which he supposed meant "thanks." In fact, it meant "scab."

So it went with attempts to maintain the electricity, the gas, the factories, the hospitals, the schools, the sawmills, the groceries, the cafés. Poole did not notice, for he was directing rehearsals of *Pinafore.* When he learned that the people of Archangel were beginning to grouse, he made a firm decision, put into action immediately.

The CIGS received a telegram from him: "Declared martial law today. All going smashingly."

In successive telegrams, General Poole asked for more troops, reminded the CIGS about the drive toward Moscow, asked again for more troops, and more or less (in the exasperated eyes of his superiors) gloated over the contents of his handkerchief every time he blew his nose.

In a paternal response, Command asked what had happened to the troops he had already been given. In addition to 5,900 Americans, he had 2,500 Royal Scots; 900 mumbling French; 350 Serbs who had scurvy; some Italians, and, of course, the Slavo-British Legion.

Poole explained he had a victory plan, and that the Allies were currently spreading out from Archangel, along railway lines, in five columns, "like the fingers of a mighty fist."

Perhaps it was as simple as that metaphor. It was decided that, for the safety of all, Poole needed an assistant. The War Office surveyed the available talent this late in the shredder and alit upon Edmund Ironside.

As soon as his name was mentioned, a faint dawn light crept up. Perhaps there was still a hero or two left. At the age of thirty-eight, Ironside had earned the C.M.G., the D.S.O., the Croix de Guerre with Palms, had received the Queen's Medal with three clasps, and was an officer of the Legion of Honor. He spoke German, French, Swedish, Dutch, Italian, and had learned enough Russian, he said, to get his face slapped, an improbability considering that he was in love with his wife.

He was rumored to have strangled a Boer soldier to death with his two bare hands. This wasn't quite true—he had done it with one hand. His nickname was "Tiny."

And where exactly *was* Ironside? A stride toward the walls of the War Office, where gray-and-green topographical maps were spread across the cork walls, and then out came the ledgers to cross-reference troop locations, and then a finger fell upon a pushpin, mauve, driven into the Marécage Gris sector. Here he was. Call him home.

7

Lee Duncan's job was to maintain the machine guns for a DH 4 airplane called *Lenore*. The observer seat had a pair of Lewises mounted on a Scarff ring that allowed them to swing up, down, and approximately 270 degrees. Unfortunately, their arc of fire included the empennage, the plane's own tailpiece. DH 4s could shake off the enemy, only to shoot themselves down. For the pilot, there was a pair of Marlin .30-calibers, which fired through the arc of the propeller via the amazingly precise harmonics of Constantinesco synchronizing hydraulic gear. It was Lee's duty to ensure, every morning, that the hydraulics were intact; otherwise, the pilot, Lieutenant Ripley, could turn his own propeller into splinters. On most rainy mornings, or even mornings with a spot of dew to them, the hydraulics were a wreck.

Lieutenant Ripley had shipped out illegally and underage to fly with the French Escadrille. He had once flown pursuit, and had shot down several Germans, though he never mentioned this. He had coarse black hair, and a mustache unique among officers in that it wasn't cultivated in the

British manner. Instead, he looked as if he had once been the marshal of a recently subdued mining town.

He had a sweetheart from the United States, whom he had convinced to come to France. She was impossible. On a particularly harsh leave during which he concluded he had nothing to live for, Ripley married her. This is why he had named his difficult and unreliable airplane, the DH 4 with machine guns tended to by Lee Duncan, *Lenore*.

The DH 4s used by the 135th were the first with entirely American parts in their engines, and were thus newsworthy. One morning in August, newsreel photographers showed up at dawn to record their launch. There was no real reason to fly that day—it was drizzling, and no offensives were planned—but headquarters at Toul wanted to indulge the Signal Corps, so all planes were ordered into the air.

The planes were carefully filmed coming out of the hangar, with the last few left in the shadows, as if there might be hundreds more in reserve. There was a great deal of commotion and drama as one, two, three, four— all fifteen aircraft lifted gracefully, one by one, and disappeared into the clouds, while the cranks turned and newspaper men wrote hymns to describe the first sight of American planes becoming one with the vault of the heavens, winding in ever-widening spirals into the ethereal blue to drive von Hindenburg from the skies forever.

Leland Duncan performed his duties with his head turned away from the lenses. The photographers asked if he wouldn't mind showing how he maintained the guns. Lee saluted, and after the tripods were set up, he showed off the bullets, how they fit into clips, how the clips were loaded onto belts, which were fed into Marlins, which operated on a recoil principle.

He was asked to stand behind the guns as if firing them, which he did, and then he was asked if he might wink at the camera. Eventually, he said, "No, I don't do that."

There was a village near the aerodrome whose name was Fleurey, or Flirrey—the peasants there spelled it any number of ways. It consisted of a few communal farms, an estaminet that rarely had food except egg and chips, a brothel, and several shacks by the river that housed either one large family or several smaller ones who had banded together. An old woman washed uniforms, taking them to the creek and beating them with an oar, and hanging them on a wire strung across the single, large room, where there was a fireplace.

One morning, Lee stood in the old woman's front yard while she found his uniform, and he looked two doors down, where the girls of the brothel stood barefoot in the dirt. They wore fading chiffon and satin. One lifted her skirt as if displaying the day's catch. He looked toward a cornfield.

It was late August. The harvest, such as it could be in wartime, had already occurred. The field was a wreck, some rows neatly trimmed back and others looming with stalks neck-high, yellow and fragile, like parchment. The peasants were burning the field at the far end. It was an easy fire, the winds were mild, and the leaves caught like wet cigarettes. Clouds of black smoke were arising, and rolling toward the village. Lee noticed movement among the closest cornstalks; they seemed to be trembling and parting in advance of the fire. Something rustled through them, its course tentative and confused but generally away from the flames.

Lee was not armed. He held a pile of laundry. The villagers seemed to give little attention to whatever was in the field, so he reasoned he was safe. When the object stopped moving, and the cornstalks stopped shaking, he paid the woman for her washing and prepared to move on.

He might have left the village for his barracks had it not been for the breathing. He could hear a labored sound, an asthmatic sighing through a long rubber tube. A few quick pants, and then the wheeze of an intaken breath.

Sitting in the midst of the tallest corn, weight tilted to one side, was a German shepherd. Her fur was streaked with blood, and her pawpads were black and reeked of tar. She was pregnant.

The sky behind her was all flames and soot and ash, and the crackle of burning corn was beginning to approach. But she was not moving, for she was clearly exhausted. She was panting so awfully because she was wearing a gas mask.

Lee put his laundry on a flat rock. "Banjo?" he asked.

Nothing in response. Just a continuation of the wheeze, and then the short, soft exhalations that made her whole body shake.

A crack of corn exploding, and Banjo turned her head slightly. Her head was shaking. Someone had taken her and used her badly. The gas mask was filthy, with splashes of blood on its olive-drab canvas. It covered her head, including her ears, and came to a point at the top, making a triangular tent. There were round holes for her eyes, which were behind protective glass, and a hose dangled below her jaw. It seemed heavy.

"Banjo," he said again. It was unlikely she could hear. He didn't know how far she had traveled or how long she had been wearing the gas mask.

He took a step forward, and another, and she continued to stay still. Her head teetered from side to side, perhaps trying to see more of the landscape through the eyeholes, perhaps trying in vain to hear or smell something, somewhere.

When he was two feet away, he crouched down. He nabbed her behind the head, where he guessed there would be a rubber gasket for the gas mask, just like on his own. She jerked against him, trying to pull away, but the attempt was weak, and all it did was make her legs skid out from under her.

He felt around the gasket, tangles of moist fur against his fingers, until he came to the buckle of a leather collar. He fumbled with it, almost losing his grip, until he released the catch, and the gas mask came away in his hands.

Banjo shook her head, tall ears making a rushing sound like sails billowing with wind, and Lee stood up to see her better, whispering, "Good girl," as she jumped for his throat.

Her jump was simple, up and then down, connecting on the ascent with Lee's forearm, which he had pitched over his windpipe. Something tingled on his side and his knee, and only when she was again on the ground did he realize she had bitten him three more times before landing.

With a growl, she launched again, and Lee went down on his stomach, lacing his fingers behind his neck, and the thought of losing them made him close his eyes and cry, "Shit! Shit!"

The attack did not come. Lee could hear Banjo panting.

He opened his eyes. Her legs were tucked under her, and she was lopsidedly leaning on her front paws, adjusting them again and again. Her face looked calm but alert, almost anticipatory. For, having heard his cry, she had done the best she could, and had tried to sit.

Lee fed Banjo some M&V rations and led her to the river, where he washed her down with soap and disinfectant. She did not like his touching her, so he tied a strap around her snout to keep her from biting. As he washed her, he told her that one day she wouldn't need the strap, and they would be friends. He kept her in a four-foot cage that had once belonged to the Signal Corps, for carrier pigeons.

The men of the 135th were curious to see her back, but not overjoyed, in that she hadn't been much of a dog in the first place. That she was about to have puppies struck them as a terrible idea. Still, after meals, men tended to throw her some grub, and now that she was boxed up in plain sight, they talked to her or banged the heels of their hands against her cage, to make her startle (for luck), as they passed to their airplanes.

There was a packing crate inside the cage to protect her from the rains that washed over the whole of France that summer. Once, Lee was crouching down and talking to Banjo, who had taken to lying on an old horse blanket in the crate, when he noticed that Lieutenant Ripley was nearby. He stood and saluted, and Ripley saluted back as if it ruined the moment. Ripley, leaving, stopped himself.

"Corporal?"

"Sir?"

"Perhaps, one day, we should go flying," Ripley said. When Lee said nothing in response—he wanted very badly to go flying—Ripley blushed. "If you like that sort of thing."

There were rumors of an Allied advance. The infantry had made many advances over the last four years, over the same four hundred or so yards, matched by retreats and routs, but this one was rumored to be different. Such was what the American infantry kept saying, and the British, French, Canadian, and Australian troops kept telling them that advances were always rumored to be different.

Another rumor spread from unit to unit: peace, whenever finally at hand, would be announced with the launching of three dark-blue flares at midnight.

Universally, the doughboys looked up at least once at the evening sky, trying to imagine the sight, and instead realized the inherent cruel joke—of course, the sign would pass invisibly. You couldn't see three blue lights at night.

Lee considered and dismissed the rumors just like anyone else. He nonetheless wobbled toward hope. He whistled to himself for no reason, and once he played baseball with children in the village. The old woman who washed the uniforms found a ham hock on her front stoop. When he wandered back to the barracks, he felt that a strange, second, phantom self walked alongside, jauntily, unburdened, and eager to greet the remaining day. Even when it rained, as it did every day. Something in his face wavered, as if a good-enough shove would send him to the side of the angels. "Hello, Banjo," he said, even when he wasn't near the dog's cage. "Hello, Lieutenant Ripley," he whispered to himself. "Look at that view."

He was on the verge of once again discovering his reflection in windowpanes. He did not notice that Banjo had begun to dig a hole below her doghouse, one that would lead under the mesh of her cage.

8

Chaplin later referred to the summer of 1918 as the happiest days of his life (he also nominated earlier days sometimes). He returned to the studio from the Liberty Loan parade fired up to be a soldier onscreen. He had, on the train ride from San Francisco to Los Angeles, sketched out a classic three-act story, which surprised him. Normally, he improvised, but for this film—he called it *Camouflage*—he wanted to know in advance what the scenario would be. It was like fulfilling a promise to the young doughboy he'd seen in San Francisco, the one looking fearfully onto the stage while Chaplin thrashed around, doing the Inebriate routine.

The ideas seemed to flow from one to another. In the first act, the Little Fellow was a henpecked husband, dodging plates, drinking to forget he'd married a shrew, and excited to get his draft notice. He imagined the dance of joy he would do upon receiving his registration, how counterintuitive the reaction, how great the laugh. Then he would have a physical (the business that would entail!). In the second act, he would be in the trenches of France. It would rain every moment, there would be gas masks used for Limburger cheese, a race Over the Top to retrieve a missing dog who has run off with the secret plans, a chase through No Man's Land. He would meet and romance a French girl, alternately wooing her and hitting Germans over the head with a sausage. And in the final act, he would become a hero for some ridiculous reason, receiving medals at a state dinner—why not put the Little Fellow up against President Wilson? General Foch? Lloyd George? "Mistaken identity," he wrote. "Little Fellow is a waiter at the banquet, he saves the day, and is elevated to hero. Those who would not even spit on him now must pay attention." *A Dog's Life,* everyone agreed, had been a pleasant half step up from the earlier comedies; *Camouflage* would fulfill his promise.

On the first day of shooting *Camouflage,* in June, he decided the whole thing was wrong. He walked into Wardrobe and asked Rhiannon to make him a tree costume. When she asked what sort of tree, he said, "A dead tree." There was something about having fallen over at that beach party, a sort of accidental humor of which he wanted to take ownership. He was drawing sketches for Rhiannon when Syd looked over his shoulder.

"A tree costume?" asked Syd, cautiously. But he had larger battles: "Charlie, the second act—the trenches—you can't do that, you know."

"Why not?"

Syd looked as if he were being tied to a stake. "Laughing at soldiers?"

"It won't be like that."

"They can destroy you, you know. They can throw you right out of the country."

He wanted to say, "I've just made the government millions, and I'll make them millions more." But that wasn't how he felt. "Sydney, I had a revelation. I feel great sympathy for those in the trenches. I won't be making fun of them."

"I can't see it."

"It's simple—it's the same as ever, except the cops are Germans. Yes?"

Syd was shaking his head in elder-brother disapproval, and so a smile crept up on Chaplin. "Rhiannon," he said, "hold the tree costume for now." The moment Syd relaxed, Chaplin continued, "Make a Kaiser costume. Tailor it to fit Syd."

He tended to shoot scenes in order, and in the first month, he filmed the whole domestic scene, the children, the throwing of plates, the physical, and he hated it. He felt as if he had been attuned to wonderful stories in his dreams, but when he turned his attention to them too carefully, they dissolved, spun candy left out in the rain.

He began again with basic training. He drilled, and made tremendous mistakes with his rifle, with his attempts to obey orders, and with the huge, floppy boots. He wasn't creating ideas so much as listening for them. Yet he was not quite talented enough to use them. Then he built a trench.

He thought about all the things that made people miserable. He filmed the Germans stealing cigarettes from the Americans, and then, because they were starving, eating them. He imagined them so hungry that they ate their uniforms. He had a shoe made of licorice and toyed with it, then put it away. How far could he go? Cannibalism?

He returned to the American side and elected to flood the trench with water while the soldiers were trying to sleep. Syd told him that this wasn't funny.

Chaplin asked Eddie Sutherland, who was assisting, "How's the water?"

"It's freezing."

"Good. Syd, get in the water."

Syd gaped at him. "You're putting the Kaiser in the trenches?"

"No, you're getting two roles in this film. You get to be a doughboy. Get in the water."

Throughout, when Syd complained that he felt new symptoms of influenza, Chaplin told him to be quiet, that many young men would kill for just one part in the new Chaplin film, and he was giving him two, out of love, so just sit still in the water and try not to behave like a baby.

His earliest films had taken a week, maybe two, and then they had taken a month. *Camouflage* was taking longer, June into July, and then August. He imagined soldiers attempting to storm a building. He imagined an enemy inside, or perhaps Edna was in there, a nurse waiting to be rescued. Setting the Little Fellow the job of entering, he imagined a perfect forward flip, ending with his skull pressed against the barrel of a tank gun. Hands up! Immediate surrender on the Tramp's part.

Every day's shooting that Chaplin threw out caused his crew to wonder whether their boss had finally lost his mind. And every day that he kept—showing smoke bombs exploding, trench foot, boredom, filth; showing the German infantry excited and pleased when the Little Fellow spanked one of their officers; showing the men holding track races between competing sets of body lice—made them wonder whether they were all going to be arrested.

"Was that good? Did it work?" Chaplin asked. The response was muted: everyone was still worried that this picture would never see the light of day.

But Chaplin was not asking them alone. He was also asking the opinion of a man who had taken to walking around the studio and observing how they worked. This man nodded, absently. No one on staff recognized him, for he did not work in Hollywood. It was Secretary McAdoo, who was taking an extended look at the filmmaking process before he returned to Washington.

The summer of 1918 was unusually warm in Los Angeles, with a swampy oppressiveness no one could remember from previous years. Actors did not want to work, afternoon breaks lasted hours, scenarios were rewritten for all the scenes to occur at dawn and dusk. Production slowed, cafés flourished, there was much praise for ambitious creations such as tequila mixed with orange syrup, lime, shaved ice, and gossip. For the first time, local newspapers provided commentary on actors' comings and goings. In August, the *Los Angeles Examiner* reported the following:

CHAPLIN MARRIAGE RUMOR IS DENIED

Despite rumors that will not die down to the effect that Mildred Harris, the dainty screen favorite, has won the heart of Charlie Chaplin and soon is to be his bride, the petite actress denied last night the last half of the double-barrelled allegation.

"No, Mr. Chaplin and I are not engaged," Miss Harris said last night when she returned to her quarters in the Wilshire Apartments after an evening at his studio. "We're just very dear friends."

Mrs. Harris was much surprised by the report, she said, and added that her daughter was only seventeen years of age and too young to think of marrying. Chaplin, currently lensing his next comedy riot, *Camouflage,* was unavailable for comment, but sources at the studio scoff at the reports. "Charlie is working sixteen hour days, his eye is on the money, and he has no time for romance. People are eager to see him married, but they shall have to wait."

An hour after reading this, Chaplin was sputtering in front of Carlyle Robinson. "Why is this in the papers?"

It was late in the morning, and the slightest motion made Chaplin perspire. The effort of facing Robinson was heroic. Robinson was cool, as if he had never sweated in his life. "The *Examiner* had a much more salacious story, which they squashed for the exclusive."

"What exclusive?"

"That would be the unnamed source telling them you had no time for romance."

"Who said that to them?"

"I did. I mentioned money so it would sound like Syd."

Chaplin was standing in the doorway of Robinson's office, which was by the studio entryway, and which was only large enough for a desk, on top of which the local newspapers were heaped. He was torn between anger and admiration. "Why Syd?"

"People expect that if it's your brother he is keeping you in line."

"I don't need to be kept in line."

"Are you going to marry her?"

"Of course not."

"Because, if you do, you should tell me first," Robinson said, calmly. As ever, he had not a hair out of place, and Chaplin could not tell how he felt about anything. But the suspension of judgment had the reverse effect of making Chaplin feel highly judged, as if there were something he was doing that required Robinson to stand back and not express opinions on.

"Marrying means to grasp blindfolded into a sack, hoping to find an eel out of an assembly of snakes," Chaplin said, raising his eyebrows.

"That's fine. Always thought Mr. Schopenhauer had something there," Robinson said with a tight, unimpressed, and still somehow judgmental-without-being-judgmental smile.

Chastened (who had actually read Schopenhauer?), Chaplin noticed Robinson tapping his pencil on his legal pad. "Yes?"

"The article was important. I placed it to establish one fact." Robinson tilted his head slightly, as if suggesting that Chaplin, a genius, should be able to determine this for himself.

Chaplin remembered that everyone took pride in his own work. "We're not getting married?"

"No. I've noticed that everyone denies they're getting married. Even married people. Just saying it aloud like this, it gets people thinking you're lying. So: no."

Chaplin scanned the article again. "That I'm working?"

"No." Robinson tapped his pencil quickly on his pad. "The article is there for one reason only. It establishes beyond the shadow of a doubt that Miss Harris is seventeen years old."

Chaplin said nothing, but he wanted to. Mildred was not seventeen.

When he had paused long enough, Robinson filled in the silence. "But it's there in the papers," he said, with a singsong inflection.

Chaplin wanted to give him a raise, but by now he'd learned the importance of the right kind of silence. He walked toward his office, pausing in the courtyard, as a typist and an accountant and some of the soft touches who constructed his sets were gathered around a girl wearing a tam, a sash, and a pleated khaki skirt. He almost passed by, but something reflected off of her blouse, popping like a Klieg light, which made him wince.

"Heavens," he said, mildly.

"Hello," she said. "Would you like to buy Girl Scout—"

"Oh," he said, "I already have cookies."

"We're not selling cookies," Rebecca said. She passed Chaplin a flyer printed on glossy paper.

He read it. It struck him as unlikely. "When did the Girl Scouts start selling meat?"

"It's a new program," she explained. "With so many things being rationed, we reasoned that the people in the area with special needs might wish to purchase high-quality cuts of meat without worrying they could injure the war effort."

It sounded almost plausible. There was quite the small but fascinated crowd around her, each member of his crew surveying with interest what a pound of flank steak or rump roast might cost. Chaplin realized what had caused the glare in the sunlight: a badge, a silver fish. Rebecca's sales pitch had been remarkable. "How old are you?"

"Fourteen and one-third."

"Ah, not fifteen-sixteenths."

She smiled to acknowledge that a genius had told a joke. He could not take his eyes off of her. She was attractive, in the way that running one's finger down the edge of a knife was attractive. He had the uneasy sense she knew how many dollar bills were in his wallet.

Handing her flyer back to her, Chaplin wished her good luck, and told her to come again when he had more time; he did not wish to be described as turning her down flat.

So he went back to work. For an hour, he sat at his desk, opening and closing the blinds, as Rebecca made her way from department to department, taking orders.

9

At Archangel, it was beginning to snow. The townspeople shrugged off all questions from the Americans about how cold it would actually get with the phrase "You know—same as last year." The Allies felt they were dealing with morons. But to the Russians, the question itself was stupid: it *always* got cold, and only a fool would bother with *how* cold. Cold enough to kill you. Idiot.

Because governments had been rising and falling every time a door slammed, there were Nicholai rubles, Kerensky rubles, State of Archangel rubles, and finally Bolshevik rubles, which were every one of the previous rubles stamped with the word "Bolshevik" in red ink. Private Hugo's company had been required to exchange their dollars for Kerensky rubles, which, it turned out, no one would take.

Every individual in Archangel was a black-marketeer. Complex trades were made of sable for sugar, eggs for Scotch, and sex for food, the latter with the exchange rate of one Hershey bar and one tot of whiskey for a nimgimmer special at the bathhouse.

Even the Red Cross, which was supposed to be free, began to charge ten cents for a doughnut. Cigarettes, also free, were two dollars a pack. There was no explanation.

Hugo was favored by the ten-year-old boys who appeared at the American barracks every afternoon with rolls of money and offers of goods and services. He was a perfect mark, in that he believed he would learn from his mistakes. He bought eggs that turned out to be spoiled. He traded away a perfectly good kilo of butter for a watch and a compass. The watch broke the first time he wound it, and the compass pointed southwest. After he threw it away, he learned that above the Arctic Circle all compasses pointed southwest.

Most days, he made do with his British rations: bully beef canned in Argentina. Sinews of rabbit that had been, according to its tin, killed and frozen in Australia in 1910. He ate M&V—of which there was no "M," just stewed vegetables with a glob of fat. Every day he was given another biscuit that was four inches long, two wide, and invulnerable to chewing. The jam he was supposed to spread on it was seasoned with pellets of lead.

"There are no rewards to being here," he moaned to Gordon.

"Your reward is to kill," Gordon reminded him.

"Oh, everyone says that," he said, "but they don't *really* mean it."

"It's going to get better," Gordon said. "Ironside is coming," he said; that explained nothing, but it was what everyone was saying.

Hugo drew guard duty at a warehouse near the cathedral. It was cold, he was always hungry, he did not know what he was guarding, and, worst of all, his partner was Wodziczko.

Hugo—train engineer, trolley-car wit—had become Wodziczko's hero. Wodziczko was astounded that Hugo knew French. And read books. And could dance like a cotillion escort. None of which Wodziczko understood, but all of which made Hugo displace Lieutenant Gordon in Wodziczko's worshipful little heart.

To Hugo, the hours of lonely sentry duty, the long, dull minutes dripping by, were heartbreaking. But Wodziczko remained peppy, certain that Hugo would soon vanish fifty-cent pieces and juggle fire.

A week into guard duty, Hugo and Wodziczko were standing the requisite six feet apart, the lonely single bright spotlight overhead casting the pine trees nearby into a pitch-blackness. Hugo had been playing breathing games, watching the jets of his exhalations turn to steam. He pretended he had been invited to dinner and a dance by a charitable organization in Grosse Pointe, and he had to avert social blunders by less fortunate comrades who drank from the soup bowl or insisted on dancing mazurkas.

Wodziczko turned away from the pine trees every so often to fix Hugo with a bright, happy smile, as if nothing better in the world would ever happen. Hugo could feel what was coming. There was no stopping it.

"There's a place in France," Wodziczko declared, "where the ladies wear no pants."

This in and of itself was not so awful. It was how he then looked to Hugo for approval. Hugo spoke French, and so would understand the arch wit involved.

"You think? Yeah?" Wodziczko enticingly waggled his eyebrows. Hugo looked stone forward, and silence returned. For all of three minutes, until unable to help himself, Wodziczko said, "There's a place in France where the ladies wear no pants."

And so it was bound to go, for many hours, as it had all week, Hugo interrupted from (say) an imaginary petite waltz with Miss Belinda Worthington by Wodziczko's recitation, and eventually the sun would come up on another day in Arctic paradise, and they would go to sleep and wake up, and the whole process would begin all over again.

But there was an unexpected shift in the routine. Around two o'clock in the morning, Hugo was thinking of a recipe for brioche, because in his fantasies a hostess had asked him to critique her pastry chef's accomplishments. His breath was coming out in little puffs of cotton. The sounds of Russia were the slow creaking of trees, the warehouse settling on its wood foundations, barn owls fluttering between rafters.

And then Wodziczko said something.

"There's a place in France," he said, "where the ladies wear no pants."

"Oh, dear God," Hugo moaned.

"I wonder what we're guarding," Wodziczko said.

Hugo prepared to let loose terrifying invective, but then he hesitated. What *were* they guarding? "They didn't tell you?"

"No. You?"

It turned out Wodziczko had apprenticed with a locksmith once. Impressively, he was able to use a piece of wire and a flattened copper shim to open the padlock. There was a click, and then the two privates threw open the huge shuttered door to the warehouse.

There were crates stacked eight feet high, in rows of ten, with narrow aisles between them. Each crate was stenciled "Cadbury's Dairy Milk."

They were guarding chocolate bars.

Wodziczko drew the doors closed again.

"Wait," said Hugo, holding his arm. "Let's look again."

"We shouldn't be looking."

"Yes, we should," Hugo said, thinking of ten-cent dead doughnuts, boiled horse stew, rotten eggs, his worthless rubles.

"I don't want to get in trouble," Wodziczko said. "They aren't ours."

"Certainly they are."

Which stopped the conversation. For Hugo had not said it.

The light overhead threw down its harsh glow, circular, hazy, and making Hugo and Wodziczko targets to enemies outside its radiance. The only place for cover was straight ahead: the forest. The voice was coming from there.

"Put up your hands and approach slowly," Hugo ordered. His rifle was parallel to the horizon, and his index finger, poking through a hole in his mitten, wrapped around the trigger. Silence. Not a creak of a tree, or a snapping twig. Then, from perhaps ten yards away, the voice continued.

"Soldiers of Detroit, you're in Russia. Why is that?"

"You tell us," Hugo said defiantly.

When the voice started again, it had moved five yards left. "Could it be that the pockets of the industrialists need to be lined with yet more gold?"

"No," said Wodziczko.

"We don't know and we don't care," said Hugo, realizing that he should move away from the light.

"Maybe the man next to you doesn't care. You've read Molière, though, soldier. You tend to think."

Hugo hadn't quoted any Molière this evening. He had done so several nights ago.

"You wonder if the chocolate is actually yours. We both know the answer. It would be a reward."

"Our reward is to kill," Wodziczko yelled.

Hugo swallowed. On the one hand, the enemy was speaking to him, and thus needed to be eradicated. On the other, he liked this disembodied voice more than anyone in his company.

"We mean no harm," the voice said. "Unlike your officers."

Hugo's eyes were adjusting. "How do you know so much English?"

"Tell me you respect your British commanders."

Hugo was silent.

"We hate them," Wodziczko cried out, and Hugo shushed him, which confused the tiny private.

The spectral voice continued, "General Poole is gone, and they tell you there is someone named Ironside coming who will make it all better. There is no Ironside coming. The patriarch doesn't fix your messes anymore."

Wodziczko looked with anticipation at Hugo. "Why aren't you shooting him?" he whispered.

Hugo put his finger to his lips, still squinting down his rifle barrel. He needed the Bolo to speak a little more, and to stay in place. Also: he was curious how this argument ended.

"Your officers with their every order demoralize you. The party, however, it salutes you. Just as workers are the means of production, and management attempts to control it, so do officers attempt to control those who actually do the work on the ground. But now is the time to grab the broom of history and sweep away—"

Hugo's rifle cracked, there was an echo and a report, and somewhere a crashing sound, dead weight collapsing into piles of pine needles and mulch.

Wodziczko's eyes shone like those of a boy on a porch in moonlight. He finally said, "Gee."

Hugo gazed his way. "I would like a chocolate bar."

"Yeah. Yeah!" Wodziczko tottered into the warehouse, and began fumbling with a crate. Hugo squinted into the night.

Then, from a great distance, Hugo heard something disheartening. It was the same voice as before. It hissed at him: "Shooting at the truth won't stop the truth, comrade."

10

If in September 1918 you had a god's eye view of the Saint-Mihiel salient, in a once-beautiful if swampy region of France, it would look like a fifty-two-mile-long tear across the landscape described by the perambulations of the Meuse River. Even though there were still clumps of fertile ground left—some woods, a stray vineyard or two—the weary locals in the villages of Flirey (or Fleurey) and Thiaucourt referred to this decimated triangular wedge of battlefront as the hernia, *l'hernie*. It was mostly a land of churned mudflats supporting the occasional blasted kiln or toppled church, burnt-out pyres, former stables, barns.

As for *l'hernie* itself, the dividing line between armies, it was a scar knitted with loops of rusted gooseberry wire laid down years before by Germans who, like their French counterparts, had long ago begun to grasp the meaning of "never."

The 135th was on the edge of *l'hernie*.

On the first moonless evening of September, it rained. Up and down the Meuse, rain fell into the river and along the banks and into the bombed-out farmhouses, and it beat against the canvas tents in which twenty thousand Germans slept the exhausted, shallow sleep of the starving.

Shortly after midnight, spotters noted in their logs the sound of thunder, and they turned their eyes from the skies to stopwatches to determine how far away the heart of the storm was. And then, one by one, as flashes from the ground illuminated the sky, logbooks were dropped into the mud, and soldiers raced to sound alarms.

It wasn't thunder. Instead, it was an introduction to a new adversary. The artillery of the U.S. First Army had launched a barrage of shells. Among actual raindrops, the explosive rounds rained down on trenches, command posts, ammunition dumps, and nests of machine-gunners. A single shell came down upon an overtimbered roof on a building near the village of Corny, with an explosion that blew bricks and wooden framing across a courtyard. Moments later, the hiss of sand pouring down from the hole in the roof, and then into the rain, one, two, three, four, a half dozen, a dozen dogs leaping out of the building and bolting through the nearby vineyards. They ran, panting, some of them in gas masks, others fluttering with the satchels containing cigarettes they delivered.

They fanned out among the bombed and ruined grape arbors, then ran across the local farmyards, in a pack, in the dark, over rising hills, illuminated through rain showers by explosions and farmhouses set alight. They dodged the freight spilled from railway cars, skittered over moldering grain stores; barnyard chickens in coops shrieked when they passed. They were shepherds, the most noble of dogs. They had been trained, but now they were just running, and soon they loped off the battlefields, bounding with the grace of dancing royalty into the woods, never to be seen again.

The shells continued to fall. The Germans began to hope that the enemy would perhaps run out of shells—after four years of battle, that *any* factory had *any* shells left was somewhat amazing—but it became apparent to their seasoned ears not only that the Americans had brought shells, but that they came in a new and depressing variety of sizes.

At five a.m., the noise ceased. It was replaced by a rumble of engines, the squeals of metal treads turning: Allied tanks. Built in France and Britain, these were, unlike their American counterparts, real. There were hundreds of them, moving awkwardly through the mud, and behind them, in a line extending the length of the salient, a sight no one had ever seen: 660,000 fresh American troops. It was a line that stood shoulder to shoulder for fifty-two miles.

They brought out cutters and Bangalore torpedoes, and sliced through the loops of *cheveux de frise,* and laid chicken wire atop the old barbed wire spools; then the Allied infantry, a mass of angular faces under metal helmets, began to walk forward.

Camouflaged machine guns and Krupps howitzers mowed them down by the thousands. But the beauty of the American forces was that there were hundreds of thousands to replace them.

And though this was a baptism, and the Americans had wanted a baptism, it was not a battle anyone would write songs about. Saint-Mihiel was not a name that would call for reckoning; it wasn't Verdun or the Fields of Flanders or the Somme. It was important only in that, for the first time, the application of overwhelming force, in the form of average men and machinery, pried the enemy out of their trenches. The doughboys were getting the hang of war.

The German troops destroyed villages as they left, blowing up railways and bridges, and throwing dead horses into wells, as *Stosstruppen* used flamethrowers to set fire to haystacks.

And that was when the Indians were turned loose.

There were a dozen of them—two Lakota from the 351st Infantry Regiment, three Cree from the 146th Field Artillery, and the rest of them from the 142nd Infantry, the heart of the Oklahoma melting pot. They rode shirtless, bareback, with long black wigs of real human hair covering their army haircuts, and their riding was tentative and embarrassed. The army—working on a hunch—had asked them to consider wearing war paint and bonnets, and in the hours before the battle, they had stood in a canvas tent as shells exploded in the distance, staring at the bows and arrows, the makeup, the feathers, shaking their heads, and reconsidering with every passing moment how deeply ran the rivers of their patriotism.

Finally, after a captain's raw appeal to their loyalty ("You aren't tribesmen anymore—you're Americans! Are you going to run from a fight?"), they decided they would ride the horses and wear the wigs, but they weren't swapping their Springfields for bows and arrows.

By the time they took the field, the battle had fallen so far in the Allies' direction that they rode quietly for miles, slowly, avoiding the huge ruts and potholes in the once-level ground, looking fruitlessly for the enemy. Germans unlucky enough to see them immediately surrendered, or stripped off their packs and ran or prayed. But the spirit of absurdity kept the team going, and when one of them was about to give up, he would catch the expression on another's face—and they would both laugh in confirmation that fate had dealt them yet another hand no one would believe. Plus, there was something to be said for fighting on the winning side.

All in all, they fired their rifles only five or six times each, never at an actual target, always at the command of the men hand-cranking the moving-picture cameras on newly engineered swivel-mount tripods atop the trucks that followed them.

☆ ☆ ☆

Lee was awakened before four a.m. by the sounds of war, and on his way to his post he saw that Banjo's enclosure was empty. Scrapes against the soft earth, piles of dirt pushed outward. She had dug under the wire. He called for her, drowned out by the huge basso rumble of cannons, and then had to run to prepare the guns for *Lenore.*

By six o'clock, dawn was breaking, and the weak autumn sun cast faint light into the towering cumulonimbus clouds, doughy and thick and unnaturally busy, dotted with airplanes that maneuvered in spirals as if caught in a whirlpool. The observation planes of the 135th were in the heady mix of things—finally!—scanning for troop movements and adjusting the battery fusillades by radio transmission.

Ripley flew six times. At the end of each sortie, Lee felt the Marlins and found them warm. His first reaction was a stab of wonder, not at all pleasant, and then he realized it was his job to restock the bullets and attend to the hydraulics. All day long he was at the aerodrome, listening to howitzers in the distance, the cracks and whistles of weapons just over the horizon. It was like standing outside a music hall and hearing an orchestra tuning up. There was some smoke, the occasional smell of cordite, and, three times, a Boche plane was thought to be approaching, so he had to throw himself into shelter.

He was thinking of troubled eyes, ratty ears, rough fur, the sound of a distant animal drinking water. He kept looking back at the enclosure, as if she might be hiding cleverly in the doghouse, and he looked all around the camp, including the garbage dump, in case she was hungry. He told himself there were many dogs in the world, and even in this desolate corner there were many pregnant shepherds, should he want another.

The Saint-Mihiel offensive was proclaimed a success after two days of fighting and a third to take prisoners into custody. The 135th had lost three planes: one to the Fokkers, one to an unfortunate incident involving their own artillery, and one to an "accidental" landing in Switzerland. All in all, the squadron was quite pleased with how it had come through, and could now, having four fallen comrades, complain about war as convincingly as anyone.

After the push across *l'hernie* ended, there was silence at the aerodrome for several hours. Lee was more awake to any noise now, listening in vain for distant barking.

11

The Supreme Council housed Edmund Ironside at the Savoy. Later, he wrote, "The first moment I understood the gravity of this mission was when I saw that the War Office had assigned me a suite with a view of Parliament and Tower Bridge, a room just above the memorial to Sir Arthur Sullivan, all guarantees that the reminders of Empire would be fresh in sight." The tailors fitted a winter suit, a hooded sealskin parka that belled over his massive form in one piece. He said to his wife that he looked like "an enormous, unscrupulous baby."

He had his valet, Pishkoff, called to duty, which made him glad. For three days, advisers for the Imperial General Staff came to the Savoy in shifts, sometimes taking tea in the rooms, sometimes strolling along the Embankment with Ironside. He was six foot six inches tall and weighed 270 pounds. He always walked with his head at a slight incline, listening and simultaneously apologizing for being so much taller than he needed to be. His tone when speaking was apologetic, as if he understood that the world was mad to have made a man of his slight qualities a general—but since it *had*, he seemed to imply, why not see what you and he could do about all this business?

The tide was turning in the European theater. "In Russia, too?" he asked, just once, the question disappearing like a penny down a well. He was to assist and advise General Poole, nothing more. "Nothing more" was said so often that Ironside understood that it was anticipated he would need to do something more. "Am I to replace him?" he finally asked, and he was told no. He was told that, in spite of the late date in the war, he had the finest available troops to carry out their mission. He later summarized his briefing as follows:

Myself: How many troops are there?

Staff Officer: 2500 Royal Scots, 5900 American, assorted others. All under the command of General Poole, of course.

Myself: Yes, as for the British troops, how many are A1?

Staff: None.

Myself: None?

Staff: No, the A1s are on the main campaign against Germany, in the most vital positions. Realize we've given you the best remaining troops.

"A2?"

"None. Still, you will have the best."

A3 were men fit for combat duty, but only under close supervision, not to be trusted with heavy arms. "A3?"

"None, I'm afraid."

So down the line he went until he got to B2, "fit for base duty abroad."

"Ah, yes." Fingers scrolling down a clipboard. "You . . . have . . . none of the B2-grade troops, either."

"What grade have I got left?" He was worried he would get C2s—those fit only for sedentary duty overseas.

"C3."

He hadn't known there *was* a C3. Men whose ears came off when they coughed. Alcoholics whose stomachs were made of glass. Men missing fingers (though not their trigger fingers, it was pointed out). These were his worker bees.

He inquired about his forty-eight hundred Americans, and was told they were excellent combat troops unspoiled by previous duties. "I was told to celebrate," he wrote.

And what was the mission? He pored over the diplomatic essays explaining the command structure—General Poole at the top, the bizarre Mr. Chaikovsky summoned to lead the populace, the Allied troops for defense. (Was it for defense? Were we really going to graft democracy onto another country?) He combed through the recruitment goals for the new Slavo-British Legion, and then a summary of the mission objective, a folder that he ultimately took to the Embankment Gardens and closed, hand to his brow, before that monument to Arthur Sullivan.

He hated monuments. All the boles celebrating the German side of the royal line had been covered, the family name changed to Windsor. Soon there wouldn't be an inch of unconsecrated ground upon which to build, and the statues would be left to salute one another.

The mission objective for North Russia bothered him. War was like opera: the plot could be as complex as a spiderweb, but if you could not explain the point in a heartbeat, you were lost. He wrote down, in the margins of the blue-and-white-banded paper, "We are in Russia because ___," and he intended to get an answer before he boarded his boat.

He wasn't the first to think Sullivan could never have conceived of Ypres. The bust of the lyricist was atop a stele against which a bronze muse, life-sized, nude from the hips upward, bowed her head, the effect *vertkitschen.* It could have been any muse, for she held Euterpe's flute, and Thalia's mask and Erato's lyre were at her feet. *With the passing of this man,* Ironside thought the muse was sobbing, *my efforts come to nothing, and never again.* Naïve provincial girl.

He regarded with his infinitely sad blue eyes the remaining mission papers. There were now five columns of Allied troops strung along tentative supply routes, some of them three hundred miles deep into Russia. Why? It was complex, which was a problem, because people would not stand for complexity. It went back to Thucydides and the Hellenes: any truth, if burdened with a dependent clause, would be castrated in the market of discourse. There were the real reasons for war: fear, honor, and self-interest, and then the gratuitous *casus belli.* Ironside had seen enough of men and war to know that sometimes men simply want to go to war, and that desire was the chalk outline into which various cuts of meat were hurled until a body of well-reasoned justifications was declared to be found within it.

Ironside wrote "Slavo-British Legion," and tried to commit its particulars to memory; this was the key to whether the North Russia campaign would be a success. The Allies could fight Bolsheviks forever, with troops occupying territory from the Black Sea to Siberia, without actually gaining a single foot of land, unless the populace was willing to fight for itself.

He wrote: "Is Russia our ally or our enemy?"

The next day, he was pleased to see Pishkoff in his hotel room. Pishkoff was some mysterious age between thirty and seventy, tended to lean to one side even at the rare moments when at attention, and could be described as "leathered" if that process included fermentation.

"You're going home," Ironside said with enthusiasm.

"Where?" Pishkoff asked.

"Russia."

Pishkoff sat on an ottoman. "Oh."

12

It was September 15, and the Battle of Saint-Mihiel was over. The squadron was at work with welding equipment, saws and hammers, miles of canvas, sail-repair kits sent from Nantucket to restitch the DH 4 wings.

Lenore was on the field, nose pointing into the fair but constant breeze. She had been gassed up, and Ripley and Lee ambled along in their teddy-bear suits. Lee's was too tight and too short, coming to his calves. It was fleece-lined, with a leather shell, and he wore his uniform beneath it, and silk drawers below that. He carried his Springfield.

"Surprising I haven't taken you up," Ripley said. "You can't walk ten feet without someone wanting you to take him up."

Lee pulled at the yarn roped around his neck, so the puppets came away from his skin and now rode atop the teddy bear. Ripley glanced at them.

"Any idea where you'd like to go?" he finally asked.

"I don't know, sir," Lee said.

"People tend to go souvenir hunting. That would be fun." Ripley walked until he and Lee were next to *Lenore*.

Lee knew that Ripley, like most pilots, had made alterations to his cockpit. It was where pilots worked, and it was where they might die, so the officers tended to bring with them pages from the Bible or good-luck charms, or they might paint slogans to cheer themselves up.

But Lee hadn't paid attention to what Ripley had brought with him—he had just a vague impression of newspapers shellacked to the framing. Now Ripley asked him to sit in the pilot's seat. Lee straddled it carefully. Rudder bar, throttle, control stick—yes, he had known these would be here. What did Ripley want him to see? He was submerged to the shoulders in a collage.

All around him were French postcards and models cut from the racier editions of *L'Etude Académique*. There were cyanide prints of nude dancers in mid-jump from Alo Studios and Alta Studios, smuggled via international mail, and exquisite silver-tint odalisques in harem poses, breasts bare above beaded midriff corsets, in postures of supplication.

All of them looked just a bit sad to Lee. He had seen—especially since his trip overseas—nude models who seemed excited or shameless or frozen in the staid spirit of classicism, but Ripley had not chosen these. His models had children at home. They knew they had to walk home after dark. They worried what their parents might think.

Ripley was looking at him expectantly, and Lee smiled, and Ripley smiled in relief, as if they both understood something powerful about what one would like to be enveloped by while battling through complex skies.

"Oh," Lee said, for there was one photograph over the magneto of a fully dressed woman with black bangs, looking straight at the camera with no discernible expression. She looked as if she were empty, as if the picture were out of focus, even though she was shown in crisp detail. She also looked familiar, more than familiar, eyes piercing those bangs with a challenging gaze much like those of the woman who had given Lee the finger puppets. The hairstyle was popular in Paris, so the coincidence was—

"What do you think, Duncan?"

"I like it, sir," he said, looking at Ripley again.

"Shall we get those souvenirs?"

"Yes, sir."

Lee stepped out of the pilot's cab, where Ripley had pasted the photograph of his wife right over the controls to his Marlins. When he shot at the enemy he was staring directly into her matchless eyes.

It wasn't as simple as jumping into the plane; the Liberty engine required three normal men to swing the prop. Starting it today was a relaxed affair, since the flight was looked upon as a practice run. Lee was asked if he would settle a bet and start the prop by himself, and he shook his head—it was widely believed, and equally disbelieved, that he was tall and strong enough to do it.

"There's ten bucks in it for you," said the sergeant, who had thirty riding by now.

Lee declined, for perhaps the hundredth time, in this case remembering a legitimate reason: he had not entirely loaded the plane with its necessary ordnance. So he trotted in his teddy bear back to the officers' quarters as the field filled with men attempting to start up *Lenore*.

A sergeant sat in the pilot's cockpit, priming the engine, and with the throttle a quarter open, gave the signal to the first man, who turned the propeller with one rough hand, and extended his other hand, which the second man grabbed firmly, and then the third man took the second man's other hand in his own, so they made a human daisy chain, ready to pull in a tug of war.

"Contact!" yelled the first man.

"Contact!" yelled the sergeant, and then all three men began to sway together. To the left, and then to the right, with vigor. It was a piston motion and a Russian dance, and when they were almost carried off their heels with the rocking, the first man pulled the prop with all his might, and then, with the weight of the others coming to his aid, the propeller swung upward, the men sprawled onto the field, laughing, and the engine caught on the very first try.

While the engine warmed, Ripley and Lee were engaged in conversation.

"How are the guns, Corporal?"

"They're perfect, sir. Loaded and ready."

"And the hydraulics?"

"Mysterious," he said.

"So we're taking our chances. As always."

Leland had imagined his life in Hollywood would be filled with friends. They would have dinners together, play jokes on one another, buy each other expensive automobiles, and have early-morning cookouts in the hills, and while the sun rose, they would bare their hearts' desires. He had never thought how he would get from where he was now (no friends) to there (many friends).

"Thank you for taking me up, sir," he said.

"You're welcome. Did I mention it would be fun?"

Lee thought, like realizing he was walking on a tightrope, that Lieutenant Ripley liked him. "I liked your décor. Very smart." Men, he decided, probably did not compliment each other's décor. "I haven't told anyone the story of these," he said, touching Nanette and her companion.

"That's been a spot of mystery, to tell the truth," Ripley replied.

"It has?"

"A pilot or two feels quite jealous of you, you know?"

"They do? Well, I'd just gotten off the train—"

"Near Montmartre?"

"Gare du . . ." He thought about it. "Nord? It's the one with the café across the street, the one with the black pillars."

"Onyx Noir." Ripley chuckled. "So black they named it twice. A little crammed with doughboys. And you went to Pigalle?"

"I didn't. I went on the Métro—Botzaris, not that far. My pack was heavy, and I'd just gotten off a car that smelled so much like horses I was embarrassed, so I went into one of those washrooms and scrubbed down a bit. When I came out, I walked another block and noticed a woman by that park." He paused.

"Parc des Buttes-Chaumont."

"That's it."

"The women there are of a higher class, I've heard. Not at all professionals at work. Very good of you."

"She asked if she could paint my portrait."

"My goodness," Ripley said. Parc des Buttes-Chaumont was the place for amateur lady painters. Many of them were beautiful, and most were Frenchwomen, married, who had money. He folded his arms, in admiration. "She had other talents."

"Yes, sir." Lee laughed.

"French talents?" Ripley asked.

"She had picked up more than the basics, even though she was American," Lee replied.

"And she had— American? Really."

"Yes, sir."

Ripley kicked at the ground a bit. "Those women who sketch, they don't usually take after soldiers. I've seen them doing flowers and whatnot."

"Well . . ." Lee shrugged.

"So she did a charcoal sketch of you, and the rest was history, I suppose."

"No, sir."

"No?"

"No, she used egg tempera."

Two of the ground crew signaled—the engine was plenty warm. Ripley looked from Lee to the plane and back again. "Egg tempera?"

"I hadn't heard of it, either."

"I've heard of it," Ripley said, but without intonation. He stubbed his cigarette out on the bottom of his boot. "It flourished in the Byzantine Empire." The stubbing continued until the cigarette had splintered like rotten wood.

"Oh," said Lee, not exactly paying attention to the fate of the cigarette. Officers tended to know things. "None of the other girls I saw there were using it."

"It's rare." Ripley opened and closed his jaw, as if testing his bite. The propeller was turning furiously, the sergeant was signaling that he and Lee could board now. Still, Ripley continued. "It's not done in Paris much, but in England, there's a special order, they recently reissued *The Art of Cennino Cennini,* and—"

"She had that book."

"Did she?" Ripley said.

"Sir? You know they're ready for us over there?"

The men were waving, for the plane was burning fuel and the engine was getting warmer by the minute. Ripley seemed to be unable to move.

"Was it the edition with . . . the red cover?"

"Actually, she'd made her own cover," Lee said brightly. He had hoped that by now he would be further into his discussion of how he had been given the puppets, and didn't want to be caught on this digression. "She'd painted a portrait on it, a man and a woman—I mentioned it to her, in fact. It almost looked like a wedding portrait. Anyway—"

"You know, Duncan, I'm sorry, you're right, we should go." Ripley walked toward the airplane, taking great strides.

Lee caught up to him before they reached the twin cockpits. "Anyway," he said, "it was quite a ride."

Ripley said nothing. Lee had heard other men bragging and knew the rhythm to it.

"She even had a trick with an ice cube," he said, and Ripley walked away, to the cockpit. "Sir? Lieutenant? You need this before we get airborne."

"Need what?"

Lee handed over what he had brought from the officers' quarters: Ripley's pistol.

Ripley climbed over the wing and into his cab, and Lee did the same, settling onto the bench of the observer cab, where he strapped himself in and lowered his goggles.

Then he raised his goggles.

The propeller was chewing up the morning air; the plane was now rattling across the grass as Ripley opened the throttle slowly. He revved the engine so that it roared, and the rocking was more severe, for, no matter how smooth the surface was, even if it had been combed by fairies, it seemed that the wheels of a DH 4 would find every stone and hole in all of France. Lee felt himself bouncing on his bench uncomfortably. It no longer seemed like such a good day to fly.

The tail lifted; the plane leapt up like a salmon, bounced, then went airborne, up, high up, over the treeline. Lee felt his stomach dropping, but this was not quite the reason for it.

Turbulence tossed the DH 4 around like a god's cocktail shaker. To go straight on takeoff or landing was to be called a sissy; the point was to show a little style, and so there were banks and spirals and loops, normally. But not today. Ripley seemed to be set on going straight up, full pressure on the stick, drawn into his stomach.

Lee could not get his attention, though he banged twice; still, they simply climbed vertically, dangerously, taking the plane to its limits. Lee looked behind him, at the ground. Below was the three-fingered lake at Lachausse, the V cut through Le Bois de Mort-Mare, and flanking it, the miles of ground pockmarked by shell holes, the lengths of wrecked railroads, overturned carriages, and then, spreading around them, the trenches that zigzagged crazily, as if interlaced by drunken spiders, tinier and tinier. The engine was groaning, it was beginning to make the sounds of pinging and popping that meant the carbs weren't adjusting to the great shift in height.

They were climbing too quickly. The wings twirled in the breeze, spiraling, the propeller pointing straight in the air; they pierced the clouds, vanished into the sheets of crystal and ice, and then, on the other side, were into the blue, where it was colder, and still no change in velocity; it was as if Ripley were going to take them to the edge of space, where the stars would always shine without twinkling.

Then the plane was horizontal again.

Lee could breathe again. Wrapped around him on the walls of his cockpit were mosaics of bones and skeletons, memento mori, thanatopian lithographs, and, as in the pilot's cab, there was a single image in the dead center. But this one was not of an alluring woman. It was a wedding photograph. The groom wore an observer's uniform, and a Statue of Liberty badge. The bride wore white. But both of their faces had been replaced by skulls. Which was disturbing enough, but Lee knew with a certainty that made him ill that he had seen this photograph before. Except as a painting. As egg tempera.

They flew on toward the horizon line, which from this great height showed the curvature of the earth. The war was below them, the arcs of occasional shells lofting and falling to earth: black puffs of smoke were the Huns, white bursts were Allied. The wind was brutal here, the air thin, and as Ripley throttled back, the radial popped, a burst of blue flame whipping from the exhaust stack past the cockpit. He and Lee were miles and miles away from anyone else who might harm them.

To see the planet from a great height leads to thoughts painted with broad strokes. From the perspective of the observer's seat in a DH 4, above the smoke and cinders of fires, with the cold reaching around his goggles into his skin, Lee was trying to come to any conclusion other than the most obvious one.

She was a good ride. The ice cube.

And Lee had handed Ripley his pistol.

Lee's Springfield was in the cockpit, which was a good thing. It was strapped down, a leather braid around its butt. He stared at it.

Life means nothing, Lee thought. They passed over what was once a village, and in the center, a red brick smokestack, which Lee saw was flanked by ruined buildings and delivery wagons that were now splintered. He'd seen—he thought—huge sacks, flour and sugar maybe, and he said aloud, in words swallowed by the engine's mighty wailing, "See, that man just wanted to have a bakery."

Decades later, in Vevey, Switzerland, dictating his life story, Chaplin asked Ingrid Etter, his amanuensis, if she had made sure to write September 15, 1918, in especially dark ink. When he read his manuscript aloud to visitors, he would pause on that date, and his guests, hesitant to interrupt their thickset host, felt they should not even breathe until he resumed. Sometimes he picked up the story again, but more often, he called the recitation to a halt, and retired early, knees cracking with every step up the marble stairs. The published version of his autobiography omits the date entirely.

By September 15, Chaplin had shot most of his film, which he decided wasn't called *Camouflage,* because that was secretly a bit snide. That went along with his early ideas, dogs dragging soldiers' bones across battlefields—clever ideas, idealistic notions the average soldier would bayonet him for. He cut the darker overtones, the starvation, the dogs, the lice, and played up the slapstick of capturing the Kaiser. And he slapped on an ending that, even as he was shooting it, struck him as the worst of any of his films: The Little Fellow wakes up. It's all been a dream. Dear God.

He finished this edit early in the morning of September 15, around five o'clock. He was entirely alone at the studio, having mastered the art of splicing film years before, when he realized that no one else was capable of staying up by the light table several nights in a row, and no one else had his eye for telling the difference between a shot that lasted eighteen seconds and one that lasted eighteen seconds and three-sixteenths. Upon finishing, he walked to the swimming pool and stood on the end of the diving board, bouncing in place. The sun was coming up; the morning birds—different kinds of songbirds whose names he didn't know—towhees? finches?— were flitting in the ficus trees; and he pinched together his thumb and forefinger against the skin of his palm until his nails left a divot.

He had fifty-six minutes of the following: him fouling up some randomly ordered infantry drills that any doughboy would know were inaccurate; him doing business in the trenches (the mail scene seemed to go on forever); taking thirteen Germans prisoner ("I surrounded them"—why had he found that funny?); the tree-disguise faction; romancing Edna while the Kaiser visits her farmhouse (why was he there?); Edna overacting to the point of gnawing her knuckles bloody; some business with Syd and Edna disguised as German staff that was actually rather good; capturing the Kaiser; Charlie wakes up, The End.

He had lost track somewhere. A *Dog's Life* had been better—the Little Fellow had changed from the beginning to the end—but in this one, no. Chaplin bounced up and down on his diving board, hands in pockets, looking into the salt waters his career had paid for. The picture was a loss of nerve. He had taken out the hardest parts, and in doing so had removed its tusks, leaving behind a saber-toothed tiger made out of soap. He had scheduled a screening at one-thirty for Doug. If Doug had reservations, he would destroy the print.

He listened for the sound of the new milkman (they took eight quarts on the front doorstep from the Golod Dairy, which had just opened shop with very competitive rates), the rattle of bottles, and he awaited the single shot of a sniper that would pitch him forward into the pool, where blood would ooze like an oil slick upon the water.

Sunnyside

He wanted to talk to Syd about the futility of love and about his coming death, but at nine-thirty the Russians arrived.

They had no appointment; the front office was filled with them. Two limousines disgorged approximately fifteen men and women in furs, with attendants and ladies-in-waiting and a silent three-year-old child of indeterminate gender that sucked its right thumb and walked with its left hand lodged in the nanny's waistband.

The procession was headed by Prince Vasily Vasilievich Meshchersky, a slender, bearded man who witnessed the commotion around him with his head tilted slightly backward, and his fingertips placed perfectly against the seams of his trousers. With him, his wife, their attendants, a few counts, a countess; Chaplin nodded with each ornate introduction. They were in Hollywood for an indefinite period, Chaplin was told. They had heard that all royalty in—the word the translator used was "transition"—should visit the Chaplin Studios.

"They love your movies," the translator said. She wore her black hair in a chignon that almost touched the collar of a black silk dress that fastened on the front with large braid buttons. She was a narrow woman, far more beautiful than anyone had ever told her, and her frequent glances at the floor made him want to pull her into bed by her hair.

"Pardon?" He hadn't heard the last three things she'd said.

"His Excellency the Prince asks about the ending of *Praztoi Ulitza,*" she said. "Of *Easy Street.*"

He remembered now that he had been up all night, editing his terrible new film. "Yes?"

"He is pleased that you defeated the villain at the end."

Chaplin tried to remember that far back. In *Easy Street,* he had defeated the monstrous Eric Campbell by sticking his head in an extinguished gas lamp, a gag he was proud of, but then he remembered there was another villain. "The anarchist?"

"The Bolshevik."

"Well," he said, "it was an anarchist, but I can see how . . ."

The prince spoke again, making sweeping motions with his elegant hands, hands whose most strenuous act in the old country had been to knock over the king of his Fabergé chess set. The translator, in a rush, said, "His Excellency the Prince enjoys that you cleverly saved Miss Edna from the Bolshevik menace which now threatens the world. It was a sophisticated outcome."

Chaplin grinned at him, and the prince put up two fists, swinging them and nodding in appreciation of the scene. He then frowned, and gestured that the translation should continue.

"But he wonders why, in the criminal's lair, there were postcards of the Tsar and Tsarina."

It had been a two-week shooting schedule. He had simply declared that Russian thugs should have Russian things on their walls. That someone would pay attention hadn't yet occurred to him, not in late 1916.

"Bolsheviks may protest otherwise, but everyone secretly loved the Tsar and Tsarina," he said, and waited for it to be translated. When it was, and there was gracious laughter all around, Chaplin turned Prince Meshchersky loose on the desk register, telling him please to sign his full family name, if only because that would buy Chaplin time before they asked him to do the walk.

While the prince dipped his pen in an inkwell filled with ruby-red ink ("Lord of Pokrovskoe and Petrovskoe; Heir to Lotoshino; Duke and master of the Vesholi-Podol palace," and so on), Chaplin went to his office, with strict instructions that he was not to be disturbed except for Syd.

Chaplin had done his office with leather padding on which he displayed framed playbills of the Lancashire Lads and Gillette's *Sherlock Holmes.* There were scrapbooks and piles of mail on the floor, and books angled at the edge of an ornate Louis XIV desk that might collapse any moment. It was cavelike, and when Syd finally did come in to sit, he had to dislodge one of the studio's orange-marmalade cats, who nested atop Chaplin's overcoat.

"How's the war movie?" Syd asked.

"How's the war?"

"It should be over by Christmas, they say."

"Is that a fact?" Chaplin poured himself a glass of water from a pitcher he kept on the floor behind the desk. "I was thinking. Comedies end with a marriage. What about tragedies?"

"Death?" Syd wished they weren't discussing tragedies. Tragedies made no money. He suspected his brother had no mind for them.

"No," Chaplin said. "Every story ends in death, if only you follow it long enough."

"Every story is a tragedy, then. Can we just start rolling on the next picture? What's the setup?"

"No setup." Chaplin was feeling a new vein of energy. "No story ends happily. The happy ending is only about knowing where to end on a smile, at the very moment where fortune is still on the ascent. The open road. The wedding."

"I guarantee you, when the war is over, we'll all be happy."

"Something will come along to replace it."

"There will be dancing in the streets."

"Until there isn't."

Syd tugged on his nose, a habit he had developed in the last year or two of these conversations. "Then something good will happen again. Eventually."

"Puppies. The lovers reunited. Or it's all been a dream. It's annoying."

"Yes, Charlie, but you're better than that. You'd never just have it be a dream." After a moment, Syd said, "What?"

Chaplin drummed his palms on his desk. "Say I kill the Little Fellow at the end of this picture," he said, and he watched with satisfaction as Syd swallowed hard. "Say we end with a bullet through his head."

"You didn't do that," Syd said quickly.

"You're right. That would betray the audience—they walked in looking for a comedy. So it will have to be the next story, maybe, or one after that. The one about Napoleon."

Syd sized up his brother. His unshaven jaw. "Have you cut it together yet?"

"I think it's called *Shoulder Arms*. That's a British command. No dough-boy would ever hear it, so it's unrealistic, but—"

"And you were up all night?"

"It's a puzzle, isn't it? You end a comedy with a marriage, because everyone wants to see a marriage. But how about a tragedy?"

The secretary, Helen, was standing in the doorway again. She had to lean to be seen around the bookcase. "The Russians," she said, and bit her lip.

"Yes?"

"They had heard from their friend Prince Henry of Greece that some-times a souvenir—"

"Oh, dear mother of us all." Chaplin winced.

"—film is made, as a token of—"

"No more princes," Chaplin said. "Let them meet Doug. Let them meet Pickford. No more tokens, not ever again. Tell them . . . tell them I'm dead, something, I don't know what."

She shimmered away like a mirage. Chaplin faced his brother with both fatigue and stamina; it was odd, the longer he went without sleep the less he seemed to need it. He hadn't been hungry for hours, and he couldn't imagine wanting food again.

"You know, you should rest," Syd said.

"I've ended the new film with me waking up. It's all been a dream."

Syd couldn't tell if he was joking. "So it's a comedy."

"With a bad ending. It lacks courage."

"I'm sure it's good," Syd said. "When do I see it, then?"

"You're sure it's good." Said with suspicion. There was an uncomfortable moment, for Charlie recognized in Syd the careful gaze, the reassuring pat to the back of the hand. How he always knew to sing harmony on "As the Church Bells Chime" when their mother reached the second verse. Chaplin wanted to clear the air of such things, so he said, "Syd, have you ever felt like you're on the verge of something larger?" He wanted to say it precisely. "Have you ever felt that if you get past the sound of your own voice, you might somehow become . . ." He opened his arms and threw back his shoulders and took in a deep draft of warm Hollywood air that had coalesced in his stuffy little office. "Like that day two years ago, when everyone thought they saw me. Like that."

Syd, lost and a bit frightened, said, "Why don't you show me the film? I might understand more that way."

"The film after this will capture it," his brother said. His voice, while not getting louder, was getting faster. "I sometimes wonder if I might just be a radio receiver for the world's thoughts, and if I am careful, I might just hear them. I'll make a film as good as—well, you know?"

Helen was at the door again, before he'd had time to truly build on these ideas, and he was angry at the interruption.

"Yes?"

"It's one-thirty," she said. "Mr. Fairbanks and Miss Pickford are in the cinema."

Syd was standing up and out the door before another word could be said. He was worried. Syd always worried, but now he was worried about his brother's moods. They walked together across the courtyard, and Syd said, "I wonder when they'll let Mum come over."

This caused Chaplin to break stride. Syd wasn't joking. He truly didn't know. In rapid succession, Chaplin felt pity and admiration for Syd, and he felt like the worst son in the world, again, and then he said, "Yes, I wonder."

14

They were heading north to no particular place. The war had moved eastward, and the sky was more or less empty. Every so often, a vibration pinged up Ripley's rudder control, which was mated to a secondary control in Lee's cabin—a type of improvised Morse code—as Lee pointed out good places to land. Then he was asking if they were going to land soon.

Ripley put the nose down, increasing their velocity, then pulled back on the stick with a kind of steady joy, sending them into the beginnings of a loop.

As they ascended, Lee didn't enjoy the carnival-ride feeling. Thrown backward, blood rushing against gravity, he ticked off his faults, beginning with ambition, and they climbed upward until they were inverted and Ripley cut the engine.

Lee lurched up at the ground, his shoulders squeezed against the narrow leather seat straps. His scalp tingled, and his palms went slick and cold. His Springfield clattered out of the cockpit until it was also hanging in the air, secured by its strap, and then—it wasn't.

They came out of the loop, upright, engine firing. Lee looked below him, as if he might see his only means of defending himself piercing cloud after cloud as it fell to earth, but it was already gone. He sat back in his seat and stared straight ahead at the gasoline tank. Then he put his head into his mittens.

The DH 4 continued on its uncertain way. Ripley was descending now like a falling leaf. He leaned into the throttle. Down they went, passing numerous likely landing sites near air hangars, machine-gun nests, bivouacs, and such. They circled a vineyard that had gone to the rambles, its hillocks and fields chaotically spotted with wildly growing autumn grapes. A single wattle and daub building stood in the flats. Its roof was mostly intact, enough of a rarity to invite exploration.

Landing would be quite the stunt, in that even here, away from the main battlefield, there were more crater holes than patches of level earth. And as they drew closer to the ground, it was apparent that the clearest part of the field itself was dotted with the stumps of former grapevines, small mushrooms half concealed by weeds. Landing was dangerous. Taking off would be almost impossible.

Ripley threw the plane into a vertical bank, and dropped sideways, killing all forward speed. They fell a thousand feet.

Lee was thrown half out of his seat, and hit the edge of the cockpit with a grunt. The ground was rushing toward him, green earth ascending far too quickly; there was no way they would land safely.

Just before his wingtip would have touched the ground, Ripley brought the plane level. With a series of thumps that were no more or less startling than falling out of bed, several times, they were coasting among the weeds.

He had put them in a clearing not more than thirty yards across, dotted with severed stands that were once grapevines. He killed the engine, unstrapped himself, went out of the cockpit and over the wing, and touched the ground, blandly smiling.

Lee went more cautiously.

They stripped off their outer layers, leaving themselves in their field uniforms. Lee switched to his simple wool cap. It hadn't rained all day, which meant it would have to rain again soon.

They stood still on the ground for a few moments, the way fliers did— in the air, they lost track of all sense of motion; returning to earth meant some adjustment in equilibrium.

"Sir?"

"Yes, Duncan?"

Lee had no idea what to say.

Ripley carefully checked the snap on his pistol, and smoothed out his uniform. He wore his thousand-yard stare. "Your rifle, Duncan?"

Lee shook his head.

"You put it in the plane."

Lee nodded. "But I enjoyed the loop otherwise."

Ripley squinted. He dusted his hands together. "Hmm."

Lee wondered what that meant. He surveyed the ruinous space between the plane's nose and the nearest stand of trees. It was studded with stumps. He saw rabbit holes. He wanted to ask a question, but he was afraid of the answer.

"How do we get out of here?"

Ripley put his hands on his hips and made an easy surveying of the field. He shrugged. Then he began walking.

It was a small vineyard, just one barnlike storage building with a horseshoe of hills behind it, patchworked with terraced rows of yellowing vines stretched in the Guyot method along wire trellises. Most of the tendrils were barren, but here and there, grapes—Chardonnay—had gone wild, overplump, and leathery among the turning leaves.

There hadn't been wine here in years—the bottles had been seized and the oaken barrels emptied. The main building looked as if it had been used until recently for something. Half timbered in oak, it was thick-walled, whitewashed, with a primitive cement binding together hazel or oak branches. It had been bombed, Leland noticed with some disappointment, but only once. From the ground, it was easier to see the damage—tiles had jarred loose from the roof, and two walls been blown out. Wild tarragon and purple dandelions poked among the debris.

The pathway there was short, but slow going because of the tall weeds. Lee and Ripley walked haltingly, eyes on the ground, searching among the pennyroyal for unexploded shells.

Ripley hummed to himself tunelessly, and Lee was thinking in circles, until the sound of humming was beginning to drive him mad. He felt airsick. He wanted to say, "I didn't know."

They were out of the weeds and on the dirt path to the courtyard. Lee's eyes narrowed.

"Yes, Duncan?" Ripley said.

The winery was as simple and friendly as a country barn, flanked by wings that created a sheltered courtyard, the entirety of which they saw only now that they were standing within it. Concussive force—bombs—had blown holes out of the flanking walls, eye sockets in a clean white skull. There were small piles of rubble—brick and stone and cement—in the courtyard, along with a weathered bench, a dead elm tree, and an oak whose branches lifted far above the roof. Under the oak, there was a motorcycle on its stand.

Neither of them said a word; they were staring at the olive-drab machine. There were no obvious markings. It was heavy with mud, and there were two leather pouches hanging over its rear fender. It didn't look American. Might it be British? They had trained in recognizing enemy airplanes by sight and sound, and either of them could identify a German tank from many yards away, but not motorcycles.

"Sir, do we know where the front lines are?"

"We're on our side. I think." Ripley turned on his heel, looking for the sun. "Or not."

Lee padded toward the motorcycle. He put his palm against its engine, and flinched, shaking it in the air. He trotted back, grabbed Ripley, and tugged him behind a pile of rubble. Lee gestured toward the bike. He held up one finger, then pointed to his eyes. One pair of goggles on the handlebars.

The rubble and the motorcycle stood between them and the exposed parts of the winery. Lee listened for sounds from within the building, which had a few small shattered windows. If a sniper was nearby, he had heard the DH 4 engine—unmistakably a Liberty—and had ample time to find an adequate vantage point.

"We could go back to the plane," Lee whispered. "We have machine guns; maybe—"

"The Marlin is pointing the wrong way," Ripley said without intonation. "And if you fire the Lewis at a target on the ground, you'll hit the empennage." He yawned. "Also, if we retreat, he could shoot us in the back."

"He doesn't have a gun." Lee dug at his collar, which suddenly felt tight. "Do you think he has a gun?"

Ripley nodded. He spoke calmly, the way water flowed downhill. "I'd rather be shot—well, if the only choice is to be shot, I'd rather be shot in the chest than the back." He shrugged. "What about you?"

Lee searched Ripley's eyes for signs of warmth or irony or even jaded savoir-faire, but all he came away with was a hint of an abyss. "Standing up," he whispered. He remembered his sergeant yelling at him to focus his breathing. He breathed through his nose. Lavender, grass, oaky smells, earth, and the way he himself always smelled: damp wool and gasoline.

They were surrounded on three sides by walls. The wall straight ahead had cross-braced doors, like a barn. The doors were padlocked. But a man could dodge left or right and scramble into the holes made by the bombs. "He hasn't shot us yet," Lee noted. He yawned; it was contagious.

"Perhaps he hasn't got a gun."

"Then we shouldn't be afraid of him," Lee said. "We have guns."

"*I* have a gun," Ripley said, which chilled Lee into silence. Ripley continued, "But there might be gas. Somewhere."

"We have respirators, I guess."

"Another reason for going forward. Zero for leaving."

They needed an immediate plan. So: Lee would go through one of the holes in the near wall. Ripley would circle around the back of the building and find another entrance. They would meet inside, and attempt to subdue anyone they found there.

"Does that sound fine?" Ripley asked.

"Yes, sir." It was a terrible plan.

"Good."

"Sir—when you get to the other side of the building?"

"Yes?"

"Be careful if you shoot."

"Of course."

"Because—"

"I understand," Ripley said. "You're worried I'll accidentally shoot you. Where's your knife?"

It was on his belt. Leland looked at it for a moment. "How will you start the plane?"

"Pardon?"

He had been so tense for so long he was almost drunk. "We might be able to turn the propeller over together. But without me, how would you get back home? You couldn't." This was like snapping a puzzle piece into place; it made him feel crafty.

"I don't know what you're on about," Ripley whispered. He hunched down and, with a spiderlike hunched-over scramble, trotted away, out of the courtyard. He was gone.

The screening room was spartan. Pushed to make it as plush and extravagant as Zukor's, with overstuffed velvet seats, perhaps four rows of them, a mixing bar, tasseled ropes, carpets, a mural or two, Chaplin scrapped all those plans. He didn't want responses to his films at all governed by how grand the setting was. Plus, there was the expense to consider. When the Galaxy opened on Fairfax, they had ordered too many seats, so Chaplin bought several of the extras. Sixteen chairs, two projectors, wooden floors, and in back, for mood music, an old church organ that you could pump with your feet, no fuss.

Entering, he was nervous to the point of being insensible, and he signaled that the film should start immediately. And so there was a moment of confusion, himself appearing just as the film came on, projected across his chest, Doug and Mary standing to greet him, and, oh dear, he couldn't really say a proper hello, how had this happened, the film had started, let's all sit down, apologies, we'll say hello afterward.

Chaplin recognized the footsteps of Alf, Rollie, and Albert Austin, and then sensed perfume and heels, meaning a girl or two had slipped in, perhaps from Wardrobe, perhaps someone Albert was trying to impress, and then another tread, careful yet heavy, that he couldn't place. Ten bodies in the theater, eleven with Eddie, who was manning the projector. Chaplin was biting his nails, a filthy habit that he wished not to have.

Laughter. It began with the opening scenes of training, and continued throughout the scenes in the trenches. Chaplin saw Pickford's hand go toward the crease of her eye. He looked carefully for how the light was hitting her cheek—was it wet?

After the first reel, he closed his eyes and just tried to listen to the reaction, feeling again as if he were on the verge of dissolving, casting off the lens of his own perception, actually feeling what the rest of the universe felt.

The laughter did not build, but, rather, there were short, sharp chuckles punctuated by a sort of holding-the-breath-with-worry. There was a question of whether Charlie, the slacker, would insult the troops, and that seemed to slip away, and in its place was the thrill of whether he would capture the Kaiser.

By the time Edna, Syd, Chaplin, and the others were standing among the AEF troops in France (actually at Fairfax and Santa Monica, on the airfield side of the street), and the Little Fellow had kicked the Kaiser in the behind, and soldiers all around were carrying him on their shoulders, funneling champagne into their mouths, slapping him on the back, there was actual applause in the tiny room. Douglas was the first to stand, but somehow his motion distracted from the final shot revealing it had all been a dream, and then there were hands on Chaplin's shoulders, tousling his hair, cries of pleasure, a strange moment in which he was being celebrated now as the Little Fellow had been, onscreen, and he wondered if he would wake up from this, too.

"Thank you," he said. And then, "Thank you."

The lights were up, and he was shaking hands with everyone, and wearing his filmmaker's smile of humility, which he genuinely felt. Syd punched him in the shoulder and told him to stop worrying. Chaplin was being told from all sides that the film was a success, he had managed to get laughs from the war without a single ill feeling toward the men who fought it, it was a small miracle.

Eventually, he noticed that behind the ring of well-wishers, to the side, spinning one heel back and forth and poking her tongue in her cheek, was Pickford. Waiting her turn.

When roughly half the room had cleared, she finally spoke. "Germans equal cops," she said. "Brilliant. You cracked it."

Knowing how much that had cost her, he took her hand and kissed it. But his eye was also going to the corner of the room, where Bill McAdoo lingered.

Chaplin asked, "Did you enjoy it?"

"Oh, yes. Yes, I did." McAdoo was staring at him in surprise. When Chaplin, a smile seemingly stapled to his face, continued to look at him, McAdoo said, "Very much." He had already seen other people tell Chaplin how good the film was.

"Do you think it will make money?" Chaplin asked.

"Huh. That's interesting." The proper answer to this would have been "yes," said with exclamation points tripping from the back of the throat, but McAdoo was in this way, too, an innocent. "I'd have to think about that."

Chaplin felt a jab of panic, but then Doug put both his hands on Chaplin's shoulders. "Charlie," he said, "let's celebrate."

"I have a three o'clock meeting, so—"

"Fine. Then I," Doug responded, "am going to the toilet." After which he strode away. Chaplin's eyes met Pickford's, which were narrowed as if to scold her man, but then she saw Charlie, and she blushed. Then they were laughing together.

"Doug," Chaplin said.

"I wonder if he has a private life," she murmured. "If he's even aware there is such a thing."

"You know, I've wondered, too." Charlie glanced across the room. Syd was talking quietly to McAdoo, leaving Chaplin and Pickford alone together, and the silence began to hum. Chaplin had to leave at any moment. But he did not want to insult Mary now. "How is Frances?"

"She's well. She's in France, I understand. She's writing a documentary about women's role in the war."

"Ah."

"And she's in love."

"Really?"

"With a man named Fred. He's a chaplain for the 143rd."

"A priest?"

"No, not that. Fred's a confessor for the men"—she made her voice gruff—"the *conscience* of the regiment. Morally he's beyond reproach, but mostly he's six foot five inches tall, looks like a god, and he was in the Olympics."

An Olympic athlete who was also a priest. "How tall did you say?"

"Six foot five." There was more news about Frances, news of nurses and drivers and Hello Girls, but Charlie could not hear it. He wanted the day to end. He needed Doug to come back so he could leave gracefully. Mary was hesitating.

"Yes?"

"I noticed something about this one." She inclined her head toward the projector, rather than the screen, as most people would have. Her eyes were careful. "He doesn't change."

"He changes," Chaplin said, as automatically as if someone had fed a nickel into him, but he saw something forgiving in Mary's face. "Well, you're right, I suppose. I couldn't actually have him be a hero. You know, the role of heroism is no longer understood in this complex—"

"I agree with you," she said. As if she were sharing a secret, she leaned in, and even in the weak light of the little theater, the bounce of her curls made Chaplin's wary heart melt a fraction. "It's an odd trick, Charlie. You play the Tramp every time, and every time he has to stick up for himself, and by the end he's changed. And then you make the next one, and he's back where he started."

"Well, he's the same all the time and he's different. He's a pooka," Chaplin said. "That's a kind of spirit—"

"I know what a pooka is," Mary whispered. "But he doesn't change this time."

Chaplin swallowed. The way she said it, she sounded like a physician who had just thumped on his chest and found something wanting. "No, he doesn't. I hope that's still all right."

"It's all right," she said hazily. "Tell me, does he have a family, ever?"

"Oh! Well, originally, I had given him children and a wife, and he joins up because they're so horrible."

"A mother? Does he have a mother?"

"Mary, I don't know."

"It's just an odd thing, fifty or sixty movies into it, and you don't know if he has a mother."

"Oh, for goodness' sake, that's nonsense, why would he have something like that?"

She didn't respond. The question had not been probing or cruel, he now realized. She had been offering him the services of an expert story-teller. When had he started yelling at her?

But then Doug was behind him, expelling a sigh of satisfaction, having returned from his trip to the Chaplin Studios toilet as if he'd been leading a safari. He threw his arms around Mary and was telling Chaplin how much he had laughed, how *Shoulder Arms* would make a mint, and was inviting him out again, telling him to cancel his three o'clock.

"Say," said McAdoo. He looked around the room, and his accountant's eye was just counting heads. Chaplin, Fairbanks, Pickford, and Syd were the only ones left. "Could I talk to you folks for a moment?"

"I do have to leave," Chaplin said. "I owe all of you so much, and I feel all of your love and support for this film so . . ."

McAdoo was oddly circumspect. "If you can stick around, I've been digging for the last few weeks," McAdoo said. "And this has nothing to do with me, but there are some subterranean conversations you'll want to know about."

It was the word "subterranean" that caused Chaplin to listen. It was more poetic than McAdoo's normal speech.

"Famous Players, First National, Metro, maybe a few others—they're talking about forming a kind of trust."

Chaplin had no idea what this meant, but he saw Sydney standing up straighter, and exhaling through his thick lips. So it meant something bad.

"How are they organizing?" Syd asked.

"They want to consolidate their business."

"Horizontally or vertically?" Pickford asked.

"Both."

Her eyes became fiery slits. "Damn them," she whispered.

Syd was shaking his head. "Both," he said.

Chaplin would never let on that he was confused, but his eye caught Doug's. Doug, because it seemed like the right thing to do, put his hands on Mary's shoulders.

Mary looked up toward Doug. "They want to produce, distribute, and exhibit films. Which means they're buying up exchanges and theaters. Is that correct, Mr. McAdoo?" When McAdoo nodded, Pickford continued. "I should own theaters," she said, but then she came back to the earth. "The troubling part—"

"The horizontal," Syd murmured.

"There's only one reason—"

Mary was cut off as McAdoo explained: "It won't be a formal monopoly, but more of a gentlemen's agreement. They want to cut you all out of it. If they all agree not to pay you, then you're through making all this money. Oh, Warner. I forgot them, they're involved, too."

"They'll never . . ." Chaplin said. But he didn't finish. "I have to go."

"What, is it three o'clock?" Pickford asked, like jabbing him with the point of a knife. "It behooves you to—"

"It behooves me? It behooves me?" Chaplin began to laugh, and, continuing with laughter, left the room.

He trotted back to his office, where he freshened up with a splash of water and a spray of breath mist, murmuring, "It behooooves me," and he combed his hair again. When he was finished, the assistant secretary was standing awkwardly near her desk.

"Yes?" He checked his watch again. He was late.

"The Russians," she said.

"They're not still here, surely?"

"No, I sent them away," she said. "They might come back."

"What's the trouble, then?"

She was biting down on her lip. "They have some pride," she said, "but finally they asked if there might be paying work, too. They all felt they might be supporting players."

"Oh." He froze, his hands straightening out his cap. "Honestly?"

"The duke was less interested in supporting roles," she said. "He thought people might want to see him in a more central . . . you know. Apparently, he has family in hiding in some monastery in Russia, and they need to earn money to get them. So supporting roles or 'even in background,' Olga said. She didn't know the word for 'extra,' so I had to tell her."

"All right, then," he said. Paper hat, paper hat. He shook his head. "But still. Dear God." He straightened his jacket, grabbed the unusually thick stack of afternoon papers off the receptionist's desk, and was out the door, where Kono awaited him at the car.

· · ·

He fumbled with the headlines in the backseat. There was news of the Saint-Mihiel offensive and its assorted victories, which he read but did not, strictly speaking, see. He was trying to unravel the afternoon's events, peeling back first the awful thoughts that led to a knot in the pit of his stomach.

He drummed his fingers on the seat, which seemed strangely unyielding, and he realized that, in his haste, he had taken not just the papers but the studio guestbook. He opened it. The last lines were filled out by Prince Meshchersky. He was surprised to see they were filled out in English.

15-Sept-18

Meshchersky. V. V. Lord of Pokrovskoe and Petrovskoe; Heir to Lotoshino; Duke and master of the Vesholi-Podol palace in Poltava; entitled noble ruling the estate of Petrovskoye-Alabino; humble penitent at the monastery of Solnechny Strana.

Chaplin marveled at the world so easily lost. Lord of what? Heir to which? The Meshchersky line was over, the revolution had left them in permanent *transition,* and in the search for work as an extra, the résumé item of ruling an estate did not count nearly as much as the ability not to look into the camera.

He thought of Samuel Goldwyn conspiring with Zukor and the rest, and he wondered if, indeed, all was vanity.

"Humble penitent at the monastery of Solnechny Strana." Its placement at the end announced pride in humility. If the prince could have but one honor back, would he choose that place, or the palace, the lordship?

He decided that Prince Meshchersky longed most for the place where he had been neither ruler nor noble, but humble penitent, and Chaplin chose to believe that the monastery stood awaiting his return, even if the revolution said otherwise.

He should have been nicer to Pickford. When he heard the word "mother," it was like "igloo" or "Portugal," something he could imagine and which he knew other people had a homespun fondness for. He wished *Shoulder Arms* had this feeling in it.

He looked up. The car was not moving. Kono had actually parked at the curb long moments before. There was a broad and flat lawn surrounding the Georgian municipal building, alone on its block, a massive and crushing structure with a red tile dome at its center, and rising from it the American flag. There was a great emptiness around it, just wild and untended fields of poinsettias, as if it were the last remaining castle on a great chessboard. Which made Chaplin stay in his automobile, for there were no shady spots or places to remain inconspicuous, and this was Hollywood High School. He should not be here.

They had an arrangement—if he was intolerably late, Mildred was to wait in the nook by the pergola, just down the block. He scanned the lawn, checked his watch again—he wasn't that late—and when he realized she wasn't going to appear on her own, he left the car.

He did not look about. Instead, he walked straight ahead, toward the pergola, attempting to radiate a sense that he belonged here. He was a teacher, an older brother, a coach, or he was Charlie Chaplin, here to give a pep talk to the boys about the importance of making your best effort.

When he had reached the timbers of the pergola, he could see the alcove ahead, and, against the herringbone brick, just the points of Mildred's black shoes.

Her mother was sitting next to her.

"Ailene," he said. He thought of social words to say—"Hello," to begin with—but it was obvious there were to be no niceties. Still, he said it: "Hello."

Mildred's knees were together, her feet apart, toe tips pointing toward each other. She did not look up. Her mother, Ailene, was holding a handkerchief, crumpled, in her hand. Her face turned its awful radiance at Chaplin.

He did not need to ask why Ailene was there. He did not need to ask what was coming next. It was coming at him with the force of shotgun pellets. It was a gaze, atavistic, that would not be tampered with.

Lee stood with his back pressed to the wall. The hole he was supposed to tumble through was just to his left. In the absence of thinking, his mind was wide open to music.

Sunnyside

That's the wrong way to tickle Marie
That's the wrong way to kiss

He tried to stop it, but that of course just made the song root like ivy. He imagined putting his head slowly around the corner, into the darkness. He imagined doing it, imagined singing loudly, "That's the wrong way to tickle Marie," then being shot in the throat.

There was some debris by his foot, a twisted sheet of metal that might have once been part of a drainage tank. He could just heft it with both hands, which meant he had to sheathe his knife. Had Ripley made it to the other side yet?

He heaved the scrap metal away from him, past the hole, into the line of sight of any snipers; it fell to earth with a clatter, but nothing further happened.

If I were a sniper, he thought, I would shoot at the *second* blur in the doorway.

He repeated his exercise with another, smaller, less satisfying-to-lift piece of metal, with similar results.

It was quiet.

Good bye to your Aunt Tilly
Hello, savoir faire
If you want to know the right way to tickle Marie

Heroic actions are taken sometimes just to keep annoying ditties at bay. He was too lanky for a good tuck-and-roll; nonetheless, he launched himself over the rubble. But when he stumble-stepped upright, his trench knife followed his arc, sailing out of its sheath, turning end over end. It hit the ground softly.

Lee was inside the building. And unarmed. His eyes weren't adjusting. He listened—nothing. He could smell overwhelming rot and some deep animal stench, but where was the enemy, if anywhere? He stopped breathing. In the dimness, from the light that streamed from the rafters, where the tiles had been displaced, he could see a tank. The gun was pointing at his head.

It looked like an ugly thirty-foot metal-studded packing crate someone had slammed around a gun barrel. The barrel was a single dark eye, all pupil. A 57mm cannon, he remembered, and then, yes, this would be an A7V tank. One of the main crossbeams that had supported the roof was splintered and leaning against the tank's main hatch. A splash of sunlight showed dirt and grime and, finally, a bird's nest. Disuse. The tank hadn't moved in months.

He heard boots on rubble. His eyes were doing better now, the winery was giving up some but not all of its secrets: splintered oak barrels, hay bales, a jumble of what looked like athletic equipment, and Ripley was picking his way carefully among a row of casks.

Then: a scuttling, the rustle of fabric, padding feet on the ground, and something in a drab, beaten-looking uniform raced across the floor and threw itself out the other hole in the wall. The sound of feet pounding against the dirt outside, racing away.

"Hey!" said Ripley. It had happened so quickly, neither man had had time to react. "Duncan?" Ripley called, sounding relieved. "We seem to be alone now."

Lee exhaled. "Good?" He couldn't help the inflection.

"Where's your knife?"

"I lost it."

"I see." He sounded disappointed.

And then, outside, a metallic wheeze, once, twice, and then ignition: the motorcycle starting. Ripley and Lee listened as the throttle opened and the bike raced away.

"Are you all right?"

"Yes. Yes, sir."

He stood with his back to Ripley. Was Ripley trying to make up his mind what to do? It was driving Lee mad. His eyes had now adjusted to the light, which was fairly helpful in that he could now look for his knife, but not helpful enough: he couldn't see the other German soldier, who was leaning against a bale of hay about fifteen yards away.

The soldier was squeezing his eyes shut, furious and sweating, horrified that his comrade had run away. He had no rifle of his own.

He did, however, have a flamethrower.

He had little training with the weapon—he wasn't a *stosstrupp*, simply a private, seventeen years old, who'd found it strapped to the motorcycle. He and his comrade had been starving, and they'd heard rumors that this building would have food in it. They'd found the food, but it was in cans, and they had no opener, so one of them had been quietly sobbing, and the other touching his shoulder to comfort him, when they heard the low drone of an enemy plane and realized they had no idea what side of the line they were on.

Sunnyside

While Ripley explored one side of the building, and Lee descended to one knee to sweep along the ground in search of his knife, eyes on whether Ripley had holstered his pistol (he hadn't), the boy was silently churning about what to do.

He had a second weapon, which he'd found here, but he didn't know how to use it, either. And it was far more dangerous and unpredictable than his flamethrower, so he turned back to the silver canister.

It was a portable model, a *Kleinflammenwerfer*, worn on the back, with straps. When ignited, its propellant would shoot a flame of petroleum about twenty feet long. He hadn't eaten in so long his arms were shaking. He couldn't determine how to use it without himself being burned to cinders. The whole of the building was dotted with hay bales.

Lee was still exploring, pistol out. The building didn't quite make sense—it hadn't been used for ammunition storage or sheltering troops or stables. The supplies didn't add up. Gymnastics equipment. Hurdles. Leather straps. Chains. On one wall was a shelf with dozens of gallon-sized cans. Each had a white label that showed a smug-looking butcher folding his arms, with a slogan below it, which Ripley read aloud, "*Rindfleisch-därme: tägliche Zuteilungen für den Kriegshund.* That's rough," he added. "They make Hans and Fritz eat beef intestines."

Lee said, "What?"

"*Kriegshunde.* War dogs. That's what the poor infantry Boche are, right? And what have we here?" There was a leather strap on the ground. He picked it up, whistling as he realized how long it was: thirty feet, perhaps. One end was tied to the tank tread.

Lee realized that no tin of food would use slang, and he realized what the leather strap meant, for its other end, which Ripley now held in his hand, terminated in a length of chain. He shouted "Hey" just as a figure leapt over a hay bale with a hose aimed high, letting loose a jet of flame at Ripley.

Ripley stood stupidly, and as Lee knocked him down to the dirt, he swore the lieutenant was grinning. Fistfuls of dirt, patting him down, rolling him on the ground just to make sure nothing was aflame, good, Lee stood up. "Hey!" said Lee again, and then, pointing his finger at the boy with the flamethrower, "No," not pleading, but as if reasoning with an irascible child. "*Nein,*" he said. "*Nein,*" calmly. The flames died out against the rafters, just as the boy fired off another blast—he aimed at Lee, but since no souvenir from a battlefield more complex than a canteen ever worked properly twice, the hose backed up, leaking oil onto the boy's uniform. He screamed in a clear, lofty contralto, and frantically beat at himself, panicked. He fumbled with the buckles on his flamethrower, and as he shifted from foot to foot, the weight toppled him over; the heavy metal canister hit the ground. The hose twisted and bucked like a snake, there was a spark, and petroleum fire spat in arcs and waves, touching the sawdust, the hay, the tank, and Lee himself.

It was a quick wash across his chest, leaving a streak of soot, but he didn't get burned—it had gone by too fast. Oil was squirting across the floor in strings and puddles.

Ripley, on the ground, looked at Lee. "Should we run?" he asked. He still held his pistol, as if it were a vestigial limb.

"Shoot him!" Lee swept both hands through mounds of sawdust, hoping he could blindly find the knife as easily as his knee could find a bedpost in the dark. Ripley stared at him with curiosity. "Your gun," Lee yelled. "Shoot him."

Ripley had about one and a half seconds to look doubtful. The boy was crying to himself, *"Jetzt! Jetzt! Jetzt!,"* and then, with an unveiling motion like pulling a cloth off a picnic table, let the other weapon loose.

Smoke was rising to the rafters, and sunlight shone down through the haze, filtered through the burning straw. Lee's fingers found the handle of his knife just as he became aware of motion, right here, suspended in the air, something dark and huge and horrible, lobbing toward Lee, something with fangs and wings fluttering on its back. The knife was in Lee's hand, and pointing, and for the remainder of his long life, he never forgave himself for swinging it upward once, right at the center of the dark, man-sized form that bounded at him.

His blade hit the flank squarely, right between two ribs; it drove in to the hilt, and suddenly Lee's hand was touching fur. He knew what he'd done, even before the dog collapsed on top of him. She tumbled once, paws splaying, then went limp.

Smoke was filling the air; somewhere, a structural support made an awful sound: teetering, then splintering. The German boy took this opportunity to scoop up as much food as he could carry. Then he was gone.

"Ripley?" Lee called.

There was smoke. Lee crawled to the dog, whose lip twitched. It was a shepherd, mostly black, with a tan bib and paws. There were straps around its midriff, and on its back, two small cages in which fluttered small white carrier pigeons. He placed a gentle hand on her neck, uselessly—*foolishly,* given the smoke and flame. He felt the ridgeline of a scar across her throat. *That's where her vocal cords were slashed,* he thought.

"There are carrier pigeons on her back," Lee announced. "Ripley?" he called again, but there was no response. Then he said, "I killed her," aloud. The words were echoing, as if they'd come out of a tin can. As he glanced at the distended landscape of the dog's belly, he understood he had a mission. His breathing thickened.

Smoke clouded his view. He pulled his shirt up over his nose, then remembered his respirator. There were nine steps to deploying it properly; Lee skipped most of them. He could breathe, a bit, through his mouth, but smoke leaked in around the goggles that were supposed to protect his eyes.

The dog had landed facing the rear of the tank, where she had recently been tethered. Lee felt bile rising in his throat, for something terrible was happening—he was watching her try to lift her head. She couldn't quite manage; she trembled and let out a small squeak. Her body shook again. Lee followed the direction her snout had been pointing: directly under the tank.

The fire was spreading, flickers and crackles and pops were growing, but he couldn't make himself leave.

"Ripley?"

He crawled a foot or so, toward the tank. As he did, he heard a soft, chick-peep kind of noise coming from between the massive treads. He could just barely see though his goggles, with hazy, watering eyes, that there was a hole below the tank. A pit. Its edges were raw and grooved, dug with claws. He reached forward.

Something against his heel. He looked behind him. In the bitter light, he could see that the mother dog's jaws were on either side of his boot. Her eye was determined, bright, and able, the upper and lower lids almost meeting in final concentration. Then the eye went cloudy and the jaw collapsed.

"Good girl," he whispered.

He pulled out the first puppy. And then another. Two could fit in his palm. They were moist. Their eyes were closed, their bellies plump, and their limbs floppy afterthoughts to their giant heads. He brought out another puppy. Two or three days old, maybe. The Saint-Mihiel offensive. The full-press assault, the armies fleeing, bombs falling, and in desperation, every weapon brought to bear. A dog trained to find wounded men, and fitted with carrier pigeons so they could signal for help; there was a war on, so they put the rig on her back and the straps around her enormous belly. In the retreat, she was tied to a tank and forgotten. And she waited for them to come back. They didn't. She dug the only place she could to whelp her litter. And there, lying on her side—how could she do it? Straps around her, pigeons on her back. The puppies, born into a world where the first sounds around them were gunfire and their mother's heartbeat, the first smells cordite and milk.

He could hear more sounds under the tank. At least a couple more dogs to rescue. He reached for the fourth puppy.

Which was when the pool of oil around the flamethrower ignited.

The explosion blew a hurricane of metal shards, throwing Lee from his crouch and the concussive blast knocking him over sawhorses, against the ground, over flaming hay bales, he ricocheted like a bullet down a crooked rain gutter; the air filled with liquid fire, raining onto the ground, pouring like lava between the tank treads, making a heartbreaking sizzle, a sound like wet fingers snuffing out a match.

Ripley stood outside, as black as a chess piece in the field of clover and elephant grass. He was completely unmoving, hands palms outward. Before him, the winery was burning, huge clouds of black smoke going into the air. He was holding his pistol, arm extended toward the ground.

His mouth was moving. He began to fantasize aloud: when they returned to the aerodrome, they would learn that the war had ended in their absence, that everyone had had enough and it was time to go home. He said he could hear the announcement that the war was over. "Three blue lights. Ta-dah."

Lying on the ground, with cans of dog food around him, was a filthy dead boy he had shot once in the head.

Lee stumbled out. He was a wreck. His boots were smoking, his trousers torn, the knees bloody, and his respirator had been blown off, leaving his head bare. He was caved in, shoulders bowing to shelter his chest, arms crossed, the unbuttoned flaps of his wool tunic pulled around him. He kept his jacket closed even as he raised his face to look at the lieutenant. Salt tears had left two tracks in the black ash on his face; he was panting, half panicked, trembling.

"Lee?"

Lee didn't answer.

"I've been wrestling all day with rather awful thoughts, I have to confess." Ripley holstered his pistol, finally. "Have you ever wondered whether this all means anything? Were you really meant for this? Or myself?"

Lee was shivering in place. Ripley reached a hand toward his shoulder, and Lee flinched away.

"Duncan," Ripley said quietly, "I want to say I'm getting a divorce."

"I'm afraid," Lee said, "to open my jacket."

"What? Why?"

"I had one in my hand, but—" His hand was empty.

"One what? Lee, you escaped, you're safe."

"A puppy. I had a puppy."

"Then perhaps you dropped it," Ripley said.

"Either the other two are in there . . . or they're not."

"Did you hear me about the divorce?" When Lee nodded, Ripley said, quietly, "Then let's take a look." His eyes went level with the corporal's chest.

If you want anything badly enough, Lee thought, *it's dangerous.* He remembered the puppy in his hand, then the explosion, and he knew, with a clammy and terrible heat, that he'd rolled over its body; he could feel the slight yielding between his hips and the ground; that feeling traveled with him, he could feel it now, here, standing with Ripley. Carefully, with his eyes closed, with his left hand, he eased his jacket open. In the crook of his right arm, lodged in his sleeve, was a puppy. Ripley gently took it from him.

Eyes still closed, Lee asked, "Is it alive?"

"No. Oh, wait. Yes, it is."

"Either there's another one," Lee whispered, "or there isn't." He took off his tunic entirely, leaving him in his flannel underdrawers. He laid the tunic on the ground, and sadly felt its lining. There was a loud pop, and a new flame jumped out a window, inside the building.

"Your union suit, perhaps," Ripley murmured.

Lee felt along his chest. His buttons had ripped off. He reached down toward his belt line. He found it pressed against his stomach. "Oh," he said.

When he pulled it out, it lay motionless in his palm. A girl, he thought. Maybe. She was tangled in something, string, and then he realized it was the finger puppets he'd worn around his neck. He started to remove them from her, but then, slowly, like a complaint, her front paws began to wriggle, and her rear paws batted the air. She was the size of a potato.

He stared at this girl, as uncomprehending and confused as he'd ever been. Ripley passed the other dog to him. This was a boy. He seemed to be asleep.

"Your souvenirs. Call them Hansel and Gretel."

Lee shook his head. He was already becoming enchanted, and they didn't need fairy-tale names. It would be several days before he decided the girl would be Nanette, named after the puppet she'd been wrapped in, but when he was telling the story of finding her, he would always make it sound instantaneous, hand in glove, the flicking on of a lightbulb.

It wasn't as simple as that, of course; he didn't even know if he would keep the animals. All he knew was that he'd found orphans. Like him.

17

Ironside and Pishkoff boarded H.M.S. *Attentive,* which began its zigzag journey behind the siren of the leading ship. It was deep into autumn, winter rehearsing, the afternoon rain showers now bracketed by pellets of hail. In all weather, Pishkoff stood on deck for at least a quarter hour in the afternoons, glumly playing "Turkish Song of the Damned" on his pennywhistle. Ironside meanwhile read Waliszewski's *Peter the Great,* the better to understand the Russian people, and a stack of books about Napoleon, just in case the Allied campaign had a different historical precedent.

On the fifth day of travel, there was an extraordinary piece of news: Poole was being recalled to Great Britain for "consultation." Ironside was to proceed to Russia, however, and would be in charge temporarily.

This had been the curtain for Poole. Pilots had repeatedly told him, beginning in October, that it was no longer safe to fly the Russian skies. Their machines could bear freezing temperatures at high altitude, but on the ground, the ignitions had to be babied, the carburetors wrapped in hot towels, cold traitorous to the grease used on release mechanisms.

But Poole didn't believe this. An RE 8 was sent up weighted down with four Cooper bombs under each wing, plus a single big-bellied two-hundred-pound bomb attached to the undercarriage. When the pilot, for the last time in his life, hit the release lever, the weather had done its work; only the bombs under the right wing released, causing him to flip over and—still holding all the remaining bombs—collide with the steeple of a local Orthodox church.

The explosion killed the sole priest in the village of Pinega and burned the church to the ground. Though the villagers accepted General Poole's sincere apology (and he *truly was* sorry), and allowed Lieutenant Whyte and his engineers of the 310th to build them a new church, headquarters decided he should return home.

Ironside read the news blankly, then went out into the squall and allowed himself to be beaten by sleet to wake himself up to his change in duties. Pishkoff somehow found him (they were enough like a married couple by now that he did not ask how) and said, "You're top kick. Again."

"Again," Ironside murmured.

"History repeats itself," Pishkoff said, because it would annoy Ironside.

"Thank you, Pishkoff. The rules of my landing have changed now. Someone might try to assassinate me, I suppose."

"And if you die, you get a statue."

"Good night, Pishkoff," Ironside said, dismissing him. Alone with the howl of the northern seas, Ironside understood he was, again, sailing into a historic occasion, and he hated historic occasions. He imagined that, somewhere nearby, a ship was passing in the other direction. He waved, as if to General Poole, whom he would never meet, now that he was in charge of the destinies of fifty thousand civilians, five thousand Slavo-British Legionnaires, and many Allied troops, including forty-eight hundred Americans. Had he ever seen an American? Tom Mix. All the doughboys he'd seen off duty, feeding pigeons in the square. But had he ever talked to an American? For a moment he couldn't decide if he had or not. With rising anxiety, he wondered if he'd seen an American in combat. Newsreel footage.

Back at his cabin, there was a telegram from Mr. Nicholas Chaikovsky, supreme commander of Archangel. He congratulated Ironside for his promotion (Ironside noted Chaikovsky's quick work). He also indicated that Ironside would be met by the entire Slavo-British Legion at dockside. "They will be in full parade dress and will demonstrate their superior techniques at formation. They will march, turning both right *and* left," he promised, a phrasing that did not set Ironside's mind at ease.

Ironside read weather reports (the highest recorded temperature this week was ten degrees below zero Fahrenheit), and he issued a coded telegram, his first order: the Allied men at the farthest post, Verst 455, should build a strong defensive position with barbed wire, and Supply should ship all the available machine-gun sandbags from the warehouses to the troops hunkered down in blockhouses. If there were any native Russian troops—he thought he'd seen such mentioned in the Canadian artillery—they should be rotated from outpost to outpost to share their knowledge of battle and survival in the snow. He ordered tea shipped to the British men and coffee to the Americans. "Build all further block-houses under forest cover; in the open, they're deathtraps. Recruit obvious parties for espionage, ferret out those who will play for both sides, feed them bad intelligence." He added, "For the men in the field, make sure there is entertainment. Decks of cards, musical instruments if we can find them. Newspapers from their hometowns, as long as they aren't demoraliz-ing. The picture show. Comedies and romance—nothing with a message."

That night, he was called to a dance in the *Attentive*'s cramped ward-room. He attended, head bursting with reportage. The Russian guests wore frayed and repatched gowns or sad, oily Savile Row dinner jackets. Some wore the khaki jackets and blue breeches piped with red silk of former officers; some had sewn back approximations of the great gold lace epaulets ripped from their uniforms in harsher times.

Ironside was pulled into corners all night long. A small man with whiskers the color of carrots showed him land grants and sable farms that could be his should all go well. No one was quite sure what "all" or "well" meant. A Russia that was safe for them that was neither tsarist (they were sentimental but not idiots) nor Bolshevik?

After the umpteenth former baroness had attempted flirtation across the room using all methods short of a pickax, Ironside asked the orchestra leader to play that silly old chestnut "You Belong to Me." He was thinking about his wife, about their last night at the Savoy. He hummed a few mea-sures ("You know, 'But tonight, you *be-long* to me' ").

The old conductor furrowed his runaway eyebrows and consulted for translation with his players, some of whom had better acquaintance with English than he. Finally, he clapped his baton against the stand twice to order silence, and announced to the audience in his fearsome high-caste St. Petersburg diction, "Our new military leader requests a song. It is apparently called 'I Own You.' "

There were gasps. The guests eyed the exits. For the rest of the evening, no one tried to bribe Ironside.

18

In France there were fifty-seven types of weather, as long as you liked rain. Lee and Ripley had flown in a rare cluster of hours between storms, but now, with the afternoon coming, storm clouds were piling up, and the first raindrops would be falling soon.

They were miles away from home, in unspecified territory, next to a building that was rapidly being consumed by flames. A DH 4 needed at least thirty yards to attain flying speed, and they had but twenty yards of unbroken field, the rest of it dotted with hacksawed grape stalks. And there was the matter of needing three men to turn the propeller.

Lee paced around the plane, making a complete circle. He regarded the field with eyes like scythes, as if a straight line thirty yards long might appear if only he stared with enough force. He was talking in a small, reassuring voice. "We'll all be fine," he was whispering.

A bead of rain hit his cheek. His arms were locked in cradle position, dogs pressed against his chest under layers of clothing. He worried that they didn't have enough air, and when he unbuttoned his jacket slightly, he worried that they were too cold. He whispered *Kriegshund,* because it was so rare that in wartime a word meant exactly what it sounded like. Generally, things were named ironically, as if to annoy you and harden you to misfortunes. The thought led him to reimagine how he'd skidded against the other puppy, which he felt as a phantom pressure as real as that of the other two now in his shirt. He wondered how he would feed them, and that led him back to the too-stifled/too-cold conundrum, which deposited him at another whisper of *"Kriegshund."*

"Duncan?"

With a swallow, he asked, "How do we get home, sir?"

"We don't have thirty yards, do we?"

"And the engine is stopped."

"I wasn't really thinking then," Ripley said. "I am now." He put his hands on his hips, and drummed his fingers against his scorched wool tunic.

The clouds were thickening. When had his orphans last eaten? Lee's gaze fell on *Lenore.* "We lighten her."

Ripley, too, looked her way. Raindrops pelted her canvas wings, and the winds brought down cinders and ash, which stuck to the men's faces. "Lighten her? That's a fatal idea," he said. Because, with the gasoline tank already half empty, there was only one way to lighten the airplane.

"We lighten her, and take off in twenty yards," Lee said.

"The propeller—"

"I'll start it."

"You can't possibly do that," Ripley said.

"I have to."

"But if you can turn over the prop, and we lighten her . . . and then we get into the air—"

"Where it's raining," Lee said, with a dry chuckle that Ripley acceded to.

"Yes. That, too."

Lee nodded. Flying through storm clouds. Enemy planes. This was impossible.

"Two hours ago, I might have let fate roll over us," Ripley said. "Right. Off we go."

Lee climbed into the cockpit and brought out the set of spanner wrenches. He apologized to the puppies for jostling them as he leaned over the Scarff ring mounted on the rear. As he reached out to loosen the first bolt, Ripley waved a hand.

"Duncan?"

"Yes?"

Ripley ran his fingers over his mustache. Lee was puzzled, until he realized: Ripley was nervous. For Lee was, to save them weight, about to detach the Lewis machine guns. And then, for balance, he would also toss the Marlins away. Which would leave them without weapons.

Lee attacked the bolts, which had frozen into place long ago. Twice, the spanner skidded off the slippery metal, and he skinned his knuckles against the Lewises' central housing, and then, suddenly, the guns tumbled onto the ground.

He dumped the ammo next, and then skittered into the pilot's cockpit, where he dismantled the Marlins' foundations under the relatively dry shelter of the top wing. There was a tumble, the smack of metal against stone, followed by the snaking of the length of ammo to the ground. Now the plane was several hundred pounds lighter.

"Sir?"

"Yes?"

"I need you in your seat. So I can start the propeller."

"Have you ever—"

"No."

"Has anyone—"

"A couple of times. Someone in the 94th, I hear, started one by himself."

"All right." Ripley climbed onto the wing. "When you've finished, I need you to do something else. Let me think this through. All right. All right. Run to the back of the plane, and hold on to the supports for the empennage. I'm going to say this now, because when the engine is on you won't be able to hear me. Good?"

"Of course, sir."

"Then I'm going to open the throttle. The plane will try to lift. You hold it down."

Lee looked confused.

"You hold it as long as you can. Longer. When I give the hand signal, let go, and run as fast as you can, so you can get into the pit. You'll have to run quickly, because the plane will be lurching forward, and if you can't climb aboard I have to leave you here. Do you read all that, Corporal?"

"Yes, sir."

Lee wrapped the dogs in his teddy-bear suit for warmth and left the bundle on his seat in the DH 4, for he was about to perform highly athletic duties and he didn't want to hurt them.

He faced the plane. Behind him was a grove of trees, and in front of him, the winery was still burning. The weather had fully shifted now, and rain was coming down in his face. The wind was blowing sideways, a poor condition for takeoff.

The hub of the propeller was a few inches over Lee's head, and the blades had stopped with the arms parallel to the earth. He knit his fingers around the tip of the closest blade and rocked it up and down, to try and get momentum going. This would be like rowing a boat, the same full extension of his arms. With a full groan of effort, he threw the blade downward, willing it to catch on the first try, and only when he let go did he realize where he was standing; he cried out as the next descending blade arm struck him on the back of the head with a terrible clout. He stumbled away, both hands to his head, moaned again like a child, then staggered and fell.

"Duncan?"

"I'm fine, sir." He returned to his feet, massaging his skull. He opened his mouth, moved his jaw, his teeth having slammed down with the impact. His vision doubled, then returned to normal. He had never been hit that hard. His hands wandered to his skull in search of broken skin or blood; they came away dirty and wet with rain, a lump already rising.

This time, he stood more carefully, to the front and outside of the blade's sweep. Rain peppered down, making a grip hard to maintain. The temperature was dropping. Lee rocked on his heels, keeping the propeller in his hands, and he threw it down violently, to no effect. There wasn't even a sputter. Another swing down, and another flutter to a standstill. He changed his posture, glaring at the plane and imagining the engine's infernal workings as if they were children who needed to be disciplined. He knew how the plane worked.

Again, a broad sweep of his strong arms, and this time, a spark, catching, the brief plateau of an engine engaging, and Lee, carried off balance, slipped backward, tripped over a grapevine and smashing chin-first onto the ground.

The Liberty engine was making its ear-splitting roar as Ripley opened the throttle. Lee stood, and limped toward the plane. His ankle. He had sprained it. He gave Ripley a tentative wave as he lurched toward the tail of the plane. He shook his head. There was a ringing in his ears—because of the engine noise, or the blow to the back of his skull. When he was in position, hands gripping the plane's tail section, he nodded at Ripley, who slowly opened the throttle.

The plane began to pull forward, so Lee dug in his heels. The idea was a simple one: forward momentum needed to build to a critical level so that they could lift into the air in twenty yards, not thirty. Thus Ripley would increase the power until it dragged Lee off his feet. The longer Lee could hold on, the more likely they would make it.

At first, it was like a gentle tug of war, an easy win, but in the course of a minute, Lee felt as if he were holding back an ox by its harness. There were twelve cylinders in a flying V shape to fight against, and he was going to lose. His only hope was holding out long enough that his fight had mattered.

Lee reset his feet in the soil, and pulled in his elbows until his forearms were going to explode. All those days he had rowed to exhaustion were just rehearsals for this moment. The engine's roar took on new depth as Ripley upped the rpm, Lee shaking to remain still, *Lenore*'s wheels beginning to turn in place on the wet earth, kicking up a foam of mud.

He hadn't considered this. If he held on too long, the plane would bury itself in mud, and be unable to release itself, the way gunning a truck engine only dug you deeper into a ditch. Still he held on. He felt that phantom pressure on his thigh, the ghost sensation of having rolled across a puppy. The plane slipped through his fingers.

The rear bounced, the wheels caught, *Lenore* roared forward as if launched from a slingshot. Lee tripped through the mud, his ankle twisting again under him so he stumbled, breaking his fall with his wrists. Then he was up and running again, the plane just within reach.

As he ran, rain pelted him and broke against his face. His uniform was ruined, wet, torn, and blistered and charred. His legs pumped forward, his arms furiously reaching forward. And he was crying from fear of missing the two puppies that were slowly, by the second, jolting and bouncing out of his reach.

Then his hand was on the fuselage, the plane was leaping, and he threw himself against it with a final embrace. The rattling was violent and awful, they were five feet, ten feet, twenty into the air, but he could not so easily fall into his seat—he had to ease down carefully, avoiding the teddy-bear suit, and as Ripley pulled the stick toward his stomach, there was a lurch, *Lenore* jumped up abruptly, and then there was a sound like playing cards riffling as the treetops scraped against their wheels. They were airborne.

At fifteen hundred feet, they burst through the low clouds and into the cold blue autumn sky. Lee had settled on his bench with his teddy bear in a bunch, the fleece pressed against his skin. It rested in his lap as if he had skinned an animal and were bringing its pelt home. His teeth began to chatter. He was soaking wet, and now it was freezing, and the wind rushed past the scrapes on his skin like the serrated blade of a knife.

Ripley knew the general way home, given the position of the sun, and how the clouds below were opening up. There was something that looked like where the Blackbird Forest had once been, and then a cluster of buildings that was the remains of the village of Corny, most likely. If Lee was right, they would next pass a railroad yard with a small lake beside it, the site of the Dépôt Roi Blanc, and, yes, there it was. They would be home in fifteen minutes, perhaps less.

Lee craned his neck, the wind freezing him into shivers, as if icicles would form on his skin. He looked for enemy fighters. It seemed unlikely to him that fate would allow them simply to find their way to the barracks without a squadron of Fokkers on their tail, now that they were unarmed.

He knew little about dogs. He had wanted one, but his mother had told him about the keeper family that had tried to bring their dog to the Reef in their boat, and how it had been slung overboard, and had drowned, and how she couldn't risk such a terrible thing, and could Leland wish such a fate upon a helpless creature?

Yet he had just rescued two puppies in the midst of a war. This meant far more dangers than taking them out to sea. He was shivering violently now with red-faced misery. The village of Fleury—the dead cornfield, burned to stubs, the brothel with its women standing in front, waving at them—sent him into a dim nervousness. As the plane began to descend, he was certain Ripley was landing too steeply, and when they were just feet above the field, he was sure the DH 4 would crash, and when the wheels were on the ground, he was afraid to touch the girl dog or her brother, knowing in his heart they would have frozen, and when he felt the rise of their bellies against his palm, he knew he could never find milk for them.

A few minutes later, he had left Ripley with the plane, dashing toward his bunk for blankets. He put the puppies down his shirt and cradled them as he trotted along the camp's fairway. It was late afternoon, and the chill air was darkening. And there was Banjo, back in her pen. He could see her ragged ears drooping forward, her brown snout against the mud, the tips of her paws by her eyes, as if she were trying to hide. As he knelt before her, she didn't move.

Had she run off because of the noise of battle, given birth, and then lost her litter? Perhaps someone had borrowed her puppies, to show them off to a visiting ace, and Lee imagined a good-natured presentation, "For valor, here is a future *Kriegshund*," and then he admitted that the battlefield wasn't so well behaved, and that her litter was probably stillborn some-where under a barracks, or in a ditch.

But would she accept two strangers?

He felt down his shirt, and carefully laid the girl, then the boy, down by her side. They simultaneously raised their heads as if smelling the breeze, and made small swimming motions with the spoons of their undersized paws until Lee scooped them closer to her belly.

Lee looked directly at Banjo's eyes, which remained dull. That she was nursing didn't seem to faze her. It was soon apparent she would neither reject nor accept her new charges, but would allow fate to roll over her.

He stood up, conscious that he was still wet, bruised, and filthy. He brushed at the back of his neck, and his hand came away with a smear of black. His ankle throbbed; how had he just run across the camp? A black fatigue settled down on his shoulders, pressing him until he began to wobble.

Just then, Lieutenant Hart walked past the mess tent, stopping on his heel when he saw the puppies. Lee smiled at him. But Hart did not smile back. His face twitched, his eyebrows went together in surprise, and he put his hands on his hips.

"I say—I thought we'd drowned those loafers."

Only a second later, with a broken afterglow to his knuckles, and Hart sprawled on the ground, did Lee realize what he'd done.

As he was grappled with and subdued, he looked toward Banjo, hoping for some kind of understanding, or a thanks-to-you, in her eyes, but she just stared dully into the distance while the puppies remained next to her, and he was dragged away, into the stockade, where his education would begin.

The *Attentive* crossed the Arctic Circle at three in the afternoon, and shortly thereafter, Archangel Harbor came into sight. Long purple shadows stretched from the rusted buoys, which stuck at mad angles through the slush and ice. On deck, on the windward side, Ironside and Pishkoff fought with his uniform, clutching at his hat in the wind, tossing aside his riding crop, and finally pinning his medals back into their silk-lined ebony cabinet box.

"Returning to Russia," Ironside said. "This must be quite exciting for you."

"Hmm," Pishkoff replied.

When Ironside let loose a low, quiet sigh, as he did now, it carried its own oceanic current, the melancholy of Poseidon. Though he was now dressed as a lieutenant, with the goal of confusing snipers, his disguise felt idiotic to him, a six-foot-six-inch peacock stuffed into a pigeon costume. His true rank was recently complicated. A major in the Gunners, a lieutenant colonel in the army by brevet, he had just two hours before been commissioned a temporary brigadier general. The men of the *Attentive* had wanted to celebrate, but it only made him nervous. General Ironside, in charge of a chronic situation.

So he removed signs of rank. He was a man in his enormous, unscrupulous-baby overcoat. He and Pishkoff strode around the deck until they faced land, which was as dismal as when the *Olympia* had approached, but darker, deserted, and even more exhausted-looking. Ironside reached his hand toward Pishkoff, who was already passing him the field glasses. The ship was slowing down in the harbor, meaning it was to dock soon. No Chaikovsky. No Slavo-British Legion. Something could be wrong.

Ironside looked through the binoculars as Pishkoff buckled and unbuckled the snaps of their leather bundling case in exactly the time signature of "The Blue Danube." The very moment this sound became annoying, before Ironside could complain, Pishkoff ceased. He held out the case, cocked and ready.

"Right," Ironside said, relinquishing the binoculars.

Pishkoff spent most of his life in a state of bemusement, aided by twelve daily glasses of wine. Now he let out a disappointed little moan. For he understood the tone behind "Right." "You mean, 'If there's a problem, we let someone else handle it.' No?"

"No." Ironside removed his wedding ring and handed it to Pishkoff, who folded it into a handkerchief in his palm. "Please, if I don't return, please tell my wife—"

"I'll give her the note."

"Thank you." He struggled with the clasps of his small box respirator, hooked to his belt; since it had been custom-made for his gigantic head, he didn't want to lose it. "Store this for me. It's too cold for gas."

Knowing it wouldn't change his mind, Pishkoff continued. "You know, if it's Bolsheviks, they could see you when you're coming."

"Mmm."

"Lots of places to hide on that dock, I think."

"I'm not skulking into my command. Arms, please."

Pishkoff checked the Webley and his Colt and pressed two packets of bullets into Ironside's pockets. "All righty."

"And, Pishkoff, honestly, about my wife—"

"What is this, the time, eighth time since Passchendaele? At Passchendaele, maybe twice, too. History repeats itself."

"Tell her that—"

"You're coming back. History repeats itself."

Really, it was the single phrase in the world that most exasperated Ironside. "Pishkoff—"

"Yes, if you die, I look forward very, very much to saying hello to her." Pishkoff flicked an ice crystal from Ironside's lapel. "How beautiful did you say she was, again?"

This wasn't a form of humor Ironside had brought to the war, but he'd learned to recognize it. "I quite intend not to die now."

On the endless and desolate quayside, in the encroaching darkness and cold, a military band had emerged from parts unknown to play a medley of "Rule, Britannia!" and "God Save the Queen," since the Russians weren't quite sure which was the British national anthem. When the gangplank was drawn down, and swept clean by four bluecoated sailors, Ironside strolled to shore. The band ceased. He craned his neck for uniforms— there wasn't a soldier in sight.

The headlights of a limousine flashed on, then off, and the back door was thrown open. A hat came out of the car, followed by its wearer, a magnificent-looking man with long silver hair. He stood upright, approaching jauntily and smiling, looking to Ironside at least seven feet tall, eighteen inches of it hat.

This was Nicholas Chaikovsky. Belling out like the business end of a hammer, shimmering as the afternoon breeze ran among its many kinds of fur, Chaikovsky's presidential hat was said to have involved four complete Siberian minks and an otter.

Chaikovsky ambled along the dock. Ironside understood he wouldn't be assassinated today. That would require energy. "Greetings," Chaikovsky said.

"Likewise from the Imperial Staff in Britain," Ironside said. "My adjutants have letters and so forth, all the administrative . . ." He gestured. "This is my man Pishkoff."

Chaikovsky said, "Greetings, Pishkoff."

"Hello," Pishkoff said.

Ironside was distracted by the strange, echoing emptiness of the docks.

Beyond Mr. Chaikovsky and the band, it might as well have been tundra. "Mr. Chaikovsky, you're alone."

"Ah," he said, laughing, "we have a mutiny!" He announced this with pride, as if it were a kind of raffle. "The Slavo-British Legion we have recruited. They were supposed to be in formation here, but all we could round up was the band. Do you like the band?"

Ironside frowned. "Are you serious about the mutiny?"

Chaikovsky nodded. "There was a medical exam. Only three hundred men didn't have the syphilis." As if that explained the mutiny, he added, "Would you like to see the palace? There will be an excellent dinner. The chef—the chef is from *Paris*."

"Actually, Mr. Chaikovsky, we should investigate this mutiny, don't you think?"

"I should tell my chef we will be late," Chaikovsky murmured. "You know, he has that Parisian temper, and . . ."

"Mr. Chaikovsky, would you perhaps like to go to the palace with Pishkoff while I see to the mutiny?"

He visibly brightened, hat swaying. "That would be best."

"I'll see to the rooms," Pishkoff volunteered.

"And, Mr. Chaikovsky, have you anything else to equip me with?" There was a long, silent moment during which Chaikovsky looked toward Ironside with increasing puzzlement. "Might you direct me to the Allied forces?"

Blinking from Chaikovsky.

Ironside said, "I don't aim to suppress the mutiny alone."

"Aha! Would you like some Americans?"

"Yes, please. Perhaps more than that, some of each army? Thank you. Let us go now."

Shortly after decking Lieutenant Hart, Lee was thrown into the makeshift jail at the edge of the aerodrome. Since the concept of a standing American army was evolving, lines of demarcation were writ in water. Matters of rank and discipline were intermittently enforced. Lee could knock an officer ass-over-teakettle and be brought to the stockade without much sense of how long the punishment would last. He was, however, charged for his missing rifle.

He was deposited with a washbasin, a new uniform, and requisition papers to fill out to pay for the new uniform, into a clapboard barracks. His cot was called a butcher's table. The frame was made of iron piping, and the springs yielded and spread quickly; a doughboy who sat nude risked unspeakable injury.

The other cots were unused—at least, on his side of the room. But chicken wire ran down the middle of the barracks, and on the other side were German prisoners. It was a housing situation that made no sense, an unarmed, unobserved American soldier within arm's length of the enemy. But there was an overstock of Germans. Trench raiders from the 166th had deposited gaggles and clots of defeated Boche with every available way station.

Since Lee was outnumbered, he set up his cot as far as he could from the wire, and planned to sleep with one eye open. He pretended he had surrounded them. The Germans didn't look at him. Instead, they lay on their bunks, played cards, and seemed only to come to life at six o'clock, when supper was delivered.

Lee lay back, looking at the ceiling, which was discolored and moldy from the rain. He was counting backward through his life, taking experiences and subtracting them from a list of accomplishments. All he had done right was to rescue two puppies and deliver them, in their need, to a mother whose puppies had been drowned.

"Your favorite pet?" "Gin and tonic."

At seven o'clock, Lieutenant Ripley came to see him. He was surprised to see Ripley holding a dog in each extended hand, flinching at their vague wriggles as if they were trout long out of the water.

"Here you go, Duncan."

"Wait, wait, wait." Lee went up on one elbow from his full recline. "They're probably hungry."

"I'm afraid you have to take them," Ripley said.

"They're supposed to be with Banjo."

"She's gone."

"If you put them with her, she'll be good to them. Right?"

"I just walked by. She wasn't in her crate," Ripley said patiently. He put each dog down on the cot. "I know they mean something to you, so . . ."

The puppies were nut-brown dinner rolls. Neither one could move much or make a noise yet, but hunger urged them to show their open mouths in hopes that something good would happen.

"What do I do with them?" Lee asked. He imagined, without wanting to, Banjo walking away from them. "I don't have food."

Ripley shrugged once. "The wind has picked up. You can keep them warm at least."

Lee looked at them miserably. "Where did Banjo go?"

"Try to give them a few good hours."

When Ripley was gone, Lee lowered his hands to their backs. He stroked their fur. He put each of them in his lap. He could feel them breathing, the tiny vibrations of their heartbeats. He could feel them failing.

"Pardon me."

Leaning against the chicken-wire fence, from the German side, was a figure so slender he was almost transparent. He wore the telltale prisoner's gray woolen underdrawers with red piping. His head had recently been shaven as part of delousing, and his cheeks were hollow, making his pale-blue eyes, which did not move, mesmerizing.

Also: he was holding a four-ounce tin of milk.

Lee picked up a puppy in each hand, and approached him cautiously. "Yes?"

"Might I trouble you for a cigarette?"

"Maybe I don't have one."

"Maybe I'm not holding a can of milk," he replied.

"How did you get milk in here?"

"I'm sorry, old chap, is that what we should be discussing?" His accent was British. It wasn't the schoolroom rote drummed into German officers. Lee had heard British soldiers, the enlisted men and otherwise, and though he didn't understand every nuance, he recognized that this German prisoner's accent came from somewhere above them, aristocrats.

"My name is Harry," he continued.

"Good for you."

"Five cigarettes for this milk," he said smoothly.

"Why, what did you do to it?" Lee said.

Harry flashed a look of quiet disappointment at Lee. "While you were talking to your officer friend, I crumpled up some hardtack, and I added about an eyedropper of sherry and egg white." He spoke as if the explanation made perfect sense. Lee began to ask why, and Harry continued: "Because dog milk is richer than cow milk, and you want to let them know there's such a thing as solid food as soon as possible. And six."

"Six what?"

"Cigarettes."

The remaining prisoners were otherwise engaged, some of them just staring up at the rafters, others in a loose circle of chairs, playing Boston. Lee noted how Harry stood with his body hiding the milk from his *Kameraden.*

"Cigarettes fit through the wire just fine," Lee said. "A can of milk, though . . ."

Harry smiled. He slid his foot forward and then flexed upward. The wire came with it. When the exchange had occurred—Lee had two puppies and a can of milk, and Harry had secreted the cigarettes somewhere—Lee looked back toward Harry, a tide of anxiety beginning to rise in him.

Harry said, "You need to dip your fingers in the milk, and smear it over their noses. They'll get the hang of licking the milk off. Find an eye dropper and put it into their mouths if that doesn't work. And you need to find them actual mother's milk—if not from a dog, then perhaps a pregnant cow or goat."

"Why?"

"And, I say, you should get your chocolate rations."

"For them?"

Harry's eyes re-evaluated Lee. "You know chocolate is poison to dogs? Tell me, then, are the fliers still eating white chocolate with nuts? Jolly good."

Lee looked at the milk tin, and then the wire again, realizing he wasn't going to sleep tonight.

"Don't worry, Corporal, the rest of the men haven't a clue about the wire. And if they did, what, do you think they would murder you in your sleep?" Harry chuckled again. "Perhaps all of us could escape and win the war after that. Goodbye."

"Wait." Lee had a number of questions to ask, but the flat blue eyes seemed to indicate that, the longer Lee kept Harry away from cigarettes, the more miserable his life would be. So he said, "But—who *are* you?"

"Tell me, Corporal. Did you find the dogs in a winery?"

"No," he said, and when Harry kept staring, he said, "Yes."

Harry showed off an open-lipped smile that made Lee think uncomfortably of aged porcelain and fragile, gold-etched dinner plates. "Keep them warm. They're only puppies, and they don't know anything yet. Soon you must train them."

"How do I do that?"

"In order to train a dog, first you must know more than the dog. Goodbye."

The Alexander Nevsky barracks, which housed the 1st Archangel Company, heart of the Slavo-British Legion, was a three-story concrete structure by a snow-covered training field spotted with the unhappy treadmarks of Shackleton boots. This field had been the site of drills in bayoneting, marksmanship, and coordinated exercise. Because equipment was hard to find, items from children's playgrounds had been conscripted. When Ironside approached, he noted from the back of his staff car one set of football goals, a wooden carousel, a pair of sawhorses, and a lonely-looking tetherball banging in the wind against a metal post.

His car drove slowly—marching speed, in fact, since it followed three companies on foot: one British, one American, and one French. Behind Ironside was a team of horses pulling a battered French 77mm field gun. The idea was to come with adequate firepower, but not so much as to be alarming.

It was dark, and so Ironside directed his C3 Tommies to rig lighting while he stood, hands in pockets, craning his head toward the third floor of the barracks building. It had small, barred windows. The mutineers waved their weapons in defiance, but when they recognized that waving wooden rifles was unimpressive, it was back to a muffled chant of dissent.

Their main concerns were that no one had told them what they were expected to do. Or what would happen when the Allies left. The drills with the children's play equipment had been demoralizing. The mutiny had been the first thing since their incorporation that actually made them feel happy.

Ironside sighed, folding his arms across his stomach. He touched the tip of his tongue to his mustache, and thought that he would have to learn not to do this when winter progressed. "What's the roof made out of?"

One of the Royal Scots squinted. "Wood shingles."

Another asked, "Shall we use the gun, sir?"

Ironside regarded the field gun. "If we wanted to kill them all, then, yes, I suppose, but no. Might I have seen a Stokes mortar kit somewhere here? Yes? Yes?"

The American company had brought one. The Stokes was simple and small: a three-inch-bore barrel about four feet long, supported by a bipod. Unfortunately, in the cold, its hand crank froze into place, and no amount of grease or cursing could budge it. Which embarrassed the two Americans in charge, who elected not to mention its shortcomings right now.

One of them was Hugo and another was Wodziczko.

"Private."

Hugo looked up. Towering above him was the general he had only seen at some distance. "Sir?"

"How go your preparations?"

"We're good, sir," said Wodziczko, whom Hugo wanted to shut up. Not so much for the lie as for the diction. Hugo wanted to say a great many things to Ironside. Wilkie Collins is quite the treat, sir. Don't we both miss Darjeeling at four?

"Private?"

"Sir?"

Ironside's gaze seemed to be made of granite. "Have you been eating chocolate recently?"

"No, sir." But Hugo's hand went to his mouth.

"Because I am not aware of chocolate being in the ration."

Hugo's eyes stole toward Wodziczko, whose face, he now realized, was also smeared with the Cadbury squares they had liberated from the warehouse.

"I'm with you, sir," Hugo said.

General Ironside blinked at him. "I'm sorry, Private—"

"Private First Class Hugo Black, sir."

Ironside turned away, for he could settle later what "I'm with you" meant. "Do carry on."

With an air hammer, four square bolts were drilled through the plate that secured the Stokes to the ground, and by consensus (no one really wanted to discuss in front of Ironside how unprepared they were), the weapon was pronounced ready to fire. Hugo pried open a crate of shells, and brushed the packing pellets aside.

"That guy?" Wodziczko whispered.

"Shh," Hugo said.

"That guy reminds me of Lieutenant Gordon."

"No, Wodziczko."

"That guy is exactly like him." His eyes had gone dreamy.

"Help me with these." Hugo added, "Please." Laid fin to nose like exotic fish were the eleven-pound bombs, painted around their bellies with the flashiest red and yellow stripes. They had received training in the form of advice: drop one in the barrel and get the hell out of the way.

"Private, are we ready to fire?" Ironside stood with his hands clasped behind his back. He regarded the barracks as if he owned it.

"Yes, sir," came simultaneously from Hugo and Wodziczko, who Hugo realized was now in love with Ironside.

"Please aim for the roof."

"Yes, sir," said Hugo, who was too intimidated to tell him that since it had frozen it couldn't actually *be* aimed.

Meanwhile, in the barracks, the mutineers noted from their third-floor window the preparation of the Stokes mortar with nods and approval—it was a very good bluff. Any second now, negotiations would begin.

"Please fire," Ironside said, covering his ears.

Hugo dropped his shell down the tube with a pneumatic rush of air and the snap of ignition fire, and the mortar round was sent sailing overhead with a low twang reminiscent of a single plucked harp string. It contained about two pounds of nitrostarch explosives, adequate to start a ruckus. The shell sang high into the night, spots of rust flying from its tiny fins, and then it came down with great speed, missing the roof, and vanishing from sight on the opposite side of the building.

A moment later, there was a distant explosion. Followed by a familiar, closer sigh.

"Excuse me, Private First Class Hugo Black," Ironside said. "Might you explain how we have entirely avoided hitting a three-story building?"

"The hand crank, sir," he responded weakly.

"Please make it work, and then fire again."

Hugo nodded. While he and Wodziczko dug up the base plate and repositioned it, a French scout performed reconnaissance and reported that the first shell had destroyed the playground equipment, and the tetherball was burning. Furthermore, a pack of wild dogs living under the carousel had been displaced.

Wodziczko whispered something that Hugo found disgusting but, finally, agreed to: use some of the lard from their rations to grease the hand crank. It seemed to work, and the elevation could be adjusted—though neither man was quite sure how many turns of the crank were correct to aim for the roof.

Ironside inquired if it was possible please to fire again.

Without responding, Wodziczko dropped the bomb into the shaft and ran off. Hugo held his breath, and his fingers went over his mouth. He tasted chocolate. The round went into the Russian sky and then came down soundly on the roof. The top floor erupted into flames.

At once the barracks was emptying, mutinous legionnaires scurrying like ants evicted from their nest.

Ironside turned his back on them. He walked some distance as the Russians flooded onto the field, dozens at a time, until the full three hundred of them stood in clumps. His promenade continued long after the last mutineers had come to ground, staring toward the great, distant man who had flushed them out and who stood alone, thinking saddened thoughts. There had been many nights in his life like this, and since he was still alive, he supposed he had learned from them. What was the lesson here, and were there still lessons at this late date? He wanted the war to be over; he wondered what "over" meant, and when the next war would begin.

History repeats itself, he thought. The problem with that nostrum was, you never knew what piece of history you were in. There were a limited number of outcomes, and yet there never seemed to be a way to learn a lesson. You were never at the beginning or end of anything. You were always at the middle, in a mist, and it was always up to someone else to announce later what your time on earth had meant. There was a thin line, for instance, between tenacity and stupidity. A mutiny was a stroke of genius or it wasn't. How sad to make the effort.

Unspoken, as if able to overhear his troubled thoughts, the mutineers began to feel *shame*.

Finally, a lieutenant in the mutinous Slavo-British Legion, a man who until moments before had preached resistance, called upon his men to fall in. And this they did. Under the floodlights, all three hundred of them together fell in, marched as well as they ever had, and came to attention in ten rows, thirty men across, with two aisles between them, to await inspection.

There were sounds like leaves stirring in a breeze, and a jump of flames as the timber roof of the barracks caved in.

Ironside turned. He walked toward the mutineers. The sound of his 270 pounds approaching, his boots crunching in the snow, promised punishment. Then, into the arc-lamp brightness, he was in the mutineers' line of sight.

"Gentlemen," he said. "I am General Edmund Ironside from Great Britain. You are Russia's best hope for self-defense. I'm not sure anyone has explained why this is." His Russian was, for a man who had studied briefly, excellent. He had memorized a speech he supposed he would have to give at some point, and had enough vocabulary to fill in the rest. Thus he had some rhetorical weight as he chopped the air with his gloved hands. The fight, he said, was against Bolshevism, a blight on their country. In theory, he explained, it spoke of equality, but it was in fact a panacea that did more damage than good. "In Bolshevism, surpluses are confiscated from the industrious and redistributed to the lazy or ineffectual," he declared. "I am sorry that it promises otherwise." His tone was so heavy with sympathy that the men were helpless but to feel sorry with him. "Of course," he said, "I come to you as a representative of the British Empire, and our Allies, which many of you do not trust. It is up to us, with our actions, our values, and our humanity, to compete with an exciting rhetoric that so moves you. I humbly take on that challenge. We have our own values of industriousness, decency, and above all responsibility for our own actions, which Bolshevism disavows. Now, will the leaders of the mutiny please step forward?"

Hugo had watched him speaking, not understanding a word, but understanding the tone: authoritarian humility. Now he looked toward the Slavo-British Legion for a reaction. There was no reason Ironside should be obeyed. Except that he was a man whose natural authority was equal to his rank.

There was eye lowering, head shaking, exhaling, and embarrassed shuffling from foot to foot. Thirteen men detached themselves from the rest.

When they were separate, shrugging at one another, Ironside nodded. "You are men with dignity, and your acceptance of responsibility is admirable." He switched here to English. "Is my adjutant here?"

Sunnyside

The adjutant trotted up, a strong and olive-skinned miner from South Wales. He saluted with his good hand. "Sir!"

"Very good. Execute them."

Hugo, standing at ease behind his mortar, among his company, thought he heard Ironside say this, but he told himself that "execute them" must mean something other than the obvious. But as preparations began, each step leaning in a certain direction, he felt sick.

There were rules to an execution wherever civilization saw the Union Jack. The thirteen doomed men were given paper to write letters to their loved ones while a detachment of men from the newly reconfigured Slavo-British Legion ran as fast as they could to find a priest to take last confessions. Much stalling occurred, however, as the prisoners consulted with each other. And the word "Dostoevsky" was murmured with increasing hope. They asked the few Allied troops who spoke Russian whether they were really going to die or if this was just a bluff. The questions percolated up command until Ironside himself answered that, as he had just explained, had they been listening, in a democracy, there were certain responsibilities to be taken for one's actions. And to start writing their families quickly. Please.

Ironside then sent for a field generator to power a fleet of high arc lamps that sent a hundred yards of battered snow into shockingly white relief. There weren't enough handcuffs to go around, so the prisoners were led to the execution with their hands tied behind their backs by short linen straps torn off discarded bedding. Each prisoner was sprinkled with holy water and kissed by the harried and puffing priest, who looked over his shoulder with alarm, worried that he was accidentally standing before the firing squad himself.

The firing squad consisted of twenty men selected by Ironside, five each from America, Britain, France, and Russia itself: a truly multinational force. Hugo, who had been picked, glanced backward at Wodziczko, who hadn't.

The firing squad formed a flying V of two rows. A British officer provided each man with a single cartridge.

The priest stood with the prisoners, putting cigarettes into their mouths and lighting them. Though some of the men had streaks of tears on their cheeks, overall the mood was Russian: nostalgic, with ill-suppressed laughter at life's ironies.

Hugo watched the events as if he were being drafted into a game of tackle football, with rules and preparations unfolding before him that he barely understood. He wished he hadn't said, "I'm with you." Who says such a thing to a general? He was told to stand in the back. There would be men on one knee ahead of him. There was a countdown, and he remembered well, from training, all the motions from loading a rifle to firing it. He was told to shoulder arms. He did so.

Regulations allowed for four men at a time to be executed, and so four posts—one of them the scorched pillar from the tetherball set, with the tetherball still attached—were dragged into place, and the first four prisoners were brought there, their arms retied behind them.

One of them was a blond-bearded lieutenant who had the merry devil in his eyes. His stripes were torn off, and he shrugged. "I never liked them anyway," he said.

Tied to the pillar, the lieutenant scuffed his heels on the ground during the blessings of the priest, in whose authority he did not believe, and during the letter writing—he had no family—he produced smirks and dark humor. He laughed as one British sharpshooter was leaning against another's back, using a ragged pencil to make small circular bull's-eyes. The lieutenant even laughed when a bull's-eye was pinned onto his chest, right over his heart. "Target," he said. "My new rank."

Ironside ordered a sergeant from the Slavo-British Legion, one who had not mutinied, to raise his sword and to drop it as a signal for the execution. As soon as he realized he would be the one to cause his friends to die, the sergeant laughed, too.

There was a Russian joke that had been popular for as long as anyone could remember: Two boys jump into a lake in summer. Neither knows how to swim, and both of them sink. Both realize they are the prisoners of fate. One of the boys thinks, "I trust in my ability—I'll fight my way to the surface," and he struggles and thrashes. The other says, "I will put my faith in the nature of things," and chooses not to struggle, but just to relax and find the surface by floating. The next day, both their dead bodies are found by the village elders, who say, with relief, "They both made it to the surface—they learned well!"

Which is a punch line that, if you happened to be a sergeant in an army that has just been recruited, holding a sword to signal the execution of your friends, might be hilarious.

From the high arc light, the field was brilliant, with long shadows behind the prisoners. The flying V of executioners had loaded their rifles and chambered the cartridges. Around them, at attention, were the Allied soldiers and the Slavo-British Legion. The low wind brought the smells of burning wood, a campfire smell that gave the scene a flavor of intimacy. Ironside recognized something else in the air, an ill sensation between a smell and a sickening dread. It was fear, the onset of civilizing influence.

There was no drumroll. Ironside only gestured to the Russian sergeant. The sergeant raised his sword, and a hush fell on the field. He had no interest in letting his friends be killed, and yet he had no idea how to free them. He looked everywhere. He looked to the sky, which was black. He looked to the barracks, which were turning to embers. He looked toward Ironside, who was gazing back with mild indulgence.

Fate, when taking its time, was never kind. The smirking blond lieutenant, arms behind his back, target on his chest, now burst into sobs, his caustic attitude vanished, and then his friend the sergeant, who realized there was no such thing as finding the surface of the lake, that life was all about the underwater, brought down his sword, and Hugo, one of many, wondering, "Is this a dream? Am I waking up?," fired his rifle.

Lee wasn't so much tried and forgiven as he was needed to work on the Marlins on the DH 4s that had flown over Saint-Mihiel. He was released from prisoner detention but told he should return there after duty. While refitting minute hose clamps, he thought of his dogs. They had taken the milk greedily, emptying half the can, one smear on the nose at a time. He was not allowed to dawdle in the camp, but he asked if anyone had seen Banjo, and no one had.

When he returned to the prisoners' barracks, the dogs weren't on the blankets he'd put on the floor. Instead, they were on the other side of the barrier, in Harry's lap.

Lee leaned against the wire, poking his tongue into his cheek. He considered telling someone to nail the wire back down, but then remembered he'd been trading cigarettes with the enemy. "All right," he finally said, "they're yours."

"I've been using a warm cloth, like so, to run over their tummies and their bottoms," Harry said. He was wearing spectacles now, and the cloth he held up was soft cotton. "Watch. Like so." He explained that this stimulated their bowels, and told Leland he would supervise the first few times Leland attempted it. "I'm sorry, Corporal, does this make you uncomfortable?"

"Well—"

"The alternative is to use your tongue. Which they might prefer, but there are limits. I was going to trim their dew claws, but I'm afraid they're too weak for such a thing. This one"—Harry held up the male—"is adequate. The female, however, is most likely going to be an extraordinary animal. She's more alert at three or four days of age than any other dog I've had the pleasure of meeting. You should keep the boy to amuse her. What are you going to do with them, old chap?"

"I don't care."

"I'm afraid you do. You've named the girl."

"That was an accident."

" 'Nanette,' yes? From the finger puppets, the young lovers, that romantic story. Surely you could name the boy after the other puppet. Why not?"

Lee had to stop himself from trying to reach through the wire and removing the dogs from Harry, who continued talking reasonably, as if they were on the same side.

"Have you managed to find a pregnant animal?"

"No."

"You must. And then return with them to America as soon as possible."

Lee stepped backward and folded his arms.

"Have I said too much?" Harry asked.

"You keep telling me things I need to do."

"I should say they might survive without mother's milk, but the girl in particular will never be robust. She might be prone to infections and colds. In America, they still have veterinarians to help you. Not so much here." For a moment, Harry's diction had become more Teutonic and fractured, as if his concern had overshadowed rules of grammar. "So, Corporal, what exactly do you want? Afterward?"

He didn't need to explain what "afterward" meant—it was all anyone talked about.

"I'm not mocking you. You seem like a good fellow. We both seem to be interested in dogs, which is a start. I'm curious about their future."

"Who are you?"

Harry considered this. "I always wait to see if a puppy will survive before naming her."

Since this wasn't what Lee had asked, he decided to play a game of patience. Finally, Harry smiled at him.

"It's a courtesy of war. Speaking about oneself can so often go badly. Let us just stipulate: I know dogs reasonably well. I've trained dogs to be sentries and couriers and scouts and guard dogs. If I'd trained with chemicals, or munitions, I could be a millionaire when this is over, but, sadly, I know dogs and only dogs. And wine, of course."

"Of course," Lee said. It had been Harry's vineyard. He considered telling Harry that the main building of his vineyard was on fire the last time he'd seen it. It struck him as wrongheaded, so instead he just watched how Harry handled the pups. He put Nanette up to the light and sighted down her side as if he were checking a pool cue for bowing. "She is truly going to be a fine dog," he whispered. "At two months she will be as coordinated as a six-month-old puppy. At a year—well, I can hardly imagine."

Lee threaded his fingers through the wire. "I wanted to be famous."

Harry regarded Lee as if checking him, too, for bowing. "You 'wanted' that. In the past. Why?"

"I don't know." He watched the puppies breathing in Harry's lap. He heard a strange, primal chirping sound. "They're hungry," he said.

Harry repositioned the pups, turning them over and staring at their bellies. The heads both lolled backward, flowers too heavy for their weakening stalks. "I can be honest with you, Corporal. They're going to die soon," Harry said. He was not being cruel. He was speaking instead with compassion, and Lee realized he was the only other person in the world who cared about these puppies.

"What can I do?"

"Ah," Harry said, looking up. He met Lee's eye approvingly. "At this late time, you care, and perhaps that's what you're built for."

"Please, just tell me."

Harry's explanation was brief: it wasn't just milk they needed, but beestings, the first milk given after birth. "What about the bitch who lost her litter? Did she reject these two? Yes, that happens." Harry said that no one knew what chemicals were at play, but unless an animal drank the milk from a mother who had just given birth, or expecting, it would never thrive. "You must find such an animal and have them feed from her."

"But there aren't any."

"I saw one as I was being marched into camp."

"I just told you there's not."

Harry wrapped each puppy separately in a faded olive cloth. Then he leaned forward, pulled up the wire, and, as carefully as if delivering souf-flés, slid the dogs to Lee. "This is something you have to want. Their survival."

"I want that."

"You'll have to want it more than anything you've wanted. You can't just play at wanting it. It takes a commitment."

Lee remembered a saying about the difference between involved and committed, like eggs and bacon. The chicken was involved, the pig was committed. "What do I do?"

It was early evening. Lee left the barracks without asking for leave, just nodding at the single guard posted by his side of the building. There was a frosty wind that whipped the autumn mists, which hit his face like pecks of glass. Men stood by oil drums that salvaged wood burned in. Though it was cold, the mood was exuberant, for in the last few days the Allies had advanced deeper into German territory, and it was becoming clear that Berlin would fall by Thanksgiving.

Lee wore his campaign hat to stay warm, and had thrown his woolen coat over his shoulders. Underneath it, his arms cradled the puppies, and as he walked, he could feel with each bounce of his step their loose skin, the sparse fur, the stubs of their toes that weren't yet claws.

The town of Fleury was also celebrating, that an influx of Allied soldiers had brought in money, and someone had, through means no one wished to know, located bolts of Moroccan silk. Each had a different pattern, and so the women of the town had unrolled them, had already planned dresses they would make, and had given the children scraps to play with.

When Lee arrived, he stood by the dead cornfield, and looked into the pasture, where the workhorses were grazing. He was quickly surrounded by little girls, who ran in circles around him, their tufts of silk held high in the air as if they were kites about to catch the wind. They were playing "nomads," a concept that had just been explained to them. If they had no home, they reasoned that someone had to be chasing them, and it was probably Corporal Duncan.

Here was a narrow stable, and next to it another pasture (both empty), and beyond it, his destination. It was a house of whitewashed plaster, cracked and patched, with burnt-looking areas of exposed brick.

Outside, there was a pigsty. A lanky woman was throwing the evening's bucket of feed into a trough, which she managed without backsplash. She admired her animals' hunger for a moment, and then looked up at Lee.

"Ah! *Pardonnez-moi*," she said, and, wiping her hands on her apron, disappeared into the house. Lee listened to the sounds of the pigs eating, and the children playing behind him, until the woman returned. She had applied rouge and makeup. She wore a navy wool jacket that was distressingly like his mother's. "Hello, Corporal," she said.

"Hello," he said.

She smiled. "Do not worry for you. It is all—okay," she said. Her call was as precise and rhythmic as a bugler's: "Yvette! Marie! Michelle! Irina!" And then the girls appeared on the porch.

It wasn't until all of them were awaiting him that Lee realized how difficult this would be. War made a woman three times as beautiful. The girls looked him in the eye, and then looked down. They were still young enough to be bashful.

"And who would you like to spend some time with?"

He felt ill. He had a old-style five-dollar bill folded lengthwise between his fingers. He felt as if he were asking to throw mud on someone. "Isn't there another girl?"

The woman smiled—all inquiries were met with a smile—and said, as if it ended the conversation, "Natalie? Ah, a popular girl, but she pays the price for that, and so, yes, you understand. Who else?"

"Natalie," he heard himself say.

"Look how pretty—Irina. Very pretty."

"Yes, she is. I'm sorry. But . . . Natalie," he said.

"*Natalie est enceinte*," she explained, the smile wavering for the first time. "*Trop enceinte*," she added.

"*Je pense.* No, I mean *Je sais. C'est pourquoi je veux*, I mean, *je elle*—Oh, damn." He looked at the woman with agony in his eyes. He understood that he had once looked sweet to her.

He felt the money slowly tug out of his hand. The woman was regarding him as if she had just hired a criminal to do simple chores around the house. "*La bouche, et c'est tout. Comprenez-vous? Oui?*"

"*Ce n'est pas*—that's not what I . . ." he said, and then he had nothing to add. The other girls were leaving, each of them casting glances his way as if they had met for the first time in their lives a grave robber, an offal eater, someone who drank blood.

It was a peasant house—no parlor, but a warm, white kitchen that smelled of rosemary, with a large stove, and a long birch table at which sat a toothless woman who had been kneading dough until one of the girls whispered in her ear. Now she stared with full hatred at Lee. He wanted to say that her headscarf, which was new and fashioned from sabra silk, was lovely, but he did not know the word for "scarf," and Irina tugged on his hand to lead him toward the back of the house.

Natalie's room was off the corridor, no door but a beaded linen curtain. Irina knocked on the frame, and exchanged a few quick words under her breath, and then she took Lee by the biceps and, as if pitching him away with tongs, deposited him through the curtain.

It was dark in here, illuminated by a single oil lamp that flickered when Lee passed. The room was perhaps four paces across, half of it taken up by a lumpy mattress. The window faced the river, which rushed by in darkness. Natalie was propped up in bed, drawing the covers against herself. She had been reading magazines by the light of the lamp.

"Bonsoir," she said with a ditch-digger smile.

She had thick black hair, a single eyebrow, and the smear of a mustache. She withdrew against the wall, and Lee was aware of being far taller than she was, taking up all the air in the room.

"Mademoiselle," he said, and then she was naked, just like that. He hadn't even seen her move.

"I am your girl," she said. "I want your bad. Right now so good, soldier." It was as if she were reading ingredients for a recipe she would not be eating herself. The magazines had slid off the bed, and she attempted to wriggle. She was reaching toward a washbasin with soap next to it, but she could not quite get out of bed to reach it because she was eight and a half months pregnant.

She said, "Very good all night."

"Wait," said Lee. *"Un moment."* He opened his coat. He pulled out the puppies.

The sight of them stopped the drone of her monologue. *"Les petits!"* She put her hands to her face. *"Petits, petits, petits. Petits pois. Oh!"* She reached for them, and Lee handed them over. Her face was pretty, he realized, by the light of the lamp. She had a wonderful smile. She was cooing into the puppies' faces, singsong country French, baby talk, the tone unmistakable: he had made her happy.

"I need you to . . . *Il faut* . . . *Il faut* . . ." he stumbled. He demonstrated. He took one puppy and put it to her left nipple. She shook it away with a quick shiver, and looked to him with puzzlement. He did it again.

She did not flinch this time, so he took the other puppy and put it atop her domed stomach, against her right nipple.

She watched, curious and not yet understanding. The puppies' heads were moving now, noses flexing and sniffing. The closest one to Lee, Nanette, was bolder, and opened her mouth. She began to nurse. Natalie flicked at the dog like it was a mosquito, but she was confused and so her wrists mostly just trembled in weak outrage. Lee put the puppy back onto her.

He expected Natalie to look down—the sensation must have been strange, dogs at her breast—but instead he saw some kind of light in her eyes—understanding—that dimmed.

He had things to say to her. But it was as if he were looking into the windows of an empty house. The puppies wriggled, the loose flesh around their mouths pulsed as they swallowed. "You see, I *care*," he wanted to say, because apparently that made him a hero at this late date in this small muddy dot of 1918. He wanted to tell her the war would end soon, and peace would feel better than today felt. He wanted to tell her that the women of Irian Jaya suckled their hunting dogs, that they did it in Kamchatka, in tribes found along the Orinoco, areas he had never heard of but about which Harry seemed to know. It isn't so terrible, he wanted to say. It really was done for love and to bind the animal to humans. A dog treated so well was a friend for life, Lee wanted to tell her. Here are your friends, he should say, *ce sont tes amis*.

There was nothing to say. The dogs continued to nurse. The magazines on the floor were colorful. On the covers were Louise Lovely, the newest Australian siren; then Helen Holmes, Queen of the North, looking resourceful; and Alice Joyce, who Leland had always thought seemed intelligent. He imagined having his own projector, and showing a Chaplin film on the wall. "Do you know Charlie?" he might say, and then might come the first ray of hope that Natalie's spirit could be saved.

She looked with doll eyes toward the window. The river outside gurgled in the darkness, and inside the house, children were running with their silk toys through the hall, and there was the smell of bread baking. Really, Lee was thinking of saying, all they had to do was hold on a few more weeks, and things would be better.

23

Engstrom Hotel
Los Angeles
October 26, 1918

Dear Charlie:
    Tried to beat the rain today, so I saw your *Shoulder Arms* this afternoon at the Trio Theatre in Hollywood—I cannot tell you how good it was—everybody was thrilled, although there were not many people there. I know you were just a "wee" bit discouraged, but please forget that, as it is wonderful and *very pathetic* when you did not receive a package. A "bump" came to my throat as it did with everyone else around me— Just one thing I did not like especially—when the German shook your hand in the trenches and you accepted it—this might not be liked in foreign countries. Of course no one else noticed it, but I being one of your most true and sincere critics tell you this.
    I am happy to know you are married now. Please give my congratulations to Mildred.
    Always
    Edna

Shoulder Arms was released in October 1918, during the height of the flu pandemic. Across the country, local health departments ordered people to stay in their homes. If they had emergency errands to run, they faced fifty-dollar fines should they fail to wear white cotton breathing masks. Sporting events were canceled. Tumbleweeds rolled down theater aisles.

Into this marketplace came a comedy about the European War in which, at the end, the Little Fellow woke up. Morgenstern, the First National executive who had signed Chaplin's million-dollar contract, needed to breathe into a paper bag as he considered the disaster to come.

"Advertising Aids" went to cinemas. "You could offer a prize to the best-equipped soldier." And "Essay contests: funniest story you know about the war." And "Hire real soldiers to march before the theater; encourage patriotism."

On the first day of release, in Omaha, when the Stella Theater failed to open promptly, doors were torn from their hinges in the stampede to enter the house. In Chicago, police were called to contain the audiences, who so badly manhandled them that they each needed a bottle of Omega Oil to recover. In Los Angeles, the lines were so long for the evening shows that people began to appear early, as much as an hour beforehand, and queue on the sidewalk, cotton masks in place, careful not to stand too close to their neighbors.

When *Shoulder Arms* played in Manhattan, the managing director of the Strand Cinema encouraged people to throw caution to the wind. He wrote to *Motion Picture World*, "We think it a most wonderful appreciation of *Shoulder Arms* that people would veritably take their lives in their hands to see it." The letter appeared next to his obituary, for, immediately after posting it, he himself dropped dead of the flu.

From the moment the titles appeared, with Chaplin's hand, in mock pretension, writing out his own name on a chalkboard, then making a pistol of his fingers and pointing them at a figure of the Tramp, the laughter at every performance popped and sizzled like sparks off a wildfire. In some theaters, the bolts on the seats needed to be retightened, and in others, the straw stuffing needed to be repaired where patrons had dug their fingernails into it.

No one cared that he woke up at the end. No one cared that it wasn't as good as *A Dog's Life*. The white feathers ceased to come in the mail. The editorials about Chaplin-the-slacker stopped. The country equated his film with the war's being on its downswing, as if, by containing it, projecting it, and pointing out its risible parts, Chaplin had caused the war to be won. Through some magisterial process like increasing mercury in its flagon, Chaplin had by his own wit become a hero, and made the country feel like a nation of heroes for appreciating him.

Shoulder Arms was a massive success. With one artistic stroke, he had been vindicated in every conceivable way. People assumed he must be happy.

On November 4, he announced that his new film would be called *Jack of All Trades* and would feature the Little Fellow as handyman on a farm. "We'll have a pastoral," he explained. "It will give him a whole new land-

scape to find trouble in." But he could have set it on the moon, for all anyone cared. First National invited him to spend as much time and money as
he needed, on whatever scenario he wanted. *The New Republic* noted that
this was one of the rare times in history when an artist could work without
the slightest restraint; who knew what wonders would come of a genius's
unfettered imagination?

On the first day of work on *Jack of All Trades,* Chaplin arrived at the
studio at eight o'clock. As his car came down De Longpre, someone cried
out, "He's here!" and the whole crew lined up to flank the car and to yell
out encouragement.

He brought along a talisman. When his studio opened, he had started a
list. He kept it folded in his desk drawer, annotating it as necessary, and
now, married, he kept it in his pocket, and he touched it when his car
drove past the gates.

> Sid
> Rob Wagner, my secretary
> ~~Terry Ramsaye, publicity~~
> Carlyle T. Robinson, publicity
> ~~Henry Caulfield, studio manager~~
> Alf Reeves, studio manage [sic]
> Tom Harrington, My Valet
> Rollie Totheroh, my cameraman
> Eddie Sutherland, assistant director
> Henry Bergman, to tell people "Mr. Chaplin is busy go away."
> Toraichi Kono, chauffeur
> Constance Collier, coach for acting, speech and deportment
> Loyal Underwood (actor)
> Adam Austin (actor)
> ~~Eric Campbell (heavy, foil)~~ RIP Dec. 1917
> Granville Redmond, painter
> Helen Orlando, studio secretary
> George "Scotty" Cleethorpe, master of properties
> Charles Levin, Superintendent of Laboratories
> Rhiannon Powell, wardrobe mistress
> ~~Ed Brewer, my technical director~~
> Douglas Tuck, my technical director
> Vincent Bryan, ~~gag man~~ my assistant

Maverick Terrell, ~~staff writer~~ my assistant
~~Jocasta Brownlee, hair and make up~~
~~Karin Wessel, hair and make up~~
~~Maybonne Mullen, hair and make up~~
~~Maggie Chascarrillo, asst secretary~~
~~Clair Knightley, asst secretary~~
~~Hopey Glass, asst secretary~~
~~Irvington Temporary Agency:~~ Hair and make up, asst. secretary
Find new Temporary Agency
Edna

A story conference was held at a pair of pushed-together card tables onstage, around which sat Alf, Eddie, Scott, and Eddie—and Vincent and Maverick, who had the most difficult jobs in all Hollywood. It was known around the world that Chaplin was a genius and did not have writers.

"I was thinking we'll open on the town," Chaplin said, bluff with energy. "And I think, since it's a pastoral, I might milk a cow."

"And you could ride a bull," said Maverick.

"I was just thinking that," Chaplin replied. "I'll ride him right through the center of town, into a schoolroom."

Vincent, who had been with Chaplin longer than any other assistant, plotted a course. "Then you could step on the parson's toe when you got off the bull."

Chaplin looked annoyed. "I don't think so."

Vincent cocked forward his shoulders and tucked down his head, sipping coffee. "I just thought that, when you said you would ride the bull into church, it might be funny if—"

"No, I don't think so. Let's not stray from my first idea yet. It can be a Sunday, and everyone will be streaming into church. The Little Fellow runs a bull right in among them."

And so it went for a pleasant hour, almost as if he weren't married, Chaplin having many good ideas that seemed somehow to get better when exposed to the air. "I want everyone to be kind to each other in this one," he said. "The Little Fellow will be overwhelmed, and they will tread on him, but I want the mood to be of kindness."

Since there was no overarching conflict binding the film together, no escalator, no bully, no dog in peril, no war, but instead a general mood (kindness), there was not much story. This bothered no one—Chaplin films always came together, eventually. They discussed bits and factions: berserk farm equipment, belligerent goats, something with a scarecrow.

"He could herd the cows and slip on a banana peel."

"No, he won't," said Chaplin.

"The farmer takes a wife," said Vincent.

"He and Edna could even have a baby, that could be . . ." This was the unfortunate Maverick, who was only on the road to saying what everyone was thinking about. Instead, the staff was now fastidiously looking at buttons coming off their threads, problematic fingernails, patches of distant sky that might contain enemy aircraft.

"We'll do a bit with shoeing a horse," Vincent said.

"And those cows," someone said, and then there was agreement around the table—"Cows, surely"—nods, glances to other team members to look for affirmation: cows were funny.

It was like a locker-room pep talk for a team that was going to lose this season. "Yes," Chaplin said. "Well. We can at least know we'll open on the Bible verse and the steeple."

"And we can close the same way," said Maverick, who hadn't quite Vincent's trick of knowing how to pretend one wasn't making a suggestion, "the Bible verse, the steeple, the town, only by then our understanding of them will have changed, it's epanalep—"

"No." Chaplin shook his head. "You can open on landscape, but you can't close on it. You close on something human."

A shuffling of notes and a checking of pocket watches, the sounds of chair legs sliding against the floorboards, but Chaplin didn't move, and, like a class that realizes the bell has not in fact rung, the company remained in place.

He jammed his hands into his trouser pockets, looking at the pine planks of the stage. He was trapped on the thought of marrying Edna. Foil the cops, find food or money, marry the girl—the three legs of the comedy tripod. Meet, court, lose, win, fade out. The ending was inevitable and pointless.

"Yes," he said, though no one had asked a question. "I have an idea," he said quietly. "We're going to fade out on my death."

24

That night, Chaplin sat on the top tread of the grand steps of his newly constructed home, a wide mahogany staircase that curved from the entryway to the fleet of bedrooms on the second floor. He ghost-fingered the strings on his violin, C to E. He recalled how he used to do this when voices were drifting upward in the Athletic Club ("What's he like?"). That had been two years ago. He was trying to decide whether all the rooms he had lived in before the age of twelve could fit in his living room.

His new home was a Spanish-style spread on the best block in Laughlin Park. It was touched with florid and playful details that turned it baroque: wrought-iron railings, Moorish arches between rooms, tremendous Barcelona sconces with bubbling glass blown in the Alhambra's finest studios, high roof beams stenciled with gold-and-green leaf patterns, fireplaces that could host an auto-da-fé, other empty rooms with no known purpose. One, Mildred had turned into a nursery. There were touches of blue paint on one wall and pink on the other. Chaplin always closed the door if it was standing open.

The house was always dark. There were gargantuan chandeliers in the main hall that seemed to give no light, and great paned windows with grand arching peaks that faced the morning sun, and they gave no light, either. One evening, he brought Rollie over for dinner, in the small dining room, to ask him seriously if they could install white-flame carbon arc lights, Cooper-Hewitt mercury vapors, or if they might paint the floors white and hire Friulians to stand in his hallways; Rollie only said, "Your house is plenty light, Charlie."

The staircase comforted him. He brought the piece of paper from the pocket of his bathrobe, and though the light was too faint for him actually to read it, he knew much of it by heart: Sid. Rob Wagner. Carlyle Robinson.

The war was ending. At three o'clock in the morning, with another day's work about to come, and with no ideas on hand—why was a pastoral funny?—the war ending struck Chaplin as getting the girl had once struck him. They were both question marks masquerading as exclamation points.

He thought of showing Frances something new. This was not from a hostile place; he imagined showing her a movie that would make her cry. *A Dog's Life* had a moment or two in it; *Shoulder Arms* was audacious, but he knew to his marrow that Frances Marion wouldn't have been impressed by audacity. He imagined taking her hand. No seduction inherent in the gesture, just kindness between two friends who knew the same things. "I did it," he was thinking. "I became better." He was thinking about refugees returning home. He wanted to organize a benefit. He wanted to call Mary Pickford, just to tell her he liked her.

"Charlie?"

"What?"

"Are you coming to bed?" Mildred had her silk half-kimono on, and her long legs showed beneath it. She glanced away from her husband and toward the view he was taking in, the entryway, the beaded glass in the sconces, the trowel marks on the walls, the timber rooflines that belonged on an Andalusian castle. She was regarding the house as if she couldn't quite believe she lived in it. She was standing on the balls of her feet because the tile was so cold.

"Hmm?" he said.

His stare seemed to fix her in place. She was fearful and a statue. Galatea. Here, then, the wicked side of the Pygmalion legend: getting exactly the girl you have carved.

"Go to bed," he said.

She turned her lips inward, biting down on them. As if she were letting herself go aloft in a balloon, she eased back her shoulders and dropped her kimono to the floor. It pooled about her toes in a slippery pile. Outside, an owl hooted twice, a soft, low, curious query. Mildred swallowed, her eyes luminescent, a rabbit caught by firelight.

"I told you to go to bed."

Her eyes were warm, they were almost overflowing, and when she spoke next, she said, "Please," with a slight lisp.

"Oh, God, you aren't even as smart as clay."

"Charlie?"

"Clay knows how to obey the potter."

"But—"

"Go. To. Bed."

The next morning, he went to the studio ("He's here!") and impatiently gave a winning smile to everyone, then called Alf, Charles, and Eddie into his office. There was no reason to do a pastoral. A pastoral wasn't *better*. He wanted a museum set. Find some photographs of the Louvre and build it.

"What paintings do you want on the walls, then?"

"Gainsborough," he said. "No, get me a book on the history of art. We'll have a survey. The Little Fellow will interact with everything from Praxiteles to my friend Picasso. We need to hire life models. Consult the local art schools. And tell the musicians to prepare suitable music."

"Suitable music, my son?" Alf asked. Alf, like Chaplin, was small, but, unlike Chaplin, was wizened. He had worn the same battered derby since 1903, and the same black suit since 1911. When he made points, he illustrated them by gesturing with a cigar, a stogie like an extra knuckle. "Suitable for what?"

"The history of the world shown through artistic ambition."

"Right-o." Alf knew enough not even to exchange glances with the other men. Instead, he left before the orders could be rescinded, and he walked into the courtyard. There he found the members of the septet that had been hired to play mood music. "So how much music do you brilliant chaps know, then?"

Back in the office, Syd was sitting on the other side of Chaplin's desk. Chaplin was drumming his fingers restlessly on a pile of books.

"I was going to have them strike a copy of *Her Friend the Bandit* so we can re—" Syd began.

"No. No, no, no. I've been thinking," Charlie said. "We know how comedies end, but what about tragedies?"

"Oh, Jesus, Mary, and Joseph," said Syd. "Haven't we— Oh, sweet Mother Mary. Yes, all right, what about them?"

"He dies at the end of this."

"Who? Oh, no. No."

"It doesn't mean he can't come back in the next picture. He's hardly even real, you know."

"He's plenty real," Syd said, nose to nose with disaster.

"What do we know about him?"

"The world loves him."

"Love is only permanent because we say it is. Eventually, it stops.

Every picture I've made before this one, every one of them, *lies* somehow." Chaplin stared at his shoes. "He's Jewish."

"Pardon?"

"Wouldn't that at least be interesting? If he was Jewish?"

"They say the early ones are still making money. Can we make a new print of *Her Friend the—*"

"We're not talking about that now."

Syd bit down on his thumb. He looked into his brother's eye as if gazing down the barrel of a mugger's gun. "You know I like Mildred."

"What does that have to do with anything?"

"I'm just saying she's a bit of a prize."

"Maybe, but I'm still going to kill the Little Fellow."

"You're going to make him Jewish, send him into a museum, and then kill him?"

"Oh." Chaplin hadn't thought this through. "I suppose those are three entirely separate *idées fixes.*"

"Put him in a museum, Charlie. Kill him in the next picture." Sensing an exit point, Syd stood.

"Don't you want to know why I want to put him in a museum?"

"No." Syd was out the door and in the hallway. For he, like Alf, knew when to leave.

"Statues," Chaplin called out. The screen door swung shut with a bang. "They'll come to life," he said. "The censors will never know what hit them," he added.

A few minutes later, Chaplin was behind his desk, eating orange segments and being careful not to get juice on some photographs. He had hired day players in the past, those not as innocuous as extras but also not bound to be in his stable of actors—from the Krotona Academy of Artistry & Talent, a school for live models that also had some spiritual bent—your body is a temple and a breadbasket, something like that. Kindly old Mrs. Dunbier, who wore a beret and still referred to his business as "the pictograph," sent him sets of matte-finish studio photographs that showed a full-body image, and three facial close-ups to demonstrate expressive range.

However, Krotona had closed up shop (Chaplin wasn't sure what that said about the spiritual side of Hollywood), and he had something new in front of him: binders of photographs, each in its own sleeve, and each with a sheet of typed statistics showing height, weight, age, hair color, etc. There were separate books for juveniles, handsome men, ingénues, "character" actors, and a slender, single binder marked "old."

They still came from the Academy of Artistry & Talent, but the new dean, Harvey Golod, explained in an accompanying letter that classes were being phased out in view of the overwhelming studio demand for "types." In effect, they would be a talent agency not unlike those for the theatrical stage, only focusing on cinematic needs. Prices for models would remain the same as before, even those with extras listed under "skill sets."

Chaplin dawdled over the book labeled "Ingénues," noting that something subtle had changed since the days of Mrs. Dunbier. There had been a battle then for who could look the most wholesome. Some of those girls were still included, toward the back, but now the eyes of quite a few others promised a great deal more than their list of skill sets could legally describe. He turned the pages carefully, only realizing that he was still holding his orange in his hand when there was a knock at his door, which was open. He was surprised to see McAdoo.

"Oh. Bill. I was just—" He flipped shut the book.

"May I?" he asked, indicating the door.

"Certainly."

McAdoo closed it. He sat down in the visitor's chair of the tiny office.

Chaplin said, "You look well," putting his fingers to his lips. McAdoo was tan. Further, he had lost several pounds and had stopped wearing suits with vests.

"I like it here," he said. "Oh, and congratulations on your marriage, by the way."

"Yes. Thank you."

"Marriage is swell," McAdoo said. "And here, at the studio, is everything going well?"

"Of course." Something in McAdoo's tone caused Chaplin to say, "Shouldn't it be?"

"Maybe." He wiped off his glasses, breathed on them, and wiped them again. "I just wanted to tell you that they are not going to play fair."

"Who?"

"Your enemies." He said this slowly, settling the glasses back on his nose. "Goldwyn, Zukor, Warner, the rest. This is going to get ugly."

"I have six pictures left on this contract. They can't interfere with that."

"I have it on good authority, Charlie, that if they have it their way, they can."

Chaplin swallowed. "What does that mean?"

"Well, gee, I don't know." He chewed on a knuckle. "Do you trust everyone in your studio here?"

"You keep saying these vague things, Mr. McAdoo. If you're trying to worry me—"

"I am." McAdoo looked at his watch. He stood. "I'm glad you trust all of your people. You're going to need them."

It was hard, then impossible, to work for the rest of the day. The list, his team, took on new import. He wondered who would betray him. No one seemed likely, and then everyone did. It was early when the cry of "He's leaving" went up, and the Locomobile burst out of the gate and up the street.

In the car, Chaplin was so nervous he folded the newspaper in his hand and smacked it against his thigh. When Kono didn't turn right on Sunset, he opened his mouth to correct the course, and then remembered he no longer lived at the Athletic Club, but near Beverly Hills.

He wanted to tell Mildred he was doomed. He wanted to tell her to pack her bags, to flee with him. Suddenly the fact that he owned things excited him in a way it never had before. The world was coming to an end. Money gave him something to defend. Syd was right about Mildred. She was funny and intelligent, and there was something more: she was a demon in the sack.

Chaplin envisioned her tied to a brass bed, a villain (himself) who hovered over her, laying his hand to her cheek, throwing his head back and cackling. Without warning, the villain is clubbed over the head and the hero (himself) is rescuing her. Her arms around his neck. Gratitude.

He recalled all the questions he had asked her, all of the "Have you ever . . ." questions, and how, the first time she had heard them, she had blushed so vividly it was like viewing her skin through the light cast by a wineglass. And then she began to answer them. "I will, with you. With you, I will. All of those things. Teach me the French word again. With you. Tell me about Nazimova. With her? For you."

The meanders of the front drive made him impatient for his rococo house, and Kono hadn't even opened the rear door before Chaplin flew out and up the staircase to the bedroom.

He woke Mildred from her nap and threw her nightgown to the floor, and she was almost weeping with pleasure, she was apologizing for the night before, and he was saying to her "my angel," and at the moment when they were rising toward crisis, he thought that there was another person inside of her and that was that.

The next day, he told his company to strike the museum set. They were returning to *Jack of All Trades.* He did not dismiss the life models who had come to the studio; he arranged for them to be villagers, and he ordered Wardrobe to find them gingham dresses or plaid workshirts. Make some of them farmers, and give others stations at butter churns. Alf complied, surprised when a representative from the Academy gave him a one-page contract agreeing to the change. They'd never had contracts before. No difference in price, just keeping track, it was explained.

When they were all dressed, he asked his carpenters to make the T-intersection that he'd used since *Easy Street* into a village block. He put on his trousers, his vest, his shoes, and stood on the lawn, tapping his cane against the cement curb. The septet was playing Strauss. He tapped his cane out of time with the music. This went on for an hour, but he still didn't have an idea.

His eyes fell on one serious-looking girl curry-combing a horse. "Excuse me, aren't you—" He could swear he'd seen her in a Girl Scout's uniform, but after a while, everyone here began to look like someone else. That was rather the point.

"Did the Academy send you?"

She nodded, and then he nodded, and then Rebecca returned to combing her horse and watching everything.

There were some real clouds overhead, but they were of the Los Angeles sort, sheeplike and embarrassed-looking. Chaplin would have put better clouds in the sky. And by the way, the Tramp was now Jewish.

Only a few miles away, a solitary passenger slouched inside a trolley that was approaching barren Sunset Park. This was a park in its kindergarten: tiny king palms dwarfed by new, shining lampposts; pathways still fresh with gravel; a fountain with lily pads that might attract actual frogs.

One hand went up to the cord and pulled. The trolley stopped, and the passenger stepped out. When the streetcar rattled off, what stood revealed across from the park was the massive and unlikely Beverly Hills Hotel.

Three hundred rooms, no waiting, the locals had joked. It was a monstrous Spanish-style faux mission, with classical façades, roof tiles the color of mud, lengthy arcades with high arches, midget king palms that matched Sunset Park's, and mighty casement awnings providing shade for exactly no one. Until five years earlier, this had been a beanfield.

The acreage surrounding it had been carefully replanted, and gardeners had to remove tendrils of bean plants from the otherwise spotless lawns and tennis courts. It was hoped that people from the East Coast would find it, and that houses and business districts would grow in its shadow. Advertising in New York newspapers celebrated its perfect location "between the mountains and the sea," as if that might make a destination out of the nowhere between two other nowheres.

It was, today, the perfect place for Carlyle Robinson. No one from Hollywood would come here. He walked across the lobby, nodding at the many bellmen alert to his presence. The manager plumped up when she saw him coming; then her shoulders sagged when she saw he had no luggage.

His destination was the Tea Room, which served tea six days a week. On Sundays, it was converted into a chapel, and prayer services were held for the local farmers and ranchers. Robinson found the table he was looking for. It was far from the entry, pushed all the way into the corner, where the windows overlooked the mound of earth that was scheduled to become a swimming pool.

He had never met these men before, which was important, for he could always claim he did not know who they worked for. Each of them was well shaven and slender and young. As lunch progressed, and drinks were ordered, some of them quoted what he had written years ago, toasting him, and saying, "Good work, my friend." They toasted the health of Chaplin early in the lunch, and praised his work, and then said, "Of course, he had a great deal of help," and after the third drink, Robinson was aware of himself saying the words "You don't know the half of it."

One drink later, one of the men said, thoughtfully, "What's astonishing is that the man is such a tower of strength. It's as if he has no weaknesses."

"Oh?" said Robinson. *"Oh?"* He wiped the corners of his mouth.

And from there, the afternoon became a blur.

25

Life under the new occupying force (which stressed, like many occupying forces, that it was planning to leave as soon as something-or-other happened—citizens of Russia had learned how to hum along without learning the lyrics) found its own daily rhythm. Along the bustling Troitsky Prospekt, three blocks from the wharf, the buildings had saloon-style doors, and wooden planks that extended over the open sewers. The streets were made of mud, and atop that, slush, and atop that, ice and blotches of something brown that smelled like shrimp that had died in an old boot. Citizens shuffled by, eyes tearing in the wind, red hands in bruised gloves, and they carried mackerel dressed in newspaper. Knots of White Russians hovered around café chess games, looking up whenever a pretty girl walked by, in case she was an heiress who needed marrying.

A saying spread among the 339th—"If I owned Russia and hell, I'd rent out Russia and live in hell." The snow was different from Detroit snow: It was malevolent. It smelled like ketchup and melted like syrup. The men swore it had a soul, and that the soul wanted to kill them.

They walked through the evil snow in cursed footwear.

When the British War Office realized they were launching combat operations within the Arctic Circle for the first time in human history, they turned to Ernest Shackleton, Antarctic explorer. The Shackleton boot was the result of all the explorer knew about snow, mated with all he guessed about combat, a match-up like any shotgun marriage. The arch and heel slid in opposite directions, as if they argued. Each step was like scurrying across an icy pond.

Perhaps this would have been bearable to the Allies had they known where they were going. The topographical maps purchased from locals omitted swamps, for instance—"because everyone knows about them." The rivers they waded through began to ice over.

And no one quite knew *why* they were going anywhere. When the men were on civic patrol, they turned their eyes toward Ironside's office window, wondering what was going to happen to them. Town Hall, near the desolate town square, was a hive of switchback breezeways crowded with refugees, builders seeking permits, tradesmen with licenses stamped by the wrong administration, spies, thieves, and a glowering Cossack who sat on a captain's chair, clearing his throat with a terrible hack as chilling as the final stroke of the clock at midnight.

The bureaucracy lived in tiny, grimy rooms whose location did not match up to the maps Ironside had commissioned. Room 516, for instance, was next to Room 22A, and both of them were on the second floor, which in certain areas was called the third.

Ironside's office was the largest, and the quietest, the walls insulated with cow manure, his several windows overlooking the village square. Today his guest was a highly agitated Felix Cole, the U.S. envoy. Cole, of the St. Louis Coles, had inherited his post in better times, but had stepped up to the plate (an American term, Ironside discovered, meaning he was admirably living up to his responsibility) during the counterrevolutions, and was generally liked. Unfortunately, Cole was now attempting to explain Russia to Ironside.

"History is repeating itself," Cole said. "We aren't—"

"I'm sorry," Ironside said. "Not to interrupt, but I find that phrase less helpful to the situation than others."

Cole hitched his trousers. He had lost weight. "How about this? The population doesn't trust us."

"Yes," said Ironside. "It makes sense, doesn't it?"

"I've heard you're a historian, General—"

"Bill. And people say that 'repeating' phrase as if it's a law of thermodynamics."

"Bill," Cole said carefully. "Given humanity's infinite capacity for getting itself in trouble, there's a surprisingly limited number of outcomes. How's that?" His voice was harsh and low, as if he had been shouting for days against the roar of a river. "Russia doesn't want us here. Two groups would like us to stay: intellectuals and those few who were having a better time of it before 1914. The very men who now pray for our guns to restore them to power are the ones who did more to ruin our cause with the Russians than the Bolsheviks will ever do."

"That's well said. But we aren't here to stay."

"When are we leaving?"

"When the Russians can defend themselves."

"Against whom?" Cole put his hand over his eyes.

"Have you been sleeping, Felix?"

"You know we aren't in Russia, right? We're in the *idea* of Russia." Cole shook his head. "It's no longer clear who my cook and my maid are working for. You wonder at suppertime why your maid wants to watch you eat your soup."

"I understand."

"May I speak frankly with you, Bill? I've been a diplomat for twenty-two years, and I never speak frankly." He coughed into his fist. "Diplomacy is about irony. The irony in our present situation is completely out of our control."

"You're speaking philosophically, Felix, which isn't—"

"No, I'm hugging the shore here. Really. Irony equals saying one thing and doing another. Tell me that's not diplomacy." Ironside could see in his eyes glimmers of another place as Cole verbally wound down. "The truth is, the world would be a better place . . . if we destroyed the Bolsheviks. But we didn't say that . . . and we didn't prepare for that . . . and we aren't fighting that war."

Ironside had never seen a man struggling so hard to finish his sentences. Cole's battle was against screaming or despair or needing to sleep, or perhaps all of them.

"You need to request," Cole said, and his voice broke. In a whisper, he continued, "You need to ask the CIGS to withdraw all forces immediately. I want to send a telegram to Washington requesting the same. I'd like to save some lives."

Ironside's massive hands played against the blotter on his desk. His fingernails felt for the sharpest edges, which were already worn down from similar thoughtful passes. "I've inherited an impossible situation. But I understand what you're requesting, and I'll take it to London if you will do one favor."

"What is it?"

"I want you to have my men move you out of your apartment and into a place you can sleep untroubled for the next several nights." He waved a folder of papers over his desk. "The local sanatorium, it turns out, is empty save for a few doctors."

Cole laughed. "You'd think it would be filled."

"It will be quiet, and you can gather yourself. I understand there are mineral springs of some repute."

Cole looked out the window. He stood and then touched his fingertips to the glass, as if proving it was real. Then he extended his hand. "Thank you," he said.

As Cole passed into the hall, Ironside stood and went to his window. He waited until he saw Cole outside, crossing the town square, and being escorted to his well-earned rest. Then he called for his newest ADC, a pale Bristol lad who tried never to speak, for he had perpetual singultus.

"Is Mr. Cole being relocated to the sanatorium? Yes? Good. He's going to be sending a cable to his superiors providing his opinions. I would like you to delay his for several hours, but send one for me now, please. As follows: 'Felix Cole exhausted, stop. Has withdrawn upon observation to mental hospital, stop. Hoping his faculties return soon, stop.' " Ironside paused here. " 'Am allowing him full use of diplomatic channels as sign of respect.' "

Ironside thought, "That, Felix Cole, is true diplomacy."

26

The puppies woke up in the middle of each night to play their wobbly games, which did not yet involve walking. They slept beside Leland's bunk in a small wire enclosure about two feet by two feet, stuffed with blankets and scraps of ruined uniforms, with a dish of water. Lee was glad there were two puppies, because it allowed them to learn how to be dogs. For instance, when they were three weeks old, they discovered they had teeth, and that it was interesting to bite things (such as Lee), which is where the lesson might have ended for Nanette had her brother not been there to bite back. The first time Nanette yelped, Lee jumped up in bed, finding Nanette already exacting revenge on her brother's ear.

He listened to their tiny snarls, the warrior challenges of elves, and tried to relax. They were just puppies. Nanette and he called the other one Boy, which was hardly a name. "Boy" meant Lee hardly cared, still. They meant nothing more to him than that. Everyone loved stories about puppies. *The war,* he said to himself in his best *Photoplay* magazine-interview voice, *it was a horror, of course, but also a crucible of heroism. For instance, and this is quite the amusing story, I once had a fifteen-year-old whore suckle puppies.*

The close rafters of the ceiling, the radium dial of his watch: three-fifteen in the morning. The rest of the men, able to sleep. And devious mewling of two hungry animals wrestling in the dark.

"I have to give the puppies to someone else."

"But you haven't. I think you want them."

"No," Lee said. "I can't handle them they're too much," which came out in one breath.

Harry was impressed to hear about Nanette biting Boy. "She already knows aggression. That is quite early."

"Harry?"

"Yes."

"Is there something . . ." He barely knew how to ask. He had vague fears, knowing there was something mysterious about the dogs' origin. Harry had been unfailingly polite and informative. But wasn't that always the way with villains? "Are the dogs . . . are they normal?"

"Normal?" Harry's expression was the textbook definition, in High Gothic font, of scoffing. "Hardly."

"Oh," Leland said quickly.

"Dog breeding is a careful sport. It's like winemaking also. It's science and art, with much brutality and heartache behind it." As if offering a biscuit, he added, "There is also love." Harry continued: There were bloodlines in place extending to the 1890s, stud books with lineages as pure as kings'. Every weakness had been accounted for; every strength mated to strength came with great difficulty. "I was part of a vision, yes?" Harry had made himself comfortable on the edge of his cot by sitting with his back upright, one arm braced against his knee. Several days had gone by since he could shave his head, so silver hairs made a stiff glaze across his skull. "We wanted to make a race of perfect dogs."

Lee thought there would be more. The words seemed to have great import. Harry looked to Lee for a reaction.

"And what happened?"

"We accomplished this."

Harry's hard blue eyes checked Lee's to ask if he understood. A cold feeling crept across Lee's chest. Sitting down, he took his tiny dogs into his lap.

Harry swallowed. "My wife and I, we managed."

"What does 'perfect' mean?"

Harry looked as if he was trying to remember something he'd seen outside his bedroom window once, years ago. His knuckle was in his mouth. Then his hands were before him, and he was counting off on his fingers: "Loyal and kind and protective and intelligent and strong and brave and selfless and attentive," which left him with both thumbs. He put them atop his head as if they were dog ears. "This was our joke, I'm afraid." So the creeping worry that he'd been harboring monsters was wrong. They were just good dogs. Lee arranged himself so Harry could touch two tiny foreheads. Harry said, "Dogs make me believe in natural orderliness. They can't exist in chaos, and they thrive with direction. You can teach them."

"I don't think so," said Lee.

"The girl will be remarkable, as I say, her coordination extraordinary even by my standards, and the boy will give her company. That you have become their mother so soon means they have bonded with you, and—"

"They have? But I don't—I'm not—" He had wanted only one thing in his life. This was not it.

"And feeding at a human breast will make them even more bonded to people, I think. They will always know they are dogs, but when they look at you, they will see no difference between you. You've become a pack leader."

Lee felt a serious stone turning in his stomach. "Really?"

"They expect you to be better than they are. And if you train them, give them order, that provides them with some hope. Say, old chap, perhaps it's like acting. You're asking them to behave civilly. Isn't that just acting? Even now, people think civilization means order." A dry chuckle. "No, it starts like this." He touched each dog once on the flank. " 'You do this, you do that, then come back to me and we eat.' Every day you decide to train your dogs and not eat them is another good day for order and a bad one for chaos. Have they sneezed?"

He had never heard *any* dog sneeze. It was like trying to imagine a person baying at the moon. "No."

"Good. That would be the first sign of oncoming death."

"Wait, what? I thought they—"

"Taking the beestings might have saved them. Winter is coming. You must keep them warm, exercise them well, and keep them covered when they rest. And train them two to four hours a day."

Lee beheld the sleeping lumps, the quick rise and fall of fur. "Harry, I don't know."

Harry seemed to chew on his next words. "What happened to you, Corporal Duncan? I think you once had a confidence that you no longer have."

Lee petted each dog once, in turn. Nanette's fur was finer than her brother's, but she was motionless and he reacted to each stroke as if it were praise.

"I've seen terrible things, Duncan. You cannot shock me," Harry said with measured tones, a performer trying to tempt an audience member onto the stage. "Please tell me."

"Well," Lee said. He had never said this. "When I was in San Francisco"—he scratched the boy under the chin, which made him lean into it—"I auditioned to be a Four Minute Man."

"And what is a Four Minute Man?"

"It's a—you give speeches that—it doesn't matter. What matters is"—and he blinked—"my mother laughed at me."

On the other side of the wire, Harry was regarding him. It was a continental look, a patient one. "Yes?" he finally said.

Lee redoubled his efforts under the boy's chin. "Laughed and laughed."

After a profound silence, Harry finally said, "The war has caused many terrible things to happen."

Lee expected the arbitrary end to the conversation. The enigmatic quip. Instead, Harry slipped something from his pocket and kicked it under the wire. With some adjustment not to disturb the dogs, Lee leaned over to pick it up. It was a hard rubber ball, perhaps two inches across. "Yeah?"

Harry made a motion, flexing his thumb and forefinger together. Lee mimicked this, squeezing the ball. It let out a small, quick, bleating sound. Boy slept, but Nanette's ears popped upright and her still-rheumy eyes popped open. Then, gradually, they drifted shut. For the first time, her tiny body, with its football belly, had gone stiff with interest. And now it relaxed.

"As I have said, Corporal. She is a very good dog."

27

In the first week of November 1918, rumors came. The Kaiser had resigned (false); the Social Democrats had sunk the royal yacht (false); the German navy had mutinied and joined the socialists at the town of Kiel (true). General Ludendorff had been sacked (true), Hindenburg assassinated (false), the Kaiser assassinated (false). Germany no longer controlled its armies, Bolsheviks had infiltrated every government office, the workers were uniting under red flags flying in Bremen, Hamburg, and Cuxhaven. The Kaiser had left Berlin and was taking a holiday at Spa.

The last rumor was true. The Kaiser and Kaiserin had taken a cottage that was covered in roses at the end of an old brick path that was slippery with moss. There was a birdbath in which late autumn sparrows bathed. He requested that there be no demands made of him. Instead, he made tea with the mint from the garden, and sat in the afternoon facing the sun, which was weak and shrouded in November mists. His wife played old, sad songs on the upright piano, and neither of them sang along.

Countries were still declaring war on them. Once upon a time, the Kaiser had greeted each day's list of new adversaries, scoffing. The Duchy of Grand Fenwick? *Latecomers!* Seychelles Islands? *Phaf!* Nicaragua, Costa Rica? Let them man their leaky boats and cross the ocean.

But then came the Onondaga Nation. They delivered their sovereign declaration of war against Germany.

He had no quips about them. The Red Men, the unstoppable, implacable creatures of the forest who showed no mercy and no weakness. He understood trench warfare and evolution of gases, clash of tank against tank. But it did not seem possible that his soldiers could fight against wraiths. It had been a hard war, and his closest subordinates had already noted the perspiration, the palsy, the sudden interruptions of council meetings to demand that the music—there was no music—cease.

So he went to Spa for twenty-four hours. In the evening, he asked that newsreels be shown. The films seized from American couriers made him chuckle at first: *Pershing's Crusaders* was clumsy propaganda. The sight of himself watching a parade juxtaposed with a few dozen tin-plate-hatted doughboys bayoneting his effigy struck him as perfect comedy. Not one of those men knew him. Neither did the man who ran the camera, or the man who had put the mustache on the dummy. He, Wilhelm, was just the necessary villain, a role as ritualistic as Pulcinella's in *commedia dell'arte*.

The evening lifted his spirits so much that the projectionist put on a second film. This maneuver took four minutes, during which Wilhelm elected to use the water closet that the projectionist had used earlier.

There was a magazine on a small stone gargoyle that crouched between the sink and the windowsill. *Photoplay.* An edition from February with the lovely Alma Rubens holding a powder puff on the cover.

Inside were glamorous photographs of the Talmadge sisters, the comic Bebe Daniels, followed by a profile of Mary Miles Minter, who, the Kaiser learned, was fifteen years old and whose name was once Juliet Shelby, named for the Shakespeare heroine. There was a full-page photograph, exquisitely composed, of her feeding swans while attended by her mother and grandmother. The accompanying story had a sentence that he realized he was reading and rereading as if it were a coded telegram.

> She has quick, intuitive likes and dislikes and, as soon as she meets people, associates them with some color or combination of colors that seem to suit them most.

He flipped to the cover of the magazine—it cost twenty cents—then back to that sentence. He had no understanding of why someone would pay twenty cents to learn this. The young Miss Minter felt Maude Fiske was beige, Mary Pickford marigold with a narrow stripe of violet, and Marshal Foch was red and blue. The page ended here, and for the briefest second, the Kaiser wondered, should he turn the page, if he might appear in her thoughts. What color did Mary Miles Minter think he was?

The idiocy of having been sucked into this thought caused him to fling the magazine away. It landed on the tile with a skid. Alas, nature was not to be hurried, and with a sigh he used his toe to shuttle *Photoplay* back into his grasp. A story about a stenographer who was now an actress. Another story that won five hundred dollars for its author, who was now going to be a scenario writer for Metro Pictures. Then photos of Eileen Percy, a beauty, knitting a scarf for servicemen, followed by Roscoe Arbuckle, apparently a fat comedian, showing how he had lost weight by conserving food for the war effort. And a page of prose by Douglas Fairbanks, or so it was said.

He understood the subtext: those people onscreen weren't that different from you, and here was your chance to commune with them as they pretended to be people. And you had a chance, whether stenographer or scenario writer, to elevate your station. We are not so different, it promised, which made him chuckle.

Then he turned the page. What he saw made no sense, and then it made all the sense in the world. It was a two-page spread of a woman named Alice Joyce, nine photographs, nine different outfits. She was of Vitagraph Studios, a designation that likely meant something to American readers, as if saying she were *schwäbisch* or from the court of Ludwig.

A light, inquiring knock at the door, from Dona.

"Yes!" he exploded. "Yes, yes, yes, *yes, yes*. One sacred moment of peace, please."

Below each of Alice Joyce's outfits was a speculation about what it might mean. "This navy-blue gabardine suggests she is combining business with pleasure." And " 'Our initial appearance will score a success at the club,' whispers this black charmeuse afternoon frock." A velvet frock said: "No Ingénue Parts, for my temperament is modest and I am taken." At the bottom of all this text was a list of department stores where the frocks in question could be purchased.

His head was swimming. Once, a million years ago, 1914, his subjects had watched him take off his cloak to interpret what his mode of dress might mean: war or peace or something in between. Viktoria Luise had been studied for her hairstyles but never equaled, always one step ahead of her admirers. For the meaning behind the gaze was the unbreachable gap, that's what made civilization. But here, in this twenty-cent magazine, logistical analysis worthy of Ludendorff aimed at an actress, an actress rather than royalty. With the promise that you, too, could dress as she did with the proper outlay of capital.

He felt ill. The knocking at the door continued, and with another response of "Yes, yes, yes," more defeated and sallow, he washed his hands and dried them four times and returned to the main room, disturbed. The next film awaited him.

This was a newsreel that was unadorned and unshaped. It did not bear the stamp of the United States government, and claimed in its titles that it presented the latest, truest footage yet shot, at the Battle of Saint-Mihiel.

"Stop!" The Kaiser stood. The images were projected across his back. "Rewind this. Immediately."

And the images, ghostlike, silver, moved backward. Horses galloped in reverse, and their riders receded with them.

"Again. Show me."

This time, standing, he watched carefully as the American soldiers stood aside and let loose their allies the Indians. The images were smudged and vague, and when he asked that the projector stop entirely, he could not see them clearly. Every frame was a blur. With a sinking heart, he could tell from their riding styles that these were not actors. These were his beloved Red Men. Their outfits were wrong, their headdresses ridiculous, their reins and tomahawks entirely inappropriate to their tribes. As with the cavalry-campaign outfits, might not the inappropriate be accurate now? Their backs were ramrod-straight, their understanding of how to take a gallop across the potholes and tree stumps of a battlefield indefatigable.

This had been done for his benefit. He understood this. He also understood that the propagandists were playing on his alleged childlike fear of Indians. But he saw more, much more. And what he saw made him sink down on his slipper couch and clutch a pillow to his chest. A low moan escaped him. Dona came in from the next room to ask what was wrong, and he just shook his head.

For the first time, he understood his enemy. The Americans were not just relentless, not just clownish and insulting without a shred of respect for three thousand years of continental history. How could he explain what was wrong? They had grabbed on to something sacred and had determined how exactly to pervert and diminish it in a way that broke him. Once, he had seen Indians paid to re-create their glorious battles for sport, and that had hardened him. But now, in front of him, onscreen, there were Indians, not re-enacting their lives but pretending to be Indians for the golden calf that was the *motion-picture camera*. In a month, they would be in *Photoplay* magazine with commentary on what color they thought President Wilson would be, if he were a color.

This was the future. It was inescapable.

He ordered the household packed, the automobiles readied, the roads cleared for his departure from Spa.

He had dreams so terrible that night that he confessed them to Princess Cecilie, who told her astrologer, who told the newspapers. And that game of telephone simplified his fears and prognostications: Indians were coming to kill the sons of the fatherland. The American newsreels had survived a 360-degree revolution in how they were understood. The next day, all Germany read the illegally printed broadsheets announcing his visions of half-nude savages moving soundlessly in the moonlight, through trenches, floating over barbed wire, immune to the gas and the bayonet, scalps draped over the infantry's now useless helmets, arrow shafts poking through the roofs of staff cars.

Marines would land on every shoreline, the British navy sail unopposed up the Rhine to occupy Cologne, the French take Strassburg, the Italians run through Bavaria. Accompanying them would be Indians, hawk feathers slicked back in the rain, wampum beads flashing by the light of thunderbolts, and as they swung their ash-colored clubs, rendering their enemies into broken bits of bone and meat, there would be launched into the ether one dark flare like a comet, then two flares hanging like medals on a vest, then, at midnight exactly, another pitch and launch into the air, and there they would hang, three blue lights.

A telegram from the Deuxième Bureau was intercepted by the American Liaison Service, which forgot it was spying on its allies and telephoned the cipherists at Deuxième to ask if it was true: an armistice had been signed? The French asked the Americans how they came by that knowledge, and the Americans sent back the telegram they had decoded, and the French were helpless but to confirm, for now they had the same information from *two* sources.

It was agreed that neither side would discuss this, for it seemed so fragile, like a birthday wish. But it was too late: the telephone call had been relayed by a Hello Girl, who promptly phoned the head of the United Press, who sent a telegram home to New York City while simultaneously the contents of the armistice were typeset and thrown onto broadsides meant to be pasted onto the buildings of Paris. Instead, they were thrown into the air, since pasting took too long, and, besides, Parisians were grabbing them and running: the war was over!

The news ricocheted around the world, with a sound like factory whistles kissing church bells. Schools emptied; stock exchanges closed; delinquent boys launched fireworks in Central Park, and when they ran out of matches, the cops gave them more, while Dalmatians ran in circles, barking.

On the former battlefields, men slathered in mud shredded their orders and threw them into the air, and then they grabbed at the walls, and flung heaps of mud, for it was the only thing left to throw.

It was not midnight, but the skies were dark enough at seven p.m. The first sighting was by spotters above the deathly St. Quentin Canal. Standing with their feet on the backs of decaying bodies, they threw off their respirator masks because the eyepieces were so scratched and smudged. They beheld a sight no one had believed could exist. But there they were: hanging like stars, three blue lights.

Chemists understood flares and fireworks and how to provide the proper colors, and there were several variations. Over Bellenglise, someone had launched three aqua-colored rescue flares that arched and plummeted within a minute. Someone deep in the tangle of Charleveaux shot a modified trio of mortars that did much the same, indigo fizzles that sent the Allied and German soldiers into parched, exhausted tears.

Telegrams began to reach the White House, and one of the first came from a mother in Florida, who wrote, "Thank you for my three sons' deaths not being in vain."

But no one at the White House had heard of the armistice. The operator called the navy, which had also heard nothing, and together they called General Pershing's secretary, who had also heard nothing.

Finally, a cable came from Chimay. There was no armistice. It had been a mistake.

Never before had the entire world shared a single mood. It was like watching a rescue boat torpedoed in the harbor.

The *New York Tribune*'s headline the next morning was "JOY DASHED UPON THE ROCKS," and its editor asked in his column, "When the real news of peace arrives shall we have another celebration as good as those first hours? Hardly, we think. The edge has been taken off."

For the men who fought, those who had seen three blue lights understood: the promised land did not fulfill its promises. Any attempt to find a symbol (three blue lights) and give it meaning (a climax!) was not just doomed but punished. The war was worse than a farce. A comedy ended with a marriage, and a tragedy had no end.

28

When the puppies were almost two months old, Lee awoke with a weight on his chest. It was Nanette. She had somehow gotten out of her kennel (he'd fitted it with a wire top and a latch) and was now patiently sitting on him, front paws placed symmetrically, rear legs tucked under. When his eyes were open, her eyebrows fluttered, as if registering that he had reported for duty, and then she returned to what she had been doing while he slept: staring at him. Which was disconcerting. Shouldn't she be playing or chewing on something?

Lee ran a hand down her back, which caused her to readjust fussily—she had no patience for that—and she licked her lips. Her eyes were brown, lucid little measuring wands that seemed to take Lee's temperature. He had the disturbing sense that she was judging whether the balance of power in the pack had shifted overnight. "Are you sure you're two months old?"

As Harry had taught him, Lee took his pointer finger and drew it downward, mouthing "down." Nanette continued to stare, so he knocked her front legs out from under her. Then she relaxed, and put her head down between her paws as if he were confirming her understanding of how the world worked.

He glanced down at the kennel to look for her brother. He could see Boy in the dawn gloom, belly upward, paws outstretched, asleep to the world.

That morning, mail call was at ten. He had once hovered during the delivery of packages and envelopes, and when each man had retreated to a chair in the mess or to his bunk, he had watched the range of emotions on their faces, and then had gone back to whatever he had been doing before. Now he didn't want a letter from home, and people who relied on them weren't self-sufficient.

Today, ten o'clock was dog-training time. Nanette already knew "sit" and "down," which Harry told him was astonishing (Lee suspected that Harry would say everything Nanette did was astonishing), and he was working on "stay" while walking backward across the muddy causeway of the aerodrome. It was a perfect area for training, in that there were many distractions: rain drizzling; men crossing to and fro, some running and laughing, others carrying equipment, and still others pushing wheelbarrows full of sand toward the landing field, where the noise of engines gunning and sputtering was a constant background music.

"Stay," Lee said, walking backward, and Nanette watched him from her "down" position, unblinking. The wind ruffled her fur; she narrowed her eyes but still did not blink.

Boy was tied with a piece of rope to a fence, because he was capable of learning exactly nothing. Lee had tried teaching them together at first, and then separately, but when Lee made hand gestures, Boy only followed his fingers with curiosity, and when he spoke—Sit! Down!—the expression changed to fear.

"Oh, come on!" Lee cried during one frustrating session. "Down!" And he knocked Boy's legs out from under him.

There was a quick yelp. Lying on the ground, in the mud, Boy showed his stomach in supplication, and his eyes rimmed with tears. He had urinated on himself with fright.

"I'm sorry," Lee said, rubbing the dog's face. "You don't understand yet." Boy licked him.

Lee turned his attention fully to Nanette, thinking it didn't really matter what Boy was called. He wouldn't come yet in any language, Allied or enemy. But: walking backward, crouched over, intoning "stay," he saw Boy lurch upright from the ground and begin to walk slowly to the end of his long lead. He was limping.

"Oh," Lee said at exactly the same time that someone behind him cried out, "Oh, little puppy!"

It was Pfc. Thomas, who worked in the mess, stirring pots of boiled and stewed meats. Thomas had just left his shift and was returning to the barracks. "Nanette is limping," he said.

"That's Boy," Lee said. "He must have . . ." He walked to the puppy and picked him up and cradled him.

"I have a dog," Thomas said. He began testing Boy's paw pads, tapping on each of them. "His name is Firefly, and Mom says he waits by the mailbox every day."

"That's great," Lee said.

"Got a letter from him today. Well, it's from her, but she pretends—"

"Yeah," Lee said. "Right."

Neither man could find anything wrong with the puppy, so Lee put him down, where he commenced to limp again, his right forepaw bothering him.

"He wasn't injured a minute ago," Lee said.

"Are you sure?" Thomas rubbed his chin. "Yesterday I came by and he was limping."

"Really? When?"

"Around this time."

Lee wondered where he'd been. Yes, he'd tied Boy to the fence and taken Nanette to the other side of the metal shop, to test her ability to stay with the noise and sizzle of the welding torches.

"Here you go, Boy," Thomas said, and he dangled a finger-sized piece of ham fat over the puppy's nose. In a second, it had been snapped up, and a pink tongue had explored the feeding hand, just in case there was more.

Lee put Boy down just as Thomas started walking away. Something occurred to him. "Hey-ya, Thomas."

Thomas stopped.

"When he was limping yesterday, did you give him anything?"

"A little gristle, yeah. Is that all right?"

Lee nodded. A moment later, Thomas was gone. Lee kept his eye on Boy, who casually walked the full length of his lead, about ten feet, back to the fence. He was no longer limping. If anything, he seemed to have a little swagger.

"Son of a bitch," Lee whispered. Which is when he remembered. "Nanette. Come!" She sprang from her place on the ground and rocketed toward him as if she were going to leap over barbed wire. Instead, she halted, and looked up expectantly. Lee gave her a piece of hardtack, which she accepted. He gave her a second piece because he'd made her "stay" for an unconscionable amount of time, and this she held in her mouth before laying it down in the mud. Her eyes indicated that the contract she'd signed had stipulated just one piece of hardtack.

"It's okay," Lee said. He fed it to her directly. He felt, with every movement of her jaw, that his standing was diminishing in her eyes. He stared at her brother, who was licking his lips and closing his eyes as if ready to dream about ham fat. Lee wondered: had Boy just *lied*?

"Corporal Leland Duncan," said an unfamiliar and annoyed voice. The man, a corporal, wore a blue campaign hat with an insignia of Mercury on it. He carried an overflowing leather satchel. It was the postman. "Here you go."

"What?"

"What?" The corporal rolled his eyes, shoving a postcard into Lee's hand, muttering, "Should have just thrown it away," and then he was gone.

It was a sepia-toned image of a man dressed in olden-times gear, Stetson, fringed leather jacket, goatee—or Vandyke, Lee wasn't sure. He held a rifle. Until he read the name Wild Duncan Cody, Lee thought the mail was meant for someone else.

On the back were his name and his unit, and in the "message" box was just one sentence.

Is it harder to be the parent of a child or the child of a parent?

It was his mother's handwriting. She hadn't signed it. The photo looked to be twenty or thirty years old, and, based on the length of the rifle, Duncan Cody was a tall fellow. His expression was courageous and ready for action, rifle aimed high, one eye in a squint, as if the photograph had been taken not in a studio but in a settler's hut on the edge of a cliff, where Apaches were sawing out the foundations so that it would teeter and fall into a den of rattlesnakes.

My father, he thought, and then, with relief, *thank you.* Then he wondered how long she had held on to this souvenir, and if she had others.

He took the postcard and sat down, and his dogs were on him—Boy for pats and Nanette to keep him from getting any. He couldn't tell if he looked like his father; the image was small, and there was the goatee to consider. His father seemed proud and had worked hard to look like this, as if it was important. Lee stared at his mother's inscription and thought, "Dear Mom: the child, of course," and as if a bright sun were bursting overhead, he realized he was not just her son but this man's. The word "father," which so many people used so easily. Perhaps it was harder to be Duncan Cody's son than what she wanted for him.

His father looked young and able. It was starting to rain, so Lee put the postcard in his pocket. He put Nanette on her leash and scooped up Boy (he didn't know how to walk on the leash yet) and walked back to barracks for his last moment of rest there.

He wanted to tell someone about the postcard. He and Ripley had spoken only in passing since the day at the winery. Ripley had gone to Paris and delivered papers against Lenore, which was helpful in that, the following week, he met another deadpan, startling beauty who seemed to torture him.

Lee put his dogs back in their wire kennel (he put a stack of books on top of the hatch), and he took the postcard back out again. He noted how perfectly the fringe of his father's jacket fell, just so, looking effortless and yet far from slipshod. The vest had damask-pearl buttons, the kind you had to order from London, utterly nonfunctional for a lawman or scout, but lovely in a photographer's studio light. He knew the look in his father's eye, for he had feigned it a thousand times. Picture a terrible danger, and know you will protect anyone looking at this photograph from it. Go!

He had a growing feeling his father had been rather a rogue. But the flip side of rogue, too: a tiresome bastard. His mother had been in the lighthouse when he was a child, and her presence was like sitting on a knitting needle sometimes. But she had been there. *"Dear Mom . . ."*

That evening, when the rain had stopped, the weather that remained was arctic and crisp; the stars were trembling in the ink-black sky. Men stayed in the barracks, gathered around the stoves, lobbing chunks of wood into them, and listening for the crackling as they burned. In Lee's, there were twenty men engaged in rounds of poker and drinking.

Lee was playing a game with Nanette. He had given her a rope with a knot at one end, and was teaching her to let it pass by without biting it. If she did it three times, he gave her a hunk of bread. He dragged the rope across his cot, and she watched it like an African explorer studying a python slithering into a river. "Get it!" he cried, and Nanette pounced, shaking the rope until it was dead. Then: treat.

It was too complicated a game for her brother, whom Lee had to put back into his kennel. But Boy tended to whimper if not paid attention to, so he, too, got a small treat when his sister did well.

Lee was making a list of questions for Harry. When would they both know not to make messes indoors? Was there a supply of squeaky balls somewhere? When would everyone be safe?

In the middle of the night, he always woke four or five times, just listening to them breathe. Was that a cough or a sneeze? Tonight, at two and at two-thirty and at three, they were sleeping, perhaps the slightest of wheezes in Nanette's exhale. And at four, as every night, they began playing mysterious games involving pouncing on each other in the forest of shredded woolen uniforms and underdrawers he cycled into their little kennel. *Bang!* went the kennel as one puppy flew into the other. Nanette's voice growled, followed by a high yelp from Boy, and then Lee needed to separate them, one under each arm, under his blanket, in a vain attempt to calm them down.

A few minutes later, they were dancing across his chest, flopping off the cot, there was a skitter of toenails on the floor, and then the launching of a small body directly into his solar plexus. He huffed upward, and then the puppies were carrying on with guttural protests like drunken friars.

He was laughing, and could not remember the last time he had laughed. Something lurched behind him, his cot bounced, and he felt something cold and smooth against his cheek.

"Duncan," someone hissed.

"Hey!"

"Duncan," he said again, and now Lee recognized the voice as Temple's, a bearlike corporal from Oregon. He also realized Temple was holding a hammer. "I want you to take your fucking dogs and get the fuck out of this fucking barracks for the rest of the fucking war."

"But—"

"Now."

"They can't—"

"If one of them makes another fucking noise, I'm going to flatten it. Move."

"Temple, they could die from the cold."

"That a problem?"

Lee walked with his puppies squirming under his arms, and a blanket thrown over him, poncho-style. He found himself walking toward the mess tent, where perhaps someone friendly would spot him some coffee (no), then toward the barracks, thinking he might reason with Temple (he reconsidered).

He remembered the shed at the edge of the field, where they stored the wooden tackle used to brace the DH 4s when they were at rest. Inside was a small space among the beams and supports, just long enough for him to stretch out on the wooden floorboards. The windows were wire mesh. As he emptied his duffle, he noted that the door barely fit the hinges.

He struggled to make a bed out of his spare uniform and drawers. He pulled his animals toward him, wafted the blankets over them, and found he had made a tent—his duffle, his boots, his knees propped up the blankets under which he and the dogs could sleep. They had had enough excitement, and after realizing there would be no more playing, they each walked in circles a few times and nestled against Lee, Nanette under his knees and Boy between his arm and his body.

It had begun to snow. It wasn't the sticking kind, but there were flurries outside the window, and he could hear the angry whistling of the storm.

His mother had tried to spare him the pain of a pet and a father. You can't save people you love from having their hearts broken, because sometimes they want things, regardless. *Dear Mom: I've been a terrible* . . .

Sometime later, he woke to find Nanette standing on top of the blankets, staring at him as she had the night before. Her breath made small jets of steam. This time, he said, "No," firmly, and swept her under the covers. "It's cold out there," he whispered. "Go to sleep."

When he awoke, the sun was shining, the light giving a listless sheen to the walls. He stood and threw open the door. His dogs bounded outside to relieve themselves in the field.

Immediately he understood something was wrong. Both of them were putting their moist noses into the breeze. Their ears, which normally flopped over, were standing. Boy made a cautious, catlike siren, a suspicious snarl, and then he was silent again. The cold wind ruffled their fur.

Lee drew his blankets around his shoulders. Ever since he had landed in France, he had felt a subsonic rumble, Olympian-sized earth-pounding equipment striking the horizon line. It was there day and night. It invaded his dreams.

No guns. No distant bombs, mortar fire, shouts in enemy voice. No distant airplanes, or mass movements of troops over barbed wire. He was alone. His dogs raced in circles, crunching through the ice sheets on the ground. They stopped, pointing in opposite directions, and then they ran again, making small woofing sounds, since they had not yet found their voices.

"Hello?" he cried. Dogs at his heels, he made it to the center of the base, which was deserted. "Hello?"

Then to the prisoners' barracks. The door was open, chairs were knocked over, bed linens scattered. He was reminded of the *Mary Celeste*, and how his mother had frightened him with stories of abandoned ships, rigging upright, becalmed, the captain's dinner table set and untouched.

It was two o'clock in the afternoon of November 11. As the world would later commemorate, the war had ended—a real armistice this time—at eleven that morning. Lee had slept through it. The men of the 135th had abandoned their posts en masse for the village, to drink, to dance with the townspeople. But Lee did not know this. He felt a viselike fear in his stomach that the world had come to an end.

Sunnyside

He grabbed his dogs—they were looking at him with curiosity about what he was going to give them to eat—and put them in his lap as he sat in the open doorway of the empty prisoners' barracks. They tumbled off, and dashed inside to snuffle through the detritus left behind.

He sat down on Harry's cot. He saw a cream-colored envelope. It was addressed to Lee. Inside was a letter.

Dear Corporal Duncan:

I have been a terrible, or perhaps a mediocre teacher. But thank you for listening to me. I think you will keep the dogs. I think you have kindness in you. It is not true that anything you want badly enough will be taken away from you. It is only true nine occasions out of ten.

They are good dogs. They want to please you.

You are looking for where your talents may take you. I think you would be good with the dogs. Take them on your stage with you and give demonstrations of their worth. Show they are loyal, kind, protective &c. and show that heroes exist. Maybe at the end of the day you will turn back a little darkness. For yourself, for them, for someone who has met them.

Of course, I must go now.

Thank you for not describing to me how my winery must look.

Harry

There were shouts outside, soldiers returning to camp. The puppies had found an open ration of M&V, and were burying their noses in it while the container scooted across the floor.

Lee would keep the letter alongside the postcard of his father, for they had arrived within the same twenty-four hours. It was the last day of the war.

"Nanette," he said. "Come." She dropped the bite of food in her mouth, jumped over the piles of sheets, and skidded to a halt before him. Boy continued to eat. Outside, the celebration was rolling back to camp, with the sound of car horns, bugles, drunken men banging on empty copper pots. Lee willed Nanette to ignore them. It was early, but it was also late. They had work to do.

On the last day of that war, three hundred men from companies of the 339th were pinned down under heavy fire in the village of Toulgas. They were surrounded on three sides by Bolshevik infantry and, worse, on the Dvina River, to the west, there were gunboats lobbing three-inch shells into the village.

The day before, it had seemed peaceful. There had been a delivery of scarves from the Red Cross, one for each Allied soldier, six-foot-long wool gray-and-red lifesavers knitted by the women of Detroit, who had heard their men were cold. It had caused joy, nostalgia, tears, then depression among the 339th.

The local topkick had declared that, since the paths were marshy, Toulgas was unapproachable by the enemy. Which was true during the day, but at night the marshes froze over, and it turned out the Bolos could bring not just themselves but far heavier guns than the light artillery the day-traveling Allies had acquired.

And so, for sixteen hours, rockets had been flying overhead, crashing into the snow, and sending it up with sizzles and pops. Bullets whined and sang past the men's ears: the Springfields that most of the Bolos had fired with a high-pitched twang like piano wire. Occasionally, dumdums thudded against the walls.

Hugo was among those trapped in a blockhouse, face covered in sawdust and sweat, ears long since sent to tinnitus by the sounds of falling bombs. Machine guns chattered like percussion against the whizzing and breeze of incoming mortar fire. The whole of Hugo's sight seemed to be blackened snowdrifts. Every so often, a particularly close explosion threw slush and dirt into the room, causing Hugo to spit to clear his mouth of the taste of cordite.

The blockhouse was packed with thirty men. It was made of felled trees notched together like a pioneer cabin, with slits for windows, and a stove in the center whose chimney pipe was now a ruin of twisted sheet metal that Bolo sharpshooters had taken, in the last two hours of slow dusk, to shooting at, for it made an amusing noise.

And so: on one side, thousands of Bolos, well armed, with a small navy, and on the other, a few hundred Americans. The 339th was scattered over a dozen blockhouses that were meant to protect Toulgas. Bolo collaborators had cut the telephone wires. And night had crept in around one-thirty.

"We are *not* out of ammunition," Lieutenant Gordon said. "Oh, holy Christ almighty. Are we?"

By a single veiled lantern Hugo could see his fellow Polar Bears (they had named themselves this recently) sizing up the situation. They were waiting for Gordon to say more. He rubbed his chin, blew out his cheeks, and shook his head.

It was at such moments that Hugo knew they would all be rescued. He was as brutal a cynic as any of them, but some part of him flared up at desperate times and decided all was darkest before the dawn.

"Oh, God," he whispered.

"What?" said Wodziczko.

His exhausted eye sockets spiked with tears, which then retreated. He could not explain this, but during each day of combat, when he could think, every so often he thought, "I am thinking," which was simple, and then "And I'm thinking that I'm thinking, and so I'm not yet dead," which ballooned into "And because I'm aware of these thoughts and they haven't yet fled the earth, I must still be here, and be here in a coming moment to remember it, and thus, because I'm thinking, I will survive."

Idiot. Humiliation. Now he was seized by the idea that every man had thought that way, including the dead ones. Because everyone died. Even if there was a cavalry now, there wouldn't be one when his number was up. Also: *there was no cavalry now.* His last package from home had been a scarf, the same thing everyone else had gotten.

"Hey," said Wodziczko. "Hey. Hey."

"What are you doing?" asked Hugo. For Wodziczko had adhered himself to one of the openings between the logs, and was peering out, his hands shading his eyes.

"It can't be."

"What?"

"Hey, everyone," Wodziczko croaked. "It can't be."

Hugo wanted to hit him over the head for not coming out with it. "What do you see?"

Wodziczko's face glowed as if he had just seen angels dancing at the hem of God's robe. "Three blue lights."

Hugo hadn't expected that. "You saw . . ."

The whole of the blockhouse rushed to the front windows. The lanterns were extinguished so that they wouldn't be seen by snipers. For there were indeed three blue lights flashing on the distant other side of the Dvina, almost two miles away, where there was an outpost of British command.

Some of the men were shoving others away to see for themselves, and the rest were exchanging questions—"Did you see that?" and "Are we saved?" and the like.

Hugo could hear everyone plainly, for the aerial bombardment had ceased. "Are we saved?" he asked, feeling embarrassed for asking the same question as everyone else.

"Don't," said Lieutenant Gordon, but it was too late and his instruction too feeble: two of the men had thrown open the front door and had raced outside, the better to see the array of deep-blue flashing lights that shone over the Dvina, frozen slush illuminated in streaks as the lights pulsed on and off.

Hugo was one of the men who rushed outside. He could hear excited Russian being spoken among the trees, in the dark.

"Is it over?" Wodziczko asked.

"Peut-être," Hugo whispered.

There were three blue lights, but they were flashing in code. The message was relayed to Lieutenant Gordon, who wrote it down by moonlight, letter by letter, word by word, with the nub of a broken gray pencil. "Attention 339th at Toulgas, stop. Need immediate accounting of supplies, stop. Misallocation of sixteen dozen Red Cross scarves without authorized quartermaster invoice, stop. Return scarves, stop."

The lights continued to flash, as the message was being repeated.

"Scarves?" someone yelled. "They want our scarves?"

Miserably, Hugo murmured, both hands hanging within his scarf, "Isn't the war over?"

And another person was crying, "Scarves?" when the first new salvo of three-inch shells was launched with an exhale and a whine and a blast into a nearby snowbank that sent the men of the 339th back into their blockhouse.

Speaking of clothing: on November 12, the quartermaster at Archangel ordered five thousand new pairs of Shackleton boots. The British War Office dutifully billed the U.S. War Department for five thousand pairs of boots, in a transatlantic cable that caused the master-sergeant recipient in Virginia to put down his champagne glass, displace the Hello Girl from his lap, and wipe the confetti from his Serbian-style overseas cap (a memento from his timid time Over There). The war was over. Why were fresh battle supplies needed? He telephoned his export-supply liaison, who telephoned the support staff of Secretary of War Newton Baker to ask: Were there American troops in Russia? Should they still be there?

And here the interrelation of irony and diplomacy went into full play, as each governmental department could in turn claim to be shocked that men committed to guard warehouses, or support local troops within the city, or serve as liaison or something with the Czech army, were burrowed in snow almost three hundred miles into a country with whom the United States was not at war. There were a great many documents composed, all in strict passive voice. Orders were given.

Hugo and the rest in Toulgas knew nothing of this. On the fifteenth of the month, there was a blizzard that lasted most of the night. With it, an artillery barrage meant to cover the Reds' retreat. Trotsky himself, it was said, directed the fusillade from his train car, and decided there were more important theaters for his new army. He said he knew they would be back. On the sixteenth, the sun rose as much as it could, at the edge of a clear, dim purple sky, a sky that called for ice-skating or hockey or making snow angels. Hugo was among the first to spill out of the blockhouse and into the clearing in the woods that made the village of Toulgas.

There were furrows and banks of snow, deep craters surrounded by strangely shaped humps. At first, Hugo thought these were scurf, flash-frozen pits from four days of artillery barrages, but then he saw that the snow had hands. The village was filled with dead Bolsheviks. As the 339th slowly left their quarters, clutching their rifles, they walked past the dead men, who were as motionless as sculptures. Each had an etching of snow across his face.

Hugo stared at a bearded man sitting up, white face sparkling with frost, chest bare, a tree branch having fallen in a serpentine way across him. "Laocoön," he thought.

He and the other men of Detroit, the Polar Bears, kept walking, directionless, fanning out stupidly and without strategy. The Shackleton boots slipped under Hugo's feet, which would normally cause him to curse. Some seabirds, squawking, cast vague purpling shadows on the Dvina.

When he looked at the river, Hugo stopped in his tracks. Some Russians had tried to cross while it was frozen at night, and had fallen halfway in. Hugo found the sight of a man's arms in the air, beseeching, to be awful enough. But it was another body that made him finally sit down atop the snow on the riverbank. It was a pair of legs sticking up from the ice, bent at the knee, one ahead of the other, as if he'd toppled over in a full dead run. The body vanished at the hip, the rest stuck under the frozen sheet.

Hugo regarded this dead man for several minutes. He could not imagine drowning upside down while freezing. But this was not what kept him here. Instead, it was that the corpse was barefoot. And someone had stolen his trousers.

There, under the mildest wisp of sun, ice glowing and reflective, the legs of the corpse were splayed and heavy with snow, like tree branches, and Hugo clutched at himself. He did not know about Armistice Day. Looking at the bare, frozen shanks in front of him, he realized the war was never going to end. Everyone would die and be replaced by people who needed the clothes you died in. This was the future.

A few yards away, other men of the 339th had discovered the body. They were laughing. For it was also a comic sight, as if the deceased had slipped and fallen into a vat of whipped cream. One of the men paddled with his arms, miming how his legs must have kicked, and the other roared with both hands on his empty belly. Hugo watched this, and thought that this was the future, too. He almost wanted to die, except for knowing that men like these would survive him, and take the things from his pockets.

That morning, the answer came down through the bureaucracies in Washington and Great Britain. It was agreed that the experiment in democracy had not yet been given a chance to flourish. The Armistice did not apply to the North Russian Allied Expeditionary Force. They were to continue the fight for freedom until Bolshevism—Communism, as it was now called—had been strangled in its crib.

30

November 11   Did Not Shoot. War Over. Mr. Chaplin rehearsing.
November 12   Did Not Shoot. Mr. Chaplin rehearsing.
November 13   Did Not Shoot. Mr. Chaplin ill.
November 14–29   Did Not Shoot. Vacation.

Sunnyside

November 30   Did Not Shoot. Mr. Chaplin rehearsing.

December 2   Shot 2000 feet, Mr. Chaplin in bed.

December 3   Shot 1500 feet, Mr. Chaplin in bed, Mr. Wilson as antagonist.

December 4   Shot 400 foot test, Edna hairstyles.

December 5   Shot 1500 foot test, goats and chickens.

December 6   Did Not Shoot. Mr. Chaplin ill.

☆   ☆   ☆

Chaplin thought of each movie he made as a sea voyage, perhaps because Syd had once been a seaman, and his letters home had a rhythm to them—set sail, drama on the ocean, return to port. On every movie, his creative spirit followed this arc: absolute certainty, doubt, dread, horror, despair, new certainty (sending him into a new compass heading that was 45, 90, or even 270 degrees different from where his first certainty had sent him), and then the Sargasso. Then something saved him. Then he was home.

Sixty-five times he had set out, and sixty-five times he had come to port, each time with a finished negative. He burned to return to port, forgetting that port made him restless.

He had learned to trust himself. He would film factions that had little to do with one another, knowing that some great force—perhaps his own ego—would cause them to have dramatic unity. He saw the scenes as little rafts he had flung over the waters, and he jumped and struggled and swam and dove across them, and somehow they made a bridge back home.

When he was younger, he might have run out of ideas for an hour or two, but now, approaching age thirty, he might spend a week, two weeks, three, in the doldrums. There was no specific way out. If he cared to list his previous solutions, they would look like this:

1) The Aolian solution. Lying on his back and watching the clouds, barefoot, sometimes with a kite tied to his big toe. Among variations were picnics on set, joshing with the crew, card games, reading fan mail, picking lemons from the orchard and making his own lemonade. Now, December 1918, he wasn't sure how this had ever worked.

2) The brute force of yoking his slaves to their oars: just executing routines from beginning to end, without the slightest inspiration except the knowledge that continuous motion was like striving

toward adequacy. These times kept everyone on set, under the command that the cameras grind, day after day.

3) A Trojan horse. He would have Kono drive to Bullock's with twenty dollars, with orders to purchase a basket of odd items in the hope they would inspire comedy.

4) Sometimes he felt better after seducing one of the girls who worked in hair and makeup.

5) He tried to put the sailing metaphor to literal use. Twice, he had chartered a boat and fled to Mexico with Rollie and a camera.

When he did not work, but instead avoided the studios ("rain," read the studio logs; then "clouds"; then "chance of clouds," by way of explanation), his crew forgave him. He was in a hard marriage. The financiers and fiefdoms of Hollywood were conspiring to drive him out of business. Someone in his company would betray him. Though all this was true, there was something else wrong, and he could not name it, and this made it still worse.

"You always think it's the worst one yet," said Syd on his last day in California. With the war over, Syd was going to the Continent with an armload of contracts to sign with Gaumont, Pathé, Kino, e/o, and Cinematia for distribution of Chaplin films internationally; the world was starved for motion pictures, and the foreign studios hadn't yet rebuilt. He also had a hunch that, with all the newly unemployed aviators and their JN 4s, establishing a service whereby important mail was flown by airplane would be very profitable.

"I've lost my spark," Chaplin said. They were standing in Syd's house, in Syd's bedroom, where he was packing his suitcase. "I don't know how stories are shaped anymore."

"I'm sure you do, Charlie. It's, what, not 'automatic,' what's the word I'm looking for? It's a part of you."

"Innate?"

"That's it. Stand up—you're on my trousers."

Chaplin stood. "But that's the thing. I no longer believe in the whole game. He finds a dime on the street, he eats a pie, he doesn't eat a pie, boy meets girl, boy loses girl, I don't care."

Syd folded his arms. "You've been paying too much attention to *The New Republic* and Robert Benchley and all that lot." He belted his suitcase shut and hoisted it off the bed.

"When are you coming back?" Chaplin asked miserably.

. . .

Later, Chaplin walked across the courtyard, studiously examining the grass and the flower beds, for there were two dozen day players milling around the stage ("@ 10/day," as per Alf's invoices, which were beginning to menace his desk). No one knew if it was a museum day or a farm day or something else, so they were all in their street clothes. When Chaplin breezed past, he gave an awkward smile their way and they waved back, unsure if they should be seen playing cards or if they were supposed to be rehearsing, so they settled for looking alert.

In his office, Chaplin called the Los Angeles Athletic Club. When Hans, the operator, answered, tears stood out in Chaplin's eyes. "Hello, Hans. It's Charlie."

"Mr. Chaplin!"

Chaplin hadn't meant to have any sort of reaction, but he began asking questions: How was Hans's sister? Did they ever take that trip to Pennsylvania? How was the Club these days? Not so good with the Drys? Ah well. And Chaplin answered Hans's questions: Yes, he was enjoying being married, Mildred was wonderful, and living in a large house was quite a change. And what was that? Oh, yes, he still played his violin.

"Well, Hans, I'm actually calling for Bill McAdoo."

"Ah, what a nice man he is."

"That, too. Yes. Take care."

Immediately after the war had ended, McAdoo had resigned from the Liberty Loan Committee, and he was tinkering with leaving his other government jobs behind. Now he took Chaplin's call with his usual good spirits, and they discussed, as always, the clement weather, and Chaplin asked, "Bill, has there been any word?"

"Word?"

Operators could be listening in. There were no secrets in Hollywood. "The Big Store."

"That? It's been quiet," McAdoo answered.

"Too quiet?"

"Too quiet?" He laughed. "How is something 'too quiet'?"

Chaplin's shoulders dropped. If McAdoo wasn't worried, then he shouldn't worry, either.

"I think there are developments, and I think we aren't hearing about them," McAdoo continued.

After he put the phone back on its cradle, Chaplin was so nervous he had his septet play Brahms, and at the end he asked them to add a harpist and a piano.

A few days later, the studio feeling like an empty circus tent with Syd gone, Chaplin received a telegram from First National. Friendly, professional, the model of support, it was an inquiry as to his progress into the untitled (as far as they knew) Chaplin production number three of his contract with them. A second telegram was sent to Accounting, asking what expenses had so far been incurred.

That afternoon, Chaplin brought Doug to the screening room.

"This is your pastoral?" Doug asked.

"Yes. *Jack of All Trades.* There might be something linking it to a museum piece," Chaplin said. Doug wore a tennis sweater around his neck, and had taken to wearing white shorts, and yacht shoes with canvas tops. "Are you cold?"

"I expect I'll laugh hard enough to warm up."

Chaplin ordered the projector to roll. He had just upgraded to a ground-mirror screen, which made the images more luminous than the old white plaster, and the projector now used an incandescent lamp, which also increased the brilliance, and when Chaplin pointed this out, Doug was duly impressed.

"This is just a rough assembly," Chaplin whispered.

"I know."

"I'm not sure we've calibrated the throw with the new projector."

"That's why there's a focus. Let's see what you've got."

"And remember, it's not edited properly."

"Quiet, old man."

The iris opened on a toothpick-thin cross atop a steeple, widening to show a church in a muddy village, a few shacks with laundry swaying outside, the broken fingers of a eucalyptus tree, a shabby hedgerow, a single brick building with wayward awnings that looked orphaned. In the foreground were two pigs, one sitting up and blinking over his shoulder, the other rooting in the muck.

"We also shot it with a duck."

"Shh."

The iris winked shut on the cross, and then it opened again on a tatted sampler that read "Love Thy Neighbor." Then a slow tilt downward to show Tom Wilson in a rumpled brass bed. Even in sleep, hands drawn into fists, he looked like an angry hatchet. The clock read three-thirty, and in the theater, Chaplin imitated the shrill noise of an alarm bell. Wilson opened his eyes, sat up to reveal his nightshirt, and, with murder in his eyes, grabbed a boot in his hand.

"This is going to be good," said Doug. "Your boss?"

"Shh," Chaplin said.

A few ragged moments later, Wilson was standing over a sleeping Little Fellow. He put on his boot, and gave the Little Fellow a good one in the backside. Doug laughed, and Chaplin let out a breath. His character, onscreen, sat upright and began dressing, as if beginning the day with a boot to the rear was perfectly natural.

Chaplin watched with his thumb between his upper and lower teeth. Contractually, he needed to deliver a two-reeler, twenty minutes. He had assembled eight minutes forty seconds for Doug, and had in mind another eight or so that he hadn't yet shot. Onscreen, he had ceased dressing and tried to go back to bed, only to have Wilson boot him again. This led to a back-and-forth, Wilson thinking each time he has finally gotten the Little Fellow awake, only to realize there'd been yet another scheme to fall between the covers. He imagined Frances seeing this.

When the Little Fellow went out the door and came back in the window, to slip back into bed, Doug laughed heartily, and then Chaplin heard it, a death rattle: one and a half extra seconds of forced laughter. They were two minutes in.

"We can stop here."

"No, no," said Doug. "I'm enjoying this."

Chaplin remembered waiting in a dirty hallway outside a flat when he was eight years old and had to tell his landlord he and his mother didn't have the rent. "Come in," the landlord yelled, and instead of knowing what to say, Chaplin was swamped by the sight of his toes poking through his shoes. He wriggled them, he wanted to talk to them, he wanted to found whole new civilizations with his toes, his best friends. We can all be poor together, he told them.

The projector was taking the reel of film. Kick, up, dodge, yawn, back in bed. Repeat. Four minutes, ten seconds. After the bedrest faction, it was breakfast, and the Little Fellow needed an egg, so he went into the yard and wrestled chickens and tried to get one to lay, but it was a rooster, and then he wrestled another, and that was also a rooster. He brought a hen into the kitchen (six minutes in) and put her in a pan on the stove and told her to hurry up and lay an egg. His eyes rolled, he poked his tongue into his cheek, he chewed as if the mere fact of its being him doing so rendered the moment amusing.

By the time the assembly of shots had crawled to a conclusion, Chaplin's eyes were closed. A flurry of black, unexposed positive film, scratched, and then the sheer white of the incandescent bulb hitting the mirrored screen.

"Isn't there more?" asked Doug. "Was that ever eight minutes?" The lights came up, and Doug saw Chaplin's face, and he didn't say anything else.

"Please," Chaplin said. "Tell me what's wrong with it."

Doug stood. He put both hands on the seats in front of him, and for a terrible moment, Chaplin thought he might vault onto them, and run on the arms of the chairs out of the theater and across Sunset. "They don't all have to be genius, you know."

"Oh, God."

"Really—the important thing is, just bang it out, old man. Set up a problem, throw a monkey wrench, give 'em a hill of beans to climb over, and fade out."

"But—"

"It's so simple. What's the film about, Charlie?"

"He doesn't want to get out of bed."

It had been said as if he were a schoolboy idiot with chalk on his sleeves. Doug's hale response was sticky with discomfort. "Ah, yes, well, anything else?"

Chaplin leaned forward, forehead touching the wooden back of a chair, fingers rubbing the velvet seatback.

"Love and temptation, or heroics and villains and . . ." Upon his friend's silence, Doug considered. "What's it called?"

"*Suicide*," Chaplin moaned.

Because he was Doug, he could not hear such a thing; he had actually heard something quite different. "*Sunnyside?*" he asked. He was touched. "Really? *Sunnyside?*"

Chaplin looked up slowly. He had no idea why his friend was grinning. Doug patted him on the back.

"*Sunnyside*. That's awfully sweet, I think. Turning that Little Fellow loose in Sunnyside. Ha!"

It was a misunderstanding neither man ever got to the bottom of, but

Chaplin grasped toward providence and decided the title would serve as ironic counterpoint, and from that day forward, the hopeless production formerly known as *Jack of All Trades* began each new and hopeless slate with the name of *Sunnyside*.

31

December 9   Shot 400 feet, bull riding. Home early.
December 10   Shot 600 feet, Edna, "the Romance." Home early.
December 11   Did Not Shoot. Mr. Chaplin talked story.
December 12   Shot 600 feet, Edna, Henry, "the Romance."
December 13   Did Not Shoot. Players sent home early.

☆   ☆   ☆

The Golod family had taken several houses around Fairfax and Beverly, among Jews. Mordecai's branch lived in a stucco bungalow newly constructed in an ersatz Spanish style that none of them, save Rebecca, paid much attention to. Since she spent days at the Chaplin Studios, where sets were constantly being built and struck, and since she walked home past construction of duplexes with arched windows and decorative tiles that suggested Morocco or Barcelona, she saw the link immediately: unlike in Texas or San Francisco, homes here didn't have to make sense. They were diversions, happy little movies that people lived in.

She was beginning to understand the concept of pride. It was, for instance, a blessed responsibility to be Jewish, and Texas was of course as proud of itself as San Francisco. Jews, San Franciscans, and Texans were all the Chosen People, apparently, but in Hollywood? It was taking her some time to find what they were proud of here.

"Papa," Rebecca said, "who negotiates for Chaplin?"

She had been sent home from the studio early, and had found her father in the backyard, next to their orange tree. In five years, he said, he could sit under it. For now, it was like a pet at his side. "That is an excellent question. Do you mean his business deals?"

"They say he makes a million a year. Did he . . ." She frowned, looking to be as clear as possible. "Did he walk up to the bank himself and say, 'I would like a million a year'?"

"I believe his brother negotiates that sort of thing."

Rebecca considered this. "Oh. And Pickford?"

"She negotiates herself. Though her mother also does."

"Oh. Does Fairbanks negotiate himself?"

"No, his brother does it, I think."

She nodded. "Oh."

Mordecai watched his daughter carefully. The proceeds from the jewelry-store enterprise would keep them in clover, but he was preparing for his next job. Whatever it was. He was a little tired, and was thinking, as he occasionally did, of going straight. To that end, he had a stack of books on the grass next to him, and he was currently keeping his thumb and forefinger in a text on Bolshevik theory, which struck him as having interesting applications. "What are you wondering, Pumpkin?"

"No one negotiated for me. I make ten dollars."

"Oh, sweetie." He put his book down and gave her a hug. "You're worth more than ten dollars." Then his smile faded. He began to see what she meant. "Hmm. That's a tough row to hoe."

"What about Betty Blythe? Someone like her? Helen Chadwick?"

"What's to negotiate?" He put his hands over his head in a protracted yawn. "The studio offers a contract. They take it."

"Hmm," she said.

"I thought I saw what you were driving at, but now I'm not so sure. If one of them says no to terms, then Alice Joyce or someone will come in and sign. It's supply and demand. Uncle Harvey does a little skimming, of course."

She said her "Oh" and then, without further comment, she kissed her father on the cheek and went to her room, where she lay on her bed and stared at her dolls.

Since there was not much to do at the studio, she had become bored, and it was unwise to let Rebecca be bored.

The next day, Chaplin called the day players back in and sent them to Wardrobe. He assembled the others, his core troupe, those few who had been in film after film with him, on the main stage, which was empty of props. It was a windy day, with the underbellies of thick clouds jutting by overhead. "We are going to turn the Little Fellow loose in a museum," he said.

"Roller skates?" Loyal Underwood called out.

"No. How many of you are familiar with tableaux vivants?" Most of them were, since they had been to vaudeville shows. There was some laughter as people realized the excellence of this idea: the Little Fellow loose among the School of Athens, or pushing clumsily on Fragonard's swing.

Waiting quietly near him was a girl he'd seen three nights before, in *How Could You, Jean?*, a terrible Pickford film whose rare critical drubbing had caused him to stand on the tips of his toes and spin in ecstasy. The girl, however, interested him. She was frail and ugly and stole every scene.

"Come here," he said, his eyes taking in the boy's cap, the sagging blouse, the sad tweed skirt. Her name was Zasu Pitts, and her body was like a bucketful of coat hangers. Her secret weapon: her face.

"Now, Zasu," he said, "this is the saddest part you've ever played. Your fiancé has just died. In the war."

"Yes, sir."

" 'Yes, Charlie.' Show me sad."

Her face collapsed. Tears the size of porterhouse steaks popped into her eyes. You could see them from the fourth balcony.

"Except you've received a telegram—he's alive!"

Unmitigated joy! She lit up like God's chandelier, and, impulsively, she did a small jig.

"No dancing," Chaplin said. "And that's not the right kind of joy. More like this." And his eyes beamed like those of a child who has just heard a disturbance in the chimney on Christmas.

She did a reasonable imitation of this, and he said, "He was your first love," and her face went as bland as oatmeal. He said, "You never even kissed him," and she seemed to shed five years off her face. He said, "Younger. More innocent. Gullible. Yes, no, no, not like that. Yes. Good. Now that 'Papa, what is beer?' look. Now just watch me."

Zasu followed him, ready to flinch, as if he might punch her. He expressed sadness—it looked like his sweetheart had died. Then joy. Then—and this is when her skin began to show goosebumps—he was a girl who had never kissed her first love. He became more innocent, more gullible, and then Zasu realized he wasn't just a girl, he had become *her*. He was Zasu Pitts, acting at all those things. For a frightening second, she thought the exercise hadn't been to see her range so much as it had been to steal her soul.

But in a Chaplin story, all the characters were him. So a successful induction into his world, and onto nitrate, meant that Zasu should imitate him imitating her imitating him imitating the character and so on, approaching something like real life. It was like sitting in a barbershop chair between two mirrors and seeing infinite faces that were only one face. It was like firing an arrow that never quite reached its target.

Her head was spinning, of course.

"Zasu, are you aware of tableaux vivants?"

"Yes, sir."

"Now how old are you?"

"Seventeen?"

She looked twenty-five. But that was fine. "Good. Now, you'll go to Wardrobe and take off your clothes."

"Sir?"

"A nude statue is permissible, of course. It's fine art. So we have the Little Fellow in a museum, admiring, say, an Eve of some sort. You can't argue with such a thing. Then, in the next shot, we've replaced Eve with you, painted white."

"Painted—painted—"

"Well, no, not actual paint, more like, it's a cerise paste, sort of, anyway, pay no mind to that, the point is, it's a statue. The censors can't argue with that. But then you move! Can you imagine the reaction?"

Apparently, Zasu couldn't imagine the reaction: she said nothing before Chaplin dismissed her.

Chaplin had Zasu slathered in enough cerise paste for her to photograph like marble. Not a streak of flesh tone registered, which was brilliant, but for the first hour, she insisted on poses that covered her chest, until she had a stern talking-to by Alf's wife. The best news was that even her tears didn't ruin any takes: the makeup set off the illumination of the radium lights, so there was no flare.

He made Zasu a water bearer, and had her stand against composition board painted to look like the walls of the Louvre. The set was more crowded on this day than any other, and Chaplin had to ask Alf to clear a dozen people whom he did not recognize.

He had the day players called in, and Alf and Maverick explained to them that they were patrons at the museum. Among them was a serious-faced girl of fifteen whom Maverick asked to stand in back. She looked at Zasu, who was on her mark as the water bearer, as if she were witnessing history, and it made Maverick uncomfortable.

Chaplin went into costume, and returned, and, upon the clack of the focusing board, set about admiring the water bearer. He leaned on his cane, walked closer, then farther, used his fingers to make a rectangle to look at her. He called for a cut, then had Henry Bergman and Albert Austin come in as patrons of the arts. He discussed some simple business with them ("You are perfectly middle-class, with pretensions to under-standing the finer things in life, which you don't actually understand, but which makes you highly judgmental"), then sent them off to wait for a cue. "Action! Camera! Grind!" Clack went the focusing board, and he returned to his admiration of the water bearer. Only this time, the longer he looked, the deeper went his admiration. Just as he began to approach her from behind, to examine her bottom, in came Bergman and Austin, who looked first at the statue, then at the frankly lecherous Little Fellow. As if feeling the heat of their gazes, he sprang from his place and pretended to admire the discus thrower instead.

This seemed to go well, so Chaplin did another take, and another, and so on, and on the fifteenth take, the water jug slipped from the Zasu girl's hands and cracked against the floor. It was just papier-mâché, but she cried out in shame and the noise caused Chaplin to jump in place, which embarrassed him, and then he decided there should be a way to use it.

It came so fast he couldn't say the words in order. He collared Maver-ick and spoke aloud, gesturing with each idea, making sure he was writing it down: the water bearer and the discus thrower were thieves. They were hiding in the museum. Their plan was to steal everything when the museum closed. The Little Fellow would be trapped there with them.

This was good. This was excellent. At the end of the workday, when the light had gone, Chaplin was not yet ready to finish. He wanted to keep rehearsing under the arc lights, but there was a build-up of ash, and then, when Henry and Albert and Zasu and everyone else was tired, and they could no longer play their parts, he told them he was very proud of them. They were going to torment the censors, drive crazy the blue-haired ladies of Indiana, for who could say where art ended and the obscene began?

The day players were dismissed, and most of them changed and ambled out the studio gates, happy to have done something, finally.

Rebecca, however, went to the invoice desk in Accounting and said she was Zasu's sister and was here for her paperwork.

Overstuffed chairs were dragged from the prop room. Edna, who hadn't been in a shot today, took off her shoes and rubbed her feet and finally leaned against Albert, who was trying like grim death to hold back a fatal yawn. Zasu, who was in not just the clothes she'd come in but several layers of sweaters and jackets, and was sipping hot tea, stared straight ahead, her wounded eyes looking as if she'd been through a stampede. Chaplin admitted he was asking her to do outstandingly difficult work, and he apologized, and she was wonderful, and there was a great conservation of effort on his part.

"What do I mean? It's like this. The theory of humor that no one else seems to understand—have you seen an Arbuckle film? He's quite good, but he doesn't understand—you don't just throw a pie. No, you have me attempt to throw a pie at an enemy"—he made the necessary motions as he narrated— "and instead, on the wind-up, it drops behind me, and I shade my eyes, take a step backward to see where it went, and I slip on it, and it shoots like a watermelon seed to hit a passerby, who knocks his glass of water over *on my enemy,* which causes *them* to engage in a fistfight. That gets four separate laughs from one piece of business. Harold Lloyd doesn't understand any of that. Lonesome Luke! Wherever did he get the idea to have baggy trousers and a toothbrush mustache?"

So it went until Alf gently put his hand on Chaplin's shoulder and told him they could continue tomorrow.

When he arrived the next day, bright and early, the whole company was there—except for Zasu.

Chaplin was furious. Then he learned they had only signed her to a day-player agreement, and she was free to take any other job she wished today. It only took four phone calls to learn she had been hired, again, by Pickford. Who was very sorry to say that she was unable to explain when Zasu would again be available. It could be months.

☆　☆　☆

December 14   Did Not Shoot. Talked Story. Orchestra. New set: museum and angels. New camera.

December 17   Did Not Shoot. Mr. Chaplin rehearsed. Orchestra. Enlarged set again: museum, angels, horses, cows. New camera, new dolly mechanism. Crane tested.

December 18   Did Not Shoot. Orchestra. Enlarged set again:
              museum, angels, horses, cows, history of the world in art,
              etc. Captive balloons tested.
December 19   !!!

☆   ☆   ☆

Which is where the logbooks for the production of *Sunnyside* ended for
1918. The kingpins of the industry, having taken the measure of the situation, finally brought their plans to fruition, with the result of stopping the
already wobbling Charlie Chaplin dead in his tracks.

This was the Russian dance: Allied forces advanced along the Vaga River,
and when their forward positions became untenable, they retreated along
the same frozen banks. Then orders would come to advance, and the
process would start all over again. The force was known as the Vaga Column, which caused many chuckles, for it implied that their position was as
straight and sturdy as Doric marble.

About two hundred men bivouacked in Solnechny Strana, which was
friendly to them, townspeople tearfully saying goodbye as if they were
their own children every time they left, and greeting them hello, without
irony, on each return.

Pfc. Hugo Black was trying to make the best of things. He was even
experimenting with getting along. He started by being pleasant to children—nodding at them, for instance—and then worked his way to his fellow soldiers. He had pumped his hand in the air and cried, "My reward is
to kill," when it seemed appropriate, and when he caught his reflection in
a windowpane, rather than burst into tears, he elected to turn the corners
of his mouth up into a meatless-Friday smile.

Hugo had a week of sentry duty in front of a former schoolhouse, now
the "A" Sector billet in which thirty of his fellow men were resting or
playing cards. Before him was the width of Solnechny Strana, easily the

cleanest and best-constructed village he'd seen in his whole tour. The townspeople who walked by, waving and inquiring in broken English about his health, wore plush coats made from animals that were neither cat nor dog. Inspired, Hugo had purchased a new hat from a man with a table on the sidewalk. The man had said "sable," but it had only been a dollar U.S., and after he'd bought it, Hugo realized it was distressingly tabby-colored.

One purple, dim day much like the rest, a villager appeared at the edge of the double apron-wire. He was a small man, tiny even, his feet making deerlike tracks. He walked thirty feet away, seemed swallowed by snow-banks, then returned with a tenacious shuffling gait to stare directly at Hugo. He removed his gloves. Hugo watched him bite his thumb.

"Yes?" Hugo said, raising his rifle barrel.

The man raised his hands over his head. Fully extended like that, the tips of his fingers were about as high as Hugo's shoulders. Hugo noted the lines on his beefy face and decided that he not only looked fifty years old, but probably *was* fifty years old. He had somehow managed to live a Russian life whose hardships aged him only a normal amount.

"Amerikanski?"

Hugo jerked his mitten westerly, to point out the American flag flying outside the barracks. *"Dah,"* Hugo said.

The small man quickly fell into a rush of language, eager to share something.

"I can't— Put your hands down— English? Speak English?"

The man dropped his hands. *"Sprechen Sie Deutsch?"* he asked. Hugo shook his head. There were a few other attempts—perhaps Czech, perhaps Polish. *"Italiano?"* the man then asked, brimming with hope, but Hugo had to shake his head again. The man snapped his fingers. "Ah! *Parlez-vous français?"*

"Oui, je parle français toute la journée et toute la nuit longtemps." Hugo said it more through his nose than his mouth, as if the whole world spoke French, and spoke it better than his interlocutor.

The man lit with understanding. *"Alors, vous êtes parisien?"*

Hugo couldn't tell if the man was making fun of him. He rubbed his red hands together and spoke to Hugo rapidly, with a precise yet accommodating accent. He sounded learned but not conceited. The man praised the French language as one of fraternity and liberty. As for equality, that led to contempt, but he could bear it.

Soon enough, he was talking to Hugo about Solnechny Strana, the views one should try to see from the timber drive, the best place to find a coffee, the honest tradesmen Hugo could purchase herring from, should he be so inclined. Hugo was reminded of taking afternoon tea in Grosse Pointe. The man—his name was Aarne—was being *polite* in a way that Hugo missed.

Hugo felt his own personal judgments were acknowledged as merciful and precise, and he and Aarne were only a few gambits away from discourse on music and art and psychology and the poetry of dreams and ballet. Ballet, especially: Hugo had never seen Nijinsky, though he felt qualified to critique him. Then Aarne shook his hand goodbye.

Aarne was delighted to have met such a cultivated young man, he said, and under different circumstances, they could perhaps have talked all afternoon long, perhaps even of Paris, but—he turned up his palms in a gesture suggesting mutual sadness, lack of alternatives—he had to leave now to keep some women from being raped and killed.

He wished Hugo good luck, put his hands in his pockets, and limped away, head down.

"Wait!" Hugo trotted toward him. *"Expliquez-moi,"* he said.

Aarne looked up at Hugo with sadness. His story was simple: he knew three old peasant women who cooked and cleaned at the local monastery. The monks had long ago fled, leaving them with enough supplies—flour, tea, sugar, and so forth—to live on. There was an underground river they got water from, there was plenty of firewood, and so they hadn't left in months, and their existence was hardly known here. And the monastery was secluded, as was the wont of monasteries, Aarne said, with a chuckle, so no one had yet robbed it.

However, the grapevine said Bolsheviks had finally realized it was there and were going to storm it this evening, when the moon was high. Again, he wished Hugo a good evening, for he had to go make a stand with the women, for their honor. Even though they had no weapons. And Aarne had rheumatism. And was approximately three feet nine inches tall.

It was a great deal of information for Hugo to take in. He didn't want Aarne to go away. He told Aarne to wait while he thought this through. One idea jumped to another, and then—a thousand-watt inspiration!—surely *he* and his fellow soldiers could help. Aarne told him not to bother with such an outlandish idea. Hugo was insistent. Making his new friend promise to stay by the razor wire, Hugo trotted into the barracks, where he was briefly arrested by the earthen stink of unwashed men wearing soiled uniforms.

Lieutenant Gordon, caught in a hand in which he had accidentally found himself drawing toward an inside straight, happily threw down his cards to curse Hugo for deserting his post. There was an argument, but a brief one, as Gordon began to understand that Hugo was volunteering to leave. Thus the assignment was made with Gordon's blessings—had Hugo explained he was going into the forest to build his own monastery, Gordon would have responded the same.

There was the question of who would join him; Hugo hoped Gordon wouldn't call for volunteers, but would let him pick his own support.

"Hugo, what you're describing is a very dangerous mission," Gordon said, placing a hand on his shoulder. "So I would like you to go alone."

"I'm sorry?"

"And it's a fabulous good-will gesture toward the locals. I think that's fabulous."

"Even Wodziczko could—"

"Private Wodziczko is on an important mission to secure barley and hops." Gordon wore a sable hat—honestly sable—stained with malt paste from a gruesome prior attempt to make beer. He touched the heel of his hand to his hat, signing off on Hugo's fate. "Your reward is to kill, old sport. Enjoy." But then, as if irritated by a pang of conscience: "You know, Private, take the Springfield."

This was a rare order. It was like asking him to accept filet mignon in place of bully beef. "Is there ammo?"

"I can spare a clip. Two clips. No, take one clip."

Hugo was touched. The Springfield, however sparsely furnished, would actually hit its target. He took it from its case and placed his stripper clip of five bullets in a leather pouch that he dangled down inside his shirt, to keep them warm. He had the company Springfield!

Before he left, he announced to the whole company, "Men, I won't embarrass you," but no one looked up.

When Hugo reappeared outside, Aarne looked past him, toward the closing billet door. It latched, and they were alone together in the faint afternoon light. Hugo adjusted his hat and shrugged the weight of his patched greatcoat around, until he was relatively comfortable. Aarne looked around Hugo, toward the door, as if he were going to ask it a question.

"*Alors,*" Hugo said, and then, with a sigh that he hoped sounded jaded, "*on y va!*"

Sunnyside

They walked side by side, passing the British field hospital, Union Jack snapping in the breeze (since it was ten degrees below zero, this was accomplished with the application of benzene). They passed the many barracks housing the 68th Battery of the Canadian Field Artillery, whose eighteen-pounder guns stood under a thin layer of frost. Next door was the billet for eighty fearsome Cossacks, whose leader, Colonel Dilatorfsky, had once punched an ox in the head "to teach it manners."

And yet Aarne had asked neither the Canadians, the British, nor the Cossacks for help.

It was perhaps three o'clock, and the purple light was already deepening. Solnechny Stranaians had an exquisite vocabulary to describe gradations in faint illumination—they would say now that it was light enough to see a friend but dark enough to miss the cunning of his shadow.

As they walked to the edge of the town, treeline thickening, buildings falling away, Hugo thought to ask why the Bolsheviks were attacking tonight of all nights, and Aarne admitted it was hard to know the ways of Bolsheviks.

"But," Hugo continued, thinking of stores of flour and sugar, "how do they know about the women? Weren't they hiding? And how do you know these women?"

The snow crunched under their feet. An owl hooted, and Aarne hooted back at it. Then a longer silence. Perhaps he was in awe of Hugo's skills with idiom. Finally, Aarne said, "Maybe they want liqueur."

"Pardon?"

"They think the monks made liqueur. You know, some monks do that. These monks in Solnechny Strana, not so much."

"I thought they were coming for the women."

"Or they want the women," Aarne murmured.

Hugo's chest, below layers of wool and cotton, felt an unexpected, untidy chill. "The women, how do you know them?"

"The liqueur, it simply isn't there. The Bolsheviks don't know that, or they don't care. They are savages, completely unlike you or me." Then Aarne dug into a pocket. "See. Look!"

Hugo recognized the blood-red border, an inch thick, that always graced Bolshevik propaganda. Always a Garamond typeface when it was in English. Peasants, rise up; soldiers, join your true brothers; workers, realize the power that lies in your hands. Wasted on Hugo, who rather enjoyed the lost ages of royal rule, if only for its vast inequalities.

Aarne clapped his hands together and declared he had a fascinating story about the town's coat of arms, a blazon, the upper part showing God's hand extending an alb from a cloud; the lower part showing—a badger. Badgers were incredible creatures, Aarne continued, key to the hagiography of St. Barlaam, and Hugo realized Aarne wasn't answering about the women. He thought about underground streams of water, women dipping scuppernongs into them, women thick and heavy as bread loaves, catching trout in midair, swiping at them as if they were bears. He wondered if he would be killed.

But his feet padded forward in the Shackletons, and when the pathway narrowed, and he had to follow Aarne into the pines, he had tranquilized himself into a low, dull obedience.

It grew darker ("light enough to see your hand before your eyes, but too dark to see the thief who drives the knife into your back"); Hugo was led along switchbacks that folded in on themselves until he could no longer sense what direction he walked in. He tossed the broadside onto the ground, just for the pleasure of littering.

Hours after they'd started, they crested a low hill within view of the crown of another hill, and, tucked between them, half hidden among the trees, turned blue by the rising moon, was a buttressed wall interrupted by odd little arches. The wall was all that was immediately apparent, as if it were the last fortified remnant of a fallen town. But if you looked twice, you might finally notice behind it the shape of a single, low tower with a round roof domed like a grain silo. The wall, the tower, the arches, the entirety of the structure was whitewashed, and seemed to blend into the snow around it. It looked in no way, to Hugo, like a monastery.

"Here is the monastery," Aarne said.

"What happened to the monks?"

"We should hurry—when the moon rises, well, I don't need to say. Where is that broadside?"

Hugo patted himself down. "I don't know."

"You don't have it?"

"I guess not."

"You guess?" Aarne barked it out again—"You guess?"—and for the first time Hugo was frightened of him. "I apologize. I don't like leaving rubbish in the forest. It could make the forest angry. But come along."

The night was already getting brighter. There was a straight cobblestone pathway flanked by pine trees that had once been trained and trimmed, and at the end was a gate, the key to which Aarne produced, stepping up on the balls of his feet to reach the lock. It opened with a shriek like a startled donkey. Hugo approached cautiously, his steps stiff and awkward. There were obviously no women here. Who was this mysterious dwarf he was following? He had no idea what was beyond the gate, or how he could defend himself against it. The depth of his despair? He missed Wodziczko. He had a rifle and a detached bayonet and five bullets that were in a bag around his neck. He was doomed.

Early on December 19, there was strangely mournful music hanging in the air around the intersection of La Brea and De Longpre. Automobiles were parked along the curbside, dozens of them, and trucks and buses and coaches extending as far as Sunset. There were men around the trucks, men with broken noses, dirty caps, and rollneck sweaters. They had been playing cards, but with the rising music, they stopped what they called work—for they were stagehands—and were silent.

The music was coming from behind the gate of the Chaplin Studios. If you were to walk past the old woman who tended the gate, you would see that she, too, was transfixed. Cross the courtyard, where the gardener had paused, shears in hand, from tending the rose beds, and then pass the swimming pool, where extras dressed in farm clothes were cooling their feet. Here was the stage, open to the air, with racks of radium lights among the diffusers. There were day players (but not Rebecca—she'd moved on) pressed stomach to back here, players dressed like Roman statues or still in their street clothes mingled together, some on the lawn, some by the makeup tables, some hanging in midair, others standing in clusters in the few places where there was still room to stand, what with the livestock that had been imported.

Alf Reeves, who had been sick two days with stomach flu, had returned this morning and had spent the entire time silent, occasionally shaking his head, and looking at today's invoices.

As he listened to the single violin, whose tremulous notes spoke of failed crops, loneliness, wide autumn winter skies with no sign of rain, Alf understood he was unable to write a memo to Accounting in New York that explained how elaborate the set had become in his absence. The stage—once a simple museum—had expanded to reflect Chaplin's idea that there should be a fantasy sequence, and so its borders had dropped away, the walls extending upward and east and west, incorporating classical types of architecture, ziggurats and Doric columns, before winding around a corner and exploding into even more bizarre shapes and forms, Cubist in motif, to which the carpenters were now adding another wing, using pegs and gravity, because Mr. Chaplin did not want the sound of hammering today.

The village had been half disassembled. The church, with its ramshackle steeple, was still up, serving as a backdrop for the musicians. They sat in comfortable chairs, in a semicircle, and at the front were (all silent) a piccolo player, a pair of flutes, a pair of oboes, an English horn, and the remainder of an eighty-eight-piece orchestra. There was also a cannon, for Chaplin had decided that, in order to concentrate better on *Sunnyside*, he would be conducting the *1812* Overture.

Now it was just the opening measures, based on the heart-rending, quiet hymn "God Preserve Thy People." Chaplin himself was taking lead violin, and he had requested that the orchestra not yet join in, except for one cello, there in the third row. When he nodded, the other cellos joined in.

He played dressed in the shoes, the trousers, the tattered shirt and vest, but no mustache, no hat. He closed his eyes and felt himself dissolving into simple, reflective longing. The horns played a call and response with the strings, which began to build to the first crescendo—the timpani player raised his mallet—and Chaplin broke.

"Hold on," he said. "From the beginning. At my count."

Meanwhile, Rollie Totheroh was attempting to wrestle the new camera setup into workable order. They had recently purchased a Bell and Howell, which they had mounted on a dolly. But to get the proper angle on the new set, Chaplin had declared at dawn that the camera would need to start high in the air, which meant the railroad tracks might be seen.

Especially because he needed to get the angels into the frame. There was now a host of angels, mostly girl art-school students fitted with wings and wearing harnesses under their togas, all hanging on wires from telephone poles.

"We can get them easily," Rollie had told Chaplin earlier that morning.

"Not if you're going to get the statues at the same time."

The statues were on their pedestals, caked with (because the cerise paste had proved unstable) a flour-based makeup that gave them the appearance of marble.

Rollie had turned his head from the statues back to the angels. "Is putting them right as crucial as—"

"We need to coordinate it with the chariots," Chaplin had said.

"Chariots?"

"Weren't you here? Chariots. When they move, they'll startle the statues into life. Which is why you'll be focusing on the ground, and you'll see the dolly's tracks. So up you go," Chaplin had finished, pointing with his violin bow.

Rollie had looked with misery at the balloon. Sausage-shaped, strapped with dozens of wires, a dinky basket under its belly, it was an observation station recently used to protect Los Angeles in case of invasion. Now it had been converted for the use of the Chaplin Studios, and a full crew of AEF boys was ready to take him up for his overhead shot of the set.

"But can they really do a smooth-enough descent to—"

"Up you go," Chaplin had said, now heading to begin conducting the orchestra, and leaving Rollie, who had taken a tug of whiskey from his flask, and then ordered a magazine of film brought to the balloon.

Upon the twenty-fifth iteration of the opening measure of the *1812 Overture*, Chaplin allowed it to continue, the mood of the tune changing from melancholy to low anxiety and yearning. The horns came in like the edges of a distant storm, the timpani brought in lightninglike strokes of punctuation, and the rest of the set could now continue its work.

The chow wagon was serving coffee. The angels were let down from their perches, for it was discovered that their harnesses had never been tested before, and the fishing line—though tolerably inexpensive—was hardly safe. Then they were sent back up.

The overture continued, Chaplin lost in the shifts from war to peace, from brutality to sentiment. It told the story of the French army taking Moscow, their momentary triumph, the Russians burning their own city down to the ground. The finale proclaimed Russia ascendant (and destitute), Napoleon and his soldiers forced into the brutal winter, which finished them off. It was a piece of music Tchaikovsky had found useless, all noise and drama and arson and explosions.

Chaplin thought he detected a few measures of a Russian wedding dance, something repeated on flute, then clarinet, and he closed his eyes, conducting, imagining his pastoral, kindness, and he was back at the beach house, a different life, in which he had kept his mouth shut and bedded Frances.

Dancing at their wedding. Toasts. Nuptial bed. They would build a bassinet together even though neither of them would be handy, and she would scrape her knuckles because she insisted on doing it herself, and he would be in the other room, painting blue on one wall and pink on the other, and hear her cry out, and he would kiss the skin on the back of her hand. He would lie in bed and hear her brushing her hair, and when she felt a snag he would feel it, at first. They would enter that odd year of the marriage, the fifth, when it went from looking at your loved one to over-looking. She would have rashes and ask him what that smell was, and he would say he didn't smell anything, and he would misplace the natural pearl stickpin she'd given him, and she would think it meant something more than it did, and they would also love each other's work and make it better. This is your best, you are making art as good as you are, Frances, and you are, too, Charlie. He would buy flowers and notice on the way home that petals had fallen out and would be torn between giving her damaged good and nothing at all. She would think of leaving him, and every time she didn't, it would be her deciding to fall in love again, and that would be a miracle.

He stopped the music. He told the orchestra to take a break, and he walked back to his apartment, and closed the door and sat on his sofa, his fingertips pressed to the bridge of his nose, eyes on the bulbs of his size-sixteen workboots, newly scuffed to hell.

Mildred was sitting in the overstuffed wing chair.

"Oh," he said. "Darling. How long have you been here?"

She wore a wonderful smile. "I didn't want to disturb you while you were working."

"Not disturbing, not in the slightest. What's wrong?"

"Nothing." She smiled. And then she laughed.

"Are you sure?"

"Of course I'm sure. Things are terrific." Another laugh.

"I just—" It was good to see her. He felt the desire for Frances slip away like a lover hiding under the rug. "You know, it's funny—just now, I was just thinking of you. The boys screened *Borrowed Clothes* last night. It was quite good."

"Thank you," she said.

"You have talent. I know I don't say that often enough, but it's true." When her smile continued, radiant, he laughed. "Why do you look so good today? You have a secret."

"I do."

"Tell me!"

"I don't know," she teased. Her eyes went hooded, as if the secret were saucy indeed, and then she exploded with it. "I joined a new church."

Chaplin laughed now, good and hard. Then, "Oh."

She was still beaming, so apparently it hadn't been the worst reaction. "It's on Hollywood Boulevard. I found out about it from Dorothy and Lillian—"

"Did you?"

"Yes. It's a great place," she said, and she began to describe the interior: not stuffy, like normal churches, but warm and friendly and devoted to serving the unique spiritual needs of those who have succeeded in the film industry. "I won't get in your hair so much. They have a women's group."

"I see," he said.

"Are you mad?"

"Are you?"

"No, Charlie." She risked another laugh.

"And what does it cost?" Chaplin asked.

"That's the good part—nothing."

"Unless you choose to donate?" It wasn't even a question he had wanted to ask.

Mildred's smile slipped away and reappeared like a star peeking from behind a late cloud. "Of course, Charlie."

"And what's it called, this church?"

"Saint Lawrence the Divine. They believe in laughter."

Chaplin was suddenly aware of Mildred's mink. She had several of them now, and this one was gray, and ended at the hips, and had a matching hat, which she was not wearing. He was not judging the expense, the way he often did, and he was giving himself a great deal of credit for being so rational.

She handed him a brochure. The paper was slick. Chaplin read it, but his eyes bounced off as if the text were made of rubber, and all he could think about was Frances.

"You see, they believe that laughter is the best solution to life's problems."

"Do they?"

"So we're encouraged to respond to adversity with a smile," Mildred said, but her voice was beginning to turn in on itself, as if she had walked into a cul-de-sac she hadn't known was there. "Charlie?"

The brochure was open in his lap. " 'Saint Lawrence,' " he read, " 'our patron, was burnt to death on a gridiron in A.D. 253. He is said to have called out, in the midst of his agony, "Turn me over. I'm done on this side." This rare example of humor from a saint sets our example for . . .' " He skipped some paragraphs. " 'The unique spiritual challenges for a successful player in the film industry . . .'

"Mildred," he said. Within himself, he felt buildings collapsing, and people crushed at their desks, the sun blotted out, landscapes thrown into shadow.

"I just," Mildred said, swallowing, "wanted to make you happy with me."

He shook his head.

"I thought you, of all people . . ."

"Take the car, and go buy the baby something, a blanket or something. Then go laugh. Go find some people to laugh with."

He left the apartment and stood on the porch, surveying the half-destroyed set, the orchestra at rest, the new museum set to which new risers and canvas backdrops were being pegged, the throngs of extras, and he walked sightlessly toward Alf.

"We need to stop all this," Chaplin said. "I just want a small, small . . ." His voice trailed off. "I just want something small," he whispered.

"Back to the pastoral, then?" Alf asked. "Right-o. What should I do with the angels?"

"Angels? What angels?"

Alf took out his cigar stub and used it as if it were chalk and the sky the board. "Up there."

Chaplin looked at the dozen or so telephone poles that seemed to have appeared of their own accord, each with its own dangling girl. Some of their burlap harnesses had slipped, and they were fighting to remain upright; others were spinning in the breeze, and one looked unconscious, and young John, a simple boy from the property department, was desperately throwing water from the ground in the direction of her forehead.

"Take them down. Pay them. Keep them here for the day."

"Send back the orchestra, too?"

"Yes. No, have them play the tune, all the way through."

Chaplin sat on a bench, drawing his knees to his chest. The baggy trousers pressed against his face; his hands wrapped around the bulbs of the idiot shoes. As the *1812* Overture began again, he thought: Courtship. Obstacle. Rival. Wicked father. A big rock in the middle of the living room. He didn't care. Life was essentially a scattering of torn ticket stubs on the ground that we found morals in because the emptiness of the universe was too horrific to contemplate.

Still, Chaplin thought, I have to go on. The overture was now at the part that sounded like Icarus slowly being brought to ground, hawks swooping in descent, dark forces gathering for one last raid upon the enemy, the intersection of the French and Russian national anthems, and he wanted to crack the music open like a thighbone and suck out the marrow. For it was the sound of impending triumph. He had not considered until now that, from another perspective, it was also the sound of impending defeat.

A limousine was pulling up at the gate.

The driver was agitated, his brocade cap gleaming in the sunlight, and the rear door opened, and out came two men who had never been to the Chaplin Studios before. In fact, they had never been to America. They made gestures toward the car; the woman at the gate stood from her stool, put down her tea, and walked cautiously toward the smoked glass of the rear door.

When the window rolled down, the woman attendant burst out in a chirp of laughter, and then a second sound, the distilled essence of pure wonder, half drowned by the orchestra. Up went the gate, and the limousine rolled onto the lot, displacing a grumbling crowd of angels, who were rubbing at their chafed sides and underarms.

The orchestra was a whirlwind now, the grandeur of the horns sharpened by the hammering timpani, counterpoint provided by violins and violas spinning so vividly that the players were beginning to perspire, a glitter of church bells behind them as, for the last time, "La Marseillaise" was smashed flat by the Russian anthem played on brass that stomped forward, Cossacks waving scimitars, fires bursting out from every doorway in Moscow, and bang went the cannon, slightly off time, but that could never be helped, and then bang again, and arms reached into the back of the limousine to help a small, stout figure.

The music finished out like a series of sneezes, and then came a silence like an afterglow. The woman wore a cotton dress with a white lace collar, and as she stood, she smoothed her skirt over her stockings. Her face had thickened, but it was still beautiful, with pleased and confused intelligence.

Chaplin, who had been engaged by the orchestra, was aware that the overture was over, and the entirety of his studio was regarding him, awaiting instruction. But there was another kind of anticipation in the air as word had started to circulate.

The lead violin was approaching him, damp stains from perspiration on his bib. "We also know the 'Slavonic March,'" he said. "Very pathetic song, if you want."

But Chaplin shook his hand limply. He now saw the woman standing by the limousine, and he felt as if the flowers in the flower bed beside him had begun to strangle him by the ankles.

One foot, then the other, walked forward. He had in the last four years known how to walk in the enormous boots perfectly, and how to force a stumble. Now, however, it was as if he were being dragged forward by the terrifying pull of gravity.

As word traveled, a crowd formed, statues, angels, laboratory technicians, doors slamming open, and secretaries striding down the stairs and into the courtyard, to see with their own eyes, and everyone was smiling.

Chaplin now stood ringed by his people, and before him she stood with her two attendants. She was fifty-four years old. Her white hair was dyed blond in patches, in the way of a woman who has not had a mirror handy. There was a burst of wilted sweet pea pinned to her dress.

"Hannah," one of the men holding her hands said. He enunciated as one would for a foreigner. "This is Charlie."

Chaplin couldn't breathe. *Say hello,* he thought. *People say hello,* he thought. But the wind had been knocked out of him. His jaw ached from clenching it.

"Really," the man said, "it's Charlie. Your son."

He felt her sizing him up. Her eyes were merry and then doubtful, and then she disregarded what they saw. She looked to her attendant. "And you're Jesus Christ."

Once they were inside the monastery of Solnechny Strana, the gate locked behind them, Aarne intoned, *"Deo gratias—benedicite."* When Hugo looked apprehensive, Aarne shrugged. It was levity, he explained. The Cistercians used those words to greet travelers. They would drink with them, then force them to pray. Aarne said. "I will deny you, monsieur, the embarrassment of the latter, for I no longer believe in God."

They were in a deep cobblestone courtyard. Their steps echoed, a lonely sound made eerie under the rising light of the moon. Hugo relaxed slightly upon seeing his first cross—it indicated that at least part of the story wasn't a lie—this was a monastery. The cross was a fat, bullying stone-and-mortar Russian Orthodox type, outside a stable sandwiched between a dormitory and a chapel.

"I apologize for not believing in God. If you need to cross yourself, I understand."

It seemed unlikely that a monastery so large would have actually avoided discovery. Aarne took him quickly past the abandoned smithie's, then a dormitory for the novices and lay brothers (empty, boarded up), the cloisters, the calefactory, all of their façades lifeless. The whole construction was like fairy-tale kingdom, its citizens evacuated from a giant, a dragon, a curse.

Because he needed to speak, Hugo said, "The monastery is large."

Aarne looked at him as if he was quite stupid. *"Oui."*

There was one especially large building at the end of a long pathway flanked by enormous, jutting, oil-filled flambeaux which were not lit. Its many windows were lined with thick curtains. Hugo imagined that the women were real and were in that house, roasting partridges, peeking through the keyhole, whispering to one another about him.

"What's that place?"

"The abbot's house," Aarne said.

"Are they in the abbot's house?"

"Who?"

"The women."

"They're in a secret place. Very secure. Don't worry about the women."

"I'm asking because—"

Aarne smacked his palms together. "A soldier with a gun and bullets is asking where are the women?" He shook his head. "You are better than that."

Hugo looked toward his battered boots. He could hardly admit he'd been hoping the women were beautiful.

"The tower," Aarne said. "There is a balistraria up there." Then he stopped. "But I'm not a soldier. I shouldn't tell you how to do your job." He explained what he knew of the coming attack: the Bolsheviks would come up the main path, because it was the only approach. They walked along an arcade, pausing before a huge metal door. Aarne slipped a key into the lock. On hinges the size of fists, the door creaked open. There was a low stone archway, then blackness.

Hugo swallowed.

"Up those stairs," Aarne said.

"Let's go."

"I'm going to hide."

"You aren't coming with me?"

"There's a weapon up there for you. Perhaps God will show you how to use it." Aarne winced as if he regretted sounding so cynical. "Just because I don't believe in him doesn't mean he can't help you. No?" He rolled his eyes, then added, a consolation, "This is for you, too."

He was holding out a silver flask. Hugo grasped it in one outsized mitten. "Gin? Vodka?"

"No. Drink it when you need courage. Take small sips."

"Is it whiskey? I don't drink much—"

"And don't drink until after you've started fighting."

Hugo stared at the mysterious potion. "But why—?"

"Please go up the stairs. There's no time."

"When this is over . . ." Hugo began. He had desires he could hardly name, even to himself, feelings that embarrassed him. Not just that he was defending real, lonely, beautiful women, but . . . "Perhaps we can—"

"We'll talk of Paris, of course," Aarne interrupted. "Go." He touched Hugo's arm.

Hugo readjusted his rifle, and ducked under the archway. There was a clatter as Aarne shut and locked the door behind him. The sound froze Hugo in place.

Aarne's muffled voice came through the door. "You're not walking up the stairs."

"You locked the door."

"Would you rather I leave it unlocked?"

Grudgingly, Hugo returned to walking up the staircase, a cochlea of stone stairs winding around a pillar. The light was dim, less a solid glow than many adjoining slivers, beams thrown off a prism. Soon Hugo realized the illumination came from an ingenious series of slits in the great stone walls, which captured and refracted the incandescence of the snow.

The top room of the tower was squat and wide, with rafters in which there were dozens of old bird's nests. Facing the courtyard were narrow windows running floor to roofline, and oak flooring littered with hay bales. There was a medieval slit of a window, and a man was standing in front of it.

Hugo threw himself to the ground, face-first, colliding with hay dirt. He groped for the bayonet on the Springfield, spitting bristles out of his mouth. Looking up, sensing a curious lack of motion, he regarded the man in the room again.

Frozen in place, one arm over his head as if about to throw a pineapple grenade, feet seemingly too large for the pint-sized body. And flat. Hugo could see him in silhouette, and as he stood, he realized it was a cardboard cutout of a man. Drawing closer, he brushed at his dirty sleeves and tugged at the leather strap for his rifle, asserting dignity.

When he was three paces away, he lit a match, the better to see what he was looking at. There was a quick flare of light that he sheltered so that no one outside in the snow could see it. And then the features were revealed. Hugo was standing next to a standee of Charlie Chaplin.

He stared in utter bafflement until the flame found his fingertips, and he flicked the match out. The Chaplin standee was leaned against the wall, right where the window was, a lone sentinel and last agent of defense. His vantage point, a balistraria, a slit cut through the stone and designed for archers.

Hugo moved Chaplin aside, and patted the edges of the opening, which curved up at the ends like a smile. The lower jaw was equipped with what looked like twin sets of stubby wooden teeth, one interior, one exterior. Hugo passed to and fro, watching how, with the change in perspective, one could make them seem to mesh like gears, and then he said, "Oh!"

If you happened to be armed, and looking out this tight slit, the twin sets of teeth were a marvelous way to spot your target. In other words, it was a medieval gun sight. He wished his father were there to see it.

He stood by the balistraria to study the landscape, the clearing in the snow flanked by trees, and then, needing a place to sit, he dragged a hay bale toward him.

Outside, snow fell, a clump of it.

Hugo startled. It was the curse of the sentry to realize that the Arctic night was never really silent, that it meant nothing when snow fell from branches, branches snapped, the crust of snow collapsed with strange, phantom groans.

After removing the clip of bullets from the pouch around his neck, he sighted down the barrel of the Springfield, awaiting a skulking, spidery presence.

A single figure approached, bundled in a thick, lumpy coat. He waddled like a penguin, dressed in so many layers that his arms came out at a twenty-degree angle. His rifle was slung over his shoulder barrel-downward, indicating he was an idiot. Making no effort to disguise himself, he ambled to the center of the clearing. He turned in a gentle circle, 360 slow and confused degrees. He scratched his face. Then, hands on his hips, he yawned.

Hugo wasn't sure he could shoot a yawning man. The target had the shambling fatigue of a Bolo. He dressed in disgusting, patched clothing like a Bolo. But in this light ("a traitorous moon so bright as to confuse both kings and fools") anyone could look like a Bolo. He was three-quarters sure it was a Bolo, which meant he was one-quarter unsure. Shouldn't there be at least five or six of them if they were storming the monastery?

There had to be more to this story. He stared miserably at the Chaplin standee, which also had no business being here. Hardly the first time since his enlistment, Hugo felt as if his destiny had been adumbrated in a broom closet by several distracted simpletons while, miles away, lesser men with grand ambitions were allowed to plan their successful futures as their feet were rubbed by trained Swedish masseuses. He decided that if the figure in the snow left he would let him live. If he tried to get in, Hugo would shoot him.

The man—Bolo? not?—ambled backward, staring at the monastery, hands on hips, as if wondering whether to purchase it. Then he found a fallen tree trunk. He sat down on it. Since this was neither retreating nor attacking, Hugo was flummoxed. "Oh, *please*," he whispered.

Then the man, just a plump, squat silhouette, took out a sheet of paper and smoothed it on his knee. The moonlight reflected on it. Amazing how, in the moonlight, all color bleached out of everything. Except a telltale red border. Bolo propaganda.

The rifle barrel fit perfectly within the wooden teeth of the loop. The Springfield was easy to sight. Hugo counted down three, two, one, and squeezed off a round. In the clearing, a cry, the man put his hand to his ear and toppled over backward, off the log.

But then, as Hugo ejected the cartridge, the bolt came off with it. As easily as pulling the stem off an apple. "Oh, God," he whispered. This did not happen to Springfields. It happened to Russian rifles. And apparently to Hugo's rifle, which was now useless. If he'd killed the Bolo, it wouldn't matter, but—

A staccato sound, like pebbles spraying against the outer wall: Hugo could see the Bolo crouching, rifle out, firing it at the stone walls. The bullets would never hit him—this was futility itself, a show of anger—but, given how unlikely the entire evening had already been, Hugo threw himself to the floor.

It went quiet. Hugo raised his head slowly and looked out, into the night. His Bolo stood in the clearing. He was holding his hand to his ear, where Hugo had shot him.

If someone had just been shot, it seemed logical he should seek shelter or attack. But most men in wartime spent most of the time waiting for something to force them in a given direction, which is what Hugo's enemy was now doing.

Hugo cursed his destroyed rifle. He would probably have to pay for it. Shooting someone in the ear was just a pip, a Blighty, not a killing shot. He peeked at his enemy again—still standing there—then sat down on his bale of hay. There was a strange object resting nearby, all wood and metal, heavy like a crucifix. Hugo felt around it, fingers finally jamming painfully against something pointed and sharp and cold.

A crossbow. He understood: this was the weapon Aarne had promised him. He lifted it by its cherrywood butt and, knowing nothing about crossbows, stupidly admired the carving on its tiller—dancing nymphs and a satyr—while its prod was pointing directly at his chest.

He made a gargling sound as he twisted it away from him, noting then that it was fully cocked, with a wicked-looking bolt in its channel, ready to loose. He had almost shot himself.

He remembered the flask. His palate was immediately awash with a sweet, intense flavor, cinnamon and anise and something bitter. It was like trying to taste all the colors of a sunset, in summer, in the company of lyrical poets.

Hadn't Aarne claimed the monks here had made no liqueurs? And yet, clearly, here was a flask of liqueur! The following taste from the flask was a kiss on a summer evening, fireworks. Aarne! A man of secrets! He had very likely eaten excellent cheeses in Paris! If Hugo had asked, "Are the women beautiful?," Aarne would have said, "Of course," because women in need of rescue immediately became beautiful.

The crossbow had a simple trigger. How much of an expert did Hugo need to be? He aligned the weapon within the twin sets of teeth that rested in the balistraria's jaw, aimed at the man, and—shooting while drunk—released the string.

Loosed into the nighttime air was a *quadrello* fashioned from yew, with leather wings that caused it to rotate in flight. Its tip, sharper than a razor blade, screw-shaped, hit the target in the side of his head, where his hand was touching it, tearing through muscle and bone like a drill bit.

With a little yelp, the bundled man in the snow stood up. He turned left, then right, hand pinned to his head, arm moving in peculiar obedience as he turned. And then he toppled.

Hugo looked at his crossbow as if it had just prepared a four-course meal for him. He brought his hands into the air and threw his head back in silent exaltation. It had worked! He took a grander mouthful from the flask, which brought less of a revelation than he'd hoped. As if trying to kindle a fire, he thought, *Oh, you clever bow!* He looked again at the body in the snow—yes, definitely dead. He looked at the Chaplin standee, then punched it in the chest so it fell over, flat. Take that!

The enemy hadn't particularly fought well, and, further, now that he thought about it, he still wasn't sure the man had been a Bolo. Would the prospect of ravishing three begrimed, stout, trout-catching loaves of bread in dun-colored kerchiefs and workboots motivate *anyone* to attack the monastery? He had been lied to, strung along with promises of discussions of cheese, poisoned with something that tasted like sunsets, and handed a broken rifle; if he was going to die, he might as well have more of that strange liqueur.

A wrenching sound of metal dragging past metal, from not so far away—the door to the tower opening. Hugo stepped toward the top of the staircase.

"*Bonsoir,*" Aarne called, his voice echoing upward along the spiral of the cochlea. "*Comment allez-vous?*"

"*Oh, comme ci, comme ça.*"

35

At the center of a crowd, here was Hannah Chaplin's face, smiling inexhaustibly, at nothing really.

There were, Chaplin thought, four ways of fading in. You could open the lens diaphragm, but that's never a complete fade. A better way was using a dissolving shutter, and Rollie had an easy finger with the graduated arc lever, a smooth and even way to fade in. He wanted to talk to Rollie, who was still in the balloon. He wanted to think more about the other two methods of fading, they worked equally well fading in or fading out, but he could not remember when he had last breathed.

He saw an audience.

The banger-shaped balloon high in the air was slowly descending, courtesy of the Air Service doughboys who were pulling on the ropes, and Rollie was peering down to the ground to see what all the fuss was about. The newest hair and makeup girls were huddled together, getting it all explained to them by the property master. The English-horn player was looking with confusion to Albert Austin, who was saying, "It's his mother. His mother!"

Chaplin knew to hug her—that was obvious. She was shorter than he remembered. Her hair touched his nose. She smelled dusty, as if she had been stored in a locker. The dress was new; it still had a hem pin from the store. Her arms patted his sides quickly.

"Are those marigolds?" she asked. She wasn't looking at him.

"Sorry?"

"Marigolds."

He didn't understand. *Already,* he thought.

"Careful with your big feet, son," she said, causing a delighted cry through the crowd, and people repeated what she'd said. He felt as if he were running behind a carriage that was racing downhill. She was looking at the crowd with confusion. Why were they laughing?—then pleasure—they were laughing! Then she was hiking her skirt and hunching down by the lacy border of flowers just outside the bungalows. "And that must be mignonette. I've heard about that, haven't I?" She was looking up with delight. "Real mignonette."

"I don't know about flowers," Chaplin said. "Mum, I can't believe you're here. How." He meant it to be a question.

Luckily, he was rescued: one of the men attending her introduced himself. He worked with the Bureau of Immigration, and explained that the paperwork that had been lost with the associate general counsel had been located, his mother was in fine health, she'd lived in Peckham as a model patient without many incidents, except of course on the nights of the zeppelin raids, but, then again, all of the unfortunates were affected similarly on such nights, and it was an honor to meet Mr. Chaplin, and his wife would never believe he was meeting Mr. Charlie Chaplin today, was it true he had learned the funny walk from Billie West, and as he was talking, Chaplin watched his mother use a stubby finger—when had her hands lost their shape?—to test the California soil.

"Mignonette," she said, and stood.

"I didn't know." He touched her upper arm. She was as stout as a bottle of beer. That was the scrim across his thoughts, like a *graduated screen*—the third method for a fade, a long piece of glass, clear at one end and subtly growing opaque, until you drew it along to utter blackness. He had a few of these in the lab, but he worried about them, they could break; he could feel nothing else yet.

"Aren't we the main attraction," she said. She smiled with terrible teeth, wrinkling her face, and he wanted to sweep her up, put her in the shade somewhere.

"Mrs. Chaplin, your son owns this studio," said someone in shirtsleeves and garters, a young man Chaplin did not recognize.

"Oh," she said.

"All of it," the man continued. "He's successful."

"He should know the names of his flowers, don't you think?"

Chaplin regarded the crowd with his royalty smile. He imagined throwing her into the car, riding on the buckboard himself, having Kono drive them into traffic while the crowd chased them. He knew she wouldn't budge. He wondered, with fear, if she'd brought presents for him.

She patted him on the cheek. "You're a good boy, Charlie. Even if you didn't know the names of the flowers, you make your old mother proud."

He could meet her eyes, but only as though he were tapping his fingers against a hot stove. They were still a deep hazel, cloudy and merry, for now. He craned his head, looking for an ally. Why did this need to happen when Syd was gone? The mood in the courtyard was festive, far lighter than on any day since he'd started shooting *Sunnyside*.

"Oh," said the man from the Bureau of Immigration. "I'm supposed to tell you this was arranged by friends of yours."

"Pardon?"

"This. Having your mother come." He had a folded sheet of foolscap in his hand, and he ran his finger down it. "Yes, compliments of Goldwyn, Fox, Zukor, Jack and Harry Warner, and, well, a great many others—it's quite a list. They send their regards."

Oh, God.

Standing on the cement top step outside his bungalow was Mildred. She shaded her eyes. Chaplin willed her to walk away. Nothing to see here, he thought.

Mildred had never looked younger. Her face had taken on the look of Fluff from Oz, as if she were about to spread the stalks of corn and find a solid-gold beetle that would take her to the moon. She stepped down the three stairs to the courtyard, and his mother, who had told him since he was four years old that she could read vibrations in the air, sliced through the crowd with her violet eyes to pay close attention to the beautiful young lady approaching them.

"Are you," Mildred asked, "are you Charlie's mother?"

Hannah touched her fingertips to her cotton dress, stroking the spray of sweet pea. She looked at Mildred, from fur cap to her cocoa kid-leather suede shoes. "Hello," she said in a throaty voice. "You're going to have a baby."

Mildred looked to Charlie, who was aware he should say something. She extended her hand. "I'm—"

"Mignonette?"

"No, I'm—"

"Of course not. I suspect Charlie knows *your* name."

"Everybody, break," Chaplin said. "Everyone, we'll reconvene in an hour. Goodbye. Thank you for your concern for our privacy," Chaplin said. *Please*, he thought as his mother silently beamed at the gathered people, *please don't let her have brought presents*. He did not speak again while the players returned to their break spots, and cigarettes appeared. His eyes fell on one young, dark-haired angel, and he imagined ravishing her, then filming her face in close-up, her flush, her embarrassment.

He was standing with his mother and Mildred, who hadn't dared say another word. His stomach hurt. He realized he was supposed to introduce them.

"Mum, this is my wife, Mrs. Mildred Harris Chaplin," he said. His voice sounded as if he were reading to the blind. "She's from Wyoming, and she's an actress. A very good actress with a bright future."

"You're a sweet one," Hannah said. She took Mildred's hands in hers.

"Thank you."

"My boy Sydney has a wife, too."

"We're great friends," Mildred said.

"And you have very soft hands. Do *you* know the names of the flowers here?"

"Some. Have you seen bougainvillea before?" She indicated a great waterfall of it, red and showy, by the archway over the entrance gate.

"Bougain—what? That's impressive. Is that real?"

"Yes," Mildred said. "I know it looks too good to be real. They planted it outside my school," she said in innocence.

"Oh, your school?"

"Yes. When did you get here, Mrs. Chaplin?"

Hannah's fingers played against her sweet pea as if she were playing an instrument. Her eyes hadn't left Mildred's face. Her mouth was open slightly.

When Mildred got no response, she continued: "Could I call you Hannah?"

Chaplin could see his mother dialing years off herself as she looked at Mildred. "Call me Lily," Hannah said.

"Okay," Mildred said, which made Chaplin love her. "Have you had lunch, Lily?"

"What a funny thing to ask me," Hannah said, staring at her son as she said it. It woke him up; he had slipped into a dream, a sandstorm around him, scarves over his face, holding perfectly still.

Men were unloading the car and, he now saw, a truck behind it. His mother's luggage: Two buckled steamer trunks with sagging leather straps around them, stacks of corrugated boxboard, hatboxes, parcels covered in brown paper with sticky-looking stains on their bottoms, and several open-ended sacks with apparel falling out. There was a giant oak wardrobe with a shattered door that swung open as it came off the truck, revealing shadowy forms that could be pelts or taxidermy or sacks of grain. She was staying. She was talking to his wife.

Hannah said, "I brought you both some presents."

"That's thoughtful, Mum, but you don't have to."

He saw a ripple go across her perfectly pleasant face. "Nonsense." She toddled back to the car, her weight shifting from knee to knee as she walked.

"I didn't know your mother was coming," Mildred whispered.

"I want you," he whispered.

"Shh," she said. "Is her name Lily?"

"Yes. No, no, it's her stage name from— We can excuse ourselves for just a minute."

"No, Charlie. Your mother."

"It will only take a minute," he said.

"Luckily, the house is big enough for her."

"The house—we shouldn't have her there," he said, mouth gone dry. Mildred now looked at him the way she did when he spoke French to her. She had become bossy and sure of herself, Chaplin thought, since her pregnancy. His mother was bent over her parcels, rooting through them and casting aside small items he couldn't quite make out.

"She's nice, Charlie. She's different than how you said."

"You don't know about her."

"She's fun. I thought she had a cockney accent."

"No," he said. "She always spoke well. She's not fun."

"She is. Really." And then Mildred laughed one of her Saint Lawrence the Divine laughs. With confidence, she continued, "She's your family. Of course we'll have her."

"Here they are, my loves." His mother paced back toward them, legs bowed as if she were walking around a drainpipe. "Presents," she announced.

As her hand reached out, weighed down by small, moist-looking brown paper sacks, Chaplin thought that other people were feeling things right now, even in the mildest situations. He saw people flirting, and he knew what that felt like, and no doubt someone in the office was on the phone to New York, arguing about money, and he knew what that felt like. He stood as rigid as a tree; not even the strongest breeze would shake his branches.

Hannah reached for Mildred's palm, and turned it upward. "Close your eyes, lovely." Mildred did so.

"Mum, Mildred doesn't need anything. Mildred, you don't need to . . ."

Hannah waved her hand over Mildred's like a conjurer, and then forced something into her palm and folded it over. Mildred's mouth turned up. Eyes closed, she stroked one finger against it. "It's metal."

"Open, Mildred Harris So and Such."

It was a piece of metal. Unpolished silver, fitting neatly in her palm. Smooth on its concave size, engraved with peacocks on the convex. "This is the back of a watch," Mildred said.

"There's more," Hannah said. "Close your eyes again."

"She doesn't need to close her eyes, really."

Mildred rolled her eyes in mock exhaustion. "It's fun, Charlie. Okay, Lily." She closed her eyes and put out her hand. "I'll bet it's the rest of the watch," she said.

It was not. Mildred opened her eyes, feeling a waxy black rectangle in her palm. "Oh," she said, "it's cheese."

Hannah was beaming.

"It's been opened," Mildred said, noticing its end had been re-bound with electrician's tape.

"It's very good," Hannah said. "Now, one more gift for you. Close those pretty eyes."

Mildred did so, puzzled by the cheese, but curious.

"Do you believe in Jesus Christ?" Hannah asked.

"Mum, you shouldn't ask people—"

"I do," Mildred said, eyes still closed.

"Good."

"I have a new church," Mildred continued. "You could come if you—" And then she screamed.

"What is it? What?" Chaplin reached for her—she was swatting at something. All four of her limbs twitched as she danced in place. People were staring, but no one came forward; actresses often screamed.

"Oh, really, now," Hannah said, her eyes amazed. "He was my friend on the boat," she said.

"Where is it? Where is it?" Mildred was shaking her hands as if flinging water from them; the silver watch backing had flown from her grip and bounced across the courtyard.

"Where is what?" Chaplin cried. "Who was your friend?"

"He's the same color as your sable. Or is that mink?" Hannah reached out to Mildred's shoulder and gently plucked off a mouse. "He's gray, you see. Not going to bite you, dear."

Mildred's hands went to her stomach. Her face was pale, her mouth open slightly; her lips were bowed, eyes watering. She caught her breath. "Your mouse—"

"*Your* mouse now, dear." Hannah extended her hand, thumb and forefinger locked down, and between them poked a small, whiskered face. "He goes with cheese, you see. And with the watch, because that's time passing, you see. You can take him later for practice loving."

"Practice . . ." Mildred didn't reach for the mouse. But she said it again, "Practice," and this time she understood.

"Is it all right if I give you more gifts? Some of them might have gone off, but you can cut those parts away."

Mildred softened. "Oh," she whispered. Her eyes went from Hannah to Charlie, as they had many times. Chaplin was slowly coming back into his body, his knees unlocked, and he flexed his arms, feeling blood returning into them. He understood what Mildred was trying to: when Hannah explained, it almost made sense. Or it made perfect sense, as long as you watched it through the tiniest, most arcane optical-glass eyepiece.

His mother petted the mouse. Her own pink tongue tip was sticking out. "No fuss, really," Hannah said. Mildred felt for Chaplin's hand. She pulled her coat closed with her other hand, and Chaplin understood what she was thinking.

"I'm sure he likes cheese," Chaplin said, which was like tumbling down a hillside.

"I'm sure he does," Mildred said. "Thank you." She took the mouse in hand. "Do we have a cage for him, Charlie?"

He likes cheese was like stepping away from his eyepiece and taking on his mother's kaleidoscope. And for Mildred, *Thank you* was *Thank you*. It doubled and redoubled on Chaplin, the feeling of it being three o'clock in the morning and everyone in the world around him asleep with smiles on their faces. If he tiptoed past a crib, would the baby be asleep, or looking back at him with its own anxious gaze?

Hannah was shading her eyes, head tilted back. "Do you own that man, too?"

"What man?"

"In the melon. The sky. The, the, the sausage."

Rollie was still in the captive balloon, descending, uniformed men in a square formation below grabbing at the ropes and pulling him down.

"I don't own him, but, yes, that's my cameraman," and Chaplin brightened to the idea of showing her the studio, which would take up time. But his mother made a small noise in the back of her throat, a hard swallow, and he remembered the sound from his childhood, like the shutters of a room fastening. "Mum? What is it?"

"That's bad." She put her hands across her face, palms out. The noise again, a click, the sound made in a nightmare, the frustrated cry of a child. "Zeppelin."

"It's not a zeppelin, Mum."

But it was too late, she was now crying. She turned her face under her sleeve and hid her eyes, as if that would keep them from seeing her. "I don't like the zeppelins."

"Shh, shhh," Chaplin said. He patted her wrist from a great distance. Hannah buried her face in Mildred's mink. Mildred held her. Chaplin didn't understand how someone knew at sixteen, seventeen to offer a shoulder.

"We should get you home," Mildred said.

Hannah sniffled. "I don't want that."

"It's a large house, very comfortable."

Hannah, who was shorter than Mildred, poked her head up. Her neck was surrounded by the mink sleeve. Charlie touched his fingers against the backs of her hands, which she didn't move. She had ruined them long ago when she had threaded needles by lamplight. "I must look a fright," she said to Mildred. "I'm sorry. I just want to be helpful."

"We'd like you to stay with us," Mildred said.

"I'm hopeless," Hannah whispered.

"You're not hopeless," Mildred said.

The three of them walked toward the car. Hannah clutched Mildred, stroking the mink, and Charlie walked next to them, his hand extended toward his mother as if he were blessing her. Now he considered the fourth kind of fade, one he never used: the chemical method. Potash of cyanide and tincture of iodine, combined. *Fade out,* he was thinking. *Fade out. Fade out, fade out, fade out.* And yet he was still there, awkward, walking near but not with his mother and wife, realizing he would need to give directions to Kono, and perhaps a truck-driving member of the crew, on how to take all of his mother's luggage to his house. Cyanide and iodine. How perfect that the chemical method of fading was half poison, half cure.

36

Aarne invited Hugo down the stairs, explaining in a voice that rang with increasing excitement that he had watched the attempted siege—he called it a siege—and Hugo's tremendous defense, and really, Aarne said, Hugo was quite marvelous.

Hugo left the rifle on the floor. He picked up the crossbow and padded, step by hopeless step, down the spiral stairs. He hiked his trousers—the months in Russia had left him thinner. There were many compliments awaiting him. That Hugo had chosen to shoot a gun, then use the crossbow, had been a special kind of genius, Aarne cried out, for it had obviously confused the Bolshevik into thinking there were many defenders. Further, using one shot each time—Aarne made a noise, *zuhp, zuhp*—fantastic restraint. Hugo wasn't just a soldier, he was quite the sniper.

"Are you sure that was a Bolo?"

"Sure? Pwfff." Aarne made a petulant, avuncular exhalation through his nose. He was speaking rapidly, recounting Hugo's heroism from different angles, and then Hugo heard Aarne say something odd.

"Monsieur Aarne, what was that?"

"Nothing, Private Hugo."

Aarne had said the evening had been very surprising, for he hadn't even known a Bolo was actually coming, and then, *zuhp*, there one was.

To stay was a mistake.

In the corridor, Aarne was using an elegant-looking candelabra to light a number of torchères along the wall. "Now to your reward, monsieur."

"My reward is to kill," Hugo replied.

"Hmm." Aarne shrugged. "Well, beyond that, the women would like to thank you."

Hugo politely declined, explaining that he should get back to his billet in Solnechny Strana.

"Oh, but, monsieur, that is such a long way. Wait with us until the morning."

"No, really, I can't."

"Oh, but Monsieur Hugo! They are so beautiful."

That was how they trapped peasants in fairy tales. Hugo opened his mouth to make a bland announcement about what regrets Aarne should give the old women. Then he cocked his head. Faintly, so faintly it might have been the heartbeat of rabbits in a distant warren, he heard—a tune. A joyous, rhythmic melody carrying across the snow. "Is that . . . Johann Strauss?"

Aarne sighed. "The impatience of the young, monsieur. They were to wait for your entrance. It was to be a surprise."

"I'm sorry—are they playing instruments?"

"There was also discussion of baking you a pie. With fruit," he added. "But if you need to leave—"

He hadn't heard Strauss in a year. Without thought, he was walking toward the sound. Aarne lit his candelabra again.

There were drifts on either side of a cleared cobblestone pathway, the snow lent a flickering orange by iron flambeaux. Ahead of Hugo stood a round building of whitewashed brick. Leaded-glass windows, with the yellow-and-orange light of candle fires dancing behind them. The door, two stories high, stood ajar.

"Isn't this the abbot's house?"

"Oui, monsieur."

"Didn't you say they weren't in the—"

"I lied, monsieur."

The music was the insistent and festive melody of "Die Königin ist fünfzig Fuß hoch," played with enthusiasm on piano, violin, and double horn. It was the music that children of a hemophiliac upper class would dance to at Shrovetide.

Hugo took a deep breath at the door, intending only to compose himself, but he was also rewarded with a magnificent and mouth-watering smell. "Cinnamon?"

"They baked," Aarne murmured. "I wasn't sure they could."

With the same fear any man would show upon finding a gingerbread house in the woods, Hugo stepped inside. The room was oval, with tower walls as sturdy as battleships. There were two stone fireplaces to shame Hollywood's: draft horses could have been roasted on spits. The room was warm without being stuffy, a luxurious feeling Hugo had long ago forgotten. The shadows in the corners were deep and black and could have hidden goblins. Hugo was positive he felt eyes upon him.

But that passed through his mind quickly, for to his right was a carving table made of stone and heaped with food—a pig surrounded by greenery, but also latkes, blini, cheeses, and, at the center, surrounded by beeswax candles and set atop a wreath of dried flowers, a single pie.

To his left, playing piano, violin, and horn, were three beautiful women. They wore gowns of lace and satin, simple but appropriate for the season opening of the Opéra-Comique. They had swanlike necks, and skin as white as Alseid marble. The oldest girl, perhaps twenty, played the piano with a smiling, relaxed ease that reminded Hugo of a yachtsman at the tiller. She had red hair in a tight *chignon définitif,* capped with a tall comb that bobbed in a 6/8 signature as she gazed at her sisters serenely, willing them to stay in time with her.

The horn player, slightly younger, hair as black as a raven's, played with obedience, her hand hidden in the bell, shoulders hunched as if in anticipation of an explosion. Which could perhaps be provided by the third member of the orchestra. The violinist, who was at most fourteen years old, had excitable hazel eyes that flickered back and forth from her oldest sister, where they were supposed to be, to Hugo, of whom she obviously expected a great deal further.

A smile was stitched to Hugo's face. He was quite literally unable to proceed. His most explicit thought was that the women were not wearing potato sacks. "Where—where are the old peasant women?"

"Mmm. I lied about that, too," Aarne said.

They were not old. They were not peasants. That they were Russian was undeniable, but this meant that, for Hugo, *Russian* meant far more than he'd ever known.

The music reached its final merry chord. The red-haired woman at the keyboard turned and stood.

"Private Hugo Black of Detroit, Michigan," Aarne intoned. "May it please you to find yourself in the exalted presence of the Ladies of Pokrovskoe and Petrovskoe; Heirs to Lotoshino; Princesses of the Vesholi-Podol palace in Poltava; entitled noble heirs to ruling the estate of Petrovskoye-Alabino; humble penitents at the monastery of Solnechny Strana. May I present the Princesses Anna, Maria, and Vasilisa."

Princesses. Hugo felt as if he had been handed a heavy chalice brimming with fine wine. The word itself, the confirmation of *princesses,* iced his blood with diamonds three feet thick. He saw, now reaching back over a decade, the powdered and corseted form of his cotillion instructor, Dame Gladys du Lac. Her pince-nez.

Each princess in turn inclined her head with the subtle significance of a dealer at the faro table. Hugo's smile trembled. "If called upon to court," he could hear his instructor saying, "you must bahh bahhhh lllahhhhhh," her voice fading and indistinct, taunting him with its absence, along with the fourth Latin declension and Ceylonese trade routes.

He bowed. His cat-fur hat dropped off of his head and onto the floor. He straightened.

Popping and crackling from the fire. Hugo once again felt mysterious eyes watching him from the shadows.

Aarne plucked his hat from the floor. "Might I take your coat? I'm afraid I should take that crossbow as well. If only for your comfort."

He handed Aarne the crossbow and began the operation of shrugging off the enormous, stained greatcoat. With it came, attached by white canvas straps, his mittens, and into his pockets he tucked the broken and torn and fingerless inner gloves.

Hugo was left in his grotesquely oversized trousers, his Shackleton boots, and a filthy jacket that was far too tight. He thought of the great houses in Grosse Pointe, how his mother had prepared for an invitation that never came to dine with the merchants in oil and rubber and automobiles. He was living not just her dreams, but beyond her dreams' broadest, most glorious horizons. With this smugness (oh, the letter he would write Mother) came a wave of terror. These women were not social climbers. This was actual aristocracy, the system America had fled in order to admire from a safe distance.

As ever, there was something about that old blue blood that stymied the new. Hugo was flummoxed. He wanted to say something witty, but the only jokes he could think of hinged on regicide.

He was watched with great interest; the princesses had never seen an American before. Ever since their parents had fled to the New World, they had pinned great maps of the wild continent in their rooms, and as time had passed and their prospects dimmed, the word itself, "America," meant both the promise of heaven and a curse.

That Aarne had found Americans were actually *in the village* seemed like the best of God's blessings; they had spent most of the day discussing what their coming American soldiers might be like. When they learned there was just one, but he was definitely American, he took on Goliath-like proportions. Vasilisa, the youngest, was prone to ecstatic speculation about his brutality: he would wear chaps, and brag about having murdered many Indians. Anna, the eldest, suggested this was unlikely. Having, of the three, best grasped the sense of noblesse oblige, she explained to her sisters that if he wanted to, the soldier who saved them could crawl on all fours like Igor the Fool and walk a chicken on a leash. It had been unfortunate to lie about Bolshevik attackers, but he *was* going to save their lives if all was considered on a larger scale.

Aarne was hurrying back, then fussing with Hugo's jacket, brushing it off with a horsehair paddle and then pulling on his sleeves to even it out. He began, with a damp cloth, to wash Hugo's face. The soul of discretion, he would never mention the family now traveling in America, or the princesses' plan, borne of necessity, should—merciful God forbid—their parents not find success as regal presences in Hollywood motion pictures. The fact was, there had never been the slightest threat of a Bolshevik incursion; Aarne had gone to find them an American. That the American had actually killed to defend their honor was exciting beyond all measure.

The cloth went into a silver cup, and Hugo was allowed to dab his cheeks dry with another linen. He ran his hand over his face, which was now cleaner, and he waggled his upper lip to confirm that his mustache no longer made him itch.

"Ceremony is difficult, monsieur, especially now that the maids and courtiers have been shot," Aarne said. "But . . ."

Near one fireplace was a table illuminated by a candelabra whose multiple stems were capped by copper shades. The table was outfitted with a damask tablecloth bearing a crease as straight and sharp as the edge of a sword. The centerpiece was a full-rigged silver frigate with a mahogany bow and silk sails, atop a bed of white porcelain waves and flanked by tall Venetian lanterns whose mica shades produced flickers that gave the ship the illusion of continuous motion. There were four place settings, each with its own white drawn-work coarse linen napkin folded to look like a rose next to a scalloped fingerbowl. There was a single drinking glass, but also salad fork, entrée fork, meat fork, fish fork, the interruption of china plates, then meat knife, fish knife, soup spoon, oyster fork, and grapefruit spoon. Each shone as if buffed against clouds. A single paper card rested at each setting, three of them in Cyrillic and one to the left, reading, in neat Roman letters whose sweet attempt at precision made his throat clench, "Hugot."

It was a full formal dinner. Tears beaded the corners of Hugo's eyes. To have come from the barracks of Camp Custer in Detroit, then to the mess halls and bivouacs of the ANREF—the horrors of M&V and bully beef eaten shoulder to shoulder with lice-infested idiots—then to find this! For the first time since his enlistment, he had been issued an invitation to duty for which he was born and bred. This was like inviting a quarter horse to gallop.

What he did not know is that he had been invited for a very specific purpose. The princesses had been left alone for two years, and though it was sinful to doubt their parents' ultimate ability to rescue them, they were certain it was *not* a sin to rescue themselves, just in case. Each one of them had declared to her sisters that afternoon that she intended, by the end of the evening, to have ensnared Private Hugo Black in matrimony.

The decision was that Hannah and Mildred would ride with Kono to the house. Charlie would supervise loading into a truck the broken sacks of clothing, the Victrola and recordings, the newspapers, the fairy lights, the rusty candy-drop machine, the Chinese fishing basket, the old men's clothing she had brought that he might want.

Chaplin picked up a picnic basket filled with rough hand towels embossed with the name H.M.S. *BELLEVUE* that were wrapped around drinking glasses, and stood upright, smacking his head full-force on the underside of the truck's rear gate. Stars! A taste like the ocean in his throat. He cried out and put both hands to his head, dropping the basket of glass, hearing shattering sounds, and he was at once trying to massage the knot on his head and wipe away the blinding tears. He shuffled in his enormous shoes out of the radius of the glittering blue-green shards.

He rubbed his head, checking for blood. He was hunched over, hands against his thighs, elbows locked. There were heaps of clothing on the ground, some of them striking him as inexplicable. Uniforms? An engine roared beside him, his touring car was pulling away, and his mother was in the backseat, passing, her face as blank as a screen, and then she was gone.

His mother's chemises and skirts and underthings were spilling from the corrugated suitcases and hemp satchels. But one pile was separate, well organized, and smartly folded on a tarpaulin, blazing with metal buckles and tasseled epaulets and rich Highland wool tunics. His wardrobe mistress, Rhiannon, was fussing with an ornate trio of buttons on one sleeve. "Why does my mother," he said slowly, "have a hussar's uniform?"

He knew there was no reasonable answer. Rhiannon shook her head heavily. "Not your mother's, Mr. Charlie."

"Whose is it?"

"Those Russians a couple of months ago? They came back."

"They wanted extra work?"

"They asked if we would buy their clothing. I told them there weren't Russians in the new film, but they told me they had been to Metro and Famous Players and Fox and Warners, but no one would buy them. Don't ask about Universal."

"What about Universal?"

"They didn't have carfare, so they sent their translator to Universal City, and she had to ride back on the streetcar with all their uniforms. She begged me to take their clothing. I gave her forty-six dollars fifty cents."

"For all . . . That's a good . . ." He touched his forehead, which was aching. "Why that amount?"

"That's what the translator asked for. It's enough to get them all train fare out of Hollywood." Rhiannon put the first jacket—a naval officer's coat—onto a hanger. She brushed at it with her palm.

Chaplin rubbed at a blue worsted suit that had probably been sewn in Moscow by tailors from France, perhaps worn by a humble penitent at Solnechny Strana. People had been streaming into town to try their luck. Of course, some would eventually leave broken-hearted.

Now Rhiannon was deliberately not meeting his eye. She put a stiff ballgown on a thick hanger, and regarded how the sunlight hit it. "I should put these away."

"Rollie," he said, for a rubber-legged Rollie Totheroh was approaching, looking slightly greenish from his trip up in the captive balloon. "How's the light?"

"Better through the bottom of my next glass of ale."

Chaplin explained what he had in mind: how he wanted to end the film. Everything they did from now on would aim directly toward this.

When he was finished talking, Rollie wet his thumb and stubbed out some dirt on his lapel. "Tomorrow," he said.

"I'll still want to do it tomorrow."

"I know. Tomorrow. We'll go to Phelps Ranch, shoot it in the afternoon, good shadows until they go bad."

Chaplin squinted at him. "I'm quite serious about this."

"See you tomorrow at Phelps Ranch."

"I'll see you." Chaplin shook his hand, and they parted, and Chaplin hadn't gotten ten feet before Rollie called to him.

"Charlie?"

"Yes?"

"If you do change your mind, have the boys call me before first light tomorrow."

"I won't."

Rollie growled his deep laugh, took a slug of bismuth, and kept walking.

On the way home, Charlie stopped at Pearl's, a louche café out in the wilds of Wilshire Boulevard, where younger actors and actresses of some talent tended to gather without gossiping. There was no other place like it, and no sentence on any set had ever begun with "Do you know who I saw at Pearl's last night?"—for no one, especially the speaker, had any business going there. It had lasted eleven months so far, and Chaplin knew it could not last much longer.

He was there, in the back room, checking his watch—plenty of time for supper—and sipping soda water. He tipped scales back and forth in his head as girls with short hair and ropes of beads that went past their waistlines took turns attempting to get his attention. He wondered who had thought of ropes of beads like that and why no one had ever thought of them before, because they forced the eye to wander. Short hair, bobbed like Irene Castle's. The very opposite of curls, of course. He wished more women would bob their hair.

He wondered where Edna was. He wondered where Frances was. The gang at the Athletic Club. He used to go to boxing matches or Barney Oldfield's. It struck him that he was old enough to have lived his life in layers; when he left one place for another, the residue of friendship only existed like scars or wrinkles.

It wasn't just friends; he shed old *qualities* of life. The contest for the Twelve Immortals of film—had that ended? Were the winners ever announced?

The back room was strangely empty. He heard laughter from the main part of the café, and, finishing his soda, he stood, fitted on his hat, wincing (he'd forgotten the bump on his forehead), and walked past the bar, where about a dozen women were in a loose circle around one leather stool whose occupant was leaning back and allowing himself to be admired.

Chaplin recognized him: it was a man called Max Eastman. His silver hair was slicked into place, his nails were buffed, and he somehow made his fifty-cent tie and one-dollar shirt and six-dollar jacket look as if they cost a mint. Eastman was a bohemian, a poet, a leftist, a psychologist, and not quite a cad, but highly successful with the ladies. Chaplin had seen him lecture once on politics, and had found, to his discomfort, that Eastman also had theories on humor. But the several times they had run into each other, he had never brought them up again.

Eastman caught Chaplin's gaze, and his eyebrows went up. But he did not invite Chaplin, no "Char-lee, how-are-ya." No fictive kinship. Instead, Eastman gave a microscopic shrug of acceptance. It said that if Chaplin wanted to help himself to a stool, he was welcome.

Which was how Chaplin missed dinner. Eastman had been describing his trip into Germany, which he downplayed as hardly worth mentioning.

"Why were you there?" Chaplin had to ask.

"I was selling stolen musical instruments, actually."

The girls laughed beautifully, and Chaplin had to say, "Oh, do tell."

Tell he did, ceding to Chaplin at the right moments. "Eastman, you're a crook and you're in the right town for it," Chaplin said.

"Well, of course, that was when I was under arrest," he said in answer to something Chaplin had said, and soon they were discussing the inequities of the Sedition Act, Upton Sinclair's *The Profits of Religion*, the imperial nature of the U.S. postal system, and whether Eastman's old journal *The Masses* was progressive or essentially conservative (with Eastman taking the latter position).

By the time they looked up, the girls were gone. The thrill had dissipated at roughly the moment when Chaplin had ignored a pretty redhead's empty glass while arguing that, in negotiations for the terms of peace with Germany, self-determination, the root of human dignity, was incompatible with punitive indemnities. Eastman, who had made this point earlier, agreed. Chaplin wrote Eastman a check, "for bailing out your magazine, its blues and woes." The check was for seven dollars, but Chaplin explained Eastman could use it to build on. Eastman folded the check and put it in his pocket.

"I think I might send my films to Russia." Chaplin put his chin in his hands. "I know I'll never get them back, but it would be a gesture."

"To whom will you send your films?"

"To Russia," he said, as if Eastman hadn't just heard something perfectly simple.

An hour later, Chaplin had expressed every political and social opinion he had, and he still didn't want to go home.

"The new film is going to surprise people," he declared.

"What's it about?"

"It's set on a farm," he said, which sounded weak, so he added, "It's about a worker who is terribly mistreated."

"By his boss?"

"It's about his revenge by being sleepy and lethargic."

"Such is a man's right."

"Exactly!" With rising certainty, Chaplin told the story of *Sunnyside*. It began to make sense: an indictment of management, a vindication of the worker, followed by exposing the opiate of religion via riding a bull into church. The Fellow's mind would be expanded by visiting a museum, where the hypocrisy of the bourgeois would be exposed when the statues came to life. Nudity! Allowable on statues but never on actors, imagine the enlightenment, not just for the audience but an infectious incident for the Little Fellow. He would return to the farm and lead a rebellion. "The whole film will be a savage crucifixion of the foibles of our time, but it will be a comedy."

"I feel goosebumps, Mr. Chaplin."

Chaplin swallowed his lemonade heavily. His breathing was shallow, and his heart thumped as if he'd just won a race. He drummed his hands on the table.

"Well," Eastman said, "if you're going to tell the truth, you should be funny. Otherwise, they'll kill you."

"Exactly," Chaplin said.

"This will keep them from calling you the Mob God again."

"Right. What?"

"You know, *The New Republic*."

"Oh. Really?"

"Something about the public reception of *Shoulder Arms*. But this should shut them up."

"Hmm," Chaplin said, "yes. Well, yes."

Thirty minutes later, still not interested in home, he was explaining that his mother was in town, and that, contrary to what the world seemed to think about mothers—

"Sentimentality about one's mother," Eastman said as if it were a thesis, "is a bit of a mirage. It's inflicted upon the bourgeoisie to stifle their feelings of rebellion."

"Do you think so?"

"Certainly," Eastman said.

Chaplin gave a small snort of appreciation. There had been a bowl of peanuts before them, and now there were shells. "Mother, son, family. It's arbitrary, isn't it?" He was absently trying to rebuild a family of them with mismatched parts. "I had thought things would be different by now," he said.

"What do you mean?"

"It's 1918. As a race, we've reached the apex of sophistication. I thought so many problems would be solved."

"Like what?"

"Is there always going to be stupidity?" Chaplin asked. "When the war ended, I thought—"

"The war's not over." Eastman drained his beer.

"What do you mean?"

"There are troops in Russia."

"I distinguish the revolution from the war, Eastman."

"So do I. I mean there are Allied troops fighting the troops of Mother Russia right now."

"That can't be so. We would have heard about that."

"It's in the papers." Eastman patted his lips. "But it's on page twenty, you know. American troops are engaged in battle against Bolsheviks."

"But why?"

"I could parrot the party line, Charlie. The Bolsheviks think the Allies want to control Mother Russia, take her resources, keep the people of Russia from their self-determination. That the United States and Britain fear the inevitable spread of workers' revolution so much they want to strangle its progenitor. If I hadn't had that last beer, I might have told you that."

Chaplin was prepared for some con to fall on him. But:

"You're a man plagued by his family right now. You don't need me to go doctrinaire on you. The truth is much more disturbing anyway."

"What's the truth?"

"Do you know why we're in Russia?" When Chaplin shook his head, Eastman shook his head, too. "There is no reason."

. . .

Chaplin had Kono drop him off at the curb, at the bottom of the driveway. There was a light on in the foyer, where he removed his shoes, and the entryway was filled with his mother's boxes. Another light was on in the dining room, where a plate of roast beef waited.

The table was set for one. Overhead, a single hanging light wreathed in wrought iron gave a faint glow. The chair was wooden, with carved arms, like a throne. Chaplin put the napkin in his lap, poured himself a glass of water, and took up his utensils in silence. The dinner table half vanished in gloom, the other end perhaps lost over the horizon line. There was a small bowl of salad—lettuce and tomatoes—and on the main plate, beside the roast beef, were two dinner rolls. He stuck his dinner fork in one and salad fork in the other, and had them do a little dance, while his face feigned lack of interest.

There was a large moon casting crooked and scattering beams through the leaded-glass window beside him. Music. His mother was playing songs on the Victrola in her bedroom: " 'E Dunno Where 'E Are" and then "Opportunity." And then the first, again, and the second. Once, when "Opportunity" had been finished for several long moments, he thought she might have gone to sleep, but then he could hear, through her door and down the stairs, her voice reaching him. "Miss Lily Harley sings 'Opportunity,' " and then the song began again. He could hear the cobblestonelike clatter of thick leather soles on her floor, and he knew she had rolled up the rugs and was dancing.

He went to the garden and stood in the moonlight. He still didn't know which ones were marigolds and which were mignonettes.

In his bedroom he could hear tiny squeaking sounds within the long shadows cast by the moon. The mouse was in a cage by Mildred's side of the bed, burying itself happily in wood shavings. Mildred was awake, knees drawn up. When Chaplin put his hand on her breast, which now filled his hand, she neither blocked him with her elbow nor arched back her shoulder to give him better access.

"Hello," she whispered.

"Hello."

"Are you okay?"

"Of course." She was wearing his pajamas, which meant he was familiar with the buttons. He ran his hands lightly over the bow of her stomach, glancing at her eyes, which were looking pensively at the moonlight.

It caused him to hesitate. "What?"

Mildred shook her head. But she was thinking *something*. "She's your mother," she finally said. She said it as if answering a question.

"I know. She's here," he said, kissing her ear.

"No, I mean"—she touched his cheek—"you're being sweet. No, I mean something different." She said it with two syllables instead of three. "Diffrunt." The Gishes said it the same way. He realized that a year ago, two years, there had been the birth of a Hollywood accent. "When the maid turned down her bed, she found bread under her pillow."

"I don't want to talk about it."

"Okay," Mildred said. He nuzzled at her throat, kissed her high collarbone. "When you think of your mother, that's the woman you're thinking about." He held her breast again, squeezing it. Mildred slipped her knees apart. She was looking at him with those luminous eyes. "Poor Charlie," she said.

Maria sat at the piano bench, her sisters standing and holding hands. "In place of the opening prayer," Maria announced in French, her voice slight. She raised her hands above the keyboard, and began to play.

The chords were simple, and the hesitation between notes would have been clumsy if not for her sincerity:

> *My country, 'tis of thee,*
> *Sweet land of liberty,*
> *Of thee I sing;*
> *Land where my fathers died,*
> *Land of the pilgrims' pride,*
> *From every mountainside*
> *Let freedom ring!*

The pronunciation was phonetic. But even if she didn't know the meaning, she had learned it to impress her future husband. She would love America when she and her sisters moved there.

Hugo, in the dark about her intentions, kept a polite smile. He would never sing about America, for it had sent him to a ridiculous war it had already forgotten. When he thought of his country—as an idea—he saw a capitalist, overstuffed, top-hatted and suspender-wearing, silk trousers ballooning, and fingertips sticky with ice cream, presiding over mechanized production lines of smudged rubber tires fitted onto ill-made automobiles purchased on credit by ill-dressed families who drove on Sundays to shabby public parks, where they listened to Sousa marches and played baseball and sang with knowing smiles, "There's a place in France where the ladies wear no pants," and ate ill-prepared meatloaf surprise while reading to one another, in shrill voices, the barbarities of the full-color comics section, *because they wanted to.*

But now here was Maria, singing:

> *Let music swell the breeze,*
> *And ring from all the trees*
> *Sweet freedom's song;*
> *Let mortal tongues awake;*
> *Let all that breathe partake;*
> *Let rocks their silence break,*
> *The sound prolong.*

"Amen," she said.

Maria glanced Hugo's way with a desire not to be found wanting.

Her sisters hated her.

Drifting toward the table, fanning themselves with wide lacquer fans, they schemed to knock her down. Aarne pulled out their chairs, and one by one they sat, laying their gloves across their laps.

Hugo took his chair last. As he drew his seat out, he thought he saw something in the distant, dark corner. He was being watched. Very well— he would behave perfectly. He thought, while tucking the napkin into his lap, "Silver must never touch silver. Turn the conversation from right to left, and when the courses change, from left to right. Rings around food are to be eaten; platforms under them, no." He was going to be the best dinner guest in all Russia.

Alas, there was wine on the table. Anna held her drinking glass aloft, and said, "*À votre santé,*" and the others murmured assent. The wine was delicious, Hugo noted. Aarne reappeared, all four plates ready, each with a sprig of parsley. Hugo anticipated what delicacy would fill the rest of the plate, and while so waiting, missed the cue to pick up his fork. Aarne said, "The pantry is rather dissipated, Monsieur Hugo. We apologize."

Hugo's head, with no effort, turned toward the buffet table, where the cheeses and pig still lay.

Aarne continued, "Alas, some things, in the chaos, spoiled. Though they make excellent decorations." Before Hugo could entirely weigh this feeling, Aarne said, "Another casualty of the chaos, Monsieur Hugo, is that manners have been sporadic. Allow us this chance to use ours. Please, drink and eat."

There were four pairs of eyes upon him as Hugo had his first bite of parsley. He was unsure how long to chew, when to wipe his mouth, if compliments were in order.

"My sisters and I thank you for coming, Monsieur Hugo." Anna had spoken. She spoke French with a throaty hoarseness, almost a whisper, as if she wanted not to overstate anything. Which she did not, for she didn't want to scare him away from marrying her.

"To serve you is my pleasure," Hugo replied.

"You serve us in more ways than one," Anna replied. "You help us observe Lord Chesterfield's rule that a dinner party, excluding one's self, should not fall below the number of Graces, nor exceed the number of Muses."

He had to think about that as he took a long sip of wine. In one sentence, Anna had justified her title. "Quite."

The parsley was replaced by the second course, a clear broth atop which floated parsley. The new course meant Hugo should talk *à droit*, with Maria, the middle princess. Maria had been born with dark-brown eyes shaped like narrow crescent moons, as if Tartar blood had floated to the surface, which had made the question of nubility loom over her since childhood. Because she had no suitors, and did not fool herself that anyone could like her face, she wore spectacular frocks.

Since he was a soldier, she felt he must know Paris. She fought against shyness to ask if there had truly been a bomb thrown through the showroom window at Premet Couture, destroying the spring 1919 line.

Hugo couldn't understand what she was getting at, and he was again distracted by something. "Pardon—Princess Maria, do you feel like you're being watched?"

She didn't understand what he meant. Since she was a princess, she always felt she was being watched. Further, Vasilisa was interrupting with short sentences, hardly even full questions, just names he wasn't sure he heard pronounced correctly.

"Buffalo Bill?" Vasilisa said, or so Hugo thought. He was having increasing trouble understanding, so he sipped more wine.

"Pardon?"

"Est-ce tu connais Monsieur Buffalo Bill? Il avait massacré beaucoup des Indians. Est-ce tu et il des amis?"

"Do I know . . . Buffalo Bill?"

The broth left the table, and was replaced by a single silver herring for each of them. The herring plate was whisked away the moment it was bare, and replaced (along with a refresher glass of wine) by popcorn. Maria explained how popcorn was made, as if it were a great delicacy. Hugo, who had never before eaten popcorn with a fork, nodded as if learning.

To make up for the sparse food, Hugo drank. His experience with alcohol, like his experience with women, was largely theoretical and based on brief, inconclusive encounters.

He was aware of how, reflected in the carafe, his face had character he had never credited himself with; further, he loved everyone in the room. But why were the princesses pushing back their chairs?

Hugo watched Aarne removing the dessert plates, which indicated not only that dessert had been served, but that Hugo had eaten it. He remembered it had been pie and ice cream. He had been overwhelmed, upon sight of the apple pie, with love of America, a feeling that surprised him, and he wondered how America had changed so much in the last few minutes.

The women understood it might be best for Private Black to lie down in a guest room for an hour or two, perhaps even spend the night in a feather bed. But Hugo had stood, and wobbled like a surprised stork. His mood shifted, like the flipping of a card, from euphoria to regret. He was on the verge of becoming more than he had been, if only he could be very, very good.

"A toast." He considered it. He was choking back tears. The princesses toasted, a bit frightened of the toasting. "And," Hugo said, wine sloshing over the rim of the glass, "let us cement our friendship with—a dance."

Before breakfast, the maid tried to open Hannah's door to bring her a newspaper and tea, and the doorknob came away in her hand. When she went into the room from the other door, on the far side of the bathroom, she found the bed made, Mrs. Chaplin's clothing folded and stacked atop her dresser, and a ribbon tied to the no-longer-working doorknob. She thought better than to remove it, and reported to Mildred that Mrs. Chaplin was very nice, and wanted to help her tidy the house, and that Mrs. Chaplin said she had tied the ribbon on the door because cats like to play with ribbons. "She asked if I believed in Jesus Christ and I said I did, and she shook my hand just like my minister does. She's funny."

Mildred, holding a cup of coffee very still, said, "She had a ribbon on the doorknob? How did that make the doorknob fall off?"

The maid furrowed her brow. "I don't know."

"Do you think Mrs. Chaplin did something to the door?"

"I don't think so."

"Tell me the part about cats again?"

Later, Chaplin was dressing for work. He stood on the sleeping porch to see what the weather was like, and saw below him, in the garden, his mother. She was on the nearest bench, the morning paper beside her. She had her head back and her eyes closed, and he thought she had never felt sun like this.

She had a ribbon in her hand. She opened her eyes, and she was dragging it across the grass, shaking it. She made it dance like a snake, and he could hear her making cooing sounds, trying to coax something from the bushes. Chaplin had only one cuff buttoned, collar standing off his shirt like the wing of a gull testing the wind. His eyes swept across the close hedge. He thought he saw something in the shadows.

"Charlie?"

He jumped. It was Mildred. "Just a moment," he whispered. He leaned against the wall and watched his mother playing with the long silk ribbon.

"Can I ask you—"

He put his finger to his lips and escorted Mildred inside, then returned outside and closed the door. He was only gone for five seconds, perhaps, but when he returned, Hannah was gone. Had he missed the cat? He stood perfectly still, long after Kono had started the car, and several times he thought he saw something playing in the shadows of the hedge, a stealthy form prowling as quiet as a memory.

Kono took Chaplin to a dusty ranch of 160 acres off Sunset. It didn't quite have a name yet. Occupying a gentle canyon, it had long ago been purchased by a man named Phelps whose widow hoped that having Chaplin film there would lead to a fantastic sale to a real-estate company. Her ranch was close enough to the Laurel Canyon trolley tracks that you could hear the bells clamoring in the distance. The grounds were planted with an acre of badly tended grapefruits, and there was a weathered barn, a riding ring, and a foreman's house.

Here they would shoot the finale of *Sunnyside* out of sequence. Rollie ran a test strip of the scene, focusing on the mountain ridge. Chaplin corrected the angle. "We won't fade out on landscape—you must never fade out on landscape."

The hand-focusing board read "Chaplin—Sunnyside—RT—Scene 145," a boy held up a train schedule for Rollie to focus on, the clapper went down, and Chaplin immediately called, "Cut."

Rollie was relieved, for he did not like the shadows being thrown. He ordered his umbrella pushed back. The blond nature of the dirt was uplighting Chaplin as in a courtship scene.

Chaplin sat in the backseat of his car with Maverick and Vincent so he could explain where the story was going. The Little Fellow, jilted in love, walks down this path alone.

Maverick and Vincent waited for there to be more to the story: How was the Little Fellow jilted? How did this relate to the eight minutes they had shot? Something with Edna—was that going to end badly? Chaplin told them to go away.

He left the car and, leaning into the driver's cabin, directed Kono to drive up the road a few hundred yards. Then he waited by himself, swatting at his trousers, for there seemed to be mosquitoes.

Chaplin was in the full tramp costume—hat, coat, vest, trousers, shoes—for the first time since *Sunnyside* had begun. He had been experimenting before with leaving off elements—one scene without the hat, another without the familiar checked vest, and so on. Today the jacket was a new one found at a jumble sale, far too small, and wrinkled beyond repair.

His eyes went to the horizon, from which the automobile was approaching him. He began a limp kind of walk, as if every step was taken in mud. Clouds of dust were kicked up behind the car's wheels as it passed the single oak tree far ahead of him. Chaplin arched his back and threw his arms out, yawning, then continued his walk. Here it was, alone again, into the sunset, his comment on the folly of all such endings.

The touring car was thirty feet away, then twenty, and then Chaplin spun on his heel until his back was to the road. He crouched down and put his fingers in his ears. He waited, eyes clamped shut, and heard the shuddering squeal of brakes being applied. The end.

He stood. He shaded his eyes. "Did you get it?"

Rollie yelled back, "Yes, Charlie."

"Did you use the dissolving shutter?"

"Not on your life. We'll do it with the cyanide and iodine. Like you said." Rollie swallowed a capful of bismuth.

"Again," Chaplin said, and then, "Places," sending Kono back to his first mark, down the road.

They shot eighteen takes that afternoon, six to eight seconds of film. Each time, Chaplin felt the melancholy of his imaginary rejection make his step a little more heavy, and each time, he spotted the oncoming collision with more relief. In one take, the walk was longer, and he paused to pick at some road trash with the tip of his stick. In another, he lay down on the ground with a daisy on his chest. Another—he jumped in the air, keeping his hat in place. Another—he rubbed his chin as if reconsidering, then concluded, Yes!, and faced the onrushing vehicle with a brave little wince.

There was a thing said in taverns around Hollywood that took some thought to grasp: "You can't impress me; I work for Chaplin." His crew had long ago inured themselves to his genius.

But Edna was there today. Though she was not on call, she had come to the set, as she often did, to knit, to read poetry. When she heard what he was shooting, she decided to watch, and around the fourth or fifth take, she was reminded of that terrible day two years before when she had thought he was lost at sea. She approached the road, standing behind Rollie, who glanced at her twice—more often than he ever did.

With every new slate, word spread a little farther, and by the end of the afternoon, when the shadows were threatening to finish it, Edna was surrounded by the crew.

One last try for luck, as Chaplin sometimes said. They rolled. The board clacked. He flashed a beatific smile and ambled onto the road, no longer melancholy or resigned. With the agent of his death approaching, his body was limber. He leaned forward as if the wind could support him. His face radiated bliss. Had she ever seen his face like this? Yes.

Chaplin's eyes were closed. He was acting. He pretended that he was off his mark. That the brake cables had been slashed. That Kono was out of control. His arms were high in the air, his knees slightly bent; his torso was tilted forward to accept full impact. Twenty feet, fifteen, ten, and then impact implied, impact imagined, dissolve, dissolve.

40

The plan to marry Hugo was a plan made by princesses, bold in intent and rather fuzzy about details. They had rarely done anything for themselves. So now the invitation to dance startled them into stillness. What to do?

Hugo straightened out his uniform, which seemed to take an unnaturally long time, perhaps because alcohol made his actions much more precise. In anticipation of bestowing the required corsages on his dance partners, he steadied his hand and aimed to pluck flowers from the porcelain compotiers, which dated to the time of Ivan the Terrible. "Oh, no, that's all right, I don't need your help, Monsieur Aarne," he said.

When Hugo had been removed from the compotiers, the women whispered about what, exactly, to dance with him. It was obvious Hugo was best suited for a ländler, if only for the stamping in hobnail boots. But no one wanted to hear him yodel.

Vasilisa campaigned for Anna and Maria to play the exciting "grosser Ausgang," while she and Hugo danced or perhaps—her eyes grew round with excitement—a hesitation waltz, followed by the violent and criminal Apache dance, with which Maurice Mouvet was said to have confounded the chorus girls of the Ziegfeld Follies. Anna and Maria were uninterested in serenading any lovers on the dance floor, and bickering ensued.

Then something unexpected: a calibrated eruption of clapping in 6/8 time. From the palms of Private Black. He stood at twelve o'clock on the herringbone floor, head thrown back, chest out, arms akimbo, and a line of three flowers tucked into the folds of his jacket. He struck up a graceful *posture droit*. On the distant stucco walls, heretofore unnoticed, were trompe l'oeil flowers and trees and birds painted in the seventeenth century and now somewhat decrepitly peeling, but warm and welcoming, as if the dance floor were a quiet glade.

As the red-tailed hawk fluffs up the ruff of feathers on his neck, his hunting eye angled toward the female, so Hugo had issued a challenge. He launched into the galliard, a dance best attempted by virtuosos. It hardly seemed possible for a man who had sloshed through a toast and spilled wine on his torn and soiled trousers, a man in slippery gunboat-sized boots, but there it was: a cunningly graceful *pied gauche en l'air avec petit saut,* which even their dance teacher had looked like a frog when executing. But he was Nijinsky, he was a loping faun, he was Douglas Fairbanks leaping over a table. Then Hugo's legs scissored so that the floor appeared to ripple beneath them. He descended with the weightlessness of an angel.

Once in a *posture gauche,* he began a new *cinq pas,* the delicate fore-and-aft galliard. He extended his hands, clapped them again in that irresistible summoning, and then came to his senses. He wobbled, blinking. He had been audacious and foolish and, for a moment, happy. What chance was there of that continuing?

He watched his princesses watch him; his heart, in his throat, was not his own.

Though it is true that history does not exactly repeat itself, some patterns are eerily familiar. Such as courtship. There are doorways into other, friendlier places that seem to open simply by the kindness of happenstance. So, even if Hugo was not quite Douglas Fairbanks carrying Mary Pickford across a stream and into Sunnyside, he had just heroically defended something more real than movie-star royalty against something more dangerous than wet shoes and slippery rocks. And now he was inviting them onto a dance floor surrounded by a pastoral of painted birch trees and distant, warbling finches, where the war and its deprivations might—if only for a moment—slip away into grace. Was his good intent enough to move them?

Oh, yes. The three princesses glided across the floor and toward their instruments.

Aarne, who had maintained a discreet distance, preparing coffee and a tray of *digestifs,* picked up his old shakestaff. Hugo handed Anna (since she was the eldest) a flower, led her to the center of the floor, and bowed toward Maria and Vasilisa. Aarne suggested, with all humility, that Maria switch to recorder and they play "Der Kuninc Rudolf." Though it was more of a troubadour's song, its rhythms were simple.

Red-haired Anna stood opposite Hugo, hands to her hips, a suspicious smile escaping her. When the feisty little tune launched, Aarne keeping syncopated time with his staff, Hugo shifted to the lavolta, taking her hand and moving into closed position without tangling his legs between hers. Then, with flashing eyes, he put one hand on her back, touching her just above the hip. She gasped—his was proper form, but done with such audacity! His other hand went to her busk, as if he owned it.

Together, they stepped, and sprang into the air, hopped for a measure, returned to the ground—with the greenery on the walls, it felt as if they were in a field. Anna caught her breath, for she knew what was coming, and Hugo lifted her, held her there, not just with his hand but with the support of one strong thigh, the contact brief, and then it was over as he allowed her back to the dance floor for the final measure.

They separated, and continued an improvised galliard that lasted not five steps, or eleven, but *seventeen.* By the third step, Anna wanted him to spare the gift of white doves and gold-leaf papyrus when he proposed to her; by the seventh step, she wanted to skip the church wedding; and by the thirteenth step, she was ready for more, immediately, now, please.

The music ended, Maria putting down her recorder and pretending she needed a drink of water. Her sister Anna had danced beautifully, and the light had caressed her red hair as she spun in Hugo's arms, reminding Maria that no man would ever love her.

But now Hugo was standing above her, extending his forearm. It was a posture as curious to her as if he were asking her to admire the fabric of his uniform, but then, swallowing, she realized he had returned Anna to the piano, and was asking her to dance. He handed her a flower.

"Shall it be a waltz?" he called over his shoulder. Red-haired Anna, flushed, glowing, confused as if she'd been kissed on the neck, struck up the opening of Tchaikovsky's Serenade for Strings. Vasilisa joined in, and Aarne, returning late with the pitcher of water, hurried to measure out time with his shakestaff.

Hugo swept Maria around the floor, supporting her in full, muscular turns. She had not had a partner like this since Monsieur Turner, the dance instructor, had gone to gather wood and been butchered by the Red

Army. Hugo propelled them forward, and into the air, with the relentless-ness of a piston engine, and yet he was sensitive to her dizziness, slowing imperceptibly and leading her when necessary. The roaring fire was crack-ling and sizzling, and throwing wonderful shadows and light over his beaming face.

The tune ended. Maria had a light sheen on her brow and lip, which she hoped seemed, under the lights of the candle and the fireplace, like a glow rather than a mustache.

When the silence became unbearable, she whispered, *"Monsieur Hugo? Où avez-vous appris à danser? Paris?"*

"Detroit," he declared. *"Detroit, la ville du Stokowski."* Because he was now feeling pleasantly arrogant, he added, *"Et le plus grand fourneau du monde."*

He released Maria to her sisters, where she sat, dazedly stroking her flower. He put his fists to his hips, and then beckoned Vasilisa with one fin-ger. Her eyes went wide, and her sisters put their hands to their mouths in mock horror for her. Vasilisa smoothed out her dress. She stepped toward Hugo as if he might eat her.

"Monsieur Hugo," she said quietly, *"savez-vous danser comme Mouvet? Maurice Mouvet?"*

"Tango?" he replied, but before she could respond, he continued, "Or . . . Apache," pronouncing it "Ah-*pash*," as did the French. Under his breath, he added, *"Oui. L'Apache."* And he feigned the opening posture, tilting back on his heels, thumb below his chin and finger caressing his jawline in a manly appraisal of his partner. "Waltz time, please," he said, for he was in the final moments of being able to do no wrong.

But Anna, Maria, and Aarne did not strike up the band. Had Hugo picked the tango, they might have complied. Even though the tango was dark and sultry, it was late enough in the evening for a saucy kind of lark. But the Apache? Did Hugo really think he was about to perform the Apache with Vasilisa? She was but a child and could be forgiven her token whims, but Hugo, a soldier, an adult—

The Apache dance told a scandalous story of the Marseilles under-world. Hugo, thumb under chin, was now in the position taken by the pimp, and Vasilisa, were she actually going to follow through, would soon be toppled to her knees, to clutch his thighs in supplication.

But the action of the Apache dance would truly begin when, upon the girl's refusal to pay him, the pimp would slap her face, drag her by her hair, fix her arms behind her back, and in perfect accord with the music, smack her head against the floor in waltz time. Women who danced the Apache at night pioneered the daytime use of pancake makeup.

Unfortunately, Hugo's powers of analysis were now hobbled. "I have killed a man and now I am dancing among princesses," he thought. The wine had unspooled a whirlwind Möbius strip of cause and effect: the women's greater interest in him as a savior and warrior and dancer, and as above all a *man*, caused him to become even more proficient and more arrogant, which in turn propelled them to hold him in even higher regard. *He could do anything.*

Young and moody Vasilisa felt the room begin to swim. A curious, dizzy pleasure began at her knee and ignited upward until her whole body tingled, as it had only once before, when as a child she had determined she would run away to the land of fairies said to live underwater and she had dived deep into a pond on a summer day with the intention of never returning to land. Her lungs seemed empty, her vision began to dissolve. There was Hugo awaiting her. The last flower—he offered it solemnly in both hands and, as the Apache demanded, when she reached for it, he tore it from her fingers and rent it in half.

Vasilisa collapsed dead away in a faint.

Her sisters and Aarne leapt to her side. Her head lolled backward, a broken puppet's, and she let out a moan, the sound of a small animal helpless on the forest floor.

Hugo moved to attend, too, but Aarne, impossibly swift, was in his path. "You have done enough, monsieur."

It hardly mattered that Aarne was so small. In fact, it made Hugo feel even more like a brute as he watched the scene before him, the distressed princess laid out and supported by her sisters.

"I'm sorry," he said. And then, "I'm sorry. No, truly. We were having fun."

Such a thing was hard to assert when one of the party had collapsed. He knew it wasn't his fault. *She* had been the one to suggest Maurice Mouvet.

Vasilisa waved away her sisters, gesturing weakly at the dance floor. "Monsieur Hugo, thank you," she whispered, eyes closing. "Thank you very much." And she seemed to slip into a light slumber.

"You know," Anna sighed, "she does like her scenes."

Maria chuckled. "Vasilisa? Are you making a scene?"

Vasilisa declared, eyes closed, "I am *not* making a scene," which caused her sisters to laugh anew. Aarne joined in, and then, carefully, Hugo, too.

Sunnyside

Anna called out, "Ah, Monsieur Hugo, Monsieur Hugo," as if he were a dear and frequent guest.

Vasilisa, with her sisters' help, reluctantly stood. The wood in the fireplace made a mighty crack, a gasp and hiss following as the logs burned a little more brightly.

What followed was subtle, a small shift in position: the three women stood together, Vasilisa supported in the middle, in almost a semicircle, with Aarne facing, in case they had needs. Hugo thought that you could connect all four of them as though they were stars in a constellation, three in a row, one before them like a stem, and they would make a kind of anchor. Or you could connect the five of them, if that was a legitimate pattern, and this thought made tears stand in his eyes.

Hugo's face was open, an innocent question written upon it for any of the girls in the room: "Since I saved you, will you please love me as well?" Incredibly, he saw the answer: *yes.* All of them. Any of them. He was loved. He wished he could hold on to this moment. He tried to remember it as it was happening, as if this were a guarantee he would *always* remember it. "I am remembering now so I will never forget." This was not unlike how, in the combat at Toulgas on the day of the Armistice, he had been aware of his own thinking and thus assured of his immortality.

Which was a sad kind of thought. It was not really how most stories went.

It dawned on Hugo what it would be like to be married to a princess: a blessing, a pain, a blessing again. Love was never the end of the story, but the beginning, and the rest was compromise. He could do it. He was good enough, right now.

And on the other side, three beautiful, virginal faces awaiting a passport to the mythological United States, where people could be elevated by opportunity and talent. All Hugo had to do was ask aloud, and any of them would be his. The air smelled deliciously of just one course from the menu: popcorn.

If only Hugo could have turned away then. If only he could have been genuinely haughty. Then, maybe, counterintuitively, he would have had a chance at his Sunnyside.

Instead, Hugo reached out, and, breaking free from her sisters, the wayward Vasilisa came forth.

"No," Anna called, for she had seen what was written on Hugo's face, and she felt disappointment, jealousy, happiness at her sister's boldness.

Hugo's heart leapt. Of all the three, Vasilisa had the most frightening spirit, and at his best, he understood that fear, tempered by faith, became love. Having stepped closer, Vasilisa glanced behind her. She did not really know what to do next. Finally, she bit down on her lip and extended her hand, palm cupped.

Hugo smiled. "For me?" he asked.

She nodded quickly.

Hugo stepped closer. His boots slapped against the floor, his woolen trousers rubbed like sailcloth. When he was close enough, he realized he must smell like an animal, but if anything, that seemed to ignite a fire in young Vasilisa's eyes. He put his hand out gently.

Vasilisa withdrew her hand. She tried to be crafty. "All of us want to go to America," she said. "Our parents are there. They might be in the photoplays by now. They love us terribly."

"All right," Hugo said. He had no idea what she was talking about, but he didn't need to understand.

No matter that the Meshchersky family—father and mother and nieces and brother and governess—were now in Elko, Nevada, attending to their jobs at a Basque restaurant, and the father would soon be fired for pilfering just a bottle cap of potato vodka and need to find work at the gasoline station, where he would wear coveralls and smell of aviation fuel and stare down the desert highway, a long, straight, perfect line of dust, working his jaws as senselessly as a cow chewing cud. Really: that was of no matter. For, even so, Hugo, lit by the sepia shine of the torchères, was close to getting what he had always wanted.

No matter. Hugo put Vasilisa's hand atop his. Hers was cold to the touch, tiny, softer than any other girl's. It was folded over loosely, not quite a fist. There was a single freckle on one knuckle, and she wore two rings, silver, on her index finger, and the nail of her thumb had gone ragged from biting.

She uncupped her hand. "For you," she said. It was her dowry. The only thing she had left on earth, and in fact something she had received herself only a few minutes ago.

It was a single, foil-wrapped square of Cadbury chocolate.

The dancing had caused Hugo to perspire. He could see again, outside the immediacy of the light, how the walls were painted with tree trunks and the timbers of the roof with leaves. He felt as if he stood on a bridge between his real life and one promised. Something was coming to an end. "Vasilisa," he said quietly. "Is this yours?"

She shook her head. She pointed to him. It was his now.

"I—I don't—it's lovely, but where did it come from?"

From a distance, Aarne cleared his throat. "In a sense, it was yours already, Private Hugo."

Hugo looked at him blankly.

"Spoils of war. I gave it to the child after liberating it from the Bolo outside." Aarne patted Hugo on the sleeve. "She likes you, and so she gives it to you freely."

It weighed nothing. Hugo could smell flowers, the fireplace, he could taste the ice cream that had caught in his mustache. His eyes blinked, and the chocolate candy went into and out of focus, and he knew beyond knowing that he had killed Wodziczko. The tiny man, lovesick for Hugo, must have volunteered to follow him, and Gordon had probably opened the door for him. And Hugo had shot him in the ear, and then shot him through the head with the crossbow. He saw it now from the perspective of memory, which was merciless, for it had as many angles as there were stories to tell.

Hugo was aware how much the house they were in weighed—tons of timber, tons of stone—and how the paint on the walls, the pastoral scene, weighed almost nothing.

His mouth trembled. Vasilisa, round and lucid eyes blinking, looked up toward him. Carefully, he took her hand, and placed the chocolate back into her palm. He held it there, no matter how hard she tried to give it to him. And then her eyes left him. For such a spirited girl, her eyes filled with tears surprisingly quickly. She returned to her sisters, who swept their arms around her.

Poor children. The evening was drawing to a close, and their stories to a close soon after. They were whispering to one another in Russian that they were still safe, for their parents were undoubtedly negotiating with many interested people. They were wrong. They were all going to die. Hugo first, the princesses next. Months from now, not long really, all three princesses would die horribly, never rescued. Is it important to know which was strangled, which hanged herself, which had things far worse done? Or is it more important to look away?

Above the room now, looking down—its timbers and floors and the sylvan glade painted on its walls—this small group was beginning to fall apart. Aarne was tidying dishes, knives, and forks without a single clatter. There were only moments left. This evening would disappear, and no one would ever know about it.

Here was Hugo, facing the sisters, the two eldest kissing Vasilisa at the edge of the dance floor in their own, learned, shared, wavelike rhythms. Goodbye, they were all thinking. Hugo could feel the lateness of the hour.

How Wodziczko had just stood in the courtyard, neither retreating nor attacking. Standing. The impact. The flight of the bolt. Hugo could see the door through which he'd entered. He knew how cold it would be outside. Goodbye.

The princesses claimed, separately and together, that their guest's charm and vigor had made them stay awake longer than they should. A groom would take Hugo back to Solnechny Strana via pony sleigh. As he was being told he'd been delightful to come, Hugo saw Wodziczko put his pawlike mitten to his ear. The princesses were telling him he was so brave to have saved them, such a dancer, so graceful, they were forever in his debt. They filed to the end of the room, and each curtsied toward Hugo, made the sign of the cross, and left, Anna first, then Maria, then Vasilisa, each of them using motions identical to her sisters. There wasn't a hesitation among them.

Hugo was left alone.

The room seemed especially empty now. It seemed to be so late the clock didn't actually have an hour for it. Aarne returned with Hugo's vast coat, which, now that he had been separated from it for several hours, he realized stank of garbage. He could hear the bolt leaving his crossbow. He could feel how the tiller quivered.

Outside, they were once again beside the Greek Orthodox cross in the courtyard. The pony was being harnessed.

There's a pony, Hugo thought. *And a groom.*

"I'm sorry there are just two gifts for you," Aarne finally said, indicating the crossbow and the flask. "Tradition calls for three gifts." He didn't say the obvious: that Hugo had declined the most precious gift of them all.

Hugo snuffled wetly. "Why did you think there were Bolos coming tonight?"

Aarne said, "Here, maybe this handkerchief can be the third gift, Monsieur Hugo. Your nose . . ."

"I'm sorry," he whispered.

"For what?" Aarne chuckled. "You rescued princesses. *Zuhp, zuhp!*," he said. "Take your handkerchief and your crossbow and your flask."

Hugo asked, "What's in it?"

"Didn't I tell you?"

"No."

"Just a little Chartreuse."

"Chartreuse?"

"The liqueur is called Chartreuse. In the grand scheme of all the troubles, it's nothing, it's . . ." Aarne looked directly at Hugo for the first time since they'd come outside. He did not understand why this soldier was so miserable, or so stupid as to leave, but he decided to show him some mercy. "Well, I suppose it's quite special." He continued: It was made by monks, but not the monks who had once been here. There were over 130 herbs involved, and every monk knew only a handful of ingredients. Rather a delicacy, but he had managed to hold on to a few bottles throughout the troubles here.

Hugo looked at his flask with new respect. Aarne tapped it with his fingertips, and nodded: yes, this was quite a treasure. In fact, they had Chartreuse in France, but it wasn't the real thing. If one were in Paris, what one had to do, of course, in the right places, of course, where there were no menus, one would never order *Chartreuse,* for you would be brought an inferior imitation. No, one would ask for *Tarragona,* which was the name of the secret distillery in Spain where the monks now toiled in isolation. That was what Hugo had in his flask, Aarne declared. It was said never to be the same for two consecutive sips. It was the taste of possibility.

When Aarne had finished, Hugo impulsively hugged him. Aarne bore it stiffly, patting Hugo on the side the way one would a dog who had hunted well, then poorly.

"You're actually going?" Aarne said.

Hugo nodded.

Aarne looked back toward the abbot's house as if it might shimmer away like a mirage. He blew on his hands sadly. "Well, I suppose this has all been *une fausse idée claire.*"

It had been the first time all evening Hugo had been unable to understand a phrase. *Fausse?* He asked what Aarne meant, and the tiny man stumbled around a definition before landing on "a beautiful idea that doesn't work."

There was a large, barricaded gate, which Aarne opened, and then Hugo's pony left the compound. The gate slid shut behind him. The groom flicked his whip, and the pony began to trot, but almost immediately Hugo asked him to stop.

They were in the clearing where he had shot Wodziczko. "Hold, stop, stop!" he cried. The groom understood only when Hugo grabbed him. Hugo left the cradle of the sleigh, crunching across the hardpack until he found the area most trampled and soiled. But there was no body. He could see marks in the snow. Wodziczko had been dragged away. He would be stripped, just like the bodies Hugo had seen in the river. There was nothing from him except a single sheet of paper, its red borders glowing under the wicked moon.

ALLIES AND AMERICANS: WHO IS YOUR ENEMY? THE WAR MONGERING BUSINESSMAN? OR THE RUSSIAN WORKING MAN?

With both hands, Hugo scooped it up as if it were bound for a reliquary. He squared its edges as he trudged back to the sleigh. A perfect gift from Russia.

The bells on the reins jingled, and the pony went back to its trot. As the monastery was pulled back into the forest, it felt less and less real to Hugo. Had he actually killed Wodziczko? Had there really been women there? Had he broken their hearts? Over the long minutes when the sleigh slid over the snow, Hugo felt growing an anger that had no specific source that he could trace. It was a simple stone-cold sense that he had always hated the world. And that he hadn't honestly known this until now.

The motion of the sleigh was gentle. The horse occasionally snorted, and the bells on the reins sometimes shook, but the rhythm hardly distracted Hugo. The shadows on his face were flinty, as the moonlight that night was brilliant. As the peasants would say, it was as bright and cruel as the awful eye of St. Cassian, whose glare turns the flour bitter in its sack. And under this moon, Hugo began to read the broadside, first aloud and in a mocking voice, and then silently, with a curiosity formerly reserved for the rules of high society.

41

February 1919 in France. The rain changed to sleet. Lee Duncan spent hours insulating his shed, where he now lived with his puppies, with newspaper and leftover canvas. He brought in a stove, and at night he heated up bricks and put them under the dogs' bed. One night he accidentally set fire to his finger puppets, which was all right, in that he'd had two furloughs, so he already had a second pair, and a third.

The puppies were now five months old. Boy was wild, and had stead-fastly refused to learn anything more complex than housetraining. But his sister was different.

"Thomas," Lee said to the man who had once fed Boy some ham fat. "Watch."

Thomas wiped his hands on his apron.

"Okay, Nanette. Come. Sit." Lee laid down a piece of biscuit. "Nanette, this is a gift to you. From the Kaiser." She glanced at the biscuit, then glanced away, offended. "Wait, I'm sorry, girl. It's from General Pershing." She fell on it as if she meant to kill it, and a second later it was gone.

Duncan looked at Thomas, who didn't know he was supposed to have a response. "Firefly wrote me another letter," he finally said. "Do you want to see?"

There was a festival in the village, something that went back to pagan times, involving burning cedar logs from a distant forest and throwing in bundles of herbs, and then everyone would get drunk. The enlisted men of the 135th came that night, and they brought instruments. Duncan brought his dogs.

Since there was dancing, Boy was particularly excited, whimpering (he hadn't yet found his bark) and paddling at the air, as if hoping to cut in. Nanette ignored the distraction, focusing on her owner, who had a half-constructed plan in mind.

The center of town, where the two roads crossed, was more or less a heap of mud divots that was home tonight to a pyre of logs around which the carousing clustered. Enlisted men drank with the women of the brothel, whose sour looks Lee endured. The smell of burning rosemary was intoxicating. When a girl flashed her underskirt, the men cried out, *"Magnifique,"* which became three syllables of a happy song.

"Sit," Lee said, and Nanette sat. "Stay. Stay. Stay." While he spoke, he was walking backward. "Stay." Her eyes were on him as if he were about to unveil a roast. One by one, the villagers and soldiers stopped what they were doing, and looked with amusement at the serious dog whose owner was walking backward around the fire pit. "Stay," he said, which caused some spontaneous laughter, for he was now completely out of the dog's sight, and on the other side of the flames.

When Lee was directly across from Nanette, with only the eight feet of fire separating them, he said something no one expected to hear. "Come."

She was up like a shot, sprinted toward the flame, and stopped dead. Then, seeming to size up her opponent, she trotted back, licking her lips. Brief laughter—the dog clearly wasn't stupid—and then the laughter stopped, for Nanette was only backing up to get enough momentum.

She sprinted, her body lengthening and going low to the ground, and then she launched herself through the wall of flames, landing at Lee's feet.

"Good girl," he said, and gave her the squeaky toy.

A cry of amazement, and now Lee was congratulated, for no one had seen anything like that. The villagers surrounded him to pet his dogs (both of them were overwhelmed and shy), and some of the whores seemed to give him slightly more approving looks. He decided to close with the big finale.

"Nanette? Catch." He lobbed something her way, and she threw her head back to catch it in her mouth. It was a pineapple grenade. Gently, she placed it on the ground.

"What the hell, Duncan?" cried one of his squadron. Nanette had one paw on the grenade, pulling out the pin between her teeth. She looked up with satisfaction. As a unit, the village screamed—people ran in every direction. Mayhem.

"It's not armed," Lee called into the chaos. "It's a gooseberry." But he was not heard, and the screaming continued.

The impact of the evening was that his rehabilitation in the eyes of the village would never be complete. The enlisted men, when they forgave him, thought it had been an excellent prank. They would forever remember it as their comrades rather than themselves panicking. A few of them collared Lee and told him of an upcoming competition he should try out for. It wasn't for a few months, but he was bound to win.

When he returned to his shed, he put the stove alight and started to warm the bricks up. His dogs were collapsed together on their cot. He enjoyed what he'd done. Except for the screaming. But he was growing confident that his ideas were good, and that he and his dogs had a future.

He had in mind a new trick Nanette could do with proper training. For the next few weeks, he and his dogs worked at perfecting it, but only the competition would prove whether it was genius or another generation of battles between settlers and Indians with giant rocks.

42

February 10   Did Not Shoot. Mr. Chaplin ill.
February 11   Did Not Shoot. Mr. Chaplin ill.
February 12   Did Not Shoot. Mr. Chaplin ill.
February 13   Did Not Shoot. Mr. Chaplin ill.
February 14   Did Not Shoot. Mr. Chaplin ill.
February 17   Did Not Shoot. Mr. Chaplin ill.

☆   ☆   ☆

Chaplin dressed the ponderous bulk of Henry Bergman as Edna's father. After three days, Chaplin decided he was Jewish, and he sent Bergman to be fitted with a yarmulke and had the Hebrew newspaper brought to the set. Then he couldn't think of anything. He decided to go home.

The next day, he found a telegram from Associated First National Pictures Exhibitor Exchange, Inc., on his desk, beneath the marmalade cat, who protested when he moved her to read it. The telegram reminded him that the corporation had planned four weeks for *Sunnyside,* and he was now four *months* into shooting, and a shocking $18,300 over budget. The telegram ended PLEASE ADVISE.

The cat jumped back into place, and Chaplin stroked her cheek. It was eight o'clock. The crew was waiting. But William McAdoo was walking across the courtyard. He hadn't expected McAdoo. A moment later, Chaplin was in the courtyard.

"Bill!"

McAdoo drew up short. "Hello, Charlie. How's *Sunnyside?*"

"It's fine."

"Are you finished with it yet?"

"Almost. To what do I owe the visit?"

McAdoo rubbed his chin. "Honestly . . ." His eyes wandered toward Edna's bungalow, and then, because he hadn't the soul of a criminal, he looked away. He could not have been more conspicuously *not* looking at Edna's bungalow had he started whistling.

Chaplin folded his arms. "She isn't here, you know." And as he said it, he hoped this meant McAdoo was just a suitor with no particular understanding of Edna's schedule.

"No? No, well, right, I know that." McAdoo looked slightly red. "I just wanted to, to— I'm not very good at subterfuge here, and—"

"Oh, that's all right. Would you like a cup of tea?"

"I don't really have time, Charlie, but . . ."

The discomfort delighted him. McAdoo seemed about twelve years old. Chaplin forcefully led him to the stage, which was now converted to the dingy *Sunnyside* hotel set, floorboards interrupted with clumps of grass. There was a check-in desk smeared with dirt, a general-store counter dotted with preserves and tins of food, and four broken chairs around a pot-bellied stove, next to a shabby excuse for a barber's chair.

The stove was a working one; Chaplin put a kettle atop it and indicated that McAdoo should sit, which he did, with difficulty, on a chair that might not hold his weight.

"How goes the Big Store?" asked Chaplin.

"Golly, it's bad."

Which Chaplin hadn't expected. "Is it?"

"These are ruthless folks, it turns out."

"Well. I can play that game," Chaplin said.

McAdoo took off his spectacles, fogged them, and put them back on. "Yeah. Huh. I don't think so."

"Perhaps you underestimate me," he said, while staring at his teapot.

"No, it's not that. It's just math, is all. Your films bring in, what, four million a year, maybe five? Well, they want an industry that's about a quarter billion a year when they're done." McAdoo put his hand high in the air. "That's them." He put it near the ground. "That's you. And that's not to scale."

"I understand."

"I could do it to scale. . . ." He shrugged. "They'll crush you."

"They can't keep me from making movies," Chaplin declared after a moment.

"If they own the means of production and distribution, sure, they can."

"Production and . . . Oh."

And there it sat. Chaplin knitted his hands and cracked his knuckles. The spout was beginning to go warm with steam. He had the terrible feeling he'd been playing cards and hadn't known it and had just woken up to an unfortunate hand before him. He wanted to say, "If all they can do is bring my mother here . . ." but he knew McAdoo wouldn't understand how having his mother in California could be bad, or part of a scheme. The neck of the kettle was sweating, and the base was beginning to glow. He felt a net beginning to draw shut around him.

"Try not to think about it," McAdoo said, and gave Chaplin a friendly pat. "You've got your farm film done, and a lovely wife, and, golly, a baby soon. Your mom is here, you can finally take care of her. That's a kind of satisfaction no one can take away from you."

"Yes," Chaplin said, fingers swimming back and forth in the steam.

The conversation wound down, and McAdoo said he should really let Chaplin get back to work, and Chaplin agreed, and they shook hands, and Chaplin pretended to go into his office, but simply watched where McAdoo had gone.

Chaplin gave McAdoo five minutes, exactly, and then darted to Edna's bungalow. He rapped on the door and, without waiting for a response, twisted the knob and threw the door open, like a husband returning from a business trip.

"Well," he said, before seeing anything. His fists were on his hips, and he was ready to lecture on all the ways he had been disappointed. The room was cozy and tidy, a mock cottage, with flocked wallpaper, two bouquets of flowers (he paid for them to be changed twice a week), and a pair of ornate, weathered velvet wing chairs flanking a Batchelder-tiled fireplace. McAdoo was sitting, tie still noosed within his collar, legs crossed with ankle over knee, showing a length of black silk sock, a sheaf of papers in his lap.

In the other chair, in a simple velvet dress, hunched with concentration, glasses on the end of her nose, was Pickford.

43

"Oh," Chaplin said. And then "Oh!" For coming upon Pickford and McAdoo in a tête-à-tête led his mind to horrific images. And Doug!

"Charlie," Pickford said. "Sit."

"I'm not—I'm not your lapdog, Mary."

He noticed a traveling projector and screen set up. She tossed down a folder of legal onionskin. "You're involved in this. Bill wanted to wait until we had run some figures."

"What are you talking about?"

McAdoo had said nothing. A man profoundly uninterested in surprises, he looked off balance.

"If you'd like to leave us alone, Bill? Please, sit down, Charlie," Pickford said. McAdoo folded up his papers. He hesitated by the door, as if searching for a good parting word, but couldn't find one. The door closed quietly behind him.

Chaplin watched him go. "What are you doing here?" He imagined that McAdoo and Pickford, in postcoital bliss, had hatched some crazed scheme to steal Edna's services away.

"I'm attempting a levelheaded solution to this." She handed Chaplin an envelope.

He did not open it. "I want that girl Zasu back."

"Charlie, the heads of every studio are meeting in three days. They're going to forge an alliance with the exhibitors and the owners of about seventy-five percent of the motion-picture houses in the country. They have all their plans in place. In six months, every actor, writer, and director in the business will be at their mercy." She had said all of this as if reading names from a city directory.

"So you and Bill were just meeting here?" His voice was a full octave higher than usual.

"Oh, for God's sake," Pickford cried. "Are you completely— What are you talking about?"

He looked down at his large hands, which were playing with the envelope. He opened it, and looked at the few sheets of paper inside, which probably confirmed everything Mary had said. Thinking was very difficult right now. In his mind's eye, all he could see was Doug waving at him from below his bedroom window, months ago. He wanted to tell Pickford how he hated crowds, how difficult it had been to speak at the Liberty Loan rally, and wouldn't it be clever to have statues come to life? He wanted to be in an audience watching wonderful things.

"Charlie, how many films left on your contract?"

"A thousand."

"Please."

"*Sunnyside* is number three. I have five more."

"If your life depended on it, how quickly could you finish those?"

"Never?"

She stamped her foot on the floor, which caused Chaplin to jump. "How soon can you finish your contract?"

"Two years, maybe."

"That's too long."

"These things take time," he cried. "You can't rush inspiration."

"Fuck inspiration," she said. Chaplin heard a gasp, and looked carefully at Mary, who was still staring at him. Which is when he realized that *he* had gasped.

"Charlie, how many movies did you make last year?" Her voice was piercing and yet light, like a sparrow's.

"Three."

"Three?"

"Two? I'm still working on the third."

"Last year, Harold Lloyd made thirty-four films."

"Oh, Harold Lloyd." He stood and waved his arms. "That third-rate—Lonesome Luke, golly, Mary, I wonder where he got that from? A poor bloke with a mustache and big shoes who gets into trouble, who—"

"Thirty-four films. In one year. And he isn't Lonesome Luke anymore. He has a new character that isn't based on you. And you know what? He's good."

"He's not that good."

"He's good enough." She chewed her lip. "Arbuckle. He's doing features."

"So what?" Chaplin sputtered. "So— Features? You can't carry a comedy over six reels. It's impossible."

"Zukor is showcasing him. Arbuckle is going to make three million, guaranteed. If the films work, he could make six million."

"Three—" Chaplin stopped. "Six? To make features? I thought everyone was getting cut out of the money."

"Arbuckle is the proof that the new trust will be generous to those of us who play well with others," she said.

He felt as if he were dissolving, as if someone were leeching the life from his body. He sat back down. "I can't . . ."

"I think we can fight them. Bill does, too. We have an idea, but we can't do it without you."

"Mary, I'm having a very difficult time right now. I don't know if you've noticed, but I'm . . ."

"Just calm down. Can I show you something?" Her eyes were soft behind her spectacles as she thumbed through the folder on the table. "Here." The way she said it, childlike, soothing, he imagined she was going to show him a photo of a kitten, a drawing of a castle.

It was a mathematical formula. The hand was familiar. It took up most of the page, with delta signs, functions and integrals, imaginary numbers in strange repetition, like place settings at a table, and tucked among them like dinner guests were odd words like "stand-in," "ego," "audience," "diegetic effect," "fear," "pleasure," "earning capacity."

Pickford explained: McAdoo had been working on this since the Liberty Loan campaign. He felt there was some function to movie stardom that had its own value beyond simple dollars. It was based in part on work by a German psychologist, she couldn't remember the name. " 'It was the darnedest thing,' " she said, imitating McAdoo with a precision that annoyed Chaplin. " 'I thought I found an integer these producers don't know about. And *they found it and they use it every dingdong day.* Golly,' " she finished. "Well, you know how he gets."

Chaplin laughed meekly. "Squirrels and pigeons and . . . Gosh . . ."

"He says our whereabouts are a commodity. He says that's something new."

This was the moment he was supposed to turn around and launch an offensive. Scrappy. But Chaplin felt like a hollow log, no heart, just a quiet urge to decay alone somewhere. "Can I explain something?" He knew she was the one person on earth it was important to tell this to. "*Sunnyside.* It ends with the Little Fellow's death," he whispered.

Pickford sat back in her chair. She moved her jaw from side to side, an old exercise from her theater days. "I don't think so."

"It's inevitable. It's— What do you mean, 'I don't think so'?"

He waited for her to say more, even as she was waiting for him to understand. He tried to put what she was saying in a positive or negative light, and he could not.

"Finish your film."

"I want it to be good."

"I've seen what you've shot."

"You have?"

She indicated the projector. "I had it screened."

"Oh, God."

"You're a genius," she said, and that *should* have sounded fine, and then she added, "so you'll pull through. But the problem is," she said, and she hesitated, "there are two ways to be a genius. One is to be a genius and hope the world notices. The other way is to show contempt for your audience. They'll mistake that for genius. If you make them feel bad for not understanding, they'll figure the fault is their own."

"All right," he said, knowing something worse was coming. "I hope you enjoyed the— Well, the farm scenes aren't inspired, but the museum is obviously, that's—"

"You have to get rid of that."

"Pardon?"

"The museum business is all about contempt."

"No," he said meekly. "No, I'm not doing it like that. I'm doing it for the world." With confidence now, he continued, "To combat all the blue-stockings from Northumberland and stick up for all the artists who are being eternally censored."

Until she spoke, he was sure she was going to be wrong. "What artists?"

"Well—"

"No. Really. Who? Who are you defending?" Mary shook her head. "Don't make this movie. Not like this. Get rid of the museum reel, stay on the farm."

"But the farm is no good."

"Then make the next one good. It doesn't matter."

"Stop saying that. I don't know what that means. Stop pointing at that formula. I don't know what that means, either." There were tears standing in his eyes. He felt, even though it was clear Pickford was not attacking him, like the stupidest boy in the world. "I just want to go home."

Quietly but stubbornly, she continued, a nurse making a bitter and frail old man take his pill. "People hear there's a new Chaplin and they come see it. If they enjoy it, so much the better. But if they don't, they'll see the next one. It's something no one has really understood how to capitalize on yet. That's what this formula is saying."

He felt dull and hollow and he could not sit up straight. He was almost proud of how easily Mary had pronounced the word "capitalize." "Mary?"

"Yes?"

"Does Frances ever talk about me?"

"What? Frances—does Frances—" She regarded him with confusion. "She's with her fiancé." Mary's gaze went around Chaplin's face as if she were sorting out a map, finding north. "What happened between you two?"

It was a strange feeling, having Pickford's best and only friendship in the palm of his hand. "Nothing," he said.

"What kind of nothing?"

"I . . . just . . . thought she was amusing."

"Fine," Pickford said. She played with her glasses, tugging them. Chaplin was a bit dazed. Had he just done something for Pickford's benefit? "We have an urgent situation here," she said. "I don't tend to lose. It behooves McAdoo and me to work with you on the larger project. I think Doug will be involved. Perhaps Bill Hart. Others, maybe," she said.

"What are you thinking?"

She shook her head. "You need to do something else first."

"Yes?"

"Finish *Sunnyside.* Do whatever that takes."

When Chaplin left the bungalow, he saw McAdoo back on the stage set, holding a teacup between his big, soft hands. McAdoo gave a brief nod. Chaplin's hand was on the doorknob behind him for longer than he meant, and then he broke contact.

It was nine-thirty in the morning. Chaplin stood in the courtyard of the studio built upon his popularity. He started walking. Quickly.

There was trouble at the mill, but there was always trouble at the mill. And it was never flax thieves, or a sabotaged conveyor belt, or fire menacing a poor, deaf servant girl. No, it was the owner himself, wondering if he was meant for a different life. Perhaps, with each turn of the mighty mill-wheel, the owner thought of the sole moment of stolen joy when he kissed the millboy, and how the shameful moment of passion blossomed in his chest until it felt as if it would crush him.

Oh, Mary, how can you fix that ache? There's no medicine you can speed across the frozen river to cure that pain. All the winsome orphans it takes to scrub a foster mother's kitchen floor are shot once in the back of the head by sheer existence.

Here's how it worked in pictures: The Little Fellow is down, and a cop fingers him unjustly. He spends fifteen minutes pulling himself out of the soup, until the end.

But in life, it actually worked like this: diphtheria.

There was no end to trouble. There were only the moments in between.

When he reached his office, he stroked the cat on his desk. There was a typewritten plea from a group of Four Minute Men, now unemployed, that someone hire them in the motion-picture industry. The cat rolled atop it. Frances never thought about him. His hand was trembling.

"Helen?"

His secretary appeared at his door.

"Do you know about girls' clothes? What kind of things my mother would like?"

"I can ask Rhiannon."

"Did she shop for her?"

"When she came." Helen smiled. "Hannah loved it. She bought yards of silk. She said she just wanted to unroll each bolt and lie down, which I thought was so—"

"I want a wardrobe for my mother. Several of everything, hats, gloves, coats, dressing gowns, whatever she needs. Have Rhiannon go to Bullock's and put it on my account. Oh, shoes, of course, and underthings, toiletries, and so forth."

Helen excused herself.

Chaplin checked his watch. "Helen?"

It took a moment, but Helen reappeared, a telephone in her hand, earpiece to her ear.

"Get Alf, please."

Five minutes later, Chaplin was telling Alf to pack up the bread trucks with lights, reflectors, cameras, and film and take them back to the Phelps Ranch property. They were going to rent it again this afternoon. "Oh, and, Alf? How many angels do we have on payroll now?"

Out came the cigar. He counted on his fingers. "Six, I think. Maybe four."

"Have them come to the set."

"Is this for after you're dead?"

"I want to finish this."

"Right-o." The cigar went back into the mouth.

Chaplin spent another half hour on the telephone. His mouth moved, he wrote down times and figures, he laughed when necessary, and expressed urgency at times. It felt like nothing. By ten-thirty, he had planned out the afternoon, including the shoot at the ranch, with all its contingent problems.

He waited in his office. He watched the courtyard. As time passed, it was sunny and then sunny and then sunny, as if the quality of light in this part of his world did not age.

44

When she arrived, Hannah was greeted by the new friends she had made. The checkerboard and a table and two chairs floated her way, for she was the best draughts player anyone had met, and when she was told this, she smiled and stuffed the ends of her scarf in her mouth. Today Maverick sat on the other side of the board, and said he was surely going to win this time. Sandwiches were brought to them. Twice, Hannah asked Maverick what that was, over there, and when he looked, she filched a sandwich into her pocket.

Chaplin watched this through the window. He was in street clothes. He ran his fingers along the band inside his cap. He asked Helen to remind Rollie to bring his new lens, the Zeiss Tessar, to the shoot.

The game lasted hardly five minutes. Hannah slaughtered Maverick, who had tried his hardest. A moment later, Chaplin was behind his mother's chair. "Mum? Should we take a walk?"

She looked up at him, shading her eyes and squinting.

"I think I can promise there will be ice cream."

"Shall I get my things?"

"No, that's all right. It's just down the block."

Chaplin and Hannah walked into the office, where he waved to Helen. "Maverick fancies you," Hannah said to her. Helen blushed, for this was true, and she looked toward Hannah for some further comment, but she had already opened the front door and stepped down the three brick risers onto De Longpre. Once on the sidewalk, she turned in place, a full circuit, unsure of where to go.

"This way," Chaplin said, pointing toward Sunset. She had to walk slowly, not so much from infirmity as in a constant amazement at her surroundings. He saw her taking them in, and then it was as if a veil were falling. It was too sunny. She walked with one hand shading her eyes.

"Oh," he said. The sun reflecting on the mica in the newly poured sidewalks was indeed painful. "Wait here, Mum. I have something."

He stepped back into the studio. He asked the electricians if he could borrow some accessories they had just purchased. The Klieg lights were so bright that an hour or two under them sent many actors into temporary blindness. The remedy was to balm the eyelids with castor oil or tea leaves. When Doug finished a film, he spent a week that way. The American Society of Cinematographers, in conjunction with Bausch & Lomb, had come up with a better solution, and this is what Chaplin returned to the sidewalk with.

"Here, Mum."

She held what Chaplin gave her with puzzlement. It was a pair of spectacles, but the lenses were opaque.

"Sunglasses." He put on a pair, to show her how it was done. She burst out laughing.

"They'll think we're blind."

"You won't have to squint," he explained. Hesitantly, she, too, put them on.

"Better?" he asked.

She leaned over a Cadillac parked at the curb and cocked her head to see the woman wearing sunglasses. "Doesn't seem right, somehow," she murmured.

"Let's go to Taylor's," Chaplin said. He checked his watch.

"Is it very far?"

"It's on the corner."

"These sunglasses aren't that nice, really."

He could not remember the last time he had walked up the street. There were few people in view. The orchard across the street was empty; a real-estate company had purchased it and planned to put up houses. There was a line of stores on La Brea that he had once shopped at. The clothes in the window were of a fashion he no longer recognized: beaded purses for women, large, overbearing fur coats—was that raccoon?—for men. Why?

"The little mouse, he seems to enjoy his wheel."

"You know, Mother . . ." It interrupted her, which made him feel awful. "That's Helmen's barbershop, over there. I used to go get my haircut there. About a year ago, I had to stop going, and I have a man come to the studio instead. It's social—I have him do it in the courtyard, and I sign papers, and people joke with me—but it's lonely, you know. Even so, it's lonely." Helmen's, the brick façade, the transom over which a young boy had once slithered on a truth-or-dare, spending the night crying among the fallen hair. Helmen's with the four chairs, discussions about how the ponies were running—all out of Chaplin's life now, because when he last sat in the chair for a shave, by the time the hot towels came off, there was a crowd outside. They didn't seem to want anything except to see him, which made it more frightening.

It had gotten warm in the last few minutes. Chaplin was beginning to sweat. Hannah's pace was slow but steady. She's not that old, Chaplin thought. She's only fifty-four.

"Here," he said.

They were by Taylor's Market on Sunset. There were heaps of oranges and apples and pears in bins along the front, and inside, where it was warmer, there were long shelves stacked with cans of food. To the side was a delicatessen case, whose metal racks were groaning with meats and cheese. His mother raised her glasses. She fell silent.

"Would you like ice cream?"

She nodded.

"Two ice-cream cones," Chaplin said with an easy smile to Mr. Taylor, behind the counter. Then he put his hands in his back pockets and rocked in place on his heels.

"You should take those glasses off, Charlie, when you're indoors."

He did so.

"They won't be penny licks?"

"No, Mum."

She watched the grocer half vanish into the standing freezer, digging his scoop into the ice-cream bin.

"Excuse me," she said to him.

He looked up. He was about Chaplin's age, with tired eyes that had red rims to them. He smelled not of alcohol but of a life hard-lived.

"It's not a penny lick, is it?"

"What?"

"Hey," Hannah said, "a penny lick? Or something diffrunt?" With an ease that sent chills down his spine, Hannah had just used Mildred's intonations perfectly.

"What's a penny lick?" Taylor asked.

"No, Mum. I'm sorry, Mr. Taylor. My mother is from England. A penny lick"—he tried to use his hands to describe a flower vase—"it's a type of glass instead of a cone that— It makes the ice cream look larger and better than what you actually get." Then, "No, Mum, here in Hollywood it's not about penny licks—it's all waffle cones."

"Yeah," Taylor said. A moment later, he handed Hannah the first cone and went back to the bin, digging more.

Hannah leaned into her son and whispered, "He fought with his wife last night." She had adjusted her sunglasses so they sat atop her hair. She flicked her eyes sideways and touched the side of her nose. Chaplin looked where she wanted him to: there was a cot behind the counter, with a blanket thrown across it. "If she made him sleep here all the time—"

"Mum, shh."

"—he would have made the bed, don't you think? Plus," she whispered, "the toothbrush?"

Then Taylor returned with the second cone. "Thank you," Chaplin said, handing him a dime.

"Thank you," Hannah said. As they left, she was regarding Taylor with a smile that likely mystified him. She put her sunglasses in place when they reached the street corner. "I've changed my mind. I like sunglasses."

"There's a bench by the trolley tracks." There was a pepper tree behind the bench, giving them shade. Hannah took licks of her ice-cream cone, dabbing at the creases of her mouth every few moments. He could feel her full engagement with the ice cream. Part of her mind had eased away, the part that judged and processed information, and she was left relaxed, just the animal in her that recognized when something was sweet. "Mum?" He checked his watch.

"Charlie?"

"Did I tell you that I used to describe things for you, but silently?"

"Whatever does that mean?"

"When you were away, and I was alone, when things would happen, I would tell you about them."

"When?"

"I don't know when it started. But I only noticed myself doing it when I was onstage and I was fourteen or fifteen. I don't remember the show, but I remember, as I was acting in it, I was also narrating it. Not aloud, just . . . It was as if I was telling myself about what was happening to me but I was also telling you. Because I knew that when you were safe you would want to hear."

She cocked her head at the word. "Safe?"

He nodded. He wanted some sign she understood, but she was looking forward, and then glancing down at her cone, and then looking at her hand through the glasses as if worried she could see her own bones.

"I used to think that when you were finally safe I could tell you about all that I'd done. But I don't do that anymore. Do you think that's pathetic?"

She considered this. "I don't know."

"When I was directing, the first few times I did it, I was narrating it for myself. I was saying, 'Here I am, directing Mabel Normand, and now I'm telling her to use her eyes to show us the burglar is hiding in the cupboard.' And when I was walking to work, or having dinner with the crew, I used to say, 'Here I am, feeling wonderful,' or 'Now I'm frightened.' I did that for you, because I thought that perhaps you could hear me. Was that pathetic? Or is it pathetic now that I don't do that?"

She did not answer. Instead, she raised her glasses up. Her eyes, surveying his face, reminded him of a place he had read about in books. A foreign jungle village ringed by a high wall that would not give up secrets because it did not speak the same language as anyone else.

"Are you feeling sad?" she asked.

"No."

"Come here and give the old crone a hug, then."

On the bench, under the swaying pepper tree, Chaplin hugged his mother. She stiffened. He let her go.

"It's okay if you don't love your mother," she said.

"Of course I—"

"No, don't say it. You don't mean it, Charlie. That's all by the wayside now."

"But I do." He could see, a block away, a red car from the Long Beach Line. It was seven minutes past twelve. The car was taking on passengers. Others were stepping off, even though it was an express and they were technically between stations. It always worked like that: the train conductors were so friendly and understanding, and it was always their neighbors they were helping, or so Chaplin remembered from his few trips. He had eaten his ice-cream cone, and it was gone. The trolley launched forward, down the tracks.

"Mum," he whispered.

"Charlie." She, too, had finished her cone. Her head tilted back as she yawned. She looked as if she might be sleepy behind her glasses.

"If you were to travel, how would you go?"

"What do you mean?"

"If you were taking a trip, would you go by airplane?"

"Oh, no, not that way."

"Take off your glasses, Mum. There you go. Now, close your eyes. Are they good and closed?" he asked. She was smiling; she liked the game. "Would you travel by boat?"

She shook her head, eyes closed tightly.

"By motorbus?"

She shook her head. She had broken her nose when she was only a girl, playing with some older, meaner children, who told her to run straight, that the tree would move out of her way. Another day, she had chipped her front teeth, and he could never get the proper story from her about that. She had always looked concerned, he now realized, as if she had never relaxed a day in her life. Even when she was telling him stories to put him to bed, her lips were clenched as if she might have to interrupt at any moment to fight murderers. But also she promised she could throw it off. If only the money came. If only the man brought the food he promised. If only the stage manager would send for an act at the last minute to fill in. Then it would be all peaches. A contagious feeling, too.

"Mum," he whispered. The trolley was easing to a stop before them. His people were on board. "Would you like to travel by soap bubble?"

Her eyes popped open, and she was wearing a tranquil smile. It was a look of pure benevolence—I remember that game, it said—which slowly, over the course of a full second, retreated into a pleasurable judgment: she looked as if her son were quite mad. And she still loved him.

As the trolley doors opened, Charlie gave Hannah his arm. He walked her two steps forward, to the bottom rung of the metal stairs. She padded up, one foot above the other, helped into the trolley by hands she did not, at first, question. There was a small crowd around her, greeting her and attending to her carefully, as if she were about to be stored in a reliquary, and men were leaning down to hand him some documents.

In the harbor of San Pedro, a half hour away by trolley, was a ship, and aboard the ship were brand-new leather steamer trunks filled with the finest accessories and clothes available from Bullock's, Seventh and Broadway. The ship was bound for Southhampton, United Kingdom, and its third-finest stateroom was now festive with local flowers (bougainvillea, for instance, on a wood trellis and packed in its own planter) and equipped with a Victrola and a dozen platters of dance-hall tunes.

It was a beautiful day. The trolley's windows were all open. The doors closed. Chaplin wriggled his sunglasses in place, for the glare against the metallic car was fierce. He could see silhouettes inside the cabin, calm, patrician men with mustaches and bowlers all surrounding Hannah, asking her to have a seat; he could hear them saying they were going to be friends.

The cop in the intersection blew his whistle and motioned for the trolley to move forward. It creaked and sang with a metallic whine, wheels turning one full revolution before Hannah poked her head out the window.

Chaplin walked beside the trolley. He waved. All was well. His mother had taken her glasses off, and she looked at him, wheels below her turning once again, then twice, then again, with increasing speed. He went into a trot. He waved.

The motion awakened something in her. She threw both her hands out. They cupped and released the air. She was saying something he couldn't hear. He was now waving goodbye and running beside the trolley, which was about to vanish around the curve of Sunset. She had something in her hand. She was flailing with it, trying to pass it to him. Hands reaching down, she was straining, stretching, and it was too late, the Red Car was gone.

Chaplin slowed down. He was panting. He bent over, hands against his trousers. There, in the dusty street, was what his mother had been trying to give him: what she had stolen during her checkers game. White-flour bread and some cheese and meat between them. She had saved him a bit of sandwich.

Chaplin walked up Sunset to La Brea, where he got into the back of his touring car, which had been waiting for him. He composed a cable to send to Syd.

```
Mother returning England STOP Good seaside
resort STOP Good may come alone STOP
```

Kono drove him to the ranch where they had filmed the Little Fellow's suicide. In the interim, the land had sold for an outrageous sum, and sold again, and it was rumored that it would become one hundred two-bedroom bungalows.

Film had come to Hollywood because of the light, the 350 days of good weather a year, and as the films were released around the world, they proved how beautiful Hollywood was. And so the land was vanishing as quickly as they could film it. The landlocked poet in Collins, Illinois, and the frustrated beauty of Teaneck, New Jersey, saw where they could live in tune with what they had always wanted to be. It was obvious, upon seeing the beaches and hills and palms, that your current self was just a stand-in for someone not yet arrived. If only you could live in such a beautiful place, the rest would change. People at their weakest, most trusting, and childlike moments believed there was out there for them somewhere a Sunnyside. Which meant the place was eventually one hundred two-bedroom bungalows. The mystery not yet solved was how to love a place when your mere presence destroyed it.

Chaplin walked a wild canyon, with culverts and brush and chaparral that would be subsumed by concrete foundations, brick chimneys, red-wood framing, appliances, automobiles, sewer pipe, and the immeasurable weight of a whole world's anticipation. With each step he was reminded of dreams he'd had where he could fly. All he needed to do was speed up his step, which he did now, and lengthen his stride, and let the sky take him.

As the crew watched, Chaplin began to skip. He waved his arms, he bounced from a *demi-plié* to a *tour en l'air*, then a series of *chassés*. And then he pretended to be a chicken.

He was going to finish *Sunnyside* before Zukor and all his lot had their meeting. He was going to finish it today.

Orders were being barked. Film canisters were eased from canvas satchels. Boys with brooms were sweeping away dust. Four women had been costumed in lengths of gauze, and they were currently having garlands of flowers sewn onto their outfits.

Chaplin surveyed the land. There was a road leading into the ranch, and it ran across a narrow bridge, not twenty feet long, over a dry riverbed, and on the other side was the wilder, more remote acreage. He was attracted to the bridge, which was raw plywood nailed to unfinished slats, just sturdy enough for a horse pulling a wagon heaped with hay.

"What's the sky like?" he asked.

"Clear today, mushy tomorrow," the dayboy said.

"If we don't get it today, can we pick it up?"

Shrugs. Then Rollie leveling with him. "Not a chance."

Chaplin ordered the brush trimmed back, and he directed Rollie to find a good place to film so that the dry riverbed and the span of the bridge would be visible.

Rollie followed him as he walked toward the wardrobe tent. "Okay, Charlie, what do you want to rehearse?"

"No rehearsal. What time is sunset?"

"Five-thirty-one today," Rollie said. "Except there's a ridgeline to the west. Let's say five."

"I want to dance," Chaplin said. "Let's have, what, three women I can dance with."

"The agency just sent four."

"Then four. Dress them as— No, better. Goddesses."

And he closed the flaps of the tent. He carefully put his trousers and jacket on wooden hangers, and removed his chambray shirt so that he was in his undergarments.

On went the Max Factor No. 30, and over that, light powder, eyeliner. Then a filthy-looking collarless shirt, a pair of trousers that would swallow a hundred Arbuckles, newly battered size-sixteen shoes that laced up with twenty eyes each. The plaid vest of the Akins tartan, two buttons missing. Spirit gum for the mustache. He wiggled his upper lip. Hat on.

When he returned to the bridge, Rollie was set up on the bank, a two-foot square of black velvet mounted behind the camera, so that he would not lose the pupils in close-up.

Chaplin stared at the bridge as fiercely as if his eyes were welding its joints. The awful little village where the Little Fellow was booted in the behind was to the left, and the sheer wild wonder of paradise was to the right, and the bridge was between them.

Four lovely girls appeared for him, barefoot, one blond, three brunette, in flowing white diaphanous gowns. They introduced themselves—Willie Mae, Olive, Helen, and another Olive, who laughed and said today she would be Olive Ann—and as they spoke, he watched how the sunlight caught their hair. He liked how each of them wore a headband of large white roses mixed with smaller buds of star jasmine, each headdress unique in the rhythm of its design.

"Has any of you seen Nijinsky's *L'Après-midi d'un Faune*? Oh, did that sound pretentious?" He put his hand to his mouth; they all laughed. Good. "He dances like this." Chaplin extended one arm north, one leg south in a lazy arabesque.

It was one o'clock. The first twelve minutes of *Sunnyside* had taken him fourteen weeks to shoot. He had four hours to shoot the eight minutes he needed for a two-reeler. Clearly, it was impossible.

The footage he shot that day began in the ditch, with Chaplin asprawl as if thrown by an explosion. On the bridge above, by magic of double exposure, four nymphs, transparent and then delightfully solid, dance with charming abandon, each girl tethered to the next by a chain of flowers. One happy beast, eight arms, eight legs, and moving with the winds. The togas promote diegetic effect, in that they allow the audience's eye to travel to mysterious and arousing places without shame, for the outfits are classical.

Olive Ann, of the longest brunette hair, tips the flower chain link by link down to Charlie. The flowers tickle his nose. How delightful to awaken when the rescue comes like this. Fluttering his hands like gills, he allows himself to be brought up from the riverbed and into the company of these dreamy fisherwomen. They love what they've caught!

Chaplin swoons, hands to his heart, he pirouettes, and then—a lunge!—they bound into a crescent field, nymphs and satyr, Chaplin's elevation almost supernaturally light as he takes *grands jetés* through bristles of unmown grass. He has quadriceps like a golden Pan, his bones are hollow, his arms are wings, he could leap nine feet in the air. The girls dash away quick as a school of minnows, and he, maintaining the grace of Nijinsky, pursues them with his cornering move, bounding three times on one leg, kicking little puffs of dust behind him. For sixteen frames—a second—the frame is empty except for the transient land-scape. In the background, oak leaves reflect like tiny mirrors when the breeze runs through them.

Then, in the center of the frame, like an asp, is a prickly-pear cactus, its flattened paddles fraught with narrative pull. The Little Fellow chases after Olive Ann, who bows down before him in invitation; he bows back and loses his balance, planting his behind directly into the devilish prickly pear. When he springs up, his dancing, already inspired, is now manic, double-time, and he dashes away; it's time for the girls to pursue him.

Then a curious moment: him rubbing his sore behind, and seeing himself being seen by the girls. He looks into the camera for the only time in all *Sunnyside*. He registers with the audience that it and he both know that there are rules: they are beyond him, time is running out, this will not end well. He shrugs, as if asking, *In that case, why not make the best of it?*

He nabs Olive Ann by the hand. The rest come with, skipping together through the tall grass. When they have left the screen, there is a full sec-ond of the landscape, a perfect day preserved, a place still beautiful with-out them.

Back on the bridge comes the finale. It is as if suitcases are put on beds, candles are being blown out, drapes drawn closed. The Little Fellow dances with Olive Ann again. They bounce like bunnies on the bridge, feet pounding against the plywood. She has sweated through her gown, the roses droop in her hair, but he is as fresh as Narcissus. Behind them is the better part of *Sunnyside,* and ahead of them the village and the world.

Chaplin falls to one knee, hands to his heart, declaring himself; she swoons, she accepts, they're in love, final embrace between them, because now that they're to marry the end is coming.

He throws his head back with a smile, and he addresses heaven. There is no title card to interrupt him. His lips do not move.

We all die alone.

But, of course, no one can hear him.

He makes a lustful and doomed lurch toward Olive Ann, who side-steps, and— ! —he falls off the bridge.

There he is, in the riverbed again, and the girls make a human chain, pulling—again—on a rope made of vines and flowers. He jerks with the motion, he's unconscious, the girls fade away, replaced by a midget, a fat man, a dirty yokel, and the evil boss, who haul him up, boot him in the rear, shove him across the bridge, and laugh until they can hardly stand up, for reasons that are not entirely clear, except cruelty.

By the time they finished, the sun was disappearing behind the hills. Chaplin was trembling. His body ached. His throat was parched. How long was that? he asked. But no one was sure yet. Was it eight minutes? Was it longer? No one knew. He could not remember anything about it.

His hair was mussed. This was the best day of work he had done in months. Three of the four nymphs asked if he was free for dinner. While his crew packed up, he lay down on the floor of the backseat of his automobile, drifting in and out of a daze, one hand on his chest, the thumb and forefinger of the other pinching his nose. He did not know if he was happy.

A touring car picked the nymphs up. The car went down the road from the canyons toward Sunset without anyone from the Chaplin Studios waving goodbye. The four women inside laughed with one another and passed back and forth a flask of gin. They lit cigarettes. Their feet were killing them. Who had a date that night, who most needed a bath, who needed to stop at the blind pig for more gin, did anyone have a hairpin? When the car vanished around the curve, it was gone.

That was the end of the day. Helen never appeared in another moving picture. Nor Olive. Willie Mae was in the background of a handful of one-reelers. Olive Ann played a dancer once or twice and later appeared in photographs taken for artistic purposes and sent from a San Francisco post-office box to hobbyists and enthusiasts across the country. Who can tell if she was happy?

The lovely land of oaks and meadows where they danced with Chaplin would be bulldozed for bungalow housing, but its silver-and-black deep-focus stand-in could be seen, though not lived in, any hour of the night or day forever. And in that way it was like a memory, but not the way memory had worked since the dawn of time. The odd thing about memory now was that it no longer needed a rememberer.

Later, when the footage was developed and assembled, Chaplin edited the scene together. It was exactly two minutes. He still needed to shoot another six minutes to fulfill his contract. He had failed.

In the spring of 1919, with flowers beginning to grow for the first time in five years without threat of being torched to the ground, Elsie Janis, the Sweetheart of the Doughboys, came to France again. When there had still been a Western Front, she was the first girl entertainer allowed up among the razor wire, and her wholesome show—singing, dancing, impersonations, acrobatic kicks, humor, good-natured ribbing—was the standard by which all morale-boosters were judged.

Her 1919 tour ended in Mandres, once a village, now a way station for troops who knew not where their next destination was. As with any stagnant pond, Mandres had grown into a *threat* of a town, with crepuscular entertainments that no commanding officer much wanted to investigate.

No man wanted the Belle of Ohio to see such squalor, and the moral swamp was drained. The saloon became a tearoom. The brothels became barracks, hotels, and cafés. There was a good deal of white paint.

Companies of men were arriving at every moment, from the Air Service, the artillery, the Medical Corps, the marines. At one o'clock, a faint whisper went through the crowd, now over ten thousand strong. The murmur was a command to hush, and as much as they could, they hushed. Then there it was, a prolonged basso hoot, the call of Elsie Janis's train.

At the platform, she leapt off the caboose and turned one of her handsprings and, when she was upright again, cupped both her hands around her mouth and shouted, "Boys, are we downhearted?"

In response, a roar of men thousands strong: "Hell, no!"

The AEF band struck up "Ohio, Ohio," the football-rally song, with extra percussion delivered by doughboys banging wrenches on their pie-plate helmets, which they held at arm's length while Janis led the final cheer from the platform: "Wah-hoo-wah-hoo—rip, zip, bazoo—I yell—like hell—OSU."

When the fuss died down, she shouted, "Is it time to quit?"

"Hell, no!"

"Maybe when the moon and stars butt in?"

"Hell, no!"

"When the bugler calls reveille?"

"Hell, no!"

"Then it's *never* time to quit," she said, and handsprung her way through a zippy rendition of "Delirious."

Thus she held the men until it was time for the talent show. It had been a long winter, and certain of the doughboys had grown obsessive, working the short days and long nights, honing abilities that would bring pride to their companies.

The show began at four o'clock, and Janis led the men there herself, pumping her knees the whole way, with her band playing bugle-fife-and-drum songs behind her. They funneled into an open field at which a grandstand had been erected, so everyone had a better view of the contestants who were now lining up before them, straining at their leashes, and occasionally nipping the air.

The entrants included the following: Sampson, of the 148th Aero Squadron; Blazes, of the 13th Artillery; Tiger Boy, of the 185th Infantry;

Killer and the Black Shadow, both of the 88th Aero Squadron; and Stumpy, whose trainers at the 24th Engineers hadn't realized their dog was supposed to have a frightening name.

As the dogs paraded by, men from each unit walked up and down the grandstand, collecting chits and shouting out odds, because no demonstration of talent was complete without wagering. To this end, legends of feats of strength, endurance, and intelligence were circulating with the passion of Homer recounting the tales of swift-footed Achilles. The Black Shadow could jump six feet from a standing position. Killer could ride on the back of a motorcycle at thirty-five miles per hour, and walk up a tall ladder to fetch a frankfurter.

Lee Duncan stood with his dog amid the rest of them. When attention turned his way, there was some pointing and harsh looks, in that this dog in no way lived up to the reputations of the rest. Whereas Killer and Tiger Boy had to be physically separated after lunging at each other, Lee's dog simply looked bashfully at the crowd and the other contestants, ears folded down not in aggression, but as if she were lost at the circus. Further, the name Nanette was in no way interesting, though the men should have at least suspected something, given that the dog in front of them was clearly male.

But the great sea of khaki was a one-thought-at-a-time lot, and so the odds against Lee grew higher and higher, and by the time he let his dog off his lead, and the dog bolted after a butterfly, stumbling over his outsized paws, the whole crowd roared with laughter. The dog turned and looked at them as if tears were welling up in his eyes. There was a fresh round of betting.

Janis stood on a platform draped with American flags and shouted through a megaphone that it was time to simmer down, that Blazes would now show what he was made of. Blazes, whom the program called a purebred, was at least somewhat shepherd, to be fair, and his performance was more comedic than vicious, in that he jumped through a hoop wearing a *Pickelhaube* helmet. His trainer bent at the waist, and Blazes sprang up and over his back, which led to applause, and then, when given a strip of dried beef, Blazes barked on command.

It was a strong act with a weak finish, and Janis, who was a kindhearted sort of judge, said, "Congratulate Blazes—he's in first place," and then it was Sampson's turn. He sprang out of the contestants' tent, also wearing a *Pickelhaube,* and his trainer followed, wearing an embarrassed smile that was still firmly cemented in place by the time a chorus of booing cut his performance—jumping through hoops, barking on command—short.

It had taken Lee a while to get his dog onto his leash, because a distant part of the field was awash in orange-and-yellow butterflies. Lee had finally to pick him up and carry him, cradled, back into place. He was a large dog for his age, seven months, but he still went slack in Leland's arms, licking his face once and smiling.

Lee sat cross-legged outside the tent, his dog lazily half across his lap, accepting stomach rubs. Lee watched the action in the stands, and thought, craftily, "Keep betting. Just because I'm showing you this dog doesn't mean it's the dog who's competing." He had invested every penny of his savings and had borrowed a hundred dollars from Ripley to invest in winning today.

He sized up his competition. When Killer trotted by, Lee squeezed a rubber ball in his pocket, and it made a quick, rusty-hinge kind of noise, something like a woodland creature's chuckle. Killer startled, ears pricking up, but then he kept going as before, bounding up the slats of a stepladder atop of which waited a sausage.

It was an impressive feat, but Lee was unafraid, in that he knew Killer hadn't been trained with the secret weapon of a squeak toy.

By the time Killer had ridden on the back of the motorcycle—Lee clocked him at fifteen miles per hour, not thirty-five—it was apparent to him that Nanette had no serious challengers on the field. She could do all those tricks and, as the crowd would soon see, much more. Barring unforeseen circumstances, a great deal of money would soon be his.

Tiger Boy walked along a narrow beam between two sawhorses; when asked what two plus two was, he barked four times; and when his owner made a pistol of his thumb and forefinger, the dog fell over, feigning death. Based on the resulting applause, Janis announced he was tied for second place.

She read off of the program, "Last, we have Nanette, trained by Corporal"—and here she choked, but she was a professional, and no one save Lee himself noticed the sudden change in inflection, the veil of control lowering onto her voice—"Lee Duncan. Crescent City, California."

Lee ambled up toward the platform, dog trotting with him, and then paused. He looked at his wristwatch. "This is going to take about two minutes to get started," he said to Janis, who nodded.

"Okay, boys, take two minutes to stretch and hoot and holler," she cried through the megaphone. "Corporal Duncan promises us a good time then."

Laughter, and calls to begin settling the bets. It was obvious Lee was not a player today. There were some romantic holdouts, the kind who never left a farm auction back home until the final animal was led around the pen, but overall, the stands were aflutter with cash changing hands.

Lee stood silently; he'd become acquainted with patience. He saw Janis staring his way. He caught her eye.

She was a plain woman. All of it—the fame, the wild adulation, the genial welcomes around the camps—came not from her face but from how people imagined it. Without the whoops, without the song in her heart, Janis was pure Ohio plain, she said, when in private and with her chestnut hair down.

"So, Corporal. You still think I'm a sucker?" Janis whispered.

In response, Lee tucked a finger down his collar and showed off the latest dolls—slightly ratty, but still there. He smiled at her, an easy smile, a share-the-wealth smile, a you-taught-me-as-much-as-I-taught-you smile. Here it was a couple months later, that smile said, me with my dogs and the puppets you gave me, you as the judge, and ain't it grand?

Only when Janis's face showed nothing did Lee realize how profoundly he had just shot himself in the foot.

"I guess you do think I'm a sucker," she said quickly, with the calm of a woman who has survived yet another heartbreak. "Those two minutes are up," she added, just as a faint drone began somewhere in the distance.

This was the late moment when Lee concluded that, though it might work for other men, he shouldn't keep leading with that "sucker" business. He tried to apologize, but she was interested in the grandstands, the sky, the ground, and then her megaphone went to her lips, and she called, "Okey-dokey, gents and blokies, we're gonna wrap it up," but there was enough distraction in the stands that she had to repeat herself, and by then the drone had become differentiated: it was a pair of DH 4s, flying low and slow.

"That would be me," Lee said, as well assembled as he could manage. He was beginning to sweat, so he stood with his hands in his pockets, one hip cocked out, slouching, and then occasionally pointing westward, until the men in the stands began to catch on.

The two planes flew a hundred feet above the earth, not ten feet separating them. Deep in a knot of men arguing over a distribution of winnings, one private threw his arm forward and pointed, yelling "My God!," which brought his comrades to crane their heads. Heads turning everywhere swept the motion through the stands and down the fields where the overflowing crowds stood, thousands of men starting to call out, some audibly, most only issuing astonished gasps, as Nanette was clearly outlined on the wing of one plane. She wore a sporty leather helmet and, more functionally, goggles.

The sight of a dog on the wing of a moving plane caused fists holding money to clench involuntarily. And then the planes passed directly before the stands, not fifty feet from the ground now, and there was wild clapping, which lasted until each plane made a graceful cloverleaf turn and began a lazy path back toward the stands. Applause ceased, for it was beginning to dawn on the men what, exactly, was promised next.

Lee, for his part, was rapidly losing the pose he had set himself in, that of a man too jaded even to stand up straight; on the one hand, he was floating in the crowd's reaction, giddy with it, but mostly he was becoming terrified. Some reservoir of care had broken loose in him, as if Janis's iron gaze had cracked him open. Great portions of his life had been a terrible mistake. It was like sitting on the limb of a tree and rapidly reassessing all the steps by which he had decided to saw between himself and the trunk.

He realized that his idea had been terrible. Not brilliant. He was going to get his beautiful dog killed. Deep in his bones, he knew it. As the planes returned, he knew he couldn't stop the stunt in progress, and so he watched, powerless, as an amazing display occurred overhead: Nanette stood up on the wing. She began, wind whipping her fur back on her haunches, to walk toward the edge. The other plane fell back and down slightly, for a horizontal gap of six feet and a vertical gap of a yard.

It wasn't worth it. The applause wasn't worth it. The ambition wasn't worth it.

The roar of the engines at low throttle was almost unbearably loud. The planes passed directly over the stands, and at the moment the men had to throw their heads directly toward the sky to see, Nanette leapt off the wing.

There was a moment of her hanging in the air, long and lean body illuminated from above, and then she descended. She landed between the wing struts on the second plane, which tipped away briefly, to find a better balance, and she scampered quickly along the wing and into the second cockpit. Perfectly executed. Only Lee noticed her immediately resurfacing with a squeaky toy between her jaws. The planes circled once again, waggling their wings as if taking a bow, Lieutenant Ripley waved from his DH 4 (she was now called *Emma*), and then they descended together onto the field, and even as they bounced awkwardly to a stop, men were roiling toward them, to stand in stark admiration.

Lee had his hands to his chest, leash wrapped in one fist, Boy straining against it, frightened enough to bolt all directions at once, but Lee was unmoving. He was measuring the beat of his heart. *Never again.* No force on earth could compel him to endanger so casually a creature that trusted him.

There were many eyes on him, and hands slapping him on the back, but he felt the intense interest of one particular pair. Janis. She ambled toward him, taking her hat and tossing it into the air, spinning it by its brim. "Soldier, if there was any way I could keep you from getting first prize ..." she said, and then chuckled. "But that's the way the ball bounces."

She waited for the retort, but Lee still hadn't even unclasped the hands from his chest.

"Hey," she said gently, sizing up how he trembled. She patted Boy on his flank. She slapped her hat back on her head, and looked up the foot or so to Lee's face, which looked fresh and raw.

"She can do other tricks," he whispered.

"Yeah?"

"I'm sorry I said you were a sucker. That was uncalled for."

"That's okay."

"I taught her a lot. She can take a pin out of a grenade."

"Well, holy smokes, Corporal," Janis whispered.

Lee smiled a little. She softened. She glanced at him, but couldn't hold the gaze—it was like struggling against a horse starting to trot, then canter. He reached out and straightened Janis's hat, which had small red silk flowers on its crown. "Hey," he said, and so she looked back at him, and, with the same helplessness she'd felt under the weight of his eyes, she couldn't break the gaze. She shrugged, as if admitting that she, too, was sometimes a mess, and it was as if the rest of the field was fading into faint shouts and blurs, and that was really all it took.

At two o'clock in the morning, Mandres was a village of music and firecrackers and rowdy shouts. Men had passed out against the buildings that had so recently been converted; when they awoke, they would be stuck to the fresh paint. Leland walked on loose limbs, his eyes half open. He didn't walk like a man with $1,282 on him. Whenever he was recognized, drunks expounded to him about his dog's prowess. The planes were fifty feet apart and two hundred feet in the air. The dog was twelve feet tall, and was it true she was half wolf? He was hugged and handed bottles of gin, which he began merely pretending to sip. There were only so many times he could say thank you.

He walked past a canvas tent through which weird shadows were emanating. When he heard the mutter of a field generator, and occasional choruses of rough laughter, he returned to see movies being projected against a white sheet draped across one wall.

It was a newsreel several months old, showing the first planes with engines from America. In other words, the 135th. It was just starting. Leland hadn't seen it before.

Leland walked among four rows of church pews, splintered at the bottom, where they'd been ripped from their former home. The men in the audience had tin cups, and the front of the tent housed a tureen whose brutish aroma made Leland flinch. He sat next to a British Army sergeant, who had obviously been in the field: he was sitting up, back straight, head bent slightly forward, and snoring. Outside, a furious burst of firecrackers ignited, which jolted him awake.

"Very rude of us," he muttered.

Lee looked at the flickering images in front of him. Planes in the air. Bursts of antiaircraft fire. Then—he had been there that day!—all the new DH 4s with Liberty engines coming out of their hangar.

The next image was of Leland. There was his face, in close-up, six feet tall of pure silver nitrate. He showed off the band of bullets, and then put his hands on the Marlin as if firing it. Then he was gone.

"Hey," Leland said. He looked around the room—he was the only one paying attention. He pointed at the screen. "That was . . ." He couldn't bring himself to say it. That was me. That was my dream. My dream just happened.

He wanted to see himself again; he stayed through the newsreel and the travelogue and the beginning of the two-reel comedy, trying to recall how he had looked onscreen. He felt a fading disappointment that he couldn't dissect. He wasn't sure if it was seeing himself that was so sad, or if it was that he'd had such a small dream all his life. Who could he tell he'd fulfilled it? He yawned.

Sunnyside

The comedy was a Mack Sennett, *On His Wedding Day*. A bride and groom were racing from room to room. A great deal of tripping was involved. There was a bad splice after the first minute, and then there were men in striped shirts and domino masks skulking outside a hotel room.

Leland reasoned that the thieves were after the bride's engagement ring, or perhaps her dowry, but between them and their goals were banana peels, workmen who carried ladders on their shoulders and who turned 180 degrees to answer questions from cops who were suspicious of the groom for reasons likely to have been explained in the missing few minutes. Nonetheless, he could fill in possible causes himself: a twin brother; an innocent action, misconstrued; a jealous rival; whatever was necessary.

He began to doze, and the action of the movie started to fuse with his dreams, which seemed to involve large, soft pillows filled with cash, and then he was jolted awake by laughter. Onscreen, the groom had dressed his dog as a ghost. Since he had previously tucked a soup bone in the thieves' satchel, they were now being pursued from room to room by a romping four-footed sheet with eyeholes and holes for his witch-hat ears.

"Hey," Lee said. Then "Hey"—this time to a private in front of him—"what kind of dog is that?"

"I'm sleepy."

Soon the sheet came off, caught in a closed door, and the dog, loping and barking, was revealed as a Great Dane. The dog stood up on a thief, knocking him down; he wagged his tail hard enough to topple a pot of glue parked at the edge of a table; he jumped into the bathtub, soaking the groom; and at the end, he was dressed, for reasons unclear, identically to the reverend marrying them.

A couple of the men in the audience said, "Awwww," before they were sufficiently laughed at. The film ran out, and Leland was in the aisle, next to the projectionist, tapping him on the shoulder until he woke up.

"You have any more of those?"

"More what?" He yawned, brushing Leland's hands away.

"The dog."

As soon as the projectionist realized Leland wasn't going to leave no matter how evilly he was stared at, he searched through reels of film. The dog was called Teddy. He starred in a second one-reeler, *Apple Pie Annie*. This one was about a poor girl hired by a wicked debutante to bake treats secretly for a boy she was courting. In between several sets of romance, Teddy once again romped and chased and knocked things over.

After ten minutes of this, Leland stood, put his hands on his hips, opened his mouth as if to speak, but found himself unable. He strode to the back of the tent, paused in the flap, and turned. "My dog can pull the pin from a hand grenade," he exclaimed. "She can uncork a baby pineapple just like that. She can jump through fire. She can jump between DH 4s! Do you know how hard that is? And that dog up there"—he pointed at the screen—"that's just . . ."

But no one was listening, so he let the flap drop, and he stalked off, into the unwinding nighttime revelry.

It was dark.

Ironside privately referred to conditions under his command as "terrifying." The skies were now black, with sunrise and sunset being amorphous notations on official charts. No one ever saw the sun. Sentries stationed outside the barracks were driven to screaming that they wanted their shadows back.

The Dvina had frozen, and no manner of ax or hammer could burst the ice enough to free the Allied ships that dotted the harbor, their hulls now imprisoned in ice, side by side with the wooden masts and paddlewheels from the eighteenth and nineteenth centuries that served as unplanned memorials to beautiful ideas abandoned.

With the Allies bunkered down in blockhouses along the five fingers of the "Hand," the enemy was launching ever more coordinated attacks. In Dubya, it was reported that Trotsky's Bolsheviks were using skis and had begun to cloak themselves in white garments so that they were invisible.

The temperature was frequently fifty degrees below zero.

Metal tools couldn't be used, as they stuck to the skin.

If a sentry broke an ankle one hundred yards from the field hospital, he would freeze to death.

Mr. Nicholas Chaikovsky held frequent meetings to forge the new constitution, which never seemed to be ratified. The Slavo-British Legion had been disbanded, except for a force just large enough to protect Mr. Nicholas Chaikovsky, who had trouble going outside without someone throwing a rock at his hat. It was evident that democracy had bloomed as it always did when forcibly planted, in a kakistocracy of the worst possible men.

One day, a dozen films arrived at Ironside's offices: Chaplins, a Pickford or two, a melodrama with Mary Miles Minter, a May Allison comedy, the first six episodes of *The Exploits of Elaine,* and a final reel marked "Officers Eyes Only." It was a short reel on 9.5 safety film. Ironside stood behind his desk, reading the explanatory text that came with it. He was being sent a print of the only known motion-picture footage of Trotsky. It was a segment spliced from *My Official Wife.*

Pishkoff stood at Ironside's office door. "Sir?"

"Pishkoff."

"General Ironside, sir, your presence is requested at the infirmary."

"Very well," Ironside said. They walked to the first floor, where they entered the snowsuit room. The general began to dress quietly while his valet stood at ease, but at a reserve. Ironside put on a sleeveless sweater, felt-lined leather tunic, fleece-lined overcoat, and then a pair of mittens, and another, each with thumb and trigger finger free. He topped off with a balaclava cap of white duck.

Thus prepared, Ironside allowed Pishkoff to open the door to outside. A wind like a punch in the face brought tears to Ironside's eyes. He blinked carefully, to keep his lashes from freezing together. He waddled next to Pishkoff in the darkness the half verst to the infirmary. Pishkoff's pace was steady, and his boots made very precise tracks in the snow.

"What do you hear from the people, Pishkoff?"

"Everything is adequate, sir."

Pishkoff was dressed to regulations, and he now shaved every day. His skin was healthier than it had been in years, and he had lost his paunch, for he seemed to have stopped drinking. Ironside wasn't sure of this last point, for Pishkoff did not confide in him.

The infirmary was a single-story clapboard building heated by many stoves, its walls several feet thick. Generators hummed just outside to power the bright surgical lights.

Once they were inside, and had stripped off their outermost layers, Ironside let Pishkoff lead him to a cot. A soldier was lying in it, eyes closed.

"What's his condition?"

"I think you should talk to him, sir."

Ironside eased into the chair beside the bed, testing the legs, for he didn't want his weight to collapse them. The scrape against the floor caused the soldier's eyes to open.

"Good afternoon," Ironside said. "I'm General Ironside."

"Sir," the soldier said.

"Please do be at ease." They talked for several minutes. The man was American, a corporal named Hedges from Detroit, and he had a girl back home who he hoped was getting his letters. His father worked assembling automobiles. His mother hated to cook, and on some mornings he and his sisters had to wake her from deep, black sleeps that they called "the bends," and he had learned to make her coffee when he was only seven years old.

"Where were you just stationed?"

"Onega, sir."

"And how is the weather out in Onega?" Ironside asked.

"It's so cold, sir, you can hear your spit crack when it hits the ground."

To which Ironside replied, "Quite."

Corporal Hedges was on morphine. There wasn't a mark on him, not a bruise or a scratch. Ironside shook his hand, they exchanged salutes, and then, with a groan, Ironside stood.

Wrapping themselves up again, he and Pishkoff left the infirmary and returned to the darkness outside.

"Yes?" Ironside said.

"He was captured at Onega three days ago. A cart dropped him off here this morning, early. The enemy has executed him."

The tense was undoubtedly accurate, and not meant to sound dramatic. He listened to the snow crunching underfoot.

"The Bolsheviks greased a pinecone, and then used a hammer and a stone chisel to lodge it point-up in his rectum. There's no way to remove it. He'll die of tenesmus."

Ironside continued to walk. He could hear the phrase "your spit crack when it hits the ground" again. He would arrange for morphine, a great deal of it. He had never heard the word "tenesmus," but realized that Pishkoff had. "Terrible," he said.

"There was a note from the enemy in his pocket," Pishkoff continued, uninflected. "It gloated a bit, but the point was, there is at least one pinecone in Russia for each Allied soldier."

They had reached headquarters, and they trotted up the front steps to stand inside the snowsuit room, where they both began unwrapping their many layers. They shook snow off themselves. Ironside had to navigate through signing documents even now, and then again up the marble staircase to his office, where he was stopped by petitioners, by reports from the field, by women who wanted him to call on them. It took long minutes to get inside the office, and at no time did Pishkoff speak.

When they were alone, Ironside said, "I never thought this would be easy."

"Sir, may I ask you a question?"

"I wish you would." He ran his hand along the schedule for today. The film of Trotsky next.

"What if that"—Pishkoff swept his scarred right hand to indicate everything outside the room—"what if that is what order actually looks like?"

"Pardon?"

"We're here to bring order. I know. But what if this mess is the natural state and what we're doing is ridiculous?"

"You can't believe that."

"I think people get tired of fighting, and for ten years, twenty years, they agree: let's stop. You have some silk, I have a cow, your daughter marries my nephew, we'll drink, it's good, happily ever after, the end. But it's not the end. It's always chaos and shouting and homicide in the end."

Ironside shook his head. "I don't think that's right."

"Why are we fighting now?" Pishkoff presented a well of intelligence behind eyes cobwebbed with despair.

"Honestly? For our lives," Ironside whispered. He missed Pishkoff.

Unexpectedly, Pishkoff snorted.

"There we are," Ironside said. "I was worried you'd lost your sense of humor."

"You know what the peasants believe? They think the devil gave man a sense of humor."

"Why would he do that?"

"So we laugh at our problems instead of solving them."

Ironside looked at his schedule. "Would you enjoy an odd assignment? We have a moving picture to watch."

"I think the peasants might be right."

"Pishkoff, we've inherited an impossible situation. We're fighting against anarchy. The railroad doesn't work, industry is shattered, other states can't have relations with Russia, and the internal life here is completely disrupted. Justice is truculent, human life is losing its value, and the power is in the hands of a small group of people, mostly Jews, who have led the country into full chaos. There isn't a sane man alive today who would argue against strangling Bolshevism in its crib."

Pishkoff's eyes went to Ironside's desk. He reached out for the letter opener, which he spun on its tip. The opener dragged across the blotter, leaving a divot.

"Watch the moving picture with me. Please."

"What is it?"

Ironside explained the unlikely situation: the antic comedy, Brooklyn, *My Official Wife*, 1914, the two minutes of Trotsky hectoring from his stump.

"Wait," Pishkoff dropped the letter opener. "Show me."

Ironside handed him the documentation, which Pishkoff glanced over. Then he tossed the sheets of paper to the desk.

"This was made in 1914. Trotsky was in the United States of America two years ago. March 1917."

Ironside blinked. "Are you sure?"

There was an intake of air on Pishkoff's side of the desk. It seemed to inflate him to a more formal posture. "Everyone in Russia knows, *sir*. He was only there once. March 1917."

"Again, are you sure of that?"

Pishkoff seemed to hold on to the next words, shaking dice until they turned the way he wanted. "Unless, of course, history repeats itself." He threw a perfect salute, and when Ironside returned it, Pishkoff left the room.

49

Leland bunked one night with engineers, who loved his dogs without self-consciousness. They had never been mistaken for marines or frontline trenchmen. No one could drink so little as an engineer and yet get so drunk. "We're efficient," one of them explained at the local estaminet, where they took Lee for battery casings of beer. They managed to order without looking their server, an Alsatian girl, in the eye.

"Three fifty, three seventy-five, tops," whispered an engineer.

"No, five hundred and five at least," declared another.

"Do I have to explain the concept?" demanded the first.

Lee squinted at them. "What?"

Never a group to bless women with actual conversation, the engineers instead gazed across file rooms and city streets with hypnotized longing through their thick and smeared and rimless spectacles. Seeing a painfully diverse group of nurses and Salvation Army volunteers and journalists and French girls, they came up with a unit of measurement by which to discuss beauty. It was the *millihelen*. This was the amount of beauty it took to launch one ship.

The measurement worked through the visible spectrum from infrared (the American Quaker volunteers), to missionaries, then army nurses, Red Cross nurses, and then dieticians and cooks, journalists, heiresses who took exciting tours of the front lines, then up around the ultraviolet range came chauffeuses, for in a country where gasoline was scarce, a service-station owner would fill a tank only for the most attractive woman.

The most beautiful women in France, women literally beyond the visible spectrum, were the AT&T-trained Women's Telephone Unit, a 233-member division of the Army Signal Corps. Their job was to run the old-fashioned magneto switchboards of France.

It was amazing to the average doughboy that when you called in coordinates from the front lines, you picked up a telephone receiver and, with explosions and mud around you, you could hear an American girl's voice. This made her "Hello" as dazzling a presence in your ear as the breath of Aphrodite. They were known as "Hello Girls."

And then, one day, they were gone. With the end of the war, the systems were staffed by men. The empty sheds in which they'd served were quickly overrun with spiders and mice, yet men still walked toward them hesitantly and knocked, hoping to be greeted with a female hello.

In May 1919, Leland's papers came through, and he began the trip across France in a 40 & 8 troop train, so named because each car was designed for forty men or eight horses—meaning that the accommodations were hay bales, blankets, and body lice. The train lurched at a walking pace from station to station, doors on each side open for ventilation. Men tended to lean through the frame, watching the countryside, where families and their wagons of belongings were returning home.

Leland made time pass by playing with his dogs and thinking about money. Sometimes he bounced the squeaky ball across the car, causing Nanette to scamper over hay bales and sleeping soldiers, until craps games were supplanted by plots to murder Leland and his charges. So instead he tied Nanette and Boy to the frame of the open door, which stunned them. A hundred passing miles of cow pasture was like a tour of the Louvre.

Whenever the train stopped, even if it was between platforms, villagers seemed to arise from between rusted tractors or in furrows of wheat fields. They were hungry. If Leland was sleeping, he knew when they were coming: Nanette would spring up and furiously wag her tail, eventually issuing an efficient single bark. She cared not for the adults, but had some primal spot, in her otherwise careful canine heart, for children. When a flock of tattered urchins surrounded the train, Nanette bounded to the ground and barked until Leland relented and put her through her paces. Sit. Down. Come. Stay. Roll over. Speak. Crawl. Beg. Shake. Jump. Higher. The first time, he tossed his dummy hand grenade, and she uncorked it and threw it with a toss of her head, but the resulting wail and scatter of hysterical children made him shamefacedly strike this from the program. Again.

Once or twice, he let Boy off his lead, which resulted in his sprinting to random and interesting-smelling places until Nanette caught up and herded him back to the train.

By the time Leland and his dogs reached Bordeaux, he was close to broke but, more important, beginning to worry. Anyone he met with a rank over sergeant had announced he wasn't getting his dogs home with him. Dogs were fine in France, but not on a boat. Killer, Stumpy, and the rest would be left here. He began to understand the danger of allowing himself to want something. When they slept, he took to bringing his ear to his dogs' chests, and listening carefully; with every day that passed, they were closer to America. And the film industry. Nanette was going to be a star in motion pictures.

Bordeaux, departure point for the troops, was a hothouse where red tape grew. Leland was told at noon that he would depart at midnight, and then, at midnight, that his departure had been delayed. He was put through the cootie mills twice, given a short-arm inspection, told that the captain of the *Hermione* loved dogs and had instructed the ship's carpenter to build them a kennel, and then that the *Hermione* had sailed without him.

At Remount Station, the captain in charge of agriculture and associated animals told him the dogs were military property and would be removed from him, and then, after Leland gave him twenty dollars, he found a memo rescinding that order. He then confided that if Leland bribed a sailor properly, the dogs might be smuggled on board in a sea bag, though the captain of the ship would be likely to throw them overboard when they reached international waters.

A makeshift Kasbah had set up near the docks, rugs rolled out on the ground under canvas awnings, each one with its own merchant hawking souvenirs—postcards, belt buckles, cuckoo clocks, even propeller blades, though it was unclear how anyone could carry something like that home. Leland drifted among the merchandise one evening. He had his dogs with him, as ever—since they'd taken to stealing socks and boots, he'd taken to sleeping outside the barracks, and now that the weather was good, he no longer needed to pack a tent.

He was developing a blind philosophical acceptance that something would work out, and that if it did, it meant only that his time had come. It made no sense that a man would be born only to get nothing that he wanted. He thought Harry would be proud of that. "Dear Mom," he thought.

He passed a black velvet blanket dotted with jewels, and he paused only because he wondered how quickly, if he owned it, that velvet would get covered in dog hair. This was long enough for the hawker, who produced a ring for him and waved it under his nose as if its fragrance were intoxicating.

"Opals, opals, opals. From Australia. Look," the merchant said, excitedly. He pointed into the ring's band.

Leland could just read, by the market lights, an inscription. *Yes.* He laughed.

"Antique! It is an antique!" the merchant yelled. He was short and round and pale-skinned, a heavy beard bristling around his jowls, and he could have been from France or Spain or a thousand miles away. "At least older than you are."

Leland closed one eye. Three small opals surrounded by crushed . . . something . . . something that sparkled, perhaps actual diamonds, set in a band that was perhaps gold. And inside, that *Yes.* This struck him as ridiculous and corny. Yet he was already counting on his fingers. He had $105 left. The ring was $150. Then it was $120. He had no business buying a ring, and no one to give it to, and it was as likely to be made of ground glass and painted brass as of anything else. It was the *Yes* that tipped him. A small purchase would be an act of faith that, one day in the future, he might have use for it.

"Seventy-five."

"One ten."

"Seventy-five."

"One hundred."

"Sixty."

The merchant shrieked like a schoolgirl and then, in a polylingual monologue beginning with Russian, announced he was being insulted, robbed blind (French), that turkey buzzards were surrounding his house (Farsi), that the temple was missing its lemons (his Greek wasn't that good), and, finishing in English, that shame should befall the man with the dogs. And eighty dollars would close the deal.

Less than an hour later, the captain whom he had bribed handed him ducats for a ship leaving at noon the next day, a reflagged German ocean liner, the S.M.S. *Sonnenseit.* It would take eighteen days to get home, a bit longer than was routine, but since it wasn't strictly a military transport, the rules about animals were slightly more lax. The passengers weren't American Expeditionary Force, but associated groups and volunteers; would Leland go?

Leland pled poverty, but the officer had been thinking about it, and if Leland successfully bred either dog back in America, he wanted the pick of the litter. Leland considered it, and then, with a weird ray of hope beginning to glow in his chest, he shook on it.

That night, Leland and his two dogs retired to a straw mat just inside a livery. The pass to the boat was solid—it couldn't be taken away from him. He worried for several seconds about Stateside customs, and then he felt calm, for no particular reason. The sheer unlikelihood of having gotten as far as he had suggested to him that perhaps life was a series of challenges to overcome rather than be murdered by.

So he celebrated impossible odds: the dogs were on either side of him, curled up tightly, as if ready to be lowered into hatboxes. On one side, Nanette, who was faster and smarter and tougher than anyone had ever seen, a dog who might just make his fortune. She still had sweet puppy breath, brilliant white teeth, and a photogenic halo of hair by her ears. On the other side was, well, yes, another dog. An amiable dog. Boy.

Leland patted him on the head. Boy was sweet. He had an engaging smile. He could run quickly, and what else? He wanted to do right by his owner, even if the details eluded him. He seemed to *lie* sometimes. Leland considered the smile again. Perhaps the world would love to see a smiling dog.

Boy was smiling now. When Leland frowned, Boy frowned. Leland thought of how Boy had limped when he sensed he was going to be fed ham fat. Leland wasn't sure what to make of that.

He lay back and held the ring up to the sky, which he could see through the open doorway of the livery. Bordeaux had a unique species of tree, a blue palm, whose papery leaves rustled all night, with sometimes a crack and a crash as a frond broke and fell to the street. The night was warm, the moon hadn't yet risen, and the animal smell that surrounded him somehow made him feel like part of the world. He would ride tomorrow on the *Sonnenseit,* named after a popular song that translated more or less exactly as "Sunnyside," and what were the odds of that trip's not having a happy ending?

It was so dim he could barely see the light catching the gems; in fact, he might have just imagined it. He ran the three opals in soaring arcs past the deep-blue velvet spread of stars, making his own announcement, through sheer force of will, that the war—what war? every war, everything that felt like a war—was finally over.

Boy slept on; Leland slowly drifted into a happy sleep; Nanette sneezed once, and then she, too, fell asleep.

Word from the Chaplin Studios was grim. His new comedy was said to be a disaster. Outside of a two-minute scene of dancing nymphs, the remainder was a bizarre construction of false starts and feints in strange directions. Chaplin had finally capped off shooting and was determined to hew a story line from whatever he had, which apparently ended with his death by suicide.

All this was true. And excellent news for Adolph Zukor, for whom the end of the war had been one week after another of good news. The Paramount Studios umbrella was casting more shade by the day. The European film industry was a shambles, so American films were hungered for over there. Burton Holmes had sold his catalogue to them, a purchase Zukor had made shrewdly, for he knew the audiences would consume the travelogues the way they did spinach. In other words, as long as there was dessert. And an Arbuckle comedy was dessert.

Further, his vision of horizontal integration was proceeding at a pace no one had predicted possible. Buying the number of theaters he had in mind cost more money than Zukor or anyone—or everyone—in Hollywood had. But "everyone" lacked basic understanding of how the world had changed since the days of the nickel dumps. Over tea at the Waldorf= Astoria with Otto Kahn, Zukor arranged a ten-million-dollar line of credit from Kuhn, Loeb, of an area no one had dared approach before: Wall Street. Zukor had known actual money was involved in Hollywood, but this was the first time actual money had allowed itself to be located and leveraged into a plan for the future.

In three weeks, his fellow studio heads and their many representatives would have a breakfast meeting that would end the reign of actors' and directors' salary demands. Chaplin and Pickford and the rest would be brought in line.

There was, however, a *glitsh,* as they said in his old neighborhood. Bolsheviks.

It was a rare rainy weekend. Rain had started Friday night, and now, Sunday evening, it was continuing. When it rained, people tended to stay inside, and if it lasted more than a few hours, they went to the windows and looked at the sky as if it were a spouse that had deceived them. At eight o'clock in the evening, Zukor left his hotel suite, lurched into his private car, and was driven to meet with, he seethed, *Bolsheviks.*

With every piece of real estate reclaimed from wilderness, and every folly becoming standard practice, Los Angeles was evolving along its own logical course. It was not entirely clear yet whether studios were closed or open shops. Zukor loved the phrase "open shop." It sounded so welcoming.

There had never really been a strike in Hollywood, except once, when Bolsheviks (this would be Zukor's view) convinced the extras to demand that their pay be increased to two dollars a day. But recently ideas had been passed around with the same effectiveness as influenza. Actors were unionizing. Nice fellows seemed to join Actors' Equity. Bolsheviks seemed to join the Photoplayers Union. And everyone from Bolsheviks to nice fellows to those who were easily influenced to those who knew no better to those who enjoyed the parties (Zukor surmised) joined the International Alliance of Theatrical and Stage Employees, the sheer, polysyllabic bulk of whose name Zukor loathed. His son-in-law Goldwyn had been very clever when he lined up actors with single adjectives. There was discomfort in a complex name; it hid conflicting ideas.

There was talk of a new union called the Amusement Federation, which would represent all studio unions. *They* had it right, Zukor thought. A very simple name, and it had the word "Amusement" in it, which showed that the organizers understood irony. Zukor was on his way now to meet with their business agent.

Adding to his respect, and a certain ill-ease, Zukor could find no information about the business agent. His network of informants could turn up not a shred of information about the man, as if he had dropped out of the sky.

The automobile was now idling on a residential street in an area Zukor did not recognize. "Are you sure this is it?" he asked his chauffeur.

A business agent spoke on the union's behalf in negotiations with management, and made sure employers honored union contracts. He also sold employees on the idea of union membership. And handled grievances. And collected dues. Zukor was not sure what sort of house he would be visiting; his imagination played between mansion and shotgun lean-to. Would he be taken prisoner by frothing men in overalls?

His chauffeur walked him to the curb under the umbrella. It was one of a dozen nearly identical places recently built on the block. A duplex, it had a front lawn now sodden with rain, and a tiled entryway. The front door was painted a Barcelona blue. Zukor could not hear the doorbell when he rang. The problem with unions was that they could easily stand in the way of the consolidation Zukor had in mind. He didn't understand whether they were motivated more by greed or by desire for anarchy.

The rain continued. The door opened.

"Hello, Mr. Zukor." Zukor's thin eyebrows shot upward. A young girl had answered the door. She had black, straight hair and probing eyes. She was, of course, Rebecca Golod. "My father is in the living room."

She took his coat. The entryway was lined with bookshelves, and the bookshelves, full to bursting with odd volumes in several languages, were also lined with small craft projects, postcards, shells from the beach, animal bones, and so forth. The rooms were overheated, and the living room even had a fireplace, before which Mordecai Golod stood.

"Sit, sit, please, Mr. Zukor," he said. He had shaved his beard, had his hair fashionably slicked back with pomade, and was dressed in blue serge. "My daughter will bring us tea."

As Zukor carefully chose an overstuffed chair to sit on, Rebecca went to the kitchen to put the kettle on. She stood without moving by the stove, setting two cups on a tray, with sugar, milk, teapot, while the flames veered around the bottom of the kettle.

She was listening to her father and Zukor. She was listening not for words but for tone. She had let the world's most suspicious man into their house, and that had immediately relaxed her, for suspicious men were the best marks. But her father's tone had puzzled her—as she had been puzzled all month by what his new scam actually was. Skimming? Bribes? Each time she had tried to wheedle it out of him, he had shrugged. "I'm concerned about the desires of the common man. His aspirations," he said one night.

Maybe. He was now saying roughly the same thing to Zukor. So, whatever it was, it was a long con, something involving wheels within wheels. Which was fine. She had time.

Though she had enjoyed moving Zasu from Chaplin to Pickford, she wasn't sure if she would try it again with someone else. She was more concerned about this "love" business, which had bothered her since San Francisco. She checked the kettle. Watched pots did indeed boil when you were as patient as she was. And—

She startled; something seemed to move in her peripheral vision. She looked toward the window and saw just her own reflection. Outside, it was dark and raining. The leaves of the cypress tree next door rattled and tacked against the glass. How had her reflection moved when she hadn't?

A couple of days before, she had taken the trolley into the canyon and then walked a little into the hills. She wanted to get a view of the city, but the pathway she chose was fenced off with barbed wire. She could hear a grinding noise—definitely a motor—getting closer. But what kind of motor was in the hills? It was too steep for an automobile, and no truck could make it this far. Patient and ponderous and strong, it was guttural, sounding as if nothing would stand in its way.

It was not an automobile, but something like a steam tractor. Except that its wheels had been replaced with endless tracks, exactly like a tank's. It was called a bulldozer. Its blade lowered, tearing up the topsoil and brush and weeds, scattering rocks that had lain in place for a million and a half years. The engine growled and whined but hardly complained, its treads turning easily, for they had been taken from tank design, and they worked far better in California than under fire in France.

Her mind made the connection between this and the end of the Liberty Loan Drive immediately. But there was a strange, subtle difference to the message now, which she could not sort out yet. Real bulldozers based on ersatz tanks, and they weren't here to build morale, but—what?

A reservoir. Why were they putting water up in the hills? Where was it coming from? Just then, a man wearing dungarees yelled at her to leave, so she did. For now. They had roused her curiosity.

As she walked back on the trail along the hillside, she tried to suppress a fear she had of running into herself. She dressed differently every day (except wearing her Silver Fish badge, no matter the outfit) in the vague superstition that her double would not be able to keep up. In the Bible, there were always stories of people running into themselves coming in the other direction, and it always ended badly. Demons, dybbuks, tricks played on you, prophecies.

So now, in the kitchen, she regarded her reflection as if it might not actually be her, as if her image might be a separate creature.

In the living room, Mr. Zukor was saying, "But sometimes the image actually is separate from the person. In fact, Mr. Golod, I'd say always." Now, *that* was odd; the hairs on Rebecca's neck stood up. "Take Chaplin, for instance. . . ."

When they'd lived in Beaumont, there had been that day when Chaplin was seen everywhere. What if that happened all the time? What if people's images were suddenly all over the planet, thousands at a time, and this had been going on for years? Maybe there were times a person was projected when there was no projector, and people we met on the street were just these strange modern *ibburim* invested with living souls, and that's why the movies were so compelling; it was part of our collective memory. Maybe that was why acting was so attractive: you got the chance to be everywhere at once, and you could pretend to be many different people, the way nature intended. No one would have known about these *ibburim* until now, because now certain people were famous. If, for instance, she, Rebecca, was everywhere, and there were thousands of Rebeccas in cities and villages and in the ocean and on mountaintops, who would know? No one except her, and only if she ran into herself.

She had never found what she loved. Not yet. The boys at the studio and at the socials sponsored by the synagogue tended to fall to pieces when she spoke. She was still waiting. For now, she wanted to be useful. She wanted to help those in need. If she could be a saint, she would be a saint, but that was problematic.

The air above the stove started to bend and sway. Vapor hit her hand, leaving it satisfyingly moist. She heard the sound of a dry piece of toast breaking against its will into small pieces. That was Zukor laughing. Her father was reeling him in. She closed her eyes and waited for the whistle on the kettle to go. It was starting to sigh.

Maybe she really was everywhere. Maybe many small things that were wrong were being set right by her. Maybe she was what the world was reaching out for now. For her to play parts wherever she was needed. Any moment now, the kettle. Here it comes.

51

The next morning, Leland approached the docks with his dogs on leashes, and a set of explanations, in case he needed them. But those rehearsals died in his throat; he was the last person in a line that made him dizzy. Before him was a mass of blue wool coats and ankle-length skirts, women milling around, uncomfortably hot in the sun, fanning themselves with their departure papers. Leland didn't even need to count to know there were 233 women standing ahead of him. He was shipping home with the Hello Girls.

He was not the only man aboard—there were sailors, of course, and a few other doughboys. But he was the only man who was over six feet, and whose impassive gaze and quiet nod tended to make the women collide with each other. Also: he had two puppies. Oh, and he was taking them to Hollywood, by the way. Never had an ocean voyage begun with such promise.

He said hello many times, dozens, as he boarded. Nanette and Boy were petted and praised, and Lee was asked by several women if he would be walking the dogs on deck anytime soon. And where he was bunking.

Leland was given a supply closet instead of a room. It lacked portholes, the nearest latrine was at the other end of the deck, and the sink's water, when it ran, was a greenish trickle. He had a cot and a blanket, but sleeping was nearly impossible because of the infinite variety of noises that the engines—which seemed to be in the closet with him—made as the ship's screws spun in the dark gray waters.

There was a slop bucket for the dogs, and no promises of meals for them, and the moment the ship first took a heavy roll at sea, both of the dogs lurched into sickness. He took them onto the decks, but the sea spray was cold and wet, and Nanette began coughing hard enough to frighten him, so he brought them back to their closet.

He left the room on the first night and immediately found several girls in the corridor who would be pretty enough to kiss, and several others whom it would be no crime to see naked. He wanted to begin talking so he could say, casually, I'm bringing the dogs to Hollywood. Nanette is the world's best dog, and I'm going to make her famous. But there were diesel fumes belowdecks, which made everyone feel queasy, including Leland, and this limited his ability to find repartee. He lay in his cot, running his fingers over his finger puppets and thinking that if he was lucky enough to find a sweetheart or two on the voyage he would not say anything about her being a sucker. He was ready for something different to happen.

In the first two days of the crossing, he learned that the Hello Girls were in the flesh exactly what a reasonable man would believe: the full spectrum of millihelens. Some of them grandmothers, some plump, some too thin, most of them exhausted-looking, and a handful of them perhaps incredible. Leland caught brief glances of a few girls who certainly deserved a second look before they were parried away into private quarters. The most beautiful were the most chaperoned.

After four days, he had gotten startled glances from some of the women but had made little progress. The reasons were relatively clear. He was at a disadvantage to any beau who *didn't* live in an airless room with sick dogs.

Boy seemed to mend gradually, and regained an interest in food, but Nanette's expression took on a profound ennui. Her eyes were glassy. She drank water at first, but refused all meals. When he encouraged her to walk on deck, her gait was unsteady; her ears went back and she shivered, even when the sunlight bathed the forecastle, and the girls were playing badminton. Leland considered joining them, but each time he brought his dog back to the sleep-in closet, he decided to stay with her instead.

At the end of the week, Nanette no longer wanted to leave the cabin. Her brother liked to be taken out and jogged among the other passengers, and he returned in high spirits that Leland hoped could be transferred to Nanette. She seemed to stop sleeping, too, hanging her snout over the edge of the cot instead, and staring at the bulkhead.

He took to brushing them both for long minutes, and talking to them as if they could understand him. He had an idea: now that they were on the boat, the war was over, they were safe, and life could actually begin. He started to say the word "love" aloud. "I love you, Nanette. I love you, Boy."

Harry had encouraged him to reason with the dogs, but now Leland was just lonely, and so he told them about the lighthouse, and the bungalow on the beach, and what Hollywood would be like, and their famous grandfather. "The truth is, I always wanted him to come see us. I loved him, but I didn't know him at all. I used to hope that was enough, loving him like that. I used to think, if only I was good enough, if only I wanted it enough . . ." And he stopped here, for he thought he was depressing the dogs.

Thirteen days into the trip, Nanette took a little solid food, but no more than a mouthful, as if she was trying to please Leland in some way but had run out of opportunities. Her hair was losing its luster. That afternoon, Leland went alone to the mess, just to stand by himself for a few moments outside the room; he was beginning to worry how this would end. A Hello Girl walked up and asked him what he was thinking, and he said, "Not much," and apologized and went back to his supply closet.

Around sunset, Leland lay back down on the cot and stretched Nanette out next to him. She didn't resist, and her expression was slack, as if she was concentrating elsewhere, a sailor staring to the horizon line.

"I should tell you about your name," he tried. He pulled out the puppets on their string, and held them in front of her nose. "A girl gave them to me, Elsie. Well, there were a couple of girls before that. The first, her name was Lenore, and she was married. Anyway, they relate to a fairy tale, and so, once upon a time, there was a girl from France named Nanette, and there was a boy who was crazy about her." He rubbed her flank for a moment. Her muscles had too much give to them. The fur moved as if she were an old woman in an oversized coat. "And there was an air raid on a subway station where they'd hid themselves, and the next day the only survivors were herself and her fellah. You see?" He was quiet again, listening to a wheezing sound, some new part of the ship that sounded mechanically tortured. It occurred with the rise and fall of Nanette's chest, and Leland realized that each new breath was becoming a decision for her. "Nanette, you see how the girl looks a little light-headed, and how the boy is flat-out, all-gears in love with her? Most guys, they think she should look in love with him. But it makes sense. See, that's what love is. The only way to make you come back home safe is if she keeps you awake nights, worrying."

He laughed. He closed his eyes, and quickly that laugh was gone, as if someone else, in some stateroom far away, had done it. He had a vision of his mother falling on the rocks and his father in a diving suit rescuing her. Which had never happened. Deep in him, he knew there was yet more to the story, a feeling so painful he couldn't even touch it, a bruise long ago gone bad: the hope that if you loved someone enough it would make them stay for you. And you could be together in a little house somewhere, smoke on the rooftop, where you were safe.

He awoke with his mouth dry, and the dim light in the cabin was sour and glazed, as if he'd been drinking. He was still holding Nanette. He ran his hand over her soft head, and then realized his clothes were wet.

Her body was limp. The whole bed, he realized, was wet. *But she's still warm,* he thought, but, no, that was just where he was touching her.

She had died while he was asleep. "Nanette," he said softly, and then he bit down on his lower lip, hard. Boy was awake and watching, curled at the end of the cot. He looked up at Leland's voice, then settled back down and closed his eyes.

Leland sat on the edge of the bed with his dog in his arms. He wanted for just a moment to smell her breath, and when he realized he couldn't, he bit down on his lip again, until his whole body shook with it.

He might have sat that way for an hour. It was hard to measure time. There was that strange throb of giant engines all around him, and a mechanical percussion that was terribly like a heartbeat.

When he couldn't take it anymore, he brought his canvas duffle bag onto the floor, and lowered Nanette into it, careful that she wouldn't hit her head. Her brother sprang up with the sound of the zipper, shaking himself, and diving to the deck. He wagged his tail furiously, eyes darting from Leland to the hand on the zipper. Leland paused.

"You should say goodbye, maybe," Leland whispered.

Boy took a couple of small, prancelike steps forward, tail beating against the bulkhead, and then he sniffed his sister's chest, and gave a quick lick to her lips, and jumped away.

Leland gently finished closing the bag. The moment he put the strap over his shoulder and stood, Boy erupted into furious barking.

"Quiet," Leland said.

He didn't stop. He was pressing into his front paws and barking upward, snout pointing at the bag, as insistent as if there were an enemy in the camp.

"I know," Leland said, "I know. Quiet." But he could never make this dog mind him, that he knew. So he turned on his heel and left the room, locking the door and putting one foot in front of the other.

. . .

There was music coming from the foredeck, and, mindlessly, he wandered away from it. He wanted to be alone the moment he put Nanette to rest. So he went to the aft deck.

There was one woman standing against the railing. He could see her outline in the moonlight. She was bundled up against the cold. Behind her, the moonlight spilled across the water, sparkling like a promise of jewels. He stood for some time, quiet, unsure of himself. He wanted more than anything for a moment of kindness. He stood on the deck, shuffling his feet and projecting dire human need so loudly she seemed to sense him, and turned around. Embarrassed to be caught looking, he nodded at her.

He stepped closer. She was young, just a girl; her hair might have recently been in braids. But it hung straight and long and black around a serious face he thought he'd seen before. She was looking at him in an evaluative way that made him uncomfortable.

"Hello," he said, clearing his throat. He hadn't spoken to another person in days, he realized, and surfacing into company so abruptly made him want to leave.

"Hello," she said in return. Her eyes dipped down to his duffle bag. He took it off his shoulder, lowered it to the deck, and watched the wake the boat was making. Foam chucked out to the sides, and the moonlight played on that, too, making little glimmering kisses of it. The wind blew against Leland so he had to lean into it and the rail, just to stay upright. The ocean looked infinite.

"It's pretty," he said.

She nodded, looking over the ocean now as if determining that he had not in fact lied.

He wanted to tell her she was pretty. "I," he said, "I have to just say . . ." And there was a catch in his throat that stopped him. "When we were over there, I got a dog." He was ready to be teased, so he said, "A pure-blooded shepherd."

"A dog," the girl said. She was so serious Leland didn't know how to react.

"Yeah," he said. "She just, well, she died a few minutes ago," and the words sounded strange in his ears, the wind sweeping around him, and he hoped she was going to prove him wrong. Maybe she knew about dogs. If Nanette were all right, he could think instead about whether this girl was pretty, or if she liked him. Instead, he followed her dark, lucid eyes as they lowered to his duffle bag, and he nodded when they looked back at him. "I can't bring a dead dog back to the States," he said, hoping he sounded at least a small bit gruff.

She fell to one knee and put her hand on the bag. "Was she a good dog?"

Leland said, "The best," and he looked toward the lifeboats. "She could do tricks." And he was about to say that she could jump from airplane to airplane, and uncork a pineapple, and that he'd hoped to take her to make his fortune in the movies, but all of that sounded pathetic, and the crushable hopes he'd had made him fall silent, and then he hefted the bag up to the railing.

"Wait," said the girl. "We can say something about her first."

Fifty feet below them, the water churned, and Leland was eager for the moment when he would be walking away. "Sure."

The girl paused. "What happened to her?"

"She got sick," he said. "She wasn't that strong."

"Those that He makes perfect, He makes fragile."

"Yeah," Leland said, feeling a thud in his heart. "Is that from the Bible?"

She shrugged. "My uncle says it when things go wrong."

"Oh." He wished he'd gone toward the music on the foredeck. They could have played "Sweet Briar" for her. But there was no music back here. Nanette would have an imperfect service.

He tried to think of some final words, but his mind was jumbled and tired. "I had this idea," he said, then faltered.

"You wanted to be happy?" she asked.

He nodded. He was so exhausted, suddenly, he couldn't even wonder whether it was strange that the girl knew this.

"And you thought it might happen here, with your dogs," she said.

He nodded. There was a long silence. When he felt that too much time was passing, he whispered, "Good girl," and let go of the bag. It was consumed by the boat's wake.

The girl looked over the side, and then back to Leland. "I'm sorry for your loss," she said. "But you'll make it."

"Oh. Good night," he said. As he walked away, he remembered he'd meant to send Nanette off with the finger puppets. Both hands flew to his neck and he looked behind him. "I meant to—"

He was going to explain to the girl what he meant to do, but she was gone.

He returned to the cabin, to his living dog, who sniffed at his trousers for sea salt and for the patches where Nanette had wet them. Leland ran his hands over Boy's head, and tried to get his deep-brown eyes to focus on him.

Abruptly, Boy sat up at attention, and looked at his master, his brow narrowing with something like concern. Then it was gone, the attention dissolving, and a grin appearing in its place.

"You're a good dog, too," he said, and then his shoulders started quaking, as he remembered that this one didn't even know how to sit.

The tears seemed to startle Boy; he stood and began licking Leland's face. Leland hugged him, and looked into his eyes, which reflected intelligence perhaps, but trust—yes—and emotion. Perhaps his Boy wasn't the best dog, but that was how life worked, it gave you obstacles. "Can you," Leland whispered, voice creaking like a half-broken hinge, "can you be good?"

In response, he received full attention, and glimmers of steadfastness, empathy, love, and then the focus broke again, and the dog was sniffing all over the room.

Leland watched him. "Come here," he whispered. Then he pulled Boy toward him with three fingers in his collar. "I'm so sad, Boy." Boy's eyes welled over as if in response. "Really, really sad." Leland felt it to his core, and Boy dropped down to the deck. Hesitantly, feeling as if he were in a dream, Leland said, "But wait—what if we're okay? It's okay, Boy, things are okay."

Boy leapt up, smile returning. He licked his lips, turned around several times, and dug his teeth into something bothering him on his flank.

Leland watched him, overwhelmed. His whole body tingled with the feeling that he now understood Boy's odd potential. He pulled the finger puppets out from around his neck. Rubbing his thumb and forefinger along their bodies, he pinned his hopes on the next-best, the dog that would have to do.

He reached under his bunk and pulled out the rubber ball that Nanette had wanted so badly she would chase it through a campfire or from plane to plane.

He tossed it lightly against the wall. Boy watched him, and then the ball as it rolled to a stop. He made no effort to chase it.

"You can do it," Leland whispered. "You just don't know how yet."

A half hour later, Leland had the bed and the slop buckets and his clothing packed into the corner, and he covered the pile with a sheet. There
were no distractions. He tossed the ball again. This time, Boy followed it
with his eyes, then looked back to his master with confusion, the desire to
please, and utter lack of responsiveness.

"Okay, Boy, we'll do it again," Leland whispered. He tossed the ball.
Hesitantly, looking back for reassurance, the dog walked toward it, just
three steps, and then sat down and looked again at Leland.

"Okay. Okay. That's a start." Leland smiled. Reaching for the ball, he
paused, staring intently at the only dog he had left. "We're going to do
this," he said, "you and me."

The idea was this: People had already made actors famous for emoting.
And the audience was always only guessing at what the emotions were.
And need for communion was so strong they ignored stunt doubles and
stand-ins and all the evidence at hand, to believe for a moment that they
and the actor onscreen understood each other.

So why not a dog acting? Leland could teach Boy stunt work, probably,
eventually. Many dogs could do that. But that was spectacle, the big
sweep. Emotions were the narrow gesture that made the experience feel
true. Boy was going to be the first dog that could act. He would be beloved.

Leland put the ball against Boy's mouth, and Boy opened up and held it
in his jaws. Quietly, with the same kind of gentle pressure you'd use on a
blindfolded friend, guiding him along a mountain trail toward a magnificent
surprise vista, Leland pushed his jaws closed, and the ball let out a squeak.

Boy, shocked, dropped the ball, then immediately picked it up again.
Squeak. A pause. Then *squeak squeak squeak squeak squeak.* His mouth
went up into a smile, and his whole body went alert; his world had
expanded suddenly, and could just barely contain the wonder of this
unknown pleasure.

Leland sat back on the cot and folded his arms. Once, there had been a
girl named Nanette, and she was perpetually about to be swept away by the
next breeze, save for the love of her sweetheart. Once, there was an air
raid, and the only ones who survived were these two, a boy and a girl. The
girl was not long for this earth, and the boy was a fool for her. She could be
kept cleaved to this earth if her boy was strong enough and loved her
enough. There was Nanette, the girl, and the boy was named—

Harry, long ago, had guessed right. For Leland to invoke the other name meant to lose a bit of himself to eternal hope, to a destiny just out of reach. He now accepted his fate, and in this raw moment, his living dog was going to change. "Okay, so I'll name you after the boy puppet. Get ready. It's a stupid name. I mean, really." The dog had earned the foolish boy puppet's foolish name, and Leland would have high and foolish hopes, and somehow, together, they could maybe generate nobility, at least, in their defeats to come. Giant rocks? An acting dog? Maybe they were the same, but maybe the point was always to try. There was only one way to find out.

In a tiny supply closet that all but pulsed with the constant noise of the engines, alone at the end of a lower deck, on a steamer chugging across the endless ocean, Corporal Lee Duncan took into his heart the fathomless future he would share with his only dog, a sweet and untested dog, a dog who would from now on bear the strange, drumlike name of Rin Tin Tin.

When he was standing before the great marble fireplaces at headquarters, listening to the petitions of one politician or another, Ironside's mind wandered toward his men, who were isolated in the vast, silent forest, and it broke his heart to imagine their weariness.

There was no safe way to visit them, but after days of what he called "well-meant hand-wringing," he elected to begin unannounced trips to the farthest troops as a way to boost morale. But how? You couldn't walk. Flying in the frozen twilight was impossible.

For several weeks, the supreme commander of the Allied forces in Russia traveled by pony sleigh. It looked like a cradle on finely turned runners. Made of light pinewood lashed together with the weave of a basket, it was filled with hay, which kept the rider warm, and fed the pony at night. Ironside traveled lightly, with a tot of rum, a Mosin-Nagant rifle, and an automatic pistol in a reindeer-skin bag under his newest absurd greatcoat. It was sable fur on the outside, layer upon layer of mohair on the inside, and it had no zippers or buttons. Getting it on or off required movements that looked as if the wearer were having a seizure.

A large group of sleighs would have made intriguing targets for snipers.

Sunnyside

So Ironside traveled with just one escort, generally a local groom, a native who handled the stops at distant relay posts with discretion. There was never any talk with the master of the post about the rider or his business, just negotiations for a samovar of tea, polite questions about each other's families, switching of the drivers.

He rode up and down the five fingers of the many fronts. The visits' qualities varied according to the personalities and wherewithal of the troops. In Solnechny Strana, morale was excellent right now. But in Obozerskaya, he succeeded only in frightening the French commanding officer, who plucked at his frozen mustache and moaned about not knowing what the enemy was up to.

"Have you asked for volunteer patrols? Talked to the locals, perhaps?" Ironside spoke French with a Normandy accent. The question led to the homesick major's bursting into tears, which froze on his face. Then, returning to manhood, he broke them off and flung them to the snow.

"General Ironside, the morale is wretched."

"Yes. I see. What if I might find you some Americans? They make excellent patrols. Quite a lot of energy, you know. Ah, they have the latest films from America, too."

The major showed several brownish teeth. "Eh . . . *Bon.*"

And so forth, visit after visit. With every company, in every bivouac, and every clearing, and every village, he found fatigue and despair. But among Americans, he found something else, whose specifics eluded him until just after his luck finally ran out, on the outskirts of Seletskoe.

☆　☆　☆

Seletskoe was exactly the *idea* of a Russian winter village: two dozen houses on the north and south banks of the frozen Vaga River, with a strong bridge dusted with crisp snow connecting them. The stars were out at eight and at three and at six, and at seven o'clock in the evening, it was thirty-six degrees below zero. There had been a storm the previous day, and every rooftop was crystalline, and every eave had icicles that reflected like razor blades. The crust of snow was unbroken beneath every tree, except where some wolves had chased one unlucky deer.

Over each rooftop in the village lay a cradle of smoke, which did not rise in such cold, still weather, but which gathered and bunched, as if jealous of the life below it.

If you stayed still long enough, you could tell it wasn't exactly quiet.

Branches creaked. Piles of snow fell from great heights into the snow below. And there was music.

There was a party within one low house. It was a squat bunker with outer walls made of felled pine trees, insulated with horse manure, then inner walls of fine spruce paneling on which hung medallions for St. Nicholas and St. George, and small bits of felt to keep the restless and invisible *domovoi* spirit from knocking over the stewpot in the middle of the night. Festive reels from the accordion and balalaika and domra were now echoing across the walls, and there was stomping and dancing, which made the medallions jump.

The center of the house was a mammoth, steaming iron stove on which huge kettles were kept boiling day and night. Over the stove was a large bed. In the bed was Grandma, covers drawn up to her ears, a bonnet over her head, her tooth exposed in a grin, and a jar of *peevo* in her gnarled hand, which she was now swinging back and forth with the music, not spilling a drop.

The peasants were dancing with Americans of the 339th. That afternoon, a soused Lieutenant Gordon had had men drop Mills grenades onto the ice, and then dash across the river after the resulting explosion to catch the stunned trout in buckets. There had been fish for dinner.

There were lanterns hanging high on the walls and others on the pine tables, which together cast a lukewarm yellow light that tended to emphasize the sweat and dirt on the celebrants' skin. It smelled of a local ponderous incense that was not unlike a wet stack of moldering Bibles. The incense was used because the livestock had been living in the house since January.

There was one man not dancing, a man who no longer danced, and this was Pfc. Hugo Black.

Since returning from the monastery, he had been a changed man. Wodziczko was assumed to have been picked off by Bolos, and so he wasn't questioned about this. While on guard duty, he no longer quizzed himself about the rules of debutante engagement. Instead, he read furtively the propaganda nailed to trees, and he recalled things the voice had murmured to him from the woods outside the candy warehouse. Here was an interesting question, one he considered cautiously: what if the workers of the world *did* unite?

As the merry music continued in the house, he knew he had to leave soon for his next assignment. In a fittingly horrible, epanaleptic assignment of duties, he was now projectionist *again*. He traveled from outpost to outpost with reels of film. He had also tried, timidly, to speak to the local populace about Bolshevism, and somehow he had never been successful. Tonight he hadn't even bothered. He had sat on the floor (all the chairs were taken), and within a few minutes, a goat and two pigs had found him and were lying against him for warmth.

The animals' adoration was intriguing to the villagers. Ptor, whose house it was, thought this might mean Hugo was blessed by the *domovoi*. But after excusing himself to use the privy, Hugo did not touch the cross, which was offensive to Elijah, and which was punishable by having the saint stab him with a knitting needle.

Ptor worried about Hugo, who seemed unaware of what might happen to him, so he sent his cousin and neighbor Ivan to watch out for him. The privy had been designed for the needs of only a few people; the influx of American soldiers had overburdened it. Waste froze the moment it left the body, and so peeking above the hole in the wooden planks was a cinder cone of solid fecal matter that had to be chipped away every morning. Ivan watched Hugo enter the privy and apparently not use it. Instead, Ivan could see him staring out the privy window and wiping at his eyes, and a few moments later, he left and closed the door without saying thank you to the *domovoi* of the privy, who would undoubtedly punish him by tickling him to death.

Back inside, Hugo also knocked over the linens and then restacked them himself rather than allowing the oldest woman in the village to do it (a terrible, terrible punishment of being tickled to death awaited that transgression). Most men on the verge of being tickled to death would be weeping, begging forgiveness, making sacrifices of grouse or house rabbit, rubbing icons on the doorstop, bringing unplucked chickens to bury below the stoop in front of the bathhouse, but not Hugo. He seemed innocent and helpless, and that this man would so soon be tickled to death made the peasants at the dance feel sorry for him.

He had learned some Russian—the words for "worker," "grain," "collective," "struggle," "landowner," and a sentence or two that conveyed that the person to whom he was speaking was the means of production. Tonight he had the ear of both Ivan and Ptor, who leaned forward, nodding their heads sympathetically.

He had to shout to be heard over the music, and he wasn't sure he was using the right words, but they did nod, and Ptor did sadly offer him a cigarette. It seemed to be made not of tobacco but of dried grasses and perhaps some rye berries.

Across the room, two doughboys of the 339th and two young peasants were having a religious discussion. The fact that neither nationality spoke the other's language was mitigated by heroic amounts of *peevo*. There was a great deal of pointing at the crosses that all four of them wore, and then hand gestures indicating slashes of the throat, arrows in the chest, scalding lead thrown in the eyes.

The Americans were trying to explain that saints only meant well, they forgave, were so generous they might even bake cookies for you (or so their pantomime seemed to indicate). The Russians were puzzled, then frightened that the Americans were missing an important piece of information: a saint was a horrifying, terrifying, all-powerful spirit who would skin you as soon as look at you. They were reminding their new American friends of—for instance—merciless St. Cassian, whose feast day was February 29, a day so dangerous that no one dared leave the house.

In return, the Americans were sure there was just a small misunderstanding that could be worked out if they spoke openly for long enough. And the Russians were similarly sure. There were still smiles, but also sideways glances, faltering gestures, more drinking of *peevo*, longer silences.

Hugo finished his cigarette. He displaced the goat, who had fallen asleep on him again. He stretched and yawned. The music was suited for two o'clock in the morning, slow and dirgelike, just the accordion playing a desperate folksong, "Dark Eyes." The peasants knew the words and moaned along.

Hugo stood by the door. He had a bundle of film canisters in a canvas knapsack that he held in one hand. His crossbow was on his back. He looked inside. The fires had gone low, and the household retired to their straw mats to hug brothers, sisters, or livestock and to settle in for a few hours of rest, and the soldiers of the 339th were moved to wonder when they were going home. Lieutenant Gordon, asked to address them, mumbled a few phrases about loyalty and then burst into tears.

When the accordion was finished, Hugo said goodbye and left. Before he'd even closed the door, the remaining men of the 339th began to sing the most miserable song in the world.

As Hugo dropped his film canisters onto his sled and pulled it into the evening blast of shocking Arctic cold, he could hear voices behind him singing their version of "Auld Lang Syne."

Sunnyside

We're here because we're here because
We're here because we're here
We're here because we're here because
We're here because we're here

The house was smaller and smaller behind him; the voices were like a choir at first, but quickly shimmering, as if—like the smoke—even the sound of human singing did not want to go into the black vast wilderness.

The next village was just one verst away, and it had no name. Or it was also Seletskoe. Either way, it was across the bridge. Hugo pulled his sled along, sighing to himself about *une fausse idée claire.* Once, he had danced with princesses. Once, he had been in Detroit.

He walked among the spruce trees, around which the local women had wrapped long silk scarves to appease the *rusalka,* a beautiful, friendly, naked girl who tended to entice young men to chase her, then beat them to death. This was said to happen mostly in summer, but the entire winter had passed without such incidents, so the scarves were obviously successful even now.

He shuffled along the road, absently brushing at his face, where the local cooties were bothering his mustache and beard. There was a solitary figure standing on the hilltop. Short and bulky in layers of sealskin, but also wearing just a simple felt cap and scarf: it was a girl.

Hugo stopped. He felt for his rifle, and then for his crossbow.

She was in silhouette. A little wind coughed fresh snow into the air, then across the path, where it was sent prismatic by the cold lunar light.

"Zdravstvuite," he said carefully. And then, "Hello."

He pulled his sled with him, up the hill. The moonlight cast strong shadows across the divots it left in the snowpack. The girl watched him, her hands buried in her pockets, her face absent of any expression, as if she were waiting for her portrait to be taken.

When he was closer, he saw she had black pigtails and dark eyes that blinked slowly. Her skin was a brilliant white, with a luminous quality, as if light were actually shining through it.

"Dobry," Hugo said, unable to remember what time it was. It seemed it was always the same time, but he remembered: it was night. *"Dobry vyecher."*

Her little village was behind her. Smaller than the actual Seletskoe, it still looked almost identical, with a few houses flanking the river, and smoke curled against each roof. There was a church. Near it, stables.

"*Kak vashi dela, tovarishch,*" he said casually. He guessed she was fifteen years old. She was looking at him now as if taking an inventory of his qualities, and he stood a little straighter, thanked God he had washed recently. Her eyes flicked over the ruins of his uniform and alit upon the sled and the canvas sack upon it. Then she returned to looking openly at his face. He smiled, showing off teeth. He wanted to ask her if she'd heard about the revolution. But it was late, and it was so difficult to string up all those unfamiliar sounds. The flask was in his hands.

He had preserved just one last taste of Chartreuse. There had been a last swallow, which left behind a last sip, and then, after that, he had put his lips to the threaded nipple when anxious, if only to inhale what had once been there. The girl watched him touch his tongue to the flask. Her eyes had lit up upon seeing the silver in the moonlight.

She still hadn't spoken. Hugo thought she was the most beautiful girl he'd ever seen. It was a different sort of beauty from the princesses'. She reminded him of other girls he'd known, only fresher and better.

She was pointing at him.

"What's that?" he asked. "Oh. My crossbow? You want to see my crossbow?" She did not nod, but she was reaching out for it. "It's quite valuable," he said. "You'll have to be careful." A quiet crackle traveled up his spine as he slipped the tiller from its case, and then lifted the crossbow by its leather cord off of his neck, like slipping off a bridle. "Have you fired a crossbow before? These are called fletches. They're like arrows." He held the crossbow himself. "You draw the string back like this, and this is the nut that holds it."

She looked at the weapon, then at him, enchanted. She pointed at the bow again. He shook his head.

"I'm sorry, I can't let you touch it. It's too dangerous."

Her gaze returned to his eyes. If he expected her to well up with tears, he was disappointed.

She was extending, between a bare forefinger and bare thumb, a small silver badge the size of a quarter. On it was stamped a tiny silver fish. There were raised letters on the back, G-S-A, but Hugo could not read them in the moonlight.

"Your badge for my crossbow?" He laughed. "I think not." But he laughed again, which made her smile. He realized how tense his shoulders had been for months. "Oh," he said, "I'm with you, miss." He performed pantomime: pretended to hand her the crossbow and take the badge, and then, a moment later, pretended to exchange them again. Not a trade. A loan.

She nodded, once.

Hugo looked down the hill, toward the town whose name he either knew or didn't. The doors of some houses had opened, and yellow lights from within made silhouettes, the shapes of people. Some were bent into old age. Most were upright, stout, and walking with arms extended from their sides. One or two were black cutouts in the shapes of children. He gave them a gentle wave. And then, as if sharing one mind, they began their approach together. He waved again. No one waved back.

Hugo handed his crossbow to the girl, and he took her badge between his callused fingertips. The exchange reminded him of something from a distant time and place. As Hugo watched the girl sight down the tiller, he knew he had to instruct her in its use. He should find her a proper target. But he was so tired. The thought a few moments ago about his shoulders made him relax them again, and then he realized he'd been clenching his stomach since he'd landed on this continent.

The people who were approaching must have been making noises. They must have been tromping through the snow, they must have been yelling a *Dobry vyecher* his way. The hoes and shovels they were carrying, the rusted pitchforks that shook up and down with every step they took, must have clanged against one another at least once or twice.

How strange it was, so deep into a winter that would not end, to find a perfect moment of quiet. He knew it would lift in less than a heartbeat, less than a second. If he could only take a snapshot of this moment and make it last, he would remember that he had felt it, and it might mean something later. He breathed slowly. He smiled. He closed his eyes.

☆   ☆   ☆

Ironside spent that evening in Shredmehrenga, where the billeting was American. Yet another man characterized the weather as so cold you could hear your spit crack when it hit the ground. After the cuckoo clock (a rarity, and in fact a gift from the village blacksmith, who had trained in Lucerne) chirped midnight, Ironside had the pony sleigh set up. Then, because he had a heart, he dismissed the groom, who had taken a shine to a young widow nearby.

Ironside traveled alone behind his pony, reclined like a baby in bulrushes.

It was a clear night. This one was illuminated by that fantastic full moon as bright as if hewn from polished silver, and swollen, looking ready to burst. Ironside recalled childhood astronomy lessons. There was the Sea of Tranquillity, there the Sea of Serenity. The rhythm of the pony trotting ahead of him along the flat and comfortable trail, the way the sleigh runners made an amiable rumbling along the hard-packed snow, left him drowsy and reflective. He missed his wife. He was muffled entirely in furs, except for a small band across his eyes.

Ironside was asleep. The pony stumbled, and, simultaneously, there was a pinging like a hammer rapping against a stone block. The sleigh went off its course, startling Ironside upright, and his animal, with a groan, fell into a shallow bank of snow.

Ironside's hands went to his rifle. The pony let out a small gasp, its lips chattered, and its forelegs shuddered in the white blanketing of snow, and then it set to panting miserably. There was a patch of frozen blood on its neck. A shaft of wood, thin as mistletoe, jutted out of its hide.

The moon overhead gave the surroundings a stark blue light, harsh penumbrae behind every hillock of snow and every tree. Ironside, rattling his sleigh onto its side to make cover, crouched next to the dying animal and peered outward. The forests were of pine, spruce, and aspen, and the snow covered meadows, lakes, rivers. The sounds in the woods would mostly be harmless. Deer, rabbits, sables.

It was impossible to tell where the shot had come from. He was in a clearing perhaps a quarter-mile square. Stumps of trees made button marks in the snow. This meant habitation nearby. Shallow breathing was recommended at such Arctic temperatures; he took a chance and breathed deeply through his nose, a punishing, burning feeling. But, yes, he smelled smoke, which confirmed there were people somewhere.

He could not see them. His horse let out a groan, and tried to lift its head. Ironside put down his rifle. His pistol was in a fur-lined bag strapped to the inside of his leg. It took some burrowing and blind finesse to reach it. Within a few moments, he had the gun in one hand in his pocket, glove off, undermitten still on. But he could only keep his gun outside and exposed for a few seconds before the oil would freeze, turning it into a paperweight. He could shoot his horse, but then he might have no bullets for the enemy, except in his Mosin-Nagant, which was useless anyway.

"I apologize, old thing," he whispered to the pony, patting him on the flank.

There was a stand of trees in the distance. This would provide protection, though the odds of making it were slender. Staying with his pony meant a likely death, however. He wore peasant boots—he'd long ago given up on the Shackletons—and he broke into old snowpack, feet sinking deeply through the crust, as he zigged and zagged toward the pines. A return to shallow breathing, the air scorching his lungs. Running awkwardly with his hands in his pockets, taking care not to shoot himself in the leg, a humiliating way to die.

There was a structure ahead. A thick woolen cap of smoke hanging over a chimney, some kind of light from within. He hadn't seen it because of the trees. He paused.

At such low temperatures, time and space and physics are subject to terrible pressure—ten yards might as well be a mile, a minute could be an hour. Ironside listened. There was some kind of mechanical noise coming from within the structure, sprockets engaged, a low purring noise, and underlying that was an essential human murmur—coughing, low voices— a crowd. But it was ahead of him by some distance, and as his hearing grew more acute, he heard a cleft made in the hard-packed snow directly to his rear. A crack. *It's so cold, sir, you can hear your spit crack when it hits the ground.*

He rolled downward and left, bringing his firing arm out of his pocket, and aiming behind his fur-bulked form, shooting twice directly into the chest of a boy holding a pitchfork. The boy toppled over backward, pitchfork bouncing once against his forehead. Then all was still.

Ironside continued to breathe. There was a kind of reverberation up his right arm, and he looked at his pistol in amazement. What had he done? He tromped through the snow toward the boy, who looked to be about twelve or thirteen, dressed in the layers of wool and fur and mohair of any peasant.

There was blood on the snow, the moon rendering it black. Ironside had killed a child. *I was defending myself,* he thought, without consolation. *The pitchfork,* he thought. *He might have been coming after me with the pitchfork,* and that his mind would pathetically generate this defense in his own internal court of inquiry made hot tears form and freeze in his eyes.

The boy had a pitchfork. Someone had shot his horse with a crossbow.

The snow was a fossil record of shoe prints. Dozens of people had been here. The whole village?

He looked again toward the building that the noises had been coming from. There was still smoke atop the roof, and the whirring of small machinery, but the crowd inside had stilled. There were no windows, but a pair of doors at one end, and a cross mounted overhead. It was a church.

He threw the pitchfork down. He walked carefully, boots crunching, following the trail of shoe prints.

Thirty feet away, at the top of the hill, was a dead soldier. His coat and uniform and shoes were gone; he was in his drawers. The face had frozen into a grimace. A single bolt stuck out of his chest. His arms and legs had frozen into a posture of self-defense, and there were tripartite sets of wounds all over his body, for, after being shot with the crossbow, he had also been stabbed repeatedly with a pitchfork.

Ironside tried to close the man's eyes, but the vitreous had frozen, as had the lids. He found the dog tags, and snapped one off, and pocketed it. He glanced at the face again and saw, in profile, the beaked nose, the lack of dignity.

There was next to him a stone chisel and an ominous pyramid of pinecones. Ironside's imagination, which had been held at bay so far, was beginning to return. There was no way to impart ideals to these people, who were equally friendly and savage to those who'd come to help them.

The dead American's supplies were scattered around him. A broken sled, empty ration tins, a deflated canvas sack, a pack shorn of its tools, a web cartridge belt looted of its ammunition. A few feet from the body, Ironside found circular canisters whose purpose he couldn't quite place. Tin, larger than pie plates, shallow, and with edges reeded like coins—there were a dozen of them, all opened, all empty. Finally, he held one up and could see by the metallic blue light of the full moon the large block lettering on its side: JOHANNA ENLISTS.

The doors of a Russian peasant church were not made to lock. A simple push, and anyone could come in and be welcome. Ironside stepped inside quietly and carefully, and found himself in a large crowd, most of them sitting, everyone facing the same direction. It was mostly dark.

Ironside doubted he would be killed in a church, but to stay outside in the cold would definitely kill him. He stood in the very back, towering over those who stood near him. Slowly, he stripped off his hat, his coat, his undercoat. He saw, leaning against the wall, a crossbow. His eyes flicked from person to person, backs of heads; it could have been anyone's crossbow, everyone facing the altar, before which a sheet was draped. Then he realized the rules of this new, grim game: it was everyone's crossbow. The families around him acknowledged him with light smiles, but when he attempted to talk—he had concocted a story that might pacify them—they put their fingers to their lips, mildly. *Shhh.*

The projector continued its low sprocketing noise. It was run off of a small battery; nonetheless, a narrow-shouldered priest stood nearby with a small candle to illuminate its mechanical mysteries, attending to it with a cloth as if a speck of dust could run it aground. Beside him were reels of Chaplin films—the first ten minutes of *The Rink,* the last of *The Adventurer,* and then *Work* and *Shanghaied* in their entirety.

The screen was a bedsheet hanging down in front of the altar. Mary Pickford's luminous face spilled across the sheet. Ironside had seen *Johanna Enlists* before, of course, too many times. He stared at it without much thought except rescue, but it was hard to concentrate, for the audience was finding delight in every motion Mary Pickford made.

She played Johanna, a clumsy farm maiden sent chowderheaded by romantic thoughts. She fed the hogs with a clothespin on her nose, she fainted when she saw a weevil on her potatoes, she tried to dance on the lawn like Isadora Duncan, ending up tangled in the clothesline.

This caused chuckling that built as Johanna rolled back and forth on the ground, attempting to free herself gracefully, while the man she loved, a handyman, shook his head in disbelief. There were high, asthmatic gasps as she finally extricated herself, only to fall into the pigsty. The priest laughed so hard he dropped his candle, and it winked out cold.

Ironside rather lost track of the drama. He hadn't slept, he needed to leave, and it was hard to think as his limbs went numb from standing upright.

Mary Pickford was praying. She clasped her hands to make a heart in the space between her thumbs and forefingers, asking the Almighty to send her a beau. A beau who could truly excite her. Her eyebrows shot north—a sound! What could it be? A bugle! The Lord sent her not a man, but a regiment!—the 143rd Artillery Brigade!—which, this moment of all moments, elected to train in the very pasture outside Mary's window. The images of soldiers drilling, of Johanna reacting with enthusiasm to the cold and obvious propaganda, made Ironside nervous.

Mary found a handsome captain, played by Douglas MacLean. As he courted her with sweet nothings, her tender, flushed face regarding his with infinite joy, you could hear a pin drop.

Ironside, who had seen many things in his life, and who would live to see many more, had no words to describe this. He had a vision that carried with it no emotional weight whatever: the sun rising at the cradle of the Tigris and Euphrates, carrying with it the light, passing west, and currently, at this very moment, sending America into ascendance, with his own little kingdom drifting from its apogee.

He would find safe passage to Archangel for himself and the dead American. And soon he would oversee a withdrawal from Russia, an evacuation of troops, an end to the democratic ambition in this part of the world. But for now, he struggled to understand what he was beholding: dozens of silent, upturned faces awash in the glow of Mary Pickford's youthful radiance. Her face was open to the camera, and there were no secrets there except how the happy flame of her soul so easily shone through her brilliant eyes. She was the most beautiful woman he had ever seen.

Mary sat in a swing with her suitor, who grinned at some empty point at the horizon, an arm around her shoulders.

In the audience, a bearded man cupped his thick palms and shouted, "Kisssszzz! Kissssszzz!" In English. It was a sound that made Ironside freeze in wonderment. "Kissssszzz!"

Mary stood, clutching her lover's hands between her own; as the camera found her in close-up, her eyes were misty. Through mere proximity to the manliness of the 143rd, her confidence was no longer that of a tremulous schoolgirl one step less agile than a barnyard animal. She was awakened. Her beau brought into the frame a ring set with a tiny, modest diamond, whose facets cast reflections everywhere, and the audience shouted out their appreciation. Would she marry him? Her mouth pumped open and her fists went into the air as she yelled, "Yes! Yes!"

"Kiss!" The audience yelled. "Ma-ry Pick-ford! Kiss!" There were tears in Mary's eyes as she finally brought her mouth to her man's. A pair of women in the front row were crying, and Ironside could hear sniffling from the darker corners of the church. And he knew that, all around the world, in grottoes and houses and mudflat huts, it was the same: there were groups watching Mary Pickford find her man, they were welling up with tears in all parts of the globe, from the port of Bar in Montenegro to lean-tos on the plains of French West Africa to the darkest recesses of Indochina.

Sunnyside

The iris of the camera blazed outward, and then drew in, a tightening circle on the happily-ever-after kiss, a goodbye kiss that brought tears in a tiny church in Russia, in New York City, in the Dutch East Indies, and as far away as the cradle of civilization itself, where young, amazed nomads in tents watched and wiped tears from their eyes, there on the desert sands of Mesopotamia.

Sing-Along

"Smile"

. . . .

Interviewer: Suppose you were going to take a long vacation—then what?

Chaplin: Russia. The thought of it fascinates me.

—Picture Play Magazine
December 1916

Smile
What's the use of crying?
You'll find that life
Is still worthwhile
If you just smile

—lyrics by John Turner and Geoffrey Parsons;
music by Charlie Chaplin

. . . .

So ends the larger story. But you never want to fade out on landscape alone. And so here are faces, dozens of them, chubby or gaunt, serious or pleased, all belonging to prosperous men who had dressed that morning to impress one another, men who were now shaking one another's hands as they arrived, then asking questions, then shading their eyes and peering inside the bronze-and-leaded-glass front doors of the most magnificent hotel in Los Angeles. Which for reasons unknown was closed to them.

They were hungry.

When the Alexandria was launched in 1906, the newspapers emphasized its grandeur by—as was the style—citing its European chefs, its British concierge, its dining-room ceilings designed by Tiffany of New York City. But of late, when people discussed the Alexandria, they discussed the carpet.

The Alexandria lobby was home to a twenty-seven-foot-long Sultanabad with a deep-blue frame and red interior, decorated with yellow flowers and intricate latticework vines, and its quality was mediocre. Knots came loose, rips appeared in it and were poorly sewn together, only to rip once again the next time someone tripped across it. However, so many film producers had shaken hands on deals here, the awful Sultanabad was known as the million-dollar carpet. It was one of the first objects that Hollywood had grown attached to, and so, every evening, a girl handy with needle and thread undertook another patch job.

This morning, a Sunday, the dining room was officially closed. However, a secret memorandum had been sent to the highest levels at the studios. A partnership-agreement draft proposal had been approved, a massive merger program that would create a $250-million corporation. In the collapse of Europe, and with it the European film industry, America had stepped in with a superior product that would now, starting today, flow with more efficiency than ever. There were also unstated goals: controlling the feisty actors and the writers and directors who acted.

Zukor had quietly booked the Alexandria dining room for the announcement, which was to occur over breakfast. Outside of the men standing with him, and their assistants, news of the meeting was supposed to have a quality that did not yet have a name. It was supposed to be both secret and known to all, and thus seasoned with primordial fear, like the true name of God.

But the doors of the Alexandria were not open, and ten minutes had already passed. The sidewalk outside was buzzing. Here was Goldwyn, looking nervous and about to explode into tears of joy; and there was William Fox, who spoke to no one; and next to him a fatigued-looking Albert Smith of Vitagraph; and then Carl Laemmle and Merrill Montgomery of Universal; Al Christie of Christie Studios; Robert Lieber of the First National Exhibitors' Circuit, NYC; Charles Eyton of Lasky; Maxwell Karger, director general of Metro; David Bernstein of Loews; Morris Kohn, president and treasurer of Realart; and of course Zukor himself, who had thought to bring bodies with him: Jesse Lasky (Famous Players–Lasky), Emil Shauer (assistant treasurer), Elek Ludvigh (from the old country, assistant secretary), four general managers, two production managers, three business managers. There were perhaps fifty people on the sidewalk, not one of them an actor. In other words, had a family from Omaha set down their bags and wandered among them, not a single face would have been familiar.

Captains of industry, they were on the cusp of their largest triumph. If only they could get into the hotel.

"Can you explain the meaning of this?" asked someone; it hardly mattered who. "Why are the doors blocked?"

And now, inside the hotel lobby: four waiters, young and graceful and excited. They were rolling a giant oak tabletop down the length of the hotel. Seconds later, they were met by another team of waiters carrying its heavy base, which they attached with quick spins of bolts onto threads.

"What's going on?" asked one executive.

"They're building a table," announced another.

The table was being set up on the million-dollar carpet. Out came a linen cloth, white and clean, catching the air and billowing like a sail before settling, and then the crew of waiters rapidly set out place mats, knives, spoons, forks, plates, coffee cups, and glasses. For five. A hubbub outside now on the sidewalk, men jostling to see better, as, inside, smiling and joking, walking arm in arm across the carpet, toward the table, toward the crowd outside helplessly watching the table, came Charlie Chaplin, Douglas Fairbanks, Mary Pickford, and D. W. Griffith. Behind them, a fifth person, whom no one except Zukor recognized. It was Bill McAdoo.

The three most famous movie stars on earth and the world's most famous director and the former treasury secretary sat down to breakfast, snapping their napkins out of their rings.

Chaplin, Pickford, Fairbanks, and Griffith had decided to form their own corporation to distribute their productions. There was even a manifesto—

> We believe that this step is positively and absolutely necessary to protect the great motion picture public from threatening combinations and trusts that would force upon them mediocre productions and machine-made entertainment . . .

—and so on. Their general counsel would be McAdoo, who was curious whether his theories about the power of stardom would hold up in financial practice. If it turned out that there was some spectral force more important than money, he wanted it. To show both solidarity among their bickering personalities, and the value they placed on their chief assets— themselves—the company would be called United Artists.

But the announcement of the name, the theories, the breast-beating, the new competition, and in fact the wet firecracker of Zukor's trust idea (over before it started, for now), were all for later. For now, on the sidewalks of the Alexandria, peering into the windows and gossiping like washerwomen on the Liffey, the many executives jostled for position, fighting for a chance to watch how natural and ordinary the stars looked.

Inside the hotel, the bell captain ordered the pins taken out of the doors so they could be flung back. At the table, McAdoo looked at the others, waiting so he could nod with parental concern and tell them they would be fine. But no one was looking his way. Instead, Pickford, Fairbanks, Griffith, and Chaplin, coffee cups raised, halfway through buttering toast, holding a section of grapefruit, watched their audience about to approach. In the air, the feeling was like that of an alpine village about to meet an avalanche.

☆　☆　☆

Sunnyside

Several months later, early summer of 1919. The daily hubbub at the sun-dappled maternity ward of Kaspare Cohn Hospital, on Whittier. Expectant fathers put their wives into wheelchairs, nurses sternly shoo them away, men pace down the lengthy hallways, men anxiously finger cigars in the lobby, and huge heaping baskets of freshly laundered pink or blue blankets are waiting to be used.

"Kaspare Cohn" was unwieldy, so it was nicknamed "Cedars of Lebanon," which was more mellifluous. And since the name went back to Gilgamesh, it suggested that Los Angeles had anchor chains and ballast and would not just float off into the air one day.

A touring car pulls into the circular drive. It belongs to a very wealthy man, a comedian who owns his own studio, a tragedian in the making, a terrible son, an awful husband, a romantic, a brat, a dancer, a mimic, and a genius. It halts at the curb. There he is, inside the car, but it is impossible to see him, for the eternal rays of sunshine are reflecting against the window, rendering him into outline, and who could pretend to read his mind?

Today is July 7, 1919, the day Mildred Harris Chaplin gave birth to a boy, whom she named Charles Chaplin.

Chaplin had spent the long morning before the birth at Russo's Toys for Girls and Boys, on Santa Monica Boulevard, selecting and setting aside stuffed animals.

They had closed the store for him, and he sat fitfully in the aisle with badgers and tigers and bears and skunks (skunks!), making them move across the floor, and arranging them in tableaux in which predators and prey all stood together with large, doped smiles on their faces. What was the use of stuffed animals?

He was imagining that Mildred would not birth a child but, with screams and agony, a lead-weight, bitter-smelling skull. He imagined that, wherever he saw it, wrapped in swaddling clothes that made it into a horrendous parody of all he might hold dear—a wife he actually loved, a life he actually wanted—it would grin back at him in triumph. It would reek of sulfur or phosgene or the vile chemicals in the nitrate bath, and he imagined Mildred wanly passing it to him, asking him to love it.

He asked what other stuffed animals they had, and after rejecting cats and dogs, he spotted something standing beside the display case that made him laugh, that *heh heh-heh* that belonged only to him. It was a giraffe, but this was the largest giraffe in the store, with a long neck and a trunk you could almost ride on, its tiny hooves made of wood, and able to stand upright on its own. Plus: its fur was soft, and as Chaplin packed it into the Locomobile, and rode to the hospital, he stroked it and imagined tiny fingers finding it for the first time and concluding that the world was a soft place. It made him understand a little better: stuffed animals, yes, of course.

The hardest part of filmmaking was showing the moment of change. The secret was: people did not change. Instead, they changed and changed back. You only grew to know them better, and then, at some key moment, you realized they had been bound to disappoint you from the beginning. Such as himself? Oh, yes.

On the road to Cedars, he began to run his fingertips across the lengthy spine of the giraffe, where two planes of fur cleverly met to form a plush ridge. He felt his heart opening. There would be a baby, and it would be half him, half Mildred, and in his better moments, he remembered that Mildred was rather a prize. He tried to recount her performance in that last Lois Weber objectively, and had to conclude that she had wit about her, and depth. He imagined his side of the conversation they might have: I'm sorry. You know we could try again from the beginning. I will promise to be as nice as I was that first night. Yes, I am happy about freedom and how well we smashed the trust. I am sorry for all the things I have ever done and all the things I will do in the future. Because this is our child. Mildred, I'm sorry.

A child floating in a tin washtub, the balloon of his belly, pink knees like islands in the water, his head resting against Chaplin's hand, which would support it. The idea that something would be born into the world and that it would trust him made him put both hands upon the giraffe and cling.

He had Kono pull up in the delivery entrance of the hospital, and he indicated that it was no problem, he would take the giraffe himself. Kono opened the back door for him, and Chaplin began to push the giraffe, but it snagged on the leather seats, which caused him great anxiety for his car, so he decided to take it out the other door. Alas, though its neck came freely, its overstuffed body in no way wished to leave the automobile.

It was delicate work, so Chaplin invited Kono to push from the other side, which he did, and it was an unexpected strain for both of them, Chaplin pulling, Kono pushing, each of them telling the other to be careful, and then it was free, and Kono fell into the cabin of the car. Chaplin, suddenly bearing the toy's bulk, started to topple himself, but spun in place, staggered, and managed not to drop it.

Sunnyside

Were there people in wheelchairs around him? Patients on tables? Doctors performing surgery on the sidewalk for some reason, elbows about to be jostled into performing accidental abortions? He couldn't see Kono or the car, but only fur and sky. He asked if Kono was all right, and there was a brief groan, then assent, yes, he was fine, Mr. Charlie should go visit Missus.

The maternity ward was on the third floor. The elevators were slow, as they always were in hospitals, wide enough to dock H.M.S. *Dreadnought* in, and the smell was of iodine.

A nurse sat behind a desk, some distance from the elevators, a long, whitewashed hall that was being mopped at either end. Chaplin almost slipped, but he carried his giraffe perfectly, as if it were a tureen filled with soup. The nurse had seen many expectant fathers coming down this hall, some of them in triumph, some skulking, some drunk, and more than a few bearing gifts. But none like this. It was a giraffe that wanted to float and spin its way awkwardly toward her, with splaying human legs to support its dreams.

Chaplin arrived at the nurses' station and dropped the toy carefully to the ground. "Hello," he said, grinning, "I'm here to see Mildred Chaplin. I'm her husband."

The nurse did not meet his eye, not at first, and then it was as if she felt she had no choice. She was not reacting to his identity—or, rather, she was, except she didn't care that he was Charlie Chaplin. "She's in Room 311."

Chaplin swallowed, a sound as loud as water hitting a metal pail. "Has, has it happened yet?"

The nurse nodded.

"And she's all right?"

She nodded again.

He picked up his giraffe and left.

When he saw the second nurse sitting outside Room 311, he knew his baby was dead. Unlike the first nurse, this one had some religious garb— he was never good at telling apart nuns and Red Cross workers, but this one had a black hood, and a cross around her neck. She looked through his stuffed toy, through his enthusiasm. It was at once a simple look—she was sad—and not, in that he saw her religion was giving her comfort, and she was about to extend it his way.

"Hullo," he said. "I'm Charlie Chaplin."

She nodded at him.

"Where is my wife?"

"She's resting."

The door was closed. If he asked, he could probably open it. "The baby."

"The baby is resting," she said.

"Oh." He noticed his hands playing over the giraffe. When you really felt it, the whorls and patterns were probably as soft as on a real giraffe. "The baby is resting," he said.

"You may go in, but your wife is very weak. She delivered a few hours ago, and . . ."

"And?"

"And, well, yes, she would need to see you now."

"What's wrong?"

The nun stood, and with a care not to make too much noise, allowed the door to open.

He brought the giraffe in. Its hooves scuffed against the floor. The room was white, the windows were tall and faced a garden of cedars and olives and trees used for medicine in biblical times. Inside, the room was swollen with flowers. Everyone in Hollywood had sent flowers, beginning the moment Mildred had gone into labor. There were arrangements from all the studios, from friends, from enemies, from people who didn't even know them, a pageant of smells and colors that should have been cheerful.

Mildred lay under the covers. Her hair was plastered to her head, the occasional pinwheel curl loose against the pillow. There was a terrible human smell in the air, the smell of fear, of medicines, of unwashed linens, and something sickly, like hot milk in a rubber bottle.

When he walked toward her, Mildred's eyes spilled over. "Oh, Charlie," she whispered. "Oh, my darling Charlie."

He swallowed. She was extending her arms, and he held the giraffe toward her, but she did not want it. So he hugged her.

Upon his touch, she dissolved into sobs. He could feel the hopeless effort she was making to hold him. "I'm sorry," she said. "I'm sorry, I'm sorry." She was gulping between words. "Oh, I'm so sorry. Please forgive me."

"I forgive you," he whispered. "It's all right, Mildred. I love you. Shh. It's all right."

An ingénue was most beautiful when on the verge of tears, but only on the verge. Now, her body jerking with each hysterical convulsion, Mildred was ugly. He still wanted to tell her he was in love. He would never leave her just because she had become ugly. That wasn't something he would do.

If something terrible had happened, he would stay with her forever. Her ugliness would be the price he paid for all the terrible things he had done. He remembered to kiss her face, his eyes closed, and murmured to her whatever was in his head, kind words. He was asking her if she remembered when they were happy, how they had met at the beach—oh, yes, the car before that—weren't they happy then? It was awkward, in that he had to bend from the waist next to the bed, and the giraffe was looming next to him like a lamppost.

Exhausted, she relaxed into letting him go, her hands fixed into fists, her thumbs plunged down inside of them.

"Mr. Chaplin?" It was the nun. She was holding a blue blanket. "This is your son."

Chaplin's eyes darted toward the flowers—how colorful they were!—and then the window. Then he extended his arms bravely to accept the bundle. Instead, the nun glided across the room and laid it against Mildred, so that it rested between her arm and her body. The nun glided out of the room. Chaplin willed himself to glance at the baby, and saw that the face was perfectly normal. The face of all newborn babies. He was tucked into the blanket tight as a bullet, though, with his entire body hidden, and a hood went up behind his head.

It looked very much like a baby, and that was all he could really think right now. Chaplin smiled to himself, a smile that vanished, and his eyes went again to the flowers. A dozen white roses from Goldwyn. A wreath with a cartoon drawing of a stork and some other animals on it from Sennett. Oh, it said, "Ol' Joe Stork Brings One New Krazy Kat." How nice of them.

"It's a boy," he said. He had never been so frightened. The way the bundle was packed up, the hood, something seemed out of proportion, ballooned in odd places, sunken in others. Or was that his imagination? The baby was strangely motionless, its eyes fixed, its upper lip twitching reflexively, but otherwise it lacked all vigor. "So," Chaplin said.

Mildred began to unwrap the blanket. She started with a safety pin at the chest and then peeled back the layers of swaddling cloth carefully, as if the infant might, with too much handling, come apart in her hands. When it was uncovered, visible to Chaplin completely, the father was quiet. His eyes ran over the little body, unable to understand exactly what he was seeing, looking for the familiar landscape of chest, stomach, arms, legs, and then the curtain of the blanket was drawn closed again. The baby made a strange gasp, like the pop of gas releasing from a swamp.

Then Chaplin was sitting in the wooden chair next to the bed. He was thinking simple thoughts: The giraffe was so soft, the flowers were so bright. Roses from Doug and Mary, how thoughtful. The giraffe had come with spectacles, they were in his pocket, he could put them on the bridge of his nose, that would be funny.

"Is he going to live?"

Mildred gently shook her head. Could he imitate the dour face of faith the nun had worn? No. There was a wastepaper can across the room, and he imagined dropping the child into it. He looked again at the baby. Its sightless eyes were gazing at him. Its lips twitched, a vague and weak suckling motion. Mildred would have been a good mother, he realized now, for the first time.

A giraffe, flowers, palm trees, his own troupe of players, perfect sunlight, friends to love, beautiful girls to dance with, a wife, unlimited freedom. He put his head in his hands and he broke apart into tears.

When he looked up, he saw that his son was awake and regarding him with an empty gaze. Once upon a time, all the times in his life until now, he had thought himself a sailor in an open skiff over the sea of humanity, not immune to its pull but strong enough to guide himself past any cruelty and to defeat it.

But this small body was immune to him, and, no matter what he did, the baby would die. Death was not a cop. The world was larger than he was.

When he had finished crying, it was amazing to him that he was still in the same room. Nothing had changed. Mildred was still in the bed, the baby was still propped up at her side.

He shuffled his feet, rubbed his face with his hands, hid his eyes with a handkerchief, and looked back at his family. A comedy ends with a marriage. A tragedy begins with one.

Sometime later, the light had shifted. The nun came and retrieved the baby, leaving him alone with Mildred, who went to sleep. Her dreams were punctuated with startled little gasps. Chaplin stayed in the chair. The sun set, the lights of the city came on, the night continued, the lights would wink out one by one, the sun would rise, it would set again, regardless.

Three days later, the baby died.

Mildred had called him Charlie Jr., but Chaplin had always wanted a son called Norman, and when she agreed, yes, this child had been Norman, not Charlie, it was to please him, but it was also just slightly terrible, for it was her, too, giving up all hope. There was no child named Charlie Chaplin anymore, not in body, or in name, erased in some way twice. But even directly referring to him was too painful. Then, and for the rest of her life, she referred to him by neither "Norman" nor "Charlie." Instead she called him "the Little Mouse."

There was a funeral. Chaplin did not organize it, and protested that he could not go to such a thing. All ceremony struck him as repressive, and funerals were awful, and a funeral for a baby was bound to be sentimental folly. But on the morning of the event, he could not find a reason to stay home, and so he dressed as Mildred found her way into a black dress and veil as slowly as if she were drugged. Beside her bed there was a small cage, and in the cage was a wheel, and the wheel spun freely as the tiny gray, pink-nosed mouse Hannah had given Mildred galloped, and then fell asleep in his wood shavings.

Chaplin saw her watching the mouse while she put on a pair of clip earrings. This marriage would not last. Nor would his next. Nor his next. The fourth one would. Chaplin saw himself in the mirror, as he shot his cuffs and threaded his onyx cuff links through his French-made shirt. He carried with him as if it were a snapshot the image of his dead baby's eyes, blank blue saucers, little windows into the human world. And the message he could read, when he looked carefully into them, was that life was meaningless.

He was finished with pictures. He had made sixty-six movies in five years. *Sunnyside*—finished—was not as good as he was. The Little Fellow romanced Edna without effort. He dreamed of dancing with nymphs. A city slicker almost swept Edna away. The Little Fellow crouched in front of a speeding car to kill himself—and woke up! It had been another dream. Even the scene cards ("And now the 'romance.' ") seemed bored. It made no real sense, and it was a failure, his first. No one asked to hold it over a week. The prints returned in excellent condition. Whispers began about him, that he had lost his abilities and was just going through the motions now. No one had understood *Sunnyside*, and he had to give his audience credit: there was nothing to understand.

And then he was at the funeral. There was Mildred, head bowed, eyes closed and leaking tears, and one of her hands closed around his, pressing her wet handkerchief into his palm. And Syd and Minnie, and Mildred's mother, and Doug and Mary. He stared out the window into the cemetery. He saw a canary on a gravestone, next to a broken sundial.

The night before, Chaplin, restless, had walked across the million-dollar carpet of the Alexandria Hotel and met a father-and-son vaudeville team: Jack and Jackie Coogan. They didn't know about his baby's birth or death, and he lost himself in a conversation. Jack was good enough at hoofing, but his four-year-old son was a splendid mimic, with a great sense of humor, a dancer, quite hilarious, showing off a perfect little shimmy dance, and he and Chaplin played soldiers and cowboys and Indians and for about a minute; Chaplin had considered putting him in a movie, and then he remembered he wasn't making movies anymore, and he left the hotel, knowing that in hours he would have to watch Mildred dress for their son's funeral.

The sermon was brief. Mildred's church, Saint Lawrence the Divine, had arranged the whole thing, which Chaplin expected to be a new level of insipid anecdotes and "wise old sayings." But instead a very serious young man with a clerical collar stood before the pews and spoke for perhaps five minutes. He did not smile. He said that some things happened for no known reason. It was useless to try and draw a moral from them. He said, "According to Thomas Jefferson, who helped put us on the path we walk today, he who believes nothing is less remote from the truth than he who believes what is wrong. So, when something awful happens, we must put aside needing to understand or to fit it into a system where the world's cruelties make sense. Perhaps, after life is over, it will all be explained. Or not."

Chaplin began to like him, slightly.

The minister explained that the question on his mind was this: Was life basically random, and were our agile human brains, trained in analogy and connecting dots, always making constellations out of chaos? Or was there a deeper meaning, and was it when we were in touch with the divine that we allowed ourselves to see it? Every moment of belief was actually about *choosing* belief, and that was what he called faith. Perhaps, one moment in the future, every person in this room would again have some kind of faith. Amen.

It's not as if the minister were a visionary, but Chaplin found himself moved. He was fidgeting in his seat. He wondered about Jackie Coogan, the four-year-old boy. He saw himself as clearly as if it were already projected onto a screen, himself on a tightrope over Niagara Falls, swarmed and bitten by a troupe of spider monkeys. He saw himself shivering outside a Klondike saloon. He saw himself being pulled through the gouging gears of fantastic machinery. He saw himself falling down onstage, through the skin of a bass drum, to tremendous laughter, only his heart had stopped and he had died. And then he saw himself, punished. Punished and punished, in movies he hadn't yet made.

The service was over. When had it ended? Had anyone else spoken? The few mourners were standing. It was time to walk into the cemetery, for the burial.

Stuck in armor, visor fixed down. Not just punished, but hoping and then being punished. Starving, eating his shoe. Infested by an entire flea circus. Napoleon at Elba.

The back doors were swinging closed. He was still standing in the aisle. Mildred was next to him. He looked over his shoulder, toward the altar, where there were bouquets of flowers, and the coffin.

Training not a dog but a child to break windows. Of course. The Little Fellow then comes by to fix them.

Mildred had lifted her veil. "Charlie?"

"I want to see him."

When he tried to walk toward the altar, she was holding his arm. "Please don't," she whispered.

"I'm fairly sure I have to," he whispered in return.

She nodded. "Just, please, please, don't be angry."

So many things had made so little sense recently, he did not know how to respond.

"It was Minister Jim's idea. He felt it was the right thing to do."

Chaplin felt a lump in his throat, something expanding and rising and unavoidable. He took Mildred's hand off of his arm, and then walked alone to the altar.

The light was coming in from stained-glass windows, lives of saints, both kind and cruel, through which shone the happy happy Hollywood sun. Chaplin heard organ music from a funeral one chapel away. Before he opened the lid to the coffin, he had a strange, prescient understanding of what he would find. He looked over his shoulder, at Mildred, who was wilting.

Chaplin's fingers found the brass railing around the tiny coffin. It opened silently on expensive, oiled hinges. The casket had white satin padding, plush and overstuffed, and almost lost inside was the tiny form of the Little Mouse. He wore a blue silk wrapper on his broken balloon of a body.

And then the lid of the casket slipped from Chaplin's fingers, for they had slicked with sweat. The coffin closed with a bang.

Mildred jolted in place, the echo playing against the high stone walls.

Now the chapel was as tense as if a shot had rung out. Mildred heard something. It was something animalistic, deep and rutting, a wild beast's song of triumph. It was Charlie laughing. She had never really heard him laugh. It wasn't the *heh heh-heh* of his quiet side. It seemed to come from so deep within him that nothing had ever touched it before.

His jaw was aching, the back of his head hurt like an ice-cream headache. The question posed in the sermon—was there inherent meaning in the universe? He began to frighten himself, because now, finally, after so many false starts and declarations, he understood.

The tiny corpse had been given a send-off from the human world. Fixed onto its mouth by the funeral-home embalmers, held into place with a crescent moon shaped from metal wire, there was a broad, toothless smile.

Three days later, Chaplin began work on The Kid, *about a boy abandoned by his mother, and the tramp who rescues him.*

It was his first film as good as he was.

Credits

I apologize to students of truth who find themselves arguing with information contained herein. Edith Wharton, busted for historical flimflamming in *The Age of Innocence,* wrote that slavish accuracy "must necessarily reduce the novel to a piece of archeological pedantry instead of a living image of the times." Which is another way of her saying, "I'm Edith Wharton, Jack—I can snap you like a twig."

When I wrote my first novel, about a stage magician, I was reluctant to spill which parts were based in reality and which were imaginary; as I said, it was like explaining how a trick was done. Which was another way of saying, "It's magic, Jack—I can snap you like a twig."

On November 12, 1916, Charlie Chaplin was indeed the subject of mass hysteria. And on September 15, 1918, Leland Duncan found two puppies on the World War I battlefield and named them after finger puppets. The surviving dog was the most successful film star of the 1920s, saving Warner Bros. from bankruptcy. And in 1918, the United States sent the 339th of Detroit to North Russia for reasons that are, with the passage of years, hard to fathom. Or distressingly easy.

I got some things wrong on purpose (I know *My Official Wife* wasn't a comedy) and there are probably some things you know that I don't. But the punctuation of Waldorf=Astoria belongs exactly as much as Pierre Revel belongs in their kitchens with champagne truffles. Also, source material occasionally contradicts what we think we know—for instance, contemporary military accounts used terminology that was technically wrong or allegedly not in use at the time (i.e., "top kick," "we're good, sir," "gunnery"). I've kept the source material vernacular where it seemed appropriate. Special salutes to":

Credits

Chaplin: David Robinson's *Chaplin*. *My Life with Chaplin*, by his second wife, Lita Grey Chaplin, is frequently dismissed but was very useful. The films in the DVD collections *The Chaplin Review* and *Unknown Chaplin* are an excellent introduction to his work.

Hollywood: *The Story of Hollywood* by Gregory Williams; *Silent Echoes* and *Silent Traces* by John Bengston; *The War, the West and the Wilderness*, and everything else by Kevin Brownlow; *Working Class Hollywood* by Steven J. Ross; *Pickford* by Eileen Whitefield; *Without Lying Down* (Frances Marion's biography) by Cari Beauchamp.

Hugo Münsterberg's 1916 *The Film: A Psychological Study* sent this narrative into orbit. Where it was shot at by Martian paratroopers holding my ideas hostage. A prescient man, he paraphrases Noel Burch's *To the Distant Observer* sixty years before it was written. I hope Münsterberg would like that in 2008 we're still discussing his heart's desire, Annette Kellerman.

World War I: *How We Advertised America* by George Creel; *American Indians in World War I* by Thomas A. Britten; *The Hawks That Guided the Guns* by Lawrence Smart; *The History of the 135th* by Percival Hart.

Dogs: James English's *The Story of Rin Tin Tin* and *The Spirit of Rin Tin Tin* by Allan Shields. Harry seems to have read the wonderful/horrifying *The German Shepherd Dog in Words & Pictures* by von Stephanitz. I highly recommend watching *Where the North Begins,* Rinty's first feature. Based on an idea by Lee Duncan, it's weird, dopey, melodramatic, and, when the dog is onscreen, it's wonderful. Rinty was popular not just because he was cute but because he could *act*.

Archangel: There are more than a dozen histories in English about the Allied intervention. But it remains a war about which we are largely ignorant. That ill-equipped Americans died in a war that was unnecessary and ill-advised, for confused goals and shifting political reasons in a foreign land among people who largely wished them to leave, should be the kind of thing found only in a novel. Probably the best single-volume book on the subject is *The Day They Almost Bombed Moscow* by Christopher Dobson and John Miller. *Quartered in Hell* by Dennis Gordon gives an overview of the troops' many miseries. *Ignorant Armies* by E. M. Halliday is a good read, though it dates from the 1960s. I hope that an updated popular history becomes available.

The mutiny of the Slavo-British Legion, as portrayed in this novel, collapses together details of several different mutinies. In his memoirs, Ironside looks away at the mutineers' fates, or claims that they were rehabilitated. Other eyewitness accounts, however, describe the immediate execution of the leaders.

Ironside: There is no full-length biography of this astonishing man, who shows up at key moments of British rule from the 1900s to World War II. Shortly after Archangel, he helped partition Iraq, which he took to with cunning and diplomacy. I recommend John Buchan's *The 39 Steps* and the follow-up adventures of his hero Richard Hannay, who was based on Ironside.

To paraphrase Thomas Mallon, nouns trump adjectives, so you can guess how an author's dice are weighted if he writes historical fiction. To that end, some quotations here are real, others are not; many are amalgams. Thank you in advance to *The New Republic* for being such good sports.

If you'd like to follow Mr. Golod and Mr. Pike's argument about the development of American diamond cutting, I recommend "What Did Marcel Tolkowsky Really Say?" by Barak Green, Al Gilbertson, Ilene Reinitz, Mary Johnson, and James Shigley.

Poet Amy Gerstler wrote, "Fear is a civilizing influence." Chaplin would not think as he does here had I not read *Ghost Girl,* particularly her poem "The New Dog." Also the work of Mark Newgarden.

Many other people helped, and here are some of them:

Scenario and Dialogue: Wilton Barnhardt, Lynda Barry, Aimee Bender, Owen Bly, Gavin Bryars, Mike Caveney, Bill Charman, Livia and Lucia Charman, Howard Chaykin, Dan Condon, Bernard Cooper, Henry Dunow,

Credits

Polly Harvey, Phil Hay, Eli Horowitz, Bill Howard, Jan Iverson, Peter Jackson, Michelle Latiolais, Patrick McDonnell, Maria Mochnacz, Karen O'Connell, Jill Olson, Jim Ottaviani, Alison Powell, Diana Schutz, Mike Sears, Rob Stolzer, Robert Towne, Cyrus Voris, Karin Wessel, Kathy Wittwer, and the Chaplin group on yahoo.com.

Stage Managers: Susan Golomb, Matthew Snyder.

Moguls: Sonny Mehta, Carole Welch.

Foley and Looping: Diana Coglianese.

Wardrobe: J. D. King, Andy Hughes.

Craft Services: The MacDowell Colony.

Set Design: Liddell Hart Center for Military Archives.

Special Effects: The Corporation of Yaddo and its attendant spirits.

No animals were harmed in the making of this book. In fact, some of them were fed tiny cubes of cheese. A shepherd mix named Lilly came into my life in December 1998, bearing a striking resemblance to the original Rin Tin Tin. She left in February 2008, two days before I turned in a draft of this manuscript. I miss you, Lilly. We are all siblings under the skin!

Costar, provocateur, hot-splice editor, script girl, femme fatale, scream queen, gamine, America's sweetheart, America's pariah, belladonna, suds maven, oat princess, love interest, second-act complication, barn-burner, aviatrix, Hello Girl, lighthouse keeper, orphan, angel, allied expeditionary force, terrifying saint, daughter of the revolution, peasant, *domovoi*, *vedma*, princess, one hundred bullets, twelve immortals, seven seas, four winds, three shots of espresso, two cats, one Alice.

Speaking of credits, last, most: as of this writing, there is one surviving doughboy from World War I, Frank Buckles of West Virginia. He drove an ambulance when he was seventeen years old. He aims to turn 108 on February 1, 2009. He and a handful of tommies and diggers are the last to remember the battlefield. Thank you for your service.

And for anyone currently serving in the United States Armed Services, I wish you safety and luck and I hope you'll come home soon.

If it's a hundred years from now and there are still people, bless you all. I hope you have polar bears.

Glen David Gold
San Francisco, California
December 2008

A Note About the Author

Glen David Gold's first novel, *Carter Beats the Devil*, has been translated into fourteen languages. His short stories and essays have appeared in *McSweeney's, Playboy,* and *The New York Times Magazine.* He lives in San Francisco with his wife, Alice Sebold.

A Note on the Type

This book was set in Bodoni, a typeface named after Giambattista Bodoni (1740–1813), the celebrated printer and type designer of Parma. The Bodoni types of today were designed not as faithful reproductions of any one of the Bodoni fonts but rather as a composite, modern version of the Bodoni manner. Bodoni's innovations in type style included a greater degree of contrast in the thick and thin elements of the letters and a sharper and more angular finish of details.

Composed by North Market Street Graphics,
Lancaster, Pennsylvania
Printed and bound by Berryville Graphics,
Berryville, Virginia
Designed by Virginia Tan